SENATOR MARLOWE'S DAUGHTER

and

THE GREAT TRADITION

TWO COMPLETE NOVELS

Senator Marlowe's Daughter and *The Great Tradition*

TWO COMPLETE NOVELS

by

Frances Parkinson Keyes

JULIAN MESSNER, INC.
New York

PRINTED IN THE UNITED STATES OF AMERICA

Senator Marlowe's Daughter

TO

MARY GRAY

WHOSE FAITH IN ME NEVER FALTERED THROUGHOUT THOSE YEARS OF NOVITIATE WHICH BUT FOR HER WOULD NOT HAVE CULMINATED IN DEDICATION

"Stand therefore . . . having on the breastplate of righteousness; and your feet shod with the preparation of the gospel of peace; above all, taking the *shield of faith,* wherewith ye shall be able to quench all the fiery darts of the wicked."

—Ephesians VI: 14–16.

CONTENTS

AUTHOR'S NOTE

Charles Morgan, in presenting "The Fountain" to the public, felt impelled to explain that in designating a great landowner of the Netherlands by a name typically Dutch, he had done so in order to give an illusion of reality to his story, and not because the character he had created bore any resemblance to the actual scions of an illustrious family. I feel that I should make a similar statement. For centuries, there have been von Hohenlohes in Germany and de Cerrenos in Spain, and the men bearing these names have been noble in every sense of the word. But as far as I am aware, none of them has had a career remotely resembling that of Rudolf von Hohenlohe or the Sebastian de Cerreno of my imagination. If I have wandered at times from the field of fiction to the field of fact in my portrayal of these personages, I have done so unconsciously and involuntarily.

F. P. K.

PART I

Flossie

CHAPTER 1

Faith Marlowe sat on the dim, winding stairway, her plump, square little hands clasped tightly over her breast, her sturdy little shoulders braced against the heavy mahogany banisters. It was very dark in the hallway, so dark that she could hardly see the portraits of her grandfather, Christian Marlowe, who had been one of the outstanding figures in Buchanan's cabinet, and of her grandmother, the first Faith Marlowe, though she was standing directly beneath them, beside the tall clock which had been both made and owned by an earlier Christian Marlowe, before the Revolution, and which the cabinet officer had brought with him when he came to Washington. The gold frames of the portraits glittered, and this glitter penetrated the dust and the dusk, even though the painted canvases which they enclosed were shrouded in gloom; and the brass balls with which the clock was surmounted glittered too. There was something comforting to Faith in their faint gleam, something steadying too, in the regular rhythmic ticking that tapped firmly across the hysterical tones of her mother's voice, as this rose, first in a shriek, and then in a wail, and then in a shriek again, from the closed library below.

"I don't care who hears me! I won't be quiet! I simply won't put up with it any longer! You keep telling me to be calm, and to be patient, and to control myself, until I am so sick of hearing you say all that over and over again, in your stiff, cold, New England way, that I feel as if I should scream just at the sound of your voice! I'd like to know if I *haven't* been patient! I guess any outsider who knew all the facts would say I had! I've scrimped and saved, and gone without company and clothes, and everything that a young, pretty woman likes to have, so that you could 'uphold' those silly old traditions of yours that you think are so holy, and go on with the stupid, tiresome 'career' that you consider so ultra important. And what has all my sacrifice amounted to, I'd like to know? It's been bad enough all winter, trying to pretend that it didn't matter that you had been defeated, that the humiliation of having a husband who was a 'lame duck' didn't amount to anything! But I have struggled and smiled, and been nice to all the right people, hoping you would get an appointment of some sort—and you would have, if you had any guts at all! You could have gone straight to the President, and *made* him offer you *something*. But, oh no, you settled back and sulked and waited to be sent for—as if that old fish, Read, ever *sent* for anyone! And now you sit there placidly and tell me you propose to sell this house, and go back to the farm, and *vegetate* for the rest of your life! Well, Christian Marlowe, I can tell you this much—if you go to the farm, you go alone!"

"Faith loves it there." A man's voice, the voice of a man who was tired, and hopeless, and beaten, rose for a moment, ineffectually.

"Faith!" Flossie was shrieking again now. "Do you think I'd let her be buried there? What chance would she ever have, I'd like to know, of making anything of her life? Going to some little hick public school and marrying some country bumpkin! Well, I guess I can do better for her than that! I guess I've got money enough of my own, in spite of all I've squandered on you, to take her along with me! She's pretty enough and smart enough to bother with! If she was a horrid sniveling little nuisance, like some children—ugly and whiny and stupid—I'd be glad enough to leave her with you—it would serve you right! But Faith has got the goods to make a success of herself, and when she does I intend to be right there to cash in!"

An involuntary shudder of repugnance and premonition shook the child's solid little frame. She had not meant to be guilty of eavesdropping. She had spent a rather blank afternoon in her own room, playing with her two dolls, Clarissa and Rose, upon whom she usually lavished a good deal of maternal solicitude, but who had somehow seemed unsatisfying on this sultry, ominous day that was so unseasonably hot. So she had waited patiently until she heard the big clock on the stairway strike five, because it was tacitly understood between her father and herself that at five o'clock every evening she might come to the library, and that he would read aloud to her. Even Flossie, much as she resented this "waste of time"—a period which her husband might better have spent, in her opinion, making "worthwhile" calls with her—had come to take it for granted, and seldom intruded when Faith and Christian were thus preoccupied. So, in starting down the stairs, the little girl had done so with a sense of complete security and happiness. It was her mother's voice that had halted her, first in surprise and then in horror. For a moment she had been so transfixed that she had not been able to go on. But now, aware that it was dishonorable to listen, she walked slowly down the stairs, across the hall, and out of doors, trying resolutely to close her ears to the shrill bitter tones that pierced her consciousness.

She did not know just where to go or what to do. Flossie did not consider it the "thing" for little girls to go out alone, but she could not afford to keep a governess, and she was far too engrossed with her ladies' lunches, and her "official" teas, to take Faith out herself. Indeed, she often left the house as soon as she had dressed after sipping the coffee which she drank in bed much later than Christian and Faith ate their breakfast, and played cards for two hours before luncheon. Christian took Faith to school on his way to the Capitol, and as he was busy in the "Chamber" when it was time for her to return, she walked back with two older girls who lived on lower Sixteenth Street. Then she had only Lafayette Square to cross diagonally, before she reached the tall, flat, narrow brownstone house with its black walnut front door, which had been such a center of distinction and elegance when Christian Marlowe, the cabinet officer, had lived there, but which his son, Christian Marlowe, the senator, continued to occupy only because he could not afford to move to a more fashionable part of the town.

Since Lafayette Square was the only place where she did not feel strange and ill at ease when she was unaccompanied, Faith decided not to venture beyond it. She sat down on a bench, from which she could see her own house, her hands still clasped, her plump legs sticking straight out in front of her, and tried to think things over. It was hard for her to do this, partly because she felt so confused and bewildered and partly because it was so hot and noisy in the Square. The trees about her were drooping under dusty leaves which looked heavy with the heat, although it was only April; a few shabby and antiquated victorias drawn by dejected horses and driven by dejected coachmen were wheeling mournfully past, a few bicycles, noisily though listlessly propelled, lurched aimlessly along; men and women sprawled about in various stages of disorder and discomfort; fretful children hurled themselves against their parents' knees; and wailing babies twisted and turned in their crumpled carriages. Only the White House, remote and stately beyond the growth of trees and shrubbery, loomed clean and cool and lovely in the midst of all this squalor. Faith had been to the White House several times. Her father had taken her in to shake hands with the President, Hillary J. Read, during the brief period before the public receptions, when members of both Houses of Congress were privileged to present constituents and relatives; and once Mrs. Read, who had three little sons of her own, had given a children's party in the East Room, to which the "younger official set" had been invited, and to which Faith had gone, as overawed as she was overbefrilled and beribboned. It would be difficult to say whether she had been more uncomfortable at the unaccustomed grandeur with which she was surrounded, or over the fact that she was the only little girl present who was not dressed in simple smocked silk or sheer embroidered muslin;

but Flossie's taste ran to furbelows, and Faith submitted to it even though she suffered under it. Besides these memorable occasions, there were others of lesser importance: the annual Easter egg rolling and the annual reception to the Children of the American Revolution, for instance. But on the whole the White House was inaccessible, though Faith realized that her mother's vaulting ambition had stretched to its very portals before the political fortunes of the Marlowe family had begun to tumble.

"You know my husband's father missed the Presidential nomination by a *hair's breadth*"—Faith could just remember the mincing boast—"it was his short-sighted stand on the slavery question that was his undoing, but we feel *most* confident that Senator Marlowe will sweep everything before him at the next National Convention." Senator Marlowe had not swept anything before him, he had instead been swept aside himself. And since they could not go to the White House, since—it appeared from what Faith had involuntarily overheard—they could not even keep the shabby, gloomy, heavily comfortable house on Lafayette Square, why should they not all go contentedly together to the farm, why should Mamma hate it so? It was sweet and quiet and peaceful there, never hot and humid and dirty and noisy, as Washington seemed that night. In front of the solid old homestead there were lilac bushes which would soon be in bloom, as well as the apple trees in the orchard, and the place would be pervaded with their fragrance. There were calves and chickens and colts and lambs and baby pigs—a little girl could have all those delightful live creatures to play with out of doors, instead of being shut up in one small stuffy room with Clarissa and Rose. And Uncle Ephraim, who managed the farm which he and his brother Christian had inherited jointly, and lived there all the time, was so very kind and understanding, always realizing that children like to go for the cows and ride on hayloads, while his wife, Aunt Emmeline, made such nice cookies, and always had a stone jar full of them, ready and waiting, on the pantry shelf behind the big pans where the smooth rich cream was set to rise.

Yes, certainly, the farm was a lovely place, Faith thought, and they might all be very happy there, if Mamma could think of it that way. Was there anything, Faith wondered, that she herself could say that would change her mother's viewpoint? Daddy had tried, of course, and failed. It was strange and sad that Daddy tried so hard and failed so often—not only as far as Mamma was concerned, but as far as everybody and everything was concerned.

It had begun to grow dark. The fretful children and wailing babies had worn themselves out and were quieter now; the hot, tired men and women did not look quite so repulsive in the dusk; a little breeze began to stir the drooping leaves of the shrubbery; a light, suddenly snapped on at the entrance of the White House, shed its effulgent radiance on its classic columns clustered about the portico. Something tugged at Faith's heartstrings. It *would* be hard to leave Washington, even to go to the farm; never to gaze at the slender shaft of the Monument shining white against the blue sky that it seemed to pierce; never to take the boat down the river to Mount Vernon; never to hire one of the sagging old victorias and drive slowly to the Zoo; never to watch, enthralled, the money being made at the Bureau of Engraving and Printing; never to go down to Daddy's office, and listen to the fascinating tap-tap of the typewriters and admire the neatly piled bulletins and pamphlets. Faith had seen and done all these things with Daddy, and the memory of them was precious to her; she had not realized before how blank a future would be that did not include them. But it would be blank to Daddy too, for such sights and deeds had been his familiar pleasures ever since he was a little boy and went about with *his* Daddy —and his mother too, because, apparently, Grandmother Faith had not been as busy with other people as Mamma always was, and loved to roam around the Capital with her husband and their children. How selfish she, Faith, had been not to think more about Daddy and less about herself! She must go to him and comfort him. By now Mamma's outburst would be over, and she would have rushed out of the library, sobbing hysterically and slamming the door after her, and have locked herself in her own room. Soberly and slowly, as Faith did most things, she climbed down from the dusty bench and started toward the house. Just then she saw her father coming toward her in the dusk.

He seemed terribly tired. His shoulders sagged and his head was bent; his hair was hardly grayer than his pallid face; and in his eyes, which always looked so hurt and hunted and hopeless lately, there was an expression of fear as well. But this lifted as he caught sight of Faith. He hurried over to her and clutched her chubby hand, which was already outstretched toward his.

"I missed you," he said, and Faith could hear the trouble in his voice. "I looked at the clock and it was after five and you hadn't come. Your mother had—been in the library with me, and I didn't notice how late it was until after she had gone upstairs. Then I went to your room, and Clarissa and Rose were both lying asleep in their beds, but you were nowhere to be seen. I didn't like to—disturb your mother by asking if she knew where you were, so I started to hunt for you. It's taken me quite a long time to find you. I don't believe your mother would like you to come to the park and sit alone."

"I won't do it again, Daddy."

"No, darling, I don't believe you will."

He had sunk down on the bench from which she had just risen, covering his face with his hands. Even to his child's uncomprehending vision he was a spent and tragic figure. She climbed up beside him and put her arms around his neck.

"Do tell me what the trouble is, Daddy."

He made a sound that was less a groan than a sob.

"I can't explain, Faith. You wouldn't understand. I'm a failure. I've come to the end of everything."

She waited silently, sure that after a moment he would go on, and that even if she did not grasp the meaning of his words, it would comfort him to utter them.

"My father was a great man," he said at last, "and he had confidence in me. He expected me to follow in his footsteps. He knew that my brother, your Uncle Ephraim—would never have any taste or any talent for public life. But he thought that I had. And he did everything that he could to get me started. I *did* get started, before he died. I'm thankful that he didn't live to see that I couldn't go on."

Again Faith waited silently.

"I didn't do so badly, in the State Legislature. Or even in the House of Representatives. I think he'd have been pleased with my record that far. But I ought never to have tried to enter the Senate, even though I did get in the first time I ran. I'm not Senate-size, Faith. I can't complain of being beaten. I don't belong there."

"You belong to me, Daddy. We belong to each other."

The man groaned again.

"Well, I don't know, Faith. Your mother thinks you belong to her. And I don't know that it is right to separate a little girl from her mother. If you had been a boy——"

"I could try, Daddy, to be ever so much like a boy."

Christian Marlowe laughed bitterly. "And put Clarissa and Rose to bed every night?"

"I could give them up, if that would help."

He drew her to him, burying his bent head on her shoulder. "No, darling," he said brokenly, "it's sweet and lovely and—and like you to offer, but it wouldn't help. Nothing would help. I don't blame your mother. I don't want you to blame her. I am ever so much older than she is—I wasn't young any more when I married her, though I tried to pretend that I was because I—wanted her so. She was so pretty and soft looking. And I tried to give her everything she wanted. But I couldn't. I know now that I never can. So I want her to be free to find it somewhere else."

"Daddy," asked Faith suddenly, "is it—is it usual for senators to sit on park benches and cry?"

Christian Marlowe jerked himself up. "No," he said, almost harshly, "it isn't usual. But after all, I am not a senator any more, you know, Faith. I haven't been since the fourth of March. I never shall be again."

"You might be, mightn't you, if you tried ever and ever so hard?"

"I'm through trying. I've tried all I can. I've let go. I told you, Faith, you wouldn't understand. I'm a failure."

"And you are going to let Mamma go away? Wherever she wants to? And take me with her?"

"She is going to take you to Europe, Faith," the man said pathetically, "on a big boat. You'll like it. Children always love the sea. I know I did. My father went on a special mission to France and England, just before the Civil War, and we all went with him."

"But this will be different. You said only Mamma and I."

"Yes, darling. Only Mamma and you. I'm going back to the farm. You see you couldn't stay there. Mamma wants you to have a good education, to learn languages."

"I could learn other things, Daddy, at the farm, just as useful as languages maybe. . . . Aunt Emmeline would teach me to make cookies. And I could get the cows for Uncle Ephraim."

The man did not answer. Slowly and soberly the child climbed down from the bench a second time and confronted him.

"All right," she said, gulping a little, but on the whole with much more composure than he was displaying, "I'm awfully sorry you're so sure you are a failure, Daddy, because I don't feel sure at all. I mean I don't feel sure that you *have* to be. And I'm sorry, if you are bound to be a failure that you won't take me to the farm with you, because I love it there and I love you and we could be ever so happy. But if I have to go to Europe with Mamma, and help her to try to be free, and learn languages, I guess I can. I guess I'll go in the house now and wake up Clarissa and Rose and pack their things. I want them to be all ready, so that Mamma won't say it's too much trouble to take them along. And I guess I can stand it, in Europe, just as long as she can. But some day——"

She had planted herself squarely in front of him. Through the dim light he could see her huge smoldering eyes glowing in the round rosy face that had suddenly become transfigured with purpose; her red-gold hair, sleekly parted and tightly braided as it was, escaped in springing tendrils of vivid color over her smooth brow and flat little ears. For the first time he realized that Flossie's kitten-like prettiness, fused with the dark distinction inherited from the first Faith Marlowe, had combined to produce elements of potential beauty and vitality in his daughter, the existence of which he had never dreamed before. Too startled to interrupt her, he heard her mutely to the end of what she was determined to say.

"Some day," Faith went on, drawing herself up tautly to her full height, "I'm coming back to Washington! If Grandfather Marlowe had confidence in you, and you haven't followed in his footsteps, the way he meant you should, *I guess I can do it* instead! If he was a great man, I guess I can be a great woman! Anyway I'm going to try! Anyway I'm going to pretend that I'm *not* beaten, every time I know I am! Anyway I'm not going to let go! Anyway—Some way . . . I tell you I'm coming back!"

CHAPTER 2

FLOSSIE had already begun to pack when Christian and Faith returned to the house. Two huge battered trunks, one rectangular, the other surmounted by a dome-shaped cover, stood in the upper hallway, and Flossie was rushing back and forth between her own room and these trunks, flinging wraps and dresses and underwear, negligees and hats, parasols and fans and shoes into them. Billows of pink tulle which had lost its first crispness, the froth of soiled lace ruffles, the rustle of stiff silk that was stained and spotted in places, pervaded the place; scarves and shawls which she had dropped in her haste, trailed elegantly, if mustily, across the floor; two straight-backed chairs of carved black walnut, upholstered in horse-hair, stood piled high with heavily boned corsets, starched petticoats, chemises and nightgowns trimmed with Hamburg edging and "run through" with wash-ribbon which had never been washed, and a tumbled collection of unmended silk stockings. Faith, climbing the stairs on the way to her own room, tripped on some of the fallen finery, just as her mother emerged from her chamber with another armful of it.

"You clumsy child! Don't you know that is lace, real Duchesse, you're trampling over! Do watch where you're going!"

"I'm sorry, Mamma. There isn't much light."

"No, there certainly isn't—with this horrible old gas I've had to put up with when everyone else is getting electricity! But we are going where there will be plenty! I suppose that your father has told you? Well, you needn't try to argue, or sulk, or take his side! Where is he?"

"He's in the library."

"You'd think he would come and *help* me! But of course he won't think of lifting a finger! And Lily's getting dinner, and was awfully cross when I suggested that she might help. It's Ella's day out, and Lily has to cook and wait on table both to-night, so she thinks she's just about killed. Your father doesn't realize what I've suffered trying to run this huge inconvenient house with only two servants. And servants, what they are nowadays—impertinent and thieving and everything else, and asking more and more exorbitant wages all the time! Lily had the impudence to say that if I wanted a lady's maid I'd better get one! And Ella wants a raise to four dollars a week! Well, they think

I am just going over to New York for a little trip—they haven't any idea that in a day or two they will be hunting for jobs, with no reference from the lady of the house where they worked last! I get some satisfaction out of that anyway."

"Perhaps I can help you, Mamma."

"No, you couldn't. You'd only get under foot. But you'd better try to pack your own trunk—you'll have to learn sooner or later and it might as well be now! I'm almost distracted with all *I've* got to do without looking out for your clothes too! I'm not coming down to dinner—I wouldn't sit opposite your father after the horrible scene I've had with him if I starved to death. But when you have finished the great hearty meal that you always eat, and that was absolutely unnecessary to cook this hot weather, perhaps he might condescend to get that cowhide trunk that was his mother's out of the attic for you. And there's a carpet-bag there too that you could take. We haven't any decent baggage, of course. I'll get some new trunks in Paris—and something stylish to put in them too—I certainly haven't a thing to wear, not a single thing!"

Flossie rushed ahead with almost incredible celerity. The following afternoon she and Faith took the train for New York, sitting cramped among the bandboxes and valises that were piled all around them. Flossie was very tired, and snapped at Faith every time the child spoke to her.

"Do be *quiet!* Can't you see how exhausted I am? And you sit there staring, with those two great dolls in your arms and ask questions! It's enough to drive me crazy. I don't *know* what is going to become of Lily and Ella, and I don't care! I don't *know* who's going to have our house and furniture—and I don't care about that either! I don't *know* who's going to help your father move, and I care least of all about that. He might've come over to New York and seen us off! He would have if he had any regard for appearance—ladies go to Europe without their husbands all the time now, and no one thinks anything of it, if the gentlemen come down to the steamer, and tip the stewards, and ask for places at the captain's table, and kiss their wives good-bye, several times, right by the gangplank. You would think that was the *least* Christian Marlowe could do! But no, it would be a 'needless expense' to take the trip to New York—as if twenty-five dollars more or less would matter when he is bankrupt anyway!—and a 'hollow sham' to pretend that everything was all right when it isn't! Well, there won't be any more hollow shams! He needn't worry!"

Flossie's voice was not loud, but it was shrill and penetrating. Faith saw that their fellow travelers were looking at them curiously, and was almost certain that her mother had been overheard. She was acutely miserable. As they neared New York, however, Flossie spoke to her with pleasant animation.

"We'll take a hack and go over to the Murray Hill Hotel. It's very select, and I know there'll be some lovely rooms reserved for us there. I think it would be nice to have an early supper, right in our own little parlor, and then you can go right to bed. I know you're tired. Don't you think that would be nice, darling?"

Faith was very tired, and she thought it would be very nice. But even her weariness did not prevent her from being thrilled by the hack, and by the "suite" into which she and her mother were ushered by two laden bellboys. She admired the Nottingham lace curtains and red velvet "overdrapes" that shaded the long windows, the thick pile red carpet, the heavy plush furniture, the massive bed, the shining tin tub in the private bathroom which was actually all their own—not shared with anyone else at all. She got undressed, and took a lovely bath right away, and put on her best cambric nightgown, that buttoned close up to her round little throat, and her feather-stitched blue flannel wrapper; and then, already nodding with drowsiness, she ate the nice supper that Mamma had ordered, and said her prayers, and lying down on her side of the big bed, fell swiftly to sleep.

She was awakened several hours later, by the sound of voices in the next room—Mamma's voice and another, a man's voice. Faith's heart leaped with joy—so Daddy had come over after all, on some other train! He was there with them, and would take her place in the big bed, and she would sleep on the "lounge" with Clarissa and Rose; and before they sailed he would do all those important things that would keep anyone from knowing that their family was not just like other families. She jumped out of bed, and pattered across the room, without even waiting to put on her slippers, and threw open the door into the parlor which Mamma had closed after they had said good-night to each other. But, on the threshold, her cry of welcome was suddenly hushed. It was not very light in the parlor, because in spite of everything that Mamma had said about longing for electricity, she had turned on very little of it; so Faith could not see very well. But certainly the man who was sitting on the sofa beside Mamma, with his arm around her waist, was not Daddy. Daddy was tall and slim and pale and clean-shaven, and this man was short and heavy and bearded and ruddy. Stricken with disappointment and startled with the shock of surprise, Faith drew back, and tried to shut the door quietly and creep away to bed again.

But she was too late. Mamma and the strange man had both seen her. She thought they looked startled themselves, and rather provoked too, as if she had done a stupid thing in opening the door. Then the man laughed, very hard and loud, and after that Mamma laughed too, in a funny, strangely hysterical way, and rose from the sofa and walked over toward Faith.

She looked very pretty. She had on her pink chiffon negligee trimmed with lover's knots and wide creamy lace flounces, and in the dim light its lost freshness was not evident. She smelled of the heliotrope perfume that she used on great occasions. Her soft rounded white arms and throat were bare, and the lovely turn of her breast. Her beautiful auburn hair was loose and curly all around her face, her blue eyes were shining and her cheeks were very pink. She spoke sweetly to Faith and put her arm around her.

"What waked you up, darling? Did you have a bad dream?"

Faith was confused, and a little unhappy, in spite of the fact that Mamma's voice was so unusually sweet. She felt shy about saying she had thought she heard Daddy talking, when it had been the strange heavy man. Mamma seemed to guess what was wrong, and went on talking herself, very, very pleasantly.

"You remember your dear Uncle Nelson, don't you, darling? He lives here in New York, and he's very fond of you and Mamma. He's engaged our passage on the steamer for us, and he'll come to see us off, and get us fixed all comfy and cozy. He's a lawyer, and he's going to take care of Mamma's own money for her, and send us what we need, all the time we're in Europe. Won't that be nice?"

Again Faith said it would be very nice. She did not remember her dear Uncle Nelson, but she supposed that he must have come to visit them in Washington when she was too little to remember—she could remember when she was four, but not very well before that. She shook hands with him very gravely and politely, and then she kissed Mamma good-night again and went back to bed. She could hear Uncle Nelson and Mamma laughing after she had shut the door, and presently she fell asleep again.

Next morning Mamma went shopping and took Faith with her. Then Uncle Nelson met them and they all had lunch together at the Brevoort House. Afterwards Mamma said she thought Faith looked very tired and had better take a nap, while she and Uncle Nelson finished the shopping and went to his office to sign some papers. Faith had not taken naps for a long while, not since that dim period before she was four that she could not remember very well. But she went and lay down, docilely, on the big bed, with Rose and Clarissa on either side of her, and sure enough, she did go to sleep.

It was dark when she waked up, dark and thunderous and hot. Presently it began to rain very hard, and there were vivid flashes of lightning. Faith was not a timid little girl, but somehow the storm seemed frightening. She wished there were someone in the Murray Hill Hotel whom she could ask to come and stay with her, since Mamma and Uncle Nelson had not returned, and it did not grow light again. Faith grew very hungry. She rang a bell, the way she had seen Mamma do it the night before, and a kind waiter brought her some supper, but afterwards he asked her to pay for it and she did not have any money. It was very dreadful. He muttered something about speaking to the manager, and finally he came and took away the dishes, clattering them a great deal and not looking kind any more. After he had gone, Faith lay down because there was nothing else for her to do, and by and by she went to sleep again.

When she waked a second time, Mamma was rushing around the bedroom putting her toilet articles into her valise and Uncle Nelson was sitting in the parlor smoking a long black cigar and waiting for her to finish. They told Faith that the boat was going to sail at four in the morning, so that it would be best to go aboard that night. Bellboys came and gathered up all the bags again, and they got into a hack, more crowded than ever because Uncle Nelson took up so much room, and were jolted over rough cobblestones for a long time. At last they reached a strange place called a pier, where everyone was jostling one another all around, and there was a great deal of noise and confusion. It kept raining harder and harder, and they got very wet going up a queer inclined thing that was like a stairway only there were no stairs. They walked and walked through little narrow halls, and then the dark jabbering man who was guiding them, pulled back a red rep curtain in front of a little cubbyhole, and motioned them to go in.

"You said you wanted to economize on the steamer, Flossie," Uncle Nelson was saying, "so I engaged an inside cabin. In stormy weather you can't have the porthole open anyway, so you won't miss one. And of course, you'll be on deck most of the time, so it doesn't matter if there isn't any daylight. Is this all right?"

Flossie said it was all right, though her voice did not sound quite as pleasant as it had the night before. But Faith thought the cubbyhole was very interesting. There were two wide shelves, with railings, built against the wall, one above the other, made up like tiny narrow beds; and there was a tall shiny brown cabinet that unfastened in a miraculous way to disclose a washstand. Beside this was a sponge-bag made of string, and over the sponge rack were a carafe and two tumblers with towels twisted in them. Near the door were four hooks, and a small flat stitched bag with scalloped edges. She admired everything very much.

"Get the kid into bed and we'll go up to the bar for a few minutes, Flossie," Uncle Nelson said in a low voice. Then he turned to Faith and patted her shoulder. "You're a cute kid," he remarked good-naturedly. "Here's a little present for you I hope you'll like. Take good care of your Mamma, won't you?"

Faith promised that she would, and put up her face solemnly, to be kissed; then she said if Mamma would undo the back buttons, she could put herself to bed all right. And after Mamma and Uncle Nelson had gone she opened the box that contained her present. There were several presents instead of one: a package of lemon drops; two books—"Elsie Dinsmore" and "What Katy Did"; stiff muslin bonnets for Rose and Clarissa, trimmed with Valenciennes lace; a little silver watch that really told time, fastened on a bow pin. Faith was delighted with them all, and stowed them safely away in the little hammock swung beside her bunk. Then she cuddled down between the coarse white linen sheets, and laid her head on the hard little pillow and closed her eyes. But she could not go to sleep again. It was very hot in the cubbyhole, and light shone in from the corridor beyond in spite of the red rep curtain drawn across the doorway; and it was very noisy. Baggage bumped along on its way to other cubbyholes, and above excited, rapid ejaculations in an unknown tongue, rose and fell the voices of men and women who had come to see their friends off, and men and women who were going away.

"*Hello* there, Tom! Are you with Jack and Mabel? No, I haven't been able to locate them anywhere. Number seventeen is their stateroom and it's a daisy." . . . "Well, I *did* mean to bring some flowers, but I couldn't seem to get around to buying any, and I thought oranges would taste pretty good—they're such a rarity at this time of year." . . . "For God's sake, don't cry so, Helen, it isn't as though the boy were in his grave. Most mothers would be pretty proud of having their sons win a prize that would give them two years in Paris free even if they did waste the time studying art." . . . "Know any French? Well, you better learn some P.D.Q. Most of these froggies don't speak a word of anything else. Look out there, *gersong,* you bumped into me with that trunk! *Prunnay gard!* I said, darn you!" . . . "Oh, I wouldn't think of going to bed! We're going to make a night of it and watch the Goddess of Liberty receding in the dawn's early light before we turn in. Time enough to rest up tomorrow—we'll be deathly sick by then anyway!"

Christian Marlowe had read to Faith about the Goddess of Liberty and had shown her a picture of it. It would be fun, she thought, to see it herself. She would speak to Mamma about it. But the hot rackety night wore itself away, and still Flossie had not come back to the cubbyhole when Faith fell at last into troubled slumber.

She waked to find the boat moving. It was queer, like everything else—it was queer, just to think how many times she had fallen asleep and waked up again since she left Washington, each time to discover something different. The light was still shining in from the corridor, and Faith inspected her new little silver watch. It was half-past four.

Rather clumsily she climbed down from her bunk and looked for Mamma. Flossie had come in and lay, still dressed, in the berth below, breathing heavily. She did not look as pretty as she had two nights before, and the scent that enveloped her was not sweet like that of the heliotrope perfume. Her traveling costume was tumbled, and the pins were half falling out of her gorgeous hair. Her small plumed hat and small soiled gloves lay beside her reticule, and her small buttoned boots had tumbled sideways on the floor. Faith spoke to her softly and she muttered something and turned over. But she was not really roused.

Faith dressed herself as well as she could. She did not dare to wash, for fear that the sound of unfastening the miraculous washstand would waken Mamma, and she could not reach the back buttons or braid her own hair. But she put on her sailor hat and her mackintosh, and reached for Clarissa and Rose. Then she pushed aside the red rep curtains and went out into the corridor.

It was not crowded any more. Faith found her way, slowly but without mishap, to the deck. Only a few people, most of them in little clustering groups, stood looking out toward the dim skyline. None of them spoke to her; they were absorbed with their own friends and families, or with their thoughts. Entirely alone, she stood and gazed at the symbolical figure of freedom, looming large and gray through the rain and mist, vaguely conscious of its significance, at one and the same time stirred and comforted.

"I'm coming back," she whispered resolutely, "I'm coming back."

CHAPTER 3

FLOSSIE was very seasick. A voluble stewardess who did not speak a word of English, helped her to undress and hung up her clothes; after that whenever Flossie rang, the stewardess came back and did necessary and disgusting things. But Flossie would not get up, not even long enough to have her berth straightened out, she would not try to take any nourishment, not even *café au lait* or bouillon, and she was much too ill to do anything for Faith, whom the stewardess more or less overlooked.

After she had watched the great statue out of sight, the little girl, subconsciously aware that she must try to take care of herself, had set about systematically to find her way around the boat. Now that the confusion of the night before had been eliminated, this was not difficult, and she met with unexpected coöperation from several quarters. When she reached the door of the dining saloon, she was kindly greeted in mixed but expressive language by the *maître d'hôtel,* to whom Uncle Nelson had, it appeared, spoken about seats for her and *madame* and who guided her to one of the small rectangular tables running at right angles to the long one which extended, in a narrow imposing expanse, down the center of the *salle à manger.*

"This is *monsieur le docteur's* table," he told her tactfully. "*Mademoiselle* will like it ver' well." And she was grateful to him for not making excuses about his failure to provide the more exalted places which

Flossie had coveted. "*Madame votre mère* does not raise herself so early, *non? N'importe!* Here is *mademoiselle's garçon,* Jules, and he will give her *chocolat* and *petits pains,* and *monsieur le docteur* will be here for *déjeuner* at half-past twelve and dinner at half-past six. He is altogether amiable. He and Jules will see that *mademoiselle* is *soignée.*"

The hot stimulating drink and crisp hard rolls were very good, and Faith consumed them gratefully. She was a little surprised that no cereal was offered her, but she was rather relieved than otherwise at the omission. She had always disliked it, and had eaten it at home only because she had been so frequently assured that she would not grow nor have nice teeth if she did not. There was no one else at the table when she began her breakfast, but presently a tall, homely boy with freckles and sandy hair came in and sat down opposite her, regarding her with interest as he drank his own chocolate and ate his own rolls.

"Hello!" he said at length. "Are you all alone too?"

"Hello!" said Faith. "No, I'm with Mamma. But she's asleep."

"Oh!" said the tall boy, and Faith thought it was strange that such a little word could sound so friendly. "Has anyone helped you to get your steamer chair?"

"Perhaps Uncle Nelson got it last night. I don't know."

"Well, when we finish breakfast we'll go up on deck and see. Don't hurry though, we've lots of time."

When the question of the steamer chair had been adjusted, very satisfactorily, thanks to the tall boy—for Uncle Nelson had not, it appeared, remembered about that—they sat down side by side and talked to each other. She told him that she was Faith Marlowe, that she had been named for her grandmother, and that the name came out of the Bible, in a place that her great-grandmother had loved. She quoted the verse to him proudly: "Stand therefore . . . having on the breastplate of righteousness; and your feet shod with the preparation of the gospel of peace; above all, taking the *shield of faith,* wherewith ye shall be able to quench all the fiery darts of the wicked." The boy told her that he was Sam Dudley, that he had not been named for anybody in particular, and that he had never read the Bible much, but that he had won a prize and was going to Paris to study art. Then Faith remembered about the lady called Helen who had been crying in the corridor the night before because her son was leaving her, and guessed that this had been his mother, and that he had felt badly about leaving *her,* and must be lonely too; so she stayed with him all the morning, and they had ten o'clock bouillon, and a walk around the deck, and a game of shuffleboard together; and when the bugle blew for lunch Faith bounded off to get ready, fairly bursting with all the wonderful news that she could tell Mamma.

But Flossie did not wish to listen to it. She was very seasick and very sleepy, and she roused herself only long enough to scold.

"I think instead of enjoying yourself all morning on deck with a strange boy, you might have stayed here and tried to do something for me—shut up in this stuffy little cabin! Whatever possessed Nelson Cummings to let us be shoved off into a hole like this I cannot imagine! I shan't forget it either! If I hadn't spent so much on that suite at the Murray Hill Hotel, so that he would have a comfortable place to sit when he came to call, I shouldn't have had to *mention* economy to him, and I guess he could have arranged something better than this if he had half tried. No, I can't braid your hair or do up your clothes for you. Goodness, can't you see how deathly sick I am?"

Faith went up to luncheon still wearing her mackintosh and sailor hat and feeling dreadfully dirty and disheveled. It made her self-conscious and wretched, and she did not say much when Sam Dudley and *monsieur le docteur* tried to engage her in conversation; and she ate without appetite the oily, highly seasoned food which Jules set in front of her with a flourish. There was a married couple, plump and beady-eyed and prosperous-looking, at the table now, who had two little girls about her own age with them—little girls who wore small dangly earrings, and neat cashmere dresses trimmed with rows of narrow velvet ribbon, and who drank red wine mixed with their water, and picked their teeth after they had finished their luncheon. Faith would have liked to suggest playing with them, and showing them Clarissa and Rose. But they stared at her shyly and wonderingly, as if they were surprised that she should be alone and untidy, and they spoke only to their father and mother, and in French.

Conscience-stricken that she should have neglected Mamma all the morning, Faith returned to the cubbyhole immediately after lunch, and spent the afternoon lying on her own bunk, eating lemon drops, reading "Elsie Dinsmore" and waiting for Flossie to speak to her. It was a terribly long afternoon, interrupted only by Flossie's spasms of sickness, when the stewardess, who kept growing less voluble and more glowery, came in and wiped things up and emptied other things. It had become very rough, and even in the inside cabin, the sound of the waves lashing the side of the boat, and of the wind howling and shrieking was very loud. Faith decided that she would rather go without her supper than face the neat little French girls again in her untidy condition. So she stayed very still and ate more and more lemon drops, hoping that these would keep her from being more hungry; but they did not, and all night long she kept waking up, feeling famished and hollow.

The next morning Flossie was still very sick and the storm was raging even more violently than it had the night before. But Faith had finished both the lemon drops and "Elsie Dinsmore," and she decided that the time had come to adopt desperate measures. She started out in search of Sam Dudley.

He was nowhere to be found. He had told her the number of his cabin, and she looked for him there; but it was tidy and vacant. She looked for him in the crowded salon, filled with miserable passengers in various stages of seasickness, and in the empty *salle à manger*, very formidable with long green baize covers on all the tables. She looked for him in all the corridors, which were permeated with a steamy, oily, dish-watery sort of smell. Then, wrenching open one of the closed doors that led to the flooded decks, she staggered out in the face of a gale which lashed about her and struck at her without mercy. For a moment she was not only bereft of breath but blinded; then beyond the menacing torrent of uncurbed waves and hissing foam she saw her friend standing spellbound in the shelter of a hatchway, impervious to the whirling torrent about him, his face raised in rapt admiration at the savage splendor of the sea.

She called to him before striking out toward him. Her cry roused him from his absorption and he waved to her and gave her a welcoming call in return. Then, startled by a sense of impending danger, he forged his way forward over the sluiced surface that separated them. He was just in time. Faith had been whirled off her feet, and slid across the slippery deck straight into the sucking maw of an onrushing breaker. As it surged back, it bore her violently away with it. Sam, springing swiftly after her, caught her by the cape of her mackintosh just as she was being swept across the shaken railing into the furious turbulent ocean.

Holding her with one arm and shielding her with the other, he dragged her back to the comparative safety of the companionway. From there he had only a little space to cross before he could reach the door leading to the salon. It was only a moment, actually, before he set her down, drenched and dripping, beyond the zone of danger; but it seemed to him like eternity. And appalled at the narrowness of her escape, he spoke, when he managed to speak to her at all, sharply and sternly.

"What do you mean by going out on deck a day like this?" he asked. "Don't you know that it's forbidden?—*Fermez cette porte à clef!*" he added savagely to a terrified-looking steward who had appeared with the tardiness characteristic of his kind in an emergency. "*Voulez vouz laisser noyer cette petite?*"

"You were out there," gulped Faith.

"Good God! I'm trying to be an artist! I was getting a glorious idea for a picture!"

"Well," said Faith, "I had a good reason too. I was trying to find you to ask if you had ever done up back buttons or fixed a little girl's hair."

Sam Dudley stared at her, petrified with astonishment. Faith gathered up courage to go on.

"I haven't been dressed really since I left New York, or had my braids combed out. I can't do it myself, and Mamma is so terribly sick, and the stewardess——"

Seizing her by the shoulders, Sam strode down two flights of stairs and along the narrow corridor leading toward her stateroom. Marthe, the glowering stewardess, happened to be standing in the passage, her arms folded, gossiping with Jacques, the steward who shared her labors. Sam accosted her with the fluency and eloquence which many persons, normally tongue-tied when they attempt to speak a foreign language, achieve when they are angry. Faith could not understand a word he said; but in spite of his pronunciation—the product of a small rural high school in Ohio—Marthe understood him perfectly. She answered him obsequiously, and her manner toward Faith changed suddenly and completely. She led the little girl away to a bathroom, the existence of which Faith had not even guessed before; and while Faith sat soaking in a tub of steaming water, the stewardess went into the dingy little cabin and rummaged through the cowhide trunk until she found fresh underwear and a creased but clean cashmere dress. Returning, she gave vent to exclamations of admiration as she dried the child with a huge shaggy towel.

"Bon dieu, que tu es jolie! Je ne l'avais pas remarqué! Quel peau! Quels yeux! Quels cheveux magnifiques!"

Even though Faith did not know what Marthe was saying, it was easy to get the purport of it. For as Marthe combed out the red-gold curls which hung about the child like a veil of glory, she kept spreading them over her hand as if she loved not only the color but the feeling of them. When she had finished brushing them, they looked as if they had been burnished; and instead of plaiting them in a tight long braid, she left them hanging loose around Faith's head and shoulders. Then, giving her a swift sidelong glance, she smiled as if she were pleased with a sudden thought that she had had and exclaimed, *"Attends! un tout petit moment!"* and whisked out of the bathroom. When she returned, almost immediately, she brought Sam with her; and Sam, for the second time within an hour, exclaimed, "Good God!" as he looked at Faith.

"I am very clean now," said Faith.

"I should think you were! You shine like a statuette made of ivory and copper. Good God!"

"I don't think that is a polite way to keep talking about God," said Faith.

"Listen, kid—would you be cold, do you think, if I wrapped you up—partly—in a blanket—and made a picture of you? It wouldn't take long."

"Without my Ferris waist, or panties, or anything, you mean?"

"Yes, just hair."

"Would you like to?"

"Would I like to? Good G—"

"All right," interrupted Faith.

Sam spoke to Marthe, authoritatively again. It was clear, however, that he was not angry with her any more, but highly pleased; and Marthe had ceased to glower and had recovered her volubility—a smiling expansive sort of volubility. Sam picked Faith up in his arms, and carried her, still enfolded in the shaggy towel, to his cabin; and Marthe, beaming blandly, followed them. Then she took Faith in her lap while Sam dug out paper and pencils and brushes and a big drawing board; and it was she who, two hours later, leaned over and touched him on the shoulder, saying in a voice charged with sympathy, "*Monsieur, la petite est très fatiguée.*"

Sam dropped his tools abruptly. "What a thoughtless brute I am!" he exclaimed. "All in, baby? Well, I can finish alone now. You've been a perfect model in every way.—Here," he went on, pressing something hard and round and shining into Marthe's hand, "take her away and feed her. And keep quiet about this. . . . I don't want all hands and the cook crowing around asking to see the sketches. . . . You too, baby. . . ."

"Yes," said Faith, wearily but exultantly. She was very happy because she had been able to do something to please Sam, who was so kind to her, and because she had made a friend of Marthe, who, she realized, was going to be attentive to her for the rest of the voyage; and because Mamma had been so unresponsive when she tried to confide in her before, she had no particular desire to tell the story of her day's adventures; in fact, she really felt that she would rather hug the unshared memory of them to her heart. She was glad, however, when she returned to the stateroom, clean and clothed, and replete with delicious food, to find Flossie no longer huddled up in a wretched little heap, but reclining gracefully against her pillows, looking amiable and cordial.

"Well, darling, have you been having a nice time? Poor Mamma has been so dreadfully, dreadfully sick, that she hasn't been able to get any enjoyment out of the trip, but she's glad if you have. A ship is so *fascinating!* Oh, there is a storm? *How thrilling!* Well, yes, it seemed rough, but I feel so much better that I haven't minded it . . . and of course, in this horrid little hole I can't *see* anything! I believe I'll try to take a little nourishment, and if I keep it down, I might wash my face and brush my hair and have this bed made. The stewardess has been good to you, hasn't she? Well, of course, I knew you'd have every care, so I haven't worried about you."

The next morning Flossie was so much better that she suffered herself to be supported to her steamer chair, and solicitously enfolded in rugs, though the clear and sparkling weather that succeeded the storm rendered wrapping somewhat superfluous. She smiled dazzlingly on everyone who approached her, and engaged the occupants of adjacent chairs in sprightly conversation. By evening she had already formed a gratifying nucleus of new acquaintances, and within thirty-six hours she was the center of an admiring circle, several members of which, Faith thought, bore a strange general likeness to Uncle Nelson. She was also astonished at the substance of Flossie's remarks, when occasionally she happened to be present during the course of one of the sprightly conversations.

"*She is* pretty sweet, isn't she? Yes, she was eight last December—she is always *so* careful to say she is eight and a half! I suppose I shouldn't agree with you, but I *do* think she is unusually pretty, and she is so intelligent. I feel I *must* give her every advantage, and languages are so important! Senator Marlowe is simply exhausted with the cares and responsibilities of office, so I urged him to take a good long rest at our country estate; but when he recovers of course he will join us in Paris. In fact, though I tell you this confidentially, he is expecting a foreign appointment at any moment, so naturally he must stay within easy reach of the White House, as there is no telling exactly when the President will send for him. Oh, yes, *very* intimate . . . you know his father was in Buchanan's cabinet, and . . . well, I am not sure, but possibly minister to Belgium or Holland . . . either would be acceptable to Senator Marlowe and to me."

Flossie was not greatly interested in Sam Dudley. Faith led him up to meet her mother, immediately after Flossie's first appearance on deck, and Sam sat down, balancing himself more or less precariously on the foot of her steamer chair, and grinned and joked. But Flossie found him unstimulating.

"I can't see why you've taken such a fancy to that great, lanky boy, Faith! He's homely as a hedge fence! I hear that his people are quite ordinary, and that he's never been out of Ohio before in his life, except when he came to New York to compete for this prize that he won. No one on the boat seems to know exactly what it is, so probably it doesn't amount to much anyway. If it had I don't see how an uncouth creature like this could have got it. Of course it's quite all right for you to amuse yourself with him if you want to—he seems to be a good-natured soul—but *I* don't want him under foot."

Faith was delighted at not having to share Sam with her mother. She spent practically all her time with him, and he sketched her for hours on end. Much of this sketching was done in his cabin, and on these occasions Marthe was always a helpful and enthusiastic witness. *Monsieur le docteur* also was let in on the secret, and when he had looked over some of Sam's sketches, he asked for permission to show them to the *commandant*. After that Sam and Faith were both invited up on the bridge, and Sam painted and painted and painted. The *commandant* was very kind, like *monsieur le docteur,* but more jolly, and Faith grew to be almost as fond of him as she was of Sam. Indeed, she would have been entirely happy, if she had not been troubled and puzzled by snatches of talk that drifted to her from time to time, and that seemed without a doubt to refer to Flossie and herself.

"Did you ever see a mother and daughter who looked so much alike and yet seemed so different? Of course it's partly because the child's eyes are brown and the mother's the sort of feline blue that usually goes with red hair, but there's something else—you feel the child's got brains and character and the mother's a gushing little fool. Well, I don't *know* just how harmless—the child talks about her 'Uncle Nelson' who came to see them off, but Flossie Spencer never had a brother. There was a Nelson Cummings who was an old beau of hers though. I used to know her slightly, in Chicago, before she was married, though evidently she's forgotten me. She was a cheap little flirt—no breeding or background whatever, and the Marlowe family felt terribly when Christian married her. She certainly has wrecked her husband's career. There are some things the public simply won't stand for in the wife of a man holding public office—and now I've heard it rumored that she's practically deserted him. Of course she blames him for his failure—yes, she has a little money of her own, not much, but enough to manage with, I guess. Her father was quite a prosperous druggist and she's an only child. . . . I don't believe a word about this talk of an appointment—the President would probably have been glad enough to give one to Christian Marlowe if it hadn't been for Flossie Marlowe, but naturally a man with a wife like that, or separated from his wife, is done for as far as a diplomatic position is concerned."

Faith longed to confide her worries to Sam; but her very anxiety made her reticent. As a matter of fact, she talked to him comparatively little; she was satisfied simply to be with him; and the thought that she would be separated from him when the voyage was over caused her to dread the time of landing. The disembarkment, when it finally came, late one windy evening, was even more horrible than she had feared. Flossie had declined Sam's suggestion that he might be of service in seeing her through the customs, evidently because she was counting upon someone else to do this; but at the crucial moment no one appeared with offers of help, and the confusion and congestion on the wharf at Le Havre were actually terrifying. When Flossie and Faith were finally shoved by a gesticulating blue-bloused porter into a second-class carriage, already overcrowded, the train was beginning to move; and it was not until after he had gone, cursing over the inadequacy of his tip, that Flossie discovered that one of the valises was missing. She seemed to hold Faith responsible for the loss, and railed at her until the little girl was numb with wretchedness, and the other passengers, who all happened to be French, were plainly aghast at her violence. Then whimpering in an effort to secure their sympathy, she leaned back against the stiff, soiled seat, as if so limp with exhaustion she were about to faint. In the dim and flickering light of the compartment they stared at her, with repugnance rather than compassion. Then two of them turned their heads somewhat noticeably away from her, and gazed out of the windows, though it was impossible, in the obscurity, to see anything; two others went to sleep and snored; and two others began an animated conversation on the Dreyfus case, as they ate *croquettes* of *chocolat Meunier* and drippy pears. The train limped and rattled on and on through an unfamiliar and gloomy countryside. It was a dark and desolate journey, unillumined, for Faith, by the thought that a great and glittering city lay at the end of it. She felt that she had lost her only friend, and that she was a stranger in a strange land.

CHAPTER 4

FAITH's first impression of Paris was that it was a city where there was no place to live.

It was past midnight when the boat-train got in, and after a scene in a station which was hardly less noisy and confusing and hideous than the scene on the wharf had been, she found herself wedged between the bags in a strange-shaped hack, the driver of which—portly, surly, and incomprehensible as to speech—kept taking her and Mamma to one hotel after another. When the hack came to a stop, Mamma would get out and go through a lighted doorway which seemed to promise welcome, only to come back after a moment saying that this hotel was full, that there was no room for them in it, and shrilly if incoherently indicating to the *cocher* that he must take them somewhere else. It was two o'clock in the morning before they finally found shelter; and by that time Flossie was muttering angrily words that were almost as incomprehensible to Faith as the *cocher's*.

"To look as though they didn't *want* me in their old hotels! As if I wasn't respectable just because I'm young and pretty and have noticeable hair! I never was so insulted in all my life! I guess they will hear of it from the consulate! I guess the consulate will resent this insolence!"

Faith always longed to ask afterwards what the consulate did to punish the unfriendly hotels; but Flossie never mentioned the matter again, so Faith hesitated to bring it up. The hotel which finally did take them in gave Faith a queer feeling. It was very cold and dingy and bedraggled and it was permeated with a smell of dust and damp, of stale food and bad plumbing. It was on a narrow little side street where long sinister shadows cast a perpetual gloom, and where passersby seemed to slink from corner to corner. She was relieved that they only stayed there a day. Flossie did go, promptly, to the consulate, taking Faith with her, and sending in Christian's card with her own; and presently a pleasant-looking, rather stout, rather shabby, man came out into the gloomy reception room, and said he was Mr. Atkinson, and that he would like to have them come into his private office. Then he told Flossie that his wife would call on her, and set a day for her to bring her little girl to lunch.

Mrs. Atkinson paid her visit that very afternoon. It was plain that she was trying to do her full duty by the wife of an ex-senator. She mentioned Sunday the twentieth, as a possible luncheon date; and she offered to go out with Flossie and Faith then and there to find another place for them to stay—"Because," she said in a curious tone of voice, "of course it is unthinkable that you should remain here. . . . I know a number of very nice *pensions,*" she went on more brightly, "perhaps you would like one of those better than a hotel. Suppose we try the *Pension Lafitte* first of all?"

So thanks to Mrs. Atkinson, Flossie and Faith were installed without further delay in the *Pension Lafitte,* the respectability of which was unquestionable. It was a "good address"; and this address, fortunately for Faith, admitted—though in carefully limited quantities—both sun and air. The room into which she and Flossie were ushered by Mademoiselle Lafitte had three long windows, which opened—if they opened at all,—down their entire length, straight through the middle, by means of an arrangement of iron bars and knobs that were hard to turn; but drafts could be—and usually were—excluded not only by lace curtains and overdraperies of wool tapestry, but also by swinging blinds, which rolled up like rugs at the top of the windows, and came down, with the suddenness of an accordion being let out, if one released the string that was twisted around a hook. Outside the windows was a narrow iron balcony, upon which it was possible to stand, or even to sit, if one placed a small straight-backed chair sideways; and inside, the skillful arrangement of the furniture permitted an ordinary-sized room to be used to advantage both as a parlor and as a chamber. Two narrow beds of dark wood, surmounted by lace spreads and crimson satin *duvets,* stood end to end on one side; and at the foot of one of these, in front of a window, was a huge double washstand. The beds, the washstand, and the night tables were shut off from the rest of the room by two large folding screens; and beyond these screens were an *armoire à glace,* a writing table with a tassled cover, and a sofa and two chairs covered with dark and serviceable material. A gilt clock which did not go, flanked with two coy gilt shepherdesses, surmounted a black marble mantel beneath which a fire was seldom lighted; and on the wall, suspended by green cords, were steel engravings of French battlefields.

Flossie did not seem enthusiastic about the room in the beginning; but somewhat to Faith's surprise, she adapted herself to it and to conditions in the *Pension Lafitte* generally without much complaint and without apparent discomfort. She felt herself a person of importance in the *Pension*, and enjoyed her prestige. She occupied the best room, she had the most clothes, and she shrewdly suspected that she commanded the largest income of any of the *pensionnaires.* Moreover, Flossie having been introduced to the *pension* circle by Mrs. Atkinson, Mademoiselle Lafitte saw to it that this official backing became generally known. The Russian family whose clothes were so threadbare but who wore such handsome jewels and spoke such perfect English; the German Baroness who was so untidy in person and so gluttonous at table; the young Swiss bride and groom who were so primly in love with each other; the Swedish student who was such a misfit at the Sorbonne and so irreproachably courteous—Flossie felt sure that they were all impressed with her, that they were thrilled when she invited them to her room to drink sweet sticky wine and eat bonbons and *petits fours;* that they considered it a privilege to take her shopping and sight-seeing. In the evenings, when everyone gathered together for an hour after dinner in the salon and Mademoiselle Lafitte poured coffee, Flossie regaled an apparently appreciative audience with tales of Washington, of the preëminence in public affairs of the Marlowe family, and of her own intimacy with Mrs. Hillary J. Read, the charming wife of the President. She also told everyone—in confidence—about the expected diplomatic appointment, adding gaily that as soon as she was really settled in the American Legation at The Hague or Brussels—which ever it turned out to be—she should want all her friends who had been so kind to her in Paris to come and visit her. When she was asked to the embassy to lunch she kept referring to the invitation beforehand. "I'm so *sorry* that I can't go to the Louvre with you Wednesday, Baroness von Thurn, but you see I'm lunching with our ambassador and his wife. Well, no, I've never met them personally before, but we have so *many* mutual friends that I feel as if I know them well already—which of course I shall soon." No second invitation from the embassy arrived, except one for the big reception on the Fourth of July, to which all Americans were asked; but Flossie explained this to herself as well as to her fellow boarders by the fact that the Montgomerys went away early that season to their château on the Loire, and were in Paris only "off and on" after early May. Mrs. Atkinson continued to do her duty; she came from Salem, Massachusetts, and she always would do her duty, even in Paris. So Flossie, lacking the embassy, made much of the consulate in conversation, and by autumn she had succeeded in dismissing the Montgomerys from her mind almost as completely as they had dismissed her from theirs. There was really no ripple in her self-satisfaction. It was the little girl, actually, who minded much more than her mother the perpetual veal, the boiled skim milk, the pulpy prunes and pale blancmanges at the *Pension Lafitte*. She thirsted in vain for ice water, and hungered for Aunt Emmeline's home-made bread. She never had the sense of being wholly clean, washing always from a china bowl and never in a tub. She felt perpetually cramped and crowded in the confines of one close room, after the spaciousness of the house on Lafayette Square, and the one at the beloved farm. She missed her father unutterably, and aching for him as she did, she found no solace in the society of the *pensionnaires*, though they made much of her, for she was the only child in the pallid place. At the day school which Mrs. Atkinson had recommended, and in which Flossie had entered her without delay, she found no joyous companions, as she had in the friendly kindergarten to which she had gone in Washington. The little French girls with their black aprons and pierced ears were very polite to her; but they were aliens and she was a stranger in their midst. There were no rollicking recesses, no jolly games, no gymnastics with the windows flung wide open. She shared no whispered confidences and exchanged no small notes and gifts with the child who sat at the desk next to hers. She was never taken home boisterously, to share pot-luck at a family luncheon, or even invited to a child's party. Her teachers were kind and competent; she was taught thoroughly and with meticulous care, and she learned a great deal in an incredibly short time; before long she was chattering French without even being conscious that she had mastered it. But her fluency did not seem to make her any less a foreigner in spirit as well as in fact than she had been before she acquired it.

After she had gone to bed at night she lay, very still and straight under the red satin *duvet*, with Clarissa on one side of her and Rose on the other, counting over the days of the week on her fingers. "Monday, Tuesday, Wednesday—three days to Thursday," or, "Tuesday, Wednesday—two days to Thursday," or, "Wednesday—one day to Thursday!" Then after Thursday she did the same thing with Friday, Saturday and Sunday. This was not primarily because Thursday and Sunday were holidays; she did not actually dislike her school; indeed, she rather missed it during the brief summer vacation, when Flossie, who believed in alternately scrimping and splurging, "blew in" the money she had saved in the course of a three-month sojourn at the *Pension Lafitte* on a hasty "tour" of the Châteaux district, Normandy, Brittany, Provence, the French Alps, and the French Riviera, dragging Faith along with her from castle to mountaintop and from cathedral to casino. The little girl's mental horizon became so blurred, and her small body so weary during the course of this rushing about, that she was actually glad when Flossie, having spent all her surplus, returned to the *Pension Lafitte* for another period of economy and thrust Faith back into school again, tired of having her "everlastingly under foot." On the whole Faith thought school the lesser of two evils, if she must choose between that and a "tour." But she looked forward to Thursdays and Sundays because she saw Sam Dudley on those days. With no coöperation from Flossie, and as a result of considerable perseverance, Sam had discovered that she and Faith were staying at the *Pension Lafitte;* and having obtained Flossie's careless consent to this program, he came regularly as clockwork to take the little girl out with him regarding it as a matter of course that she would carry at least one of her dolls with her, and that she would need to retie the streamers of the wide hat she wore, which fastened under her chin, every block or so, while he stood patiently by, holding Clarissa or Rose, as the case might be. It was thanks to Sam that Faith made the discovery that the main characteristics of Paris were not noisy stations, or unfriendly hotels, or prim *pensions* or strange schools. She discovered that there were Punch and Judy shows in the Champs-Élysées and balloon-men in the Place de la Concorde, row boats in the Bois de Boulogne and push carts laden with daffodils and violets in the Place Vendôme, a toy shop called *Le Nain Bleu* on the Rue Saint Honoré and *pâtisseries* at almost every corner. She discovered that there was an Eiffel Tower to climb, and arcades to walk under, and merry-go-rounds to ride. But Sam, though he revealed all these delights to her, took it for granted that she would also derive enjoyment from the same pursuits and investigations that he enjoyed himself. It never occurred to him—as indeed there was no reason why it should—that she would not be happy if he elected to spend an entire afternoon sauntering along beside the bookstalls on the *Rive Gauche* or standing absorbed before the jewel-like windows of the *Sainte Chapelle.* He took her to see the Gobelin tapestries woven, to see the fountains playing in the gardens at Versailles, to see the lights of all Paris twinkling beneath the *Sacré Cœur* at Montmartre, to see "Ruy Blas" at the Comédie Française, and to hear midnight mass sung on Christmas Eve at the Madeleine. He kept her sitting for hours on end before Giorgione's "Concert" and Leonardo's "Mona Lisa." She came to know the Louvre as well as she had known the old house on Lafayette Square and to love every corner of it; she came to love the third balcony in the Opera House and the gorgeous performances enacted beyond the glittering chandelier; she came to love the forest of Fontainebleau, and the fussy little boats that plied up and down the Seine. But best of all, she came to love Sam's studio—a great messy, friendly room in a ramshackle old house with a stone courtyard, situated in the shabbiest part of the students' quarter. Sam cooked and ate and slept and painted all in this one room; and often boon companions of his who lived in similar studios, drifted in casually to cook and eat and sleep and paint with him. It was a terribly untidy place, and where it did not look cluttered it looked threadbare; but it was permeated with the warmth of good fellowship, and youthful enthusiasm and youthful hope. There were glowing colors on the smeared canvases that stood haphazardly about, a fire always smoldering on the unswept hearth, an abundance of coarse, hot food dished up bountifully at frequent if irregular intervals. There was even a great, fluffy, friendly cat, which sang like a tea kettle, and sat with its paws folded away beneath it, blinking and motionless for hours together. More than once, when Sam, who had no clock and whose watch seemed perpetually out of repair, guessed, by the gathering twilight, that it must be time for him to take Faith back to the *Pension Lafitte*, she pled with him to let her stay.

"Just to-night, Sam. I could leave early in the morning and still get to school on time. It's raining outdoors and it's so lovely and warm here. I promise I wouldn't be any bother."

"Gosh, Faith, I'd like to have you. But little girls don't belong in the Latin Quarter, except just for visits."

"Velasquez is asleep. I don't think it would be very kind to take him out of my lap and wake him up." Velasquez was the fluffy cat.

"Well, I must see if I can take him out of your lap *without* waking him up then."

These arguments grew more and more frequent. At last they began to prey upon Sam's mind.

"Look here, Faith, if you're going to fuss about going back to the *pension* every time I bring you here, I'll have to *stop* bringing you, that's all."

"Couldn't you stop taking me back instead? Couldn't you let me stay here all the time?"

She climbed up into his lap and pressed her face against his.

"You could teach me to cook," she urged. "And I can dust. It would really be a good thing if someone dusted here. Nobody does now, and Ella showed me how at home. I took care of the doll-house and the piano legs myself. I could be very helpful to you. I am sure if I had been here to help, you would have had a picture in the *Salon* this spring. You know how disappointed you were because you didn't. If I stayed you could paint me whenever you felt like it and by and by the *Salon* would take a picture of me."

"Don't you know bribery is a crime?" asked Sam, running his fingers through her hair.

"Yes," said Faith confusedly, "what is a crime?"

"Sometimes it's hard to tell exactly," admitted Sam. He drew out her curls to their full length, bunched them up, drew them out again. "Wouldn't you be sorry to leave your Mamma?" he asked at last.

"Not very," replied Faith promptly. "Not really sorry, the way I was to leave Daddy."

"Does Senator Marlowe write you letters?"

"Oh, yes. From the farm. There are six new calves. And a little colt. And the mowing has just begun. There will be hay-rides." Her lips quivered.

"You could ask Mrs. Marlowe to send you back, Faith."

"No, I can't. Daddy didn't want to take me to the farm. I asked him."

"Then he must have wanted you to stay with your mother, Faith. And she would feel badly if you went away from her."

"I think she mostly wanted to take me away from Daddy. Because he was a failure. But she is so busy, really, she wouldn't miss me. She is busy now all the time with Mr. Lindstrom. Even busier than in the winter."

Sam winced a little. "Isn't Mr. Lindstrom going back to Sweden this summer?" he asked slowly. "The courses at the Sorbonne must be almost over for the summer."

"They are over. So he and Mamma have lots of time to spend together."

Sam winced again, harder this time. Then he set Faith on her feet, and got up, stretching his long legs.

"Come on," he said, "I'm not saying I'll ask your Mamma to let you stay here with me. But I *would* like to talk to her a little while to-night. And maybe——"

He never finished the sentence. He was very silent all the time they were on their way back to the *pension*, in the bus. Then when Sophie, the *bonne*, opened the door for them, she looked at them strangely, as if there were something the matter; and almost immediately they heard Flossie's voice, shrill and furious, piercing the stale air.

"You evil-minded, vulgar, old prude! Insinuating such things just because I was *kind* to a poor lonely boy, slaving away in a strange country! What if the door *was* locked? What if it *has* been locked before? If you weren't snooping and spying around at keyholes how would you *know* whether it was locked or not? Oh, the other boarders have complained, have they? Slandering me behind my back when I thought they were my friends! Well, you wouldn't have needed to ask me to leave! I'd have gone anyway just as soon as I could get my trunks packed. I've been planning for quite a while to take a complete tour of Switzerland, and then go to Dresden for the winter. I guess I realize I owe it to Faith, to give her a chance to learn German. I have the address of a *Pension Schneider* that is *really* select! And just you try to collect one cent of money from me and see what happens to you. I'll sue *you!* And I'll see that the consulate knows of this! You've told Mrs. Atkinson already that you were going to speak to me and she *approved* of it?

Well, I guess *she'll* get an earful from the White House. When her smug husband's been sent to Mongolia or some such place I guess she will wish she had done a little less approving! I never was so insulted in all my life!"

Faith clutched Sam's hand tightly, raising imploring eyes to his. She knew, without taking another step forward, that when they reached the closely curtained, carefully screened room that she and Flossie had occupied for so many months, she would find Mademoiselle Lafitte looking dignified and final, and Flossie looking disheveled and outraged, and Mr. Lindstrom standing mutely by, saying nothing and hanging his head. Then presently her mother's two big trunks, the box-shaped one and the dome-shaped one, and her own little trunk covered with cowhide would be trundled in, and she would be packing quietly and miserably while Flossie flew about tossing mountains of ruffled dresses and plumed hats and soiled negligees into heaped-up piles. She turned to Sam with one last appeal.

"Dear, darling Sam," she begged, "can't you save me this time too—the way you did on the boat?"

She heard Sam swallowing. She thought for one blessed moment, that perhaps he was going to take her back to the studio after all. But after the swallow came something that was like a laugh, only it wasn't much like it after all; it sounded so unhappy and so helpless.

"No, Faith, I can't this time," he said, "there isn't anything I can do. I haven't any money, or any influence—or—or anything—I'm only twenty-one myself. And anyway, little girls have to stay with their mothers."

He swallowed again, and tried to go on, speaking words of comfort and reassurance. Instead, he strangled, stifling the agonized exclamation that fought for utterance.

"I guess, perhaps, it would have been better if I had let you drown!"

PART II

Rudolf

CHAPTER 5

THE casual onlooker might have supposed the tall fair young man sitting alone beside one of the little iron tables in front of Florian's to be English. He had the well-knit slenderness, the clear bright complexion, and the complete poise of manner which are generally—and rightly—regarded as attributes of British youth and British breeding. But the more experienced observer would have noticed that he was not typically English after all: His perfectly cut clothes were too closely molded to his wide-shouldered, slim-waisted figure, his hair and eyes—unsubdued by any tinge of brown and gray—were both a shade too striking for that. So such a shrewd observer would have proceeded to guess, and guess correctly, that he was an exemplary product of German aristocracy, whose military and scholastic training were only recently behind him, and who had been sent out to see something of the world before embarking on the career which had been carefully chosen for him.

He shifted the strap of the field glasses, which, enclosed in a beautifully polished leather case, was slung over his shoulder; straightened the position of the costly camera which he had set down in front of him; and took a tentative sip of a glass of beer which he had ordered. Then disdainfully, though calmly, he set it aside. It was already evident to him that there was no beer worthy of the name in Italy, although he had been there only twenty-four hours, and he was slightly impatient with himself for having ordered it more than once. And yet, what else should he order, at four o'clock on a summer afternoon? Coffee? It was too warm for that! An ice? Insipid and ridiculous refreshment for a vigorous male creature! A heady whisky and soda, or a sweet sticky *Strega*? He was content to leave the first to the Scotchman and the second to the Venetian! Unless he could get a real beverage—bitter and brown and clear and icy-cold, and crested with foam like the top of a wave—it would be almost better to go thirsty. He pulled a pipe out of his pocket, tapped it lightly against the sharp rim of the table, filled it with swift, expert fingers, and began to smoke.

A band which was stationed near the café and to which most of its patrons were listening with evident enjoyment, was playing trivial, tinkling arias of obvious melody; multitudes of iridescent, pampered pigeons fluttered and crowded obtrusively about; beyond the piazza the gorgeous intricate façade of San Marco glittered in the afternoon sun. The traveler, too well bred to be unintelligently critical, could not entirely suppress a pang of homesickness. It seemed futile to him to leave the land of Wagnerian music, of isolated, castle-crowned crags rising above laden vineyards, of restrained Gothic architecture, in order to hear Rigoletto, and scatter crumbs for pigeons, and gaze at gold mosaic. He sat looking at San Marco and thinking about the Cologne cathedral. From time to time, allowing both his vision and his thoughts to be diverted, he regarded the occupants of a table near his with an absorption which was saved from being a stare only by the skill with which he tempered it. He was quite evidently wondering whether he might venture to go over and speak to them.

The same question had been forcing itself upon his attention, intermittently but insistently, ever since his arrival in Venice the day before. When he had presented himself at the reception desk of the Hotel Superbo he had found the manager in a state of volubility exceeded only by his incoherence. At first this functionary had persisted in speaking only Italian, of which the traveler did not understand a syllable; and having been politely, but firmly, persuaded that they might find a common medium of speech in French, German, or English, whichever he preferred, the manager shrugged his shoulders, spread his hands and rolled his eyes. The *signor* was quite sure that he had written for reservations? The letter did not seem to be anywhere about! The manager fluttered a sheaf of papers back and forth on his desk with an air of increasing helplessness. Oh, the *signor* had *wired*, also? Well, wires . . . the manager's manner seemed intended to convey the impression that no telegraphic communication had ever been known to reach its destination. Still perfectly courteous and perfectly self-controlled, the young German was swinging on his heel and signaling to a porter to gather up his hand baggage, when a young girl, accompanied by an uncompromising-looking, middle-aged woman, who had also approached the manager's desk, addressed herself to that plenipotentiary with surprising effectiveness. The eye-rolling and hand-spreading ceased abruptly; there was a final shrug, but it was one of resignation rather than of protestation. The girl, having finished, in Italian, what she had to say to the manager, began to speak in unfaltering, correct, and idiomatic German.

"It is unfortunate that you should find the mails and telegraph system so unreliable in Italy," she remarked, with a suspicion of a smile, "someone really ought to speak to the Minister of Communications. . . . So much depends on first impressions . . . and in Germany everything is so efficiently organized and run! It would be too bad if a really important, influential German had cause for complaint! . . . I have just been reminding the *signor* director," she went on more gravely, "that there is a very good room available, overlooking the Canal. It was reserved for a friend of ours, who expected to arrive to-day from Paris. But a wire has come in—yes it really came in quite promptly and safely—saying that he had been detained, that he wouldn't be here for at least a week. Apparently the *signor* director forgot about this cancellation. I am sure you will like the room—we looked it over ourselves because we wanted to be certain our friend would be pleased. There isn't much furniture in it, but it has an arched ceiling, and the mural decorations are simply superb."

She had disappeared, with a swift, friendly smile, before her beneficiary had completed the deep, formal bow with which he had accepted her intervention, before he had been able to achieve a graceful phrase expressing his gratitude. He was conducted, without further delay, to the room so providentially untenanted; and though he was not given to facile and spontaneous mirth, he laughed, as he shaved and bathed and changed, at the brief and vivid accuracy with which the young girl had described the somewhat overpowering apartment in which he found himself. An enormous bed, carefully shrouded in mosquito netting, dominated its vacant surroundings; for the rest, the room contained an inadequate wardrobe and still more inadequate washstand, a chilly-looking table with a mosaic top, and two very stiff straight-backed gold chairs. The lighting fixtures, made of the same twisted and tinted Venetian glass with which the numerous mirrors were framed, were placed at an elevation which would preclude any practical use of them; the elaborate and unrelieved parquetry of the floor shone with a glacial glitter; the walls, which appeared to be at least thirty feet high, were intersected by numerous doors, which were evidently supposed to be invisible, as the "mural decorations" were painted over them without interruption of design and subject, and there were only narrow slits in the surface of the plaster and unobtrusive door knobs to indicate their presence; while the vaulted dome which surmounted all this splendor was embellished with a fresco representing the ascension of a solid and satisfied-looking saint surrounded with phalanxes of plump pink cherubs.

Suddenly conscious that he would be late for the *table d'hôte* luncheon, and also that he was amazingly hungry, the young German descended to the dining room and fell upon the excellent *hors d'œuvres* that were placed before him with zest and thoroughness. It was not until he had devoured several substantial courses, not until he had scoured a heaped-up plate of *ravioli* clean, and washed down the *ravioli* with red *Lacrima Cristi*, that he began to look about him with appreciative interest. It was, indeed, very late; the dining room was almost empty; but near the window, at some distance from where he was placed, the young girl who had so efficiently rescued him sat eating figs and almonds with healthful appetite and enjoyment, while the angular middle-aged lady who was with her tentatively fingered a peach that apparently did not really tempt her much.

Discreetly, he allowed his gaze to wander from one to the other. There was not the slightest resemblance between them; if there was relationship, he felt it must be very distant. Possibly the middle-aged lady was a *dame de compagnie,* though for some reason which he could not quite define he thought this doubtful. Her dress was as severe as her manner, and wholly lacking in elegance or distinction. She was colorless, correct, negative; but she was not negligible; she was unmistakably a gentlewoman. The girl was very different. Her face was shaded by a large black hat; it was impossible to see her features clearly. But underneath the hat there was a glimpse of gorgeous red-gold hair which was not wholly concealed, a glimpse of lambent skin. Her sheer black dress was simplicity itself; but it was exquisitely smart, and it revealed a lovely, graceful young throat and figure. There was something about her that he seemed to recognize, something vaguely familiar. Was it possible that he had met her? Certainly that seemed unlikely, for it was unthinkable that he could have forgotten so arresting a personality. Yet the impression that this was not the first time he had seen her persisted.

He was still trying to crystallize this impression when she passed him on her way out of the dining room. There was not even the suggestion of a pause as she went by his table; but she said "*Mahlzeit*" and smiled again, with that same friendly, illusive smile which seemed to reveal so much human comprehension and sympathy, and which had so intrigued him as she stood speaking to him by the director's desk. Now it was slowly beginning to dawn on him that his failure to find Venice charming was based upon his failure to meet this charming girl. It was with this realization, and the need for thought preparatory to action which it entailed, that he had sat down beside one of Florian's insecure little painted iron tables and ordered beer; and it was with the consciousness that he was still unprepared to meet this situation adequately that he continued to hesitate, smoking, and watching the attractive young creature who was now so conveniently near him, and who this time had given no sign that she was aware of his proximity.

At last he could stand it no longer. He extinguished his pipe, placed two small silver coins beside the beer which he had spurned, and picked up his camera. Then he rose, his hat in his hand, and walked over to the adjacent table. He clicked his heels together, and bowed both to the radiant girl and to the severe-looking middle-aged lady; then he addressed the latter.

"May I venture to present myself, *Gnädige Frau?*" he asked in German, since this was the language in which the girl had spoken to him the morning before and he still felt uncertain as to her nationality. "My name is Rudolf von Hohenlohe, and I so greatly wish to thank the *Gnädiges Fräulein* for her pleasant and powerful intervention in my behalf yesterday." He bowed again and waited.

It was the girl who answered. "Mrs. Atkinson doesn't speak German," she said serenely, "but you speak English. I heard you trying it out, among other tongues, on our plausible but hypocritical director yesterday. He knew perfectly well that he had room for you, but he would have loved to brag all over Venice that his hotel was so crowded he was turning away even *noblessa.* Of course he saw the coronet on your baggage!"

"Perhaps," said Rudolf von Hohenlohe, rather formally. He bowed once more, and repeated the statement he had just made to Mrs. Atkinson, in English this time, with a Teutonic accent and Teutonic precision, but with complete grammatical accuracy. To his immense relief, the lady, though she regarded him with swift appraisal, appeared neither resentful at his intrusion nor critical of his temerity. She answered with less acidity than he had expected.

"I know Faith was very glad that she could help you," she replied, reservedly but agreeably, "and I am glad too. It is unpleasant to arrive alone in a strange place, and to find oneself without a habitation. I have had such an experience more than once myself. . . . Is this your first visit to Venice?"

"Yes, *Gnädige Frau.* My first experience in Italy in fact."

"Isn't it wonderful?" broke in the girl. "Don't you love to see the yellow sails at sunset and the moon coming up behind Santa Maria de la Salute? Don't you love the little arched bridges over the side canals that look like kittens with their backs up? Don't you love the big quiet stone *campos?* Don't you love the boats that anchor down where the Canal Grande and the Canal della Giudecca come into each other, with musicians on board who play and sing anything you like, for a few *soldi,* if you stop your gondola beside them and choose? Have you been through the Doges' Palace and the Accademia? Have you seen Titian's Ascension of the Virgin? Have you gone over to the Lido for a swim? Have you——"

"Remember that Baron von Hohenlohe arrived only yesterday, Faith," remarked Mrs. Atkinson, "and that he is not an American tourist. . . . My husband, John Atkinson of Salem, was in our consular service for many years," she went on, turning to Rudolf with something surprisingly like a twinkle in her eye, "and we had a good deal of experience with our compatriots who expected to see all Europe thoroughly in a week or so. Since you probably intend to proceed in a more leisurely manner, won't you sit down and have an ice with us? I am sure Faith intends to eat at least two before we go back to the hotel. Her capacity for ices is almost as great as her capacity for sight-seeing!"

Rudolf von Hohenlohe disposed of his camera, and this time of his field glasses as well, by unstrapping them and placing them on the pavement beside him. He forgot, or at least disregarded, his antipathy toward ices; and he was somehow unstartled by an intuitive feeling that Mrs. Atkinson had anticipated his desire to meet Faith and had been prepared to cope competently with his overtures toward acquaintance whenever he made these. Her next words, however, revealed a foundation more solid than any for which he had ventured to hope upon which to build a friendship.

"My husband was stationed in St. Petersburg some time ago," she said casually. "I remember that the German ambassador there, whom we had the honor of knowing rather well, was a Baron Rudolf von Hohenlohe. Possibly he was a relative of yours?"

"He was my uncle, my father's younger brother. I was named for him!" exclaimed the young man, with greater enthusiasm than he had ever before disclosed in speaking of his godfather, for whom he had hitherto always felt a rather tepid affection. Now he saw this uncle in a new light, as a liaison officer of priceless value between himself and Faith. He was "placed" already, as far as Mrs. Atkinson was concerned; and the fact that his position was, so to speak, ready-made for him, would save both time and trouble, though he would have been entirely willing to take a good deal of both to establish himself in her eyes. He only wished that he was equally enlightened concerning Faith's identity; but the discerning lady seemed to know what was passing in his mind.

"If you have no one here with you in Venice, perhaps it would be pleasant for you to join us sometimes," she went on. "Faith speaks such excellent Italian that it is a great advantage. She went to school for two years in Florence, but this is her first visit to Venice, and she is all enthusiasm. She and I are both alone in the world, so we have joined forces. We have invented a sort of cousinship. It is a happy arrangement for both of us. Her father was the late Senator Marlowe, of whom you have possibly heard, if you have ever been interested in following the course of American politics."

Rudolf inclined his head gravely. He had never heard of the late Senator Marlowe and he had never been interested in following the course of American politics, as he felt sure that Mrs. Atkinson was well aware. But he recognized the simplicity and skill with which she had made Faith's identity, and her own connection with Faith clear to him. Details could come later, and he felt confident that all in good time these would also be revealed in a satisfactory manner.

"Of course you have letters to the German consul here?" Mrs. Atkinson inquired. "He is a very eminent scholar—one of the greatest authorities in the world, I believe, on Byzantine art."

"That's probably the reason Baron von Hohenlohe hasn't delivered his letters," broke in Faith. "You haven't, have you? You've been *dreading* to see it with an eminent Byzantine scholar! You wanted to see it with someone young and amusing!" Suddenly she pushed back her third ice, half consumed, and rose, impetuously. Her sheer black dress obscured the radiance of her vitality and youth no more effectually than a sheath of black tissue paper could obscure the splendor of a *Gloire de Dijon* rose. Her wide black hat had somehow ceased to shade her face. It was revealed laughing, lambent, lovely, as Rudolf had guessed it to be at luncheon the day before. His first full view of it now showed it to be even more vibrant, even more enchanting than he had divined.

A little forking flame suddenly seemed to leap from his heart and to creep, darting and quivering, through every nerve of his body, as Faith went on speaking. He had never felt anything like it before.

"Well, you *shall.* You and I are going to see it together. Aren't we, Cousin Sarah?"

"I shouldn't be at all surprised," said Mrs. Atkinson dryly.

CHAPTER 6

"But, Good God, I've come all the way from Paris to do those things with her myself!"

Sam Dudley shook back the long lock of sandy hair that always hung limply over his forehead. The gesture was not, in itself, a savage one; nevertheless he seemed to invest it with a certain ferocity; and he spoke not only fiercely but bitterly.

"I know, Sam. If you had only arrived when you first planned to——"

"Yes,—if I had only turned down a five thousand dollar commission from a Youngstown magnate with a letter of introduction from the governor of Ohio—damn his smug smirking face!"

"Sam!" expostulated Mrs. Atkinson mildly.

"Sorry, Cousin Sarah . . . but you know yourself, darned well, that I needed the money. I needed it badly. And I was thinking not only of this five thousand dollars, but of all the other five thousand dollars that might result from it. . . . 'My friend, Mr. Josiah H. Seabury of Youngstown, Ohio, has shown me the portrait recently painted by you which hangs behind the mantel in his back parlor, and with which he and his daughter, Mrs. Elmer R. Todd, are both eminently satisfied. It has occurred to me that you might paint a picture of my wife that I would like equally well. I am expecting to take my first trip to Europe this summer, accompanied by Mrs. Grimes, and upon receipt of a favorable reply from you, we will call at your studio immediately after our arrival in Paris and arrange for sittings. There will be no difficulty about the financial arrangements. I may say in passing that I am the inventor of the Grimes solid porcelain bathtubs and lavatories now being installed extensively all over the United States. Very truly yours, Alonzo B. Grimes'. . . . Can't you see the letter, Cousin Sarah, and flocks more like it?"

"Yes," admitted Mrs. Atkinson with a slight smile. "Did Mr. Seabury buy anything besides his portrait?"

"He's offered me a small fortune for 'Mary of Nazareth,'" said Sam abruptly, "he's a very devout Catholic, and he wants to give it to a convent in memory of a younger daughter who died and who had intended to become a nun. I am thinking over his offer. . . . I've let all the other pictures go. . . . I rather hoped to keep the 'Mary.' I know it's the best thing I've done. But painters have to eat and pay rent just like other people, and they rather enjoy shoving a little into the bank for—for the future." He broke off suddenly. "I worked like hell to polish off Josiah H. Seabury in short order. After all, I'm only a fortnight later than I said I'd be."

"A good deal can happen in a fortnight sometimes," said Mrs. Atkinson quietly.

"Well, suppose you tell me just how much *has* happened," snapped out Sam, with a little of his former ferocity. "I get to Venice, expecting of course that Faith will meet me at the station, and she doesn't because —as you explained, having come alone—she's gone over to the Lido for a swim with a Baron von Hohenlohe——"

"Not alone," interjected Mrs. Atkinson hastily. "The American consul's wife, Mrs. Saunders, and their daughter Harriet, a very nice girl who goes to Vassar——"

"Oh, yes!" exclaimed Sam sarcastically, "I can just imagine how much Baron von Hohenlohe would notice the very nice girl who goes to Vassar when Faith was along! Well, anyway, next I arrive at the hotel and get shoved off into a little gloomy back room, and when I complain the mechanical boy-doll who calls himself a manager informs me that the room he *meant* to give me has been turned over to the Baron von Hohenlohe at the *signorina's* request; and that he himself doesn't like to dispossess so important a member of the *haute noblesse* for a mere artist, or words to that effect—set to music and motion, you know. That man's eyes and shoulders must work with springs! And finally I sit down for a quiet cup of tea with you, and you begin, with the manner of leading up tactfully to some very dark and disagreeable disclosure, to tell me you are *so glad* that dear Faith, after all the hideous experiences the poor child has had, is beginning to forget, and to enjoy herself . . . and apparently the sole source of her forgetfulness and cause of her enjoyment is a tow-headed German off on the loose! I bet his coloring is more brilliant than his intellect. I thought Faith had more sense! And . . . if you'll excuse me for saying so! . . . I thought you did!"

Mrs. Atkinson set down her cooling cup of tea on the mosaic top table beside her. "My dear Sam," she said quietly, "I must ask you to be more accurate in your remarks. Rudolf von Hohenlohe may not have brilliance. I am willing to admit the possibility. But he has breeding, which is better, and he looks something like a viking god—tailored and trained and educated, of course, but still with the unmistakable air of a young Siegfried. He's quite as magnificent in his appearance—though in a different way of course—as Faith is herself. I can understand perfectly why she should have been attracted to him immediately. But nothing could have been more respectful and more correct than his behavior—which is not surprising, considering his traditions and upbringing. He belongs to one of the greatest families in Germany."

"I didn't know there *were* any great families in Germany," said Sam gloomily.

"Well, your ignorance is appalling then," retorted Mrs. Atkinson with unaccustomed heat. "If Faith should marry into such a family as that——"

"Marry! Good God, the child's hardly out of short dresses! Has this cradle-snatcher started in talking about marriage already?"

"I don't think he has to Faith. In fact I am reasonably sure of it. But he has to me. He's asked me if I would be willing to have him address her, providing he could obtain his family's approval and consent—and he intimated that he was going to cut his vacation short in order to go home and confer with his family——"

"So you told him you *would* be willing?"

"I—Sam, don't glare at me like that! I told him I thought Faith was too young. But he more or less wrung the admission from me that I didn't object to him personally. And I don't. I . . . I think he's rather nice. Wait until you see him yourself, Sam!"

"Oh, I'm perfectly crazy to see him!" exclaimed Sam brutally. "And I'd like to know just how much you've told this young Siegfried about Faith—about her mother, rather. I've always understood that god-like dynasties had rather an aversion to family skeletons."

"Flossie Marlowe is dead, Sam," said Mrs. Atkinson quietly. "If she were not, I admit that the situation would present serious complications. As it is, I do not believe they are insurmountable. I have made no effort to deceive Rudolf von Hohenlohe. I have answered every question that he has asked me. Indeed, I have forestalled some that I thought he might ask me. I have told him that Faith is an orphan. I have told him that her parents separated when she was eight years old, and that since then she has never been back to the United States. I have told him that

Flossie Marlowe was a vain, selfish, and silly woman, fond of admiration and given to—coquetry. I think I have made him realize, to a certain degree, what Faith's life was like for seven years—that she led a neglected existence in a succession of drab *pensions,* while her mother amused herself, and that the monotony of the years was broken only by hasty and superficial 'tours' embarked upon whenever her mother decided that she herself must have a change. I did not say that this decision was sometimes made for her. I did not tell him—just how Flossie died. I must, of course, eventually—I or some other friend of Faith's. It would not be fair—either to him or to Faith—to leave him uninformed indefinitely. Meanwhile I think, that without having had Flossie Marlowe forced into the foreground of his consciousness, he has been made perfectly well aware how greatly Faith must have suffered. And that Faith should have suffered seems to him so lamentable that he feels doubly anxious to assure her a future of unclouded happiness."

Sam did not answer. Mrs. Atkinson paused for a moment, as if gathering her forces, and then went on.

"I have told Rudolf von Hohenlohe," she said, "that I happened to be in Vienna when Flossie Marlowe died there, and that as Faith was left entirely alone at the time, and as I had known and loved her when she was a child, I asked her to stay with me, at least temporarily. I told him that I was a childless widow and that Faith had grown very dear to me—as dear as any daughter of my own could possibly have been. I told him that she would eventually inherit my little competency. I also told him of Faith's legacy from her father."

Again Sam did not answer, and again Mrs. Atkinson went on after a slight pause. "Since Flossie and Christian Marlowe are both dead," she remarked, "I see no harm in emphasizing the more desirable parent of the two. The fact that Flossie died, as she had lived, selfishly and sensationally, leaving an innocent young girl crushed and unprotected, need never loom as large on Rudolf von Hohenlohe's horizon as the fact that Christian Marlowe, a former senator of the United States, and the son of a distinguished member of Buchanan's cabinet, bequeathed to his daughter not only an honorable name, but a considerable fortune. Of course he should have had the will power and initiative to take Faith away from Flossie. But when I think of that lonely man assembling the rare books and documents he had inherited, and disposing of them cautiously and advantageously, so that he might provide for Faith's future I am almost inclined to forgive his weakness. It all seems so pitiful!—I believe the house on Lafayette Square brought in only enough to pay his debts and I do not suppose the farm is worth much, though Faith has a great deal of sentiment about it. She has been—or rather *had* been—planning to go back to the United States and spend next summer there. But those first editions of Poe and Hawthorne! Those

Lincoln letters! Those paintings by Stuart and Copley!—and Christian didn't sell them all! He managed to save out enough so that Faith would not be entirely deprived of heirlooms! And besides, she has a certain income of ten thousand dollars a year, with the principal held in trust, so that it can never be squandered, as Flossie squandered her own money, or 'misappropriated'—that is the euphemistic term, isn't it?—as Nelson Cummings 'misappropriated' it for her!"

"Do you think the Wagnerian hero would want to live on his wife's money?"

"Of course not, Sam! You are perfectly absurd! But I think the fact that Faith has a dowry will enhance her desirability in the eyes of his family, less because the money would be helpful than because her possession of it would meet their standards of the fitness of things. A German *Braut* never goes to her husband empty-handed. And the money undoubtedly *would* be helpful. There are five children in all to be provided for—the two elder sons are officers in the army and that always means a large outlay—and one of the daughters is already engaged. I imagine that Rudolf will have to practice some economy in taking up that post in Madrid to which he has just been appointed—young diplomats, like young artists, have to eat and pay rent, remember!"

Sam grunted. His ferocity had quite obviously begun to subside. Mrs. Atkinson, recognizing that she no longer had explosiveness with which to deal, permitted herself to enlarge upon another aspect of the situation.

"You haven't seen Faith in a long time," she reminded him. "You'll be surprised at the change in her. She was such a serious, silent child! And then, after her mother's death, she was so tragically mute that I lived in constant terror that something would snap inside of her, that she would have a complete nervous breakdown. If she hadn't possessed wonderful strength of character and something more than that—a real reserve of spiritual fortitude on which to draw, some sort of inner exaltation—she would have, of course. Remember her finding Flossie as she did——"

"I try not to remember it. I'd rather not be reminded of it," said Sam with a return of savageness.

"I know . . . and when she finally discovered that she could turn to me with confidence she began to—unfold. Very slowly, certainly. But it happened. Almost like a flower. At first the only difference was that she was less withdrawn, less self-protective and reserved. Then gradually I realized that she had succeeded—in partly forgetting. That she had begun to be happy—for the first time in her life—with me."

"Look here," said Sam, with sudden gentleness, "don't you go getting the idea I don't understand all you've done for Faith. You—you saved her."

"She saved herself, Sam. But I *was there.* Thank God! And, after that she began to be happy, to eat and sleep and think normally again. Then just recently the unfolding ceased to be gradual. It came with a rush. Of course she is at the most formative period of her life. And now, Sam, there's beginning to be something radiant about her. She's—she's joyous! And oh, Sam, she's the loveliest thing to look at you ever saw!"

Sam cleared his throat. "I don't doubt it," he said, still gently, but with a slight tinge of sarcasm, "which makes me all the more receptive to the idea of seeing her myself. When had she intended to come back from the Lido? Because she's had time, practically, to swim the Adriatic since I arrived, and still there isn't the slightest sign of her. I have no doubt that the consul's wife and the nice Vassar girl are perfect chaperones, and the high-born viking so correct that he wouldn't touch Faith by tying up her shoe string if it came undone, and all that, but it's nearly eight o'clock. And I got in at half-past two. If you don't mind, I think I'll wade over to the Lido myself and see if I can find her. . . . Anything I can do for you before I go?"

He reached for the electric switch. A pale, apologetic gleam emanated from the fanciful lighting fixtures, sending a faint illumination over the stiff, little twilit salon. But before he could put his purpose of departure into effect, the painted doorway was suddenly flung open and slammed shut; and Faith, a swift blur of gray and gold, rushed across the parquet flooring.

"Darling Sam!" she cried, throwing her arms around his neck. "Oh, I *am* so glad to see you! How wonderful you look! How wonderful that *you're here!* How's Velasquez? Have you moved to the new studio? Did you get millions out of the magnate man? I know you put a terrible *steely* look into his portrait! Has he taken it away from Paris already? I hope not because I'm crazy to see it. I did feel dreadfully not to meet you at the station, Sam, and to be so long getting here. We'll make up for it to-morrow. But your wire came late, and Mrs. Saunders and Harriet couldn't seem to change their plan at the last moment, and go another day instead, and Rudolf and I had planned on the swim—and oh, I forgot—Sam, this is my new friend, Rudolf von Hohenlohe."

Sam had caught the girl to him with a hungry hug. Now, deliberately, he extricated himself from their mutual embrace, set her gently aside, and stepped forward. As he did so, his eyes met those of a very tall, very fair young man, who stood erectly and proudly, but unobtrusively, beside the painted doorway which Faith had flung open and slammed shut—eyes in the clear blue depths of which even Sam's searching glance could unfathom nothing but sincerity and steadfastness.

CHAPTER 7

THE afternoon had not been one of unclouded happiness for Rudolf von Hohenlohe.

This, he admitted to himself, was not Faith's fault. Faith had seemed even more entrancing than ever, from the moment when she met him in the reception hall of the hotel, dressed in trim gray flannel, her bathing suit folded into a compact, smart little gray bag, to the moment when the expedition ended at the door of Mrs. Atkinson's salon. And certainly it had not been Mrs. Saunders' fault or Harriet's. Mrs. Saunders had been up very late the night before, and had betrayed her agreeably somnolent state even before they had all left the little steamer that chugged along between the Schiavoni and the Lido; and went sound asleep before she had been settled five minutes on the silver sands. While Harriet had decided at the last moment that she did not care to swim, that she would rather sit beside her mother and read the book on Comparative Philosophy which she had been "meaning to get to" all summer and which she had brought along with her. So when Faith stepped from the Stabilimento dei Bagni, and put her hand in Rudolf's and waded out into the shallow water beside him before they took the final plunge into the breakers, he had her all to himself. And *Gott in Himmel*, but she was glorious!

He was still tingling with unaccustomed rapture when at last they strode, still side by side and hand in hand out of the water again and sank down, weary but invigorated, upon the beach. Mrs. Saunders continued to sleep profoundly. Harriet's absorption in her book had not abated. No other bathers were very near them. To all intents and purposes, Rudolf still had Faith entirely to himself.

"Someone ought to paint you as Lorelei," he said, watching the movement of her arms as she lifted them and ran her fingers back and forth through her hair, shaking it out and spreading it over her shoulders to dry.

"'*Die schönste Jungfrau sitzet*
Auf oben wunderbar—
Ihr goldnes Geschmeide blitzet
Sie kammt ihr goldnes Haar!'"

he sang in a remarkably good tenor. "Or else as Aphrodite, rising from the sea foam," he added, thinking of Faith's lovely emergence from the crested wave.

"Of course!" she exclaimed enthusiastically, "just as Botticelli painted 'La Bella Simonetta'—Aphrodite, I mean, not Lorelei," she continued hastily, "but Lorelei would be good, too. I must speak to Sam about it. He'll be awfully grateful for the suggestion. It will make up to him for not meeting him—I can't help feeling so guilty," she went on, "about not meeting Sam."

"Sam?" asked Rudolf, honestly puzzled and startled. To be sure, Faith had mentioned that she was expecting a visit from a friend, but this had escaped Rudolf's memory; and he had entirely forgotten the friend's name, and had never heard the nature of his profession.

"Yes. I told you about Sam Dudley. He is my very best and oldest friend. Even better and older than Cousin Sarah."

"You mean that he is an elderly gentleman?" asked Rudolf hopefully.

"No-o-o. Not so very elderly. He's about thirty. But he's very well preserved. When I said he was my oldest friend, though, I meant he had been my friend *longer* than anyone else."

"I see," said Rudolf less hopefully, "and he is a painter?"

"Yes. He is getting to be quite well known. Not famous, you know, but recognized."

"*So,*" said Rudolf politely, but without evident pleasure, "and just what is it that he paints?"

"Well, he does some marine pictures. The first one of his that got into the *Salon* was called 'A Storm at Sea.' I liked it because I saw the storm myself. I was nearly drowned in it. Sam and I were on the same boat, and I went to look for him on deck, and a big wave almost swept me overboard. Sam saved me. So I have a personal interest in that picture. But it was very badly hung and the critics didn't particularly praise it. So mostly Sam paints me. The reason your idea about Aphrodite was so *especially* good, was because it would be a marine picture and a picture of me too!—The first time Sam really had a *succes fou* at the *Salon*—got a prize you know and all that—was with a painting he named 'Young Eve.' It was sold, afterwards, to a very rich and noble Austrian."

Something clicked quickly in Rudolf's brain. So *that* was it—the feeling that had persisted ever since he had first seen Faith that he had met her before! Of course! "Young Eve!" The prize picture of the Archduke Stefan's modern collection! Stefan had given a magnificent dinner after it had arrived in Vienna, to celebrate its arrival and to show it to all his friends! Rudolf had been at the dinner himself! He never would forget his first view of the painting, hung, for just that evening, before being taken into the art gallery, on the crimson brocade wall of the state dining room: the picture of an exquisite child, the color of her rosy flesh emerging with a shell-like smoothness and firmness from the gloom of a sylvan background, the serpent hardly more than a curving shadow behind her white feet, her dark eyes luminous with still unfulfilled promise, her wistful mouth innocently provocative, her hair falling like radiant rain over her bare shoulders. . . . Rudolf suddenly felt as if he had been shot. The "Young Eve"—Faith!

"Did—did you pose for that picture?" he asked, quickly and involuntarily.

"Of course. I have posed for all of them. I was in Paris the first year Sam was there, you see. And since then he has spent his vacation wherever I happened to be. I posed for 'Suzanna,' and 'Lady Godiva,' and I posed last year for 'Mary of Nazareth.' That is the best one of all. It has taken a gold medal at three expositions. Sam hasn't sold it yet. The noble Austrian wants that too, but Sam says he can't bear to part with it—that it represents so much. It is the Madonna, you know, when she was very young—before the annunciation."

The Madonna before the annunciation! Again Rudolf felt that swift stinging pain. For Stefan, fulminating against the stubborn genius who had created it and would not sell it, had dragged him to admire it at the loan exposition in Munich where it occupied the place of honor. And Rudolf had stood spellbound before the slender, white-robed figure of grace and chastity, recognizing that it was delineated with an understanding and a tenderness with which he had never seen it interpreted before. The Holy Child was hardly a dream, as yet, to this future Mother, no prophetic vision of Calvary had risen before her tranquil gaze. She stood, with the slim halo curving above the sheer veil that framed her heart-shaped face and fell softly over her shoulders, half-concealing, half-revealing her shining hair and budding breast: virginity incarnate.

Rudolf tore his mind clear from the impression that he was still looking at the picture, and moistened his lips. "You—you posed for that also?" he inquired at length.

"Yes . . . a year ago last May—the month of Mary. We were at Lourdes. We hadn't decided yet what this year's subject should be . . . it's especially hard when the 'Mary' has been such a success—it would be dreadful to follow it with a failure! And now you give us this wonderful idea of Aphrodite!"

Rudolf made a great effort. "I have been trying to think, ever since I first saw you here, where I had seen you before," he said slowly. "Now I know. 'The noble Austrian' is a cousin of mine. He is the Archduke Stefan. I saw the 'Eve' at his house. And he took me to see the 'Mary' in Munich. He greatly desires to possess it."

"Oh, but you won't mind, will you, if Sam won't let him have it? Because I don't believe——"

"No," said Rudolf still speaking very slowly, "I shan't mind."

"Rudolf!" cried Faith with intuitive alarm. "You mind *something!* What is it? Didn't—didn't you like Sam's pictures?"

"They are great works of art," said Rudolf with reluctant reverence. "You have inspired a genius to rare creation, *liebe* Faith. But I must be sincere with you. I am happy about the 'Mary.' But I am not so happy about the 'Eve.'"

"Well," said Faith with relief, "of course, when Sam painted that he wasn't half the artist he is now—all the critics say he's made tremendous strides. Probably you'll be happier about all his future pictures, Aphrodite, for instance."

"It is unthinkable that he should paint you as Aphrodite!" exclaimed Rudolf with vehemence.

Faith felt baffled. She decided to change the subject, which she realized was unwelcome without in the least understanding why. "Don't you think," she asked finally, "that we have talked about Sam enough for a while anyway? Don't you think we might talk—about something else?"

"I think," said Rudolf hesitatingly and painfully, "that we must not talk about anything else just now—that we must arouse the estimable *Frau* Saunders and interrupt *Fräulein* Harriet's progress in philosophy. *Es tut mir leid, Liebchen,* but it is time that we should go back to Venice."

. . . . .

There was, as Sam had seen in that first searching glance, nothing but sincerity and steadfastness, courage and beauty and honor in Rudolf von Hohenlohe's deep blue eyes. And when, very much later in the evening, he turned regretfully away from his little balcony and crossed his small room to answer a knock at his door, to find himself confronted again with the same steadfast look that had, at one and the same time, reassured him and sent him into the depths of despair, there were no reservations in the greeting he gave to their possessor.

"Why, come right along in!" he said cordially, "I thought you'd have hit the hay hours ago. I was outside baying the moon—like the proverbial hound, you know. I'm afraid I didn't hear you when you first knocked."

"If I do not intrude, I must a little with you talk," said Rudolf von Hohenlohe very earnestly.

They had been together with Faith and Mrs. Atkinson all through dinner and the early evening. This was the first time that Sam had heard the German speak unidiomatically. He pricked up his ears. Something must have happened to shake Rudolf's Teutonic poise, and the strain of it was beginning to tell upon him.

"Sure!" he said easily. "Smoke? Drink? I wish I could offer you something to sit on beside these alleged chairs. I think they must have come out of the Doges' torture chamber. But they're all I have."

"You must at once permit yourself into your own apartment to be moved," went on Rudolf, almost as if he had not heard. "I have the manager my opinion of him told."

"Wish I'd been there to hear it," replied Sam, grinning cheerfully, "but really, I'm all right here—more comfortable than I'd be with your mural decorations. Faith described them to me. I'm supposed to be an artist, you know, and I really feel they'd be more than I could bear."

"But I must insist. I must a point of it make."

"Why, of course, if you feel that way about it. . . . But you don't want me to move to-night, do you? My traps are all thrown around, and——"

"The morning will do," conceded Rudolf, "I must to-morrow leave in any case. I must at once my family see."

"Yes?" said Sam still speaking easily, "nothing wrong, I hope?"

"It is that I must permission ask to marry Faith."

The words were out. Sam braced himself to meet them. "If there's the slightest chance that Faith will have you," he said as quietly as he could, "with or without your family's consent, you're so rotten lucky that——"

"She will have me," said Rudolf very gravely. There was a moment of tense silence. Then his words came with a rush. "It is not as you must think. I did not importune her. I know she is very young. And, moreover, I wished to pay her the tribute of giving her the same formal courtship that I would have given to a German maiden. But last night as we stood together on the balcony looking out at the water, and the moon, and the palaces, and listening to the sounds of the waves lapping against the stones, it was all so beautiful that suddenly I was overcome. I knelt at her feet. I laid my face against her white dress. I kissed her hand. She did not repulse me. And when at last I rose and looked at her, I knew that she was responsive to my feeling, though no word had been spoken between us. And knowing, how can I in honor wait to speak?"

"You can't," said Sam simply.

He was terribly moved. All the time that Rudolf had been speaking, Sam had felt the blur of unshed tears against his eyelids. And now that Rudolf stood silent before him, waiting for his verdict, he knew what it must be. Characteristically, he endeavored to hide an emotion quite as genuine as that which Rudolf had revealed.

"And as long as you're sure she loves you," he asked, almost testily, "what in hell's worrying you?"

"It is that my family may not consent."

"Well, tell your family to——"

"*Mein Freund*, you do not understand. It is because of this that I give you my confidence, that I ask your help. It is impossible that I should marry without my family's consent."

"You mean that it wouldn't be legal?"

"Legal, yes, that. But I could be stripped of rank, fortune, career."

"Well, good God, wouldn't Faith be worth it to you? Because if she wouldn't——"

"To me, yes. *Tausend Mal.* It is only that I fear, by and by, that I might not be worth it to Faith. She has said to me that you are her oldest and best friend. You know her well, much better than I. Therefore I have come to ask you, if in your opinion, it would."

Again Sam felt that bitter blur of tears against his eyes. More and more he wished, dully, that Rudolf von Hohenlohe would not force him to greater and greater respect.

"Mrs. Atkinson has disclosed to me Faith's so unhappy childhood," Rudolf went on, "therefore doubly have I wished that as my *Braut* she might have joy. Is she not too proud to be completely happy if in her breast there is the thought that her husband's family has not welcomed her, that she has cost him his position, his future?"

"But why *shouldn't* your family welcome her? Why should she cost you your position and your future? Just the opposite, I should think! She's a girl in a million!"

"That is true, but my family may not so see it; and it is not only with my family that I shall have to reckon. The foreign minister sometimes declines to permit junior diplomats to marry, because this is not in accord with his policy, unless the marriage is most suitable. And Faith has to-day told me," said Rudolf laboriously, "that—she posed to you for the 'Young Eve' which hangs in my cousin Stefan's art gallery. It is not presumable that my family and the foreign minister will feel that an artist's model should become the wife of a von Hohenlohe."

There was another tense silence. This time it was Sam who broke it.

"Not even," he said, trying to control his sudden fury, "if the model for 'Young Eve' was eight years old when she posed for it? Not even if the same model, when she was fifteen, inspired the 'Mary of Nazareth' which your exalted cousin would sell an ancestral castle to get? Not even though the man who painted both those pictures has built his whole world around that model for eight years?—By all means go and tell your family—and the foreign minister—that Faith Marlowe is my model," he went on, his anger gathering force in spite of his efforts to check it, "that she is the inspiration for everything I have ever done or been! That but for her I should still be a gawky, provincial fumbler! That but for you I might still hope that some day she would be my wife."

"*Mein Freund!* I must beg you to believe that I meant no disparagement of Faith! And that I did not guess——"

"Oh, no!" Sam raged on. "You did not guess! There are a hell of a lot of things you have not guessed! The Archduke Stefan is your cousin, is he? Then is your mother by chance an Austrian by birth? The Archduchess Victoria Luise? Was her first husband an Austrian too? Did she have a son by that marriage who was an officer in the Austrian army?"

"Yes," said Rudolf quickly. "Yes, that is all so. But what then?"

"An officer who committed suicide," Sam shouted, now entirely beside himself, "after killing his mistress because he found another man in her room at midnight? And went off leaving her lying there dead, for her child to find hours later, in a pool of blood? Oh, yes, I know there was a revolver in her hand, that the verdict was brought in for double suicide! But Flossie Spencer never would have had the guts to shoot herself! She was a rotten coward, just as she was a rotten quitter! Her husband made her give up his name when he divorced her for desertion—as he could have divorced her a dozen times for worse than that! But the woman you knew as Flossie Spencer was Faith Marlowe's *mother!* Go tell your family that! And at the same time tell Faith that your brother was her mother's murderer—and then find out, and be damned to you, whether you can get *her* to take *you!*"

PART III

Victoria Luise

CHAPTER 8

SAM DUDLEY was too healthy and normal a man to be subject to either futile introspection or to vain regrets. Nevertheless, he spent the months that elapsed between his arrival in Venice and his departure for the Straits of Magellan—where he eventually painted the greatest of all his marine pictures—remorsefully contrasting his own clumsiness and violence with the constancy of Faith, the steadfastness of Rudolf von Hohenlohe, and the finesse of the Archduchess Victoria Luise.

It was in vain that he argued with himself that sooner or later—sooner *better* than later—Rudolf and Faith would both have been bound to discover and forced to face the sordid and hideous tragedy which at one and the same time linked and divided them. That *he* should have been the one to reveal the blood-stained intrigue which formed the background of their romance, because he resented the possibility of an injustice to Faith and because he had been defrauded of his own heart's desire—this thought was bitter bread upon which to feed perpetually. It would have been better—far better—to starve.

The projectile which he had hurled at Rudolf von Hohenlohe recoiled against Sam almost instantaneously. For Rudolf, having already braced himself against shot, was, in measure, prepared against shell. And the first words that he spoke were charged, not with concern for himself, but with compassion for Faith.

"*Das arme holde Madchen!*" he cried with horror-stricken emotion.

"I ought to be drawn and quartered!" groaned Sam. Rudolf advanced and laid a firm arm around his shoulder.

"Let us try to steady each other a little, *nicht wahr?*" he said in a voice that was already under control and that was wholly untainted by hostility. "I have stepped in and robbed you of a treasure which you hoped to possess—that I feel sure you deserve to possess. This has been to you a great shock. I must be sincere and say that even if I had known you loved Faith, I should have tried to win her. Because I love her also. But I did not mean to steal. For this I must ask your forgiveness. Also if I have been indelicate of language in speaking of Faith as your model. And *mein Freund*, you have done right to tell me what you have. With a little less suddenness, if that had been possible, but perhaps it was not. And it is always better to face facts—when there are ugly facts to consider, it is not only better, it is necessary. That is one of my mother's maxims. And my mother is a very sagacious lady."

Sam, fumbling toward self-mastery, was aware that the German had already assumed command of the situation. There was no indication of either defeat or despair on his face, though its look of untested youth had been swept away from it.

"At present we can consider the situation from every angle at once," Rudolf went on earnestly, "instead of incompletely, as it would have been considered, if I had returned to Germany without knowing what you have just told me. Afterwards, even if matters had been once adjusted, further readjustment, of very painful character, would still have been necessary. Now perhaps, when I go to Germany, it may be without any story to tell, without any permission to ask; it may be with finality, not to return. As you have pointed out, Faith would be justified in declining to marry me, when she learns that my half-brother was her mother's lover. In the morning we must tell her—not to-night, for she is already sleeping peacefully. But to-morrow, *so bald wie möglich*—as soon as possible . . . we will of course inform *Frau* Atkinson that she may be prepared to give both counsel and comfort to Faith."

"Well, and what about you?" burst out Sam with involuntary admiration.

Rudolf von Hohenlohe did not even wince. "But, *mein Freund*, there can be no question of me," he replied steadily. "Even if it had been my own brother Hans—my father's eldest son whom I love with my very soul—instead of my half-brother Otto, for whom I must confess I cherished no love at all, whose ghost stood between me and Faith, can you suppose that I would hesitate? You who have known her so long? *Nein, Tausend Mal.* The first part of the decision lies with Faith. We must speak to her, we must give her time to consider . . . when, having considered, if by a miracle she finds that she does not abhor the thought of me, I must go to my mother. For I think the second part of the decision must lie with her. If by a second miracle, she finds that she does not abhor the thought of Faith, we must bring them together. With as little strain, with as little design, as possible. My mother, if she consents to the meeting, will know how to arrange it. She is a very great lady."

In the light of subsequent events, Sam discovered that he concurred completely with Rudolf's high estimate of the Archduchess Victoria Luise. A woman like her had never before come within the range of his limited vision. He had gone straight from a side street in Jonesville, Ohio, and his classmates at the Jonesville High School, to the Latin

Quarter in Paris with its haphazard, hearty *camaraderie*. Though he had occasionally come into brief professional contact with personages of note, as in the case of Archduke Stefan, the characteristics of a "very great lady" and her *milieu* were as unfamiliar to him as those of an Eskimo inhabitant of Greenland. And the acquaintance of one was now to be forced upon him. What Rudolf and Faith had said to each other, the morning after Sam's arrival in Venice, he never knew exactly; for the first time in years, Faith did not turn to him with overflowing confidences. But he knew that she had declined to let her mother's ghost stand between her and Rudolf with as little hesitation as Rudolf had declined to let his brother's ghost stand between Faith and himself. For immediately after the conference Rudolf took a train for Germany, still looking white and stricken, but still completely composed; and within three days, Faith also looking white and stricken, but also completely composed, showed Sam a telegram saying that Rudolf would return the following afternoon accompanied by his mother.

Sam dreaded the descent of the Archduchess upon Venice with unspeakable apprehension; he visualized her as being stupid, opinionated, and heavy both mentally and physically; he felt sure she would extinguish the still unflickering flame of trustfulness which burned in Faith's breast; that she would snub and slight Sarah Atkinson; and that she would give him the impression that she regarded him as an insignificant artisan of a doubtful personal cleanliness. It did not matter much, of course, what she thought of him; but it mattered a good deal how she treated Sarah Atkinson; while upon her attitude toward Faith, all creation, just then, seemed to hinge. . . .

He recognized, that in spite of his worst forebodings, it devolved upon him to meet the Archduchess and her son at the station. Certainly it would not be suitable for Faith to go; and certainly it was unthinkable that Faith should be left behind alone while Mrs. Atkinson accompanied him. He therefore set off by himself on his errand of grim greetings; but at the station he found what appeared to be a delegation of welcome: the German consul and the Austrian consul, both of whom he knew by sight, were standing on the platform conversing agreeably with an imposing-looking ecclesiastic in gorgeous raiment whom Sam rightly guessed to be a bishop at the very least; and close beside them had forgathered a sizable group of personages whom he labeled mentally as "eminent citizens," and who—he was forced to admit to himself—looked very eminent indeed. As the train swung into sight, they hurriedly clustered around the steps of a private car, emblazoned with coronets, which was attached to the rear; and when two men servants in livery, a very trim maid carrying an enormous jewel box, and a discreetly dressed young woman with a distinctly secretarial air, had alighted and had placed themselves in positions ready to render immediate service, a pale, slender, dark-eyed lady of infinite elegance and distinction glided out upon the platform at the side of Rudolf von Hohenlohe.

Her appearance was the occasion of immediate acclamation. Such an expression of enthusiasm and admiration would, Sam reflected, have been accompanied in Jonesville by the strains of the local brass band and a speech by the mayor. Here the method was different, but the general effect was much the same. Sam, a stranger to all these dignitaries, felt forlornly superfluous. He endeavored to slip inconspicuously away. But before he could make good his escape, he was conscious of the striking nearness of Rudolf von Hohenlohe and the fascinating gaze of the lovely lady.

"This is the famous American painter, Samuel Dudley, *Mütterchen*," Rudolf was saying, "my great friend, of whom I have told thee." And the slim gloved hand which the consuls and the "eminent citizens" had all been kissing with such rapturous respect was extended in Sam's direction, accompanied by a glance of melting charm. Sam had never kissed a lady's hand in his life. But he did so now, discovering, with swift surprise, that it was a fairly simple act productive of a remarkable amount of pleasure. Before an instant had elapsed, the Archduchess, with adroit facility, had contrived to include him in her circle, to make him feel at ease and acquainted. Then he realized that with the gracious acceptance of an invitation here and there, but with the smiling statement that she preferred to remain *incognita* because she was taking a little holiday with her son, most of the dignitaries were being courteously dismissed; and when the Archduchess was actually installed in her waiting gondola, Sam further discovered that he was among the favored few from whom she had not separated herself. And three hours later, after she had rested, he found himself seated beside her at the perfect dinner that was being expertly served in the salon of an imposing suite which the hypocritical manager had discovered to be providentially vacant, the moment he had heard of the impending arrival in Venice of the Archduchess Victoria Luise.

No, decidedly, Sam considered, sipping his iced Asti, after his warmed Burgundy, he had never dreamed that "very great ladies," dowered like this one with such suavity, such tactful charm, such exquisite urbanity, really existed. He had thought of them—when he thought of them at all—as the product of the flighty brain of the "dime novelist"; and he visualized them, moreover, as vain and vapid, unredeemed by either intellectual or moral stamina. But the Archduchess, sitting at the head of the flower-banked table, was a vital as well as a distinguished figure. Her dark hair was piled high above her regal head; her pearls glistened against her delicate skin; her lace dress, folded softly away from her sloping shoulders, fell in filmy ripples on either side of her slim waist. And she was, Sam realized, neither vapid nor vain. She was very beautiful and very clever; she was also very kind. They were all immeasurably better off because she had joined them. He looked across the table at Faith, and suddenly, in his heart, rose an inarticulate prayer that God would bless Victoria Luise. For Faith was gazing at Rudolf's mother with an expression that revealed her serene consciousness that in relying upon this great and wise lady to help her she had not been mistaken, and that in trusting her future to those slim, jeweled, skillful hands she was secure against betrayal.

Victoria Luise, gathering up a large black lace fan and a small white lace handkerchief was signaling to her son, with a smile, that she was ready to leave the table. As she rose, she turned to Sam with an air of interpreting and granting unexpressed wishes. "I am sure that you and Rudolf will wish to confer a little without the supervision of ladies," she said lightly. "I shall then take Mrs. Atkinson and Faith with me to my boudoir to confer a little without the supervision of gentlemen. And as I am the least trifle fatigued after my journey, shall we say *auf wiedersehn* until to-morrow morning? I am depending that then you shall show me the most beautiful vistas of Venice!" Again she had given him her finger tips; again finding it the easy and natural thing to do, he had kissed them. Rudolf also had kissed her hand; then she had raised her dark head and he had bent his blond one, and she had kissed his brow, murmuring, *"Gute Nacht, lieber Sohn—schlaf schön!"* before, with a rhythmic, undulating grace she left the room, Mrs. Atkinson striding solemnly beside her, Faith guided by the pressure of an encircling arm.

For a time, across the current of Rudolf's reassuring words, Sam could hear their three voices from the room beyond; then, after an interval, he realized that he was hearing only two voices. Mrs. Atkinson had gone. Faith was alone with Victoria Luise. In the course of the next hour, every essential of her life would be decided. Not the details of course. But everything that really mattered. He flung down the cigarette which he had lighted from the one he had smoked before that, and rose abruptly.

"Look here," he muttered with embarrassed vehemence, "I'm going to my room. I simply can't sit here talking to you while I know that Faith's in there with your mother. I guess I feel about the same way I would if I'd taken her to be examined by a doctor—even if it was the best doctor in the world—and was outside in the waiting room looking at humorous magazines six months old and all dog-eared, while I wondered how much she was being hurt and watched the clock until the doctor came out to tell me either that she was all right or had got to have a major operation. Of course if I'd had your training I could have stuck it out and talked about the weather, or the Greek tragedians, or trigonometry. You take scandals and suicides and murders and matrimony all in your stride, without showing how you feel about it, because you've been taught how. But I haven't. Good God, they don't breed or raise men like you in Jonesville, Ohio, or in the Latin Quarter! But even then you don't hold a candle to your mother. I'd bet my bottom dollar on her. When everything is all over but the shouting, and Faith has told me what's what, I'll come back and shake hands with you. And I've got a hunch that after that I'll want to get down on my four paws and lap the blacking off the Archduchess Victoria Luise's shoes."

CHAPTER 9

Victoria Luise's great, frescoed bedroom was fragrant with massed flowers and lighted with tall candles. Where the slim, multitudinous tapers which had supplemented the inadequate but glaring bulbs of electricity, with their little, candy-colored twisted glass shades, had come from, was a mystery—nothing of the sort had been supplied to any of the other guests at the Hotel Superbo. The source of the luxurious *chaise longue,* banked with small, lace-covered cushions upon which Victoria Luise lay extended, was also a mystery. But there it was. All the rigid little gilt chairs had disappeared as if by magic, and in their stead, besides the *chaise longue,* were several low, comfortable *fauteuils,* in one of which, her hands pressed rather closely together, but her manner completely composed, Faith sat facing the Archduchess. Autographed pictures, in large silver frames, of the members of various princely families, had been scattered about; there was a small basket of luscious fruit on the bedside table; there was even a cheerful fire burning beneath the austere mantel. In the course of a few hours, the stiff, bare room had been transfigured. For the first time, Faith realized how completely the personality of a woman may dominate her habitation; and looking backward, almost subconsciously, remembered that Flossie's room had always been cluttered, musty and permeated with stale scent; while Sarah Atkinson's room always seemed to bear the evidence of recent scrubbing, meticulous order, and slight chilliness.

The sound of Victoria Luise's soft voice recalled her to her immediate surroundings.

"So now that we are comfortable, and alone, we may talk together, may we not, *liebes Kind?*" the Archduchess was asking, gently. "We have so much to say to each other, you and I, that it seemed better not to wait, even until to-morrow, to begin. Or so it has seemed to me. Do you feel as I do?"

"Yes," said Faith quietly.

"And shall we begin by discussing those subjects which are hardest to mention? Then we shall not have the thought of them, the dread of them, constantly before us. We may dismiss them from our minds. At least, I believe we may, if we both try very hard to see clearly and think clearly. And I know I can depend on you to do so."

"I will try," said Faith, still very quietly.

"I know you will, *liebes Kind.* And so shall I. And because we will both try, we shall probably succeed. It is generally thus. To show you how hard I am willing to try, I am going to make a confession to you, and then I am going to ask you a question, which I hope you can bring yourself to answer. Come closer to me, Faith, and put your hand in mine. *So!* That will steady us."

Her slim, jeweled fingers, surprisingly strong, closed securely over Faith's warm, little hand. With their pressure, Faith's sense of stability deepened. She waited, without impatience or fear, for Victoria Luise to go on.

"I did not love my son, Otto, who killed your mother," the Archduchess said in a low voice which did not tremble. "He was an uncontrolled, vicious, and violent man. From boyhood—almost from babyhood—he showed traits of weakness and wickedness which wrung my heart. His death was a shock to me, a source of shame and scandal. But it was not a sorrow. Within a few weeks after it happened, I knew that it was a relief—a release. I have shown respect for death, even though I could not respect the dead. I have worn mourning, I have lived in seclusion, I have been silent. I have faced this stark and sordid tragedy with my head held high. But this has not been as hard for me as has been supposed, because I have not really grieved. I have never admitted to anyone before, not even to my husband, or to my children, what I have admitted to you. But it is true. This is my confession. I make it now because I believe it is your due. And having made it, I ask my question: Did you love your mother?"

"No," said Faith, drawing a long breath.

"She also made you very unhappy? After you had recovered from the horror of her murder—for I know it was that, not suicide—after the good *Frau* Atkinson had befriended you, your life became tranquil and lovely for the first time, did it not?"

"Yes," said Faith, drawing another long breath.

"Then should we, you and I, permit the shadow of this dreadful double death to darken our lives? Are we not both strong enough to go—hand in hand as we are now—out into the sunshine together?"

"Yes," cried Faith convulsively.

Suddenly, vehemently, she had begun to weep, with an abandonment which would have betrayed, even to a far less wise and compassionate woman than Victoria Luise, the fact that these were the first tears she had shed since she had faced the revelation of Otto's identity. Victoria Luise bent over her, and clasped the girl in her arms, drawing the bright, bowed head against her breast. For a long time, holding her so, gently, steadily, she did not speak. It was only when the deep, agonizing sobs had begun to spend themselves that she commenced, caressingly, to murmur words of comfort and endearment.

"We have passed it, *Liebchen*," she whispered, "that dangerous and difficult place in the road—that menace to our purpose together. We shall never need to turn back and look at it again. Forget that it ever existed, as I shall. For if we forget, you and I, the world will also forget. The world recalls only what the individual is so weak as to remember."

There was a long silence. Faith felt a final kiss of reassurance brushing her brow, a soft, fine, cool handkerchief slipped into her hand. Victoria Luise was freeing the girl gently from the embrace that had enfolded her.

"There is a carafe of water near the fruit at my bedside," she said gently, "go and pour yourself out a little, *liebe* Faith, and drink it, and bring me some also, if you will be so kind. And on my dressing table there is powder in a glass jar. We will feel better if we dust a little over our faces and straighten our hair. You shall hold a little swinging mirror for me, and then I will hold it for you. The woman who permits her emotions, of whatever sort, to disfigure her, even temporarily, wages a losing battle with life."

Beneath the seemingly simple restoratives Faith sensed the poise and breeding which prompted their offer. Victoria Luise was right: the time of tragedy, the time of tenseness, the time of abandonment had passed. Spontaneously, Faith settled herself on the foot of the *chaise longue*, brushing aside the violet draperies to make room for herself. Spontaneously, she reached out to take Victoria Luise's hand again of her own accord. The Archduchess smiled.

"You are not too tired, *liebes Kind*, to talk a little more?"

"I want to," said Faith impetuously. "I want to talk about another difficult thing. The thing that troubles Rudolf so much."

"You mean your relation to Sam?"

"My relation?" asked Faith in amazement. "Sam and I are not related! We are friends."

"I used the wrong word," said the Archduchess, quietly. "Purposely," she added after a moment, as if compelled to candor, "as a test."

"I don't understand," said Faith with growing bewilderment.

"I see that you do not, *liebes Kind*. But it is that which I had to find out, even at the risk of wounding you again. And since you do not understand—well, we have passed another obstacle. Suppose you take my word for it that this is so, and do not ask me to explain too much to-night, when it is growing late, and when we have both, already, been *très emotionées*. Suppose you trust me to talk to Rudolf on that point later on, telling you only, now, that you have nothing to dread on this score and venturing only one suggestion: that you should not, at least for the present, pose to Sam for the 'Aphrodite'. That you should persuade him, rather, to give Rudolf the 'Mary of Nazareth' that my son may place it where his eyes can rest on it constantly, and his thoughts dwell on all that it so exquisitely reveals."

She rose and walked over to the open window, resting her white arm on the deep embrasure and gazing reflectively out toward the quiet canal. When she spoke again it was with the manner of one whose thoughts were finding undirected release in speech, rather than as if she were addressing anyone.

"Is narrow-mindedness not a greater sin than unchastity, and prudery even worse than immodesty? *Sicherlich, Sicherlich!* And since this dear child has been guilty of no sin at all, surely I am strong enough to shield her from slinking scandalmongers."

She turned, and sitting down in one of the two great armchairs that stood on either side of a carved table, motioned to Faith to take the other.

"Let us now be most practical," she said earnestly, holding herself very erect. "You are extremely pretty, unusually intelligent, adequately educated and moderately wealthy. Your command of languages is remarkable and would be a real advantage if you should marry a diplomat. So would your little income, which, from what Rudolf has told me, is large enough to dress you suitably and still leave you enough over to take care of your other personal expenditures—your charities, your gifts, the wages of your own maid, perhaps even the upkeep of your carriage. This would be most helpful to Rudolf. He is a younger brother, as of course you know, and ours is not a wealthy family, though it is a very old one."

Faith, who in spite of a natural and youthful nonchalance about money matters had rather gathered from Mrs. Atkinson that an income of ten thousand dollars a year was sufficiently substantial to enable an entire family to live comfortably, even if not luxuriously, was amused that it could be regarded so casually. She said so, quite frankly. "But of course," she added, "I should like to use it in any way that would be most useful to Rudolf."

"I know you would, *liebe* Faith, and that would be as I have indicated—after you had purchased your trousseau. Since—if I understand the matter correctly—you are not able to touch your capital, it may be necessary for you to make economies to pay for that out of your income, as I suppose you have never had any general provision for a marriage outfit. I know, you see, that such is not the American custom."

"No," said Faith, still frankly, "it isn't and I haven't. But I can. I can begin right away. There is lovely linen right here in Venice. Cousin Sarah and I might start shopping to-morrow. We can draw up lists, the way we do for Christmas, and you can tell us whether the things I want to get would be suitable for a German *Braut*. . . . I should like them to be," she added, "*suitable,* but perhaps not exactly the *same* as a German girl would get. Because I'm not a German girl. I'm an American."

"You are quite right to feel that way about it," said Victoria Luise, smiling. "I will look at your lists, and I will make suggestions, but all the decisions shall rest with you. And there is no hurry. You can proceed gradually. Because, you know, in spite of all the obstacles we have passed, we must not make the mistake of regarding your betrothal to Rudolf as an accomplished fact. We must only look forward toward it hopefully as a glad possibility."

"Why?" asked Faith.

Victoria Luise smiled again. "I think Rudolf has told you that it is not always in accordance with the policy of our foreign minister to permit junior diplomats to marry," she said pleasantly, "and any apparent defiance of his rule is apt to cost a young man his career. But with tact and time, adjustments can often be made. . . . I am confident that they may be in this case. Especially as you are an American."

"Why?" asked Faith once more.

"Because at this moment, there is no country with which Germany is more eager to cement friendly and intimate relations. You see, *liebe* Faith, that I am talking to you as to a woman of perception and understanding, not as to a child."

"I know you are," said Faith, "that is the reason I like you so much . . . what does Germany want?"

"We shall probably find out within the next decade," replied Victoria Luise lightly, but rather as if dismissing the subject. "Meanwhile a personal element enters into this particular situation which is most felicitous. It seems that the present American Ambassador to Germany, Mr. Carolus Cavendish Castle, was a great friend of your father. I believe they attended some university—Harvard, is it not?—together, and that also, after your father became senator, Herr Castle still used to visit frequently at the house. He recalls you, as a little girl. Do you at all remember him?"

Faith considered a moment. "Is he very huge and glowery, but jolly underneath?" she inquired, at length. "Do his eyebrows and his stomach both stick out? Does he show dozens of teeth when he laughs, and knock off his glasses when he gets excited?"

Victoria Luise laughed. "I might have added that you have rather unusual powers of observation and description, when I was enumerating your talents," she said with amusement. "I see that you do remember His Excellency. I am glad, because he is going to write to you, and Mrs. Castle is going to write to Mrs. Atkinson, suggesting that you and she should come and pay a long visit at the Embassy after the season opens this winter in Berlin."

"Oh, but how wonderful!" exclaimed Faith. "Why, you arranged all this—just in those few days after Rudolf got home, and told you about me—before you started for Venice! Even before you knew whether you were going to like me! I don't see—it's simply too marvelous—and *too* kind!"

"I have tried to be helpful," said Victoria Luise earnestly, "so I have earned the right—have I not?—to ask you, in return, to be very patient, and to trust me a great deal. I will make a little holiday here in Venice, for a short time, and we shall all be happy together. Then I must go home again, and I think Rudolf must come with me. After that, he will go directly to his post in Spain. When you reach Berlin, he will be in Madrid. You will not see him again for some months. Naturally, you will write to him and he to you. But not love letters!"

"Just the kind of letters I write to Sam?" asked Faith obediently. "I mean, as nearly as possible," she amended candidly. "Because, of course, I *couldn't* make them quite the same."

"I am sure you will try your best to express yourself with reserve," said Victoria Luise, "but we cannot hope for entire success, in this or any other endeavor. However . . . for the next few months, you and Mrs. Atkinson will doubtless remain in Italy, unless, just before coming on to Berlin, you should chance to go to Paris to do a little shopping. You have natural taste and style, of course, but no one, however gifted in these directions, should fail to take advantage of the existence of *grands couturiers* when this is possible, as happily, it is in your case. . . . The Honorable Carolus Cavendish Castle will wish to take you at once to the Opera. His loge is, fortunately, very close to the Imperial Box, which is generally occupied nowadays. There is, as you have doubtless heard, a lovely young English singer who made her début last year and who has found favor in the most exalted circles—but that is beyond the point. I have every reason to believe that your pleasing appearance at the Opera will pave the way for your prompt presentation at Court, a presentation which would have been assured, sooner or later, in any case, for the gentleman who is 'very huge and glowery, but jolly underneath, and whose eyebrows and stomach both stick out a little' is very much *persona grata* with the Emperor."

"And if the Emperor likes me, too, then I can marry Rudolf?" asked Faith bluntly.

Victoria Luise leaned across the table and patted Faith lightly on the cheek. "*Gott sei dank,*" she said whimsically, "that Rudolf did not fall in love with a *Dumkopf*. You have guessed very quickly, *liebe* Faith. If the Emperor likes you, and I feel more and more convinced that he will, then Rudolf will come home from his post in the spring; and there will be a beautiful little wedding at the American Embassy in Berlin; and afterwards, a honeymoon spent at the *caseria* of our distant kinsman and close friend, Sebastian de Cerreno, near Granada, which is to say, near Paradise. With all this to hope for, can you be patient, my child, and docile?"

The expression in the girl's eyes as she looked at the Archduchess answered for her more clearly than any spoken words would have.

"There is, then, only one thing more that I must say to you before we tell each other 'good-night' and I send you away to sweet dreams."

The earnestness with which Victoria Luise had spoken a few moments earlier crept back into her voice, but this time it had a new vehemence, a greater depth.

"Rudolf loves you," she said, speaking very seriously. "He loves you sincerely. I believe he will love you steadfastly. He was ready to risk forfeiting much in the hope of marrying you. According to his lights, he will never fail you. He will be faithful to his marriage vows. Within the limits of his consciousness, he will be kind and just. But he does not understand you. He has already revealed that by his complete failure to see your beautiful friendship with Sam in its true light. And though you are much more intuitive than he, I doubt whether you will always understand him either. There will be barriers between you—barriers which would have been high enough in any case, because of fundamental racial differences, and which your divergent temperaments may render insuperable. For all your adaptability, you are intrinsically American. No matter how long you remain in Europe—and I doubt whether you will remain here without restiveness much longer—no matter how gracefully you appear to accept adoption by an alien country, no matter how many children of yours are born on foreign soil, you will never become really naturalized. And Rudolf, who is not adaptable at all, is the very embodiment and essence of the Prussian spirit. There can be no question of his unswerving adherence and allegiance *to* Prussia. He himself *is* Prussia personified."

"I know," said Faith, "and I think it is very glorious. There is something about the Prussian spirit that glistens, just as the Prussian uniform does."

"It is radiant; but it is not pliant. I believe that because you were dazzled by it just now, you do not see how inflexible it is in fiber. By the time your eyes are accustomed to its glitter, you may be aware also of its rigidity."

"I may be aware of it; but I shall not be afraid of it."

"*Liebe* Faith, a woman can experience frustration without experiencing fear; and frustration wounds her pride and breaks her spirit. But it is not only this racial barrier which I see stretched across your pathway.

There are, as I have just said, many others. Two natures are not necessarily antagonistic because they are diametrically different. Sometimes they merge and blend, producing harmony; sometimes they interlock, producing strength. But they seldom produce both harmony and strength, and I do not believe that yours and Rudolph's can either merge or interlock."

"Why?" asked Faith again. But this time Victoria Luise did not smile as she answered her.

"Because I know Rudolf's character so well that I cannot be blind to its deficiencies. I have already told you that I realize he lacks adaptability, while you do not. He also lacks gaiety and imagination and fire. He has shown great self-control in this recent crisis, but strangely enough he often shows himself lacking in that. And because I have seen him gripped by violent though transient anger, I believe he is capable of an overwhelming outburst of a still more powerful passion; but I do not think he is capable of one that is really great and long sustained. Marriage, as soon as it ceases to be a novelty to him, will not mean high ecstasy and enduring rapture. So I am afraid of this betrothal, even though I am helping to bring it about. Because I have already discovered that you do not lack gaiety or imagination or fire or the capacity of a really great and long-sustained passion. Because you will ultimately—although you are now too young to know it—not find fulfillment in a marriage unillumined by these qualities. Unconsciously, involuntarily, you will seek the high ecstasy, the overpowering rapture. And your search will be very brief, even if it is not forestalled. For both will be offered to you. By many men. By some one man whom you will love in a way you do not dream of now."

"What makes you think so?" asked Faith.

Her voice was still untroubled. It was not even eager. Her question was hardly more than a matter of form. It betrayed, completely, the misplaced self-confidence of untouched and untarnished youth. Victoria Luise answered with supreme gentleness.

"I do not think, my child. I know. I, too, gave my heart away—or thought I did—when I was sixteen. And afterwards, because I had done so, I was tempted to give my soul away. I am confessing to you again, you see. I have pledged you my assistance; but now I am begging you—for the sake of my son and for your own sake—not to accept this assistance! To give Rudolf up, voluntarily, and before it is too late! To keep yourself free for the great lover who is still sure to come!"

Again she leaned across the table, taking Faith's hands in hers. For the first time there were tears in her eyes. Afterwards Faith remembered, there was a quality of prayer in her entreaty, and at the time wondered why it had moved her so little. She answered with the same brevity, the same steadiness, which had marked every word she had spoken to Victoria Luise.

"I am sure that Rudolf loves me," she said, "and that I love him as much as he loves me. And you must not be afraid. I know he is very loyal. But I am very loyal too."

PART IV

Sebastian

CHAPTER 10

FAITH VON HOHENLOHE lay very still and straight in the narrow lower berth of a compartment on the Paris-Madrid *train de luxe,* subconsciously, but not resentfully, aware of the rhythmic metallic clatter that the car made as it jerked and jolted its uneven way along over the rough roadbed of the narrow-gauge railway. She was so thankful to be able to lie down, even on a hard and sloping mattress, that the minor irritations of travel were almost forgotten in her sense of relief. The first lap of the journey—from Berlin to Paris—had been comparatively comfortable; but this had been a trying day, very hot and dusty, and the garden-like countryside of France, usually so fresh and lovely in her eyes, had been tarnished by the glare of a relentless sun. The French couple sitting opposite her in the day carriage had objected to the amount of her hand baggage, which, as they kept reiterating, crowded them badly. They had as much as she did, and there was no reason why she should have felt remorse over their alleged discomfort; but she did, and she kept trying to rearrange her belongings, holding her heavy gold-fitted dressing case on her lap until she was so cramped and stiff that she could not keep it there any longer. When she set it down again, as close to her feet as possible, the man who was her *vis-à-vis* looked at her with increased animosity, and hissed "*Allemande!*" in an audible aside to his wife. Faith noticed that he was wearing the ribbon of the Legion of Honor, and felt a distinct surprise that anyone who was worthy of such recognition and reward should be so discourteous. It seemed to her that the frontier, where, at Irun, she would be able to change into the *wagon-lit,* and escape from the atmosphere of hostility, would never be reached.

Over and over again she thought it must be nearly half-past ten, only to find that it was five, that it was a quarter-past six, that it was twenty minutes of eight. And of course there had been veal for dinner, thin sizzling slices of it, folded down between mounds of fried potatoes. Faith often wondered how any of the calves in Europe lived to grow up, veal was such an omnipresent item on *table d'hôte* menus. She had never liked it, and now she had reached the point of almost choking over it when she tried to eat it.

Rudolf had minded all this far less than she had. He was not disappointed in the appearance of the French landscape, because he never admired it in any case; he thought veal was delicious; and the discourteous couple had not troubled him at all. He had responded to their first complaints reasonably and briefly, with formal politeness; after that he had paid no attention to them whatever, until the word *"Allemande"* had been hissed at Faith. Then he had levelled a look of such cool insolence at the offending speaker that Faith had felt something turn over inside her. . . . She had never guessed that Rudolf could look that way at anyone. She was really relieved when after a little apparently superficial conversation, which was carried on in English, and which she realized was actually designed to reveal to those who must inevitably hear it, that she was an American, he turned his head away and went peacefully to sleep, still sitting very upright, and still retaining his air of complete superiority to his would-be annoyers.

He was sleeping now, calmly and deeply, in the upper berth. Faith could hear, above the clatter of the jerky little train, the even sound of his breathing. It had taken her a long time to get to bed, for she felt too hot and untidy to lie down until she had sponged herself from head to foot in the small lavatory that opened out of the compartment; and she had achieved her bath slowly and with difficulty, owing to the lack of space and the rocking motion. Rudolf had assured himself that all her possessions were disposed as she would prefer them, and then, after kissing her with a fond, *"Schlaf schön, Traüm süss,"* had swung himself lithely into the upper berth. His own ablutions, previously performed, though meticulous, had not been extensive, and they had taken very little time. He had already sunk into a profound slumber when Faith came back into the compartment, pleasantly refreshed. She had smoothed all the tangles out of her curls, had brushed them indeed until her scalp tingled agreeably, and then she had braided them into two great plaits with a part between them which went all the way down the back, so that she would not have to lie on their bulk; and the resultant feeling of smoothness and firmness was delightful. She had also poured a little eau-de-cologne into the basin with the water, and after her bath, had dusted herself from head to foot with violet powder shaken from a ball-like puff. Even her sheer nightgown, lace-edged, monogrammed, delicately embroidered, and folded, like the rest of her linen, in sachets, was faintly fragrant. After feeling soiled and mussy for so many hours, the sense of so much sweet cleanliness was very welcome to Faith. The thought flashed through her mind that she would like to share it with Rudolf, that she would like to have him see her as she was now, after looking at her all day in her crumpled traveling dress. But of course Rudolf would see her every night now, and besides he was asleep. It would be selfish as well as silly to disturb him. Moreover, once in her berth, she found that she was strangely thankful to be alone. From childhood, she had been accustomed to much mental and physical solitude. She was suddenly aware that she needed the feeling of respite which they afforded.

Completely relaxed, she began to turn over the events of the past months in orderly review in her mind. She liked to "think things over"; it helped her to regulate her life—though, ever since her meeting with Victoria Luise in Venice, it was, she admitted to herself, the Archduchess who had regulated it. And with what marvelous success! The progress of events had been as smooth as it was steady. There had first been the "little holiday" which Victoria Luise had spoken of "making," and which they had all spent so happily together. . . . All except Sam, who was, unfortunately, called back to Paris to paint another magnate, and who had caught the express at an hour's notice one day when she and Rudolf and Cousin Sarah had gone with the Archduchess to have tea at the Austrian Consulate. He had left only a little scribbled note behind him to say good-bye, and when she heard from him again, it was to tell her that he was starting for the Straits of Magellan to paint marine pictures—and she had so counted on having him at her wedding! But aside from this, there had been nothing to regret. Even the parting with Rudolf had not been very hard because his mother made it so easy; and afterwards, the letters he wrote her from Madrid had been so completely adequate, so loyal and loving in tone. They reached her with infallible regularity, all through those golden weeks of early autumn that she and Cousin Sarah spent in Italy, although their address changed constantly, for they went, without definite schedule, from Venice to Verona, from Verona to Padua, from Padua to Bologna, and from Bologna to Lucca. It seemed incredible that Rudolf should be able to foresee, with such exactitude, when he was writing a letter, where she would be when it reached its destination. But never once did he estimate time and distance incorrectly. Her love letter lay under a bunch of fresh flowers on her breakfast tray every morning.

She saw the little cities of Italy through a haze of happiness; but when she and Cousin Sarah finally turned their faces north, she awoke to new alertness as they approached Paris. She could not afford to have many dresses, if these were to come from *grandes maisons;* but she was determined that each one should be precisely right. She insisted on visiting a dozen or more establishments of the first order; and even then she wrote to Victoria Luise before making any final decision.

"I am sending you *croquis,*" she said in the letter that accompanied the sketches. "You will see there are two *tailleurs,* one navy blue and one golden brown, and two three-piece velvet costumes for afternoon in the same shades. If I do not go into too many different tones, it will be less expensive—because of hats and shoes to match, I mean; but I would love to have the champagne-colored ribbed silk and the mauve voile for occasions when I would need to be *habillée* and still not in evening dress. The party frocks that are really *jeune-fille* are all made of such perishable materials that I have chosen three. The pink tulle is so very pale that it really is all right with my hair, and of course I did not have to hesitate over the pale green taffeta or the white chiffon. The emerald-colored evening wrap will go with all of these, and Cousin Sarah has given me a lovely set of furs, in advance, for my Christmas present, so I do not have to think of buying those. Will you please write and tell me if you approve of what I have chosen?"

Victoria Luise had not written. She had wired. "Everything charming congratulations your exquisite taste but double number evening dresses add riding habit tweeds and flannels for country eagerly awaiting to welcome you weekend Schönplatz before going Berlin hope you can arrive by nineteenth." So Faith had decided that she could do with less linen than a German *Braut*, and had gone steadily and joyfully on with her shopping, buying the extra dresses that Victoria Luise had suggested, and finally setting out for Schönplatz with everything neatly packed in beautiful new Vuitton luggage. Even for Schönplatz, Victoria Luise had prepared her, so that she was not overwhelmed when she arrived there. "Expect to see a very large house, *liebes Kind*, and acres and acres of woodland," the Archduchess had written. "I tell you this lest you should not realize how immense are many estates in Germany, for I believe you have not visited at one before. And it is necessary on such estates that there should be a great many retainers, and natural that the house servants should wear the livery of the family. The week-end party however, will be small, not more than twenty guests in all, and some whom I believe you will especially enjoy. If you do not know how to ride we will teach you—in fact I have chosen a pretty gentle horse for you—and there is no reason why you should hunt if you prefer not. My husband wishes me to extend his fond greetings to you and tell you how glad he will be to see you in our *Heimat*."

It was Rudolf's father that Faith had dreaded to meet above everyone else. She had pictured him as a rigid and relentless figure. Therefore this kindly message from him was doubly reassuring. And its sender was the first person to welcome her when she and Sarah alighted on the platform of the little station that served Schönplatz; a tall, erect man, with ruddy color and frosty blue eyes, who looked almost as young as his wife. He was dressed for hunting, with a tiny gay feather stuck in the dark velour hat that he lifted with a certain charming precision.

"*Frau* Atkinson? Permit that I should present myself. I am Hans von

Hohenlohe. It joys me to see here my brother's friend. And this is Faith, *nicht wahr?* The *liebes Kind* of whom Luischen speaks with such affection. As it is on the platform a little cold, she waits in the carriage to embrace thee. *Nein—nein*—all these luggage the footman will see to. Not to disturb yourselves. Please. If you please. This way."

Since Rudolf's father was like that, what did it matter that they were instantly surrounded by servants in livery, that there were coronets on the carriage doors, that they drove through acres and acres of forest and finally reached a huge looming house which must contain at least fifty rooms? Faith was entranced with the one to which she was shown, with the huge white puff on the bed, with the comfortable ponderous furniture, with the huge porcelain stove in the corner, with the rosy-cheeked maid who stood curtseying and waiting to unpack for her. And when she had washed and put on the amber-colored cashmere which she had brought, because she felt instinctively that it would be just what she would wish to wear for tea at Schönplatz, there was a rap at her door, and a lovely young girl came in.

"I am Elsa, the youngest daughter," this girl told Faith in friendly fashion. "The others are all below—Hans, and Heinrich, and Marguerita and her *Braütigam*, Friedrich von Mitweld. That is all, except Rudolf—*es ist schade, nicht wahr,* that he is not here too? But we hope, the next time you come, he will be. The *Mütterchen* thought you would like to come down and meet our other guests. Your—how do you say—*Botschaft* and *Frau* Castle are here—that was the *Mütterchen's* idea, that it would be pleasant if you could meet them at Schönplatz before going to stay with them. Oh, and yes—one of the Imperial Princes, only he is incognito—you are not to reveal that you know who he is, though of course everyone is well aware."

There was, with one exception, nothing frightening about any of these persons, Faith discovered, when she went downstairs, her fingers locked in Elsa's. The members of Rudolf's family and the friends they had collected to spend the weekend at Schönplatz, were cordial, simple, and wholly unalarming, in spite of the fact that they referred casually to most of the reigning potentates of Europe by their first names and seemed immune to insecurity or discomfort of any sort. It was not that they "put on airs" about their positions. They appeared, rather, unconscious of any occasion for "putting on airs." Even the Imperial Prince, an amiable and rather chinless young man, very blond and very slim, whom everybody called Willie and whom Faith soon called Willie too, was untouched by any regal tinge. He was chiefly engaged in playing with a puppy's ears and responding blandly to humorous comments that were being made about his admiration for a beautiful young English singer, Gwendoline Lamar, in the intervals between gulping down enormous quantities of weak tea.

The one overpowering exception to the general characteristics of this group Faith almost instantly discovered in the person of Mrs. Carolus Cavendish Castle. This lady had spent most of her early life in Belford, a New England manufacturing town where her father had made shoes: such very good shoes, indeed, that his continually increasing trade soon overflowed the room put aside for it in the little house where he both lived and cobbled; and he set up a neat shop which in turn was succeeded by a factory of sizable dimensions. His one fair daughter, Annabelle, who had married an apprentice, inherited a very comfortable fortune, which she had all to herself, as her husband—slightly dizzy with unexpected success—had followed her father to a comparatively early grave. She was still young, and of a commanding appearance which revealed her temperament so completely as to be deceiving—and she shortly afterwards chose a second husband. She was profiting by her widowhood to make a grand tour, looking about her in a comprehensive manner which included much besides scenic wonders; and at Monte Carlo she encountered Carolus Cavendish Castle, who was several steps above her on the social ladder, and who opportunely for her had just exhausted his letter of credit. In spite of a certain amount of will power of his own, he lacked the energy to combat Annabelle, and their marriage was not long delayed. With ripening years and an income which continued to increase by leaps and bounds—thanks to the steady demand for footwear—Annabelle was more and more conscious of the need for widened horizons; and responsive to her impetus, Carolus contributed one hundred thousand dollars of her money to the campaign fund of a Presidential candidate who, fortunately for Carolus as well as himself, proved to be the choice of the nation, and Carolus forthwith was appointed United States Ambassador to Germany.

He had been a big booming sort of boy, the adored son of rather shrinking and stingy parents, who had amazed Belford by suddenly "loosening up" and sending him to Exeter and Harvard to be educated. And big and booming he still remained, with a curious mixture of the belligerent and the benign in his make-up. He did not speak a word of German, he did not pretend to understand international affairs, he did not aspire to diplomatic distinction; but there was something very likeable about him, and he was as popular in Berlin as he had been in Belford; and Faith had talked with him for only two minutes when she was sure she was going to find him as genial a host on Unter den Linden as he had been a welcome guest on Lafayette Square.

But Mrs. Carolus Cavendish Castle was different. She was so very rigid that Faith quailed before her. Her eyes and her mouth both snapped, and she held herself very erect. She was very firmly corseted, and the bones which upheld her high-necked collar rose to her ears. Her dress had unquestionably been made by Worth—indeed, Faith recognized the model—but in some way Mrs. Carolus Cavendish Castle had contrived to rob its smooth lines of all their softness. It looked as if it had been stiffened throughout with buckram, and its steel belt-buckle was in the form of twisted, teethed dragons. Long hatpins protruded menacingly from either side of the rigid gray bows of her high-perched hat and a rigid gray pompadour bristled beneath this.

"It is simply appalling," she was saying in a cutting voice as Faith entered the drawing-room, "how many Americans are coming to Berlin nowadays. Really, if things keep up as they're going on now we'll have as many tourists as there are in London and Paris. Hardly a day passes that we don't feel forced—yes, really forced—to invite some wandering Westerner to lunch or dinner. I think senators and congressmen must keep form-letters ready to fill in for the benefit of all their restless friends who want to range through embassies. Even in summer there is very little respite. You know we took a small house in Rugen for a few months —as a *retreat*—and while we were there we had sixty visitors—for *meals,* I mean, and some of them actually seemed to feel we might ask them to spend a week-end or to stay even longer. Not that we did. There are some limits left, I hope. . . . Oh, really? So you are Faith, are you? Senator Marlowe's daughter?"

Mrs. Carolus Cavendish Castle raised a lorgnette which clicked open with a metallic sound as she did so. Faith, stunned by the thought that the woman to whose views on hospitality she had just been forced to listen was to be her hostess for the next few months, admitted her identity as briefly as possible. But before the Ambassadress could open her trap-like mouth again, Victoria Luise had interrupted.

"We all realize how heavy are the responsibilities of your position, dear Mrs. Castle," Faith heard this daughter of a hundred kings, saying suavely, "and have therefore been doubly thankful to realize that Faith will be able to lighten some of the burdens for you this coming winter. Not only with the aggressive tourists. But in so many other ways. She speaks such beautiful German! She is so *gemütlich* a person to have at hand! She has such gentleness and tact! But it is not well, is it, that a young maid should herself hear of her so great merits? . . . Willie, that puppy is not a dachshund. I do not wish its ears further elongated. And please do not drink any more tea. If you so overindulge you will lose your figure, then what will say your lovely nightingale?"

"I have been thinking," remarked the personage last addressed, calmly continuing to gulp and to pull, "that *Fräulein* Marlowe would naturally be wishing to attend the opera."

"Oh, yes," said Faith eagerly, remembering her conversation in Venice with Victoria Luise. "I—" But she was interrupted. Mrs. Carolus Cavendish Castle had by this time recovered herself. And though properly resentful of the *double entendre* in the remarks of the Archduchess, with which she meant to deal in due time, she was primarily bent, for the moment, on upholding the purity of the arts, even at the risk of putting royalty in its place.

"I shall see to it that your opportunities along those lines are not neglected," she said, addressing herself directly to Faith, "the opera, though underestimated by the ignorant, and abused by the vicious, is, properly regarded, a great educational and inspirational instrument."

"Willie will be the first to agree with you," said Friedrich von Mitweld, winking at the tea-drinker.

"I was referring to the superb art of Emmy Destinn," retorted Mrs. Carolus Cavendish Castle grimly. "I believe she is singing 'Aida' on Friday. I shall consider it my duty to take Faith to hear it that night."

"Oh, but I am sure," remarked the tea-drinker, putting down his cup at last, and transfixing Mrs. Castle with a glance that had swiftly assumed a strange authority, "that you will feel the same way about Wednesday—when Gwendoline Lamar will be singing in 'Romeo and Juliet.' Father and I will both be looking for you—and for your lovely guest. . . . You have been to see the dogs, *Fräulein* Faith? *Nicht?* Well then, let us, you and Rita and Friedrich and I go for a so little walk to the kennels. I must restore this baby puppy to his mother."

So after all, the terror inspired by Mrs. Carolus Cavendish Castle had been of brief duration. Between them, Victoria Luise and "Willie" had swiftly assuaged it; before the house party was over Faith had entirely recovered from its effects; and before another week was over she had forgotten all about it. By this time she and Cousin Sarah were safely installed at the Embassy in their own pink and silver suite, with their own pink and silver maid; and Mrs. Castle was really not inhospitable after all; she talked about the burdens of her position because this made them seem more imposing; but Faith discovered that she really liked to have company! And they did go to "Romeo and Juliet": the Ambassador and Ambassadress, Cousin Sarah and Faith, a nice young man named "Dulcey" Mitchell who was second secretary of the Embassy, and another man, Mr. Caleb Hawks, who came from Hinsboro and was "just passing through Berlin." He was really exactly the sort of man to whom Mrs. Castle had referred in her terrorizing speech, but he was "something very important in pencils," and therefore commanded consideration. And Faith, who remembered going to visit him with her father when she was a little girl, was tremendously glad to see him again, and much more thrilled by his "home news" than "Dulcey's" *blasé* observations on the performance and condescending compliments.

The Castles' loge was very near the huge central box with the shining imperial crown surmounting its crimson draperies, and it was easy for Faith to observe the occupants of this box without in the least seeming to do so: there was a gray-haired lady with a sweet smile who was handsome without being beautiful, and elegant without being stylish, and who had on almost as much jewelry as Mrs. Castle—almost, but not quite, for Mrs. Castle knew exactly how glittering the American Ambassadress should be on such an occasion, and her tiara, her necklace, her brooches, and her bracelets all bore witness to this important fact. There was a very alert-looking middle-aged man, whose mustache turned up and whose eyebrows turned up and whose very ears seemed to be pricked to attention—a man who gave the impression of being very tall, he held himself with such conspicuous and superb dignity, but who, compared to the three handsome blond young men beside him, was not really very tall after all.

The Ambassador nudged Faith. "Some family, eh?" He grunted as if personally responsible for its size and very pleased at his responsibility. "And just to think they have three more sons like those at home, not to mention the little princess, and she's the cutest kid you ever saw. Well, the throne in this country's safe, anyway, whatever happens anywhere else. I've got a rather uneasy hunch all of them aren't. Look at Spain, now, with that one poor sickly youngster."

"I know," agreed Faith, "but Rudolf likes the young King. He says everybody does."

"Well, and I guess what Rudolf says *goes* with you, doesn't it?" the Ambassador asked slyly, giving her another nudge.

"Of course. If it didn't I wouldn't want so much to marry him. Oh, Mr. Castle, do you—do you really think that I can make a good impression?"

She turned in her chair, her eyes looked imploringly into his. So she did not notice—though she heard about it afterwards—that almost simultaneously "Willie," whom she had scarcely recognized in his splendid uniform, had leaned over and whispered first to the brisk gentleman with the mustache, and then to the lady with the sweet smile, and that they had both glanced toward the Castles' loge. The next moment the house was rocking with applause, and a slim, vivid, dark-haired girl with her arms full of flowers, was taking curtain-calls, bowing in every direction, right, left, straight ahead of her—even directly toward that great crimson box that stood in the center of so many tiers and tiers of other boxes. Melody seemed to flow from her; her smile was radiant; her grace was permeated with magnetism.

"Now, if I looked like that!" Faith exclaimed with irrepressible envy.

"Well, if you looked like that, it wouldn't be Rudolf that would be your beau. It would be——"

The Ambassador checked himself, and Faith, without understanding why, felt as if a slight chill had passed over the sunshine of her happiness; but somehow she did, and she was immeasurably relieved when he went on again, a little hastily.

"Come, come now! You know you're not such a bad-looking girl yourself! That pink mosquito netting—oh, pink *tulle* is it?—you've got on is a sweet pretty dress too. Becoming. I like the way those little bunches of roses sort of pucker it together in places. And when it comes to hair, young lady, let me tell you Miss Gwendoline would swap hers for yours in a minute if she had the chance. Honestly! But we must stop gossiping and give her a hand. She deserves it, and besides, that's what everyone else is doing. Let me see how hard you can clap."

. . . . .

"Yes—yes indeed. Her father was a great collector and connoisseur of the arts, and, as of course you know, a member of the United States Senate—the most important legistative body in the world. His untimely death was a tremendous loss both to American culture and American statesmanship. Dear little Faith has inherited a remarkable library and paintings and correspondence that are uniquely valuable. As to the *fortune*—modest, but tidy, modest, but tidy. The Marlowes have been so self-sacrificing in their country's cause that they perhaps fail to think enough of the purely material necessities of life. But now the Ambassador and I feel quite as if Faith were our own daughter—oh, absolutely—and we shall treat her as such financially, officially, in every way! Oh, certainly! I'm sure everyone understands that!"

Faith hardly recognized her own background as she saw it sketched by Mrs. Castle's commending hand. Every disadvantageous detail was rubbed out. Every item that enhanced her eligibility to enter the ranks of German nobility was thrown into sharp relief. Her present position was painted with bewildering brilliance. It dazzled her so that she could hardly believe in its reality. Early in the new year she wrote about it to Sam, and wholly failed to achieve the sort of letter she intended. Still she tried.

"Dear Sam"—she scribbled hastily one evening when she was supposed to be resting before going to a court ball—"You never could believe how easy it has all been. I thought at first that Mrs. Castle would be hard to live with and hurt my feelings, but she's wonderful. She makes things happen, not in the same sort of way that *Tante* Luise does, but still the results aren't awfully different. The person I had to impress liked me from the beginning and I've been heaps to the Palace. It's a good deal like any other big house when you get past the sentries and through the long dreary halls and the Porcelain Room and Queen Charlotte's Study and the pictures of Friedrich the Great when he was a child. After all that it begins to seem actually homelike and I love to go there. In fact I'm going to-night and looking forward to it a lot. I'm going to wear a pale green dress that made me think of you when I bought it, because it's the sort of dress Aphrodite would have worn if she'd worn any dress at all, I mean. Of course, I know she really wouldn't."

"Christmas was wonderful, the sidewalks covered with trees to sell, in every size and all smelling so good, and the shop windows full of the loveliest things and wakes singing '*Stille Nacht*' in the snowy courtyards. We all spent Christmas Eve with *Tante* Luise, and that fortified us for the morrow, as it says in Shakespeare or the Bible or somewhere. She had a lovely tree, decorated with white and silver lilies and white candles. It was the most exquisite thing and I helped her make the lilies from a pattern that looked like a paper doll yet you can't think how effective they were after they had been cut and folded into place. And while we were all dancing around the tree and opening presents and kissing each other and calling out '*Fröhliche Weinachten*,' who do you think should walk in? *Rudolf!* He had not let anyone know he had Christmas leave and there he was. Well, really it was too perfect."

"Christmas Day there was a big celebration at the Embassy, dinner for the members of the staff and their families and a reception afterwards for the American Colony, you'd never believe how many Americans want to colonize Germany. It was pretty exhausting and I certainly was thankful that Rudolf was there to take refuge with, sort of, in odd moments."

"And now there doesn't seem to be any reason at all why we shouldn't be engaged, of course we have been anyway ever since August. But now it's going to be announced! Rudolf worries about my going to balls as it is, though why he should I can't imagine, because I sit with Cousin Sarah on one side of me and Aunt Annabelle on the other between every dance. My partner comes up looking simply gorgeous in his uniform and clicks his heels together and bows, and then we whirl off for a waltz, not reversing at all until I get much too dizzy to talk to him even if I wanted to. Then the music stops and he takes his arms away as quickly as if he had been suddenly burnt or someone had touched an exposed nerve in his tooth, and restores me to Cousin Sarah and Aunt Annabelle, bowing and clicking again. But Rudolf says that even with a foolproof cast-iron system like this there are sometimes accidents, so now I have my ring, which is not a solitaire diamond in a Tiffany setting, like those I have seen American girls touring in Europe wearing, but pearls and rubies and emeralds all sunk together in heavy twisted gold, very huge and ancestral."

"I do wish you could be here for my wedding, Sam, for I feel sure it's going to be beautiful and it would mean so much more to have you give me away than anyone else. No matter how much I love all my new friends there will never be anyone—not even Aunt Sarah—that I care for the way I do you. I know you told me that marine pictures are awfully important in the 'development of your versatility' and that you always wanted to go to the Straits of Magellan, in fact you said you'd take me there some day, and now I suppose you never will. But won't you come back to Europe, even if it's only for a week, and stay with us here at the Embassy, until I'm safely married?"

Faith had a very indistinct notion of the length of time it took for a letter to reach Patagonia from Berlin. Intermittently she wondered at Sam's silence. But there was a round of official life in which she had been caught up to absorb her time, and the assemblage of the all-important trousseau to absorb her thought. Mrs. Castle would not listen to Faith's suggestion that she did not need as much linen as a German *Braut.* She marched her to Mosse's and pounced upon the first clerk in sight with ferocity. He was a stalwart man with a powerful jaw who played the bass-drum in a brass band during his leisure hours; but he quailed before Mrs. Castle's onslaught. Then he collected himself and began to spread out table-cloths and coverlets, sheets and towels, with the air of a general reviewing his troops in the presence of his sovereign. The result was stupendous—so stupendous, that it accounted in large measure for the fact that Faith's worries were at first intermittent, and that she finally forgot them altogether.

Sam's answer was handed to her with a sheaf of other telegrams as she stood, draped in snowy satin, veiled in snowy lace, a myrtle wreath encircling her head, waiting to hear that the Honorable Carolus Cavendish Castle was ready to escort her to her wedding. She had slept in the pink and silver suite with Cousin Sarah for the last time. Her baggage, full of beautiful clothes and beautiful linen, was packed and strapped and labeled Madrid. Her bridal bouquet lay beside her on the bare dressing table stripped of its dainty bottles and brushes and boxes. Everything was ordered, composed, complete. Faith lifted the telegrams from the proffered silver tray without excitement.

"THIS IS A CONVICT COLONY CAN'T ESCAPE UNLESS I MAKE MONEY IN SHEEP"—she read uncomprehensively. Her gaze leaped forward to the signature, and she gave a little startled exclamation and went on reading. "SWELL SUNNY SEA AND SKY WONDERFUL COLOR BLUE PAINTING A LOT MARINE PICTURES ONLY BROUGHT THE MARY WITH ME FOR COMPANY HOPE RUDOLF FINDS THE APHRODITE I MISSED YOURS FOREVER—SAM."

· · · · ·

A strange thin light seemed to be filtering around the edges of the drawn green curtains of the compartment. Faith raised herself sharply on her elbow. Was it possible that it was dawn? That she had spent the entire night mentally reviewing the events of the past months? That she had not slept at all? Since there was nothing to worry or trouble her in her memories, how could they have absorbed her so completely? It seemed impossible, but it was true. Very softly and slowly, in order to run no risk of awakening Rudolf, who was still sleeping as profoundly as he had before she went to bed, she slipped from her berth and raising the green shade halfway, looked out of the window.

She had expected a beauty that would be almost blinding. Instead, she saw a bleak and barren landscape, gaunt, treeless, strewn with rocks. In the midst of its emptiness a monstrous building suddenly seemed to rise from nowhere, defiantly, against the sky that was already hot though as yet it was hardly tinged with sunlight. While she stood looking at it, repelled yet fascinated, she felt Rudolf's arm slip lightly around her waist, pressing her sheer soft nightgown against her flesh. He had awakened and descended from his own bed so quietly that she had not heard him.

"The Escorial," he said in answer to her questioning look. "A strange place built by a strange man, but something of the spirit of Spain lies concentrated there with him in his tomb. Some day I must take you to see it. . . . We are less than an hour from Madrid, now, *Liebchen.* We must perhaps somewhat hasten with our preparations. You look a little tired. Have you then not rested well these two nights on the train when I have slept so soundly? And have you a kiss for me this morning?"

CHAPTER 11

DURING the first period of her acquaintance with the von Hohenlohes, Faith had been both bewildered and impressed when they talked to her about their relatives. They had been quite unconscious of the effect they were producing, not only in referring to cousins scattered over the entire face of Europe—cousins whose numbers, nationalities and names were alike confusing—but in revealing casually and often tardily that these cousins were members of reigning families, even if not actually rulers themselves. Gradually, however, she became less bewildered and impressed, and ceased to feel an active curiosity in them one way or another. Therefore, when Victoria Luise told her that their "great friend and distant kinsman, Sebastian de Cerreno" had a house near Granada that would be available for a honeymoon, Faith dismissed him from her mind, except as the generous owner of an ideal estate ideally situated; and it was not until Rudolf remarked, about fifteen minutes before the *train de luxe* was due in Madrid, that he supposed Sebastian would be at the station to meet them, that she felt enough interest in him to make any inquiries about him.

"Is he your cousin on your mother's side or your father's, Rudolf?"

"On *Mütterchen's.* You know of course that she is a Hapsburg. My *Tante* Sophia—my grandmother's half sister—was Sebastian's mother. His elder brothers and sisters have all died, except one, who has entered the church."

"Sebastian wasn't at the wedding, was he? I don't seem to remember him, but there were so many. . . ."

"No, Carlos and Carlota were the only Spanish cousins who came. Sebastian hardly ever leaves Spain. But he sent the *parure* of aquamarine you liked so much."

"The lovely necklace and bracelets and tiara and brooch all to match? But those were from the *Duque* and *Duquesa* of Something. Is he married?"

"Yes, he is married. He would have sent his wife's card too, of course. But it is very sad. She is the victim of a strange malady. She has not been herself for years."

"You mean—she is *insane?*"

"*Ach, liebe* Faith, do not use such harsh words. She is a nervous invalid. There are many such."

A little shiver of horror ran through Faith, the strange feeling that in the midst of pomp and circumstance she had inadvertently touched a whited sepulchre and found it cold and ghastly. She had to force herself to go on speaking.

"Oh—I will be very careful to remember—I shall not be likely to see her, shall I?"

"No, indeed. She lives in retirement, in one of the family castles among the Pyrenees."

"In retirement? You mean? . . ."

"*Liebe* Faith, is it necessary to dwell on details? Be assured she is well cared for."

Faith, closing her mental vision to the thought of high barred windows and futile screaming, tried again.

"It must be very lonely, for Sebastian, unless he has children."

"There are no children. Fortunately, perhaps, lest they might have been strange too. Otherwise it is sad, for he is the last of that branch of the family who could have had descendants. But I do not think he is lonely. He has many diversions. He plays polo and sails a yacht better than anyone else in Spain. He is a famous whip. He has even bought one of those new horseless carriages and dashes about in it at the rate of twenty miles an hour. He raises bulls and mules, and celebrated vintage wines come from his estate. He owns one of the finest libraries in the world and half a dozen palaces, and he is very much in demand everywhere. Besides—no, I do not think Sebastian is lonely. Well! I do not know whether you will like him much or not. Sometimes he is most agreeable and at other times he seems to withdraw into himself. To those who do not know him he appears somewhat haughty and cynical. He may appear so to you."

The train had begun to slow down while Rudolf was still speaking. It had not fully come to a stop when Faith was aware of a slender man standing directly opposite the window of their compartment, as if he knew by instinct exactly where this would be. He was carrying a light cane, and was dressed in gray flannel rather nonchalantly worn. A panama hat of extraordinary whiteness and exquisitely fine weave shaded his forehead. As he lifted his hat, Faith saw that he was very dark, that the face was blade-like in its keenness and narrowness, and that a strange scar, disfiguring out of all proportion to its size, ran horizontally across his left cheek. His deep-set eyes met hers with penetrating directness and he did not smile at all. She felt herself flushing, and was annoyed that this should be so; but as Rudolf lowered the window and hailed his cousin she impulsively held out her hand too.

"Good-morning, Sebastian," she said gaily, "you *are* Sebastian, aren't you? I'm Faith, your new relative. I do hope you're going to like me."

"*A los pies de usted,*" said Sebastian gravely, still looking at her with that piercing gaze. His formality chilled her a little, and she felt herself blushing more deeply still. Probably she should have waited and taken the tone of her greeting from him, she reflected, as he bent over her outstretched hand, barely brushing it with his lips, before turning to Rudolf as if fully conscious of him for the first time. "*Qué tal?*" he said agreeably, "was it a good trip? But need I ask? All trips are good in the *luna de mielo!* . . . Now for the bags. Those are really all? Well, Manuel will look after them and we can come straight to the carriage. I am driving you up to the house myself. I thought my mules might amuse the *Señora.*"

There was a short interlude consumed by the necessary detail of arrival. When it was over, and they were clipping along in a smart open landeau, drawn by four very sleek and sprightly mules ornamented with bells and tassels, Rudolf answered the question Sebastian had asked on the station platform as if there had been no interruption.

"It was a good trip," he said speaking rather precisely, "cool and pleasant in Germany—a little warm coming through France. And we had very bourgeois traveling companions who were rude to Faith. French, of course."

"Oh, but not 'of course', *querido!* Be more just! However, it is certain that no Spaniard will be rude to her!" Sebastian turned halfway around from his driving seat, and waved the ribboned whip. "Are you interested in the landmarks of Madrid? That is the Royal Palace over there, and this is the Puerta del Sol through which we are passing on our way to the Castellana, the residential section where I am taking you now. No doubt next month when you come back from Granada you will be choosing a house of your own near that of my Cousin Carlota's—we are going there, for the moment, as my own great barracks are closed for the summer and look so stiff and empty. All the furniture is wrapped in winding sheets—the effect is quite tomb-like." For the first time he smiled a little, but Faith did not think his smile was merry, and it intensified the lines of the scar. She remembered that she herself had already thought of a tomb once that morning and now Sebastian was speaking of one. "I walked through all the apartments yesterday," he continued, "and could not find a single one that I thought was appropriate for a bridal chamber."

"Rudolf says that it is one of the most beautiful palaces in Europe," remarked Faith with an effort. She had been enjoying the bells and the tassels of the sleek mules immensely, and the smart landeau and the dashing drive through the streets. But now her pleasure was blighted. Little creeping chills began to dart through her again.

"I hope you will agree with him," Sebastian answered formally, "when the season opens perhaps you will permit me to give a dinner in your honor and you will be able to judge. Meanwhile, I am sure you will be much happier at Carlota's. The express to Granada goes only three times a week, and as there is no good train to-day I have had the necessary reservations made on it for you to-morrow night. I know you are eager to be on your way, but we are delighted at the prospect of this interval. Carlota has a lovely garden, full of flowers and sunshine, and the room prepared for you—if it pleases you—overlooks this. It has quite wonderful Louis XV furniture in it. Red and gold. We like to impress the colors of the Spanish flag on our guests. . . . Oh, and a very sumptuous bathroom—I suppose someone has told you that there are no bathrooms in Spain?"

"Oh, *everyone*," rejoined Faith, her spirits rising once more, "but then they told me the same thing about Germany."

"And still you were persuaded to marry a German?"

"I didn't even have to be persuaded. I wanted to anyway."

Faith looked affectionately toward Rudolf and reached for his hand. But Rudolf happened to be gazing in the opposite direction at the moment, and noticed neither the gesture nor the glance. It was Sebastian instead who saw both. He smiled again, and this time Faith discovered that his smile could be charming after all.

"*Muy bien,*" he said, more gently than he had spoken before at all. "*Felicitaciones, Señora.*" He checked the mules, bringing them to a smooth stop, alighted, and forestalling his groom, opened the door of the landeau himself. "Would it please you to get out?" he asked. "*Esta es su casa.*"

CHAPTER 12

FAITH had met so many of Rudolf's relatives and so briefly, at her wedding, that she retained only a very hazy recollection of most of them. But his cousin Carlos and his cousin Carlota, who were like nobody else in the world and uncommonly like each other, had made a real impression upon her, and she was glad to learn that she was going to their house and not to Sebastian's palace. They were twins, between whom a tremendous devotion existed. There was something bird-like in their appearance and manner; they were tiny, timid, and twittering; they moved their minute hands about unceasingly, they jerked their heads forward as they spoke, and they darted restlessly from place to place. In their youth, both had married according to the wishes of their parents, but without much feeling of ardor for their respective mates; both had been left widowed and childless at middle age—in fact a strange similarity shadowed their lives. In their early sixties, with a happiness they had not known since childhood, they established a joint *ménage,* and arranged to spend their last years, as they had spent the first years, joyfully together. Their house was a delightful place, permeated through and through with the spirit of their affection. Its heavy carved furniture and somber paintings were lightened by this; its marble floors and high walls were warmed by it; and Faith felt sure she would be content in it from the instant she set foot inside its grilled gate.

The twins were waiting for their guests in the garden and before the first greetings were over two grave but friendly servants appeared bearing trays laden with *café con leche* and sugar-coated rolls piled into snowy mounds, which they spread out on the little iron tables standing on the gravel underneath the oleander trees. Both coffee and rolls were consumed in enormous quantities, for fresh relays of each were constantly forthcoming; and a long time was squandered in the pleasant process of breakfasting. When at last Rudolf and Faith went up to their crimson and gold room with their "sumptuous" bath, Carlota accompanied them to be sure they were comfortably installed in it and then retired to take a short rest, being slightly fatigued after getting up unusually early and the excitement of welcoming the bridal pair. But Sebastian and Carlos continued to sit in the sunshine smoking innumerable cigarettes, the older man slightly garrulous, the younger one very silent. And when Faith came down again two hours later, after unpacking and bathing, they apparently had not stirred from the place where she had left them. They seemed completely enfolded by the fragrant languor of the garden.

"Rudolf has gone to the Chancery," she said a little shyly, in answer to their unspoken question. Neither of them had expressed the least surprise at seeing her alone. Nevertheless she realized that they were astonished at this, and that though the astonishment of Carlos was mild and undisturbing, the astonishment of Sebastian was mocking and sarcastic. "It was understood that he should put in to-day and to-morrow there, on his way to Granada," she went on. "You see he has been away nearly a week already, and work has accumulated, though he tried to leave everything cleared up before he left to be married."

"Rudolf," murmured Sebastian, rolling still another fresh cigarette between his slim, restless fingers, "would certainly leave everything cleared up before he was married. Not that he would have much to clear up. He is far too meticulous for that; but he would do it anyway. He is so different from the rest of us, who spring into matrimony irrespective of the encircling wreckage."

"You will give our new cousin a most unfavorable impression of Spaniards, if you talk such nonsense," said Don Carlos. He spoke gently, almost too gently, Faith felt, as if he were trying to shield her from something.

"I shall try not to judge them all by Sebastian," she remarked, serenely.

The two men glanced at each other. Then Don Carlos laughed, as gently as he had spoken, and Sebastian smiled again, not cynically, but charmingly, as he had when she had said she needed no persuasion to marry Rudolf.

"*Touché!*" he said lightly, "but after to-morrow, what then? What about the next few weeks? Is Rudolf to keep coming back and forth from Granada to make sure everything is in good order at the Chancery?"

"He is not to come back at all for an entire month. His only official duty will be to read the history of Spanish colonization, in Spanish, for three hours each day."

This time Sebastian put back his head and laughed outright.

"Is the history of Spanish colonization especially amusing?" Faith asked, still serenely.

"It is not. It is very dreadful and very glorious, like many other things connected with Spain. But the thought of any man reading about it for three hours a day on his honeymoon is irresistibly comic."

"Sebastian!" exclaimed Don Carlos in his tone of warning gentleness.

"*Tio mio,* admit that only a German mind, concentrated on system, culture and acquisition could ever conceive such a plan, much less carry it out."

"Rudolf has not actually carried it out yet," said Faith rather thoughtfully and Sebastian laughed again.

"I challenge you to see whether you can keep him from doing so!" he exclaimed.

"Perhaps," interrupted Don Carlos mildly, "if the Spanish mind had been capable of more concentration we might have retained in our possession those same colonies about which Rudolf intends to inform himself. It is also possible under similar circumstances that the War of 1898 might have been either averted or won."

"Perhaps," replied Sebastian, evidently without interest. "It is certainly much too hot to argue the question now. Though your words remind me of what I had temporarily forgotten: that we have an enemy in our midst. With the shadow of defeats still hanging so heavily over us and the wounds of conflict hardly healed we can scarcely call her anything else. Remember that the *Señora* is an American."

"She is Rudolf's wife," said Don Carlos speaking for the first time a little sharply and impatiently, as if he had borne with Sebastian's vagaries long enough.

"No doubt it is prudent that you should remind me of that," replied Sebastian, his voice sarcastic again, and the mocking smile which twisted his scar reappearing, "though to do myself justice, since nobody else is so disposed, I have been considering, while this more or less futile conversation has been going on, what we could do to make the day pass pleasantly for Rudolf's wife while Rudolf is at the Chancery. I know that *Tia* Carlota has invited in a few relatives for dinner—not more than ten or twelve—but that she purposely left the day free. Unfortunately she did not reckon with the irresistible attractions of the Chancery! She actually imagined that Rudolf would wish to have the day free to devote to the *Señora*. And here is the *Señora* left stranded and alone! We must find a way of helping her out. For since she is an American I am very sure of two things; first that she never takes siestas, and regards persons who do indulge in them, unless they are aged and infirm, as incorrigibly slothful; and second that her conscience troubles her if she does not begin intensive sight-seeing the instant she arrives in a strange city. Though she rather enjoys sitting here in the garden, idealizing you and dazzling me with her gifts of repartee, she really feels she ought to be galloping through the Prado, stopping only long enough in her haste to gaze soulfully at Murillo's 'Immaculate Conception.'"

"Will you take me to the gallery?" asked Faith almost angrily.

She was intensely annoyed. Sebastian with his scorn and sarcasm had rent the peace that lay over the old garden. He had ridiculed her wonderful Rudolf for being conscientious; he had goaded his gentle old uncle to rage; and his attitude toward her had been insufferable. At first she had thought that she might like him after all, in spite of Rudolf's warning. But his graciousness was so corroded by cynicism as to lose its beauty. Faith was not often easily ruffled, but she was ruffled now, and there was a taunt in her question as she asked it, because she felt sure that Sebastian would be bored by the Prado, but that all things considered he would not decline to accompany her there. She felt that it would serve him right. She resolved to spend endless hours rooted before the dullest picture she could find. His answer was a distinct shock.

"I am desolated. If I had been free, of course there is nothing I should have enjoyed quite so much, nothing that I should have considered such a privilege. Naturally I should have kept the day open if I had considered the Chancery. But I have a luncheon engagement. In fact

I must hasten away to it now. That is why I am concerned as to how you will pass the day. For naturally *Tio* Carlos and *Tia* Carlota sleep all the afternoon."

"Are you lunching with the King?" asked Don Carlos sharply; and Faith understood that he felt only a royal summons could justify Sebastian's refusal to go out with her.

"I am lunching, since you insist upon asking, with Felicidad," Sebastian said slowly.

Something like a spark of enmity suddenly seemed to flare up between the two men. But it was over in a minute, and when Sebastian had taken his leave with elaborate courtesy, Don Carlos said gravely and a little hastily that he would take Faith to the Prado himself—should he send a servant for her hat and gloves? She did not in the least care about going and she recognized that for him it would be a real effort; but under the circumstances, it did not seem possible for her to decline. Once in the glorious museum she became quickly and deeply absorbed; and after luncheon, for which Rudolf did not return, she was only too glad to lie down, making up for her sleepless night by falling into a profound slumber from which she did not wake until early evening. When at last she drifted back into a state of blissful semi-consciousness, she saw that Rudolf was standing beside the gold and crimson bed, looking lovingly down at her.

"Who," she asked sleepily, putting up her face to be kissed, "is Felicidad? Is she another cousin?"

She felt Rudolf's arm grow quickly taut around her.

"Who has been talking to you about Felicidad?" he asked indignantly.

"Nobody. But Sebastian went to have lunch with her. He said it was very important. He told me that otherwise he would have been delighted to take me to the Prado, and Don Carlos seemed very upset about it, just as you do now. Is she—oh Rudolf—is Felicidad the poor lady who is 'strange?' "

"No," he said after a moment. "The name of the poor strange lady is—Dolores. Sebastian has been known to say more than once that she is well named, that she has indeed brought him nothing but sorrow. That this is why he must look for 'happiness' elsewhere. He has found it—at least temporarily—in the companionship of a little gutter-snipe whom he has succeeded in placing in the corps of the Royal Ballet."

Faith gave a little smothered exclamation.

"*Liebe* Faith," Rudolf said, almost as if he were asking her forgiveness for something. "I did not mean that you should ever hear of this. I meant always to shield you for the rest of your life from everything sordid and soiled. I know what your childhood, what your early girlhood before the good *Frau* Atkinson took charge of you must have been! . . ."

"I always had Sam," interrupted Faith, with a rush of grateful memory.

"Yes," said Rudolf grudgingly, "you had Sam. We must be thankful for that. But—I did tell you, *Liebchen*, when you questioned me that Sebastian was not 'lonely,' that he had his diversions. But I hoped it would not be necessary to particularize, though I knew you were bound to hear soon, perhaps, to see for yourself that he is—a wastrel. If he did not have great wealth, great position, great gifts he—he would have sunk very low. He has also certain undependable elements of generosity. My mother is inclined to feel that perhaps some members of the family have judged him too harshly. But I have never agreed with her, and I am thankful that she did not hear him, on your first day in Spain, decline a request of yours, because he was going to lunch with Felicidad Gomez!"

"And he will be coming here again to-night! He may even take me in to dinner! He sent me jewels for a wedding present and I shall have to wear them! We are going to spend our honeymoon in one of his houses!"

"That is all true. But I must beg you to be calm. You have every reason to feel affronted. But you must try to put it out of your mind. I cannot believe that Sebastian will often err in judgment and civility as he did to-day."

"He said himself that no one in Spain would be discourteous to me and then he was the very first——"

"*Liebe* Faith, you must compose yourself, you must be reasonable. I was angry too, as you doubtless saw, but I forced myself to self-control. I deplore Sebastian's conduct. But at the same time I beg you not to attach too much importance to it. Above all I beg you not to permit him to guess that you attach any importance to it whatsoever."

He pressed her hand, released it and rising, reached for the electric switch.

"It is unfortunate that I could not return for lunch," he said practically and without further trace of emotion. "The arrival of some important dispatches forced me to remain at the Chancery. Otherwise we might have discussed this matter calmly before you had become so completely upset about it. We will now dismiss it from our minds, however. I am going to ring to have our tea served to us here at your bedside, that you may continue your rest—let me put some extra pillows behind you—so! While we take it we will talk of pleasanter subjects. There is still much time before it will be necessary for us to dress for dinner, even though I should like you to appear *en grande toilette.*

For it would please me greatly that you should look your best to-night. I have brought you very proudly, Faith, into a very proud family."

CHAPTER 13

Faith had cause to be thankful both for her siesta and her tea, before, completely exhausted, she sank into her gold and crimson bed at three the following morning.

Dinner, *Tia* Carlota, had informed her, would be at ten o'clock. At first Faith thought that she had misunderstood, but when, striving to sound casual, she tried, by means of an indirect question, to confirm her impression, *Tia* Carlota had reiterated her original statement.

"Of course," she added by way of qualification, "we are never too much bound by time in Spain. My sister and brother-in-law, Mercedes and Pedro de Mantoña, for instance, are always rather unpunctual. And as for Sebastian, he is incorrigible. He thinks nothing of sauntering in more than an hour after the time fixed for a repast. Of course I should like to have you and Rudolf receive our guests with Carlos and myself. But if you are in the drawing-room by quarter after ten, I am sure you need feel no concern lest you will not be there to welcome them."

This was meant, Faith gathered, to be reassuring. So she waited until she and Rudolf were having tea together for an explanation for the lateness of the dinner hour.

"But that is not late," he protested, "at least not for Spain. If this had been a formal function, instead of a quiet family gathering, the hour set would have been a much later one."

"But when do Spaniards sleep?" asked Faith in bewilderment.

Rudolf shrugged his shoulders. "Oh, all the afternoon. And every now and then besides that. They are a naturally slumberous race, particularly during working hours. Perhaps that is why they think nothing of sitting up most of the night—it affords an excuse for somnolence the following day." He paused a moment, devastated a scrap of pastry in one bite and added, "Of course you understand, Faith, that I am saying this to you confidentially. Indeed, half-jestingly."

"You are very cautious," she said, pushing back her cup. "Naturally I know when you are talking to me in confidence. I am not as indiscreet as you seem to think. You do not need to keep warning me. And do Germans always explain their jokes?"

Rudolf glanced at her in calm astonishment, and then leaned across the table and took her hand, "You must still be very tired, *Liebchen*," he said gently. "I fear we made a mistake to come straight through from Berlin. We should have broken our journey by spending a day or two in Paris. But I could not endure the idea of wasting even a little of our so precious time at some noisy hotel in a city I have always detested."

"I have had a good long sleep this afternoon. I am not very tired any longer."

"Then is it that you are even more upset than I had supposed? Certainly else you would not speak to me in just that tone of voice—almost as if you were irritated with me. It is unfortunate that your first impressions of Spain—or rather of Spaniards—have not been more favorable. I should try to change these and not to confirm them. For with all its infirmities, Spain is a very noble land. After you learn to speak its language and become familiar with its customs you will discover this for yourself. I must engage a teacher for you in Granada. While I am studying the subject of colonization, you could make real progress in grammar. The Spanish verbs are rather complicated, and it is wise to become well grounded in them from the outset."

Faith drew her hand away. The gesture was not impatient, but it indicated a lack of response which was slightly disturbing to Rudolf. Nothing of the sort had previously marred their relationship.

"You aren't honestly thinking of studying while we are on our honeymoon?" she said. "Or asking me to? Not really? Please don't, Rudolf! Can't we have these few weeks all to ourselves? Just for—for loving?"

"But, *liebe* Faith! How can the effort to acquire helpful knowledge interfere with our love for each other?" He was genuinely troubled. He was also, Faith saw, entirely uncomprehending.

"You don't understand. It's—it's only that I'd like to be able to sit beside you and talk about foolish little intimate things for hours and hours without having to say to myself, 'Now I must stop telling Rudolf that I adore the color of his eyes, because it's time to go and conjugate verbs.' I believe I want to be rather slumberous myself. I think I'd like a sort of—Spanish summer after a German winter. I've always liked the expression 'slumberous, amorous, Spanish summers!' Though I've never quite known what it meant. Spaniards are—amorous as well as slumberous, aren't they?"

"Yes," said Rudolf. "Sebastian, for instance, could be so described. But the effect he has had on you does not seem to have been agreeable, to say the least!"

He also was tired and he was very close to anger again. The effort which he made toward restraint, after his curt retort, was visible. He came around the table and sat down on the bed, putting his arms about Faith.

"Dearest," he said tenderly, "you have not married a Spaniard. You have married a German. A German who loves you very dearly. You must know this, and since you cannot doubt it, will you not let him reveal it in his own way, instead of in a way that would be less natural to him, even though it seemed more romantic to you? You shall have your Spanish summer after your German winter. A winter which I know taxed your strength and patience, and put you to a test which you met magnificently. I hope and believe it will be a happy summer for you, at your German husband's side. I shall do my utmost to make it so. But meanwhile I must not neglect my work, for it in its own small way is designed to contribute to the strength and glory of the Fatherland. I must not permit you to tempt me to do so. On the contrary, I must beg you to spur me on to it, after the manner of the ladies in the age of chivalry who encouraged the knights!"

Faith did not answer. Rudolf realized that he had still failed to strike a responsive chord. He tried again.

"Out of twenty-four hours in a day only three for study! All the rest for you! And even those three hours devoted to building up a career which will make me more worthy of you as well as of my country!" He hesitated, his consciousness shot through with a sudden suspicion. "You have not before to-day objected to this program, upon which we agreed long ago," he said slowly. "Why do you object to it now? What has happened to make you discontented with it?"

"I suppose," Faith replied rather reluctantly, "it was something Sebastian said. He made fun of it. He thought the idea of any man reading about colonization for three hours a day on his honeymoon was 'irresistibly comic.' He pointed out that 'only a German mind, concentrated on system, culture and acquisition, could conceive such a plan, much less carry it out.'"

"Oh!" said Rudolf, curtly again. "And though you have been almost hysterical in your display of aversion to Sebastian, still you have attached enough importance to his opinions to permit them to influence yours?"

"I hadn't thought it out before. Now I have. But I didn't mean to quarrel over it, only to explain how I felt. Please Rudolf—I'd rather not talk about it. Do we have to?"

Rudolf was aware that her detachment was becoming more and more complete. A subconscious fear that through such withdrawal the spiritual and physical unity of their marriage might be threatened suddenly surged through him. He drew her closer to him, almost fiercely.

"No," he said. "We are not obliged to discuss it further—either that or anything else. There is a time for everything, and this is not a time for talk, any more than it is a time for work. It is a time for love." There was a vibrancy in his voice of which Faith had not been previously aware, and slightly startled, she raised her eyes to his face. As she did so, he pressed his lips down hard against hers.

• • • • •

Never before had he dominated her completely or possessed her entirely; the violence of his emotion overwhelmed her, and left her as drained of strength when it was over as she had been powerless of resistance while it lasted. She was still shaken by the shock of it when, three hours later, she descended with Rudolf at her side to the tapestried drawing-room where *Tia* Carlota and *Tio* Carlos were waiting for them. In her agitation and exhaustion, she felt as if she had lost forever both her individuality and her independence. It did not seem as if she could be, even in outer attributes, the same person who had arrived blithely and light-heartedly in Madrid that morning. Surely, during the tense twilight which had merged so swiftly and mysteriously into rapacious darkness, Rudolf must have set his seal upon her in a way that would be visible to all the world. She was grateful for the dim light in the great room, for the soft shadows cast by the tall tapers in the branching silver candelabra; and she was immeasurably reassured when her hostess greeted her tranquilly and affectionately. Surely, if *Tia* Carlota had been conscious of any startling change, she would not have spoken with such kind composure.

"So you've decided to be punctual after all, *querida!* You are on time to a minute for our little gathering! And how lovely you look in your green and silver! I see that not even a May night in Madrid can impair your freshness! But observe that others have been punctual, too, in their eagerness to welcome you. Here are your *Tio* Pedro and your *Tia* Mercedes of whom I spoke to you this morning, slanderously telling you they were always tardy! And they are actually waiting for you!"

The *Duquesa* de Mantoña had none of the bird-like characteristics of her sister. Instead, she and the *Duque* were both ponderous and portly and both faintly mustached; and however little others might be feeling the heat, they were themselves visibly affected by it, for perspiration flattened their hair and streamed from their faces. Each was twirling a preposterously tiny fan in a futile though energetic effort to obtain relief; and they simultaneously closed these with little hissing sounds as they wiped their brows and smilingly advanced toward Faith. The *Duquesa* was wearing enormous garnets, set in heavy gold filigree, and voluminous *moiré antique* to match, neither of which tended to make her look cooler or slimmer; and across the *Duque's* ample chest so many orders and decorations were stretched that Faith involuntarily wondered why his heavy broadcloth and stiff linen did not sag under the weight of them. But she was caught up too quickly by the tide of their cordial volubility to give the elaborate medals more than a passing thought: Had she had a good journey? Was it very hot on the train? Had she seen anything of Madrid that day? Ah—the Prado—was it not *prodigioso?* Did she care to do a little shopping the next day on the Carrera de San Geronimo and perhaps visit the church of the same name, where King Alfonso had been married to the English Princess Ena? Would she like to lunch at the Nuevo Club, just another small family gathering? The real fiestas, like the real sightseeing, must await her return from Granada and especially the autumn season. But they wished her to reserve her first week-end after she got back for a visit with them at Ventosilla, ten miles out of Toledo. They would send the landeau and the mules to meet her there. . . .

"Faith has already had her first ride behind our Spanish mules," interposed *Tia* Carlota. "Sebastian met her with his at the station this morning."

"Ah, then she has begun by seeing the finest in Spain! However, we will place the best we have at her disposal—Josefina, I did not see you when you came! And have you met our new cousin?"

Josefina, Inez, Francesca, Beatriz. Vicente, Tomas, Raimundo. The *conde* of this. The *princesa* of that. Who was whose brother? Who was whose aunt? Would she ever be able to keep these involved ranks and relationships straight? Would she ever be able to disentangle herself from so much complicated cordiality? Would these kinsfolk ever stop talking to her and each other? Would they ever stop coming? No, not yet, for they were still one man short. Josefina had come alone. Faith had the vague impression that this cousin had been betrothed in her youth to a grandee who was banished, just before the time appointed for their wedding, for participation in a Carlist plot. And Josefina, who, if her *novio's* revolt had been kept secret until it was successful, might eventually have become Queen of Spain, had instead immured herself in a convent and had been prevented from taking final vows as a nun, only because the precarious state of her health precluded her from enduring the rigors of the order of her choice. Her only ornament was a huge silver crucifix and her somber draperies seemed more suited to a cloister than a hearth. She was evidently a very ill woman who had made a supreme effort to be present at this assembly; and her face was scarred with frustration as well as fever and beckoning death seemed to walk beside her.

Faith turned away from her shuddering. Would the missing man never come? It was Sebastian, of course, who was keeping them all waiting. Faith had thought in the morning that she never wished to see him again. And now she was actually longing for his arrival. At least he was not completely a stranger, and that gleaming blade-like quality of his would cut its way trenchantly through this stifling solidarity, which was as alarming in its smiling as in its sinister aspects. She found herself watching the doorway at which the heavy brocaded curtains were silently drawn back for each new arrival—the doorway through which Sebastian would enter. She had not once looked at

Rudolf since she came downstairs. To save her life she could not have done so.

It was after eleven o'clock when the curtains parted for the last time. For a whole hour the stream of Spanish, the turmoil of a tongue as unfamiliar as the men and women who spoke it, had reverberated in her tired ears. For a whole hour foreign faces and figures had advanced and receded before her dazzled eyes. Now at last someone was coming toward her whom she knew; someone who would speak to her in English.

He was all in white, except for a scarlet sash tied tight around his slender waist and the vivid ribbon on which the Order of the Golden Fleece—the only decoration he was wearing—was suspended around his neck. His garments fitted as if they had been molded to him, and there was something glistening in their spotlessness. His appearance was as striking as it was exotic. No doubt he had meant that it should be. No doubt he had planned and executed a theatrical entrance, all the more dramatic because it was so long delayed. But it had lost nothing of its intended effect through premeditation. There was something electrical in the atmosphere as he crossed the polished floor with silent grace and greeted every one of the relatives with deferential affection. When at last he paused before Faith, he spoke to her very softly.

"I come, *Señora,*" he said, raising her hand to his lips, "asking your forgiveness less for being so late to-night—though this in itself is unpardonable—than for leaving you as I did this morning. I hope you will believe in the sincerity of my repentance. I also hope that it is not too late for me to make atonement for it."

Whether Faith actually answered him she was never quite able to remember. Her impression was that she did not. For she was instantly aware that whereas no one else had noticed anything anomalous about her, Sebastian's rapid penetrating glance had pierced the brittle veneer of self-control with which she was striving to conceal her emotional and physical exhaustion; and the consciousness of his swift discernment was so startling that for a moment she was incapable of speech. By the time she had collected herself, Sebastian had given a quick order to a passing servant and was addressing her again.

"Shall we not sit down?" he suggested. "I think there will still be a few minutes before we go into the dining room. Spanish dinners are long as well as late, and I fear this one will be still another tax on your strength, which has been so greatly overtaxed, and so variously, already to-day. Manuel is going to bring us some sherry and I hope you will do me the honor of drinking a glass of it with me. I believe you will agree that it is not only delicious as a beverage, but most effective as a stimulant. Of course I should not extol its merits, but I take a natural pride in this particular product as it is an unusually good vintage, and comes from one of my own properties."

A decanter surrounded by tiny goblets and filled with amber-colored liquid was already being presented on a silver tray. Sebastian motioned to the servant to set it down. "I will pour it out myself, Manuel—" he stood smiling at the old man—"and you might leave it here. I am hoping to persuade the *Señora* to sample it more than once." He lifted the decanter, and the wine flowed down with a thick rich gurgle. "*Salud, Señora!*" he said, passing her a brimming glass and raising his own ceremoniously. "Tell me if you think I have overpraised this."

"It is very good," said Faith slowly. Her hand was shaking a little, and she found it hard to hold the goblet steady; but she had recovered her voice and spoke quite calmly. "It tastes differently from any sherry I have ever had before, and I do not think it is quite the same color."

"You are right. It is much paler—paler and more powerful—than the inferior sherry that is used for export. You are going to have some more, aren't you—just to prove to me that you like it? And this time you must pour it and say '*Salud!*' to me."

The animating fluid was streaming through her veins, flooding her tired body and brain with refreshment. When she had emptied her goblet a second time she found out she could smile at him without an effort.

"You can't imagine how much better I feel," she said gratefully.

"I must try to continue the cure. *Tia* Carlota has been good enough to say that I might sit beside you at dinner. And after dinner there is always the garden. It will be very late before the party is over. By the time you return to Rudolf I hope you will be entirely restored."

Manuel was looping back the portières that hung between the drawing-room and the dining room. Beyond, Faith could see a long table, massed with flowers and glittering with glass and china. The relatives, who, momentarily, seemed to have forgotten her as completely as she had forgotten them, suddenly surged forward again, talking excitedly. Rudolf was not in sight. He seemed to have been swallowed up somewhere in their midst. Sebastian rose and offered Faith his arm.

"The wedding feast," he murmured with a return of irony, "at which the bridegroom tarrieth. Shall you and I go into it together, *Señora?*"

CHAPTER 14

FAITH woke reluctantly, with a sensation of one who has slept a long, long while, but still feels so incompletely refreshed as to wish to slumber on indefinitely; she also woke to the consciousness of the emptiness which pervades a room when one of two persons who share it is absent. Half opening her eyes, she saw that a meticulously folded note had been neatly pinned to the pillow beside her own; and reaching for it, she drowsily read the message that Rudolf had left for her.

"*Liebe* Faith . . ." it ran:

"It is time for me to leave for the Chancery, and you are sleeping so soundly and still looking so tired—though so lovely!—that I cannot bear to wake you, even to kiss you good-bye, although I long to do so. I also wish to talk to you a little, for I am very troubled. And now I fear I shall have no chance to be alone with you to-day, since the Mantoñas have made so many plans so that you will be kept busy until it is time for us to take our train for Granada. My aunt's maid, Angelina, will bring you coffee when you ring, and she will let *Tia* Carlota know, whether you still wish to visit the shops on the Carrera de San Geronimo, or whether you would rather rest until luncheon-time, when we shall all be meeting at the Nuevo Club. Please feel free to do just as you would prefer. Angelina understands French, so you will have no trouble in talking with her. Devotedly, Rudolf."

The small enameled watch, which Mr. and Mrs. Castle had given her for an engagement present, lay on the bedside-table. Faith pulled at its long jeweled chain, swung it in front of her, and sat bolt upright, rubbing her eyes, unable to believe that she had seen the hour correctly. Then she shook it and held it to her ear, thinking that possibly she had forgotten to wind it when she went to bed; for certainly its tiny gold hands were pointing to quarter before one. But it was ticking away with a cheerful little gallop, and dismayed lest she should be late for luncheon, she laid it quickly down and rang for Angelina.

The afternoon was almost over by the time the copious repast at the Nuevo Club was finished. How was it possible, Faith wondered, for anyone to do justice to so many and such abundant courses in such warm weather? The multitudinous *hors d'œuvres* alone would have made up an ample midday meal; and they were followed by an omelet, a fillet of beef, cauliflower, broiled chicken, green salad, *meringues chantilly,* and a variety of luscious fruits. But the assembled relatives ate their way from the beginning to the end of the menu with leisurely relish, and then sat sipping their strong coffee and rich liqueurs for an additional half-hour before they dispersed for their siestas. Even though Angelina helped her, it was necessary for Faith to hurry with her packing; and then came leave-takings at the station as protracted and elaborate as if she and Rudolf had been leaving for a two-year sojourn in China, instead of a fortnight's stay at a family house in Granada. The relatives, refreshed by sleep, reappeared *en masse.* In spite of the lateness with which they had finished lunch, their first concern seemed to be to provide more food for the journey: a large hamper, from which a cold fowl, long sticks of bread, a large cheese wrapped in silver-foil, and several slim bottles of wine, could be seen protruding beneath the folded napkin which covered its contents, was stowed into a rack by Manuel under the twittering direction of *Tia* Carlota. *Tio* Carlos seemed to feel that this snack would prove inadequate; so to reinforce it he had brought chocolates in an enormous and gaudy box, which was ornamented with glazed pictures, highly colored, of a bull-fight, and tied with red and yellow ribbons. Even Josefina had an offering of plums, which she whispered to Faith were known to have special miraculous value as nourishment, since they grew in the garden of the convent of Our Lady of Perpetual Sorrows —and came from the same trees as those which had been the sole sustenance, during a long period of abstinence, of a nun who had later been canonized. To offset the somewhat overwhelming effect of the plums, *Tio* Pedro lumbered down the platform staggering under the weight of a great sheaf of humorous periodicals and risqué novels which he had bought from an itinerant vender; and unperturbed by the fact that since Faith did not understand Spanish she would be unable to appreciate either the subtle witticisms of *Buen Humor* or the somewhat salacious stories of his favorite romancer, he presented these to her with puffing pride. The billowing bundle of *Tia* Mercedes proved to be filled with down cushions; and the crackling cornucopias of stiff white paper which Inez and Francesca thrust into Faith's hands contained huge bouquets of purplish-pink roses pressed together as closely as tinned-sardines; while the temperature, which was soaring well above ninety, had not deterred other members of the family from coming equipped with travel rugs.

It was not until the fussy little train, with a pompousness out of all proportion to its size, had tooted its way out of the station, past the low row of upturned faces, and the indefatigable hands throwing kisses and waving handkerchiefs, that Faith was actually alone with Rudolf. It was evident that he had something on his mind, and that whatever this was, he was at one and the same time anxious to unburden himself of it and hesitant about how best to do so. But he could hardly be blamed for feeling that the stiff and stuffy little compartment, unconducive to physical ease, was not an ideal setting for intimate revelations. Besides, she was not only aloof, as she had been the afternoon before; she seemed actually to be on her guard against him; and her absorption in the gifts which had been showered upon her seemed entirely out of relation to their value, fitness, or usefulness. His tentative endeavors to converse with her and to caress her proved equally unsuccessful; and the fact that the conductor seemed bent on intruding at most inopportune moments did not help his cause. Finally, with characteristic Teutonic patience, he decided to bide his time.

His second attempt at an exchange of confidence had a happier ending. Though still silent and undemonstrative the following morning, Faith seemed less on the defensive; and her delight in the old vine-covered *casita,* which they reached shortly before noon, was instantaneous and unrestrained. Indeed, her mood had become more melting from the moment they left the train and started on their drive through the radiant Andalusian countryside. A stocky, swarthy servant of expansive geniality, named Felipe, had met them in Granada; and as he pointed out the landmarks of interest along the dusty highway with a beaming smile, Faith responded to him with mounting enthusiasm. By the time they came in sight of the gardens and orchards encircled by the olive groves and vineyards of the *caseria,* which was completely hidden from the highway by a tall blank wall, intersected only by one immense iron-hinged wooden door, she was sparkling with spontaneous admiration.

"Why didn't you tell me how beautiful it all was, Rudolf? I never saw such roses! Or such box-hedges—big and bushy enough to lie down and go to sleep on! I think I will some sunny day! What kind of trees are those? Pomegranate? Not really? I thought that pomegranates only grew in the Bible. I mean, I thought they were sort of mythical and symbolical like frankincense and jasper and things like that! And these are *real!* We can have pomegranates with cream and sugar for breakfast!"

"They are not usually eaten that way," said Rudolf practically. "In any case this is not the season for them, and they are rather acid. I doubt if you will care for them. And surely you know that Granada is a literal translation of the word pomegranate, so it is quite logical to expect to find this fruit in the vicinity of the city."

"I'm terribly afraid I'm not as logical as you are, Rudolf. Anyway nobody told me about the literal translation. And I *do* care for them. I think it's wonderful that they exist; and, oh, what a lovely, lovely little house!"

She leaped down from the creaking old carriage before either Rudolf or Felipe could stretch out a detaining or assisting hand. The next instant she was standing in the paved patio, tilting her head to look up at the shining sapphire sky, and then bending over to trail her fingers through the water that bubbled about the small stone figure of a chubby cherub, standing on a stone cockle-shell in the middle of the central fountain.

"So patios with fountains are real too!" she exclaimed. "We can sit here in the evenings and look up at the stars, can't we? And we can have a little table brought out and set in the corner and eat our meals here."

"We can have our luncheons and dinners here if you choose. It is cool and pleasant for that. But I think you may like the tower best for breakfast and tea. It is not hot there early in the morning, and the sunsets are very beautiful. Besides there is a fine view of the Sierra Nevadas and the *vega*."

"Is there a tower, too? I didn't notice it, I was so busy looking at roses and pomegranates and box. Can we go and see it right away?"

She rushed indoors and came again to a happy halt. What wonderful old furniture! There was nothing in *Tia* Carlota's house half so beautiful as those high-backed black and gold chairs, those tall dark screens painted with flowers and scenes of Granada, those crimson velvet chests studded with metal! But how did it happen that there were Venetian glass chandeliers in an Andalusian house? Now the red-tiled floors—those were more like what she had expected to find at the *caseria!* Only she had not realized they would be so spotless and shining. How charming to have the bedrooms all opening into a *galeria* around the patio! Were they to put their clothes in those inlaid *bagueños* instead of bureaus? Was it all right for a Protestant to use a *prie-dieu?* She had always thought she would adore it. And was there a library in the *tower?* Whoever would have thought of putting one there! Yet it was an ideal place after all. And what a heavenly open terrace that was above it, looking out on all those green plains and white mountains beyond the groves and orchards.

"Of course we must have our morning coffee and afternoon tea here!" she agreed ecstatically. "It's marvelous. Do you remember the story about the householder who planted a vineyard, and hedged it round about, and digged a wine-press in it, and built a tower? We are just like him! I haven't seen the wine-press yet, but I am sure we have one."

"Yes," said Rudolf amiably, "we have." He was infinitely relieved at Faith's change in mood. "I think you will find it very interesting to go and visit the *bodega*, where the great barrels containing the wine made on the place are kept.—But I do not seem to remember the story of which you speak."

"It's in the Bible, like the pomegranates and the jasper. Grandmother Faith used to read it to me when I was very little. I was named for her, you know, and I was very fond of her. It's strange that I remember her so well, but I do. I remember what she looked like and everything she taught me. Besides, after she died, Daddy used to read to me the same way she did, in the afternoon before my supper, in Washington and at the farm, too. He never let anything interfere with our time together."

She leaned her arms on the parapet, and resting her chin on them went on talking with Rudolf while she continued to gaze away from him toward the distant Sierras.

"I've never been back since mamma first brought me to Europe nine years ago," she said slowly. "That's a long while to be away from home.

Do you think perhaps the next time you have leave we might go there? I had been planning to, you know, when I met you."

"But *liebe* Faith," Rudolf reminded her, "Germany is your Fatherland now."

"No, it isn't," she contradicted quickly. Then seeing his pained expression she added, "Of course I admire Germany, and I understand, because you have explained it all to me so clearly, that when a girl gets married her husband's country becomes hers legally. But it doesn't seem that way to me. It seems to me that the place where you are born is really home. It seems to me that's the place you always want to go back to most. Of course just now I wouldn't want to be anywhere but here. It's like a fairy tale, isn't it? Much more beautiful than anything I've ever seen before. But just the same, it would never mean quite as much to me as home does."

"Perhaps some day I shall be appointed to Washington," said Rudolf. "It is coming to be considered quite an important place, though formerly, of course, it was looked upon as a rather undesirable post. Diplomatically, I mean. Residentially I am sure it is an agreeable city."

Having dismissed the capital of the United States courteously and concisely from their conversation, he felt the announcement that luncheon was ready to be extremely opportune. He did not wish to argue with Faith again; he feared that more differences of opinion might cast another blighting shadow over her radiant spirit. Therefore, the bulky form of Catalina, Felipe's wife, looming up before them with timely tidings about *almuerzo*, was extremely welcome. Faith, who had been too transported to take off her hat or wash her hands, went blithely off to do both, admitting that now she thought of it, she was really very hungry; and she did full justice to Catalina's oily omelet, to the fish which had been brought over the mountains from Malaga during the night, and to the olives and figs which had been grown on the *caseria*. After luncheon she very sensibly raised no objection when Rudolf remarked that he would rest for a little while in the library before beginning his work there, while she took her siesta; and when she rejoined him, several hours later, on the terrace, she told him, with a touch of pride indicative of budding housewifeliness, that, instead of taking a nap, she had unpacked and arranged their belongings while he was studying, and that she had also been through the kitchen and larder with Catalina.

"I do like a little friendly house like this so much better than a big formal one," she said. "And just two or three nice old servants instead of rows of footmen and flunkies—Did you know that the water for our baths was all pumped up by hand from cisterns back of the patio? Catalina showed them to me with very graphic signs, so that I knew that she wanted us to use as much water as we pleased. And, oh—I've had my first Spanish lesson! I pointed to things, and Catalina laughed and told me what their names were. It was great fun. I can almost order a meal already." She began to check words off on her fingers: "*pan-vino-sopa-huevos-carne-pescado-legumbres-dulce-queso-frutas.* There now!"

Rudolf smiled, but did not answer instantly.

"Your cue is to say '*Muy bien*' and whatever the Spanish word is for darling."

"There are all sorts of extravagant phrases," Rudolf answered. "Spaniards are no more given to restraint of expression than of behavior. I should prefer to go on calling you *Liebchen.*"

"But you might at least tell me what some of the extravagant phrases are. I am sure it is part of my education."

"*Dulce amiga, vida mia, alma de mi alma,* are a few of the more conservative ones," Rudolf said a little grudgingly and with a touch of sarcasm. "But I do not think, as I just said, that I shall become addicted to any of them. However, I am very pleased that you have spent your time so profitably. And is it not pleasant here now?"

"Pleasant! Oh, Rudolf, you know it is divine! Listen to those church bells ringing! Look at that color in the sky and on the mountains!"

With the first spontaneous sign of affection that she had made since they arrived in Spain, she linked her arm through his; and they stood in silence for a few minutes, while the silvery sound of the Angelus echoed across the *vega,* and the radiant rose of the sunset spread like a flame across the horizon. Encouraged by her gesture, and by a sense of encircling benignity, Rudolf laid his cheek against Faith's, and was unaccountably thrilled when she turned and kissed him. Moreover, her next words filled him with satisfaction.

"I have been waiting for a chance to tell you," she said, with a slight hesitancy which seemed to spring less from embarrassment than from a desire to speak tactfully, "that I have been thinking about those three hours a day that you want to set aside for study, and I think you are right about them. I do not care much for siestas and I shall be glad to try and learn Spanish while you are working out theories of colonization. I think if we separate for three hours after lunch to do this we will enjoy our tea on the terrace all the more afterwards. I am sorry if I have seemed unreasonable."

"I felt sure, *liebe* Faith, that when you thought the matter over you would agree with me," Rudolf said in a pleased tone of voice. "I know I can always depend on your good sense."

"And before we go downstairs to get ready for dinner," Faith went on serenely, as if in natural sequence to her remarks on the acquisition of knowledge, "perhaps I ought to tell you—so that you won't be surprised—that when I unpacked I put our things in separate rooms. We have so much space here, all to ourselves, that it seemed too bad not to use it. For dressing you know. And for times when we don't want to disturb each other."

Rudolf stared at her in amazement, his complacence completely wrecked.

"But, *liebe* Faith! Nothing could disturb me so much as the knowledge that you would even think of doing such a thing! And without consulting me at all!"

He was visibly appalled. Faith's color deepened a little, but she showed no other sign of concern.

"I did not mean to hurt your feelings. But I thought perhaps we both might be more comfortable that way. When you think it over perhaps you will agree with me, just as I agreed with you after I had thought over the study period."

"I want to talk to you very seriously, Faith," said Rudolf with great gravity.

"Yes. You said so in the note you pinned on the pillow. And I could see, on the train, that you kept thinking about it. I pretended not to notice because it did not seem to me like a good time. But this is a very good time."

Her candor was disconcerting. Rudolf was actually less self-possessed than she as he attempted to go on. His embarrassment made him abrupt.

"I was very glad that Sebastian did not come to the luncheon at the Nuevo Club," he said without preamble, "or return to *Tia* Carlota's house at all yesterday. I have not forgiven him for upsetting you so completely."

"He did upset me at first, in the morning. But I think that was partly because he is so different from any man I have ever seen before. Much more—more complex. He bewildered me. I felt that he was naturally clever and charming and at the same time that he was bent on proving himself cynical and cruel. But in the evening he did not upset me at all. He was wonderfully kind and understanding. I felt as if I had known him all my life. I did not expect to see him again yesterday. He explained to me that he would not be able to come to the Nuevo Club because he would be lunching as usual with Felicidad. He said she had grown to depend upon having him for luncheon almost every day, and he did not like to disappoint her, especially since he had so many evening engagements. He spoke about her so naturally and frankly that I did not seem shocked at all. He said that dancers were paid very little and would hardly be able to live unless they had *protectores*. He told me he thought I would enjoy seeing her on the stage next winter, she is so light and gay and graceful, and he says she has a lovely laugh—that's what attracted him to her at first. A lovely laugh and a very sweet sunny disposition."

"Oh!" said Rudolf again abruptly, "and after he had put you at your ease, partly by talking to you about his latest mistress and partly by the equally unpardonable means of giving you some very strong sherry to drink, you did not by any chance talk with him intimately, did you? About our personal and private relations? Or subjects which should never be discussed except between a husband and wife?"

The startled surprise with which Faith gazed at him was all the reply Rudolf needed. Nevertheless, after a moment of mute astonishment she answered him so quietly that he did not suspect he had wounded her to the quick by his question.

"I was very tired when we went down to dinner, Rudolf. And then—after a while—I became dizzy. Everything had been strange and confusing to me all day and the strangeness and confusion kept getting worse and worse. There seemed to be no end to them. When Sebastian came into the drawing-room he seemed to guess exactly how I was feeling the minute he looked at me. That was when he sent for the sherry. I had two glasses and afterwards I felt ever so much better. Until I did he kept telling me funny stories and by and by I talked too. That is, part of the time. But I didn't discuss anything with him to speak of. Naturally nothing private or intimate. We didn't even keep up a regular conversation. It didn't seem necessary. It wasn't awkward when there were silences, the way it is with most people. It was friendly. I don't know that I'm explaining very well, because I've never felt exactly that way before. Not even with Sam. But I hope I've made you understand what it was like, if you wanted to know.—What made you ask?"

"Because," said Rudolf, "Sebastian upset me quite as much in the evening as he upset you in the morning. When the ladies went back into the drawing-room after dinner, he maneuvered to get me away from the other men, at one of those little tin-tables in the garden. He had Manuel, who simply feeds out of his hand, bring coffee and liqueurs to us there, and kept on bringing them, so that I could not get up and escape from him without a discourtesy so flagrant that it would be evident to everybody. He asked preposterous questions, and made preposterous comments on my answers. His effrontery is surpassed only by his indelicacy."

"What sort of questions do you mean?" inquired Faith.

"He asked me how old you were."

"But Rudolf, that is a perfectly natural question!"

"It depends on who asks it, and how. When I told him, seventeen, he remarked that even in Latin countries a girl was hardly considered marriageable at that age any longer, which is of course a great distortion of fact."

"Is it?" said Faith.

"You must know that it is. Early marriages are the rule rather than the exception in all Latin countries, especially in Spain."

"Was his—his wife very young when she was married?"

"I believe so. Yes. She was. Both of them were, in fact. I know that they have been married more than ten years, and Sebastian is only just past thirty now."

"Then can't you understand why he should have a special reason for feeling that early marriages are unwise? Remember how unhappy he has been!"

"I remember how profligate he has been!" exclaimed Rudolf bitterly. "You seem determined to find excuses for Sebastian, Faith! But even so, I do not believe you would contend that his next remarks were excusable."

Rudolf paused.

"What did he say?" inquired Faith.

She asked the question with interest and without eagerness. Nevertheless Rudolf seemed to feel that there was no reason why she should have asked it at all, in spite of the fact that he had invited it.

"If you must know, he insisted upon talking about marriage as an institution. He said that Catholics were taught it was a sacrament, and that even Lutherans talked about 'holy matrimony.' And then, he remarked mockingly, that the former were apt to convert it into bondage, and the latter into—legalized violence."

"Oh!" cried Faith, aghast, "how terrible that he should feel he is in bondage!"

"Faith! I am appalled by your lack of subtlety! What do Sebastian's remarks about bondage—if they were really sincere—amount to compared to—his other expression? Don't you realize what he meant?"

Faith did not answer immediately, and when she did she spoke rather stumblingly. "I am sorry that I seemed so stupid," she said slowly. "But I honestly didn't realize—right away——"

"I am sorry to make you do so. But in view of Sebastian's hideous behavior I do not see how I can help it. He declined to be diverted, and he kept looking at me as if I were some kind of a violent criminal, instead of a loving bridegroom. I finally decided that he must be either intoxicated, or temporarily deranged, or else that you must have said something to him which betrayed—that the consummation of our marriage had been forced upon you."

There was a long silence. It was Faith who finally broke it. "I do believe that Sebastian knew exactly what happened," she said at last in a low voice. "I thought so the minute he looked at me when he came into the drawing-room. It was uncanny, almost as if he were clairvoyant. But of course I did not say anything at all. How could I? I mean, even if I had dreamed of doing such a thing? It would have been impossible. I was too—overwhelmed."

"But Faith," asked Rudolf desperately, "didn't you guess at all——? I know that young maidens are kept in innocence, but didn't you have any idea——?" His bitterness had spent itself, and there was deep solicitude in his troubled voice.

There was another long silence, and when Faith spoke again it was evident that she had been considering carefully beforehand what she was going to say, that she was resolutely trying to be not only calm but just and truthful.

"It is very hard to explain, Rudolf. I knew of course that married persons slept in the same room. But it is all so vague and—indefinite to a girl. She senses that there is something. But something so mysterious and secret that it is—sacramental. Unless it is just the opposite. Unless it—seems shameful. I had begun to realize before my mother died that there was a—a sort of close relationship between her and certain men. But I never tried to find out exactly what it was. I tried *not* to find out! I felt so—so smirched by it all the time that I couldn't bear to. Afterwards—after she died—I was stunned for a while, I suppose. Anyway, I didn't think about any—any mysteries again for a long time. And then I met you, and suddenly the world seemed like a different place. Instead of being numb and wretched I was so happy and excited I didn't know what to do. I thought you were the most wonderful person on earth. Oh!—much more than a *person*—a radiant St. Michael! Driving away dragons! Bringing salvation and strength! Surrounded by All Angels!"

"*Liebe* Faith, in one way I am glad that you thought of me like that. I am thankful that I seemed to bring you deliverance and joy. But in another way I am sorry. For I am not a saint, and it did not occur to me that you thought of me in that light."

"Oh, Rudolf, I would give anything if I could make you understand! When I said I thought of you as a saint, I didn't mean that I didn't think of you as human too! St. Michael was a very *masculine* sort of a saint anyway, wasn't he? What I am trying to explain is that I worshipped you so and trusted you so that when I did begin to wonder a little about —about mysteries again, I didn't worry over them. I felt sure they *would* be sacramental, since they were to be part of my life with you. I didn't even want anyone—any outsider—to spoil them for me by telling me too much about them beforehand. I wanted you to do that yourself. Cousin Sarah did try to have a 'little talk' with me the week before we were married. I could see that she thought she ought to. But I wouldn't let her. I stopped her by telling her that I wanted to leave everything in your hands. I told her I cared for you too much to doubt your gentleness and your tenderness—and your loving kindness."

Suddenly she clasped her hands together and gave a little dry sob.

"That is what has made me so unhappy. It is not what you did. I–I understand about that now. It is the way you did it. You are usually so calm, and all at once you were–violent. It was *all* so sudden! You did not prepare me at all. If you had I am sure you would not have needed to use force. You did not caress me; you–compelled me. You were not gentle or tender and kind. You were not even loving, though the only thing you said to me was that it was a time for love. Oh, Rudolf, why–why did it have to be like that?"

She had broken into uncontrollable weeping. Rudolf bent over her and drew her toward him.

"*Liebchen,*" he said tenderly, "my dearest Faith, don't–don't! I do understand everything now, but you must try to be understanding, too! I did mean to be very patient–to wait until we reached here. But I wanted you so much, and I felt that you were drawing away from me, not growing closer to me–that is why I lost my self-control! And I could not guess how far you had relied on my intuition and my guidance. Please, darling, tell me that you forgive me! I promise you that it will never be like that again."

She was not actually struggling against him, but still he was conscious of no real yielding to his embrace. In his real and deep concern lest he should again fail in gentleness he made no effort to hold her closely, and presently she raised a tear-stained face to his.

"What is it going to be like?" she asked.

He hesitated, torn between the passion that was surging through him again, and the insidious fear that if he erred a second time he might lose her altogether.

"You told me, when you first came up on the terrace, that you had separated our belongings," he said gravely. "I shall not ask you to place them together again. And when I knock at the door of your room, I will not come in unless you tell me that I may. I give you my word of honor."

The glory of the sunset had long since disappeared, the moon had not yet risen. But the dark sky was jeweled with stars, the terrace luminous. Rudolf could see the tense expression of Faith's face changing, almost before he was aware that she was relaxing in his arms. He took courage.

"But I shall come to it hoping you will be more generous to me than I deserve," he said softly.

. . . . .

Nevertheless, after he had parted from her that night in the *galeria* his hammering heart failed him. It was very late. Even at the *caseria* dinner never took place until after nine; and it had been delayed because he and Faith had remained so long on the terrace, where neither Felipe nor Catalina–who had a romantic regard for the exigencies of a honeymoon—had intruded upon them. Then the dinner—served in a corner of the patio, as Faith had desired—had lasted a long time; and after that they had sat, with Faith's head against his shoulder, listening to the bubbling fountain. Finally she had said it was bedtime and they had gone upstairs together. Yes, it was very late. He reached for his bedside candle to blow it out. Just then he heard Faith calling him.

He swung open the heavy door that divided the room which she had chosen for her own from his. The metal lamp suspended from the high ceiling had been extinguished; but through the long window leading out to the *galeria*, moonlight rushed in with a stream of radiance, flooding the smooth-tiled floor and high white walls with its light. In the great carved bed, set in an arched recess under a small high window, Faith lay beneath a golden coverlet, her shining hair falling over the snowy pillows, the sheer lace of her nightgown only half veiling her soft breast. As Rudolf came up to her she held out her hands.

"You didn't knock," she said softly. "You didn't give me a chance to be generous. Won't you?"

PART V

Gabriel

CHAPTER 15

A SENSUOUS quietude enfolded the *caseria.* Serene days, permeated with tranquillity and warmth, drifted fragrantly away into one translucent twilight after another. And with the descent of night, the little vine-clad house lay hushed and hidden in the embrace of poignant darkness.

Through Faith's sudden self-abandonment, Rudolf had been transported to rapturous regions of which he had never even dreamed before; and having attained them, the fear that this abandonment might not be lasting served as another spur to his stimulated senses. But she had done far more than yield to the urgency of his desire; she had surrendered to the principle that passion was his prerogative; and in doing so she had made herself wholly his. The aftermath of her supreme submission was a languor so insidious that she found she could not prevail against it; and she succumbed to it utterly. But it was a languor that enhanced her radiance, and Rudolf found her more irresistible than ever. The "slumberous, amorous summer" for which Faith had pled so artlessly had become a reality, and Rudolf, who had rebuked her for her unconscious expression of emotionalism, was himself discovering an emotional heaven.

For some time there were no intruders in his passionate paradise; and it was not until he inadvertently glanced at a small calendar in the library, so unobtrusively hung as to be hitherto overlooked, that he realized, with a shock of surprise, that he had been at the *caseria* almost a fortnight, and that in all this while he had not read a single word about Spanish colonization. He had been on his way to the terrace when he made his disturbing discovery, and feeling nearly as guilty as if he had deserted his regiment under fire, he tore himself away from Faith, the instant they had finished their coffee, with lingering and ardent embraces, but with a Spartan injunction that she was not to come near him again until luncheon-time.

Freed from his dominating and demanding presence, and with a conscience slightly troubled because of the sense of relief of which she was almost instantly aware, she went outdoors and began to divert herself aimlessly but agreeably. She watched an old man who had come out from Granada to take up the honey; she gathered and sampled a few persimmons; she transplanted a palm for the mere pleasure of moving it from one place to another. When the heat of the mounting sun drove her back into the house, she filled twenty vases with the flowers she had picked, and then she settled herself contentedly in her bedroom, sorting and mending the folded piles of freshly washed garments which Catalina had laid there. She was accustomed to keeping her own clothing in order; and she was glad to sit down now peacefully in a low chair, to weave together a tear in a fine silk stocking and close up a rip in a French seam. When Catalina burst in upon her, visibly and volubly excited, and gesticulating frantically toward the drawing-room, Faith faintly resented the interruption to her tidy occupation. She could disentangle nothing definite from the servant's agitated exclamations about *Su Eminencia.* So when she reached the *salita* she was surprised to find herself confronted by a tall purple-clad figure of great distinction, who rose at her approach and came forward with an air of benign dignity.

"I have been hoping that you and your husband would come to see me," he said in excellent English, "but since you have not, I have come to see you instead, for I wished very much to welcome you into the family. I learned from my brother, of course, when you and your husband came here."

"I am very glad to see you," said Faith cordially and sincerely. Her visitor was indeed apparently very eminent; he was, moreover, kindly and gracious also, and though she could not instantly identify the likeness, he bore a certain softened but striking resemblance to someone whom she had seen already. "But I am afraid I do not know who you are."

"My name is Gabriel de Cerreno. I am Sebastian's elder brother—much older, for I am nearly old enough to be his father. But we are devoted to each other, in spite of the difference in our ages and—pursuits. Indeed we always write to each other every day when we are separated, as we unfortunately are much of the time. We have both lost so much that we are united by an unusually close tie. Our parents and their other children have all died and we are the only remaining members of our immediate circle."

"I am sorry that you have lost so much," said Faith sympathetically. "I remember now when Rudolf first spoke to me about Sebastian he told me that there were only two brothers left out of a large family. He said that one of them had entered the church."

"Yes," said Gabriel, smiling a little, "I happen to be the Archbishop of Granada."

"Oh!" said Faith, "then I am afraid I should have kissed your ring or something like that, when I came into the drawing-room, instead of just shaking hands. But I do not know just how archbishops should be treated. I have never met one before. Are they anything like archduchesses? I should be relieved if you could say that they were, because my mother-in-law is an archduchess, and I am very fond of her."

"I do not wonder," replied Gabriel amiably, "she is one of the most charming women in Europe. She is also a devout Catholic, like all Hapsburgs. I should be very pleased if you thought, in this instance, that there was a similarity between archbishops and archduchesses. In fact I should take it as a distinct compliment. As to the questions of ecclesiastical etiquette, do not let those disturb you. I am sure you will master them very quickly. Besides, I came to see you as a kinsman and not as an archbishop, though I should have been very glad if Rudolf had brought you with him to be received in audience, and to be given my Episcopal blessing. However, I am not surprised that he has not."

Gabriel smiled, and Faith thought there was actually a twinkle in his dark eyes, as if he were perfectly well aware how complete Rudolf's preoccupation had been since his marriage and precisely what form this had taken. She colored deeply, and the Archbishop, noticing her blush, continued speaking in a manner calculated to put her more at her ease.

"Rudolf was, of course, baptized in the Church," he said smoothly, "as the children of mixed marriages always are. Perhaps you did not realize this."

"No," said Faith in genuine surprise. "I thought he was a Lutheran like his father."

"He is. He became one as soon as he was old enough to be confirmed. This was a great blow to Victoria Luise, but naturally she never mentions it. She is wise enough to know that piety is no excuse for tactlessness. In fact she and I have often agreed that Our Savior, who was a gentleman, would have been the last to tolerate ungraciousness from his followers. And certainly Victoria Luise was not to blame for Rudolf's defection, nor, to do Hans von Hohenlohe justice, do I think he was either. I have never known him to even contemplate a dishonorable act, in spite of great provocation. I am sure he put no pressure on the boy at all. I think it was merely that temperamentally, Rudolf was much more fitted to be a Lutheran than a Catholic. And, as a matter of fact, I have never felt as bitter about his apostasy as most of the lay members of the family. Sebastian, for instance, never neglects an opportunity to goad him to fury about it, though I have often pled with him not to do so."

Faith, remembering how Rudolf had recently been so goaded, and not at all sure Sebastian had neglected to inform his brother of the episode, blushed more deeply still.

"I hope Rudolf does not imagine there would be the least awkwardness about his coming to the Palace," the Archbishop went on, with such an air of cordial composure that Faith ventured to hope her increasing confusion was not too evident. "Please assure him that there will not be—unless there is a prospect that I may give this assurance myself?"

"I am so sorry. Rudolf is studying the history of Spanish colonization. He gave strict orders that he was not to be disturbed. Of course he did not expect that we would have a caller. But still——"

"Oh, yes! I also learned from Sebastian about the proposed course of study. I would not have you interrupt it for the world. Besides, as a cleric, I think you are quite right to carry out Rudolf's orders literally. From the time of St. Paul, the Church has been teaching the Gospel of a wife's submission to her husband's every desire."

Faith was rapidly coming to the conclusion that it was futile to try to conceal anything from the penetrating intuition of these Cerrenos, that it would be much simpler to tell them whatever they wanted to know in the first place, than to have them find it out, adroitly, for themselves, in the end.

"This is the first morning that Rudolf has remembered to study," she said candidly. "But I do not think he will forget about it again. Instead I think he will study doubly hard to make up for the time he has lost.—And I *am* trying very hard to do just what he wants to have me about—about everything."

"I know you are, my child," said the Archbishop gently, "and as I have just said, I cannot, as a churchman, commend your conduct too highly. But as a relative I should like to see a little more of you. Particularly as I was predisposed in your favor by a very wonderful painting for which I believe you were the inspiration."

"You were predisposed in my favor!" reiterated Faith, with an astonishment in which thanksgiving was mingled. The wound which Rudolf had inflicted in Venice by his manifest abhorrence of the part she had played in Sam's career had never entirely closed. Now she suddenly felt, as she gazed gratefully at Gabriel, that it had been miraculously healed.

"Of course. 'Mary of Nazareth' is one of the most supreme pictures of modern times. In achieving it, Samuel Dudley has made a great contribution to religion as well as to art. I am sorry he has felt, so far, that he could not part with it. You may remember that the exhibition at Seville was one of those at which it won a gold medal. It was the hope of many of us then that we might retain it in Spain."

"Sam took it with him to the Straits of Magellan," said Faith in a burst of confidence, "to keep him company. I got a cable from him about it on my wedding day. He said he hoped Rudolf would find the Aphrodite he missed. The next picture was to have been Aphrodite, you see."

"I see," said the Archbishop gravely. "I am not surprised that he took the 'Mary' with him, and I am sure it will be a source of inspiration to him, as many other holy paintings have been to many other great and rather lonely men. In fact, that splendid canvas which he has just shipped back to Europe—'Magellan Passing the Straits' I believe it is called—discloses how rapidly his genius continues to develop. It is much more than a superb marine picture. It is a revelation of the indomitable courage which drove Magellan forward and crowned him with conquest. This has never been so vividly depicted before."

"Oh!" exclaimed Faith impulsively, "you don't know how happy it makes me feel to have you talk like this! It is so long since anyone has spoken to me about Sam! And I have missed him so much!—Did you ever meet him?"

"Yes," said Gabriel with an accent of genuine admiration. "When he was in Seville I went over there on purpose to do so. But I was one of so many that doubtless he did not remember me and did not attach enough importance to our meeting to tell you about it. But I hope that he will return to Spain and that when he does he will be my guest. He will be coming, you know, one of these days, to paint you again."

"As Aphrodite?" asked Faith doubtfully.

The Archbishop smiled. "No," he said, "I do not think that Sam will ever paint the Aphrodite. Instead, as he meant to infer when he cabled you, he purposely left the way clear for Rudolf, as far as Aphrodite was concerned, and Rudolf has not had the genius to visualize her as Sam would have done—or to make others visualize her. His method has inevitably been very different. Personally, however, I have no regrets because Sam will not paint that particular picture, though I realize he might have rivaled Botticelli if he had achieved it; because I think he will paint a picture of you instead that will prove to be another divinely lovely manifestation of Mary."

"What sort of a manifestation?" asked Faith eagerly.

"I may be able to tell you before you leave Granada," replied Gabriel, looking at her intently for a moment and then appearing to dismiss the subject. "But meanwhile you must tell me—are you contented here? Are Felipe and Catalina doing everything they should and can for your comfort? Are you enjoying the *caseria*?"

"Yes. I am contented," Faith said quietly. Then she went on, with rising enthusiasm, "Felipe and Catalina are simply wonderful. I never knew servants could be so capable and thoughtful and friendly. I am learning a great deal about housekeeping from them. And some Spanish, too!" she added with a little laugh. "Though I must get a grammar and start studying it more systematically.—And I adore the *caseria.* I think it is the most beautiful place I ever saw. Rudolf is amused because I keep telling him I am sure that some fairy must have laid a spell on it. But I really mean it. It seems as if I could feel the magic. You don't think I am silly, do you?" she asked a little anxiously.

"No, my child, I do not think you are silly. I think you are very wise," Gabriel said slowly. "Probably the house *has* magical—or shall we say miraculous?—properties. Perhaps instead of being spellbound by a fairy, it has been blessed by an angel." He seemed absorbed in reflexion for a moment and then continued slowly, "Be that as it may, since you feel as you do about the *caseria,* I wonder if you would not like to have it—for your very own, I mean? So that you would be free to come at any time? I think it would please Sebastian greatly if you would let him give it to you, if you would let him make a reality of the phrase we Spanish constantly use, '*Esta es su casa.*' He has half a dozen other houses, you know, all much more pretentious than this one; he would never miss it. And besides, he is naturally generous. There is nothing that makes him so happy as to bestow presents right and left. Persons who themselves feel—bereft, for one reason or another, are often like that. I do not know how I should carry on all my charities without his help. He tells me, mockingly, that I pour water through a sieve in trying to help the poor, and then he sends me thousands of pesetas so that I may do so more freely."

"And do you think he would like to give me the *caseria?* Really and truly?"

"I am very sure of it," said Gabriel gravely.

He watched her searchingly as she turned the matter over in her mind. Certainly she was touched. Certainly she was pleased. And yet he was almost positive that she was going to decline the gift. He did not, however, guess the reason for this until she spoke.

"Sebastian won't think I'm ungrateful, will he?" she inquired. "I do love it—and I should like to feel free to come here whenever I can.—Perhaps he'd let me do that anyway. But I'd really rather not own it. Because, if I did, it would be a sort of home. And I have a home already. I haven't seen it in a long time. For—for rather sad reasons. But now I want very much to go there for a visit as soon as Rudolf can take me. And some day I want to go back there to live. It isn't very clear to me just how I ever can, but I am hoping for it somehow just the same."

"I see," said Gabriel, understandingly, as he had spoken when she was talking about Sam.

"You wouldn't think my house was pretty at all," Faith went on, encouraged to further comment by his obvious interest. "It isn't at all an important house. It's made of wood. It's painted white and it has green blinds. Inside the ceilings are very low, and there are lots of fireplaces, and there is white paneling in the parlor. It all smells very clean.—There is a walk made of cobblestones leading up to the front door, which isn't very large, and has a big brass knocker in the middle. There are lilac bushes and maple trees in the yard around the house, and a lane leading down to the river in the back. It's on a farm, near a little New England village, and further off there are big meadows and mountains. My great-great-grandfather had two sons, and when he settled in the upper Connecticut Valley, he built two houses, so that the sons would each have one after he died. There have been only two Marlowes—men I mean—in every generation since then, just as you and Sebastian are the only Cerrenos. My Uncle Ephraim lives in one of the houses. The other belonged to my father. When he died he—he gave it to me. So I'd rather not have anyone else give me a house."

"I see," said Gabriel a third time.

"I knew you would," Faith answered. She had enjoyed Gabriel's visit immeasurably; and as she began to be afraid that he might soon think of leaving she realized that she would be sorry to have him go.

"I suppose archbishops are rather busy," she said artlessly. "So it was very good of you to come and see me at all, but now that you are here I have been wondering if you could not spare the time to stay for luncheon? Rudolf will come down from the library for that, and then you could see him too."

The Archbishop rose, gathering the purple folds of his robe about him. "That is a great inducement," he said, and again Faith was conscious that his eyes were twinkling. "But I am having guests myself for luncheon, so I am afraid that I must go back to the Palace. Before I leave, however, I want you to kneel down and receive my blessing. I will show you just what to do—it is very simple. And I have been wondering—as I said before, I should like very much to see more of you as a relative. You say you know nothing of ecclesiastical procedure, and since you seem to be really interested in it—would you care to learn something about it? In connection with Church History perhaps? It might be a good way for you to study Spanish."

"Do you mean you would come here and give me lessons?" cried Faith delightedly.

"No—I did not mean just that. You are right in supposing that archbishops are rather busy. I could not arrange to leave the Palace every day or even to teach you myself, though I should be only too happy to supervise the schedule. But I could send my carriage here for you if it could not conveniently be arranged to have Felipe drive you back and forth from Granada. As I remember, the only vehicle on the place is rather decrepit. And one of my secretaries—the elder one—is a very learned scholar. I am sure he would prove a satisfactory instructor. Suppose you talk the matter over with Rudolf. You can send me a note by Felipe when he goes in to market to-morrow telling me what your husband thinks of our plan. Of course we would time the lessons to coincide with his periods of research, and I promise there shall be no proselyting. If he approves, we might begin our work on Wednesday."

"That would be wonderful!" exclaimed Faith.

The sweetness and solemnity of Gabriel's blessing made a deep impression upon her. When she rose from her knees, after he had pronounced it, she stood looking steadily up into his face, her reluctance to have him leave her increasing every moment. He laid the hand which she had so recently kissed lightly on her shoulder.

"I should not be surprised if some day you became a good Catholic yourself," he said quietly. "But Catholic or not, the goodness is there anyway.—Is there any message you would care to send Sebastian by me?"

"Of course there is! When you write him give him my best regards. And tell him how kind I thought it was of him to offer me the *caseria.* I suppose that was his suggestion."

The Archbishop was already preparing to get into his imposing carriage, beside which Felipe and Catalina were devoutly kneeling. He turned back and smiled at Faith once more.

"Yes," he said. "It was Sebastian's suggestion. I will let him know that you were touched by it, even though you did not accept it. But it will not be necessary for me to write him to that effect. He arrived three days ago to make me a prolonged visit."

CHAPTER 16

WHEN Rudolf rejoined Faith for luncheon, he commended her discretion in leaving him undisturbed, and at the same time expressed genuine regret that he had not been at leisure to welcome Gabriel.

"There is no one among our Spanish kinsfolk whom I respect and admire so much," he said, speaking almost enthusiastically. "Of course it is impossible not to be exceedingly fond of *Tio* Carlos and *Tia* Carlota. But they are simple souls. They are not of the same caliber as Gabriel. It is surprising how much alike he and Sebastian are, and yet how different. Many of their characteristics are almost identical; but the qualities which are distorted in Sebastian are beatified in Gabriel. Yes, certainly, I should have taken you to present you to him before this. You have made this fortnight a period of such delight for me, *Liebchen,* that I must atone for my self-indulgence by extra diligence from now on. I feel I must study not only between lunch and tea-time, according to our original plan, but all the morning too, as I did to-day."

"That would not leave us a great deal of time together, for a bride and groom," observed Faith thoughtfully, though not resentfully.

"We will still have the late afternoons and evenings. I can count on relaxation with you when my day's work is over. I can always look forward to finding you waiting for me on the terrace; and to long rapturous hours afterwards."

Catalina, having placed a basket of nectarines on the table, had vanished, with timely tact. She had enjoyed several honeymoons, of one sort or another, herself; and she recognized certain symptoms in Rudolf's manner which led her to believe that he was impatiently awaiting her departure from the patio to take Faith on his lap. Her surmise had been entirely accurate. She had hardly disappeared when he lifted his bride into his arms.

"*Liebe* Faith," he said fervently, "I cannot tell you how happy you have made me. I will confess to you now, that during that dreadful day in Madrid—and until you called me to your bedside the first night we were here—I was—very anxious. Besides, even while we were betrothed, I could not help having some moments of uneasiness—much as I loved you—lest we should not always be of accord. I had heard that American maidens were headstrong and willful; but no German *Braut* could have been more docile than you have proven. And besides, you are so serene and sweet! Anything that any man could hope and long to find in his wife I have found in you! I know I am blessed beyond measure in my possession of you."

Faith lay quiescent in his embrace for a moment; then she gently freed one of her imprisoned arms, and began to stroke the locked hands clasped around her waist. "I am glad that I have made you happy after all," she said earnestly. "I can understand that you must have worried for fear I might not. And it encourages me very much to have you say I am turning out to be just the sort of wife you wanted. I have tried to be, and I will keep on trying.—Gabriel encouraged me this morning, too. He really seemed—to approve of me and to like me.—By the way, he asked me if I would care to come to the Palace and take lessons in Church History and things like that. I was very informal about welcoming him when he arrived. I didn't understand who he was when Catalina told me, and even if I had, I wouldn't have known exactly what to do with an archbishop. But instead of being haughty and hurting my feelings, he made this kind suggestion. He told me to talk the matter over with you and let him know the decision. He said he had an elderly secretary who he was sure would be helpful to me. And he said my lessons would come at the same time with your research, so that they would not separate us at all, and to be sure to tell you there would be no proselyting."

Rudolf did not appear to hesitate at all. "The elderly secretary of whom he spoke must be Father Constantino," he said approvingly. "Yes, he is a very learned scholar. I fear we are rather too apt, in Germany, to dismiss all Spaniards from our minds as illiterate, or nearly so. I do not believe you could have a better teacher. It is immaterial whether you learn Church History; but it is very important that you should learn Spanish, and the proper etiquette to observe in your contacts with personages of ecclesiastic rank, many of whom, in Spain, are incidentally also members of the nobility as well. I will write to Gabriel at once asking when I may go with you to the Palace for an audience, and when he sets a time we will take advantage of his offer and accept it."

"Gabriel told me that Sebastian had just arrived to make him a long visit," went on Faith, wondering why it seemed so hard to impart this information casually, and at the same time why she felt she would be guilty of duplicity if she did not. Rudolf, however, heard the news without attention, much less acrimony.

"Sebastian often makes the Palace his headquarters while he is amusing himself in this vicinity," he remarked absently. "He has a great many friends about here. So have I, for that matter. Some of them will doubtless be calling upon us before long, and naturally we shall have to return their visits."

His mind seemed centered on an exchange of courtesies rather than on the propinquity of Sebastian. Without actually dragging the matter into the conversation Faith did not see how she could refer to his offer of the *caseria* as a gift, much less do this with nonchalance.

"I shall be very glad to have your friends come here whenever they can," she said cordially. "Are they all Spanish?"

"Nearly all. But you did not have a great deal of trouble in talking with Gabriel, did you?" asked Rudolf, with one of his rare excursions into pleasantry.

Faith laughed. "Where did he learn to speak such English, Rudolf? He and—and Sebastian?"

"At Eton," said Rudolf, rather dryly. "Their father was the Spanish Ambassador to Great Britain for ten years. Incidentally they both have degrees from Oxford. In fact I believe Gabriel has two or three degrees from various institutions. He was always scholarly as well as devout, and since his uncle was the Papal Secretary of State, it was doubly logical that he should turn to religion as a vocation. But his parents were averse to his taking irrevocable vows until it seemed certain that the family name would be carried on by Sebastian. Having lost several sons in infancy they were naturally anxious on that score."

"And now the name is not to be carried on after all!"

"No. As I said before, in one way it is perhaps fortunate, while in another it is certainly a pity. Especially as Sebastian is very fond of children. He would have liked to have them, not only as descendants but as companions. It is one of those strange contradictions of character which sometimes occur. No one, to meet Sebastian casually, would dream that he had such a leaning. But he actually dotes on babies. He is like a different person when he is in the presence of a little child."

Rudolf's complacency had reached a stage where he was ready to make favorable comments on almost anyone. He was gratified by the benign visit of Gabriel. The sunny stillness of the patio was very soothing. He was replete with excellent food and even more excellent wine. And his wife, relaxed and responsive, was seated on his knees. Faith, aware of his contentment, decided to take advantage of it by asking a question to allay her curiosity on a point which hitherto had not been clarified for her.

"Rudolf," she asked without undue emphasis, "you have never happened to tell me how Sebastian's face was so badly cut. That is a queer scar on his cheek. Is there dueling in Spain as there is in Germany?"

"Yes, there is some dueling in Spain. Not much. But Sebastian's scar did not come from a duel."

"What did it come from?"

"*Liebe* Faith, why are you so inquisitive? This is not the first time you have so shown yourself. It seems to me almost your only fault. But since you are so insistent I will tell you what you want to know. In one of the periods when her malady took the form of frenzy, Dolores attacked Sebastian. It was before her condition was really recognized as—insanity. Up to that time she had simply been considered—very hysterical. No precautions had been taken against violence on her part. But she suddenly snatched up a jeweled dagger—a beautiful heirloom that was lying on a table among other treasures—and hurled herself against him. Gabriel was in the room when it happened. If he had not been Sebastian would doubtless have been killed. There was no forewarning of her maniacal mood, and Sebastian had no time to defend himself. In any case he could not have used force against her. She was his wife, even though she was a madwoman."

Rudolf did not look at Faith as he set her on her feet. He was resentful because she had insisted on hearing this frightful story about which he had been so discreetly silent; he felt she had unsettled the serenity of the afternoon by her urgency. She was probably shocked and startled now, for which he was sorry, but it was her own fault. He hoped she would interpret his withdrawal as an unspoken reprimand. After all, she was very young and she still had a great deal to learn about finesse. He must make every endeavor to teach her for her own sake as well as his.

"I am now going to write to Gabriel," he said almost formally, "and give the note to Felipe to take into Granada at once. After that I shall return to the library. I have found a book there on the rights of neutral nations which is very absorbing. I think I shall supplement my studies on colonization by reading this work also, and perhaps preparing a report on what I have read. I will see you again at tea-time."

"Very well," Faith answered levelly. A sudden unexpected quality of maturity in her voice arrested him. He turned and saw that instead of appearing abashed by his reproof, she looked slightly scornful; and apparently she had not been frightened by his gruesome chronicle, for her expression was strangely self-reliant.

"Of course I will not ask you questions if you do not like to have me, Rudolf," she went on in the same even tone. "But I do not see how we can be really intimate unless I do—unless we ask *each other* questions. I do not see what good it will do us to come close to each other in the way you want unless we come close to each other in *every* way. Of course there will be barriers between us, no matter how hard I try to please you, if you make me feel that you are bored or annoyed by subjects which interest me. We can talk just about what interests you, but that will not change my thoughts. And anyway, I am glad I know at last how Sebastian got his scar. Also that he would not use force against his wife in any case. Even if she were a madwoman."

CHAPTER 17

Rudolf sat, staring at the closely printed pages of the very absorbing book on the rights of neutral nations. From time to time he turned one of its leaves mechanically; but he had not succeeded in making out any kind of résumé of the contents, though a plump pad and several neatly sharpened pencils, which he had placed on the desk in preparation for his important task, lay within easy reach of his long fingers. At last he shoved back his chair with an exclamation of impatience and strode across the room. For some moments he stood glaring out at the beautiful *vega,* his hands thrust savagely into his pockets, his shoulders sagging. Then he recrossed the library, flung open the heavy door, and called loudly to Catalina.

He was obliged to repeat his summons three times before he heard her willing but heavy footsteps approaching. His irritability increased with every second that marked her delay. When at last she presented herself before him, puffing and panting, he spoke to her with unprecedented sharpness.

"Is it necessary for me to wait indefinitely when I wish to give an order?"

"Disculpe, Señor Barón. I was preparing the tea. I set down the kettle and hastened the instant I heard the *Señor Barón* call. But to mount all these stairs—the *Señor Barón* understands that for this a *momentito* is required."

"It is about the tea that I wish to speak to you. Please tell your mistress that I shall be obliged to have mine here alone in the library. My work has not progressed as fast as it should. I cannot join her on the terrace."

In his exasperation, he thought he detected a shade of derision in Catalina's bland expression. He rapped out another curt question.

"Why do you look at me like that? Don't you understand me?"

"Pero si, Señor Barón. I was only wondering how you could have your tea otherwise than alone, or how I could carry a message to the *Baronesa,* since she is gone?"

"Gone!" thundered Rudolf, terror as well as rage gripping him. "What do you mean?"

"I thought of course the *Señor Barón* knew," said Catalina unctuously and mendaciously, "that she went into Granada with Felipe. The *Señor Barón* perhaps recalls that he gave Felipe a note to deliver to His Eminence, the Archbishop?"

"Of course I recall it! What has that to do with the *Baronesa?*"

"After the *Señor Barón* had given Felipe the note, Felipe prepared with great dispatch to carry out the *Señor Barón's* wishes."

"With great dispatch!" barked Rudolf ironically. *"Gott in Himmel,* when was a Spaniard ever known to act with dispatch!"

"He had just finished harnessing Pepito into the cart," went on Catalina calmly and with thinly veiled contempt, "when the *Baronesa* came into the outer patio wearing a large white hat, and made signs to Felipe that she wished to accompany him. He made signs to her that he would get out the victoria, and harness Benito instead. She made signs that she would go in the cart, that he was not to molest himself. She laughed and climbed into the cart and took the reins herself. Felipe laughed and climbed up beside her. And *presto!* They were gone from the *caseria,* both laughing and both making si——"

"Stop talking to me about signs!—Do you mean to tell me that they have not returned yet?"

"Felipe returned more than two hours ago, *Señor Barón.* But the *Baronesa* did not return with him."

"Send Felipe to me this instant!" commanded Rudolf.

He began pacing up and down the library like a caged lion. Catalina's tale was simply preposterous. Faith had put on a large white hat, she had climbed into a rickety old cart and driven off behind an aged donkey into Granada, escorted only by an Andalusian peasant! And then she had remained behind in Granada under unimaginable conditions! The *Baronesa* von Hohenlohe, the wife of the Third Secretary of the German Embassy! In the most conservative section of the most conservative country in Europe! A section riddled with exalted families, many of them related to him, whose own womenkind had never been known to stir away from their patios in an undignified manner, who were always suitably accompanied, and who wore their delicate black mantillas drawn over their beautiful creamy brows to protect them from the vulgar gaze of the curious! The incredibility of Catalina's narrative was matched only by its monstrosity.

Felipe, when he finally appeared upon the scene, which was not until Rudolf had worked himself into a ferment, was quite as calm as Catalina had been. Who was he to attempt to prevent the *Baronesa* from doing as she pleased, especially as he of course supposed the *Señor Barón* to be fully informed of her purpose? Naturally he had not understood all her signs, but it was evident enough that she wanted to go into Granada for something. And fortunately everything had been explained to him all in good time. As they drew up in front of the Palace, a group of gentlemen were just emerging from the doorway, who had evidently been lunching with His Eminence. Indeed, His Eminence was among them. He had welcomed the *Baronesa* cordially, and with no sign of surprise. He had then read the note from the *Señor Barón,* he had spoken a little with the *Baronesa,* and finally he had told Felipe that she had decided, as long as the *Barón* was so studiously occupied, to while away the period of his seclusion by doing a little sight-seeing in Granada, which she had not visited at all, except to pass through it on the morning of her arrival at the station. His Eminence had also hastily written a little note, which Felipe had hesitated to deliver to the *Barón* for fear of disturbing him; but now that the *Barón* had sent for him, *mire!* Here it was!

Rudolf almost snatched the stiff little square of paper away from Felipe.

"Dear Rudolf" . . . he read:

"I too was sorry not to see you this morning, but I shall be glad to receive you and Faith in audience at ten to-morrow. We will plan then for her lessons. I am delighted to know that you approve of our tentative program. Meanwhile, since Faith had decided that she would like to see some landmarks this afternoon, I will arrange for this, and also for her safe return to the *caseria* later in the evening. Please do not be in the least anxious about her. Affectionately, Gabriel."

Felipe stood respectfully and patiently before Rudolf, fingering with joy the two coins which the Archbishop had given him, but taking the precaution of doing this very quietly, so that they should not jingle.

He did not feel quite sure whether he was dismissed or not. The *Señor Barón* seemed to have forgotten all about him. At last he sighed, deeply and audibly, and then the *Barón* sent him off, with a gesture and an expression which the humblest hidalgo would never have used. Felipe shrugged his shoulders and went his way. He had been favorably impressed with the *Barón* at first, but he admired him less and less as time went on. It was a great pity, he and Catalina agreed, as they sat talking over the situation in the cool of the evening, that the *Baronesa,* who was not only *muy simpatica,* but, *preciosissima* as well, had not bestowed her lovely hand in marriage on some high-born Spaniard instead of on this abrupt and glowering German, who could hardly even be called a *caballero.*

"We can only pray," said Catalina piously, "that since heaven has not blessed her with a Spanish husband, it may swiftly send her a Spanish lover, to whose ardent importunities she will speedily succumb, and thereby attain the bliss which she so well deserves."

"May it so please the Blessed Virgin!" ejaculated Felipe fervently.

. . . . .

It was nearly nine o'clock before Rudolf heard the sound of horses' hoofs in the outer patio. His anger had burned itself out, for characteristically, his emotion had been as evanescent as it was intense, and he had spent several hours in searching self-scrutiny. He was intrinsically just, and the feeling that he had been unfair to Faith, kept steadily gaining ground in his consciousness. There was really no reason why she should not ask him questions, though it was unfortunate that in doing so she so often uncovered some family skeleton; but after all, it was not Faith's fault that there were so many skeletons in the family. He was even ready to admit, though the idea was novel to him, that a frank and habitual exchange of confidences might stabilize rather than shake the foundations of their marriage relationship. He knew that Faith respected his wishes and recognized his authority. Even her precipitant departure had not been, he began to realize, an attempt to escape on account of rebellion, any more than it had been a deliberate disregard of decorum. She had merely gone off, on the impulse of the moment, because she had no other outlet for her natural energy, because an opportunity presented itself for visiting a beautiful city, and she had been unaware of any reason why she should fail to take advantage of it. It was unfortunate that he had not himself suggested a sight-seeing expedition to Granada. But it had not even occurred to him to do so, primarily because his days at the *caseria* had been so saturated with sweetness that he had been oblivious to all the world that lay beyond its shielding walls. There was also another reason for his negligence: he had been to Granada so many times, in the course of numerous visits, that he was no more thrilled by the idea of a visit to the

Alhambra than by the idea of a visit to the Palace at Charlottenburg. But then, Faith had been thrilled by a visit to the Palace at Charlottenburg. He should have remembered that. Yes, decidedly, he had been very short-sighted.

It was also unfortunate that he had betrayed his surprise at Faith's plunge to Catalina and Felipe. Gabriel, emerging from the Palace surrounded by dignitaries, had quite evidently not given the slightest indication that he thought there was anything the least extraordinary in being suddenly confronted by an unaccompanied young lady who jumped out of a donkey cart and hailed him with effusion. And yet, Gabriel must have been almost speechless with astonishment—well, probably not speechless, for the Cerrenos were never tongue-tied, but certainly very much astonished indeed. And he had welcomed her cordially, giving both the dignitaries and the servant rather the impression that he was hoping she might give him the honor of coming to see him about that time.—It was humiliating to admit himself outdone in delicacy by Gabriel on the very day when he had endeavored to teach his wife a lesson in tactfulness.

Having blundered so variously and so clumsily, how should he greet Faith on her return? And who would be with her when she did come along? Gabriel had assured him that she would be adequately cared for and his confidence in Gabriel was implicit, as he kept assuring himself. Yet a little forked flame of fear kept twisting through his body. Fear of what? Fear of whom? Why should he be afraid of anything or anybody as far as Faith was concerned, especially at a time when he was fortified by the might of Gabriel's pledged word? Yet was there not one person in the world against whom Gabriel's pledged word would not prevail? Would Jacob have denied anything to Benjamin? Why had he not thought of all that in the morning? How could he have been blind to the underlying motives of the Archbishop's visit, of his suggestion that Faith should go daily to the Palace? Why had he not recognized in Gabriel the emissary and tool of Sebastian, whom, in a sudden blinding flash, he saw revealed in his true and lurid colors? Sebastian, who wanted Faith for himself, who had followed her to Granada, who was planning, with diabolical cleverness, to get her through the connivance of his saintly brother? Sebastian, who had fascinated Faith as a snake fascinates a bird, so that he was never out of her thoughts? Sebastian, who was so lost to shame that he would not hesitate to defile a bridal-bed or to stage an intrigue on the altar steps?

Rudolf was as shaken with hatred and panic as he had been shaken with anger a few hours earlier. He knew that he should be ruled by reason, not swayed by suspicions—especially suspicions that were without substance, and which were an insult even to Sebastian, and almost a sacrilege as far as Gabriel and Faith were concerned. Yet some primitive instinct continued to kindle them. It was all he could do to steady himself against the insidious dread of the circumstances which would surround Faith's return. When he heard a horse's hoofs, clattering in the outer patio, he listened, breathlessly, for the voice which he felt sure he would presently hear too, rising and falling in response to Faith's —a cultured, liquid Spanish voice, as melodious as it was mocking.

He was aware instead of a nasal twang which grated across his consciousness as harshly as a rasping file. But its tones were music to his ears. He had never heard it before; and though he had no idea to whom it belonged one thing was certain: It did not belong to Sebastian. That, for the moment, was all that mattered. The nights were dark now, except for the twinkling stars, for the silvery young moon, which, a fortnight earlier, had flooded Faith's room with delicate luster, had mellowed to the ripe gold of maturity and sunk forever in luxuriant splendor; and in the patio of the fountain, where he had come at last to wait, were only the high, swinging lanterns of wrought iron and translucent ruby-colored glass for illumination. Rudolf could see nothing more than the indistinct outline of the two figures that were approaching. But dim as this outline was it showed that the man who was walking beside Faith though very heavy, was not much taller than she was. As they came nearer, Rudolf realized that though he was rather uncouth, he gave an immediate impression of strength; and when his features became vaguely visible, they were revealed as shrewd rather than stolid.

"Say, if that ain't a sweet pretty house!" were the first words which Rudolf heard him say clearly. "Cute, I call it!" The stranger paused, and drew a deep whistle of unconcealed admiration. "Just as cute as it can be!" he exclaimed.

"It's a magic house," said Faith happily.

"You don't say!" replied the stranger whistling again. "Well, I want to know!"

"I'm going to tell you all about it," Faith assured him, "but first I want to introduce my husband to you—Rudolf, this is Mr. Caleb Hawks of Hinsboro."

"Pleased to meet you," said Mr. Hawks, grasping Rudolf's hand heartily.

"Mr. Hawks is something very important in pencils, Rudolf," Faith went on. "I'm not sure just what, but I'm sure he'll explain it to you. He used to be a friend of my father's, and I knew him when I was a little girl. I met him again in Berlin, when I was visiting the Castles, and to-day again at Gabriel's. He's touring Spain, and he'd been lunching at the Palace. He's going to have dinner with us."

"If you're sure it won't put out the hired girl any," said Mr. Hawks considerately.

CHAPTER 18

CATALINA's dinner, and the wine from the *bodega,* which she poured out with an unusually lavish hand, were both excellent, and Mr. Hawks did full justice to them though Faith saw him looking vainly around for butter as the meal began.

"I'm sorry there is none," she said solicitously, "but the only kind we can get here is canned, and comes all the way from Denmark. It's horrible in this warm weather, so as Catalina cooks entirely with oil anyway, we don't use butter at all. We have jam for breakfast instead. And just think, Mr. Hawks! There are one hundred acres on the *caseria* and we haven't a single cow! Only goats! The people in the country here think that goats' milk is much more healthful, and Rudolf has explained to me that it really is, because it doesn't carry tuberculosis. But of course the farmers aren't worrying about anything definite like that. It's just that goats are much easier to take care of than cows and much cheaper. And I simply love them. I think they are perfectly darling. There *is* one *caseria* though, not far from here, where there is one cow, and every now and then Catalina's nephew, Timoteo, goes and brings us home some cow's milk in wine bottles. He brings us our drinking water too, from a spring, in earthen jars."

"Well, if that ain't all real peculiar," said Mr. Hawks, with interest. "I don't know but what I'd just as leave have the liquid that usually goes in the bottles though, as any milk, goats' *or* cows'.—Oh, thank you kindly, ma'am. I don't mind if I do."

Having quaffed deeply of the proffered beverage, Mr. Hawks smacked his lips, and turned to Rudolf with an access of affable garrulity.

"You could'da knocked me over with a feather," he said earnestly, though considering Mr. Hawks' bulk, it would have been difficult to visualize what sort of a feather would have effectually served this purpose, "when I saw Faith here jump out of that donkey cart and come racing up the steps. She didn't take in who I was, not right off. She'd only seen me once, of course—that is, since she was knee-high to a grasshopper—at that show Cal Castle took me to in Berlin; but I reccernized her right away. I knew her father and her grandfather both well, and looked up to them considerably, same as everyone did in our state. There was pretty general regret, I can tell ye, when this young lady come along, that she warn't a boy, so we could have another Marlowe in the seats of the mighty at Washington. But land! Christian Marlowe set his eye-teeth by her and I don't know as I blame him. I sure was glad to see her again. You know how 'tis, Mr. Lowe, in these furrin' parts. You're so homesick all the time you keep your ears pricked for someone that comes from God's country and speaks the King's English, same as you do."

"Rudolf's never had a chance to be homesick," interposed Faith. "He could take a train anytime, anywhere, in Europe and get off at any station; and when he looked up at the sign to find out where he was he'd be able to say to himself, '*Ach*, this is the city where my grandfather's second cousin Wilhelm, who married the Countess of Concertina is now living. He will be delighted to have me make him a little visit. I will then up the avenue walk until I reach his palace.'—But I know what you mean. I did it hundreds of times when I was a little girl. I shouldn't wonder if it were even worse for a little girl than a big man, especially if she had just two dolls for company, and spent lots of time in dingy little pensions, or got dragged around seeing Alps and things. Of course, after I went to live with Cousin Sarah, it was different. She had lots of nice consular friends. But I *do* know just what you mean."

"Not but what everyone's treated me fine," Mr. Hawks, who was eminently just, hastened to say. "Cal Castle now. I've known him ever since we was in the first grade together. So when I decided to come to Europe, I went straight to Germany, on one of them fine new boats of yours. I give Cal the surprise of his life. He never figgered on my coming to Europe and neither had I, Mr. Lowe, and that's a fact. But Mrs. Hawks passed away last fall, and Myra, my only daughter's married. So my house was sort of quiet, as you might say, with no one in it but the hired girl and me. Of course I have my church—I'm a deacon in the First Congregational—and my lodge meetings—I belong to the Order of the Oriental Caribou and the Persian Panthers both. And then of course there's always politics. I've been on the city council in Hinsboro for fifteen years, and I kin run for mayor anytime I say the word. Mebbe I will when I go home. But all them associations don't take the place of your wife after thirty years. No sir, I was kinder lonely. So I thought I might as well come to Europe. Lots of people do. With Cal to turn to, I thought I'd get along all right. And I have. His wife was never one to hang the latchstring out, and she ain't changed, but neither has Cal. He's done handsome by me himself, and he give me letters right and left besides. Everyone has been real hospitable. But of course you can't expect to eat every meal out in company. And in between times, I've wondered once in a while if it wouldn't have been better if I'd gone to stay with Myra for a spell. As I said, that's my daughter, Mr. Lowe, and I've got two of the cutest grandchildren! I never saw such kids! Smart ain't no word for them! The things they get off! Just for instance——"

Mr. Hawks gave several examples of his grandchildren's precocious wit to which Rudolf listened with courtesy and Faith with real amusement.

"Oh, Mr. Hawks, that *was* smart! I don't wonder you hated to leave them. But I don't believe you'll be sorry you came to Europe in the end.—Don't you like Gabriel?"

"Don't I like him?" echoed Mr. Hawks solemnly. "Say, he's a prince."

"No," said Rudolf politely, "I'm sorry to contradict you, Mr. Hawks, but the Cerreno family has no more than ducal rank."

"Mr. Hawks only meant that Gabriel was a wonderful person," explained Faith, "and of course he is.—Was it Uncle Carolus that gave you a letter to him?"

"No, it was that handsome mother-in-law of yours," said Mr. Hawks, "but it was Cal gave me a letter to *her*. I don't know as I ever met a pleasanter-spoken woman, Mr. Lowe, than your mother, and that's a fact. But now, in Spain seems as if everyone was pleasant. Of course people are polite to you in other countries, but there's a difference. In France, for instance. You get the feeling that folks are sneering at you behind your back. And in Germany, well, you seem so downright dumb all the time. Not that anyone tells you you're dumb. But you get the idea. Here it's different. We've had a war with Spain a few years ago and cleaned them out of what little they had left on earth, and I ain't so sure we done right by 'em. It's a grand thing to talk about liberty and all that, but some of them Cubans are pretty slick. I've run into 'em considerable in my business. And it looks to me as if we'd got our own claws sunk pretty deep into the Philippines and Porto Rico. But be all that as it may, do you think I've met a single Spaniard that acted as if he had a grudge against me because I was an American? Not on your life! Hotel *conserges* and all, they've treated me like a member of the family. Even on the trains, all the passengers seem to want me to eat up half the victuals they're taking along with them to strengthen them for the journey. And land! They celebrate Thanksgiving every day! As for this here bishop—or whatever you call him—well, he certainly is a prince."

For a moment Mr. Hawks' enthusiasm rendered him inarticulate. Then, having drawn breath and shoveled a large portion of *pollo con arroz* into his mouth he continued.

"Say, you missed a treat not being with us to-day, Mr. Lowe, and that's a fact. I don't know as I ever seed a city I admired more than Granada. Mebbe it wouldn't have suited Mrs. Hawks the way it is. She'd have wanted to houseclean it pretty thorough. She was a great one for having everything just poison neat. But a little dirt here and there never did anyone any real harm and never will. And it certainly is a sweet pretty place. The red geraniums kinder make me think of home. Mrs. Hawks would have liked them. They grow different here from at home of course. More easy like, sorter tumbling over balconies instead of being set in tomato cans in the front parlor windows. But geraniums are cheery lookin', however you plant 'em."

"I have always thought they were very pretty flowers myself," said Rudolf politely. "Did the Archbishop take you to see the Capilla Real?"

"I should say he did!" exclaimed Mr. Hawks, warming to his subject. "I couldn't have told you its name if you hadn't helped me. But the Caterpillar Reel, that's the word. We looked at the tombs of Ferdinand and Isabella. And say, the Bishop pointed out a real peculiar thing. He said that the 'Catholic Kings'—that's the way he described 'em, though I would'da called Isabella a Queen myself—were both very wise, but that Isabella was wiser than Ferdinand. He said the man who carved them tombs wanted to make that plain, so he's got Isabella's head layin' on her pillow so's it makes a deep dent, but Ferdinand's is just as smooth as it can be. I guess women's rights ain't quite so new-fangled a notion as most people seem to think. I guess Isabella got hers or knew the reason why.—Say, Faith, do you think there's any more of that fricassee in the kitchen? It's real tasty, after all the fried veal I've choked down."

"Oh, isn't it awful!" exclaimed Faith. "Catalina, *un poco de pollo para el Señor, por favor.*"

"Would you care to smoke?" asked Rudolf, still with extreme courtesy, and extending a coroneted cigarette case, as Mr. Hawks piled his plate high again.

"Well, Mr. Lowe, I don't mind if I do, but if it's all the same to you I believe I'll have one of my own."

Mr. Hawks' right hand, which was ornamented with a massive carbuncle sunk in the deep claws of a heavy gold ring, sought his waistcoat pocket with the dexterity of long practice. He extracted from this an enormous black cigar, bit off the end of it, spat this to the ground, and, when he had scraped up the last morsel of chicken, stuck the cigar, tip-tilted and still unlighted, in the corner of his mouth as he continued his narrative.

"After we had seen everything in the Caterpillar Reel, crowns and jewel boxes and all," he went on, "the Bishop took us to another church where there was a sweet pretty saint over the altar all dressed up in silk and satin and diamonds fit to go to the Governor's Ball. I couldn't tell you the name of——"

"It is the Virgin of the Angustias," interposed Rudolf, "a very precious and ancient relic."

"That's the word," agreed Mr. Hawks heartily. "Say, it makes you feel differently about graven images, as the Bible calls 'em, to see some of these statues here in Spain, now don't it? As if they couldn't be such a symbol of sin after all, like we've always been taught. They're so downright handsome, as you may say, and then the way the folks all feel about them. Why it—gets you somehow. That church was full of the best appearing women you'd care to see anywhere, kneelin' in front of that statue, with them lace veils of theirs halfway over their faces, but not so far but what you can judge what their looks are. It tickles me to see them fan 'emselves and cross 'emselves at the same time. They're pious, all right. But they got a way with 'em just the same. I wouldn't look to find many maiden ladies in Spain."

"No," said Rudolf, "there are not many. Except for those who enter the church, they nearly all marry."

"Rudolf means except those who become nuns," said Faith, noticing Mr. Hawks' look of bewilderment. Certainly, his expression seemed to say, those ladies whom he had seen worshipping before the *Virgen de la Angustias* had entered a church, and yet he could not bring himself to believe that they were all spinsters.

"Oh," exclaimed Mr. Hawks with relief. "Well, when we come out of this church, we went across the park. To see the——"

"The Paseo?" asked Rudolf helpfully.

"That's the word. The pretty ladies that had just been praying. Walkin' up and down. Enjoyin' 'emselves. Easy, like at a church supper at home. The Bishop had to leave us when we went to the park, and so did some of the rest of his company—a Cardinal, one of them was, from To*leedo*, if I understood right. He was a pleasant-spoken man, too. So the Bishop turned Faith and me over to that younger brother of his, and say, I certainly took a liking to him. I couldn't get the hang of his title and all, so I asked him what his first name was, and that was easy. There's a young marblecutter—we've got quite a few of them in my state—named Sebastian, lives right across the street from me in Hinsboro, whose mother was born in Spain herself—yes, sir, right here in Granada. It was him give me the idea of coming here. He ain't old enough to vote yet, but he does considerable work for me among the furriners just the same. I'll always know just where he stands. I kin see he's goin' to be a stiddy supporter of mine. So I told this brother of the Bishop about my young Spanish friend at home, and asked him if it would be all right if I just called him Sebastian too. And what do you think he did? He said he'd been hoping I would, and by golly! he asked me what *my* first name was!"

"Sebastian is not without tact," conceded Rudolf.

"He asked me what I'd like to do next, and I said that if it was all the same to him I'd like to do a little shopping. I've been wanting to pick out a present for Myra, that's my married daughter you know and it's kind of hard when you get into a store and just point, and someone starts spouting a stream of something you can't make head nor tail of. So Sebastian said of course, we'd go to an——"

"*Antiquario's,*" said Faith.

"That's the word. I didn't quite like the sound of it. I was kinder afraid it would be four-posters and things like what we've got rid of lately in Hinsboro. We have nice brass beds in almost every house now, Mr. Lowe, modern plumbing and steam heat too—Well, as I was saying, Sebastian took us to a store that looked outside as if it was just full of junk, but when we got in there, if he didn't ferret out some of the most elegant ornaments I ever clapped my eyes on. I bought Myra a breastpin which I bet will tickle her just to pieces. I never would'da found it if it hadn't been for Sebastian."

"I am very glad you have secured just what you wished as a gift for your daughter," Rudolf observed.

"And then," broke in Faith, "after we had been to the *antiquario's*—tell Rudolf what we did then!"

"Say, that was the greatest treat of all, warn't it? Sebastian asked us if we'd like to go to the gypsy quarter. Up on the——"

"The Sacro Monte——" prompted Faith excitedly.

"That's the word. You see, Mr. Lowe, we were just coming out of the store I told you about, when one of these gypsy fellows—dressed just like a postal card, if you'll believe it—come up and spoke to Sebastian. An old man, it was. They seemed real pleased to see each other."

"It was Mariano, the King of the Gypsies," exclaimed Faith, unable to restrain her enthusiasm for another moment. "He's an old dear. He has gray side-whiskers, and the most wonderful teeth. And, as Mr. Hawks says, he was in full regalia. Sebastian has known him ever since he was a little boy. He—Mariano, I mean—used to clip Sebastian's poodle. We all walked up the hill to the caves together. It was very steep and very dusty, but that was part of the fun, and the road had prickly pear hedges all along it. Mr. Hawks and I had never seen any before. Had we, Mr. Hawks? Or caves with people living in them?"

"There's more than prickly pears and caves I'd never seen before," chimed in Mr. Hawks. "Say, some of them gypsy dances—Well, I don't know as they'd go too well for entertainment at the Annual Church Supper. I don't know as I'll describe 'em too carefully in Hinsboro. Of course I'll tell Sebastian I seen 'em, I mean the marble-cutter Sebastian. But Lord! His mother's seen 'em too! And she's probably told him herself. I should think it would'da been kinda a wrench for her to come away to a place like Hinsboro after she'd lived near the gypsy quarter in Granada. Well, they certainly are cute. The gypsy girls, I mean. But I kinda think the one that told fortunes was the cutest of all. And say, Mr. Lowe—what do you s'pose she told your wife?"

"I cannot imagine," said Rudolf rather formally.

"That's right, you can't. Not in a million years. Of course she strung Faith along with the usual stuff—Told her a tall dark man was going to enter her life, etc. Gypsies always pull that line, don't they? Of course that was bunk, because I don't know when I've seen a more light-complected feller than you are, Mr. Lowe. No offense, I hope. Honest, I mean it as a compliment. But that gypsy couldn't seem to let go of Faith. She clung onto her like a leech. And Sebastian, who was translating for us, said after he'd told us about the tall dark man—he told us that twice—that Chiquita—Chiquita was the name of this cute gypsy—thought Faith had the strangest hand she'd ever read."

"Indeed!" said Rudolf more formally still.

Mr. Hawks was unconscious of the increasing chill of the atmosphere. He pulled his tip-tilted cigar, now considerably chewed, out of his mouth at last, lighted it with a flourish, and leaned across the table, thumping it with his free hand.

"Chiquita told us," he said, his voice thumping too, "that she saw all kinds of terrible things hovering around Faith. Death, for instance—violent death! More than one kind! She made me think about that line I've heard somewhere, 'battle, murder and sudden——' "

"You must excuse me," said Rudolf, rising and drawing himself up very straight. "But this is fantastic. It is not seemly to dwell on a gypsy's raving."

"Well, they're weird," said Mr. Hawks, rising too, though with obvious reluctance, "but it kinda gets you. It wasn't all this talk about death that got me so much though, as what Chiquita said about violence generally. 'Violent storms, violent conflicts, violent passions. Violence of every sort,' she kept repeating."

"Mr. Hawks! I am very sorry, but——"

"But in the end," persisted the unquenchable Mr. Hawks, "but in the end, Chiquita said, Faith would 'triumph.' She even said Faith would become famous! 'Very famous and great! In a way no woman ever has before!' " He fairly shouted the prophecy which Rudolf had not been able to silence. " '*In a way no woman has before!*' Now, Mr. Lowe, I ask you! What do you suppose this cute gypsy meant when she said that?"

CHAPTER 19

Mr. Hawks' visit, which, in the beginning, had seemed to Rudolf like a reprieve, seemed, long before it was finished, like a nuisance and an imposition.

The Yankee's enthusiasm over Granada reached its culmination in his detailed description of the visit to Sacro Monte, upon which he insisted on dwelling at length, in spite of Rudolf's every effort to divert him. When his excitement had finally spent itself, and Rudolf began to feel that there were reasonable grounds of hope for his imminent departure, he settled himself so securely in his chair that he gave the impression of being lashed to it, bit off the end of another cigar, and embarked on an exposition of the complicated and corrupt condition of politics in Hinsboro, and the measures which, in his opinion, would remedy this.

To Rudolf's amazement, Faith, instead of being bored and puzzled by this recital, listened to it not only with rapt attention but with evident comprehension. The mysteries of "wards," "bosses," "machines," "gangs," "lobbying," and "plums," would, he should have supposed, be as tedious and baffling to her as they were to him. Instead, she drank in every word that Mr. Hawks spoke with avidity, and moreover revealed, by her own questions and comments, an instinctive understanding of what he was saying that was actually startling. He was almost aggrieved at the facility with which his unsophisticated bride, whose naïveté was a source of disturbance to him, mastered the intricacies of a maze which he himself could not disentangle.

It was when Mr. Hawks began a minute account of the career of an obscure young politician named Neal Conrad, a fellow member of his on the City Council of Hinsboro, that Rudolf, realizing he was growing sleepy, feared he would not be able to conceal his drowsiness. It was inconceivable to him that Faith could be really thrilled by hearing that this small town lawyer, without background or distinction, whom Mr. Hawks seemed to feel so certain would eventually become governor of his state and very likely "go even further," had a pretty young wife named Anne to whom everybody in Hinsboro had "taken a liking," though she was the product of a worthless farm "out back of Hamstead." But Faith was intrigued by Mr. Hawks' accounts of Anne's perfect housekeeping, and of her triumphs at fortnightly meetings of the Woman's Pansy Club. She was eager to hear all about the Conrads' "cute kids." She wished . . .

Rudolf gathered himself together with a start. So he *had* gone to sleep after all! Faith's light touch on his shoulder, gentle as it was, jerked him back with the suddenness of a shock from the somnolence into which he had drifted. Mr. Hawks was actually taking his leave, taking it sociably and slowly, but really taking it, and as a host, Rudolf had been remiss. He had not been on the alert to speed the parting guest with courtesy. Faith had been obliged to rouse him. Even if Mr. Hawks had remained oblivious of his negligence, Faith had not, and though Rudolf knew she would never refer to it, the fact that she was aware of it would always rankle. Besides, to-day of all days such a perception on her part was especially inopportune.

"Don't forget," Mr. Hawks was saying with heartiness, "that my latch-string's out and my spare-room bed's made up. Of course you'll be coming over soon to stay a spell at your own house, Faith, but it'd be convenient, mebbe, while you was getting settled and all, if you boarded out.—Well, Mr. Lowe, it certainly has been nice to meet you. I don't know when I've passed a pleasanter evening and that's a fact."

"But you'll come again, Mr. Hawks, before you leave Granada?" asked Faith hopefully. There was no possible doubt of it; she was almost pleading with this oaf to repeat his visit. It was with immense relief that Rudolf heard him declining her invitation.

"Say, I'd love to, Faith, and that's a fact. But I gotter get back. I don't like the look of things in Hinsboro, and they're liable to go from bad to worse unless I shove in somewheres. So I'll push along in the mornin'. But you'll be comin' to see me pretty soon. Don't you forget that."

He patted her on the arm. Rudolf saw that the gesture was meant to be encouraging, reassuring, even as well as affectionate. She put up her face and kissed him, as she might have kissed a favorite uncle from whom she was regretfully taking leave.

"Leopoldo and Leonardo will drive you to your hotel," she said, with the air of a chatelaine dealing with a social situation capably and with satisfaction, "and come back here at half-past nine to-morrow morning to take Rudolf and me into the Palace. Sebastian explained everything to them carefully. But of course Rudolf and I will come out to the carriage with you and see you safely in it before we say good-bye."

Beginning to wonder if he were, after all, thoroughly awake, Rudolf followed Faith and Mr. Hawks into the outer patio. In the dim light Felipe was revealed, sunk forward in a straight-backed chair and sleeping profoundly. A glistening new carriage, with red wheels and a ducal coronet emblazoned on its doors, to which a span of superb horses was attached, stood at the entrance. And on the driver's seat, in positions of comfortable relaxation, a coachman and a footman attired in gorgeous livery, were slumbering side by side. Faith waked first Felipe and then the man on the box, and Rudolf saw that she was doing it in much the same way that she had touched him, as unobtrusively as possible, instead of uttering the curt rebuke which they deserved for their lapse from alert attendance, and which a German *Hausfrau* would certainly have administered—though of course in the case of well-trained German servants no such a lapse would ever have occurred. He sensed too the joyous quality of the instant response to her summons—in some subtle way she had succeeded in making Felipe not only her respectful servant but her willing slave, in spite of her lack of aloofness and the gentleness of her rule; and it was evident that the mysterious new members of the retinue, whose sudden appearance on the scene was so far unexplained, were equally eager to meet her wishes with alacrity. She had proved *simpatica* to these humble Andalusians, and that she could not understand their language was of secondary importance, since she understood their psychology.

The dazzling carriage spun swiftly around, with Leopoldo cracking his beribboned whip, and Mr. Hawks waving his hat and cheering as it disappeared from sight; Felipe swung the heavy doors of the outer patio together, shot the iron bolts, and murmuring, *"Buenas noches, Señores,"* faded noiselessly away, his lantern flickering like a firefly beside him. It was, Rudolf reflected with repugnance, like a scene in an *opéra bouffe*. For the first time, as Faith slipped her arm through his, though a little piercing thrill stabbed through his body as she pressed against him, it was he that withdrew himself from her.

"Perhaps you will be good enough to tell me the meaning of all this," he said formally.

"Mr. Hawks was a friend of my father's. We used to visit at his house when I was a little girl. And, as he told you, he is a friend of Mr. Castle's too. He was a very poor boy—almost a waif—I've heard him say himself that he was just a mongrel puppy that no one wanted around and that no one quite had the heart to put out of its misery. Isn't it wonderful that he has fought his way up to success?"

"It is no doubt commendable," said Rudolf stiffly, "but he is a very uncouth person. I was amazed to see you treat him as if he were a social equal."

"But Rudolf, he manufactures splendid pencils, and he is a great political power."

"In Hinsboro," said Rudolf contemptuously. "However, I do not suppose we are likely to see him again, so there is no reason why we should argue about him at this hour of the night. I should, however, like to have you tell me where this gaudy victoria which seems to be at your disposal has come from?"

"It goes with the *caseria*," said Faith readily. "It was waiting for us when we came down from Sacro Monte. Sebastian apologized for his oversight in not sending it out before. He has had so much on his mind, he said, that he entirely forgot it had gone into Granada for repairs, and had not been returned here before our arrival. He said there was really no excuse for such negligence on his part, and he was dreadfully chagrined over it, but that he hoped we would be charitable and forgive him."

"Faith!" exclaimed Rudolf in exasperation, "are you really such an ingénue? The two jackanapes on the box were probably supernumeraries on Gabriel's staff—he has so many retainers that he could easily spare any number at a moment's notice. But that carriage is brand-new.

The paint on the coat-of-arms is not even dry yet. Sebastian must have contrived to buy and equip the victoria this very afternoon. I cannot imagine how or when——"

"He did not go with us to the Capilla Real," said Faith still readily, "he joined us later at the Paseo. If the carriage is really new perhaps he bought it while we were in the church."

"Of course he did! As an intimation that your behavior in visiting the Palace as you did was highly incorrect, but that if you were determined to run around the countryside unescorted, family pride demanded that at least you should do it with some show of dignity."

For a moment Faith stood very still. Then she spoke with a serenity which was somehow more disquieting to Rudolf than a sharp rejoinder would have been.

"I honestly do not believe that is the way Sebastian felt about my coming to the Palace, Rudolf. He and Gabriel both seemed very glad to see me. Perhaps they do not look at everything quite as you do. For instance, they liked Mr. Hawks, and you do not. But I do think possibly Sebastian suddenly realized—if he did buy the carriage this afternoon—that it would be convenient for us to have one here, especially since I am to go in to the Palace every day for lessons. You have said yourself that he is very generous—very generous, and when he wishes, very gracious. I think he felt that he was making a generous and gracious gesture in offering us the carriage."

Rudolf did not answer.

"Sebastian seemed much happier to-day than when we saw him in Madrid," Faith went on after a short pause, "something like a boy off on a vacation. Laughing himself and making the rest of us laugh too—just over trifles, but it was great fun. And he joined in the gypsy dances, and did them much better than any of the *gitanos* themselves, even the most intricate steps and movements, he is so lithe and quick. The gypsies seemed to adore having him with them, and he had a wonderful time himself. He kept scattering money around, and that was like a little boy too, a little boy squandering his allowance on candy and marbles. He gave gold pieces to Mariano and Chiquita and pesetas to the others, joking with them all the time and kissing them all good-bye when they went away. And I must show you what he bought for me at the *antiquario's*. He said that every bride who came to Granada should have Granada lace, and that every bride who came to Spain should have a fan, and a shawl and a mantilla and a high carved comb for presents——"

"From her husband!"

"But Rudolf, we have been here two weeks and you have not even suggested buying any of them for me! Sebastian asked me whether you had, and when I said no, he told me he felt much better—that if a methodical German could be capable of an inadvertence, a Spaniard who did not even aspire to system might be forgiven one. Especially as he was eager to make atonement."

"Did Sebastian mean that he was eager to atone for negligence on his own part or did he wish to infer that he was eager to atone for it on mine?"

"Why—both, I suppose, in a way! Anyhow, he bought me the lace, and a fan, and the shawl, and the mantilla, and the comb, and a few other trifles, besides arranging about the carriage. Do come in and look at my lovely presents, Rudolf! I heaped them on the table in the *salita* when I came home. I want to show them to you."

"I do not wish to see them," said Rudolf stiffly. "It is very late and I am very tired. I have had a most fatiguing day. I have not been frittering away my time with gypsies and *antiquarios*. I have been doing constructive work."

"What did you construct?" inquired Faith with interest.

She asked the question affectionately. Unsuspicious of the way in which he had actually spent his afternoon, she could not guess how embarrassing it would be to him. The vagueness and brevity with which he answered hurt her self-respect, already bruised, more deeply still. She felt not only a worshipful pride but an intelligent concern in his career. It wounded her to be treated as if she were prying into matters which were beyond her grasp and outside her sphere. Besides, her joy over her new possessions was blighted because Rudolf would not share it. Evidently he was very tired—tired and annoyed, though his vexation could not be deeply disquieting to himself, for he was asleep before Faith was ready for bed, as he had been on the train. But she knew that now his desire was submerged in displeasure instead of tenderness, for he had not even kissed her good-night; and for the first time since they reached the *caseria,* there had been no passionate prelude to slumber.

Lying wakeful beside him, her thoughts tumultuous, her body tense, she knew that the night had marked a subtle change in their relationship which was as ominous as it was crucial—a change which would perhaps have been inevitable sooner or later in any case, but which had been precipitated by forces which she could neither control nor comprehend. Instead of finding peace in the respite from her husband's urgency, she discovered in it new sources of agitation. If this bond of the flesh, which she had at first resisted and to which she had since succumbed so utterly, weakened between them, what would hold her to him? Only the loyalty she had so vaunted in Venice, for as was so poignantly apparent, the mental and spiritual bonds between them were so fragile that they might snap at any moment!

Faith had dismissed the forebodings which had inspired Victoria

Luise with such prophetic dread from her mind with the same serenity with which she had declined to be swayed by them; now suddenly they surged back into her throbbing consciousness. Were they already verging on fulfillment? A horror lest they were swept over her, for, with their onrush, the impediments to perfection in the communion of marriage, which she had so firmly believed existed only in the imagination of the Archduchess, rose relentlessly before her. She had felt wholly self-reliant that morning, when she had retorted to Rudolf's reproof with such level scorn. But the situation with which, in the daylight and sunshine, she had been so confident that she could cope, took on a sinister aspect in these dark watches. Certainly she was frustrated, and distraught with perplexity, she wondered how she could make good her boast that she could face frustration without fear. For she was trembling, trembling before that menacing future which she saw must hold in store for her a succession of "insuperable barriers" which she had only just begun to glimpse. How could she contend that she was not afraid, when she was shaking from head to foot with terror, when her very teeth were chattering with it?

In her anguish, loneliness as well as fear engulfed her, and she yearned for the reassurance that comes with tangible tenderness. If she stretched out her arms to Rudolf, if he waked to find himself encircled with them, her head against his shoulder, her tears falling on his breast, surely he would divine the depth of her dependence on him, of the despair she would feel if he failed her! Surely he would comfort her through this desperate hour by convincing her that he cherished her for all time! Surely his sensibility to her need and her happiness must be greater than it appeared! Surely he could not be so alien to her in thought, in outlook and in standards as he had seemed increasingly ever since their marriage, and most of all throughout the portentous day that had terminated in this calamitous night! Surely there was somewhere between them a neutral ground on which they could meet without misunderstanding and without conflict, some pleasant place where peace prevailed! Surely since he had wanted her to be his wife so much that he had overcome obstacles that seemed unsurmountable before their marriage, he could overcome the obstacles that now arose, even if she could not! Surely since he had honored her by raising her to his high estate, by giving her his proud name, by taking her with him into the exalted sphere which was his natural habitat but which had not previously been hers, he would not withhold his confidence or fail in fostering solicitude!

She turned toward him, searching in the darkness for his hand, and when she had found it, locking her taut fingers between those which lay relaxed at his side. Almost instantly she felt a responsive pressure, light at first, but gradually growing firm and hard.

"Rudolf," she said breathlessly.

It seemed to her that her very soul cried out to him as she whispered his name. If he failed her in this supreme moment, she knew she would never call on him again.

He too had turned. She had crept so close to him that he did not even need to draw her to him, and his arms closed, like bands of steel, around her quivering body.

"I knew!" he murmured triumphantly. "I knew that if I waited you would ask my forgiveness. All day you have rebelled against my judgment and my authority; but I was sure that when you thought of your defiance through the long night, remembrance of it would distress and grieve you, that you would be repentant. *Liebe* Faith, I do forgive you, freely and fully! We will never speak of this defiance again, for I know you will never be guilty of it again! Hereafter you will always yield to my will!"

His voice, low as it was, vibrated with the same exultation that a Roman soldier might have felt after subduing a proud and beautiful Greek captive.

CHAPTER 20

It was nearly nine o'clock before Rudolf woke the following morning. There was not time to have breakfast served on the terrace before starting into Granada. So he ordered Catalina to bring it immediately to Faith's room instead, and pending her somewhat leisurely interpretation of his command, bathed and shaved hastily, returning, with a dressing gown of dark corded silk knotted around him, to drink his coffee with his wife.

"It has just occurred to me," he said with a trace of concern in his voice, "that as Gabriel is receiving us in formal audience, you should wear a black dress of rather conservative cut. I do not suppose you own such a garment."

Faith, who had risen too, and was sitting in front of her toilet table brushing her hair, answered him calmly.

"Oh, yes, I have. Your mother told me that I should need one. It is made of that new material called georgette crêpe, and trimmed with fine tucks and little plaited ruffles. It is what the *grands couturiers* call *une petite robe très chic mais très discrète.*"

"I should prefer that you should not speak French to me, Faith, when you can avoid it."

"*Es ist ein sehr nettes Kleidchen,*" she said with equal tranquillity.

"I am relieved. But as this is Spain, that is not all you require. You should wear a mantilla instead of a hat."

"Yes, I know. Well, as I told you last night, I have that too. I am so glad Sebastian thought of giving it to me yesterday.—Shall I pour out your coffee? We have not much time."

As she took her place beside him in the new victoria, her appearance was, he admitted to himself with satisfaction and complacency, highly conventional, and—he reflected with more satisfaction and less complacency—distractingly charming. The correct and exquisite dress had been cut by a master hand; it fitted Faith's budding figure like a sheath. Her hair shone like burnished gold through her filmy mantilla. Rudolf decided not to compliment her, lest it should give her an exaggerated idea of the attractions with which she had adorned adequacy.

"I have been giving Leopoldo and Leonardo a piece of my mind while I have been waiting for you to come out," he remarked instead. "I do not think they will ever go to sleep again while they are on duty."

"We must try to set them a good example," replied Faith.

He shot a furtive glance at her direction. Was she intimating that a master who went to sleep himself in the presence of a guest was hardly a pattern to hold up to a somnolent servant? But her fact and manner were so composed that he decided she must have been speaking at random; and the decorum and dignity with which she conducted herself throughout the audience gratified him intensely. No one, watching her as it progressed, could have divined that this was the first time that she had knelt before an enthroned ecclesiastic and kissed an Episcopal ring; and the grace with which she rose from her knees, and stood with slightly bent head and clasped hands before the Archbishop while he pronounced a few words of pastoral counsel was appealing. Even after Gabriel himself had signified that the audience was to close without further ceremony, by leaning forward and laying one hand lightly on her hair, smiling as he did so, she did not commit the blunder of glancing up too quickly with a responsive smile.

"I think," Gabriel said with that slight whimsicality which had drawn Faith to him the day before, "that it is time for us to resume the rôle of relatives.—Since you have broken in on your régime of study to-day in any case, Rudolf, why do you not take Faith for a short stroll through the Alhambra? It is always cool in the more sheltered chambers. Afterwards you might bring her back here for an early lunch with me, and when we have eaten, we will talk with Father Constantino about her schedule. I think, all in all, that would make a pleasant program."

Rudolf was half afraid that Faith would burst out with an impetuous acceptance before he could reply. He decided, if she did, that he would immediately decline for them both. But though he paused for a moment before speaking again, she pleased him by standing silent and motionless until he answered.

"Thank you. I know you understand how important it is that I should not neglect my work long or often, but as you say, I have already broken into my schedule for to-day. I shall be very pleased to remain. Especially as it is very important that Faith should also get started in her studies."

Except for the fact that Leopoldo and Leonardo were again discovered sound asleep on their box when he and Faith emerged from the Palace to visit the Alhambra, and once more when they left it for the *caseria,* nothing happened all day to mar Rudolf's complacency. He knew the history of the Alhambra thoroughly; and he expounded this to Faith all the time they were walking from the Court of the Lions to the Tower of the Two Sisters, and back again, while she listened with an attentive interest which was delightful. Their luncheon, at which Sebastian was not present, was most agreeable. Gabriel suavely explained that his brother had suddenly changed his plans and decided to visit his friend Don Jaime de los Rios, in Malaga, for a time, instead of remaining in Granada. He had gone off on horseback early that morning and no date had been set for his return—he would probably be gone several weeks. He had left greetings for Faith and Rudolf, and hoped they would excuse his absence. Rudolf said, very gravely, that they would be glad to do so, and turned his attention to Father Constantino, who had been included in Gabriel's invitation. It was evident from the priest's scholarly conversation, that he would make an ideal teacher for Faith; it was arranged that she should have a daily lesson at ten o'clock, and she was given some books to take home with her, so that she might begin to study without delay. Yes, it was all eminently satisfactory. Rudolf, returning to his tome on the rights of neutral nations for a couple of hours before tea-time, found that he could not draw up the outline for his thesis competently and quickly, and became increasingly certain that the disturbing interlude of the day before had, after all, been a blessing in disguise, since it had been so beneficent in its results.

. . . . .

As the golden days flowed on, this sense of beatitude deepened. He was no longer dominated by the driving passion, which, during the first fortnight at the *caseria,* had proved so insatiable that he had begun to wonder whether it would ever be slaked. He had been like a ravenous man perpetually seeking repletion but perpetually rising, still unfilled, from a feast. Not until that supreme hour of exultation, when Faith had turned to him in the darkness, had he drunk deep enough from the fathomless cup of desire to drain it to its last drop. Now at last his senses had steadied themselves; intellect was no longer obscured by ecstasy; the student was no longer submerged in the sensualist. He was the master of his own mind and his own emotions, even as he was the master of his own house.

There were no further interruptions to his long hours of work in the library; a few more Spanish kinsfolk called, but when they did so before tea-time, Faith dealt with them alone and competently at the moment, and their visits were returned at his convenience; an exchange of dinner invitations did not disturb him, since he seldom cared to devote his evenings to research. His concentration bore rapid results; and a few days after he had dispatched his report to the German Embassy in Madrid, he came up on the terrace, where Faith was bending over her own books, holding a letter high above his head.

"I have good news, *liebe* Faith!" he exclaimed. "Felipe has just come in with the post, and in it is a communication from our Ambassador. He praises the thesis I sent him very highly—indeed he is so pleased with it that he suggests prolonging my stay here for an extra month, in order that I may continue my research undisturbed, along the same lines. You would be glad to remain at the *caseria*, would you not?"

"Very," said Faith, closing her grammar. "And I am so glad, Rudolf, that the Ambassador is pleased with your report! I felt sure he would be!"

"But if we do stay on, it will be necessary for me to go to Madrid at once to receive further instructions and assist at a brief conference. Indeed, the Ambassador's letter is both a commendation and a summons. I have sent Felipe back to Granada to see if he can secure a compartment on the express to-morrow, and I have also given him a telegram to dispatch to *Tia* Carlota telling her to expect us, in case I obtain it."

"Do you really wish me to go with you?" Faith inquired.

"But certainly! Can you imagine that I would leave you here all alone? Why do you ask so strange a question, *Liebchen*?"

He saw that she hesitated for a moment before replying, and the idea that she was choosing her words carefully did not altogether please him.

"I thought that perhaps you would not think it was best that my lessons should be interrupted, merely because you had to go to Madrid. I know how eager you are that I should make progress."

"But you *are* making progress, wonderful progress! And the interruption would be for only a few days. Besides, you could take your books with you."

"I suppose I could," she said rather listlessly. Then, with increasing hesitation, she went on, "Really, Rudolf, I should not be lonely, staying here all by myself. I should enjoy it."

"You would enjoy a separation from me?"

"That is not just what I meant——"

"Then I cannot imagine what you did mean. And I should not enjoy a separation from you at all. Nor shall I consent to one."

"Very well," she said more listlessly still. "Perhaps I had better go and start packing then." She rose slowly, and as she did so, Rudolf noticed that she was very pale and that she swayed a little.

"Faith!" he exclaimed. "What is the matter with you? Are you ill?"

She reseated herself, stretching out her hands on either side of her as if for support.

"I think I must be," she said with evident effort. "I did not mean to bother you by telling you about it, Rudolf, but these last few days I have not felt at all well. That is why I would rather not take a long hot journey just now. This morning my head ached so that I could hardly see, and I was so dizzy during my lesson that I only half understood what Father Constantino was saying to me. When I started to leave the Palace I—I fainted. I never did before, and it would have frightened me, rather, if Gabriel hadn't been so kind. Father Constantino called him at once, and when I came to myself, I was lying on a long divan in Gabriel's own study and he was leaning over to lay a cold cloth on my forehead. I never shall forget how good it felt or how gentle his hands were. Afterwards he gave me something cloudy to drink—aromatic ammonia in water I think he said it was—and sat beside me until I was better. It was nearly an hour before he would let me get up again, and then he came out to the *caseria* with me. He told me not to disturb you, because he knew you were studying."

"But Faith, I am much disturbed because you are not well! Of course if you are not able to travel—but I must go, and if you grew worse while I was away, what would you do?"

"I am sure Catalina would take splendid care of me. Gabriel told her, before he left, what had happened at the Palace, and she has been simply sweet to me all day. Sweeter than ever, I mean. Of course she is always a dear!"

Faith smiled faintly at the pleasant reminiscence of Catalina's attitude.

"Gabriel told Leopoldo and Leonardo too," she said, "and cautioned them that we must come out here 'with moderate velocity.' I love the way Spaniards express themselves, don't you, Rudolf? There is no end to their elegance of speech. Leopoldo is a dear too. When he was thoroughly awake—he was asleep, as usual, when Gabriel began to talk to him—he said '*Sanctissima Maria!*' and kept on saying it, smiling to himself and walking the horse all the way to the *caseria.*—Did you know that he and Leonardo were twins, Rudolf?"

"No," said Rudolf, "I have had no occasion to be concerned with their relationship. But I am much concerned over your health. If you are not much better to-morrow morning, we will dismiss all thought of your going to Madrid, and I will hasten back here as quickly as I can. I shall miss you very much, *Liebchen,* if I am forced to leave you; but

I do believe that Catalina will wait on you faithfully.—Did Gabriel speak of sending for a doctor?"

"He spoke of it; but he said he did not think it was necessary."

"He has probably seen such attacks before, as a result of the climate, and knows they are not serious."

"Probably," agreed Faith, "I am sure they do not amount to much."

. . . . .

But when morning came she was so much worse that it was obvious she could not lift her head from her pillow, much less get up and prepare for a journey. She set aside her coffee with aversion, pressed her hands against her throbbing throat, and then sank into a state of stupor, from which she roused herself only occasionally and with evident effort. Felipe had secured the compartment, and Faith, though visibly disinclined to talk, agreed instantly if drowsily that Rudolf should not alter his plans on her account. The chances were that she would be all right again in a day or two.

"If you are not better in the morning," Rudolf said, "I should prefer that Felipe should fetch a doctor. I will send a note to Gabriel, telling him you are not able to come in to your lesson to-day, and asking him to recommend one."

"Very well," murmured Faith indifferently.

"Is there anything I can do for you before I leave?"

"No, thank you."

"Are you sure?"

"I should like a cold cloth on my head again. I have told Catalina to bring one. I do not seem to want anything else—just to be very quiet—not to move or think or speak."

She turned away and closed her eyes. She had not actually said, "I want to be alone," but her gesture revealed her unspoken wish.

"But Faith! I cannot go away without kissing you farewell!"

For a moment she did not stir. Then she lay back, both shoulders resting on her high pillow, her eyes still closed. Rudolf slid one arm underneath her to lift her to him, and with his free hand raised her face to the level of his own. She did not resist him at all; but there was no vitality in the pliancy of her body; and in spite of the molten heat of the day her lips and fingers were cold. As he laid her back on her pillows, he did so with a sensation of having embraced a statue, which, unlike Pygmalion, he had not succeeded in animating with his own ardor.

Really disquieted, he stood looking down at her, uncertain whether to leave her after all. But her lethargy was so profound that she did not even seem to be aware of his presence; and at last, focusing his mind on the significance of the summons he had received, he went quietly out of the room and downstairs to his waiting carriage. In his anxiety, he even forgot to rebuke Leopoldo and Leonardo as he waked them. Felipe, who had carried down his bags for him and disposed them in the victoria, returned, after watching his master with apparent respect out of sight, and told Catalina of the omission, smiling broadly as he did so.

"His journey will be an atrocity in this heat," said Catalina with dark satisfaction, "*Madre de Dios!* When has there been so burning a day!"

"I fear that it will end in a storm. There are great clouds gathering."

"It would clear the air. But the thunder would disturb the *Baronesa* and the lightning might frighten her."

"I do not think so. She is a lady not easily frightened. But she needs sleep."

"*Es verdad.* What man ever let his wife sleep in peace during the *luna de mielo?*" asked Catalina contemptuously, as if in wholesale condemnation of the male race. "Now that she is rid—*gracios à Dios!*—of this German husband of hers, the *Baronesa* can have her sleep out. Afterwards she will feel better."

All through the torrid afternoon, Catalina plodded back and forth at frequent and regular intervals between the kitchen and Faith's bedroom, each time returning to inform Felipe that the *Baronesa* still slept, that so far she had not even stirred. But as the smoldering clouds, closing in over the brazen sky, plunged the *caseria* into premature darkness, Catalina reported a change.

"I carried a candle into her room, shielding it with my hand and looked at her closely. There is a little color in her face again and she has moved. She lies relaxed at least. This morning she frightened me, she was so still and white. She looked like a sheeted saint in a sepulcher."

Catalina interrupted herself to join Felipe in making the sign of the cross. As she did so, a bolt of lightning, followed by a terrific explosion, zig-zagged violently across the menacing heavens; and as if released by the flood-gates which it had torn open in its wild flight, torrential sheets of rain descended like an avalanche. The onrush of the elements had come with such swift frenzy, that though they had been waiting for it all day, Catalina and Felipe stood for an instant stupefied by it; and as a second crash of thunder rent the supercharged atmosphere and reverberated along the black horizon, the sound of a galloping horse coming closer and closer over the cobblestones rang out above the storm.

"Someone is going to try for shelter here!" shrieked Catalina. "Whoever it is, do not let him in! It might well be the devil himself, riding through the darkness!" She sank on her knees, under the shelter of the *galeria.* Felipe, no less terrified, crouched beside her. As the heavy knocker hammered against the door of the outer patio, and the shouting of a man rose above it, they hid their faces and screamed. Then they were conscious that someone else was calling, calling calmly but imperiously.

In the first grip of their superstitious fright they had momentarily forgotten even the lady of their loyal devotion. Now, as they opened their eyes and looked across the patio, they saw, through the translucent rain, a shadowy white figure beckoning to them, and mistook it for an apparition. It was not until Faith had succeeded in making herself heard above the battering at the gate, the lashing water, and their own outcry, that they realized what it was.

"Felipe! Catalina!" she cried. "Shame on you! What do you mean by such behavior? Go at once and open the gate for your master! Do you not recognize Don Sebastian's voice?"

CHAPTER 21

"ONCE, a long while ago, I went to visit a relative who was the Spanish Minister to Ecuador," Sebastian said. "We spent a good deal of our time at a country place not far from Quito, which had been put at his disposal by Ecuadorian friends. The Ecuadorians are great land lovers, just as we are. It is their Spanish heritage. Many of them have five or six estates, and spend most of their time in the country. This house where I stayed was built of pale blue stucco and had a red-tiled roof. It was long and rambling, with deep *galerias,* and it had frescos running along the outer walls, and a great bell that hung above the stone steps leading from one balcony to another. There were twenty rooms on each floor, all opening into each other with wide doors, and a splendid staircase. Really, it was charming. I was very happy there."

"It must have been beautiful.—What made you think of it just now?"

"I thought of the house because I thought of the garden, which was even more lovely."

"But, Sebastian, that is no answer at all! What made you think of the garden?"

"You did. Everything about the garden was beautiful: the little streams with rustic bridges curving over them, and the quiet pools where swans swam about, and the violets and orchids and the roses and forget-me-nots that bordered the paths and extended in beds and clustered over the terraces. But the most beautiful thing of all in the garden was a waterfall that fell in smooth broad sheets over a background of lilies. It veiled them without concealing them." He paused for a moment and then said vibrantly, "When I came into the patio, and saw you on the *galeria,* with the rain streaming down between us, you looked to me like a lily shining behind a waterfall."

Faith did not answer at once. The storm was over, for it had spent itself almost as suddenly as it had descended, and she was seated opposite Sebastian at a little table which Catalina had placed near the fountain. She had told the old servant that she was sure Don Sebastian would want some tea as soon as he had shed his drenched garments and reclothed himself. And as she hastily dressed and wound up her hair, she was conscious of a craving for the steaming, fragrant drink herself. When she went downstairs again, and found that wine, cold ham and olives had been laid out beside a great loaf of bread, but there were no tea or biscuits in sight, she was disappointed and for a moment bewildered.

"I am sure I told Catalina tea," she said to Sebastian, who had reëntered the patio just then, his black hair still glistening with moisture, and clad in corduroy breeches, a soft white shirt open at the throat, and a wide red belt. "I don't know much Spanish yet, of course, but that is easy enough to say. And look what she has brought!"

Sebastian laughed. "I am afraid she was thinking of my taste rather than yours. The true Andalusian buys tea at a pharmacy, and uses it as a medicine for colds and colic! Catalina knows that I would always have ham and olives at six o'clock and wine at any hour rather than tea, if I were free to follow my preference. But of course you must have yours just the same. I hope you have usually been properly served?"

Faith assured him that she had. She thought it was rather touching, and told him so, that Catalina should have so instinctively reverted to her natural custom, in serving her real *patron*, that she had forgotten the habits of the temporary chatelaine of the *caseria*. But she drank her tea thirstily when it was finally brought to her and ate her biscuits with relish, listening with interest as she did so to the account Sebastian gave her of his visit to Malaga, while he consumed his ham and olives.

"It is a lovely city, *Señora*," he said. "And Jaime de los Rios, whom I visited there, has a delightful house. It is reached through a long avenue of royal palms, and there are innumerable great poinsettia trees and custard apples on the place, besides of course quantities of jasmine and roses and orange blossoms."

"I wish I could see it," said Faith eagerly.

"But you can, *Señora*. Any time you like. Jaime would be delighted to have you come there."

"Sebastian," asked Faith abruptly, "why do you always call me *Señora*? We are almost relatives, aren't we? Anyway, friends and 'kinsfolk' as you say here. All the other members of your family call me Faith. I have wondered why you don't?"

Sebastian hesitated. "Do you know the Spanish word for Faith?" he asked at length.

"No."

"It is Fidelidad."

"*Fidelidad!* Why, Sebastian, that sounds almost exactly like——"

"Felicidad. Yes. Now you see."

"But, Sebastian, the meaning is not at all the same!"

"Gabriel would tell you that it is. He believes that faith and happiness are interwoven. But I have always known Felicidad to be without faith, and I doubt whether Fidelidad would grant me happiness."

His play on words confused her, and she sat silent for a moment. "But since we always talk in English," she suggested at length, "perhaps——"

"You really wish it?"

"Very much."

He reached across the small table, took her hand, and lifted it to his lips. "*A los pies de Usted,*" he said and stopped. "If I call you by your Christian name I shall claim the privilege of following the Spanish custom in such cases and using the term 'thou' also," he ended.

"Of course."

"*A tus pies* then. Do you know what it means?"

"Yes," said Faith readily. "It is a conventional expression of courtesy."

"Not when 'thou' is used. Then it has a more literal meaning. You know, Faith, do you not, that I am 'at your feet'?"

Something in his voice startled her a little, but when she looked at him, and saw the gentleness of his expression, she was reassured.

"You came over the road from Malaga to-day?" she asked, giving no direct answer to his question.

"Yes," he said, following her lead without insistence. "I love to come over it, for it is one of the most picturesque in Spain. It takes you through high clefts in the mountains, and deep gorges, which open into the fertile valleys where dates and grapes are cultivated. I stop along the way at the *ventorillos*—the roadhouses—for refreshment—when I am off on a holiday I always travel very simply. There is one *ventorillo* consisting of several arbors built up high on a hill, of which I am especially fond. I go there very often. To-day I lunched and rested there and found the whole place simply a mass of purple morning-glories."

"Oh, how gorgeous! Have you ever thought, Sebastian, that there is so much beauty in Spain—that it almost hurts?"

"Yes," he said softly, "very often.—Is it the beauty of Spain that has hurt you, Faith?"

Once more she looked at him with startled eyes, and once more was disarmed by the gentleness of his expression.

"What makes you think I have been hurt?" she asked, a shade too quickly. "I have not been well the last few days. But it is only the heat. I am always better toward evening, and this evening I am very much better. I have slept for hours and hours to-day, and I feel like a different person now."

"Faith, do you think I am blind? Can you imagine I will ever forget the look on your face when I entered the drawing-room that night in Madrid? Or when you came up Gabriel's steps that afternoon at Granada? Of course I know you have been hurt. But I do not think it has been the beauty of Spain that has hurt you. Is it?" And as she did not answer he went on, more gently still, "Will you not tell me about it, *querida*?"

"No," said Faith slowly. "There are some things we do not talk about to anyone."

"I have not offended you, have I? You must forgive me if I have. I do not mean to seem curious. It is only that I want to comfort you."

He took her hand again, this time without kissing it, and she let her fingers lie in his as she answered him.

"You do comfort me, Sebastian. And it is very easy for me to talk to you—so easy that perhaps I should be tempted to tell you secrets, whether it were right or not, if I did not have the feeling that you had guessed them all anyway! That makes it unnecessary, doesn't it—for me to say very much? Suppose you talk to me instead?"

It was then that he told her about the Ecuadorian garden. He was still holding the hand that he had taken when he asked her if he had offended her, and as he said, "You looked to me like a lily shining behind a waterfall!" he reached for the other hand also, and resting his elbows on the little table, leaned toward her above their interclasped fingers.

"But it was not only of a lily I thought," he said. "I thought of so many different manifestations of loveliness that I was confused. I thought of the Virgin in the Grotto at Lourdes, as I first saw her, very late one misty evening, when I was the only worshipper at her shrine. I thought of Juliet standing on her balcony, still unaware that Romeo was in her garden. I thought of Rapunzel of the golden hair. She let it down, do you remember——"

"Yes," exclaimed Faith excitedly. "Of course I remember! Oh, Sebastian, I am so glad that you read fairy tales! Because I believe that this is a magic house, and perhaps you can tell me if I am right. Is it?"

"I think it must be. Indeed, I have never doubted it," he said gravely.

"Tell me why you are so sure!"

"Because so many fairy stories have come true here."

"What kind of fairy stories, Sebastian?"

"Love stories. Shall I tell you about them, Faith?"

"You mean that people who have loved each other very much have been happy here together?"

"Yes. That is what I mean. One of my ancestors bought the *caseria* and built the *casita* for a—a lady he loved very much. A lady whom he could not marry."

"Why not?"

"He was married already. To a princess. They lived in the most beautiful palace in Seville, except the Alcázar. But they hated each other. It was here, in seclusion and simplicity, that he found real joy."

"And what finally happened?"

"Oh, finally the princess died. And he married the lady he loved. I told you it was a fairy story!"

A slight bitterness suddenly tinged his speech. But as if conscious that Faith was fascinated with the thought that he agreed with her about the magic qualities of the *caseria* he went on more lightly.

"Of course the family protested. But after all, it was necessary that he should have an heir, and the princess had never had any children, while the lady he loved had four."

"What was her name?"

"Doña Cecilia. Her three daughters, who were born before her marriage, entered convents. But fortunately her only son was legitimate. He was one of my great-grandfathers."

"And since then——"

"Since then the men of my family have always contrived to find sanctuary here with the women they have loved. It has been our refuge from the world, the flesh, and the devil."

"And you offered to give it to me!"

Faith's voice trembled as she spoke. Sebastian realized how deeply she was moved.

"I hoped very much that you would honor me by accepting it, *querida*. I was grieved when Gabriel told me you felt you could not, though I was interested and touched by the reason you gave for declining:—That you wanted to think of your own little house in America as your real home. But if you should ever reconsider, it would make me very happy. And you must not misunderstand what I have just told you. There is no stain of shame on the *caseria*. It has not been a bower for illicit intrigue. It has always been a sanctuary, as I said—it was a sanctuary for me to-day. It is true that Doña Cecilia was not married to my ancestor when he first brought her here. But she was not a light woman. She was a great lady. And my great-grandfather was the one love of her life, as she was of his. While in later years—" Sebastian stopped for a moment, and then went on very softly, "It was because my mother loved the place so much, Faith, that I wanted to give it to you, not merely lend it to you, as I have to so many others."

"Did—do you feel as if you could talk to me about her?"

"I feel that I cannot help talking to you about her. Her name was Cristina, and no woman was ever better named. I think her spirit lives again in Gabriel. She and my father came here together when they were first married, and as long as she lived, after that, she never failed to spend part of every year here. Even when my father was Ambassador to England, it was here that they came for his leave of absence. My mother adorned any gathering, and was as much beloved in London as she was in Spain; but she was never dependent on courts and crowds for enjoyment; in fact she was happiest of all when she could live simply and in seclusion with her own family. I can remember, when I was a child, walking hand in hand with my father, beside the donkey on which she rode, when we went on little excursions together—I suppose you have been to the Carthusian Monastery?"

"No," said Faith, in a voice as hushed as his own.

"Really? I should have supposed—but never mind! Cartuja—the monastery—is only a mile from here. It has a very famous sacristy filled with chests and cupboards of inlaid tortoise shell, and mother-of-pearl, and ivory; and I never tired, when I was a little boy, of opening and shutting those countless glittering drawers. There is a statue of Saint Bruno in the church, which I loved. I know now that it is the work of a great artist, Alonso Canaso, but then I loved it merely because Saint Bruno seemed to me such a very friendly saint."

"Tell me more," Faith urged as he paused.

"There is really nothing much to tell. It is just that I was so happy in those days and that I adored my mother so. On our way home from Cartuja, we sometimes stopped at the next *caseria* to this, where our olives were ground into oil, as we had no mill of our own. The mill was really very primitive. But to me it was intricate and exciting. And we were nearly always here for the harvest. We used to get up early in the morning to watch the grape-pickers at work. A great many extra helpers came in at that time, for we had only two old house servants here regularly, just as I do now. Nearly all the grapes were white, but there were always a few dark ones mixed in. I used to count the bunches of those. And I gorged myself on them so, as they came off the vines, that it is a wonder that I did not succumb from over-indulgence. I suppose the only reason I survived is because it is the good who die young!"

"Nonsense! You survived because your mother took good care of you, and watched you carefully to make sure that you really did not eat too much."

"*Querida*, you are right. No man ever had such a mother."

He sat so long seemingly absorbed in memories that Faith began to be afraid he would forget that he had not finished telling her about the harvest. But she did not like to break in on his pensive moods; and when he turned to her again, she was glad she had not, for she saw there were tears on his cheeks, though he took up his story calmly.

"Later in the day," he said, "the baskets, brimful, were brought up to the *casita.* Before the men emptied the grapes into the presses, they trod on them with their feet. It is a very old custom, and not at all dirty or unattractive as you might think. They washed themselves very thoroughly beforehand, and wore a special kind of sandals, called *alpargatas.* And of course they sang all the time they were working.— Some day, *querida,* would you like to see a harvest here?"

"Is it still like that? Could we watch the men trampling the grapes and listen to them singing?"

"Of course. And we could go to the Cartuja and the *caseria* of the olive mill—you on a donkey, and I walking beside you, and perhaps——"

He broke off abruptly.

"And perhaps what, Sebastian?"

"Nothing, *querida.*—Let us talk about Rapunzel again. You cannot think how instantly I thought of her when I came into the patio and saw you standing, dressed all in white, with your hair falling over your shoulders. I had not seen you with it down before. But it looked exactly as I have been imagining it would ever since I met you. I am sure it is the most beautiful hair in all the world. I have been wondering—it is a great deal to ask, I know, but I have been wondering—if you would let me touch it?"

Without hesitation, Faith bent over. They were so close together that she could feel his breath on her face.

"I may touch it with my hand?"

"Isn't that what you wanted?"

He disengaged his fingers from hers, laid them lightly on her shining head, and then let them slip softly down on either side of the part which divided the glistening waves, until they met under her chin, tilting it up a little.

"Yes, that was what I wanted," he said slowly, "in part."

"In part?"

"I hoped—I suppose vainly—for a miracle. I hoped you would also let me touch it with my lips."

Their eyes were almost level with each other. Faith, gazing into his, saw through the dusk a wellspring of light rising in them. It reflected, though she did not know it, the wellspring of light in her own. As if in the clarity of two fountains swiftly mingled, her assent merged into his quest; and though the pressure of his lips against her brow was so light that the golden tendrils framing her forehead hardly quivered, almost instantaneously she became aware that they had both risen; that the table was no longer between them; that her arms were around his neck and his were around her waist; that her face was lifted and his bent; that his kiss no longer rested on her bowed head but on her upturned mouth; that all her being had been fused with his into a heavenly harmony.

How long they stood there, clasped against each other's hearts, Faith never knew. At last a tremor passed through Sebastian's frame, communicating itself to hers, and he released her, without abruptness and without haste, stooping to brush his hair against the hollow of her throat and letting his hand linger over hers. Then, as if he were fearful of breaking his spell unless he were silent, he stood looking at her with a dark luminous gaze of wonder.

"Sebastian!" she whispered breathlessly, "what have we done? What has happened to us?" Then as he still stood looking at her without speaking, "I did not know a kiss could be like that—so gentle and—so sweet!"

"Nor I," he answered simply, "I have kissed countless women. But I have never kissed or been kissed like that before."

It did not seem to occur to him that Faith might shrink from the knowledge of the kisses that were so different from those which they had just exchanged. He spoke rather as if, after what had taken place, anything less than complete candor between them was unthinkable.

"But I do not understand—we were sitting on either side of the table and suddenly—was it you who moved or I?"

"We moved together, *querida,* impelled, at the same time, by the same force. What has happened is neither your doing nor mine. But the miracle for which I did not dare to hope has come to pass."

"And now—what are we going to do now?"

Sebastian smiled. Faith, who had not seen his face radiant before, marveled that she had ever thought his face cynical and cruel for all its charm.

"I am not quite sure. I think perhaps we had better consult Gabriel, who is an authority on miracles. I am not. This is the first time I have ever caught a glimpse of one."

There was a ringing quality in his voice as unfamiliar as the light in his face. As he went on talking, it seemed to her that it became increasingly joyous.

"But I do not think we need to consult him immediately. Do you? At least not until we have sat down and talked the question over ourselves!"

He motioned toward the stone bench flanking the fountain; and when they had seated themselves, he put his arm behind her, without trying to draw her close to him, but as if he expected her to lean against him for comfort and support.

"Do you not think we might have dinner here, together, first?" he went on. "A little *fiesta,* all of our own, a sort of thanksgiving to celebrate the revelation of our miracle? That would give us time for a long discussion. And afterwards—The moon is beautiful to-night—Have you been to the Alhambra yet?"

"Yes," said Faith. "Gabriel suggested that Rudolf should take me there. We walked all through it one morning, and Rudolf told me its history. He——"

She stopped short. For the first time it came over her that Rudolf's absence had neither been questioned nor explained.

"Sebastian! We have both forgotten—about Rudolf! He was summoned to Madrid."

"Yes, I know," said Sebastian carelessly. "So he dragged you through the Alhambra in the burning sunshine and told you its history! It is just about what I should expect of him! In a nation which describes sausages as delicatessen almost any incongruity may be looked for!"

"Sebastian!" said Faith severely, "I cannot let you speak in that way about Rudolf." She paused for a moment, and then went on, "I told you a little while ago that there were some things it was not loyal to discuss with anyone, and that anyway you guessed all my secrets, almost before I was conscious of them myself. But there is one thing that you do not seem to realize, and that I feel I ought to tell you: I wanted to marry Rudolf, just as much as he wanted to marry me. I thought, the moment I saw him, that he was a paragon. He looked to me as I think Saint Michael must have looked. He knows I felt that way about him. I have told him so."

"Oh!" said Sebastian with mild mockery. "You thought he looked like Saint Michael and you told him that! I can imagine how delighted he must have been! I think Rudolf has always rather pictured himself in that rôle, and to have you recognize him in the part must have been most gratifying to him. But now you have discovered that your idol's feet are clay, surely you may admit this—at least to me?"

"No," said Faith steadily.

He looked at her with unreluctant respect. "Very well," he said quietly. "I shall not again make the mistake of asking you to do so. But tell me, *querida*, when you met me—did I appear to you like a supernatural being also—the kind that is supposed to have cloven hoofs? I am sure Rudolf had prepared you for that by giving you a long list of my delinquencies."

Faith colored a little. "He was not very flattering," she said frankly, "but I am afraid I did not think—about delinquencies very long. Because almost immediately—as soon as I got over being angry with you for ridiculing Rudolf and for declining to take me to the Prado that first morning—I felt—so happy every time you came near me. I watched for you to come. It seemed to me as if I had been waiting for you always, and yet as if I had always known you. It is hard to keep delinquencies in mind when you feel like that about a person—

as if you could not imagine what your life would be like if he did not have a part in it."

"Do not try to imagine," said Sebastian, a slight huskiness blurring his ringing voice. "*Vida de mi vida,* can you guess what it means to have you say this to me? Oh, Faith—if I had only found you years ago!"

"You have found me now," said Faith.

"Yes. I have found you now. That in itself should be miracle enough."

For a moment he seemed almost to forget her physical presence. She had to force herself to intrude on his silent immobility.

"You must let me finish what I started to say about Rudolf," she said resolutely. "Perhaps you do not know about the tragedy and the disgrace that lay between us. How much he was willing to forget and forgive in order to marry me."

"I know that his brother killed your mother," said Sebastian almost angrily. "The more such stories are hushed up the more they spread. But I should have said it was you who had a good deal to forgive and forget. I will not—ridicule Rudolf, since it pains you that I should do so. But neither will I permit you to speak as if he had condescended in marrying you."

"Perhaps we had better not talk about him any more just now," Faith said slowly, "except that I wish you would explain to me how you knew he had been summoned to Madrid."

"Does it matter? As far as that goes, how did you know I was calling to you through the storm?"

His savage look had melted in a smile. He seemed actually ready to jest with her, so unclouded did his happiness appear. But as he saw her face lose its serenity, his own became grave again.

"*Alma de mi alma,* do not look so startled! You dreamed about me, did you not, in your deep slumber? You thought that I was calling you? And then you woke and heard my voice at the gate? There is nothing alarming in that—It is strange, but lovely, like everything else about our miracle!" He rose, holding out his hands to help her to her feet. "It is getting late," he said. "Catalina has been a pattern of discretion. She has left us undisturbed for nearly three hours. But she will be wondering if we are never going to have our dinner. Shall we call to her to bring us candles, and go to prepare for it?" Then, before Faith could answer, he asked, as if a pleasing thought had suddenly occurred to him, "Tell me, Faith, if you have ever worn the relic I bought for you the day we went to the Sacro Monte together?"

"The beautiful rhinestone cross on the long shining chain, you mean? —No, not yet. I have been waiting to christen it on some great occasion."

"*Rhinestone!*" exclaimed Sebastian. Then catching himself up quickly, he went on, "Will you please me very much, *querida,* by going and putting it on now? With your loveliest dress? Or better still, by bringing the cross here, and letting me hang it around your neck, when, but for that, you are ready for our *fiesta*? We will dine here in the patio—as neither of us has ever dined before! And later—after we have finished our feast—we will go to the Alhambra and walk together through the moonlight in Lindaraxa's Garden!"

CHAPTER 22

It was Gabriel de Cerreno's custom to celebrate mass very early every morning, as he had done when he was a young priest, instead of taking over a later service, as his age and rank would have warranted. But in spite of the fact that he was always up before dawn, he went to bed very late, even for a Spaniard. Long after Father Constantino and his other secretaries had gone their austere way to chaste and untroubled sleep, he sat in the sumptuous study adjoining his great tapestried chamber, reading by the light of a massive lamp, writing the family letters for which he had no leisure during the preoccupied day, and arranging and rearranging the priceless collection of medallions and crucifixes to which he was constantly adding, though they were already worthy of any metropolitan museum. It was his period of pleasure and relaxation, upon which only one person was privileged to intrude; and since this one person, at that time of the night, was apt to be very differently occupied, the period was almost always undisturbed. Gabriel looked forward to it with quiet anticipation, when his executive duties pressed down upon him, or when the misery of the souls and bodies committed to his pastoral care wrung his heart through some fresh example of suffering or sin with which, for all his skill and saintliness, he was unable to cope. In the tranquil and beautiful surroundings to which he retired, he recaptured the joy and quietude of spirit which so often deserted him through the troubled hours of the day, though even Father Constantino never guessed how much inner turmoil was concealed behind his calm and gracious countenance and bearing; and his hours of slumber, however brief, were permeated with peace, so that he always rose refreshed to face the "burden and heat" of another day.

He had laid aside Rudolf's letter, announcing Faith's continued indisposition and his own impending departure from Madrid, with a benevolent smile. Of course Rudolf had been right in responding immediately to his Ambassador's summons; his absorption in his career, combined with his capacity for unremitting work, would certainly assure his rapid rise, for his intellect, if not brilliant, was comprehensive —at least as far as diplomacy was concerned, Gabriel added to himself, still smiling. As for Faith, the quieter she kept the better, until her "attack"—Gabriel smiled more deeply still at Rudolf's choice of words —was over. Certainly she did not need a doctor—in fact, he doubted whether she needed, or desired, anything, except to be let alone. The conviction that she did not, combined with the complexities of the cares which crowded in upon him throughout the thunderous afternoon, caused him to dismiss from his mind the tentative idea that he might drive out to see her during the cool of the evening; and when the storm burst with such unleashed fury, he went, earlier than was his custom, to the secluded apartments which no violence of the elements could invade.

His friend the Cardinal Archbishop of Toledo had brought, when he had made his recent visit, a new treasure for Gabriel's collection: a very ancient medallion from Arequipa, made of vegetable ivory framed in carved gumwood, and representing the Virgin kneeling with a lily clasped between the hands folded over her breast, before the Archangel of the Annunciation. "It is fitting that you should have this rather than I, Gabriel," the Cardinal had said with amiable innuendo, "not only because you collect such relics and I do not, but also because your parents saw fit to christen you as they did. The papal nuncio to Peru, who has just sent it in, assures me that it is a very rare piece. Certainly it is a very charming one." Enchanted with his offering, Gabriel had awaited an opportunity to study it circumstantially; and reëxamining it now, under the glow of the effulgent lamp, he was struck afresh with its ethereality. The disposition of the draperies flowing around the genuflected figure—the veil, the mantle, the robe—had been indicated with an unusual feeling for modesty and grace; the carving of the exquisite profile had the finesse of consummate art; even the fingers encircling the lily stems gave the illusion of delicacy. Enraptured by each new detail that his minute inspection revealed, Gabriel was reaching for a magnifying glass in order to discover these still more clearly, when an almost subconscious feeling that he was no longer alone caused him to glance swiftly up from the image that he held.

The damask portières hanging over the entrance to the outer corridor were certainly stirring. Gabriel was still uncertain whether this movement was not caused by the breeze, which, in spite of the sultriness of the night, drifted, from time to time, through the open windows, when he heard the door behind them close softly, and was aware that his brother was standing on his threshold.

"Sebastian!" he exclaimed, with an affection which masked his amazement. "When did you arrive? I had no idea you had left Malaga or thought of doing so. But it does not matter—as always, I am delighted to see you." He laid down the medallion, and went toward his brother, holding out his arms. "*Qué tal?*" he said cordially.

Sebastian advanced a step or two, knelt to kiss Gabriel's ring, and then rising, laid first one cheek and then the other against the Archbishop's. "I came over the road from Malaga to-day," he said when they had embraced, "on horseback. I was caught in the storm a few miles outside Granada."

"But you took shelter? You borrowed clothing?" asked Gabriel, glancing at Sebastian's somewhat fantastic and informal costume. Sebastian appeared to be both unaware of what he was wearing, and indifferent to Gabriel's appraisal of it.

"Yes," he said slowly. "I may even say that I found sanctuary. At the *caseria*."

There was a moment's silence. Gabriel, standing immobile, permitted his gaze to wander from Sebastian toward the enameled clock that stood on his desk, and then back again to his brother's face.

"The storm was over a little after six," he said at length. "If you have just left there, your visit was rather prolonged."

"Yes. It was rather prolonged. Though it seemed, while it lasted, as if the moments were flying by on wings. I have come to talk to you about it."

"Then suppose we sit down?" suggested Gabriel suavely. "We shall be more at our ease—not that I imagine, of course, that you have anything disturbing to say." And as Sebastian did not answer immediately he continued, "You might begin by telling me how you knew that Rudolf had left for Madrid."

"He sent Felipe to the station yesterday to secure reservations on the express and to wire *Tia* Carlota. It somehow occurred to Felipe to wire me at the same time. He has the unerring intuition of the perfect servant regarding his master's wishes.—Surely you did not have the naïveté to imagine, Gabriel, when you persuaded me to go to Malaga, that I would do so without arranging to return at the first opportune moment."

"I am afraid I did. I am afraid I made the mistake of assuming that you were a man of honor."

For an instant the shaft which Gabriel had released quivered between them; then it seemed to fall harmlessly to the ground. For Sebastian recoiled from it with less violence than Gabriel had expected.

"That is not just," he said, almost entreatingly. "It is true that I was determined to see Faith alone, to talk with her without interruption. After you dissuaded me from my first plan of seeing her here, when and as I could, on the reasonable ground that you could not permit the episcopal residence to shelter such hole-in-the-corner meetings, I knew I should have to find some other way to accomplish the ends I had in mind. I have done so—not in the way I should have preferred—you cannot suppose that I would choose to approach Faith through the medium of a servant. But as I could—desperate men use desperate measures. But nothing has happened in the course of my meeting with her which you could criticize, much less condemn."

"Suppose you tell me just what has happened," said Gabriel.

He still spoke with controlled courtesy; but Sebastian was aware of a slight sting in the suave suggestion.

"*Hermano mio,* is it necessary to speak to me in such a voice? Especially when I have come here for the express purpose of doing exactly that!"

"You cannot blame me for being anxious about Faith, all things considered."

"You priests are all alike," interrupted his brother, anger beginning to master him. "I came here to confide in you, to ask your help and guidance. And instead of giving me a chance to speak, you begin to denounce me. Anyone would think I had confessed to committing most of the deadly sins."

"It would not be the first time," said Gabriel levelly. "As I said before, I am still awaiting enlightenment as to what you have done."

"I have seen a miracle. It is the first time I have ever caught a glimpse of one," replied Sebastian swiftly, repeating the words he had spoken to Faith, "so I came to ask you to interpret it for me. I have always looked upon you as an authority on miracles. I see now that I was mistaken. You are only an authority on the commandments, especially the seventh, which in this instance does not concern me in the least, however much it may have done so in the past."

He flung himself, with a sort of furious grace, out of the great chair which Gabriel had drawn up for him beside the desk, facing the one in which the Archbishop himself was seated. Gabriel rose too, laying a constraining hand upon his brother's arm.

"Sit down," he commanded, "and control yourself. I cannot help you if you rage and rant." Then more gently, he added, "Forgive me, *querido,* if I have seemed harsh. Your unexpected appearance here at this time of night was, in itself, something of a shock. Your abrupt announcement that you had been alone with Faith for many hours was a still greater one. It cannot surprise you that my confidence in your trustworthiness where young and lovely women are concerned has been badly shaken, considering certain—episodes, shall we call them? —in the past. But I am relieved that in this instance I misjudged you, and repentant that I was too ready to pronounce judgment.—What was your miracle?"

"A revelation of Faith."

"And how did she reveal herself?"

"First on her balcony. In the rain. She made me think, as I told her, of a lily shining behind a waterfall.—Do you remember our *quinta* in Ecuador?"

"Yes," said Gabriel thoughtfully. "I remember it very well, and I think your comparison is apt.—Well, and afterwards——"

"Afterwards she came downstairs and we had tea together. And later on we had dinner. That is to say, I had dinner, and succeeded in getting Faith to drink some champagne."

Gabriel moved slightly in his seat.

"I mean," said Sebastian hotly, "that champagne was the only thing that tasted good to her. She had been ill all day, and had eaten nothing except a few dry biscuits while I had ham and olives at six o'clock."

"And you urged champagne upon her when she had had no food for twenty-four hours?"

"Yes!" shouted Sebastian. "Of course I did! As a restorative of which she was in great need! You act as if you never heard of champagne except as an accessory to the seduction of a chorus girl! You, who serve it at ten o'clock in the morning to every visitor who enters your house!"

He was beside himself with fury. But his rage, instead of kindling a responsive spark in his brother's breast reassured him as no amount of argument would have done.

"*Querido,* again I must beg you to calm yourself. And again I must ask your forgiveness for misinterpreting what you were trying to tell me.—So you and Faith dined together, and sat for hours together in the starlight, talking mostly of rather insignificant things perhaps. Was that it?"

"Yes, that was it—How did you guess? I told her of our life at the *caseria,* yours and mine, when—our mother was alive. And later she told me of her own little home on a farm, to which she longs to return."

"And as you talked of these familiar things, all the secret places of your hearts were suddenly revealed to each other?"

"Yes. Yes. Yes."

Sebastian spoke with increasing intensity. His next words came swiftly.

"I had meant to take her with me to the Alhambra—to walk with her in Lindaxara's Garden, and beside the pool in the Patio de las Narangas, where you taught me to swim, when I was a child, Gabriel. But I could see that she was very tired. So, though she would have gone with me eagerly, I dissuaded her from doing so. I had proposed the plan and yet in the end, it was I who insisted we must give it up —for to-night."

"And so you left her?"

"And so I left her—and came to you."

"Is that all?" asked Gabriel searchingly.

"All except for one thing, which is everything. We kissed each other. She told me afterwards that she had not known before a kiss could be so gentle and so sweet. Of course, I had not known it either."

For an instant, Sebastian bowed his head. When he raised it again and looked imploringly at his brother he saw that there was no censure in Gabriel's expression, but that he looked suddenly careworn and stricken.

"And so you came to me for help? *Hermano mio,* what can I do to help you?"

"You can release us from bondage. You can secure our freedom. You can give us to each other."

"*Probito,* what are you saying? Do you not know that it is only in the service of God that perfect freedom is found? And that only God could give you and Faith to each other?"

The tone in which he spoke the words robbed them of all effect of a pronouncement of dogma, and made them seem, instead, like the utterance of a powerless man wrung with anguish.

"You have enormous influence with the Rota—and if the Cardinal of Toledo also pled our cause as you could persuade him to do——"

"To annul your marriage? Or Faith's?"

"It would need to be both, would it not? I do not know. But I knew you could tell me."

Gabriel's lips moved, but he did not speak.

"Are there no grounds on which my marriage could be annulled?" Sebastian asked at last in a voice so low that Gabriel could hardly hear him.

"There may be. I am not sure. But it is possible," said Gabriel laboriously, "if you went to great lengths. You would have to abandon all reticence, to dwell on the pitiful condition of Dolores as if it were criminal——"

"Is attempted murder not a crime?" asked Sebastian quickly.

"Yes. If the attempt was intentional. You know in her case that it was not, that she had no idea what she was doing when she attacked you. You would have to swear that she did know what she was doing. Are you prepared for that, Sebastian?"

A terrible silence fell between them. It was Gabriel who finally broke it.

"Let us grant then, for the sake of argument," he said painfully, "that the annulment of your marriage could be achieved. What then?"

"The annulment of Faith's should be very easy. I have already told you I know she was coerced."

"Not into marriage. She married Rudolf not only willingly, but gladly. As for what may have taken place afterwards—I fear, Sebastian, that many marriages would be annulled if every bride to whom her husband's vehemence had been a shock sought and secured release from him."

"You would condone an act of violence merely because it is often committed?"

"Never. But since I am a man myself, I would recognize how much all men are in need of forgiveness—from God, from other men, and most of all, perhaps, from the women committed to their care. Our instinct fails us so frequently—Our understanding is so incomplete—Our desires drive us headlong into such excesses! So, as a man, I would not be too harsh or sweeping in the condemnation of any other man."

Gabriel's voice, as he went on speaking, gained in volume and power with every word he uttered. Sebastian, who had been totally unprepared for such a declamation, stared at his brother with a stupefaction which momentarily submerged all other sensations.

"How dramatic you are!" he said tauntingly, when at last he had recovered enough to talk. "I should not have supposed that you would be so well qualified to speak with conviction on men's sins of commission and omission toward women. But perhaps there have been —episodes shall we say?—in your life as well as mine!"

"It will not help your cause, Sebastian, to insult me."

"The insult came first from you."

Once more a poised dart quivered between them. This time it was Gabriel who turned it aside.

"Again I must ask your forgiveness, *hermano mio,*" he said. "I know there is no blot upon your past, whatever it may be, which can spread far enough to stain your love for Faith. That is a thing apart, the greatest thing that has ever come into your life or ever will. But I must beg you to believe that I know what I am saying when I tell you that Rudolf loves her too—as deeply, as sincerely, as intensely as you do. Because you have found him lacking in delicacy, you are making the great mistake in believing that he is lacking in devotion. It is a mistake that is unworthy of you."

Sebastian hesitated, but only for a moment. "Very well," he said evenly, "I will accept your apology—this once more. And let us grant—for the sake of argument, as you said a little while ago—that in his own way Rudolf may love Faith—a stupid and barbarous way, but let that pass. What difference does it make in any case, since she does not love him?"

"I admit that she has suffered a revulsion of feeling toward him which has caused her great anguish, which she has courageously tried to conceal. Part of the revulsion might have been avoided if Rudolf had not underestimated both her intelligence and her sensitiveness—I deplore his lack of discernment as much as you do. But another part of the revulsion was inevitable. Faith had not seen Rudolf as he really was, but as her dazzled imagination had pictured him. He was bound to topple from his pedestal. Her disillusionment has hurt her terribly; but when she recovers from the shock of it, I think she could adjust herself to realities without too much pain. For her lot would be cast in very pleasant places; and she was deeply attached to him, though certainly she did not love him in the sense you mean—in the sense of a woman recognizing her mate and yearning for him. She was too young, when she pledged herself to him, to know that such a radiant revelation, such unutterable longing, would ever come to her."

"She knows it now!"

"Subconsciously."

"No, instinctively."

"And do you think she will be swayed by her instincts? Or controlled by her sense of integrity?"

"I think—after to-night—that there is nothing I could ask of her that she would deny me!"

"And what," inquired Gabriel poignantly, "are you going to ask of her? That she should commit perjury also?"

"Perhaps in her case it might not be necessary. She is not a Catholic."

"And so?"

"And so, if she cannot obtain an annulment for coercion, she might obtain a divorce for something else."

"For instance?"

"I have not thought it out. But there must be something. And after the divorce was granted—surely the Church could rule, since her union had not been blessed by a priest, that it had been in a way irregular, that there was no impediment to another marriage—especially if she should become a Catholic."

Sebastian's statement was so concise that Gabriel guessed that it was meant to be tantalizing. But he did not betray his consciousness of his brother's strategy.

"She is not a Catholic yet, at all events," he said, almost as if declining to admit the potentiality. "And the Rota cannot be bribed by the prospect of a convert, as an ignorant servant can be bribed with money. But, as you say, the avenue of divorce is not closed to her. I cannot think of any pretext by which she could bring suit against Rudolf. It would, of course, be very simple to find one by which he could bring suit against her."

There was a calmness about Gabriel's expression that was ominous. Sebastian was instantly aware of this.

"What do you mean?" he said sharply.

"Since you do not object to perjury, since you are ready to go to any lengths yourself to secure your freedom, and to persuade Faith to do the same thing, you would not blame Rudolf too much, would you, if he should divorce Faith—for unfaithfulness, let us say?"

Sebastian stared at his brother in sudden and horrified revulsion. But before he could open his lips, the Archbishop went on speaking.

"I know, of course, as well as you do, that your visit to her to-day was entirely innocent. But do you think Felipe and Catalina are so sure? You have already confessed to Felipe's connivance, and there must be a record of the telegram on file. And apparently Catalina knew better than to intrude upon you all through those long hours while you were in the patio with Faith. If they were put on the witness stand against her, have you thought that someone else might bribe them—or terrorize them—into giving testimony that would be most incriminating? And since the question of paternity would necessarily be involved, the proceedings would be ugly as well as sensational. I cannot help wondering whether Faith would have the strength to survive them."

For a moment his penetrating glance swept over Sebastian's horror-stricken face. Then, apparently inadvertently, it fell on the medallion. He picked it up and turned it over slowly.

"I had meant," he said deliberately, "to go out and see Faith in the morning taking her this little image as a gift. It has just been presented to me by the Cardinal of Toledo for my collection, which of course it would adorn. But I felt there would be something almost symbolical in offering it to Faith—under the circumstances. Perhaps you will take it to her for me. Would you care to look at it? It is really very beautiful. I do not know when I have seen a more exquisite interpretation of the Annunciation."

Sebastian snatched the medallion from his brother's hand and threw it down on the table without looking at it. "What are you trying to say to me?" he asked hoarsely.

"But surely, Sebastian, you must have guessed—and guessed that she has not? Did it not dawn upon you that Faith is with child?"

Gabriel knew that he had shot his last bolt. The effort left him so completely spent that for a moment he felt as if he could not hold himself erect another second, as if he must succumb to the strain which had taxed him beyond the limits of his endurance. The keen distinction of his features became strangely blurred and his fine face looked old and sorrowful. But steadying himself with a supreme effort, he looked straight into Sebastian's eyes.

"When you see Faith with her baby," he said, and there was infinite compassion in his voice, "you will thank God on your knees, even in the desolation of your own childlessness, that you did not sin against her. And willingly or not, you will love her son better than anyone else on earth, except Faith herself. Better than you have ever loved me."

Suddenly, and with horrible mirthlessness, Sebastian laughed. But Gabriel made himself heard above his convulsive mockery.

"You think I do not know!" he cried triumphantly, "but I do! If I had not how could I have prevailed—against you, my dearly beloved brother—for Rudolf who should have been my son!"

PART VI

Hans Christian

CHAPTER 23

A VERY erect little boy, whose well-set head was covered with short ruddy curls which gave the effect of being impervious to both shears and smoothing, stood with his nose pressed against the window-pane, looking fixedly down toward the wide bleak street below him. His attitude evinced neither impatience nor weariness, but complete absorption and hopeful expectancy. He seemed oblivious both to the two other occupants of the large luxurious room to which his back was turned, and to the dismal drizzle of rain slanting across the façades of solid, but gloomy houses on the other side of the street, and descending to the dripping pavements. From time to time, an elderly lady of great elegance, whose dark, snow-flecked hair was wound in a superb coronet of braids above her white brow, looked up from her letter writing, to glance first at the child and then at the clock; but it was not until the soldierly-looking man who had been reading the *Berliner Tageblatt* with a concentration which precluded interruption, threw down his paper exclaiming, "Surely the train is late!" that the lady laid aside her correspondence and spoke.

"Actually only a few minutes, I think—Hansel, darling, are you sure you are warm enough? It must be cold over by the window, and you have been there a long time already."

"I am very warm, thank you, grandmamma. But I think grandpapa is right. I think the train must be late."

The lady smiled, and rising, walked over to the window and put her arm around the child's shoulder.

"You have been happy here with me, while your mother has been gone, haven't you, Hansel?" she asked persuasively.

The child hesitated a moment, and then replied with evident sincerity but without enthusiasm.

"Yes. But it is not the same."

"What is not the same?"

"Nothing. Nothing is the same when my mother is away. You are very pleasant, and it is kind of you to take me walking with you in the Langelinge and to ride in the flying carousel at Tivoli. But you do not invite me into your room when you are getting ready for a party, and let me choose which dress you will wear between those that have been laid out on the bed. You do not let me take the things out of the jewel box and put them back in different corners. You do not let me watch Hilda dressing your hair—and then, of course your hair is nice, and there is lots of it, but it does not shine like my mother's. You are not such a shining lady as she is anyway."

His grandmother laughed. "No, Hansel, I know I am not," she said regretfully. "And there are other ways also in which I am inadequate?"

"You smell very good, but it does not seem as if you were made on purpose to hold little boys, the way my mother is. She is soft in just the right places. I do not fit in when I try to cuddle up to you. And you never call me your precious treasure."

The lady laughed again, and this time the soldierly-looking man frowned slightly, and throwing down his paper joined his wife and grandson at the window. "Your mother indulges you a great deal, Hansel," he said with a touch of seriousness. "She is a very busy lady and you ought not to impose upon her. You are not a baby any more."

"I am quite big, I know. But mother says it will be a long time before I am too big to sit on her lap. She says she has to make me do, because she has not two or three real babies like Aunt Rita. And she is never too busy to hold me."

As if politely dismissing a closed subject, the child resumed his contemplation of the street, which, in spite of the endless stream of bicycles and carriages wheeling past, was, to all intents and purposes, empty as far as he was concerned. At last, as a pair of handsome bay horses attached to a smart brougham turned the corner above the house, he gave a sudden joyous shout, and tearing across the room, precipitated himself down the stairway, shouting more loudly and joyously with every step he covered in his headlong rush.

The sounds attendant upon the return of distinguished persons from a journey to their own well-regulated household merged with a child's voice. Doors opened and shut with prompt precision. One piece of hand-baggage after another thudded softly against a carpeted floor. There was an exchange of greetings—respectful on the one side, courteous but slightly aloof on the other—followed by questions and answers. Yes, everything had gone well while Their Excellencies had been away—the weather had been very bad, but what could one expect of Copenhagen in April? Had it been fine in Norway—ah, that was well! And the Herr Baron's cough, was it entirely gone? The large package from Worth's which the Frau Baronin had been expecting had come in—everything seemed to be quite in order, except that point-de-Venise instead of Duchesse lace had been used on the violet satin. The Herr Baron's secretary had been waiting for him in his study since nine o'clock. A number of dispatches had come in, and there was a message from the Palace to which the Herr Baron would probably wish to give immediate personal attention. Her Serene Highness and the Herr General were in the drawing-room—Would Their Excellencies like the coffee served there?

"Yes, and at once," a somewhat peremptory voice ordered. "I must get to my study without further delay—this lateness of the train is most upsetting.—Stop jumping over your mother and asking her questions, Hans Christian! How can she answer so many all at once?"

"I only want to know if she had a good time—and if the snow was very deep—and how many prizes she won—and whether she saw the King and Queen of Norway, and if they were as nice as the King and Queen here—and if she will promise to read to me to-night——"

"My precious treasure! Of course I am going to read to you to-night! I had a lovely time—and the snow was 'way over my head—and I won two prizes, a second and a third, for skiing—and father and I had lunch with the King and Queen at Bygdo Konsgaar[1] and they are charming. Now—race me upstairs! I want to see grandmother and grandfather!"

There was another rush on the stairway, swifter and lighter than when the child had pelted down it alone; then the drawing-room curtains were flung aside, and he bounded into the apartment again, just in front of a young, graceful woman, wrapped in lustrous furs, who instantly caught him back to her in a close embrace.

"I am out of practice! I can't let you win like that!"

"Race me again!"

"Yes, darling, by and by—Oh, *Tante* Luise, I am so glad to see you!—Dear Father Hans, have you been comfortable and happy here with your namesake while Rudolf and I have been away?"

She turned impetuously first on one and then to the other, presenting both cheeks to be kissed, her arms still around the child.

"We have been very happy and comfortable. Your household runs on velvet, and Hansel has been as good as gold. But it is pleasant to have you back again, *liebe* Faith.—As Hansel says, nothing seems quite the same when you are gone.—Are you by chance going to take off your wraps and linger here a little while? Not that I blame you for keeping on your coat, for it is beautiful! Did you get it in Christiania?"

"In Bergen. I never saw such furs as they have there! I knew you would admire it—that is why I didn't take it off downstairs—I wanted to show it to you right away. It fits nicely, doesn't it?"

She detached herself gently from the little boy, drew the coat still

[1] A suburban palace not far from Christiania.

more closely around her slim waist, and turned slowly around so that the older lady could see it from all sides, before throwing it open to display a lining of rich brocade.

"Very. It is beautifully cut—and your figure does it entire justice!"

"Oh, but my figure is not a bit better than yours, even now, and you know it—I wish I could have seen you when you were my age, *Tante* Luise! But speaking of figures, the Queen of Norway has the smallest waist I ever saw.—Really, it is no bigger than that!" And she made a hoop of her hands.

"I see that Faith, as usual, is engaged in exaggeration—no woman could possibly have a waist of that size!—And is this a fashion show? Or are we eventually going to have some coffee?"

Rudolf von Hohenlohe's entrance into the drawing-room had been made far less precipitately than his wife's. His coat, although it was also new and handsome, had been surrendered to the ministrations of a footman immediately after his arrival; and he had retired to wash his hands and brush his hair before coming to the drawing-room to greet his parents. In spite of being extremely well-built, he gave the effect of a solidity that was beginning to verge on heaviness; and the seriousness of his expression did not relax as his son clambered up beside him on the sofa where he had seated himself with a certain precision of manner. He watched Faith without further comment, as she folded her furs over the back of a chair, took off her hat, and rather nonchalantly smoothed her hair and adjusted the white frills of the blouse she was wearing with her traveling suit. But if she were conscious of his unspoken but obvious criticism of her casual preparation for breakfast she gave no indication of this, as she took her place behind the shining service which the butler brought in and set down before her, just in time to forestall a second question as to when this might be expected.

"Oh—thanks so much, Johann!—You will have some coffee with us, won't you, *Tante* Luise?—Nonsense, Father Hans, that must have been nearly two hours ago!—Hansel, my precious treasure, do you want a *canard?*"

She dipped her lump of sugar into her own cup, and dropped it gaily into the eagerly opened little mouth close beside her elbow. Then as she drank her steaming coffee and ate her flaky crescents with evident relish, she began an enthusiastic account of her trip.

"It has been the greatest fun, from the very beginning—that is why I haven't written you more about it, *Tante* Luise! I wanted to tell you all about it, myself. In the first place, I think it is delightful to take a ferry at Elsinore—I looked everywhere for Hamlet's ghost! He was nowhere to be seen, but some dark night I am going back to look again! It was very smoky and foggy when we reached Christiania, but of course we went directly out of the city. Our Minister had sent Franz von Witzleben, the second secretary, to meet us and he was most helpful! He went out to the Voksenhollen Sanatorium with us, through the pine forests and snow. The air was glorious, so cold and bracing and windless, and the sunshine was simply dazzling! Our rooms were all ready for us, lovely ones with a view of the mountains and fiords, glorious too——"

"Glorious seems to be your favorite word, Faith," remarked Rudolf. "May I interrupt you to ask for another cup of coffee?"

"We have been breakfasting downstairs all the time we have been gone," Faith went on as she complied with his request. "There is no such luxury as coffee in bed at Voksenhollen unless one is really ill! That seems strange, doesn't it, for a health resort! But of course it is really not a sanatorium in the sense that we use the word, but a hotel where people go for rest and recuperation after an illness, just as Rudolf did.—His cough got better almost immediately, by the way.—You would never guess now that he had been so sick with bronchitis only a month ago! Everything was very simple. But it was the cleanest, pleasantest place you ever saw, and very attractive. The huge room where everyone sat was decorated with black rafters and quantities of carving, and there were comfortable little rooms adjoining it for reading and cards. I played almost as much bridge as I do here—while Rudolf was resting, of course."

"Did you enjoy the sports?" General von Hohenlohe asked, lighting his pipe and turning toward his son.

"I went for an hour's walk regularly every day. Holmenhollen made a good objective. There is an excellent inn there, a copy of a medieval dwelling house. I enjoyed lunching there occasionally—I cannot say too much in praise of Norwegian food. The skiing did not appeal to me. But Faith indulged in it. You doubless heard her telling Hans Christian as soon as she arrived that she had won two cups."

"I asked her!" the child said quickly.

"Certainly you asked her, darling," his grandmother interposed smoothly. "Father knew that you did.—I am delighted to learn that the Voksenhollen experiment was so wonderful. You have had some diversion, too, have you not?"

"Yes, everyone was very kind. The Prime Minister invited us to dinner almost immediately—a state function given in honor of the King and Queen, who were most gracious. There were one hundred guests, a very distinguished company. There was a musical program after dinner, very well rendered, and the drive back to Voksenhollen afterwards in the moonlight was peaceful and agreeable—a pleasant contrast to the one going in, which was quite the opposite."

Rudolf paused significantly, and glanced at his mother with the air of one expecting to be questioned.

"I am so sorry. What happened to make it so?" she asked instantly.

"When Faith started dressing for dinner—at the last moment as usual—she found she had no long gloves with her. So she rushed off to the manageress, half hooked into a conspicuous petunia velvet dress. She failed in her attempt to borrow a pair of gloves at the sanatorium, so then she started telephoning into Christiania to one shop after another. It was just closing time, but at last an obliging establishment was persuaded to send a pair of gloves to the Prime Minister's residence. The episode was certainly very disquieting, besides involving a great deal of delay, so that the drive in town, as I said before, was something of an ordeal for me."

"Mother has such lovely arms, I should think everyone would be pleased to see her without gloves," said Hansel, again speaking very quickly. "I am. I like to see her when she has nothing over them at all. And I am sure Uncle Sam does. I heard him saying, the last time he was here——"

Rudolf set down his cup, and turned abruptly toward his son. "Why are you not at your lessons?" he asked curtly. "You should have been, long ago.—Tell your tutor for me that you are to work two hours this afternoon, to make up for the time you have lost this morning."

"But then mother and I will not have our walk in the Langelinge!"

"You should have thought of that instead of lounging around here! And I must be off myself. Will you excuse me, Mother? I am lamentably late."

"My dear! As if I would dream of detaining you!"

The Archduchess smiled affectionately at him. But as he left the room, accompanied by his father and propelling his protesting son in front of him, it was on her daughter-in-law that her glance rested; for with the child's unwilling departure, the buoyancy of Faith's expression seemed suddenly blighted.

"I am afraid Rudolf is not quite himself yet after all," Victoria Luise said gently. "It takes some time for the nerves to readjust themselves after an illness. I am sure you realize this, *liebe* Faith."

"Oh, perfectly, *Tante* Luise."

The Archduchess had risen, and as she spoke, she put her arm lovingly around her daughter-in-law's shoulder.

"Tell me, my darling," she went on, "if I am not indiscreet in asking, what impression the Councillor of the Italian Legation makes upon you? Is it a favorable one?"

Faith looked at her mother-in-law searchingly for a moment, but when she answered, it was with a nonchalance that was obviously unassumed.

"Guido Bonatelli?" she said after a moment. "Why, he has never made any impression on me at all! What made you think of him?"

"My dear, he is very much in evidence, and he is not without a certain fascination, if you care for the Italian manner. And I have somehow gathered—one senses these things rather than hears them—that he has been endeavoring to attract your attention for some time—that he has been delicately trying to indicate his hope that you would consent to an *amitié amoureuse*."

"But *Tante* Luise, I do not think Guido Bonatelli is fascinating at all! I think he is a nuisance! I shall probably find half a dozen notes from him in my mail, and I shall tear them all up without even reading them—I read the first three he sent and they were all alike! You would never believe that a man would have so little to say, and say it with so little originality! If I were going to have an *amitié amoureuse*, at least I should want it to be amusing. And one with Guido Bonatelli would be too dreary for words!"

"Then you have thought, my dear, that you might like to have one? If not now, some time? If not with Bonatelli with someone else? Provided it were amusing?"

"Not really. It has occurred to me, of course. I suppose it does to most women, doesn't it, after—after a certain time? When their husbands are—very preoccupied, I mean? But it is just playing at love, isn't it? I have never wanted to do that, *Tante* Luise."

She returned her mother-in-law's caress as warmly as it had been given. Then, smoothing down the fur of the gorgeous garment which she had laid over her arm, she paused on the threshold and looked back at the Archduchess.

"Will you come in and see the new dresses that have arrived from Worth's?" she said. "Hilda is sure to have them spread out all over my room for me to look at as soon as I get there. I shall be only a few minutes in the kitchen, and I hope it will not take me long to go through my mail."

"I should love to see them. You have such exquisite taste—which reminds me that I should think petunia would be an ideal color for you. I am surprised that Rudolf cannot see that it is."

"Perhaps he is color-blind," Faith said lightly. "I thought, in Norway, that he was snow-blind. And often before this, that he was blind in other ways. But it does not trouble me any more because Rudolf does not like my clothes. He would always rather see me in a nice black dress made in Berlin.—Why are you so worried about me, darling, all of a sudden?"

"My dearest child! Why should you imagine that I am worried?"

"Because I can see that you are. Is it because I am so hopelessly American and still have so many rough corners left, in spite of all these years of association with your perfections? Or is it because Rudolf is so hopelessly Prussian, and just as inflexible, though not quite so glittering, as when you first warned me against him?"

"*Liebe* Faith, why do you talk such nonsense?"

"Because you began to talk nonsense yourself, *Tante* Luise! All because Rudolf was cross and critical, and you were afraid he forgot to get the enamels you surreptitiously told him to buy for me in Christiania! And because I have been playing too much bridge and doing too much skiing with Franz von Witzleben, and you think you must tactfully lead up to the tales that have been told you about that by sounding an Italian note first! And because I almost precipitated a diplomatic crisis between Norway and Germany by neglecting to take any long white gloves with me to a sanatorium! All this is unworthy of a lady of your fine balance, *Tante* Luise! And as to *amitié amoureuse*, you have nothing to fear—remember that Americans take their love affairs very seriously—more seriously than any other people in the world, except, perhaps, the Spaniards."

"What makes you think Spaniards take their love affairs seriously?" inquired Victoria Luise quickly.

"Oh, it was just a general impression—enhanced by some chance remarks of Gabriel de Cerreno's. Isn't it correct?"

"My dear, how should I know? After all, I have spent very little time in Spain."

Faith laughed, and drew the curtain back. "But after all, Gabriel has spent a good deal in Germany," she said, "so you have had an occasional opportunity to listen to his views. And you will admit that he speaks with conviction and authority. However, suppose we dismiss the subject of an *amitié amoureuse* for the present—I am really rather surprised that your Serene Highness should put the idea of one into my head! But if I should ever decide to have one after all, I shall certainly tell you about it before anyone else. I am sure you would have all kinds of helpful advice to give me."

CHAPTER 24

WHEN Victoria Luise entered Faith's room two hours later, she found her daughter-in-law sitting in front of her desk, still occupied with the masses of correspondence which she was sorting and stacking into neat piles as she ran through it. Her bare feet were thrust into turquoise-blue mules, and a dressing gown of turquoise-blue satin was tied loosely over a flesh-colored slip banded with cream lace. Evidently she had just stepped out of her tub, for the aroma of bath salts still clung to her, and her freshly washed hair, still damp, hung in burnished masses all around her. As her mother-in-law approached, she put down the last letter she had opened, tilted back her head, and ran first her fingers and then her comb through the coppery cloud.

"I do not wonder that Sam's painting of 'Lorelei' took so many prizes," Victoria Luise said admiringly, placing her fingers on the shining tresses. "This seems to me more beautiful every year, Faith."

Faith sprang up, laughing and laying down her comb. "It is humorous, isn't it, that it was actually Rudolf who suggested that picture, considering how he hates it?" she said lightly. "The first time we went to the Lido together! Of course he did not guess he would ever be taken literally, or he would have bitten out his tongue first. Since then he has learned to beware of the true word spoken in jest—indeed of all jesting!—How nice of you to come, *Tante* Luise! I did not hear you until you were actually beside me. I find that the household still seems to function, and so do the mails—some of my letters this morning are especially interesting.—Where would you like to sit?"

"It does not matter, so long as I have a good vantage point from which to look at my surroundings. I never come into your room, Faith, without marveling at the exotic atmosphere you have captured and conveyed to this gray Danish city. Considering the comparatively short time that you were in Spain, it seems to me nothing short of miraculous that you should have been able to create for yourself so completely the setting of a Spanish princess."

She seated herself, her gaze wandering from the great bed of carved and gilded wood, the sumptuous hangings of mellow brocade, and the splendid somber pictures in their rich frames to the inlaid *escritorio* at which Faith was sitting.

"You were so ill all that summer in Granada," she went on wonderingly, "and you were hardly settled in Madrid the next autumn before you had to stop going out because you were so far *enceinte.* Then, when you returned from Schönplatz after Hansel's birth, apparently you continued to spend most of your time in his nursery—you had only just weaned him when Rudolf was promoted and transferred! And meanwhile you had posed for three pictures! I should have said you could hardly have known whether you were in Spain or Siberia! Yet you appear to have absorbed the very essence of Spain."

"Perhaps it is just because I actually saw so little of it that I wanted to bring a bit of it away with me," Faith said still lightly. "You must admit that my essence of Spain is very concentrated—all the rest of the house, even the drawing-room, is admirably Teutonic! It is only here that I have been guilty of self-indulgence. But I did fall a victim to the lure of Spanish *antiquarios* almost immediately—even before I began to be ill in Granada!—But to change the subject—or rather to revert to one that you indirectly brought up—I have a long letter from Sam. He says Cousin Sarah's rheumatism is becoming more and more troublesome. She thinks the Paris climate is very bad for her, and I gathered that Sam believes she is secretly pining for Salem—not that the climate there is any better!"

"But, Faith, Sam would never leave Europe for any length of time now! And that joint ménage has been such a happy arrangement!"

"I know. But after all, Salem is home for Cousin Sarah. I know how she feels. Sam thinks he might at least take her over, and see her settled there among her old friends. And he could use it temporarily, as a base for more marine painting.—By the way, Sam also says that the Luxembourg is bent on acquiring the trilogy of which you first spoke."

"The trilogy?"

"Is it only three plays or three poems that can be called a trilogy? I am never sure. I thought it might refer to three paintings too. Perhaps I should have said the trinity—or is that merely a triple Divinity?"

"You mean all three of those pictures Sam painted while you were in Spain—'The Annunciation,' 'The Holy Mother' and 'The Flight into Egypt'?"

"Yes. It seems he has held out a long time. Of course it is obvious now that he will never part with 'Mary of Nazareth.' But I think he was greatly moved by Gabriel's entreating that he would permit either 'The Annunciation' or 'The Holy Mother' to be kept in Spain. Gabriel did not care so much for 'The Flight.' But of course the series would have much less value if it were divided, and it is almost unheard-of for the Luxembourg to make such an offer. It is too bad it could not have been for 'The Lorelei' instead."

"Yes. But, even if that did take prizes, you know it is not comparable to 'The Trinity'—I really think we may use that definition. There are times when I understand Rudolf's dislike for 'The Lorelei,' even though I recognize its *allure*. And it seems strange that this should have been Sam's only interpretation of you since the Trinity."

"Dearest, do not sound so tragic! It was the '*Schiffer in kleinem Schiffe*' that went on the rocks, remember—not Lorelei! She just went on combing her hair!"

The telephone beside her tinkled. She picked it up and answered the call. Then, covering the mouthpiece for a moment she flashed a smile at her mother-in-law. "Speak of the devil!" she whispered mockingly, "as you did a little while ago!—Yes, this is the Baronin von Hohenlohe," she went on, uncovering the instrument again. "Yes, thank you, Bonatelli, most delightful. Yes, I did meet him. Yes, he did teach me how to ski. Yes, I like him very much. Yes, very much better. Yes, of course, at the Chancery. Yes, five or six of them. No, I haven't read any of them yet. Yes, a great bouquet on the piano and another here on my desk, but I haven't looked at the cards that went with them, and of course I never guessed they were from you. Yes, very busy. Tea at the Citadel and the American Legation in the evening. Yes, this is the dinner the Madisons are giving in honor of the surgeon who has made such a stir. Oh, getting organized again. No, I don't see how I could. You know I always read to Hansel about that time. Yes, I found the invitation waiting for me here, but I don't know whether I shall accept. The Radens' house-parties are always delightful, but it is still so dreary in the country at this time of year. No, I shouldn't advise you to. I am really very busy, and my mother-in-law is with me. Yes, right here in my room. Yes, not for a long time yet I hope. I adore her and I am always desolate when she goes back to Berlin."

"But I must go, you know, *liebe* Faith, to-morrow," Victoria Luise said, looking at her daughter-in-law attentively as Faith replaced the telephone. "Rita's baby is due very soon now, and she was so ill when Luischen was born that I cannot help being anxious about her. Her children have come very close together, and her strength has been overtaxed. Just think! she was married after you were, and she has six!"

"I know, dearest, and I am very envious of her. I do realize how much she needs you, but I begrudge you to her. I wish you did not have to go away. I need you too."

"You will feel freer to accept the invitation to your house-party if I am not here."

"You are mistaken. I should feel much freer to go if you went with me. You see, when we are asked to the country, Rudolf always finds at the last moment that he must stay in town to catch up with some unusually important work. The first time we went to a Danish castle, it happened that the women all sat around after lunch making little sachets from the lavender which had just been brought in fresh from the garden, while the men played very languid golf. He has imagined ever since that this was typical of all house-parties. So now I go to them without him, not only with his approval, but at his express wish."

"Faith," asked her mother-in-law gently, "do you remember our first conversation together?"

"Do I remember it? Are you going to say I told you so? Or are you going to remind me that I promised to be very loyal?"

Her levity had suddenly deserted her, and her voice was edged with bitterness. Victoria Luise spoke more gently still.

"My dearest child, can you believe that I would gloat over the fulfillment of a prophecy which I have done my best to keep from coming true? And do you think you need to tell me that you are loyal, that it is only to me that you have shown your heart? But I will confess—though I would not do so when you first charged me with it—that I am very troubled. I cannot help seeing in you so much of the 'Lorelei' where a few years ago I saw only the 'Mary'."

"It is unfortunate that Rudolf has seen neither the one nor the other," said Faith, still bitterly.

"It is worse than unfortunate. It is tragic. Even though I am his mother, and love him dearly, I cannot defend him," said Victoria Luise. "My darling, I know how much deep disappointment, how much wounded pride, how much real heartache, underlies your apparent volatility. I know that your quest for pleasure rises from your failure to find happiness—that because of the intensity of your nature you seek out one outlet whenever you are denied another—even your perfect housekeeping is an indication of this. But you cannot wonder that I am anxious—as to just where this intensity may lead you."

"It is not going to lead me anywhere," said Faith. This time there was no bitterness in her voice. There was instead a hopelessness so profound that Victoria Luise looked at her in startled astonishment.

"My darling, do not speak like that. Think of all you have—of the place you have made for yourself, of the widespread admiration that you have won, of the inspiration you have been to Sam, of the confidence and respect which you know Rudolf accords you, however imperfectly he reveals it!"

"Would that have been enough for you, when you were twenty-five?" Faith asked.

Victoria Luise had never heard Faith's voice tremble before. She steadied herself against the shock that this quivering note in it gave her now.

"My darling, have I not helped you at all?"

"You know that you have! You know you have helped me in every way that my own mother failed me! That I could not have loved you any more if you really had been my mother! But you have not answered my question!"

"It seems that I do not need to," said Victoria Luise quietly. "I see that in some way you have guessed that something in my own experience has taught me how perilous is the path of the young wife who feels she has ceased to be desirable to her husband and realizes how desirable she is to other men. But I had a safeguard, and so have you—a lovely child whose very world you are." She saw the sudden tenderness that flooded Faith's face and pressed her advantage. "Thank God you have Hans Christian," she went on. "The namesake of your own father as well as Rudolf's. When a woman has a son she has a protection which is hard to penetrate. And if her own heart has never been touched, as in your case, she is doubly safe, for then there is no overpowering temptation lying in wait to engulf her."

The telephone rang again, and again Faith reached for it. This time, as soon as she had controlled her voice, there was real cordiality in it. But she was speaking in Spanish, and though Victoria Luise could not mistake Faith's tones, she could not understand Faith's words. It was a long time before her daughter-in-law turned to her again.

"That was Jaime de los Rios," she said. "It is delightful having him here as minister. He is really one of the most charming men in the world. He is very anxious to hear all our impressions of Norway, so I have invited him to lunch to-morrow. I do hope you will not leave before then, *Tante* Luise, for he especially asked after you. It seems that a treaty is about to be negotiated between Spain and Norway, and he himself will be covering the same ground that Rudolf and I have been over later on in the month. I did not gather just what the treaty was about but evidently it is very important, for King Alfonso is sending a special representative to confer with Jaime about it. He will be arriving almost any day now—in time to take part in the celebration at Odensee commemorating the one hundredth anniversary of the arrival of the Spanish troops on the Island Fijen."[1]

"How very interesting! Of course we will wait over to see Don Jaime. Did he mention whom the King had designated?"

Faith rose, smiling. "We almost forgot that we were going to look at my finery!" she said. "We grew so very earnest and intent—*très emotionées*, as you said the first time we talked together—and really over nothing! As you say, I have all sorts of blessings, and all sorts of safeguards. And I shall put you at the top of the list!—I told Hilda not to lay the dresses out until you came; after all they clutter up the room. I must ring for her, before she decides she is forgotten." Faith walked across to her golden bed, and pulled the brocaded rope hanging beside it. When the bell had ceased to tinkle she reverted to Victoria Luise's unanswered question. "Yes," she said, "the King has chosen his great friend, Sebastian de Cerreno. I wonder if he will have changed much? It is a long time since I have seen him."

CHAPTER 25

"I AM looking forward to this dinner very much," Faith said to Rudolf, as their brougham clipped smartly down Trondhjemsgade in the rain. "I had a nice little note from Mrs. Madison, besides the engraved invitation, telling me that it was being given in honor of a famous American surgeon and his wife—a Dr. and Mrs. Noble. They are passing through Denmark on a roundabout way home from Vienna. Dr. Noble was a delegate to some clinical congress there, I believe. *Tante* Luise said he made a great impression by an address he delivered about the removal of tumors on the brain—he has effected remarkable cures on

[1] This celebration actually took place a year after the signing of the treaty between Spain and Norway, and both events slightly earlier in the century than the period in which this story takes place.

persons who were supposed to be hopelessly insane—some of her relatives met him and wrote her about him. Besides, I was especially interested anyway, because I found a letter about them from Mr. Hawks waiting for me too. It seems Dr. Noble comes from Hamstead."

"From Hamstead!" echoed Rudolf. "A great surgeon!"

"Well, a cabinet officer and a senator came from there," Faith said whimsically. "Good sometimes does come out of Nazareth! You may be pleasantly surprised in him—or at least in his wife. She is half-French, a great heiress and very fascinating."

"I am not usually swept off my feet by the French, even the half-French," said Rudolf dryly. "How did Dr. Noble happen to meet anyone with all these enchanting qualifications in Hamstead?"

"You will have to ask him yourself, Rudolf. Neither Mrs. Madison nor Mr. Hawks explained that part to me."

"I should hardly be guilty of prying personal questions."

"Well, perhaps the secret will come out of its own accord in course of time!—If you find that you do not actually dislike the Nobles, we might give a dinner for them ourselves."

Rudolf did not reply, and Faith realized that his silence indicated that he was dubious as to the social qualifications of anyone introduced by Mr. Hawks. But to her immense relief and agreeable surprise, it was evident, long before the evening was over, that far from taking a dislike to the Nobles, he had not only been pleasantly, but greatly, impressed by them. And when she went to bed that night she slipped a little note under her mother-in-law's door which the Archduchess read the next morning with much amusement.

"Dearest" . . . it ran:

"I know you will be as thrilled as I am to hear that it is *Rudolf* who seems bent on an *amitié amoureuse!* Not that I believe it will do him much good, as I fear the lady in question, whose name is Jacqueline Noble, is hopelessly in love with her own husband. But at least Rudolf has taken a step in the right direction. The conquest was so immediate and overwhelming that I have asked the Nobles to waive formality and come to luncheon to-morrow. The Madisons—Mr. and Mrs. and Eleanor—are coming too, so with Jaime it ought to be a very pleasant little party.

Exuberantly,

FAITH."

"P. S.—I thought she was lovely myself. She is what the Spaniards call *encantadora.* She had on an American Beauty satin—which is apparently much less objectionable than petunia-colored velvet! But I must admit that no woman who is not at least half-French could look the way she did, whatever she wore."

"P. S. No. 2.—Of course it is all nonsense about Rudolf. He was much more excited by David Noble's conversation concerning tumors than by Jacqueline Noble's charms. And David Noble is exciting! He looks like a Sicilian brigand or something—very white teeth, very dark skin, very brilliant eyes—you know the type! And still he is wholly *homme du monde*. It was a great shock to Rudolf to discover that such a finished and arresting product could come from Hamstead. I am sure lots of ladies are willing to let David chop them into little pieces, just for the sake of being sewed together by him afterwards. Probably he creates brainstorms in order to cure them!"

"P. S. No. 3.—The Nobles are friends of Sam's too. They saw him in Paris just before they left for Vienna. And they think his work is wonderful."

This missive caused the Archduchess no uneasiness, and indeed, she took her departure for Berlin with a lighter heart than she had anticipated. The luncheon had been a great success; and a considerable portion of the succeeding afternoon had been devoted to mapping out a program for which the Madisons and the von Hohenlohes were to be jointly responsible, and which was designed to make the Danish visit of the striking surgeon and his charming wife as agreeable and as comprehensive as possible. A strenuous schedule of sight-seeing had been arranged—Victoria Luise had heard recurrently the words—Glyptotek—Thorvaldsen Museum—Rosenberg Palace—Royal Porcelain Factory—and there had been a good deal of discussion as to the best hours for visiting points of interest and the surest ways of saving time. The arrangements were eventually developed to include a supper at Froken Nimb's Tivoli Restaurant, an opera party, and several official appointments. And when the American Minister pulled out his watch with a startled exclamation at the time, it was obvious that he and not Rudolf had been the first to be conscious of neglected diplomatic duties. Evidently German efficiency and American energy had merged for once with mutually satisfactory results. It even seemed possible that an acquaintance had begun for which Faith and Rudolf might feel a common enthusiasm, and a friendship founded which might form a tie for Faith with the home she had not seen in so long.

"Faith always gives us a *déjeuner dinatoire*," Jaime de los Rios said as he bowed over the Archduchess' hand. "We have talked so long that it is almost tea-time, and we have eaten so much that we shall not be able to take any tea!"

"That is no hardship for an Andalusian!" Faith said quickly. "You know that you would much rather wait until six or seven, and then have wine and ham and bread and olives!"

"But I shall not be able to eat those either!" Jaime exclaimed in mock despair. "Meanwhile, will you permit me to escort you to the Palace, Faith—you have an appointment with the Crown Princess, have you not?"

There was real consternation in the cry with which Faith sprang to her feet. "You have saved me again, Jaime!" she exclaimed. "I had forgotten all about it, and if I had made another *faux pas* at the Palace I never should have been able to live it down!—Will you forgive me, dearest, if I fly and dress? And if I am not back in time to see you off at the station? It is not as if you were a Spaniard—you can take an overnight journey without a family assemblage!"

Faith cast a teasing look at Jaime de los Rios, embraced her mother-in-law lovingly and impetuously, and fled from the room. And she was still almost breathless from haste when, half an hour later, she entered the antechamber of the Crown Princess' apartments. There was not a single member of the royal family for whom she felt a more affectionate admiration; and yet she seemed fated to maladroitness in all her associations with this exalted lady. On the occasion of her first audience with Queen Luise, she had passed through several rooms, and at last had been received by Mademoiselle de Wimpfen, Her Majesty's lady-in-waiting, with whom she had talked for some time before her presentation to the Queen. She had taken it for granted that much the same procedure would be followed when she was received by the Crown Princess. But from the entrance hall she had been taken directly into a salon where she was pleasantly greeted by a tall dark young woman in mauve whom she had assumed to be another lady-in-waiting; and it was not until she had shaken the cordially extended hand instead of kissing it, taken a designated seat upon a tapestried sofa, and began chatting quite volubly, that she discovered she was in the presence of the Crown Princess herself!

The thought of this episode, and several others almost equally embarrassing, discomforted her intensely now, as she took her place among the diplomatic ladies who had already foregathered in the Princess' drawing-room. The circle was, she saw, with a swift glance of chagrin, already complete except for her; and there was an element in the atmosphere so alien to the tranquil stateliness with which the Palace was normally pervaded, that she felt bewildered as well as distressed. There was no stir of welcome as she slid into the chain; instead she was conscious of a suppressed, almost a stifled, murmur. It took little imagination to sense that this was critical if not actually hostile. The very chandelier, quivering icily over her head, had taken on a glacial aspect that chilled her. But the Crown Princess began to make her rounds almost immediately, talking for a few moments with the wife of each envoy as she did so; and as she paused before Faith, the amiability of her greeting seemed unusually marked. With characteristic volatility,

Faith's depressed spirits began to rebound. But after the group had been dismissed, she felt a light touch on her arm, and was aware that Mrs. Madison was attempting to draw her inconspicuously aside.

"What happened to detain you?" the American Minister's wife asked in a low tone. "We *did* stay a long time after luncheon—it is so delightful at your house that it is always hard to tear ourselves away, and the Nobles were enjoying it immensely! But surely we left in ample time for you to dress!"

"Do you mean I was late? Really late?" asked Faith in consternation.

"My dear, we waited half an hour for you! Then the Crown Princess spoke to us all, and was about to leave the room, when a lady-in-waiting went up to her and whispered that you had just arrived. So we were asked to resume our places, and say nothing, in order that you might not be upset—the comedy was played through a second time for your benefit! Really, the Crown Princess is the personification of tact. But the wives of some of our husbands' colleagues are not. I heard the *doyenne* murmuring that only an American would be so *gauche!* You know how fond I am of you, Faith—I am sure you will not mind if I beg you to be more careful. Rudolf will be really angry if he hears about this, and one of our dear friends is almost certain to feel 'he ought to know' and tell him!"

The older woman's voice was gentle, almost playful, her manner affectionate; but in spite of the kindly *savoir faire* with which she tempered her reproof, Faith turned away from her with burning cheeks and brimming eyes. If she could only have fled from the Palace and walked briskly home, she could, she thought, have steadied herself; but she could hardly leave the Amalienborg Square on foot, even if the chilly drizzle of rain which was relentlessly descending had not made such a plan impracticable: her brougham was waiting in line for her, and her costume, strikingly appropriate for a court reception, would have been unsuitably conspicuous on the street. She forced herself to take her turn at the entrance, and to keep up her end in the small talk with which she was surrounded, though conscious of the captiousness of the comment which would be unrestrained after her departure. But when she had bowed her last smiling farewell from the window of her carriage, she flung herself back in one corner of it with a recklessness that bordered on rebellion.

It was seldom that she chafed, even subconsciously, against the established order of her life; but now the incident which her tardiness had precipitated, had set her spirits seething. A sudden mutiny against the rigidity of her existence engulfed her. She saw herself rising, reclining, sleeping, waking, eating, drinking, speaking, moving, in accordance with inflexible rules, to which, despite her every effort, she failed to entirely conform. There was no challenge to a restless mind in such a relentless régime, no spaciousness for a soaring soul. If it were not for Hans Christian she would find some avenue of escape from the shackles of a system which seemed to deprive her so mercilessly of every essential liberty.

If it had not been for Hans Christian! But without this radiant child, whose loveliness was his legacy from the "slumberous, amorous summer" to which he owed his being, what would liberty of life be worth to her? Was he not only the core of existence to her, but existence itself? Why should she rebel against the usages which fettered her, when these were, after all, the symbols of a sphere where he was monarch? Her hour of humiliation was behind her, and she would rise above it as she had risen before; she would remember the Princess' tact, not the tattle of the diplomatic circle; and though she could not justify herself to Rudolf, she could bear his condemnation uncrushed, with candid apologies, and with the earnest assurance that she would not again fail to do him credit. The hour of revolt was passing too—had she not promised to be loyal? Loyal to a code as well as to a man? Could she be faithless to her own pledged word?

She straightened herself again in her dark corner, dried her eyes, and lifted her head. Then, conscious that her brougham had turned into Trondhjemsgade, she leaned forward, looking up toward the window where Hans Christian always stood to watch for her home-coming, the shade raised above his glowing hair, the light shining behind his erect little figure.

He was not visible; and as she approached her house, a swift stab of alarm, which went far deeper than momentary disappointment, smote her. Could anything have happened? Had he been taken suddenly ill? Could Rudolf, as he had so often threatened, have interfered with their precious twilight hour by imposing another lesson on his son? A dozen different fears assailed her as she mounted the steps. But as the front door was thrown open for her, she heard the familiar headlong rush on the stairway, and the next instant the little boy was locked in her arms.

"Hansel!" she cried, kneeling down and pressing her face against his. "You were not watching for me at the window! You frightened me! What happened?"

"I did watch, mother, a little while. But then a visitor came. He asked first for father, and Johann said that he was in the Chancery. And then for you, and Johann said you were at the Palace. And then for me, and Johann said I was in the drawing-room. So I came out to welcome him. That was why I was not at the window. He is very easy to talk to and I like him. He is a Spaniard, and he has been telling me about Spain—about bull-fights and *ferias*, and the little Prince of the Asturias who looks like his beautiful English mother, and the young King who plays polo. He is a very pleasant man and his eyes crinkle when he smiles.

He says he is a cousin of ours, and that he hopes you will be glad to see him."

"What is his name?" asked Faith, faintly and superfluously. For she knew that when she reached the top of the stairway, she would find Sebastian de Cerreno waiting there for her. She put her free hand on the banister to steady herself, and stopped for a moment. But even as she did so, she was aware that Sebastian would span the years of their separation with some smiling syllable, and that his facile grace would smooth away all constraint from their meeting. She looked up and saw him standing above her; and as she met his eyes, her heart gave a sudden joyous leap, and she hastened toward him.

"*Se bien venido,* Sebastian!" she exclaimed. "*Esta es tu casa.*"

"*A tus pies, Fidelidad,*" he answered gravely, "*siempre.*"

CHAPTER 26

There was something in the gesture with which Sebastian kissed Faith's outstretched hand which gave the illusion that he had knelt before he raised it to his lips. And as he released it, lingeringly, and spoke to her, she felt the quality of worship in his voice.

"Will you not come into the light where I can look at you?" he asked her gently.

"I do not need the light to see you have not changed at all!"

"No, not at all," he said, still very gravely. He did not stress his words, and yet the double meaning which he gave to them was unmistakable. "But you, Fidelidad, have changed immeasurably!"

She had passed swiftly on into the drawing-room, then, turning as swiftly, she had faced him. Hans Christian looked from one to the other anxiously.

"Mother says," he announced in a slightly troubled voice, "that she has no real elegance, like Mrs. Noble, who just came here, for instance. But I think she is lovely-looking, just the same, don't you?"

"I have always thought so, Hansel," Sebastian answered, looking down at the eager upturned little face, "and so has everyone else who has ever seen her. She is talking nonsense to you, *querido!*" He glanced quickly from the child to his mother, his narrow somber face illumined with his smile. "Why do you trifle with your son's sense of values, Faith?" he asked lightly. "Can elegance compete with loveliness? And yet, as far as that goes, what could be more elegant than cream broadcloth and sables, worn with topazes? Your taste is unerring as it always was. But I was not prepared to find it so sophisticated!"

"I am not seventeen, you know, any longer. I am afraid the lily, shining behind the waterfall, has emerged!"

"A lily is still a lily, whether it is behind a waterfall—or not, Fidelidad—and its clarity is still more dazzling when this is not veiled. . . . Are you not going to sit down so that Hansel and I may do so? And ring perhaps for some sherry, if there is any in this Teutonic household? And ask me when I arrived, and if I had a good journey, and how long I am going to stay, and so on—the usual conventionalities of welcome at least?"

Faith walked over to the bell and pulled it. "There is sherry," she said, "though I am afraid you will find it abominable compared with yours. And of course I am immensely interested in learning when you came, and so forth. I am sorry I did not ask you without being prompted. But I am remiss about conventionalities still—in fact, I have just been late at a royal reception. The knowledge of my guilt and the consciousness that the entire diplomatic corps is discussing me at this moment, combined with the surprise of seeing you several days before I expected, has made me more negligent than ever, I am afraid. . . . Sherry, please, Johann."

Sebastian seated himself quietly at the further end of the brocaded sofa on which she had flung herself down, drawing Hansel up between them, and keeping his arm around the boy's shoulder. "If the entire diplomatic corps is discussing you at this moment, Faith," he said calmly, "it is less because of your guilt than because you are young and beautiful, and an heiress in your own right, and the daughter-in-law of an Imperial Archduchess, and a great favorite with the Danish Royal Family, as all Europe knows. Therefore women less favored by fortune must vent their jealousy in some way, and the unfortunate men who are fettered to them must pretend to agree with them. What do you expect? I see that I shall be obliged to continue reminding you that you have lost your sense of values!—As to my own insignificant program, I did arrive a day ahead of schedule—it is a plan I always follow whenever I can. It never fails to furnish me with exceptional opportunities. For instance, in this case, when I reached the Spanish Legation, I found that Jaime was at the Citadelet playing bridge, instead of waiting for me at the station accompanied by various other personages of rank, all eager to engulf me immediately with tiresome talk about treaties and commemorations. I was therefore free to walk out of the house again unhampered as soon as I had washed my hands.—Tell me how you like Denmark, Faith. Does everyone ride a bicycle? And does it always rain like this?"

"Nearly everyone and nearly always," she answered, smiling in spite of herself. "But there are exceptions and interludes." Her sense of inadequacy and tension had melted away, and the old impulse to talk with Sebastian discursively and confidentially surged over her. "And there are interludes in the country itself, just as there are in the rain.

Most of the landscape is so trim and tidy that it all seems to be part of a neat pattern! I have kept hoping, ever since we came here, to see a fallen brick somewhere, or a woman with her hair tumbling down, or sunshine that really blazed——"

"The way it all is in Spain," said Sebastian encouragingly.

"Yes—and I know now I never shall! But in the midst of all this trimness, you suddenly come upon some of the most enchanting forests in the world. Those are the interludes. They are beech woods, and they are symphonies in emerald! The leaves are green and the tree trunks are green, and the sward is covered with green moss. Even the lights and shadows that flicker back and forth are green. And there are elements of magic in them; I am certain they are fairy forests!"

"Have you wandered in these fairy forests, Faith—since you left your magic house?"

"Not yet. But——"

"Mother says she is sure there are elves and gnomes and goblins in them," Hansel interrupted excitedly. "And some day she and I are going out to find them!"

"Will you take me with you?" Sebastian asked gravely.

"We would love to, wouldn't we, mother? I am sure Sebastian could help us find the fairies! You said that father couldn't find them, because he didn't believe in them, and so they hid. But you believe in them, don't you, Sebastian?"

"With all my heart. And I am glad, Hansel, that your mother still does so too—in spite of everything."

He glanced at her over the child's bright head, ruffling up the crisp unruly curls as he went on talking.

"And besides the fairy forests—what are Denmark's delights?"

"The country life is very pleasant," Faith hastened to say. "Almost all the people we know spend ten months of the year on their estates. There is a law which forces them to pay a huge tax if they sleep in the city more than sixty nights annually. Just think how funny it would seem to you, Sebastian, if every night you were in Madrid you had to say to yourself, 'Well, this is the thirty-ninth or the forty-second,'—or whatever it was—'there are only so many left before New Year's Day!' "

"It might teach me to spend them more prudently," he said with his old whimsicality, "if I could not be prodigal—prodigal with time of course I mean. You have no idea how austere I have become in other ways. It is all Gabriel can do to emulate me."

"Is Gabriel well?" Faith asked with affectionate solicitude.

"He is well. But he is not strong. He tires easily, and even minor cares rest heavily upon him. He has aged very rapidly these last years. —He sent his love to you, Faith, and said he hoped you would come and see him soon and bring Hans Christian."

"To Spain? To Granada? Oh, mother, can't we?"

"I wish we could, darling. But you know father does not like to have us leave him—and if we ever can go away, it must be to America."

"You have never been there yet—to the old New England homestead?"

"Never. But to-day, coming home from the Palace, I felt as if I could not wait any longer—to go home, Sebastian!"

"You may not have to wait much longer," he said soothingly, averting his gaze from the desperate look in her eyes. "Are you going to tell me more about this Danish country life which you say is so entrancing? I suppose its charm is not wholly confined to its efficacy against taxation?"

"No, it is really delightful. Most of the castles are very old, and have turrets and battlements and arches and courtyards and moats—especially moats. The life is very feudal in some ways; but in others it is very modern. There are splendid tennis courts and golf links, and everyone plays bridge and ping pong at the house-parties. But a watchman goes poking around with a lantern at night, and calling, 'All's well.'"

"At inopportune moments?"

"Occasionally. But the Danes are very correct. It is only their foreign visitors who are sometimes inconvenienced. . . . At one castle there is a curious old slide that was formerly used to shoot prisoners down to a dark cell. It leads straight out of the kitchen—apparently that was another old custom! And still another is to place a carafe of champagne in front of every dinner guest, and this is drunk as if it were water—no one here considers it an important wine at all!"

"And do you think there is any hope that I may be asked to see something of Danish country life?"

"Any hope! Who is being ridiculous now, Sebastian? A grandee of Spain and the King's special envoy! You know you would be asked to a house-party every week-end, and to all sorts of other parties besides, even if——"

"Even if what, Fidelidad?"

"Even if you were not the most charming man in Europe. But you are!"

She spoke with a vehement sincerity that robbed her words of all coquetry. Sebastian answered her with a seriousness commensurable with her own.

"I shall try to be worthy of this conviction, Faith, not to swerve you from it."

"You and father will ask Sebastian to dinner when the King comes here, won't you, mother?" inquired Hansel, again feeling vaguely that a moment meet for intervention had come.

Faith smiled. "When the King dines at a Legation in Copenhagen," she told Sebastian, "the Minister stands at the front door to welcome him, with the footman holding a huge candelabrum on either side. Then royalty is 'lighted up the stairway.' That is another charming old custom. It made a great impression on Hansel when he watched it from a corner in the hall. So now he wishes you to see it!"

"I am very eager to see it," Sebastian assured the child. "But I hope I may dine with your mother, Hansel, without waiting until the King does also.—Are you by any miracle free to-night, Faith?"

"No," she said regretfully, "I am never free." Then, conscious of her *double entendre*, she sprang quickly to her feet. "But I am sure Guido Bonatelli, at whose house we are dining, will insist on your joining the party, when he hears you have arrived. He is giving a dinner dance in fancy dress, and it will be very gay. Will you excuse me while I go and telephone to him?"

. . . . .

It was just eight o'clock when Rudolf von Hohenlohe knocked on his wife's door. He detested fancy-dress parties, and absolutely declined to appear in costume; but since Faith adored such festivities, his colleagues continued to invite him to them on her account. He also detested Guido Bonatelli; for though he held fast to the comfortable theory that a woman who had been married nearly ten years must necessarily have ceased to appear desirable to any man, he mentally characterized the Italian as a trivial idler, unentitled, except for the position he had unaccountably attained, to serious consideration from any other diplomat. In any case, therefore, he would have prepared grudgingly for this gala dinner; but his aversion to participating in the madcap revelry before him had been intensified a hundredfold by the tidings, which had just been brought to him, of Faith's tardiness at the Palace. If it had not been for the fact that a failure on his part to appear in public, and with her, on the evening after her lamentable breach of etiquette, would certainly be interpreted as a timorous and apologetic gesture, nothing would have persuaded him to leave his own house.

She flung the door open suddenly, and confronted him with a scintillating smile. She had put on a black dress of heavy corded silk, the low, square-cut bodice molded to her figure, the skirt a billowing mass of full and narrow ruffles edged with velvet ribbon. Over one shoulder was flung a heavy fringed shawl of black crêpe embroidered with brilliant and exotic flowers; there were roses clustered at one side of the high black comb that surmounted her head, and crimson slippers on her feet; a cascade of brilliants fell glitteringly from her ears, and around her neck, on a long dazzling chain, was hung a magnificent cross of splendid diamonds.

Rudolf stared at her with overwhelming stupefaction as she seized his arm, and began to propel him gently but urgently in the direction of the stairway. They had almost reached it before he recovered himself enough to draw away from her. And to his own amazement, the first words he spoke had nothing whatever to do with her recent lapse from decorum.

"Where did you get that pendant?" he demanded.

Faith laughed and slipped her hand through his arm again. "I don't remember exactly," she said blithely. "Somewhere in Granada at a musty *antiquario's,* the day I went to see the gypsies on the Sacro Monte. It has lain at the bottom of my jewel box, wrapped up in cotton wool, for years. But to-night I felt like getting it out again."

"It looks very valuable to me to have come from an *antiquario's,*" said Rudolf doubtfully. "Besides, I do not consider that a cross is a suitable ornament to wear with a fancy-dress costume."

"But it is a Spanish costume! Remember that the Sevillian choir boys dance the quadrille at Easter-time in front of the high altar in the cathedral! . . . Do hurry, Rudolf, or we shall be late!"

"That would be quite in keeping with your conduct, earlier to-day," Rudolf said formally and without moving.

Faith stared at him in her turn and then laughed again. "Oh, you mean at the Palace?" she said nonchalantly. "I was very sorry—but I am sure the Crown Princess understood and made allowances. She is always so sweet! I really had forgotten all about it until you spoke—so much has happened since then that is far more important!"

CHAPTER 27

THE stir of admiration which Faith's Spanish costume elicited, as she made her belated appearance in Guido Bonatelli's drawing-room, was significant in both its immediate and subsequent results. The evening was not over when her host suggested that if she would wear such a dress and dance the tango at the forthcoming Charity Bazaar in which the Princess Marie was so deeply interested, she would have a *succes fou* herself besides benefiting the cause immeasurably. Before Faith could answer Rudolf interposed an objection.

"Faith does not know how to dance the tango."

"I should be delighted to teach her. I am sure she would be a very apt pupil."

Rudolf turned with amazement to Jacqueline Noble, from whom this startling offer had come. She gave him a ravishing smile.

"My mother was a professional dancer," she went on tranquilly. "I am supposed to have inherited a little of her talent. I have often coached the dancing for amateur theatricals."

That any woman should voluntarily make such a damaging announcement regarding her maternal parentage was inconceivable to Rudolf. He nearly gasped out loud in his surprise. But he managed to recover himself enough to give a conventional answer.

"You are most kind. But even if my wife could avail herself of your offer, she would be without a partner."

"How tiresome you are, Rudolf! Do you think I spent a year in Argentina futilely? Of course I can be her partner! If Mrs. Noble will so far honor me, we might give an exhibition dance now, to show you what a vivacious addition one would be to an evening of stodgy tableaux."

Sebastian detached himself nonchalantly from the group with which he was sitting, and approached the self-confessed social pariah with a look of bland beguilement. Dinner was over, and though the drawing-room floors were already cleared, there had been an agreeable period of lingering over coffee and liqueurs, and dancing had not yet begun. No moment could have been more propitious for a dramatic gesture.

Jacqueline's response was immediate. She was on her feet almost before Sebastian had finished speaking, and there was a moment's smiling conference about music. It appeared that the orchestra was prepared to rise to such an agreeable emergency; and almost instantly Sebastian had swung her into position, and they had begun to move forward in swift symmetrical unison.

She was wearing a Breton peasant costume entirely inappropriate to the rôle she had so precipitantly assumed; but for all that, she gave it an illusion of exotic grace and fascination which stamped her performance with unmistakable genius. When at last she glided back to her seat, it was amidst cries of "bravo!" and "encore!" and a tumult of clapping. As the applause finally died down again, Sebastian slid quietly into a place beside Faith.

"You see how easy it is, Fidelidad!"

"*Easy!* To dance like that! I am only just average, Sebastian, at dancing."

"Perhaps you need practice," he suggested. "Does Rudolf dance much?"

"He does not dance at all," she said, her voice slightly edged with vexation.

"Oh—I suppose he spends all his leisure at the bridge table."

"You know perfectly well, Sebastian, that Rudolf has no leisure. And he detests cards."

"It must be tragic," Sebastian murmured smoothly, "to have such limited tastes.—I suppose you can waltz, Faith, in spite of all this vaunted inexpertness of yours! Shall we try?"

They had not gone twice around the room before she knew that the question of the tango was settled. She felt not only as if she had melted into his arms, but as if her very being had been merged into his.

"I tried to tell you how it would be," he said smilingly. "But you would not listen to me—I shall have to call you Thomasina, because you would not believe me until——"

"Sebastian! You must not be blasphemous!"

"I did not mean to be blasphemous," he answered gravely. "Shall we rest a little? You are very pale, *querida*."

"I—I think that I am going to faint."

"You are not going to do anything of the sort. You are going to tell me where I can take you without running the risk of having you snatched away from me immediately, and then we are going to sit and talk together. I am sorry to seem so unresourceful myself, but you must remember that this is the first time that I have ever been in this house."

"Guido has a—little conservatory back of the dining room."

"How thoughtful of him! By the way, you were not considering him as a possible *cavaliere servente*, were you, Faith?"

Her answer was delayed until they found the flowery enclosure toward which she led the way, her heart still hammering; and after they had taken their places on the recessed window-seat, she made an indirect reply.

"You are the second person to put that idea into my mind!"

"And who was the first, Rudolf?"

"*Rudolf!*" she exclaimed almost contemptuously. "No—it was *Tante* Luise—only she spoke of an *amitié amoureuse* instead of a *cavaliere servente*—Rudolf is sure he is the only person who ever fell in love with me."

"Whoever—what?"

"Fell in love with me," she persisted, with a little nervous laugh. "He still thinks he did, you know, and that he is the only person who ever will."

"Have you taken much advantage of this convenient viewpoint?"

"I haven't taken any at all," she answered, flushing. "I think you know that."

"I do know it. I only wanted to hear you say it."

"And now that I have said it, may I ask a question? It flashed through my mind when Jacqueline Noble said her mother was a dancer. What has become of Felicidad?"

"She has six children, twins among them," said Sebastian imperturbably. Then as Faith gave a startled exclamation, he glanced at her with an ironic gleam in his eye, and suddenly burst out laughing. "*Querida*, what a look! And how little I deserve it! The twins, unfortunately, are not mine—or any of their delightful little brothers and sisters. Felicidad is married—very happily married—to one of the doorkeepers at the

Royal Opera House in Madrid. I have seen her only once or twice in the last eight years, quite by chance and in the presence of this worthy functionary. I am afraid her dancing days are over. She must weigh one hundred and fifty pounds, and she is always nursing a baby or preparing to nurse one."

"Sebastian, you are incorrigible!" said Faith, joining in his laugh in spite of herself. "It is fortunate that you did not look for a *dulce amiga* in the ballet here—it is the finest one in Europe, except perhaps the imperial ballet at St. Petersburg; but the standard of morality for the girls is very strict. They are considered government employees and if they digress from the strait and narrow path, they are instantly dismissed."

"As you say, it is fortunate I do not live in Copenhagen," said Sebastian soberly. "I should constantly be haunted by the thought of the dismissals I had caused." Then as Faith laughed again, involuntarily, he added, "But I have really lost all interest in dancers, or thought I had. Your charming compatriot has rather revived it. Her bombshell about her mother was most refreshing! Who is she and where does she come from?"

"I only know that she is half-French—the French half was the dancer, I suppose!—and that her husband is a famous surgeon. He is delightful too."

"I thought so myself," said Sebastian idly. "I talked with him for some minutes after dinner, and found him most *simpatico*. What is his specialty?"

"He concentrates on mental cases. He has had a most remarkable success."

"What do you mean, mental cases?"

"It seems he has removed tumors from the brain, and cured persons who are supposed to be hopelessly insane—when it was not hereditary, I mean.—Sebastian, what is the matter? Have I said anything to hurt your feelings?"

He had risen with a smothered exclamation, swinging swiftly away from her. As he turned again, she saw that the expression on his face was almost savage.

"What are you telling me this for?" he asked harshly.

"But you asked me! I never thought—Sebastian—are you thinking—*that he might cure Dolores?*"

For a moment they stood staring at each other, shocked beyond utterance at the sudden insidious supposition that had darted through their mingled consciousness. Then Sebastian took Faith's hands in his and carried them to his breast.

"No," he said without a tremor in his voice, "I am not thinking that. She is incurable. A dozen different doctors have pronounced her so.

The greatest specialists in Europe. It is not possible that this American could succeed where they have failed. And it pains me, Fidelidad, to hear her name on your lips. Shall it be agreed between us that we will not speak of her again?"

He kissed her hands, released them, and offered her his arm. "I have not told you how much it pleases me to see you in Spanish dress," he said. "Except for that charming costume which the Icelandic Minister's wife is wearing, yours is certainly the most effective one here. And I am delighted that you have put on your cross of *'rhinestones'* to celebrate my arrival.—But we must go back to the ballroom, *querida*, before we are missed—in each other's company. Indiscretion is the thief of opportunity. And this time I do not intend that anyone—or anything—shall divert our destiny."

. . . . .

When the question of the charity ball and the tango was next raised, it was not by Sebastian. He left for Norway only a few days after his arrival in Copenhagen, accompanied by Jaime de los Rios, "to talk about treaties and look at cod," as he wrote Faith in a letter that was delivered to her with a big box of snowy flowers during the course of the afternoon following his departure. Meanwhile, besides making official calls, he had been playing tennis at the Citadelet and golf at the Eremitagen; and Faith had seen so little of him that she had begun to wonder to what lengths he proposed to carry his discretion. But there was a postscript to the letter saying, "This is the kind of lily that shone through the waterfall in Ecuador. I have hunted all over Copenhagen in the rain for it"; and she read and re-read her note with eyes that sparkled and then softened.

"If you will bring me some vases, Johann, I will arrange these lilies myself," she said as she glanced up at last, and saw, with a slight sensation of confusion, that the servant was still standing at her door.

"Pardon me, Excellency. I do not think Your Excellency heard me say that Dr. and Mrs. Noble are calling, and wish to know if it would be convenient for you to receive them."

She hastened down to the drawing-room, genuinely distressed because she had kept them waiting, and giving swift instructions as she went, that tea should be served at once, and that the Minister should be informed of their visit as soon as he returned from the Chancery. It was Jacqueline, who, after the first greetings had been exchanged, referred to the question of the tango.

"I have quite lost my heart to Don Sebastian," she said gaily. "He sent me some beautiful red roses the morning after Signor Bonatelli's dinner, with a note saying they were a thank-offering for the privilege of dancing with me. It is a pity Americans never learn to express themselves like that."

"I should not have thought that Dr. Noble was inexpressive," Faith answered, glancing at the surgeon, who was leaning back rolling a cigarette between his long dexterous fingers, and looking at his lovely wife with mingled amusement and affection.

"He has had some beneficial Gallic influence," laughed Jacqueline, "which has improved his technique immensely. But even so, he could never compete with your attractive Spanish cousin—he *is* your cousin, isn't he?"

"He is distantly related to my husband," said Faith, wishing that she would not blush, and conscious that for all the nonchalance of his manner, there was little that escaped David Noble's scrutiny.

"Oh—he rather conveyed the impression—he called on us yesterday at the Angleterre—that the connection was quite close; and I have heard several other persons refer to it in the same way. But I know how united most of the great European families feel!—At all events he is very hopeful that the exhibition dance of which we spoke should be featured at the Charity Bazaar. Apparently he is much interested in this—the Princess Marie received me on Friday, and told me he had sent her a thousand kroner for it. So I have come to say that if I could help you at all with your preparations, I should be delighted. I have agreed to do some Majorcan dances myself, that I learned from an old peasant when David and I once spent almond blossoming-time near Palma."

Faith hesitated. She was ashamed of the swift stab of jealousy which had pierced her at the thought that Sebastian had given roses to Jacqueline as well as lilies to her, and that he should have found time to call at the Angleterre when he had not darkened the door of the German Legation. But as his strategy became clearer to her, she could not help admiring it, and she was irresistibly tempted to take advantage of it.

"If you really feel that I should do credit to your teaching—" she began. But Jacqueline interrupted her.

"I am positive you would! When you are sitting or standing, when you rise and walk, you are very graceful. But when you dance, you stiffen the least little bit. You seem a trifle unyielding. I think that is the only difficulty we need to overcome. You must relax when you are dancing with Don Sebastian, in the same way that you relax when you pose for Sam Dudley. You are wholly natural with him, and when you are wholly natural, you are wholly captivating!"

"If you keep on, Jacqueline, Baroness von Hohenlohe will think that you are the surgeon of the family. You are very analytical."

"But the analysis is accurate, isn't it, David? And I am sure the Baroness wants me to be frank! Besides, you have probably been analyzing us both while we have been talking, so you have no right to reprove me!"

She laughed again, and turned to Faith with increasing animation. "You have a great deal of dramatic instinct," she went on. "Caleb Hawks told me so first, and I have seen it for myself here in Copenhagen. Of course Caleb didn't put it just that way. He said it was a pity you didn't have a chance to speechify for women's rights, or something like that, because if you did, you would be a 'rabble-rouser' and 'liven up any campaign considerable.' I think he cherishes a hope that some day you will do so yet. But for the moment, you certainly can't decline to dance the tango! Is eleven in the morning a convenient time for you to rehearse? The day after Don Sebastian returns from Norway? And —you do not mind another suggestion, do you? Leave off your stays! You must not barricade yourself with steel! You must be absolutely plastic in your partner's arms."

She spoke as if the matter were entirely settled, and began to fasten her furs and draw on her gloves. Faith's lips parted ever so slightly, and then she closed them again.

"I think Baroness von Hohenlohe has something to say in self-defense," suggested David.

Faith turned to him with an uncanny feeling of fear. If he had noticed even so ephemeral a movement as the one she had just made, she had been right in believing there was nothing which escaped his observation.

"No," she said falteringly. "I—I will dance the tango with Sebastian, since Mrs. Noble has so much confidence in me. She has made me understand already—how to do better. It was about something else that I wanted to speak to you, only I am not sure whether I ought to—partly because I do not know whether Sebastian would wish to have me, and partly because I realize that it is very incorrect to talk with a doctor about a professional matter when he is making a friendly visit."

"I hope you will talk with me about anything you wish," said David encouragingly. "That is, unless you really feel that Don Sebastian might prefer you did not."

He spoke with such sympathy and kindliness that Faith was disarmed. She locked and unlocked her fingers as she usually did when she was excited, but she began to unburden herself almost immediately.

"It is about a lady who is—a—relative of Sebastian," she said, her words coming with a rush. "He cannot bear to talk about her, it is all so tragic; but the night of Bonatelli's dinner, he asked me what your specialty was, and suddenly we—suddenly I—ever since then I have felt I must tell you about her, that I couldn't keep still. She has been —strange—for a great many years. She lives—in great retirement—in a castle in the Pyrenees. Once, when she was not watched very carefully, she even tried to kill her husband. But there is no insanity in her family. She is the only one who has ever been—as she is. And if she could get well—and—and have a child, it would—it would mean everything. Her husband is the last of his race."

"Is this lady Don Sebastian's wife, Faith?" David asked gently.

She looked at him in deep astonishment, too amazed to even notice that he had called her by her Christian name, and that he had spoken almost as tenderly as if he had been comforting a troubled child.

"How did you guess?" she asked impulsively.

"Doctors need to be skillful at surmise," he said more gently still, "since they are certain of so little! May I tell you what else I have guessed? That you are hesitating to say, for fear that I will misjudge Don Sebastian—though I assure you I should not!—that his memories of his life with this lady are so interwoven with bitter disappointment and horror and grief, that he shrinks from reviving them, even if there were a chance that she might be cured."

"Is there a chance?" exclaimed Faith.

"I cannot tell without seeing her. There might be—a possibility."

"And could you go to see her?"

"To Spain? It is a long journey."

He appeared to be turning the question over in his mind, watching Faith's expression covertly as he did so. At last he answered rather slowly.

"It would mean the postponement of work at home which is important. But if Don Sebastian asks me to go, I will not refuse."

"And if he didn't ask you? You couldn't go, could you, right away? Without even giving him a chance to ask you?"

"You mean, before you have a chance to regret that you have asked me?"

"I could give you a letter to Sebastian's brother, Gabriel," Faith said recklessly, disregarding David's question. "He is the Archbishop of Granada, and he is very powerful and very wise. He would arrange everything for you. No one would even find out until it was all over. Would you be afraid to—to act secretly?"

"I should not be afraid. But there is one contingency I do not think you have considered: you are thinking only of what would happen if this lady were cured. Sometimes patients die while a tumor is being removed, or as a result of the removal. If Don Sebastian's wife did not survive an operation upon which you had insisted—how would you feel then?"

There was infinite compassion in his voice, an understanding so profound that it seemed fathomless. He reached over and took one of her hands in his powerful flexible fingers.

"You are a very gallant lady," he said gravely. "I will do everything

I can to serve you. But I do not think you have a right to exclude Don Sebastian from this great decision."

CHAPTER 28

If Rudolf von Hohenlohe had not been anxiously abstracted because of certain subtle developments on the map of Europe which he knew were portentous, he would have observed that Faith was unusually silent all the evening. The Radens were in town, and had arranged a large "Dutch treat" dinner at the Angleterre, with informal dancing afterwards, to which only intimate friends had been asked; and as a rule Faith was at her best on impromptu occasions of this sort, which she enjoyed far better than those attended with more ceremony. But she sought Rudolf out of her own accord a little after midnight, and suggested that since they were free to leave whenever they pleased, they should go home.

"Are you ill?" he asked, complying with alacrity, but obviously astonished.

"No. I am like Queen Victoria. I am not amused."

"You are not in the least like Queen Victoria," said Rudolf literally. "If you are indisposed, why do you not say so?"

His manner did not invite confidences. And yet, as he bade her good-night, Faith asked him, a little hesitatingly, if he would not come into her room for a chat and a cigarette before he went to bed.

"A chat and a cigarette?" he echoed. "At this hour? When you have left a party before it was half over because you were too tired to stay until the end? You are not very consistent, Faith. Try to get a long sleep—tell Hilda not to let Hans Christian come bounding into your room early in the morning. You cannot reasonably expect to keep on burning the candle at both ends indefinitely. I hope you will feel much better to-morrow."

Even then she longed to detain him. It seemed to her that she could not shut herself in for the night alone with the burning problems which confronted her. She felt impelled to take his hand, to look candidly into his face, to talk to him without reservations. The very words she seemed constrained to speak were trembling on her lips. But as he continued to look at her with an expression of detachment which she felt amounted to indifference, she turned despondently away from him, and went slowly into her sumptuous Spanish room.

For hours after Hilda had been dismissed, Faith sat on the edge of her golden bed, her turquoise-colored dressing gown wrapped about her, locking and unlocking the slim hands toward which she looked down unseeingly.

David Noble had made a profound impression upon her: his intuition had startled her, his sympathy had touched her, his arguments had overpowered her. Yet now that she could count on his skill and his wisdom, she knew she still could not prevail in her purpose unless Sebastian could be induced to consent to it. She realized David had been right in dissuading her from her first wild project; yet how could she perfect another plan? And how could she withstand a passion to which, with every fiber of her quivering consciousness, she ardently responded? The barriers before which Sebastian once had bowed—her youth, her innocence, her imminent maternity—were not there to restrain him any longer; and such safeguards as she did have were not strong enough to repel him. She had no sooner looked into his eyes than she had known he had come at last to claim her; and when he told her that no power on earth could thwart their destiny a second time, she felt he spoke the truth.

The sound of a striking clock roused her from her tumultuous reveries. The reluctant dawn of the late northern spring had not yet penetrated through the drawn draperies at her windows; yet it was nearly morning, and she was no nearer a solution of her perplexities than she had been the night before. She let her blue robe slip to the floor, and lay down at last in her bed, falling eventually into a troubled slumber; but she woke unrefreshed, and for the next few days, she went automatically through her engagements, only half-conscious as to how she filled them. Even after Sebastian's return from Norway and the resumption of their meetings, she seemed to make no headway toward clarity. As if he guessed her intention to reason and plead with him, he kept mockingly aloof from her; and his attitude, during their rehearsals together, was so impersonal that she was almost piqued. He could, apparently, dance with her indefinitely, and still remain as detached from her in feeling as he was close to her in person. His grace, his litheness, his dexterity, were all inimitable; but she never recaptured the sensation of ecstasy to which he had so swiftly stirred her on the night of Bonatelli's dance.

She and Rudolf were invited to the dinner at the Palace given in honor of the special envoy of the King of Spain; and she saw Sebastian's eyes resting appraisingly upon her for a moment as she came into the great room where royalty received its guests. She was wearing the most superb of all her Paris dresses—a lustrous heavy white satin trimmed with rare Alençon lace and finished with a square-cut train two metres long; and she was wearing her diamond cross and earrings as ornaments. She was conscious that she was looking her very best; and yet when he finally came and spoke to her, which was not until after dinner, he made a rather cutting allusion to her appearance, and immediately afterwards began to speak of how extremely interesting he had found the court ceremonial.

"Very beautiful," he murmured, glancing at her glistening gown and jewels, "but just a little glacial, Fidelidad. Are you impersonating Andersen's 'Snow Queen,' by any chance?"

"The court is in half-mourning, as you know," she answered, with a slight tinge of annoyance in her voice. "I had to wear black or lavender or white, and I happened to choose white, that is all."

"Oh—I am glad to learn you were not trying to chill me with the rather frosty quality of your crystalline inaccessibility.—This is a delightful function, is it not? I never saw a dining room more brilliantly lighted, and the effect of the concealed music is charming. I was really much impressed with the health-drinking. *'Skaal,'* is a perfect word for a toast, and this custom of standing and looking your royal host straight in the eye as he lifts his glass and you lift yours, is most inspiring. As to those flowered headdresses the footmen wear, I could hardly refrain from asking for one as a souvenir!"

He drifted away from her leaving her vexed with him, and with herself that she should be so vexed; and again she longed to turn confidentially to Rudolf. But Rudolf apparently noticed her ruffled temper now no more than he had noticed her silence a few nights earlier. Indeed, as the spring advanced, it seemed to Faith that his preoccupation in his work had never been so complete.

Before pledging herself irrevocably to the exhibition dance at the Charity Bazaar, Faith made very sure that he did not disapprove of it. The only objections which he raised were inconsequential.

"I should think Sebastian would be too busy with this impending treaty to take time for amateur theatricals," he said coolly. "However, that is his affair. . . . I have always known he had a weakness for buffoonery. I suppose King Alfonso knows it too, and makes due allowances. No doubt with Mrs. Noble's help you will be able to give a reasonably good performance. Though I have never thought dancing was your forte."

"What have you thought that was, Rudolf?" Faith inquired.

He shrugged his shoulders without answering her, as he always did when he seemed to suspect her of seeking a compliment.

"I have learned that Jacqueline Noble's grandfather was Horace P. Huntington, the plutocrat-philanthropist," Faith went on after a moment—"You know, the man who endowed libraries and built hospitals all over the world. His only son died very soon after his marriage to Jacqueline's mother, who was a French *artiste;* and she died too. It was old Mr. Huntington who brought Jacqueline up. I thought you might like to know. You seemed interested when they first came."

"I have too many things on my mind, Faith, which are much more important to me than the background of the Nobles, to be unduly concerned about this. They seem to have settled down here rather indefinitely, and to be generally accepted."

He gathered up a sheaf of papers that were lying in front of him, and began to glance through them. Faith correctly interpreted the gesture as one of indirect dismissal. And Rudolf did not refer to the Bazaar again, in spite of the fact that he knew of her daily attendance at rehearsals, until she reminded him that it was about to take place.

"I do not see how I can possibly go to the theatricals. The dispatches which came in late last night will require hours of attention."

"Oh, Rudolf—don't you care at all about seeing me dance?"

He was drinking his morning coffee, and as she spoke to him, he set down his cup with unconcealed irritation.

"How can you be so unreasonable!" he exclaimed. "I tell you about dispatches upon which the fate of nations may hang, and you answer by asking if I do not care to see you dance! So I will say that I do not care in the least about seeing you dance. I think this whole affair is ridiculous!"

He went out leaving her chilled with the strange sensation that she had been repudiated as well as rebuked, that he did not care what she did or with whom, as long as he was not inconvenienced by it. At lunch-time he telephoned that he was too busy to leave the Chancery; and it was not until evening that he came to her room, and told her that he had just learned that the King and Queen were to attend the tableaux, and that therefore he would accompany her to the Concert Palais.

"I am sorry that you should be put to so much trouble, because of royalty," Faith said icily.

"They are very grateful to you for your participation in this Bazaar, Faith. . . . I have just learned also, that it was at his special request that you were put at the King's side for the *quadrille d'honneur* at the last court ball. That was a real compliment—both to you personally, and to your dancing."

"I should hardly have been there except by his request," said Faith with continued iciness. She realized that Rudolf regretted his rudeness, and that his attitude was conciliatory of intention; but she still felt congealed and wounded; and it was not until she had reached her dressing room behind the stage, where she found a professional waiting to help her with her make-up, that her naturally buoyant spirits commenced to rise again. An enormous bouquet of white lilacs and lilies, tied with long streamers of vari-colored ribbon, lay on her toilet table; and beside it stood a silver cooler filled with ice, into which a pint bottle of champagne had been plunged. When the professional had finished his work, she sat fingering her flowers and sipping her wine, crushing the bubbles with her lips before she swallowed them, and conscious that a welcome feeling of warmth was permeating her being.

"Are you ready? May I come in? Our cue will be called almost directly now."

She had not seen Sebastian once alone since the Bonatelli dinner, but now he had opened the door of her dressing room and glided inside almost before she could answer him. In the midst of the confusion that reigned, he had evidently contrived to slip away so unobtrusively that no one had seen him. And he confronted her now, slender and dazzling in his superb costume, a smile on his lips and a look in his eyes which she had never seen there before.

"Try to dance for once as if you were a gypsy instead of a snow maiden," he said quietly. As he spoke, he suddenly drew her toward him, one strong supple hand crushing her waist, the other lifting her face to the level of his. He had taken her completely by surprise. Nevertheless, as his mouth closed ruthlessly down upon hers, she knew that she was already straining upward for his kiss.

. . . . .

She found him waiting for her the following afternoon when she came in from a long walk in the Langelinge with Hans Christian. She had been a prey to such surging restlessness all day that she had finally sought release from it in violent exercise, and she returned to the house grateful for the exhaustion which she hoped would drug her tingling senses. When she was greeted by Johann with the announcement that the *Duque* de Cerreno was in the drawing-room, she unconsciously tightened her hold on her little son's hand as she went up the stairs.

But for once Hans Christian did not wish to remain with her. Sebastian had sent him a huge box of tin soldiers, gorgeous in Spanish uniforms, and equipped with tents, cannon, horses, and other paraphernalia. He had just finished arranging these in the nursery, preparatory to beginning maneuvers, when his mother had summoned him to go out with her; and now he was eager to resume his interrupted operations. He darted into the drawing-room and flung his arms around Sebastian's neck, thanking him ecstatically for his present; he made an appointment to go and see the changing of the King's Guards the next day with his cousin; but he disregarded Faith's remonstrance as he bounded swiftly out of the room again, leaving her alone with her visitor, who kissed her hand with his usual formality.

"I have come to confer with you about an invitation I have received," Sebastian said quietly.

"Yes? I hope it is a pleasant one?"

"Very. Countess Raden has asked me to spend the week-end at Radensholm. In spite of your confident predictions, I have not been to many house-parties after all. I have been too much entangled with cod and commemorations. But I thought I might enjoy this one very much. Especially as I have somehow gathered that you were planning to spend Sunday in the country yourself."

Faith was silent.

"Is it possible that I was misinformed?"

"No. But I do not think it is best, Sebastian, that we should spend the week-end at Radensholm together."

"Together? You talk as if it were to be a *solitude à deux!* I understand that the Radens are to have at least a dozen guests. But I did think that possibly we might create an opportunity at their countryseat—which somehow seems to have eluded us in town—to discuss a project which I know you have very much at heart."

"I am not sure I understand what you mean, Sebastian."

"I think you do. I asked you not to refer to the subject again, and you have been most magnanimous in your avoidance of it. But I know you feel I should consent to an examination of Dolores by David Noble—to an operation if he advises it. If you can convince me that this should be done—and I am inclined to believe that you can when you are not in constant danger of being interrupted—I will make arrangements to leave for Spain with him next week."

Faith's heart gave a sudden bound of triumph. This was the first reference to Dolores which she had ever known Sebastian to make; and the fact that he had voluntarily brought up the difficult subject which two months earlier he had declined to discuss, seemed a tribute to her influence for which she had not dared to hope. Yet some indefinable instinct of caution made her wary.

"Have you talked with David about this yourself?"

"No. Because I felt I must first talk with you about it. After all, the results of the contemplated operation—whether these are beneficent or disastrous—will affect you more closely than anyone else except myself. You cannot be so naïve that you do not understand that!—but Dr. and Mrs. Noble are going to the house-party also, and when you and I have had our preliminary discussion, we will ask David Noble to confer with us. I have guessed of course that you have spoken with him already. Indeed I suspect you urged him to proceed without consulting me at all, and I am thankful that his judgment acted as a foil to your recklessness! Considering how you have tried to circumvent my authority, I think I am magnanimous to treat with you!"

He smiled disarmingly and engagingly. Faith, sensible at his generosity in the face of her contemplated interference with his life, and more and more touched by his deference to her, smiled faintly in return but did not answer. When Sebastian spoke again, she was conscious of the reassurance in his courteous and guarded voice.

"Are you mistrustful of me, Faith? After all these years? Have I forfeited your confidence? Merely because I talked to you once about destiny and kissed you as I did last night?"

"I am mistrustful of myself," she said with a sudden strangled sob. "I have tried so hard to do right all these years! And now—and now—I feel as if I were rushing toward a precipice! I did ask David to go secretly to Dolores, Sebastian, but only because I thought—I hoped—that if she could get well, you might be happy—after all—with her. I never thought that if she died your—your bondage would be over. And even if it were—you know that mine would not. There is no hope of—of freedom for me. None at all. And yet——"

"And yet—*querida?*"

"You know," she said, burying her face in her hands.

For a moment there was no sound in the room except her smothered weeping. When she raised her head in a desperate effort at self-command, she saw that Sebastian was bending over her and found herself leaning against his shoulder and looking straight into his eyes.

"Fidelidad," he said earnestly, "you must control yourself! Remember that at any moment someone may come into this room—Rudolf, Hansel, Johann, another visitor! It is precisely because it is impossible for us to talk here undisturbed that I am urging you to come to Radensholm! For it is imperative—for your sake as well as mine—that we should converse intimately together. Besides, despair like this is as unworthy of you as it is needless. You are not a helpless child any more. David Noble calls you a 'gallant lady.' You are that, *querida*, but you are much more than that—you are a beloved woman. Are you not brave enough to face your fate?"

He laid his face swiftly against her wet cheek, kissed her eyelids, her throat, and at last, very gently, her lips.

"I have waited for you nearly eight years," he whispered. "I have tried, *alma de mi alma*, never to fail you. I shall be waiting for you Saturday—at Radensholm. I know that you will not fail me."

CHAPTER 29

WHEN Faith reached the railroad station on Saturday morning, she found that a number of her fellow passengers on the tidy little train were also bound for Radensholm. Bonatelli hailed her as she went by the compartment in which he was already installed with the French Minister and Madame Marceau; and a group of Danish friends also sought to detain her. But David and Jacqueline Noble had promised to save a place for her with them. So she went down the narrow corridor until she caught sight of Jacqueline's unmistakable figure, silhouetted upon the window against which she stood looking out with interest and amusement at the crowded station platform.

"Faith! I am so glad to see you!" she exclaimed, turning quickly as David touched her arm to attract her attention. "And Hansel, too!—Good morning, Hilda!—And so the Minister found, as he feared, that he would not be able to get away?"

"Yes. Sunday is often his busiest day. He was very sorry."

"And Don Sebastian? I thought he was coming, but I have not seen him on the train."

"I believe he and Jaime went down yesterday or the day before. One of the first things I learned about Spaniards is that they are not 'too much bound by time,' and their interpretation of a week-end is often a period lasting from Thursday to Tuesday."

She spoke casually, but as usual when she was in his presence, she was conscious of David's discerning gaze, and almost as soon as baggage had been disposed, and wraps arranged, she leaned forward and spoke to him impulsively in French.

"Sebastian came to see me the other afternoon," she said, "and brought up the subject of—of his wife himself. I have never known him to do this before, and I was tremendously encouraged. He has promised to discuss the situation with me at greater length while we are in the country, and I feel very hopeful now that he will consent to an examination at least. Indeed, he spoke of starting for Spain with you next week, if you would be free to go."

"Of course. I have been waiting all this time on purpose."

"And aren't you delighted?"

"I am very glad you have made some progress with the plan which means so much to you. I hope the results will be everything you could wish for."

Faith wondered whether the slight formality in David's manner rose from his inability to speak French with real flexibility and fluency, in spite of his long acquaintance with it. Languages, she had heard him confess more than once, had always been a stumblingblock to him; and Jacqueline, bilingual herself, catered to his weakness. Since Hilda as well as Hansel understood English, Faith did not wish to shift to that and pursue the subject in their presence; so she changed the topic of conversation tactfully, and talked to the Nobles about Danish coöperative farming, and the characteristics of the pleasant and peaceful landscape through which they were passing.

They reached the ferry that was to take them from Zealand to Funen a little before noon; and the party all lunched merrily together on *smørbrød*,[1] *rødgrød*,[2] and a variety of hot and hearty dishes while they paddled across the placid waters dividing the islands. As they piled

[1] Thick bread, heavily spread with butter and cold meat.

[2] A mixture of red fruit juices and potato flour, chilled and molded, which is served with chopped almonds, sugar and cream, and is a favorite Danish sweet.

into the train a second time, Bonatelli detained Faith with the plea that she would make a fourth at bridge with the Tesdorfs and himself; and she was deeply engrossed in a rubber-game, when the guard began shouting the name of the station at which they were to descend. During the ten-mile drive that followed, she forced herself to talk mechanically; but her heart had already begun to beat fast and her thoughts to wander. She was both relieved and disappointed because Sebastian had not come to the station with the Radens' two attractive sons, Valdemar and Gustav; and she found herself alternately dreading and longing for the moment, now inevitably near, when she would meet him. As the carriage swung in through the tessellated entrance to the castle grounds, she saw him standing in the family group at the doorway, with one or two other houseguests, waiting to welcome the additional arrivals. He was beside Dagmar, the Radens' only daughter; and for once, the tall fair girl, with her milk-and-roses complexion, and her ropes of honey-colored hair, was laughing and talking excitedly. Faith had never seen her smooth beautiful face alight with animation before; and the knowledge that Dagmar was already unofficially engaged to Erik, one of the guests at the house-party, did not suffice to allay the swift stab of jealousy that always pierced her when she saw Sebastian paying the casual and graceful court which was as natural to him as breathing. Even after the newcomers had been installed in their apartments and had foregathered for tea in the garden, he did not detach himself from Dagmar except to stroll over to Jacqueline and ask if she would feel inclined to play a little tennis later on; and he turned again to Jacqueline as soon as the dancing began after the choral singing that followed the late dinner. It was Jaime who suggested a walk through the orchards to Faith, and who, as they wandered back and forth in the mild dappled sunlight of the late afternoon, pulling cherries from the trees and eating them as they meandered along, told her how favorable an impression her kinsman had made upon their hosts.

"He is as firmly entrenched as if he had been here a dozen times already. Not that Sebastian has seemed to press anything at all—but you know how easily he fits into any situation.—I believe there is a plan for swimming at six—are you in the mood for sea-bathing? The water is actually very warm, warmer than I have ever seen it here before.—Or would you rather go on through the kitchen gardens? I always enjoy looking at those myself. I have never seen such ornamental vegetables as there are in Denmark—the asparagus-bean intrigues me especially!—How delicious these cherries are! I never can decide whether I like best to eat them fresh off the trees like this, or to drink them in cordial form after dinner."

When Faith went back to her rooms, she found a small rectangular package wrapped in old gold brocade, and tied with heavy silk cord, lying on her desk. Hansel, who had had his supper, and was waiting impatiently for her to come and read to him, was consumed with curiosity to know what it contained; so she permitted him to untie it, rescuing the exquisitely bound book and the note that fluttered from it, as they fell from his impetuous little hands.

"Is it a book of fairy tales?" he asked eagerly, watching her turn over the leaves with lingering fingers.

"No, darling. It is a grown-up book. The name of it is 'The Forest Lovers.' "

"I am very sorry," he said with real disappointment, but he added, with never-failing thoughtfulness, "unless you are pleased with it, mother."

"Yes, darling, I am very pleased with it," she said, trying to speak quietly, and putting her arm around him. But her eyes were devouring the written words before her. "*Alma de mi alma,*" she read. "I hope you will enjoy this exquisite romance, which I think is the loveliest of its kind in the English language. I have had it bound for you in the covers of a book once owned by my ancestress, Doña Cecilia, and I am wrapping it in a piece of one of her dresses. I have thought of sending it to you because I constantly feel in this country as if I might come across Isoult and Prosper walking down a forest path—surely it must have been in woods like these in Denmark that they found sanctuary in each other's arms! And in such woods also, for that matter, that Daphne must have evaded Apollo. Which are they going to mean to us, beloved—fulfillment or frustration? *A tus pies, siempre,* Sebastian."

The gift and the letter threw Faith into a tumult of excitement; but when the party broke up for the night, she had actually exchanged only a dozen words with Sebastian, except during the course of the one dance for which he had asked her. As they glided over the polished floor together, he expressed himself with being enchanted with the Palace: with the huge banqueting hall, all galleries and gilding; with the big kitchen where the fat old cook and eight rosy-cheeked scullery maids were bustling about; with the chapel, which, in spite of the "sterile atmosphere pervading all Catholic churches that have turned Lutheran" was really very fine; but especially with his own room, which, he told her, was hung in dark red damask and furnished in carved ebony; and from which he could look out of a bay window set in a wall three feet thick, at the most beautiful laburnum tree that he had ever seen.

"The Countess says that she always puts you in an isolated wing on the ground floor overlooking the moat, because you like to keep Hansel with you, and she is afraid he will disturb the other guests," he remarked. "I hope you are as comfortable there as I am. It sounds gloomy and remote to me."

"It is somber, but it is not gloomy," Faith answered. "There is something very regal about all the rooms here. Mine are different from yours, but they are just as magnificent. I do not object to isolation as long as I can have Hansel with me—If he slept with Hilda he would be so far away that I could not even look in on him the last thing at night without covering a quarter of a mile or so of corridor. I always kiss him in his sleep, the last thing before I go to bed myself; and I like to be able to comfort him when he has bad dreams—quite often he dreams. And in the morning we read Andersen's 'Fairy Tales' together before breakfast. Hansel feels an especial interest in those because the story-teller's name was Hans Christian too. I have thought that some day I would ask the Radens if we could not arrange to go from here to Odense to see the Andersen birthplace. I am sure Hansel would enjoy that immensely."

"I should think it might be managed very easily—we might make up a party and drive over to Odense for lunch," Sebastian said idly. "And you are not going to hurry off again on Monday, are you? Countess Raden has suggested that I should remain until Wednesday at least."

"But if you are going to start for Spain next week—" faltered Faith.

"Friday or Saturday would still be next week," said Sebastian rather absently. "I have been wandering about in the park here, Faith, and it is really charming—the little pavilions which are scattered through it are exquisite, and the beech woods are full of enchantment, just as you said. I hope some time we can manage a stroll through them together."

"I hope so," answered Faith, trying to suppress the agitation in her voice. "I was delighted with the book you sent me, Sebastian—the book and—and the note."

"I thought we might possibly read aloud together in the woods," Sebastian said, still absently. "It will attract no attention if we eventually wander off together, since we have not rushed off together. And I should like to see those regal rooms of yours, Faith. Will you show them to me some time?"

"If there is a chance," she whispered, with suddenly quickened pulses.

"Oh, there is sure to be! . . . Is there no encore to this dance? What a pity!"

The vagueness with which he spoke was somehow more disquieting to Faith than urgency would have been, and on Sunday he still seemed entirely content to let matters drift along. The guests, clothed in riding habits, breakfasted downstairs with their hosts; some of them had already been out for an early morning canter; others left almost immediately for one; and those who had ridden before breakfast, fished before lunch. At noon, the women, all in white dresses, were seated at one side of the long table and the men on the other. The program for the afternoon was equally unstimulating, though it was suggested that the guests should improvise costumes, and come to dinner in fancy dress. Sebastian joined Faith and commented on the plan without much enthusiasm as they went out of the dining room.

"Amusements in Denmark are agreeable, but they lack diversity," he said, looking as if he were stifling a yawn. "There have been a dozen fancy-dress parties in Copenhagen lately, and yet we no sooner get into the country than another is incongruously proposed. I am totally unprepared for such an emergency. I suppose I shall have to devote the afternoon devising something that I can wear."

"You are usually resourceful, under provocation," said Faith demurely.

"Yes. But just at present you are provoked, not I," said Sebastian, resorting to the *double entendre* in which he always took such pleasure. "I really think I shall take a siesta before I do anything else. I enjoy the tranquillity of my carvings and brocades and the view of my laburnum tree more than I do this ceaseless round of wholesome sports, interrupted only by tepid tea in the rose garden."

He shrugged his shoulders slightly and drifted away; and feeling almost annoyed with him, Faith went back to her own rooms, read with unwilling absorption the book he had sent her, and looked up from it with genuine amazement when Hilda appeared on the scene with the respectful suggestion that it was time the Frau Baronin dressed for dinner. But the process of preparing for the fancy-dress party intrigued her. She had foreseen the contingency which had arisen; and she had brought with her to Radensholm a costume which she had kept laid away in a trunk, ever since it had been sent to her, together with certain other unique heirlooms, at the time of her father's death. It was the dress which her great-grandmother, the first Faith Marlowe, had worn for her New England marriage: a narrow-skirted, high-waisted, puffed-sleeved, white silk, absolutely devoid of ornament. Faith had tried it on when it had first arrived, and had discovered that it fitted her perfectly; but she had folded it away, with the mesh mitts, the low-heeled ankle ties, the embroidered handkerchief, the parchment fan, and the short lace-edged veil that went with it; feeling, for some indefinable reason, that the time had not yet come when she wished to wear it. She had shown it once to Victoria Luise, who had been entranced with it, and had even suggested that Faith might wear it to her own wedding, and prove that contrary to popular European belief, Americans had a heritage and a tradition. But Mrs. Carolus

Cavendish Castle had been firmly in favor of Worth's latest lustrous creation, and had pronounced the yellowing grosgrain entirely unsuitable for a function which was to be virtually a court ceremony. Faith had been inclined to agree with her; she had a sentiment about her ancestral dress, but she thought lengths of shining splendor far more glamorous than this trainless example of early nineteenth-century severity. It was only recently that a belated reëxamination of it had convinced her that she had underestimated its effectiveness. There was actually something primly provocative about it.

As Hilda did up its fastenings now, while Hansel jumped up and down on the tapestried bed, squealing with admiration, Faith realized that she had never put on anything that became her more. She had chosen a short tight string of pearls for her ornament, and had bound her head with a wreath of small white roses, from which the sheer veil fell over her shoulders; the grace of her throat and the splendor of her hair had both been accentuated. She could not help being conscious also of the soft whiteness of her arms, revealed between the short sleeve and the short mitts, and of her neck and breast rising above the tuckered bodice; and she knew that the quaint cut of the close-fitting dress revealed the slender unconfined curves of her figure as no stiff modern dress could have done.

"I am glad Mrs. Noble gave me the idea of leaving off stays," she said casually to Hilda as she picked up her handkerchief and fan. "I should never have thought of doing it myself, but I feel like a different person without them. . . . Good-night, Hansel darling. I will come in to kiss you the minute I can get back here after dinner."

"But I will be asleep then! Kiss me again now, mother! You are beautifuller than ever, and you smell so sweet!"

"Just once more, darling! But do not muss me up!"

She disengaged herself gently, running her fingers through his tangled curls in a lingering caress; then, as Hilda held open the door for her, curtseying with admiration as well as respect, she stepped swiftly out into the long corridor.

It was dimly illumined by bracket lamps projecting from the walls at long intervals from each other; but as she passed quickly and quietly along, she saw a flickering light ahead of her, and was aware of the watchman's swinging lantern. She had not realized that he began his rounds so early; but dinner was later than usual, because of the long forest drive which had been scheduled to follow the afternoon swim; and at lunch there had been some laughing comment to the effect that if such irregular hours continued, the guests would begin to imagine themselves in Spain instead of in Denmark! As she approached the sentinel, she saw that the somber color of the garments in which he was clad made of him a dim apparition hardly distinguishable from the encircling shadows; and interested afresh at the mysterious medievalism of this faithful figure, she paused to greet him with a cordial good-evening. As she did so, he lifted his lantern; and with a startled exclamation, she stepped back, shocked at the subtlety of the artifice with which she was confronted.

"Sebastian!" she gasped. "What are you doing here? And what do you mean—mean by putting on those clothes."

"We were told to appear in costume, were we not?" he inquired imperturbably. "Without forewarning enough to prepare any? I was thankful to find a coöperative as well as a congenial spirit in the watchman. I roused him from his well-earned slumbers after my own siesta, and solicited his help. I fear that I should hardly have been as expansive myself under the same circumstances as he was."

Sebastian smiled, swinging his lantern slowly around until it made a circle of light about her. Then, in his turn, he gave a startled exclamation.

"*Madre de Dios!*" he whispered. "Where did you ever find such a dress and veil? You are the reincarnation of some seductively simple spirit!"

"I have had them a long time. They belonged to my great-grandmother—she wore them on her wedding day. I am impersonating a Puritan bride, Sebastian."

"A Puritan bride!" he echoed deliberately. "And what happens, Faith, when a Puritan and a pagan meet? Do they clash—or do they merge?"

"I—I do not know."

"But you expect to discover, Faith, do you not?"

She felt as if he must hear the quickened beating of her heart in the surrounding stillness. But she could not answer.

"Listen," he said swiftly, "after the dance is over to-night—a long time after—I will come down this corridor again. As I pass along, I will call out, 'All's well.' Then I will try the latch of your sitting-room door. If it is unlocked, I will go in. If it is not, I will go away. But if I find it fastened, I do not know to what desperate lengths I shall be driven afterwards."

"And if you do not find it fastened," she faltered, "will you promise to leave me to-night whenever I ask you to? To—to go to Spain before the week is over?"

"On my sacred word of honor! By the memory—of my mother!"

He looked at her impellingly. She bowed her head for an instant, and then raised her eyes.

"The door will be unlocked," she said breathlessly.

CHAPTER 30

A PROFUNDITY of stillness engulfed the castle. The last echoing footfall had died away hours before; the last twinkling light in the corridor had been extinguished; and from the high chest in the corner where Faith had set a single candelabrum, shadows rather than radiance appeared to stream. Outside her window, the surface of the moat shone as smooth as black onyx under the summer stars. She had sunk down among the cushions in the deep embrasure of the window-seat, her hands locked in her lap, her breath coming fast. It seemed an eternity to her since she had stirred. And still she heard no signaling call, she was conscious of no impending presence.

She had laid aside her fan, taken off her mitts, and removed her wreath and veil. As she did so, she could not help tingling with reminiscent pleasure at the thought of the admiration her appearance had roused. The Puritan bride! Why had she never thought of that rôle before? It was infinitely more effective and unique, infinitely better suited to her, than that of a Spanish dancer, or that of an Empire belle. Perhaps some day Sam would paint her wearing this dress, and give the picture the title she had just coined. . . .

Her thoughts reverted to the grandmother she had loved so dearly in her childhood, the daughter of the ancestress whom she had impersonated that night, for whom the little house she had once described so feelingly to Gabriel had been built. It had been the first Faith Marlowe's bridal home; and to her descendant's clarified vision the woman who had lived there suddenly seemed a bright and living reality. She felt that if next she could only cross the threshold of the old homestead again, she might almost see her ancestress standing there. . . .

"Two o'clock and all's well——"

The call suddenly reverberated through the silent corridor. Faith shrank back still further against the window frame, trembling all over. As she heard the sound of the lifting latch, she bowed her head and held her breath. Perhaps, hidden as she was, Sebastian would not see her. Perhaps he would think she had already gone to bed, weary with waiting for him. Then he would turn away again and she would not call him back. Perhaps. . . .

"Did it seem long to you, beloved? I did not dare come until the house was sunk in sleep."

He had crossed the room noiselessly, and was standing beside her. As she did not answer, he unfastened the long gray cloak in which he had been wrapped, and laid it quietly down on a chair. Then he sat down beside her in the wide-cushioned window-seat, sliding his arm around her waist.

"How beautiful it is here to-night!" he said throbbingly. "It makes me think of Francesca's window, at which she sat with Paolo. Have you ever been to Rimini, *querida*? Some day, we must go there together. Francesca's castle stands uncrumbling still. I believe her love made it imperishable."

"Was she not killed? She and Paolo both?" Faith asked stranglingly. "And were they not—very wicked?"

"Very wicked, *querida*? How can you say that when their names are glorified among those of the other great lovers of the ages—Romeo and Juliet, Abelard and Héloise, Jacob and Rachel, if you will!—Yes, they were killed—but then it was too late to harm them. They were one body and one spirit already."

She did not answer him. He laced his fingers between hers and pressed them.

"You do not need to say anything more to convince me that I should go to Dolores with David," he said softly. "In fact, I have told him today that I will start as soon as he is ready. The preparations should not take long. . . . I feel sure that by the end of the week—Of course I shall wire to the Castello Viejo to expect us. David says that in Dolores' condition it may be difficult to examine her. But he is confident that within a few days he will be able to tell whether he thinks an operation is advisable. If he does, it can then take place immediately."

Faith neither stirred nor spoke.

"If Dolores dies," Sebastian went on without a tremor in his voice, "we shall have a situation to meet that will in some ways present more complications than if she lives. I have thought of several ways to meet it, and have dismissed them all as impracticable. For instance, for a time I thought I might ask you to return to the *caseria*, and live there with me—as Doña Cecilia lived with my ancestor. But I know you could not be happy in that way—there would be too many lingering memories centering in the *caseria*. Inevitably you would associate it—with your marriage. And inevitably you would seek a more active existence than you could have there. You are too brilliant to be long at rest deprived of stimulating contacts. It was the quality of your mind, *vida de mi vida*, that arrested me first of all. It was only afterwards that I was conscious of your physical beauty. No other woman had ever drawn me to her in that way before.—Do you remember that first morning in Madrid?"

"I remember."

"Besides at Granada there is Gabriel—he is growing very frail, as I told you. It is unthinkable that he should be bowed down by grief because of us. And he would be—if you went to the *caseria* with me."

"Yes—it would be unthinkable that we should cause Gabriel grief."

"There might be other solutions—you might go to the United States, for instance, and I might follow you there. I have no doubt that somewhere, somehow—a divorce could be arranged for you—I find that in certain Western States that is very easy—and afterwards—we could marry. I would chafe under expatriation less than you under imprisonment, *querida!* I know myself as well as I know you. But this solution would mean scandal, with which I could not bear to have you sullied, and it would mean heartbreak too—for Victoria Luise, whom I know you love, for Samuel Dudley, who, I know, has always loved you. And —it would ruin Rudolf's career. That is what he cares most about, so I feel we should leave him that."

A shade of irony had momentarily crept into his tender tones. But almost instantly it faded away again.

"Therefore I suggest that we dismiss this problem from our minds —unless or until we are confronted with it. You would consent to another conference, would you not, if we were faced with the contingency which released me and not you?"

"Yes."

"You promise?"

"I promise."

The sense of reassurance that Faith had begun to feel revealed itself in her voice. She leaned unresistingly back against Sebastian's shoulder and waited for him to go on.

"Then we will only consider for the moment what is to happen— if Dolores recovers. And that, I feel, is the contingency we are far more likely to face. I believe you have the same feeling. Am I right?"

"Yes."

"I will not force myself upon Dolores. You would be the last to wish me to do that." He paused significantly, and then went on, "But if she recovers, and—and feels toward me as she once did, I will return to her—as her husband. That is what you think I ought to do, is it not, Faith?"

"Yes."

"If I had not known you, it would not be too hard," he said musingly, almost as if he were talking to himself. "I have not forgotten that she was once very beautiful—innocent and sweet and lovely."

"I know. I saw her picture once, at Jaime's house. He does not hide it when you are not there. It was seeing her picture, realizing what she must have been, what she still might be, that——"

He pressed her hand. "You have an understanding heart, Faith. But she is not like you. She is lovely, but she is not radiant. She is gentle, but she is not brilliant. And she is sweet, but she is not 'gallant.' There is no one like you, my darling, in all the world."

He bent his head again, and this time he kissed her lips. But even now, though there was infinite longing in his caress, there was no vehemence.

"If I go back to Dolores," he said at last, "I must not—we must not deceive her. I would be—all the world to her. It would take a long time before she could become readjusted, before she could grope her way back to security. I should have to help her constantly. She would not be absorbed in a life of her own from which she shut me out, as Rudolf is absorbed, and shuts you out. And she would be in time—we hope——"

"Yes," said Faith again, steadily.

"We shall be very hungry for each other, you and I, *querida*, in the years to come. And your life, Faith, will be even emptier than mine."

"Yes," she said once more. But now the steadiness was shaken.

"Since all this is so, may I say what is in my heart to say, darling? Without fear that you will be surprised or shocked?"

His voice melted into a poignant silence. She could not answer him in words. But she knew he no longer needed such an answer. For a moment his immobility and stillness were as profound as hers. Then, she was conscious, that as gently as he had taken her into his arms, he had released her, and that he was kneeling at her feet, his hands still clasping hers.

"It is not seduction, Faith, that I am seeking," he whispered. "It is not even largesse, or the assurance of a memory. It is—fulfillment. For you as well as for me. If I did not know you loved me——"

"You do know it."

"As much as I love you——"

"As much as you love me——"

"Then—then—I want to take you for my own, Fidelidad, to-night. . . ."

Very slowly she rose to her feet, drawing him with her. In the accustomed darkness, he could see his own infinite passion mirrored in the eyes she lifted fearlessly and unhesitatingly to his.

"I am your own," she whispered.

He was aware that her lips did not even tremble as they formed the words.

. . . . .

Hans Christian wakened suddenly crying aloud in terror. He had had a horrible dream—a dream that the shining lady whom he adored was lost, and that he could not find her anywhere. He had seemed to see her standing close beside him, smiling down at him, wearing the white dress and veil in which she had looked so lovely. Then gradually she had faded away from him and disappeared.

He sprang up from his cot, and flung himself across the great carved bed that stood beside it, calling to his mother as he felt for her. The bed was empty.

He groped his way across the dark room, his teeth chattering. As his small fingers sought for the latch, they shook so that he could hardly find it. When they finally closed down on it, still shaking, he plunged forward and threw his slender weight against the massive door.

It opened slowly. On the great chest which stood in the corner beside it, three candles were guttering in their sockets. The light was very dim, and he could see nothing in the obscurity which engulfed the huge room. Yet instinctively he felt that it was not empty.

"Mother!" he cried again. "Where are you?"

His voice seemed to echo in the silence and shadows. Almost paralyzed with fright, he cried once more.

"Mother!" he called desperately. "Won't you answer me?"

Suddenly he rushed forward. As he did so, he saw a slim white figure detach itself from the encircling gloom, and come slowly toward him. Then Faith, still wearing her bridal dress, gathered him into her arms.

CHAPTER 31

JOHANN was sure that the Herr Baron must be overwhelmed with weariness. He had not left the Chancery until midnight; and when he came home, he had gone straight to his study and fastened the door. At eight the following morning, Johann, distressed at finding that his master's bed had not been slept in when he went up with breakfast, knocked hesitatingly at the study door, and asked if there were nothing he could bring the Herr Baron or do for him. At first the answer had been negative and monosyllabic; but a little later the Minister had emerged, looking old and haggard, and had shaved, changed his linen, and drunk some coffee before starting back for the Chancery. Now it was evening again, and he was once more locked in the study.

It required all the courage the old servant could summon to intrude a second time. But if his master went on at this rate, without rest or food, he would certainly collapse. Besides, there was now an additional and imperative reason why the Herr Baron should be interrupted. Spurred on by the conviction that a crisis was impending, Johann rapped decisively.

This time there was no immediate answer of any sort. But Johann declined to be daunted by the lack of response to his summons, and at length he was rewarded. Rudolf crossed the room and opened the door himself, confronting the servant with a look of stern rebuke. But Johann forestalled him before he could speak.

"Pardon, Excellency. But the Frau Baronin is very anxious to see you."

"The Frau Baronin!" repeated Rudolf in astonishment. "Why, she is at Radensholm!"

"Pardon, Excellency. She returned to the Legation about three hours ago. And I do not think she is at all well."

"Has she gone to bed? Have you sent for a doctor?"

"She has not gone to bed, Excellency. She is packing."

"Packing!" exclaimed Rudolf, echoing what the servant had said a second time. "First you say she is not at all well, and next you say she is packing! What are you trying to tell me?"

"I am only telling Your Excellency what I have seen. The Frau Baronin is packing, and she is so pale that I am frightened. She looks as if she had not slept at all, and as if she had wept a great deal."

"Go and ask her if she will not come here," said Rudolf slowly, recrossing the room to his desk, and picking up one of the letters with which it was littered.

The force of habit was so strong that it did not occur to him that he might hasten to her instead of asking her to come to him. Nevertheless, he was intensely disturbed by what Johann had told him, and the pressure of fatigue which was almost crushing him, seemed suddenly to be redoubled in weight. As he heard the door open and close again, he glanced up apprehensively. And when Faith came toward him, he saw that Johann's concern was not unfounded. Never, in all the years of their marriage, had he seen her look so badly.

"What is the matter, *liebe* Faith?" he asked with unwonted gentleness. "Have you been seeing ghosts?"

"Yes. That is just what has happened, Rudolf."

In spite of himself, he shivered. A week earlier he had had a letter from his mother saying that the White Lady of the Hapsburgs had been seen wandering in the palace of the Archduke Ferdinand. And now . . . he forced himself to speak quietly.

"Will you not sit down and tell me about it, if it will relieve you? I did not know that there were any traditional ghosts at Radensholm."

"It was not a traditional ghost of Radensholm that I saw. It was the ghost—of a little girl I used to know."

"Yes?" said Rudolf with constrained encouragement.

"She woke in a strange place and found that her mother was not in the bed beside her. So she got up, and opened the door into the next room, looking for her mother——"

"Her mother was not in the next room, either?"

"Yes. She was there. But she was not alone. And that night was the beginning of—hideous years that ended in—shameful disgrace and violent death. It was—a—tragic landmark. I had almost forgotten about it. But suddenly—dreadfully—it was recalled to me."

She covered her face with her hands and burst into abandoned weeping. Rudolf went over and laid his hand gently on her shoulder.

"*Liebe* Faith, you must not grieve so," he said kindly. "I am not sure that I understand just what you are trying to tell me, though I am inclined to think you are speaking symbolically—that something happened at Radensholm which caused you to feel as if you were seeing a ghost, though actually you did not. . . . Something that perhaps recalled a—a painful episode in your own sad childhood. I am distressed that you have been made unhappy, especially in surroundings which you have always enjoyed so much. But you never need to go back to Radensholm again, or see—anyone who was there, if you prefer not to do so. And no real harm has been done." Then, as she did not look up or make any effort to control herself, he asked with a self-command which required increasing effort, "I am right, am I not? No real harm has been done?"

She gave an exclamation which he recognized as one of anguish. "No!" she cried, shuddering, "no real harm has been done! But it might have been! It was—almost! It may be yet! Another time——"

She was trembling, he saw, from head to foot. Suddenly she dropped her hands, grasping at his, and looking up at him with tears rolling down her cheeks.

"Rudolf," she said imploringly, "you must let me go away! At once. To-night. Do not stop to ask me any questions—now. Some day—some day after I come back again I will explain—everything you feel I ought to tell you. But not now. I—I couldn't. I—I can't."

"Of course you cannot," he said soothingly, "and there is no reason why you should. I do not need explanations from you, *liebe* Faith—now or at any other time. I have complete confidence in you." He hesitated, and then, almost awkwardly, he leaned over and kissed her. "I know that it seems to you that for a long time I have shown my affection for you very inadequately," he said in a strained voice. "I realize it myself. It—it is hard for me to be demonstrative. I am not naturally light-hearted or pleasure-loving; I have always been deliberate and reserved. And I am afraid I have begun to seem—almost stolid. Lately I have also been—very much preoccupied and worried. You have a right to feel that I have neglected you, that I have been cold and critical. I—I am very sorry. It would mean a great deal to me, Faith, if you could tell me that you forgive my shortcomings."

"If I would forgive your shortcomings!" she echoed, staring at him with stupefaction.

"Yes. If you are thinking of going away for a time, I shall not try to prevent you. I shall help you get ready—if I can—indeed, I meant to suggest to you myself, when you came back from Radensholm, that you should try to have a little change. But it would make me much happier if I could feel, after you have gone, that we had parted affectionately. Perhaps some day you will feel happier too—if this could be so."

There was an unfamiliar huskiness in his voice which she had never heard there before. It was mysteriously touching, and at the same time it was strangely steadying. Faith felt a sudden return of composure.

"You must not talk to me about—forgiveness, Rudolf," she said. "If we were to talk about that—there is much that I should have to ask you to forgive me."

"I do not believe there is anything," he said calmly. "Anything for which I am not to blame—directly or indirectly. You were very young when we were married. I was older, and I should have insisted that we should wait until you were more sure of your mind. For you were not in love with me—you imagined you were, but you were not. And I was very precipitate—very violent. I shocked you and—hurt you—and dominated you. If I had not done so, you might have learned to love me—instead of learning to love someone else."

"Rudolf!" she exclaimed aghast.

"Did you think I never guessed—because I never spoke of it? *Liebe* Faith, I have always known of your love for another man—and of your loyalty to me. Always known and always grieved. But again, I might have taught you to love me after all, if I had not shut myself away from you—if I had not been proud and resentful and bitter—if I had not made you feel that I did not love you—that all I cared for was the career to which I have given the intensive devotion I should have given to you."

"Rudolf, Rudolf, why didn't you say all this to me long ago?"

"God knows," he said gravely. "Perhaps because this is something I can understand—and so often I have not understood. Perhaps because I never could have said it—except in a moment such as this. But I hope you will remember, Faith, that I have said it now."

He turned away from her, obviously striving for composure. Moved as she was, she did not dare intrude upon his struggle for self-control. When at last he spoke to her again, it was in a voice which he was evidently determined to keep calm.

"I am sure you will be very sorry to hear," he said, "that I have had bad news while you have been away. My mother's cousin, the Archduke Francis Ferdinand, and his wife, were shot yesterday in Sarajevo by a Servian fanatic. It is very tragic. Of course the entire family has been plunged into mourning."

"Oh, Rudolf, how terrible! How terrible! Would—would it be any comfort to *Tante* Luise, do you think, if I should go to her?"

For a moment he did not answer, but stood, picking up one after the other, the papers that lay on his desk, and then putting them down again.

"When you spoke to me about going away, a few moments ago," he said at length, "did you have any definite plan—any thought of where you would like to go?"

"Yes. I want desperately to go home. Just for a little while, Rudolf, until I can—until I am——"

"Until you feel better," he said soothingly. "I understand, *liebe* Faith. I know you have wanted for a long time—to go home, and I have been wrong in thwarting this yearning of yours. Certainly, I shall not thwart it now, and I am sure my mother would not wish you to change your plans on her account. After all, Francis' death is a—a Hapsburg family matter, which does not concern you intimately. I know my mother would urge you, as I do, to—to go to America at once. As soon as you can secure passage."

"I have secured passage. On the *Frederick VIII*. It is sailing at midnight," she said breathlessly.

"At midnight! And it is past seven now!"

He looked toward the bronze clock on the mantel, and for a moment its loud relentless ticking was the only sound in the room. Then he spoke very gravely.

"That will not give you much time to get ready."

"But I am nearly ready now. There are only my own trunks to finish. Hilda had all her own clothes together before I came in here, and Hans Christian's——"

"Hans Christian!"

The paper which Rudolf was still holding suddenly fluttered from his hands. He bent over and picked it up.

"I had forgotten," he said slowly, "that you would be taking Hans Christian with you. But naturally—you would. Hans Christian and Hilda. Of course—that would be best."

"You—you will not be too lonely, will you, Rudolf, without Hans Christian until we come back? You never see very much of him really. And you will always have your work."

He laid down the dispatch upon a pile of other documents, straightening them all as he did so, before he answered her.

"No, I shall not be too lonely. As you say, I shall have my work. I think it may take me to Germany before the summer is over—perhaps even to France. It would be very selfish of me to suggest that Hans Christian should stay here—he will be much happier with you."

Suddenly Rudolf looked toward Faith with a smile that was wholly strange to her.

"I have always been glad," he said, "that we named Hans Christian for his two grandfathers—for your father, Faith, as well as mine. Both have been men of a great tradition. When he grows older he can choose —which tradition he prefers to follow, and by which of their names he would rather be known. It is not impossible that he would like to use your surname also, as many Germans use their mother's names. Hans von Hohenlohe or Christian Marlowe—it will not matter which! Both are noble!"

He came over and put his arm around her shoulder.

"That is another thing I want you to remember," he said. "If I should not happen—to be with you, and Hansel is confronted with a choice, do not forget that I should be proud to have him bear your father's name and yours."

"I will not forget. But of course, Rudolf, we would all make decisions as important as that together!"

"Of course," he answered reassuringly. Then, as if something of significance had occurred to him, he asked, "Did you not tell me, *liebe* Faith, that Sam was going to America this summer? To take Mrs. Atkinson to Salem? Perhaps you could persuade her to stay with you at your old home instead—she loves you dearly and it is a long time since she has seen much of you. And Sam——"

He paused and smiled again.

"I am very much ashamed when I recall how much I used to resent your association with Sam," he remarked. "All jealousy is ignoble of course. But this was especially despicable. Sam is not only a great artist, *liebe* Faith, he is a great man. If you had married him, he would have shown himself far more deserving of you than I have been."

"Oh, no!" she exclaimed, moved almost past endurance. "Rudolf, you must not say such things!"

"I will not say them if they give you pain. But I may say, may I not, that I am thankful to know that you can count on Sam's devotions whatever happens? And that I hope some day—in some way—it may be rewarded?" He laid down the last of the dispatches he had been arranging, and put his arm around her again. "If you are willing, *liebe* Faith, let us go now and have something to eat and drink," he said, "before we make ready to go to the pier. I have had a busy day, a—a rather hard one, and I know you have too. We will feel better, both of us, when we have broken bread and tasted wine. And we must drink together—to The Day!"

"To the day? What day?"

Rudolf lifted his head. His face, Faith saw, was illumined by a radiant light. There was about him that same magnificence which had so dazzled her when she had first seen him in Venice, and which she had not beheld for years. But now there was an enraptured transfiguration as well. She caught her breath as she waited for him to answer.

"The Day of Glory!" he answered. "The Fatherland's and yours—and mine—and Hans Christian's!"

PART VII

Caleb Hawks

CHAPTER 32

THE return of Senator Marlowe's daughter to her native village was the cause of unbounded excitement in Hamstead.

This excitement began long before her actual appearance. A radiogram arrived for Ephraim Marlowe, and Sol Daniels, the depot master, who had never before taken such a message on the ticker, locked up the station at once, and walked over to the Marlowe farm with the scrawled sheet in his horny hand.

It was generally considered that Ephraim Marlowe had "married beneath him"; and with the passing years the aura of Marlowe glory which once surrounded him had grown more and more dim, as he sank comfortably to the social level from which Emmeline, his kindly but unlettered wife, had never risen. Sol found the elderly couple, who were growing feeble, and consequently "took things as easy as they could," in spite of their "ample means," eating their dinner of fried pork, boiled potatoes, fresh asparagus and strawberry shortcake in the kitchen; and he leaned back against the door leading into the shed to watch the effect which the startling news of which he was the conveyor would have upon them.

"I can't just make out your writing, Sol," Ephraim said, screwing up his eyes. "I recall way back when we was in the sixth grade together, 'twas the worst in the class. Let's see.—'Arriving New York *Frederick VIII* Danish American Line, July 10, accompanied by son and maid. Stop. Please wire me Waldorf-Astoria whether convenient for us to stay with you while getting my house ready for long stay. Stop. Love, Faith.' Land of Goshen, Sol! It's from my niece!"

"Looks that way," agreed Sol noncommittally.

"I'm expecting my second cousin Mem Wilkins and his wife up from Lynn next week," Emmeline Marlowe said anxiously. "It's his annual vacation from the shoe factory. I don't see how I could have any more company just now—not but what I'd hate to turn your own niece from the door, Ephraim, but I haven't housecleaned the north chambers this spring, and I don't feel equal to doing it in this weather. There isn't any other place I could put her and her little boy and her hired girl. Like as not this girl's a foreigner too!"

She lowered a piece of shortcake to the plate from which she had just lifted the last stalk of asparagus to her mouth, but she did not attack it with any real relish. It was evident that she was deeply troubled.

"Emmeline's been having a lot of sick spells lately," Ephraim said in an explanatory voice to Sol. "We don't rightly know what ails her. We've been kind of biding our time 'til David got home to find out, instead of sending for a strange doctor. But land! It looks as if he was never coming. Now if he and Jacqueline was only at the Big House, they'd take Faith and her family in."

"Maybe Sylvia Gray c'd think what to do," said Sol, trying to be resourceful in an emergency. "She ain't never at a loss. I c'd take this—this telegram over to the Gray Farm and ask her. I'd just as leave."

"Sylvia Gray's just had another baby, and her first ain't more'n a year old," said Emmeline, still anxiously.

"Well, I guess I know that same's anyone," retorted Sol, stung by the unjust inference that he was not aware of everything that was going on in the neighborhood. "But she kinda takes babies in her stride, as you might say. And she always has plenty of help. I can't think of no one else, seeing as the Big House is closed. Mary Manning's willin', but she's got her hands full. And the other Mannings never find it convenient to have company. No criticism to you, Emmeline. They're fixed different."

"I know," said Emmeline. The anxiety in her voice was deeper than ever, and she had not eaten more than one or two mouthfuls of her shortcake. "It's a cryin' shame there ain't a hotel in Hamstead. Some public-spirited citizen ought to put one up. I guess you can't do better, Sol, than to go over to Sylvia's and tell her what's upon us. If she can't help out, I'll get into those north rooms the first thing in the mornin'."

But Sylvia Gray, who had lived in New York most of her life, was not in the least disturbed by the radiogram. She had been a young widow with a tragic past behind her when she had come to Hamstead for refuge, and found love there as well. Seldom as she left the country nowadays, she had never cut herself off either from contacts from the city which had been her birthplace or with the world at large; and she received Sol's tidings with genuine enthusiasm.

"Faith Marlowe—the Baroness von Hohenlohe!" she exclaimed. "Coming to Hamstead! Isn't that wonderful, Sol? You know I've never seen her—why, I don't believe she's been here in nearly twenty years, not since she was a very little girl—I must ask Austin.—You know she's been the inspiration of all Samuel Dudley's wonderful pictures.—I suppose he's the most famous living American painter now."

"Mebbe," said Sol, who had never heard of Samuel Dudley, and who had a poor opinion of artists, but who was nevertheless relieved, since he judged, and correctly, by the tone of Sylvia's voice, that the complications arising from Faith Marlowe's impending arrival were to be smoothed out.

"The tenth of July!" Sylvia went on. "Why, Sol, that is day after to-morrow! I'll send my Nora over to the Christian Marlowe house right away, if Uncle Ephraim will give me the keys, and I believe we can have it almost ready for her by the time she gets here, though naturally Austin and I will want her to stay with us while she's getting settled. I'll write out two telegrams for her, shall I, one signed with Aunt Emmeline's name and one with mine? Then you can get them off right away, and they'll be waiting for her at the Waldorf when she gets there. And Sol, I know someone else who would like to know about this—Mr. Caleb Hawks, the Mayor of Hinsboro, who was such a friend of Senator Marlowe. I'll telephone him and tell him the Baroness is coming. It wouldn't surprise me if he went on to meet her!"

By evening there was not a family in Hamstead which had not heard that Senator Marlowe's daughter was coming back there. Her expected arrival was the sole topic of conversation at every supper table. And Mrs. Elliot, the most indefatigable conversationalist of the village, voiced a general sentiment about her in her comments to her taciturn husband.

"I tell you, Joe, I can't pronounce that heathenish-sounding foreign name of hers and don't propose to try," she said with spirit. "I called her Faith when she was a baby, and I aim to call her Faith now. If she don't like it, she can lump it. She was a queer young 'un, mostly hair and eyes, and giving you a turn now and again, she'd say such peculiar things. Her mother wa'nt no better than she might have been, if you ask me."

"I didn't ask ye. I ain't got no need to," muttered Joe, who felt fully competent to recognize a light woman when he saw one.

"She turned up her nose at Hamstead," went on Mrs. Elliot, wholly undaunted. "Just as if Hamstead didn't turn up its nose good and plenty at *her!* It always seemed to me there was somethin' real strange about the way she died—we never heard no details, but it was awful sudden. And her father had about as much backbone as a jellyfish. He didn't put on airs—I'll say that for him. But, land! What did he have airs to put on about, come right down to it? I've heard tell that the United States Senate is 'the greatest legislative body in the world' whatever that may be. But it don't make me tremble none, and everybody knew Chris Marlowe never would have got into it nohow, if it hadn't been for his father. And he *was* high and mighty! He wasn't any too pleased when his own son, Ephraim, wanted to settle down and stay in Hamstead, same as the rest of us. And I bet you'll find Faith Marlowe's high and mighty too. Probably she wears a crown regular, and a red velvet dress trimmed with ermine. I understand that's the usual court cos*tume* in Europe. I shall go straight over to Sylvia's the moment Faith gets here and see for myself. But I ain't prepared to be a mite surprised."

Contrary to her expectations, Mrs. Elliot was very much surprised when she saw Faith. This was not so soon as she had expected, however. The German Consul-General had met Faith at the pier, having received a cable from Rudolf, advising him when she would arrive. He and his wife had insisted that she should stay with them in New York, instead of the Waldorf-Astoria, and had almost overwhelmed her with Teutonic hospitality. Mr. Caleb Hawks had also met her; and he in his turn had been insistent: she must, he told her with an emphasis which precluded argument, come and spend a few days at his house in Hinsboro. The latchstring was out and the spare-room bed was all made up, just as he had told her they would be. His housekeeper, Mrs. Mead, had made her currant jelly a whole week ahead of time in order to be free for the Marlowe visit; and she had her heart set on seeing what a Baroness looked like. Besides, Mrs. Neal Conrad—that nice young woman whose husband had been such a help on the City Council before he entered the State Legislature—was about to entertain the Fortnightly Bridge Club and she was counting on having Faith as her guest of honor. Mr. Hawks had practically promised. He knew Faith was anxious to get into her own house, and it was being made ready for her as fast as it could be. But it *had* been closed a long time, and there were a great many things to do to it. They could motor over to Hamstead every day if she liked; but as far as headquarters were concerned—well, she must make those with Mr. Hawks.

Faith acquiesced almost apathetically. She was eager to be at peace in her own house—if indeed peace were to be found anywhere. But she did not feel equal to arguing about the details of getting settled or even to deciding for herself where she should stay temporarily. She permitted herself to be installed in Mr. Hawks' spare room; and she went docilely to the bridge party the day after her arrival in Hinsboro. But she looked so pale and listless as she came up the front walk after this was over, that Mr. Hawks, who was sitting on his porch in his shirt-sleeves waiting for her, felt distressed.

"Didn't you have a good time at Anne's party?" he asked anxiously, feeling sure that something must be wrong, and yet unable to guess what this could be.

"Oh, yes. Everyone was very kind and cordial. And Mrs. Conrad is charming," said Faith. But she spoke without real enthusiasm, though she added with more interest, "Why doesn't her husband take her with him to Belford? I should think she would be an immense success there and a great help to him."

"Well, likely he may, some time. But it's cheaper for him, living the way he does in a single room at the Talmage Tavern than if he took his family along—there are two cute kids, Nancy and Junior too. Maybe you didn't see them."

"Oh, yes I did, and they are beautiful children. The little boy—*why* do they call him 'Junior'?—is the same one who came over this morning and asked Hansel to play baseball with him and his 'gang'; and he and his sister Nancy both helped pass salad and cake and sandwiches and candy and coffee and about a dozen other things. Why didn't you warn me, Uncle Caleb, that there would be a hearty meal served at half-past four in the afternoon, instead of tea? And that the women would all take their hats off? And that they would get up and mill around the room every time they finished playing four hands—they called it 'progressing,' but I never saw anything less like progress! And that no one played for money, or even breathed of such a thing—I asked what the stakes were, and you should have seen the look I was given! But I won first prize—'two darling little guest towels.' I shouldn't have known what they were if the lady sitting next to me hadn't gushed over them!"

She sat down beside him on the steps, leaning wearily back against the railing, and clasping her hands over one knee. Caleb could see that there were dark circles under her eyes.

"I guess you hadn't better go to no more parties until you get rested up a mite," he said solicitously. "Everyone is so crazy to meet you, and that's a fact, that I give in when Anne pestered me. But I see I done wrong to urge you and not to tell you more about how it would be—not that I know much about these women's affairs myself."

"Don't men and women ever go out together?"

"Well, yes, some—nights. But day times of course the men folks are busy, and naturally their tastes ain't the same as their wives' anyhow."

He thought he saw Faith wince, and the impression troubled him deeply. He wondered if anyone at the party had unintentionally hurt her feelings; but her next question had nothing to do with the meeting of the Fortnightly Bridge Club.

"Is there any special news? I haven't seen a paper all day."

"Why yes. The Democrats are aimin' to thrust Shaw down the throats of the American people again—there's a long piece about it here on the front page. But the voters won't never swallow him for another four years. Cotton's gone up two points—the market's kinda unstiddy. And there's a drought in Kansas—looks as if the wheat crop might be damaged. Here in Hinsboro the Marblecutters' Union is threatening to strike, and my friend Sebastian Perez, who lives across the street, is one of the ringleaders——"

"I meant, any foreign news. I couldn't help feeling, when I left Europe, that there might be—disturbances."

"Because that Duke, or whatever he was, got shot? Shucks, I wouldn't worry none about that!"

Again he saw Faith wince; but this time she did not answer him at all, and after a moment he went on, in an eager effort to say something that would please her, "Do you want we should get started for Hamstead in good season, Faith? We can have breakfast at six instead of seven, just as well as not, if you say so."

"I think seven will be early enough," she answered with a faint smile. "But I hate to trouble you to take me back and forth."

"Gosh, Faith, it ain't no trouble! It's a pleasure to have you here, and that's a fact. If I should get tied up at City Hall or the factory any time, I c'd send the hired man with you. He drives the otter real smooth and easy, though you wouldn't think it to look at him."

Involuntarily, Faith smiled again. Mr. Hawks' hired man, whose name was Silas Sims, had given her the impression of being mostly Adam's apple, red flannel undershirt, and chewing tobacco. It was difficult for her to visualize him in the rôle of chauffeur, though he had been so kind to Hansel, who had tagged at his heels most of the day, that her heart was touched.

"I have been wondering," she said hesitatingly, "whether I couldn't buy an inexpensive automobile, and learn to run it myself. I've seen a number of women driving in Hinsboro. If I had a car of my own—I—I could get out in the hills alone once in a while."

"Why yes," agreed Mr. Hawks heartily. "I don't know about hills and such, but you could slip back and forth between Hamstead and Hinsboro in two shakes of a dead lamb's tail, and that 'ud be pleasant for ye. It's kinda quiet in Hamstead, Faith, and I look to see you find it sorta dull. I think a car 'ud be a real nice thing for you to have. I'll call up my friend Will Emery, that's agent here for several makes, and trades in second-hands too, and see what he's got to offer. About what was you thinking of paying?"

The deal was settled that very night. Before supper was over, Mr. Emery and his two sons, all driving different kinds of cars, were parked on Mr. Hawks' front lawn between the stone deer and the geranium urns; and the evening was spent in making trial trips around Hinsboro and its environs. Faith eventually decided on a neat little five-passenger Dodge, which had been used as a "demonstration car" and was consequently a great bargain; and as something did "come up" at the factory, it was agreed that Mr. Emery should accompany Faith to Hamstead the next morning, and thus begin the driving lessons without delay.

She "caught on," he told her, very quickly; and she found a real exhilaration in the new experience. Before she reached Hamstead she was feeling almost happy, for the first time since she could remember. The countryside through which she passed, fertile and verdant, the mountains rising steadfastly in the distance, the quiet river winding its undisturbed course through the meadows which sloped down toward it—all these gave her a sense of fulfillment and peace. And the sight of her own house, smaller, more weather-beaten, and more isolated than she remembered it, nevertheless stirred her to sudden joy. There was smoke curling up from the chimney and the front door stood wide open; and as she leaped out of the car, and ran up the cobblestone walk, a tall slender young woman came forward to meet her with a charming smile.

"Welcome home!" she said cordially. "I'm Sylvia Gray, one of your neighbors—I do hope we are going to see a great deal of each other. Your Aunt Emmeline is rather busy with company, so she couldn't come over here, but she hopes you'll drop in to see her later in the day. My husband and I are counting on you to have dinner with us—by the way, dinner in Hamstead is at twelve! We hoped you'd stay with us while you were getting settled, but we realized that Mr. Hawks had a prior claim. Shall we go in and see how my family treasure, Nora, has been getting along? She and I have been working here together."

It was evident that between them, Sylvia Gray and Nora had done wonders. The house smelled of scrubbing and scouring, the windows shone, the carpets and mattresses were hanging on a line where a long lanky man was vigorously beating them. But Faith's first sensation, as she walked from room to room, was one of acute disappointment. She had not realized that Flossie had set her mark so unmistakably on the place. The wallpapers were garish; the old paneling had been painted in all sorts of fantastic colors; the fireplaces had been closed up, and gilded coal scuttles and bunches of dried grass protruding from hand-painted jars, stood before them. There were embroidered sofa cushions, chenille hangings, "whatnots" and "knickknacks" everywhere, a clutter of oak and wicker furniture, a scattering of highly colored, sentimental pictures. Sylvia, watching Faith's expression as she finally sat down without comment on the "parlor couch," spoke impetuously.

"I didn't dare make any changes before you came. But I felt certain you'd wish to. I suppose you know that the barn and attic are crammed full of your grandmother's possessions that your mother stored away when she 'modernized' the house."

"No, I didn't know," said Faith slowly. "I'm very glad they weren't—

destroyed. It would mean a great deal to me to—to live surrounded by them."

"I was sure you'd feel that way!" Sylvia exclaimed. "Would you care to have me go with you to see our local paper-hanger and carpenter and plumber? I'd be delighted to serve as a liaison officer! Only first I must rush home and feed my baby—won't you come with me—and meet the rest of the Grays before you go any further?"

It was just after the various calls which Sylvia suggested had been satisfactorily completed that Mrs. Elliot decided to make her first visit to Faith, who was by this time in the attic taking account of stock. Nora was in the back yard, helping the long lanky man, whose name proved to be Perley Stubbs, with the carpets and blankets, when a rap on the knocker reverberated through the silent rooms. And as her first attempt elicited no response, Mrs. Elliot redoubled her efforts with such deafening results that Faith dropped the footboard of a spool-bed which she was examining and rushed down the stairs to the front door herself.

By the time she reached it she was breathless with haste and exertion. She had tied a cheesecloth duster, capwise, securely over her hair, which was so abundant that any violent exercise was likely to loosen its heavy coils; and it was entirely concealed; while the white silk sports suit, immaculate when she had left Hinsboro that morning, was now covered with a liberal layer of the dust and cobwebs which for twenty years had lain undisturbed in the attic. Mrs. Elliot gazed at the disheveled figure before her with disapproving astonishment; and Faith's unembarrassed greeting, though cordial of intent, was not soothing in its effect.

"Good afternoon," she said pleasantly. "Were you looking for Nora? She is in the back yard."

"Looking for Nora!" snorted Mrs. Elliot with indignation. "I guess I've got better ways of passing the time of day than hunting up hired help! I was looking for—for the Bar—for her as was Faith Marlowe. If you're that German girl she's brung with her, you better go and tell her this minute that Mrs. Elliot's calling."

"Oh! I am so sorry! I am the Baroness von Hohenlohe. Won't you come in?"

"You could'da knocked me over with a feather," Mrs. Elliot said to her husband at suppertime. "She warn't any more embarrassed at being caught looking as if a cyclone had struck her than if she'd been sittin' in the front parlor doin' tattin'! An' even if she'd been clean, there warn't nothin' remarkable about her clothes—many's the time I've seen a heap handsomer right in the front of Mr. Goldenburg's store in Wallacetown. No trimmin' at all. It's queer, though. She has a sort of way with 'er, come to see her close to. And she ain't bad lookin'. Nor stuck up. I was wrong there, Joe. 'Don't forget, Mrs. Elliot,' she says when I told her good-bye, 'that the next time you come over we'll have tea together! I'm so sorry there isn't any in the house yet!' She's aimin' to move in just as soon as she can, though she's goin' to have the place all tore up. I thought myself the house was sweet pretty, the way Flossie had it fixed; but Faith's got different ideas, and of course a woman feels to do what she wants with her own house. Anyways, I shouldn't be a mite surprised if we liked her in Hamstead after all."

CHAPTER 33

By the time Faith was settled in her own house, most of Hamstead, and a good deal of Hinsboro were inclined to agree with Mrs. Elliot.

As she turned the Dodge triumphantly back into Caleb Hawks' front yard for the first time, she was conscious of a tall dark man standing before the house across the street, who was regarding her fixedly. Something about his carriage and expression arrested her; and as she covertly returned his glance, she could not suppress a startled exclamation.

"You're doing fine," said Mr. Emery encouragingly. "Just take her out of gear and put on the brake. Then shut off the engine."

Faith did not correct his impression that she had been momentarily perplexed by the mechanism of her car. But when he had taken his contented departure, she linked her arm through Caleb's and drew him down the walk with her.

"Yes, everything is going splendidly," she said in answer to his solicitous look. "I'll tell you all about it at supper. . . . Is that your friend Sebastian Perez standing over there? I want to meet him."

"Well, look here, Faith," said Caleb under his breath, vainly endeavoring to stay their progress, "it's like this: me and Sebastian's been good friends for years, but now that he's leadin' this marblecutters' strike I told you about, it makes things kinda awkward, seein' as I'm the Mayor."

"It isn't going to be awkward," she said insistently. "If you'd rather not go with me, I'll go by myself. But I want to speak to him. He looks unhappy to me. Perhaps if he could find some outlet for whatever is troubling him, he wouldn't be so hard to deal with."

Her grave and courteous, "*Buenas tardes,*" had been pronounced before Caleb could collect himself to meet the situation into which he had been thrust. For a puzzled moment he stood silently on the sidewalk while Faith and Sebastian Perez apparently exchanged compliments. Then Caleb was conscious that the slight tension which at first had pervaded the air was beginning to pass. The Spaniard's serious face relaxed into a smile and he motioned toward the piazza. Faith turned reassuringly to Caleb.

"*Señor* Perez wants us to come up and have a glass of sherry with his mother and himself," she said. "That would be pleasant, wouldn't it? A glass of sherry before dinner is always so refreshing. His mother does not speak much English, he says. But of course she and I can talk together while you and he do."

It was nearly an hour later before Mrs. Mead, whose anxiety over the condition of her waiting supper was beginning to mount to a frenzy, and who was watching the course of events with a distracted eye from her kitchen window, saw Mr. Hawks and his guest begin a series of elaborate leave-takings from the marblecutter and his mother. Hansel had joined them and had been eating with avidity something offered him on a small silver dish, while the rest of the group sipped a shining liquid from tiny glasses that were filled and refilled. Mrs. Mead felt sure that whatever the substance was which Hansel was devouring, it would "spoil his supper"; but he sounded so happy about it as he finally came rushing back into the house, that her wounded feelings were almost immediately assuaged.

"It was nice to have *mazapan* again, wasn't it, mother?" he was saying enthusiastically. "I haven't had any in a long time. I like *Señora* Perez and her son very much, don't you? It is funny the son's name should be Sebastian, because he looks a little like our Sebastian, and *Señora* Perez comes from Granada too."

"Yes, dear. It is funny. And I do like *Señora* Perez and her son very much.—Have you washed your hands for supper?"

In spite of Mrs. Mead's anxiety, the "evening meal" did her great credit, and the strange sticky candy which the Perez had given Hansel, and which he continued to devour, had not spoiled his supper after all. He did full justice to it. Besides, she could not remember when she had seen Mr. Hawks look so happy as he did now.

"I don't believe there's goin' to be a strike after all," he was saying in a voice of astonishment and pleasure. "From what Sebastian said to me just as we wuz leavin', I gathered he wuz goin' to say a few words at the Union Meetin' this evenin' that 'ud call the whole thing off. It beats me, Faith, to know how you cud o' smoothed things out the way you did, just settin' on the front porch drinkin' sherry and talkin' to that poor little old lady. As far as I know, she ain't asked any American to her house before. Fact is, 'cept to go to church regular, and to work in her garding, she hardly stirs out at all. Spaniards is sort o' sober most of the time, I've noticed—they ain't forever lettin' off spirits and steam, like the Eye-talians. But *Señora* Perez is soberer than most. She's sad lookin'. She acts to me like a person with some kind o' secret that's troublin' her."

"Yes," agreed Faith rather thoughtfully, "she does. But she isn't very old, Uncle Caleb—that is, not much over forty. I think you're wrong there."

"Sebastian can talk the King's English, same as I do," went on Caleb. He wondered, fleetingly, why Faith seemed interested in the subject of *Señora* Perez' age. Then he dismissed it as unimportant. "But I could see how it pleased him to talk Spanish to you. He's got a heap o' friends here—that's how he comes to have so much influence; but even among furriners he don't take his mother around much. I guess she ain't wanted to go. But she cottoned up to you like you wuz a long-lost daughter. I never seen her smile before—for the most part she looks like them grievin' dark-complected women mourners in the pictures I wuz druv into lookin' at in the Spanish art galleries. But she sure smiled at you, and say, she looks like a different woman when she does, don't she? All that tickled Sebastian most to pieces—that she liked you and that you liked her, I mean—well, I guess you've turned the trick for me, and no mistake. I see in Granada you had a way with you. But I wouldn't a guessed you worked so fast."

"I do really hope I've been helpful," Faith said earnestly. "But don't give me too much credit—probably the trouble wasn't serious anyway. And I was delighted to meet the Perez—the *Señora does* look like one of El Greco's or Ribera's Mater Dolorosas. How observing you are, Uncle Caleb! And—and her son reminds me of someone too."

"You mean that smooth, good-lookin' brother of the Bishop's? Well say, Faith, I've kept thinkin' of it too! It can't be imagination if you thought of it straight off, same as I did!"

Caleb paused to pour some tea into his saucer and began to drink it down with a relish that was slightly impaired because he thought he saw Faith wince. But after a moment she went on speaking so calmly that he decided he had been mistaken.

"I told Sebastian Perez that when I am settled in Hamstead, I shall expect him to bring his mother over to have dinner with me," she said. "It seems good to me to talk about Granada, about the snow on the Sierras, and the wind blowing over the *vega,* and the gypsies on the Sacro Monte, and the *antiquarios*——"

Her voice trailed away, a little brokenly. But she smiled and recovered herself quickly.

"Speaking of dinner guests," she said, "I have been wondering if you wouldn't like to do a little entertaining while I am here? I know it is hard sometimes for bachelors and widowers to manage without a hostess. Yet of course all men who are in public life, as you are, realize that it is important, as well as pleasant, to bring congenial groups together. That was one of the first things Rudolf taught me after we were married." She hesitated, and Caleb thought that her lips were quivering; but after a moment she went on again, more gaily, "I think it would be delightful, for instance, to ask the Conrads here, don't you? And several of the ladies who were at the bridge party told me that their husbands were on the City Council. We might ask them to dinner too —the husbands and wives together I mean. Hilda could wait on table, but Mrs. Mead is such a wonderful cook that we ought to take advantage of her talents!"

Mrs. Mead, who, just at that juncture, was bearing in a steamed blueberry pudding on a yellow platter, felt a glow of gratification permeate her being as Faith looked at her. She was a wizened, wiry little woman, with a grim mouth and a small upstanding nose which sometimes quivered unexpectedly, like a rabbit's. It was generally thought in Hinsboro that she was a Tartar, and that the redoubtable Caleb himself trembled before her. But Faith had not trembled before her. She had enslaved her.

"Well now, I don't know but what it would be a good idea," Caleb agreed, covertly watching Mrs. Mead's reaction to this suggestion, "though I never give it much thought before. My wife wuz kind o' like your Aunt Emmeline: she took company hard, and that's a fact. She had to start in the attic and clean right through to the cellar, even if 'twas only a member of the family or the minister comin' in for Sunday dinner. And afterwards she wuz all tuckered out. And Myra took after her ma. So I got out of the way of askin' anyone in. But Mrs. Mead says Hilda's wonderful help. So mebbe between the two of 'em, they cud manage. Yes, I guess mebbe they cud. But *you* look pretty peaked to me, Faith, and I don't want you should get all wore out with company on top o' movin'."

"It won't wear me out. It will be a pleasure."

He realized that she was telling the truth; indeed, he dimly divined, that in spite of her evident weariness and anxiety, she was eager to be constantly and actively occupied. And the first little dinner having proved a great success in every way, he himself suggested that others should be given; and by the time Faith left Mr. Hawks' house for her own, she had established a foothold of friendliness in the little city of her temporary sojourn. This foothold, however, was by no means based exclusively on her startling innovation of "entertaining at dinner"; she had also made a pleasing impression sitting beside Mr. Hawks in his prominent pew at the First Congregational Church, and an equally pleasing impression at the early Mass which she had impartially attended with Sebastian Perez and his mother. She had gone to the annual outing of the Persian Panthers and the annual entertainment of the Order of the Oriental Caribou. She had visited the pencil factory and the marble works, where she had caused a stir of real excitement among the employees, by talking naturally and fluently with them in alternating Spanish, Italian, and French. And she had also visited the day nursery which Mr. Hawks had built in memory of his wife, where her coming, accompanied by a shower of small gifts, had seemed like the apparition of a fairy godmother. When her little car was loaded for the last time with the miscellaneous objects which she was taking with her to Hamstead, and she was about to step into it herself, she found that Mr. Hawks' yard seemed suddenly swarming with the well-wishers who had come to bid her good-bye. Every rung of Hinsboro's social ladder was represented, from Neal Conrad's haughty and exclusive parents to Sebastian's "helper" at the marble works, Angelico Mendoza, who was accompanied by his wife and six children, the eldest of whom was eight years old; and the shouts and cheers which followed her as she swung past the stone deer and out into the street resounded long after she had vanished down the road leading to open country.

. . . . .

Meanwhile, the progress she had been making in Hamstead, though less spectacular, had been quite as steady. From the beginning, Sylvia and Austin Gray had recognized her as a kindred spirit; and where the Grays led, the rest of Hamstead always followed. The Mannings, the Westons, the Griffins, and the Taylors, had all called almost as promptly as Mrs. Elliot. Aunt Emmeline and Uncle Ephraim had both "worried considerable" less she should be "put out" with them because of their apparent inhospitality; but she had dwelt so tactfully on her pleasure at the opportunity of visiting Caleb Hawks, that their relief was great; and their hearts warmed at the genuine affection of her manner, even before she made a suggestion which caused them to gasp by its prodigality.

"I thought at first I might try to move into my house right away," she said. "Sylvia Gray's done such wonders with it that if I hadn't decided to make certain changes in it there wouldn't be any reason why I shouldn't. But Uncle Caleb has urged me to stay with him for a fortnight at least, and I enjoy motoring back and forth—it's a delightful new experience for me, driving a car, and the country is so beautiful at this time of year! So I'll commute for the present, until I have two or three rooms in order at least. I'm going to have them all repapered and repainted, and use my grandmother's furniture instead of my mother's, and I think it would be easier if everything I don't want were taken out of the house first of all. Don't you? Then I could start in from the beginning."

"You don't mean to say you aren't going to use any of them handsome brass beds and oak sets and elegant hangings, Faith!"

"I—thought I wouldn't. I really think there's enough furniture stored in the attic and barn to make the house look almost the way it did when it was first built. So I thought I'd give away everything that is in it now."

"Give it away!" exclaimed Emmeline and Ephraim in one breath.

"Yes. Perley Stubbs is going to find someone to help him and load everything into hay wagons early to-morrow morning. But I thought you could advise me what to do with it. There must be some needy families, right here in Hamstead, who would be glad of it. Of course if there aren't, I know there are lots of people in Hinsboro——"

Again Emmeline and Ephraim spoke simultaneously. There were indeed several families in Hamstead who would regard the gift of substantial and stylish furniture in the light of manna falling from heaven. Faith's aunt and uncle did not word their answer just that way; but Faith knew this was what they meant; and before dark the following evening she watched the last creaking, top-heavy hay wagon, laden with tinsel and trash, heave its way slowly out of sight.

She gave a deep sigh of overwhelming relief. The house was bare and empty; but she felt as if it had been thoroughly cleansed of Flossie and all that she had represented. Faith put her arm around Hansel's shoulder, and paused for a moment beside him on the wide granite doorstep in front of the disused south entrance, talking over her plans with him quite as seriously as if he had been a contemporary.

"This was the front door when the house was first built, Hansel," she said. "I think it would be pleasant to use it that way again, don't you? With a driveway curving up to it, and a garden stretching out in front of it toward Uncle Ephraim's house—that ugly old barn looming up belongs to you and me, so we can have it torn down, and build a new one in the back where it won't show. Then there'll be nothing but lovely lawns and trees and flowers between the two Marlowe places. The room on the right of the front door will be our library, facing the river and mountains, and the room back of it, the dining room, instead of the kitchen as it is now—when that huge fireplace and brick oven are unstopped, it will be charming."

"And will this be our drawing-room, on the left of the front door?"

"Yes, darling. Only here they call it a parlor. We'll have it very glistening, don't you think so? With all that paneling painted white and brasses shining in the fireplace, and beautiful old pictures in gold frames and polished mahogany furniture. Then back of the parlor, on the other side of the little passage, will be the kitchen."

"And upstairs, mother?"

"Well, upstairs, the large room over the library will be mine, with a big four-poster bed and flowered chintz hangings; and the one leading out of it will be yours. The other large front room will be our guest chamber, and back of it, Hilda's. And the two small rear bedrooms I thought we would make into bathrooms. That will give us all the space we need for now. But later on we could finish off part of the attic if we wanted to."

"Oh, mother, it will all be lovely! I like this little house! Do you think we can stay here a long time?"

"I think so, my precious treasure. I—I hope so."

"Only of course it isn't so nice for father to have us away as it is for us to be here. So perhaps we ought not to stay too long. We mustn't forget about father."

"No, darling, we mustn't forget about father. But he knew he was going to be very busy this summer, and he thought it was really best that we should come away. You know he told us so, when he said good-bye to us on the boat."

"I know he did, mother, but I didn't think he looked very happy when he said it, did you?"

"Not very, dear. But saying good-bye is always a little hard. Perhaps next summer father can be here with us. Perhaps he can have a vacation."

She tried to make her voice sound calm and convincing; but she knew that she had failed, even before she saw Hansel's eyes resting anxiously on her face.

"Father was all right when he wrote to you last, wasn't he, mother?" he asked in a troubled way.

"Yes, Hansel, right as rain! Why, you know that, dear—I showed you the letter! Of course it was sad for him, going to his Cousin Francis' funeral, and he had been even busier than usual, but he is all right."

"Yes, mother, I suppose so."

She saw that she had not wholly reassured him; and to divert his thoughts, she changed the subject.

"I didn't tell you that in the same mail with father's last letter there was one from Uncle Sam too," she said. "Father had very thoughtfully written him that you and I had come here. Uncle Sam told me he felt he had better not leave France this summer after all, though he didn't tell me why. But Cousin Sarah is coming just the same—Uncle Sam is going to see her on her boat and leave her in charge of the ship's doctor and her stewardess. He hopes you and I will meet her in New York, and try to persuade her to come and visit us for a little while before she goes to Salem. She is going to sail from Havre the thirty-first. So we must hurry and have the house ready before she gets here."

Apparently, his mother's reasons for haste were manifold; she was constantly mentioning a new one. So Hansel felt gravely conscious that he should try to help her as much as he could, that he should not spend too much time with Junior Conrad and his "gang" in Hinsboro, or with Moses Manning, the seraphic-looking small boy who had immediately tempted him to join in agreeable and diversified deviltry in Hamstead. He wished that his mother would sit down quietly every evening before supper, and read him fairy stories as she had always done before. But he stifled his disappointment of the abandonment of their tranquil hour, as he had stifled his sense that all was not well with his father, hopefully assuming that in course of time life would take on a more normal aspect again.

The speed with which Faith was plunging ahead with her program of remodeling and refurnishing was startling to Hamstead; but like Hansel, the village as a whole coöperated with her unquestioningly; and the results were remarkable. By the time she moved in the worst of the chaos was over, though Hansel was to sleep in Faith's bedroom for the present, and they were to eat in the library. And as they sat down for their first simple supper in their own house, Hansel was aware that a subtle change had already come over his mother. There was a quality of quietude in her voice which he had not heard in a long time, a repose of manner which he had sorely missed, a look of contentment in the gaze with which her eyes kept wandering over their surroundings. Hansel himself felt that these were beautiful, and understood her content. The paneling in this room was of hard pine, and scraped free from the disfiguring colors which had defaced it, there was a mellowness and warmth about it which blended richly with the russet-colored volumes extending from floor to ceiling. An ancient maple secretary stood between two windows, the wide shelf dividing the drawers beneath from the cabinet above already equipped with writing materials. Over the mantel, between two tall brass candlesticks, hung an impressive portrait of the first Christian Marlowe, clad in fine broadcloth and snowy linen. Braided rugs were scattered over the wide-boarded painted floor, and a wingback chair drawn comfortably up beside the scrubbed hearth, where a cheerful fire blazed gaily above the polished andirons; and near this stood a gate-legged table, temporarily covered with a white cloth and set with sprigged china. Sylvia Gray had sent over a profusion of sweet-peas from her garden, and clear glass bowls filled with these were scattered about; while almost every dish which Hilda brought beamingly in was laden with some delicacy donated by a kindly and thoughtful neighbor: Aunt Emmeline had contributed feathery rolls, ruby-colored currant jelly, and tomato relish; Mary Manning, a chicken pie, cottage cheese, and the "makings" for a mixed salad; and Mrs. Elliot a chocolate layer cake. And when they had finished their little feast, Faith took their well-worn copy of Grimm's "Fairy Tales" from its new nook in the tall bookcase, and drawing Hansel down beside her, began to read, for the hundredth time, the story of Snow-White and Red-Rose.

A little later, she and Hansel went upstairs together. Among the treasures which the attic had yielded was a quaintly turned trundle bed of generous proportions. For the present, this was to be Hansel's;

and he and Faith pulled it into place together. By mutual consent, they decided that it was cool enough to have a fire in the bedroom too —for late July it was unseasonably, though agreeably cool. And when they had prayed, side by side, they lay down, hand in hand, and fell asleep with the soft glow from the quiet flames flickering across their faces, and the summer moonlight streaming in through the many-paned windows.

CHAPTER 34

THEY were still sleeping profoundly when Hilda came in the next morning, and set a big tray down on the four-poster. It was very late, she told the Frau Baronin; and Perley Stubbs was insistently asking whether those old beams were really to be left in the dining-room ceiling. He would have to know before he went ahead with the queer rough wallpaper; and to his way of thinking, the huge fireplace with the Dutch oven beside it was "unsightly." Faith laughed, more merrily than she had done since Hansel could remember, and said she would be "right down"; but she did not hurry over her coffee and rolls for all that. It pleased Hansel to see her sitting propped up against big pillows again, with her hair tumbling over her shoulders, while she ate her breakfast, instead of hastening downstairs early to have it with Mr. Hawks; and he was rapturously grateful to Hilda for bringing up his milk and eggs, so that he would not be separated from his mother while he breakfasted himself. Indeed, he was not separated from her all day. He stayed with her while she reassured Perley Stubbs about the dining room, which was, after all, just the way she wanted it; and when that important point had been settled, she and Hansel went out to see how the demolition of the old barn was getting along, and Faith explained to him where the rosebeds and sun dial were to be in the garden. Late in the afternoon, she actually suggested that they should leave the scene of reconstruction, since everything seemed to be going along all right, and take a ride together; so they chugged off in the cheerful little Dodge, and poked their way over back roads until the deepening shadows warned them that it was time to go home.

Again, Faith had planned to go to bed as early as Hansel; but just as they were finishing their story, the sound of the knocker reverberated through the quiet house; and before Hilda could come trudging to answer the summons, Hansel had bounded off to the door himself. The next instant Faith heard a shout of welcome from the child; and mingled with it the compelling ring of David Noble's voice.

He had arrived early that afternoon, he said, advancing toward Faith as she sprang up in her turn. Yes, Jacqueline was well, but she was a little tired, so she was resting that evening, though she would drop in the next day without fail; meanwhile he had come to give Faith her love, and to see for himself whether there was anything he could do to help her. What wonders she had accomplished already, he said, looking about him with appreciative enthusiasm. And someone had told him, he added laughing, that she was going to put a flower garden where the old barn had stood—he would never have believed that she was so practically, as well as so artistically, minded—she would not have to buy any fertilizer for years! He had also heard that she had both mercantile Hinsboro and agricultural Hamstead groveling at her feet, and that she had settled the marblecutters' strike. Yet—news traveled fast in this part of the world. But apparently she had been traveling fast herself!

He spoke almost banteringly, but Faith was conscious that his raillery had no depth; and his unpresaged appearance set her newly calmed senses quivering again. Where had he been since she had last seen him—at Radensholm—in another world? Was he the bearer of good or evil tidings—or of no tidings at all? It took a supreme effort of will for her to betray no impatience, to sit quietly smiling at his badinage, and to eventually, with apparent nonchalance, change the topic of conversation herself. She asked him to tell her about the Cottage Hospital which he and Jacqueline had built in Hamstead: would they take her to see it some day? Was he able to use it as a center for much of his own work? His versatility was amazing to her—she had already gleaned that he was regarded as the "family doctor" by everyone in the village, for whom a substitute was chosen only during his long unavoidable absences; yet in the world at large, he was recognized as one of the leading surgeons of the day.

Faith was beginning to find suspense intolerable, when Hansel, of his own accord, confessed that he was sleepy, and said that he would ask Hilda to help him roll out the trundle bed. The door had hardly closed behind him, when David assumed control of the situation.

"I knew you would be very anxious to hear everything I have to tell you," he said. "That is why I did not wait, even until to-morrow, to come to see you.—It seemed better not to try to write—better to Don Sebastian and better to me. Especially since you left Denmark so—unexpectedly, shall we say?"

He paused for a moment as if to give Faith an opportunity to speak. Then conscious of the imploring quality of the gaze she turned upon him, he went on swiftly.

"Don Sebastian was most insistent that I should tell you first of all," he said, "that he had never intended to bargain with you—to promise that if you would do one thing, he would do another. He said you would know what he meant when I told you that—of course I did not inquire. I only know that he had pledged you his word to go with me to Spain and that he kept it. According to his own code—and there are many worse—he is a very honorable gentleman."

He heard Faith give a dry and stifled sob, quickly smothered. But she continued to look at him imploringly and without speaking.

"We traveled directly through, from Copenhagen to Biarritz," David went on. "Jacqueline and a French doctor and nurse with whom I have worked before, and in whom I have a great deal of confidence, went with us. From Biarritz we motored through the Pyrenees to the Castello Viejo, which is a very splendid old stronghold—perhaps some day you would like to hear more about it. We reached there very late one night, and early the next morning I saw Doña Dolores. She was fortunately in an unusually quiet state and I was able to examine her almost immediately. Because I wished to proceed very cautiously, I continued to watch her for a time, but I was convinced from the beginning that I might take the chance of operating. After I had been at the Castello Viejo four days I did so. The operation was entirely successful."

David laid a steadying hand on Faith's trembling arm. "I stayed on at the Castello Viejo for ten days after the operation had taken place," he continued. "When I went away, I left Norchais and Sœur Celestine—the French doctor and nurse of whom I spoke—in charge. They have kept me informed of the progress of events by wire. Sœur Celestine is still there—Doña Dolores has become very much attached to her, and besides, the period of convalescence will naturally be long. But Norchais had left. That means that the Duquesa is wholly out of danger."

"And—Sebastian?"

"Of course, Don Sebastian has remained also. Doña Dolores can hardly bear to have him out of her sight, and his devotion to her is supreme. She recognized him almost as soon as she had recovered from the anæsthetic, though imperfectly—at first she was under the impression that they were young lovers, then that they were just married—as a bride she must have been passionately attached to him. But before I left she understood the situation completely. And it was very moving—very wonderful—to see her when she understood.—You have given Sebastian's heritage of glory back to him, Faith. That is a great thing for a woman to do for—for a man."

"For the man she loves, you started to say!" Faith cried. "Oh, David, why didn't you say it! You have guessed from the beginning! And Rudolf guessed too, years ago, though I never knew it until the night I went away—the night I *ran* away! It was only a miracle that saved me from—from—if I had stayed——"

"I know, Faith. But you didn't stay. Don't give way like this—it isn't worthy of you. Don't even say that I 'guessed,' that Rudolf 'guessed.' Say we understood."

He bent over her, one hand clasping hers, an arm about her shoulder. But he made no effort to check the frenzy of weeping to which she abandoned herself, realizing that the floodgates of long repression had opened at last, and that she could not be comforted until she had recovered from the overpowering storm of passion with which she was torn. At last, as her sobs became less and less intense, he spoke to her very gently.

"I know that you feel a chapter in your life is closed, Faith," he said, "a very poignant and precious chapter. Perhaps you will never turn the pages of one like it again. I am afraid you will never love another man in the sense that you have loved Don Sebastian, and—may I say it?—in the sense that he has loved you. For you have been the great love of his life, as truly as he has been yours. Never let yourself doubt that—either because of his past or because of his future. What he has felt for you is altogether alien both to trivial intrigue—and to pride of race. Can you understand that?"

"Yes. I—I have always understood that."

"Then it will be a great comfort to you. And do not forget that for every chapter which closes another always opens. I told you that you had given his heritage back to Don Sebastian. And I believe that after a long exile you are going to come into yours. Haven't you begun to be vaguely conscious of this already—reaching home? You always felt yourself a stranger in Europe—even in Spain, much as you loved it—if you hadn't, you would have accepted the *caseria* as a gift. But here you feel that you belong."

She looked up at him in surprise. He smiled and went on speaking without waiting for her to answer.

"Now that I have reminded you of this and told you everything vital there is to say about Doña Dolores," he said quietly, "I think perhaps I should prepare you for certain world conditions which are very unsettled and which may affect you."

"World conditions!" she repeated dazedly. "What do you mean by world conditions—that could affect me?"

"Have you never thought—never feared—that the murder in Sarajevo——"

"Yes!" she exclaimed. "I have! But I haven't heard anything. I've dreaded to read—I've hardly let myself think—David, what has happened?"

"Austria declared war on Servia to-day," he said with forced calm. "Russia has been mobilizing for three days already. If there is a general upheaval almost anything may happen. France and England will probably throw in their forces with her."

"Throw in their forces with her! Against whom?"

"Against Austria—and—and possibly Germany, Faith."

This time she cried aloud. He saw that the anguish from which she had just recovered was again threatening to crush her in another form.

"I must go back!" she exclaimed wildly. "By the first boat! If Germany is going to be drawn in, this means that Rudolf—David, I deserted him—when he needed me most!"

"No, Faith. A strange coincidence took you away just as he was on the point of sending you in any case. I'm sure he does not feel that you deserted him. I'm sure he is thankful that you are safe from the storm—you and Hansel. He knows that nothing can harm either of you here. If you had stayed in Europe, he could not have been so certain."

David rose, and walked over toward the east window. Under the summer moon, the valley lay bathed in peace as with a benediction. It seemed impossible, looking out upon it, that anywhere in the world there could be war. But when he turned, there was a note of admonition in his voice.

"I imagine you will have some sort of a personal message before long," he said guardedly. "In the meantime, I advise you to read at least one reliable newspaper every day.—If you are sure there is nothing I can do for you here, I must go home now—that is, when I have told you one more piece of news."

"Is it—is it more bad news?"

"No, it is good news—that is, I believe you will think so. Jacqueline and I saw Sam in Paris as we passed through there on our way to Havre. He asked us if we would not bring Mrs. Atkinson back with us, so that she would not have to make the voyage alone, as she had planned. She is at the Big House with us now. I know that to-morrow you will wish to see her."

. . . . .

For the next few days Faith went mechanically through the process of living. It seemed to her that she always heard her own voice as if it belonged to someone else, speaking from a great distance. She felt as if she were constantly listening for a sound which did not come and watching for someone who did not appear; and at last the tension became so great that it seemed to her that it would be better to hear anything and see anybody than to live indefinitely in terrified and unrelieved suspense.

The sound which finally shattered the strained silence was only another rap on the knocker, no more violent than those of Mrs. Elliot and David Noble. But she intuitively knew that it was portentous as she flew to open the door; and when she saw herself confronted with the solid figure of Sol Daniels, the station master, she instinctively put out her hand, even before he spoke to her.

He was beaming broadly. Evidently he was swelled with a sense of self-importance that was extremely satisfactory to him. As he extended the two flimsy envelopes he held in his hand, he chuckled.

"I never took a radio message of'n the ticker 'til I got that one sayin' you was on your way here," he said delightedly. "And I figgered the kick I got out o' that would have to last me quite a spell. But land! If this afternoon two cables didn't come in from Yrrup within half an hour of each other. I hadn't got one of 'em half writ before I had to turn to on the other. You've shook this town up good an' plenty, Mrs. Er—um—Faith. Well, good-evenin' to ye."

"Good evening," said Faith, in the mechanical voice that seemed to belong to someone else.

She had torn open one of the yellow envelopes. The scrawled sentences on the limp pages which met her eyes contained the message against which she had been bracing herself.

> "WAR DECLARED BETWEEN FRANCE AND GERMANY," she read. "FATHER HAS TAKEN COMMAND HIS TROOPS MY BROTHERS WITH THEIR REGIMENTS I HAVE RESIGNED FROM DIPLOMATIC SERVICE AND AM REJOINING ARMY. WILL COMMUNICATE WITH YOU OFTEN. ALL MY LOVE TO YOU AND HANSEL.
>
> RUDOLF."

She sat down on the stone steps and leaned against the lintel of the door. The envelope which had contained the message fluttered to the ground. It was some moments before she even remembered that she was holding another. Without premonition of further shock, she opened it slowly.

"WAR DECLARED BETWEEN FRANCE AND GERMANY," she read again; and for a moment she wondered, stupidly, if Sol had brought her two copies of the same cable. Then suddenly her eyes leaped forward. "FRANCE HAS BEEN MY COUNTRY FOR YEARS I AM OFF TO FIGHT FOR HER. TAKE CARE OF COUSIN SARAH FOR ME. YOURS FOREVER. SAM."

CHAPTER 35

THE sensation that she was perpetually waiting and listening, which had been so strong from the night when David had brought her word that Austria had declared war on Servia, did not end on the afternoon when the cables from Rudolf and Sam reached Faith simultaneously; instead it gradually increased until it became almost an obsession. If she had not constantly struggled against it, it would have overwhelmed her completely.

As August advanced, there was nothing on which she could lay her finger to account for her feeling of impending and inescapable disaster. The letter which Rudolf wrote almost immediately after he had dispatched his cable, and which came through with unusual celerity, was calmly matter-of-fact in tone. It went into few details about himself, but none of those supplied sounded ominous; and it revealed meticulous interest in her own welfare.

"We all expect that the war will be over before Christmas," he stated with a confidence which carried conviction, "but since winter will probably be well along before the situation is really tranquil again here, it would reassure me if you would let me know whether you can remain in Hamstead through the cold weather without inconvenience. In the spring it might be possible for me to join you in Hamstead and stay for a time—I should like to see something of America myself, and we might come back to Germany by way of the Orient. Now that I have resigned from the Service there is no reason why I should not have a vacation after the war is over, and you and I have never taken a trip of any consequence together. Would it amuse you, *liebe* Faith, to go to Japan and India, for example?"

Sam's scribbled communications were as different from Rudolf's in tone as they were in penmanship, but they were no more alarming. Apparently he was very happy himself, and certainly he was not worrying about her. He was taking it for granted that she was having the "time of her life" in Hamstead, after hankering for it so many years. And it was a relief to know that Cousin Sarah had given up the idea of going to Salem for the present, and that she was going to make Faith a long visit. He would like to see the old house she had got her claws into, and he would, when the little scrap he had taken on was over—probably his next picture of her would be "The New England Housewife." Meanwhile he certainly was enjoying himself in the Foreign Legion—there were men from ten different countries in his company, and say. . . .

Faith smiled as she read this letter, but the smile did not last except on the surface. She wrote reassuringly to Rudolf: she was very comfortable in Hamstead, she told him, and everyone was very kind to her. Though her life was quiet, it was extremely pleasant—now that David and Jacqueline were back at the Big House there were even a few festivities in Hamstead. She would be glad to remain where she was until he could join her, and then they would have a wonderful trip together. In a way, it would be like a second honeymoon.

To Sam she wrote even more gaily, enclosing snapshots of the old house she had "got her claws into," and of herself as a "New England Housewife"—rather disheveled and beaming broadly, with a broom in one hand and a pail in the other. Cousin Sarah's rheumatism was much better, she told him—David, who was a perfect wonder, was helping her a great deal. Faith had always heard the Foreign Legion was disreputable, and she had no doubt it was more so than ever, now that Sam had joined it; but she loved his stories about it just the same. Would he please write her some more, and illustrate them with sketches? And she was as always. . . .

Hansel and Moses Manning, who had been swimming together, took her letters to the Post Office; and Faith sat down on the stone doorstep, gazing out toward the mountains, and feeling, now that these were written, that she had nothing of much consequence to do. It was becoming increasingly clear to her that there was not enough to do in Hamstead to fill her time or stimulate her mind. The house, which had temporarily done both, though still a source of satisfaction to her, was ceasing to be one of occupation and excitement; and her friends and neighbors were agreeable rather than thrilling. Her close comradeship with Hansel had been a godsend to her, but she realized that as the friendships he had formed became more and more absorbing, she would see less and less of him herself. Decidedly, Hansel's days of dependence upon her were numbered. Yet her dependence upon him had never been so great.

If time had not been hanging so heavily on her hands, her unformulated fears would have haunted her less; but now that she was no longer preoccupied, her feeling of impending disaster became more and more intense. Her days she managed to fill somehow, by one expedient or another, but the nights became increasingly dreadful. They stretched out before her in endless succession, black, hideous, vacant and interminable. And not alone because terrors which could be stilled in the friendly daylight reared menacingly before her in the darkness: her precipitate fall from the emotional heights which had culminated at Radensholm had been as agonizing as it was swift; and she could not drug or kill the starved passion for Sebastian which had been so close to consummation. David, whose brief and casual visits had become an established custom, watched her solicitously as the weeks went on. At last, with unaccustomed bluntness, the doctor made a challenging statement.

"Look here, Faith, you can't go on indefinitely like this, you know. In fact, you can't go on much longer. You've got to find some outlet for all this pent-up force of yours."

"I know. I'm trying, David, really I am. But there doesn't seem to be anything to do here, beyond what I'm doing already. And I don't know where else to go. Besides, I don't believe going away would help. I seem to be faced with something that is—inescapable."

"Nothing is inescapable," said David still more brusquely. "Work out your own salvation. I told you, when I first got home, that you'd come into your heritage here, even though you didn't realize it yet. Do something with your legacy."

"What?"

"I don't know. If I had, I'd have told you long ago. But do something."

. . . . .

It was with this recommendation that David had left her, somewhat abruptly; and while she sat idly on the doorstep, watching the sun as it sank toward the western hills, and waiting for Hansel to come home, Faith turned his counsel over in her mind, as she had done many times already. She did not doubt the wisdom of his advice; but she was profoundly puzzled as to how she could profit by it. At last, acting, as she so often did, on a sudden impulse, she went into the house and called Caleb Hawks on the telephone.

He was not in, Mrs. Mead informed her, and Faith detected a note of concern in the trusty housekeeper's voice. What with one thing and another, he was "druv almost to death." But of course she would tell him that Mrs. Lowe had "foamed." Was there something special?

"I hoped that he would motor over and have supper with me. I want very much to see him. Yes, really it is rather special."

"I'll tell him the minute he comes in," Mrs. Mead promised.

It was about half an hour later when Caleb called her back himself. He was plumb tuckered out, he said; but take it all in all, he didn't know but what he'd be glad to get out of Hinsboro for an hour or two even if he was. No one would know where to find him and pester him to death. He guessed maybe he'd better shave and put on a clean shirt—he looked like something the cat brung in; but after that he'd be right along.

He arrived within an hour, shining with heat and cleanliness; but it was plain, as Faith had already gathered, that he was beset with worries. It appeared that there had been a demand for increase of wages at the pencil factory, the second in four months; and though Ted Jenkins, the General Manager and he thought the trade in pencils brisk enough to justify this, there was no telling how long business would continue at its present high pitch; it wasn't prudent to be too optimistic. The contractor for a new pavement on Main Street had reneged on his agreement, and the city stood to lose a good deal of money by his default. But this did not mark the end of his perplexities: the School Board had had its first meeting of the season, and some darn fool had insisted that Spanish should now be added to the High School curriculum. *Spanish!* Just as if the pupils weren't studying enough languages already! There was no one he could find to *teach* Spanish now anyway, not with school opening in three days, unless some marblecutter could be persuaded to give up good wages for a starvation salary. But Sebastian Perez didn't think any of them would. In fact, he didn't even think it would be a good plan to suggest such a thing, with the threatened strike just called off, so——

"I could teach Spanish at the Hinsboro High School," said Faith suddenly. "I—I should be very glad to. Do you think the School Board would consider me? I have never had any experience, of course, but then I wouldn't care about the salary either. Perhaps——"

Caleb, demolishing his fourth ear of sweet corn, dropped it on the table edge, where it balanced precariously for a moment, and then fell to the floor.

"You!" he exclaimed, "teach a parcel of young hoodlums in the Hinsboro High School! Faith, I guess you've took leave of your senses, and that's a fact."

"No, I haven't. Really, Uncle Caleb, I think I would make a very good teacher. Won't you let me try?"

He continued to stare at her in stupefaction, absent-mindedly picking up the breadcrumbs which were scattered about his plate and making them into a little pile.

"It ain't that," he said at last. "Of course you'd make a good teacher. Land o' Goshen, you'd be good at anything! Don't I know it! But you ain't got no idea what you'd be lettin' yourself in for. It'd be hard work for you. The School Board wants there should be at least three of these dumbfangled classes a week, and it'd be freezing cold driving back and forth between here and Hinsboro every other day. And papers to correct evenin's and order to keep in the schoolroom an' 'neverything. No, it ain't to be thought of. Not but what I appreciate your offerin'."

"Uncle Caleb, you don't understand. I—I want something to do."

"You want something to do!" he said explosively. "Land sakes, ain't you got enough to do as 'tis! You do about three times as much as any woman I was ever acquainted with and here you are clamorin' for more trouble! Well, if you really want it, I'll give you some. Not in the High School, though. In the Day Nursery. I tell you, Faith, that Day Nursery is the straw that's broke this camel's back. On top of the new wage scale at the factory, and that rascally contractor that's tryin' to swindle the city, and this high-falutin' idea that boys and girls that's goin' to sell ribbons and dig ditches for a livin' has got to learn some elegant furrin language instead of speakin' the King's English same as the rest of us, what do you think I got on my hands at the Day Nursery? An epidemic of whooping-cough! An' the matron's sick herself, and all the help so druv already, and all the lady visitors so scared of contagion, I don't know whose goin' to take care of them poor young 'uns, and that's a fact!"

"I do," said Faith calmly, "I am."

CHAPTER 36

THREE weeks later, when Faith began her duties as teacher of Spanish at the Hinsboro High School, the worst of the epidemic of whooping-cough at the Day Nursery was over.

"You could'da knocked me over with a feather," Caleb Hawks told Mrs. Mead, though he had added another twenty pounds to his ponderous weight since he had annoyed Rudolf with this expression, "when I see she weren't jokin' or triflin' or nothin', but dead in earnest. She *wanted* to go to that Day Nursery and look after them poor sick young 'uns. She said Hansel had had whooping-cough anyway, so there warn't no danger of contagion. To make a long story short, there warn't a single objection I c'd raise she didn't brush off like a fly; and she's ben on hand ever since. There ain't nothin' she ain't willin' to do, and some of the work's been kinda nasty, and that's a fact. Them children is awful sick to their stomachs at times, when they cough. And the place warn't none too clean anyway. She was right down on her knees scrubbin' floors before I c'd stop her. Well, with that new matron David Noble helped her to find, and the extra hired girl she dug up somewhere out in West Hamstead herself, I guess things is goin' to run smoother from now on. I told her so, and she laughed and said she aimed to keep her finger on the trigger hereafter, or words to that effect. The kids is all crazy about her, and she sure has got a way with them; and I guess the Lady Governors is goin' to make her a member of the Board. They couldn't very well help it after what she's done, and the office of treasurer is kinda goin' beggin'. Likely, they'll elect her to that."

Mr. Hawks' prediction was fulfilled: three different ladies, separately and cajolingly importuned to take over the thankless task of acting as treasurer for the Hinsboro Day Nursery had declined to do so; but when as a last resort the Board appealed to Faith, she accepted the position with alacrity. She had become deeply interested in the Day Nursery. The situation there had not only roused her sympathies; it had challenged her efficiency; and the hard grueling work she had done there, instead of exhausting her, had acted on her as a tonic and a panacea. She had been up at six every morning, and had given competent and comprehensive directions for the day to Hilda and the still swarming mechanics, before hurling herself into her Dodge, and compelling it to eat up the miles between Hamstead and Hinsboro. Sometimes she took Hansel with her, to spend the day with Caleb and Mrs. Mead or with Junior Conrad; more frequently she left him at home, in charge of Hilda and Cousin Sarah, who was now duly established in the spare chamber; and she was always home again in time to read to him after supper and see him tucked into his trundle bed. When she finally sank down on her great four-poster, and reached for his hand, sleep did not always elude and mock her as it had been doing. The "white nights" of anguish persisted intermittently; but they no longer dominated her or tortured her past the limit of her endurance.

The Hinsboro School Board held another meeting as the epidemic was beginning to subside; and Faith persuaded Caleb Hawks to permit her to accompany him to this, and to state her own case before its members. Several of them had met her already, and the others had heard her achievements heralded. Far from encountering opposition, she found that her services were unanimously solicited; and she was even asked whether, since she would be coming to the school to teach Spanish in any case, she would consider "taking over" a few other classes: there was an incipient course in Fine Arts as well as the one in Spanish, and Mr. Hawks had revealed the fact that she "knew all the furrin picture galleries like a book"; while the director of Home Economics felt sure she would have some suggestions about European recipes which could be tried out to advantage. In short, if she would consider coming five times a week, instead of three, it would be deeply appreciated.

"It'll be ungodly cold by an' by, same as I told you," Caleb cautioned her warningly, as he thought she appeared to hesitate. "And there's an awful crowd of roughnecks among them scholars. 'Tain't as if they wuz pure-breds, same as me and you is—a lot of 'em is furriners, Canucks and Poles and Eye-talians, and Lord knows what."

"I'm goin' to buy a coonskin coat," Faith said briefly. "I won't be cold. And I'm not afraid of foreigners—why Uncle Caleb, haven't I lived with foreigners for nearly twenty years? I'm much more used to them than I am to Americans! Besides, if I were in Hinsboro every day except Saturday and Sunday, I could keep on going to the Day Nursery regularly, and I want to do that—my idea of a Lady Visitor is someone who *visits!*" she added with a slight touch of scorn, "and if I'm going to take charge of funds, I want to know exactly how money's being apportioned and spent.—But I was thinking of Hansel. It was all right to leave him in an emergency like this one we've just been through, but I shouldn't like to do it all winter. If he would be willing to go to school in Hinsboro instead of Hamstead though, I could arrange for the teaching and the welfare work too; and I don't see why he shouldn't be—it would be fun for both of us, driving back and forth together. I'll talk it over with him when I get home this evening."

"Land sakes, Faith! I never see anyone *organize* the way you do, never in my life, and that's a fact."

"You mustn't pay me such extravagant compliments, Uncle Caleb.

The Board will think you're prejudiced," she said, glancing about her with a comprehensive and disarming smile. "Will it be all right if I let you know my decision in the morning?" she went on agreeably. "I feel quite sure I can arrange to take over all the classes you have in mind. But I must confer with my son before I promise."

As she left the Board Meeting, and walked back toward Caleb Hawks' house with him, he reiterated his expressions of admiration concerning her executive ability. At the same time, he questioned her rather awkwardly.

"If you'd only ben a man, Faith," he told her, "you'd a ben in the State Legislature by now—in fact, I wouldn't be a mite surprised if you'd a ben Lieutenant Governor! Your grandpa would certainly a ben proud of you—and as for your poor pa, my, my! You got all the guts that was left out of him—beg pardon, Faith, that slipped out without my noticing.—Just the same, you still look kinda peaked to me. Are you sure you feel real well?"

"I feel very well. Except that I—I had bad news this morning. It was a good deal of a shock."

"You don't say! Well now, I'm just as sorry as I ken be. What happened?"

"I had another cable," she said in a low voice. "I—I keep expecting them all the time, since the first two came. I—I listen for the knocker in the night. I can't seem to help it. And Sol Daniels seems actually pleased, every time he comes up to the house with another message. This was from Rudolf again. It told me that my brother-in-law, Hans von Hohenlohe, who was a colonel in the German army, was killed at the battle of the Marne—the one that has been going on for nearly a week. Hans was Rudolf's favorite brother. I have heard him say that he 'loved him with his very soul.' And I know he did. This will be a terrible blow to Rudolf, and I do not know whether he is near anyone who—who can comfort him. I am afraid he is not—and that troubles me—very much. Besides, I was very fond of Hans myself. The first time I went to Schönplatz, the von Hohenlohes' country place, he was so kind and cordial to me that I have never forgotten. He was very gentle and affectionate, and he had a voice like an angel. At Christmas time it was always he who led the carol-singing. And now he has been killed—in a war—where men murder each other."

Caleb gave an exclamation of sympathy. Faith turned toward him, and he saw that she was making a supreme effort to keep her lips and voice steady.

"David Noble came in last evening and said that he had been expecting this battle, that it would repulse the German forces, and keep them from getting to Paris," she said. "He told me whole regiments were sent to the front in taxi cabs, the German advance was so close.

Of course the French have fought with desperate bravery, and I do not wonder that he admires them for defending their capital so superbly. But the Marne will never mean the place where Paris was saved to me. It will always mean the place where Hans was slaughtered and Rudolf was bereft."

"Now look here, Faith——"

"I know. I won't. . . . I think David would like to go to France himself. And I told you that Sam Dudley, the best friend I have in the world—has enlisted in the French Foreign Legion. I suppose he'll be fighting soon, if he hasn't already begun. I'm terrified for fear the next cable I get——"

"Like as not you won't get no more cables, Faith. Anyways, don't you go listenin' for 'em in the night. It ain't healthy. It'll wear you down. I'm goin' to say a few words to Sol Daniels myself."

The few words spoken by Caleb were so forceful that when the next cable came, Sol was bewildered as to what to do with it. Certainly he could not withhold it. But neither, in the light of Caleb's remarks, did he dare to deliver it. He finally decided to telephone Mr. Hawks and confer with him.

The idea was not without well-meaning merit; but it chanced that the moment he chose could hardly have been more unfortunate. It had finally been decided, after the discussion of numerous divergent plans, that Faith and Hansel should take their daily dinner with Caleb. Faith's classes at the Hinsboro High School all came in the morning; and in the afternoon, while Hansel was at the second session, she went to the Day Nursery for two hours. The noon-time interval was one of relaxation and pleasure; and the little group which was becoming more and more closely knit together had just seated itself at table, when the bell on the dining-room wall jangled, and Caleb Hawks rose to answer it.

"Hello," he said, hastily swallowing a generous portion of Hamburg steak. "Yep, Caleb Hawks, speakin'. Oh—hello, Sol! What's that? What's that you say?"

Instantly, he felt Faith's hand on his arm, and saw her white face close to his.

"Is it Rudolf?" she whispered. "Or Sam?"

"It ain't neither of 'em," he said quickly. "But it *is* a cable, Faith, *from* Rudolf. Mebbe I better let you take it yourself. There's something about Wipers and a man who was hurt there—I don't reccernize the name. Here's the receiver."

He put his arm around her, and felt her slim body growing more and more rigid as she slowly repeated the words which Sol Daniels was painfully spelling out to her.

"Heinrich—has—died—from—wounds—received—at Ypres," she said

tonelessly. "Mother—has—now lost—all—her—sons—but me. Rudolf."—"Yes—yes—I understand. Yes—I should like a copy of it. Yes—I will come in with an answer this afternoon. Thank you, Sol, good-bye."

She sank down where she had been standing, covering her face with her hands. Caleb tried to wedge a supporting hand under one of her elbows.

"You come upstairs and lay down on the spare-room bed," he said, "till you kinda get hold of yourself. You're not goin' to the Day Nursery this afternoon, not except over my dead body.—All her sons but Rudolf! *All*—why, how many more was there, Faith?"

"There were three," she said in a smothered voice. "The first one—Otto—was a son by another marriage. But he—died violently too. I never told you about that, but some day I will. Oh, Uncle Caleb,—it's too dreadful. Heinrich was like *Tante* Luise—dark and brilliant and charming, full of life and high spirits. It seems impossible that any wound could be deep enough to kill him, his vitality was so dazzling. *Tante* Luise will feel that part of herself has gone this time."

For a moment Faith continued to sit where she was, bowed and shaking, her face still hidden. Then she rose slowly, dried her eyes, and smoothed back her hair; and walking out into the little front entry, reached for her hat and coat.

"What are you aimin' to do, Faith?" Caleb called after her. She turned toward him with a determined, though pitiful attempt at a smile.

"Did you ever read Tolstoy's story about the peasant?" she said. "The one who was out in his field ploughing, and was asked by someone what he would do if he knew he were going to die the next day?—No, I suppose not.—Well, he said he would go on ploughing. I think he had the right idea. I'm going back to the Nursery."

. . . . .

The long cold winter progressed slowly. There was not as much snow as usual, and there were only a few days when the Dodge could not nose its way somehow through the rutted and frozen roads between Hamstead and Hinsboro; so there were almost no interruptions to the teaching and nursery work with which Faith went doggedly on. The schedule which she had systematized so skillfully was saved from monotony by the approach of the Christmas holidays with their attendant diversified activities: she agreed to teach the school play; and she financed and organized a celebration at the Day Nursery, drilling the children to sing Christmas carols and cajoling Caleb into acting as Santa Claus. All the parents of Faith's charges had come to this celebration; and by the time "refreshments" were being served and the distribution of presents had begun, the very walls were resounding with the hearty merriment of the factory hands and marblecutters and their families.

Then next day there was a glorious feast at "Marlowe Manor": Caleb Hawks and his daughter Myra, and her husband, Ted Jenkins, the manager of the pencil factory, and their children all came to it; so did Uncle Ephraim and Aunt Emmeline, and David and Jacqueline Noble. And when the last guest had gone, Hansel looked up joyfully from the new electric train that was already chugging its way over the neatly laid track on the library floor, and asked Faith a question which she realized concealed no disappointment beyond that which he frankly voiced.

"It was a lovely Christmas, wasn't it, mother? As nice as a German Christmas except for not having father and grandmother and the others here. I'm afraid they're missing us too, aren't you? But next year we will all be together again, in Berlin, won't we?"

"I hope so, Hansel. Yes—of course we will."

"Except, I suppose you are thinking, Uncle Hans and Uncle Heinrich won't be there? When we sing 'Heilige Nacht,' it won't seem quite the same without Uncle Hans, will it? But then, perhaps he is singing it in heaven now—just think how that would please all the other angels!"

"I will think of it, Hansel. It is a lovely thought."

She walked over to the secretary, and taking out the letter which had come in from Rudolf two days earlier, sat down in the wing chair by the fire to re-read it. He was purposely not sending her a cable, he said, since he feared that by now she might have come to regard the arrival of one with dread (it was strange how separation from her had given him the intuition which intimacy had never evoked!) but he wanted her and Hansel to know that he would be thinking of them both constantly on Christmas Day. He was happy to say that he had been fortunate enough to secure the promise of holiday leave, and General von Hohenlohe also hoped to get away from the Eastern Front for a few days. So there would be a family gathering in Berlin, and they would make it as cheerful a one as they could, looking forward to next year when everything would be different. But perhaps it would be best for her not to count too confidently on his being with her in the spring—the war might be somewhat more protracted than he had foreseen at first. However, as soon as it was over, he would hasten to join her, and they would travel anywhere she chose together. Meanwhile, he sent her his devoted love.

The unfailing regularity with which Rudolf's letters continued to arrive, as well as their loyal and affectionate tone, reminded Faith of those he had sent her immediately after their betrothal, when she and Sarah Atkinson had been visiting the hill cities of Italy together. The exigencies of life at the front seemed to present no more obstacles to uninterrupted correspondence now than her indefinite method of traveling had done with him years earlier. Occasionally, he was even adroit enough to avoid the censor, and to send communications to her through some indirect channel. When this was the case, he wrote her fully and freely, and the pages covered with his clear and forceful handwriting were absorbingly interesting to her, entirely apart from their personal element. He made the intricacy of the trenches and the horrors of No Man's Land clear to her long before anyone else in either Hinsboro or Hamstead had grasped that all time-honored methods of warfare had been revolutionized. The eyes of everyone else she knew seemed focused exclusively on the Western Front; but she understood that the impregnable line which stretched from East Prussia to the Carpathian Mountains, had begun to assume proportions of immeasurable importance to the Central Powers. Reading between the lines in Sam's infrequent and light-hearted letters, casually dispatched from the headquarters of the "Stepsons of France," she could understand his optimistic point of view. But it was in Rudolf's analyses rather than in Sam's persiflage that she placed real reliance.

She had learned, early in the previous autumn, to keep her own counsel; and though she was conscious that the United States had been neutral in letter rather than in spirit, almost from the beginning of the war, she seldom detected signs of personal antagonism in the atmosphere about her. She was aware that she was regarded less as the wife of a German officer—entirely unknown in the valley—who was fighting against the Allies, than as the daughter of an American Senator—whose memory was greatly respected and revered—who had opportunely found her way to her ancestral home. She had every reason to feel secure in her enjoyment of popular approval and popular affection.

This feeling of security became solidified as time went on and nothing happened to perturb her. Her emotions were under control at last, even though they were not subdued; the dreadful forebodings which had haunted her for so long became more and more dim as her worst fears remained unrealized; and her driving preoccupations did much to ward off introspection. In addition to everything else she was doing, she had embarked upon a scheme of landscape gardening which would engage her attention through the evenings and week-ends during the spring, and engross her intensively after the closing of school during the summer. Now that the house was completely restored to its former beauty, her mind had turned eagerly toward the improving of its surroundings: she had begun to visualize a vegetable garden and orchard stretching out behind a garage and a tennis court; and best of all, extending between her own house and Uncle Ephraim's, paths and plots bordered with flowers, and sweet with summer scent.

It was while she was vigorously spading up earth for her pansy bed one Saturday afternoon early in May that she heard Hansel calling her so loudly and intensely, that she realized, even before he came running out to find her, that her new-found sense of peace was shattered; and as she rose hastily, and went toward him with quick alarm, she saw that there was an expression of horror in his eyes which had suddenly robbed them of all childishness.

"What has happened, darling? What is the matter?" she asked, trying to speak calmly.

"It is something about a big ship that has been sunk by the Germans —a passenger ship. Uncle Caleb is on the telephone. He wants to tell you about it before anyone else talks to you. He says he will drive over after supper anyway, but this is so very dreadful that he must speak to you at once. You don't think it can be true, do you?"

"No, darling, of course I don't. Of course it can't be true."

But she knew that it was. If Caleb Hawks were calling her, when he intended, in any case, to come and see her within a few hours, it could be only to soften the deadliness of some terrible shock from which he could not save her; and late that night, when she went up to her room with leadened feet, she found that Hansel was still awake, sobbing in his trundle bed. She gathered him into her arms, and they lay closely locked together while she tried to comfort him. But nothing she could say assuaged his horror and his grief.

"When father's next letter comes, perhaps he will explain, Hansel. There must be something that we do not understand. The *Lusitania* was warned not to sail——"

"But mother, the seas have to be free—America has always said that the seas must be free. I have been learning about it in History. And there were babies on the *Lusitania*, little babies!"

It was not only Hansel's anguished thoughts that were haunted by the dead babies. Everywhere Faith turned, she felt as if she were seeing them herself, floating white and lifeless above the blue waters off the Irish Coast. And everyone she encountered was, she knew, obsessed with the same troubled vision. A sudden strain and silence shadowed all the relationships in which she had been so happy—she was conscious that her neighbors were avoiding her, that her pupils confided in her less freely, that even the mothers of the little charges at the Day Nursery shrank away from her as they came to fetch their children home. The hostile wave of rage and resentment against Germany which had swelled, almost overnight, to gigantic proportions, had engulfed her. She did not know how to struggle against its crushing and devastating force.

CHAPTER 37

As the spring and summer moved heavily forward, Faith was increasingly thankful both for the intensive labor which her garden exacted from her, and for the sense of solace and escape which its unfolding beauty brought her. She made no aggressive effort to repel the wave of antagonism which had engulfed her. Instead, she went quietly on with her accustomed tasks as if oblivious of encompassing enmity, and withdrew, when these were finished, among her flowers. Sarah Atkinson and Caleb Hawks, watching her anxiously during this crucial period, marveled at her extraordinary wisdom and patience. It was not like Faith, they said to themselves and to each other, to bow her head before a storm and wait for it to pass. But while they marveled, they gave thanks: no other attitude, they knew, could have been so effective in the supercharged atmosphere.

Until school closed, she continued her daily supervision of the Nursery; then she calmly announced that since everything was going well there, she felt that bi-weekly visits from her would be sufficient to insure its continued efficacy and progress, and disappeared from the foreground of its direction. Her fellow members on the Board of Lady Managers, some of whom had been her hostile critics, professed themselves as thankful that she had had the grace to vanish from the picture. But with the advent of dog-days, and their attendant discomforts and ailments, these ladies began to change their minds. None of them cared to give up the outings they had planned to the "shore," or the ease of their own screened piazzas, in order to minister to small wretched victims of "summer complaint"; and eventually a delegation, succumbing to the importunities of the distraught matron, called upon Faith and begged her not only to resume control of the situation immediately, but also to take over the office of President of the Board.

They found her in her garden, which by now had begun to give beautiful evidence of the care lavished upon it, seated on a rustic bench, reading to Hansel. She received them with the utmost courtesy, ordered iced drinks served to them, and listened gravely while they stated their case. But when they had done this, she told them that it would be necessary for her to think the matter over.

By the time she had finally been induced to return to the scene of action, not only the Lady Visitors, but the parents of nearly all her former charges, had been obliged to seek her out in her garden and beseech her continued coöperation. When at last she took up her former duties, it was with the knowledge that she had been thankfully welcomed back to the Nursery, and that the security of her position there would never again be challenged. Fortified by the consciousness of this, she composed a letter to the School Board, suggesting, without the least hint or rancor or resentment, that it would perhaps be well if she should resign from the faculty. This Board, having observed with alarm the course of events at the Nursery during her absence, hastened to send her its unanimous assurance that such a withdrawal on her part would be regarded in the light of a calamity. She was entrenched at the High School no less advantageously than she was at the Day Nursery.

With the resumption of daily commuting between Hinsboro and Hamstead, her limited leisure necessarily curtailed the time she could spend in her garden; but she still managed to wedge in a surprising number of hours there. And it was while she was setting out autumn bulbs one windy day in late October, that David Noble came to tell her of the birth of Sebastian's son.

For a moment she closed her eyes, to shut out the blurred vision of earth and sky which rocked around her; and David, looking down at her stricken face, saw that her pallor was startling.

"Just let the world roll by for a moment," he said quietly, brushing the fluttering leaves from the rustic bench and seating himself beside her. "And keep saying to yourself, 'I didn't lose Sebastian. I never shall lose him now. I renounced him; and this is the reward of my renunciation.'" Then as Faith did not answer, David added gently, "You hoped all the time that Doña Dolores would some day have a child, didn't you, Faith?"

"Yes—yes, of course. But not—not so soon. It is such a little while since—since Sebastian and I——"

"I know, Faith. But you must try to see the other side—to look at this whole situation squarely and sanely. Don Sebastian talked it over with me very frankly. He asked me how soon I thought it would be safe—and I told him any time, after Doña Dolores had recovered her strength. Remember that she—isn't young. If this hadn't happened soon, it couldn't have happened at all. And then you would have felt—perhaps—that your great sacrifice had been in vain. But now——"

He saw that a faint color was coming back to her ashen lips. Again he spoke very gently.

"Would you like to see Sebastian's letter, Faith? I think it was really written as much for you as for me. It is filled with joy and thanksgiving——"

"No, please—please——"

"Faith," David said abruptly, "do you know how wonderful I think you are—how wonderful everyone thinks you are? I never saw anyone so unconquerable! You've had enough to contend against, in this last year and a half, to send the average woman into her grave—or an insane asylum! And you've become steadily more magnificent! I shall never forget how you played up to me the night I got here—it was superb! Or how you flung yourself into the breach during that epidemic at the Day Nursery—or how you took the news that Hans and Heinrich von Hohenlohe had been killed—and most of all how you acted those weeks after the *Lusitania* was sunk when you didn't know how far people would turn against you, and when one false step on your part would have made them turn pretty far. You've 'kept on ploughing,' as you put it yourself, through all that. Can't you keep on through this?"

"Yes, David. I can. I'm going to. But for just a moment I think I must—'let the world go by.'"

He continued to watch her, sympathetically and searchingly, but he did not immediately speak to her again. It was she who finally broke the silence.

"Tell me something about your own plans—and Jacqueline's," she said, so calmly that he knew her struggle for self-mastery was almost won.

"You're really interested—and not sensitive? We're all for France, you know."

"Yes, I know. And I am really interested—and not sensitive. Don't forget, Sam's all for France, too!"

"Of course he is!" David agreed instantly, seizing upon the opening offered him. "Do you hear from him regularly, Faith?"

"No, very irregularly. Sam is never methodical like—like Rudolf. His letters are delightful when they do come, but they don't come often. It must be six or eight weeks now since I've had one."

There was no apprehension in her voice. David, resolutely closing his mind to the grim foreboding which crossed it, answered the question from which he had been momentarily diverted.

"Jacqueline's planning to do some nursing at a base hospital or convalescent home—the fact that she's had practical experience already, and that she's half French, has helped cut a lot of red tape. I think she'll get off before long. And I'm going over with one of the Harvard Medical Units—I've been waiting for Sylvia's baby to come before making definite arrangements. Austin's terribly worried about her, and to tell you the truth, I am too. She wasn't strong enough for this—yet. But there's something about that marriage that foils interference. If any two human beings ever achieved perfect happiness together, Austin and Sylvia Gray have."

"I've realized that. And I'm glad you haven't interfered, David, whatever happens. Sylvia would rather die, bringing Austin's child into the world, than——"

"Perhaps!" he said quickly, following the drift of her unspoken thought. "But think of Austin afterwards! And think of all the rest of us!"

. . . . .

In the desolate months that followed, Faith had tragic cause to think of Austin and "all the rest"; for the birth of her twin daughters cost Sylvia Gray her life, and the overwhelming grief of the bereft husband found reflection in the mourning of the entire countryside. When Austin finally found courage to face the world again, it was not through quiet occupations in the peaceful valley where he had lived all his life, but through driving an ambulance over the shell-shot roads of France; and within a week of his desperate departure, David and Jacqueline came to say good-bye to Faith, one bound for a field hospital directly behind the firing-line, the other for a convalescents' home in Brittany. The little brick cottage, and the Big House both stood dark and empty through the long cold winter; and Faith, deprived of these havens of hospitality and friendliness, threw herself, with redoubled intensity, into her chosen work.

It was not until late in June that the summons for which she had listened so long, and for which at last she had almost ceased to listen, finally came. She was even more preoccupied than usual, for graduation day of the Hinsboro High School was imminent, and besides teaching her own classes, she was drilling many of the students who were to take an outstanding part in the graduation exercises. Hardly a day went by when she did not find it necessary, toward the end of the morning assembly, to leave her faculty seat and come forward to read general notices, make general requests, and impart general information. She was always able to command immediate attention; even though final examinations and final rehearsals had reduced the entire student body to a state of nervous irritability, her voice and her manner seemed to have a hypnotizing effect upon the pupils. They stopped shuffling their feet the instant she rose to hers. They strained their ears to listen to an announcement that a fraternity pin had been lost and that she would keep it on her desk until the owner claimed it, or a request that the members of the class of 1916 should meet in her room at the end of the morning session, though similar announcements and requests, coming from other sources, made no dent whatsoever in their consciousness. Mr. Alonzo Markam, the principal, had observed this phenomenon with feelings of mingled envy and relief: it was humiliating to be obliged to admit that any subordinate teacher had more powers of control and attraction than he himself possessed; yet it was reassuring to be certain that as long as Faith Marlowe continued her domination, the lawless young forces under him could always be checked by her charm.

It was with the reluctant knowledge of this that he appealed to her in the crowning emergencies of the school year: Neal Conrad, now Food Administrator for the state, had agreed to make the "principal address" on graduation day; he was without doubt the leading citizen of Hinsboro, and Mr. Alonzo Markam had congratulated himself on his good fortune in securing so desirable an orator. But Neal, with the ruthlessness that characterized his political progress, had telephoned from Belford to say that he was taking a night train to Washington for a conference with the President; he was sorry, of course, if this sudden change of plan would inconvenience Mr. Markam; he was sure, however, that some other speaker, much more eloquent, could easily be found.

"But Mr. Conrad," the distraught principal had protested, "the exercises are *to-morrow evening*. I don't know where to turn, really I don't! Couldn't you possibly——"

"No," Neal had called back crisply. "A Presidential summons is a command.—Surely you know that, Mr. Markam. Well, if you can't do better, ask Faith Marlowe to step into the breach. Tell her I'd appreciate it very much if she'd pinch hit for me. I don't know whether she's ever made a speech in her life or not, but I'm sure she can. Good-bye, Mr. Markam, good-bye. I'm sorry to seem abrupt, but I'm late for my train already!"

For a moment after he had hung up the receiver, Mr. Markam hesitated. But only for a moment. The few well-chosen words which he had prepared to speak during the distribution of diplomas had already cost him hours of anguish; he could not possibly enlarge on them without prostration. The male quartet from the First Congregational Church was to render two choice selections; but these could not be dragged out to consume more than ten minutes. Mr. Caleb Hawks, as mayor of the city, always appeared on the platform on great occasions; but it was unthinkable that he should be permitted, even if he could be persuaded, to air his "King's English" before the large assembly that would attend the graduation. There was nothing to do but telephone Faith Marlowe, who had already returned to Hamstead for the night, and give her Neal Conrad's message.

There was an instant's hesitation on her part also, though this, Mr. Markam almost immediately realized, was not caused by any lack of willingness to coöperate with him. But she had never made a speech, she said—that is, not a real address—she had just talked casually to the pupils now and then. And for a graduation, of course, he would want something much more formal in character. She really didn't know whether—what subject did he have in mind, what sort of a slant would he want her to give it?

"Oh, I'll leave all that to you," Mr. Markam said airily. "Something inspirational, of course—some kind of a special uplift message. I know you'll handle it beautifully. I can't tell you how relieved I am."

. . . . .

As Faith advanced toward the center of the platform the following evening, the students gathered before her were conscious that there was something unusually arresting in her looks and manner. She had detached herself quietly from the side of Caleb Hawks, who had accompanied her when she came into the hall; and now she was standing and speaking as she always stood and spoke. Yet there was a subtle change in her poignant voice, an exalted expression on her face, of which her pupils had never been aware before. They watched her breathlessly, as if in the presence of a phenomenon unaccountably appearing upon a familiar scene.

"Last night, when our principal asked me if I would speak to you in the place of our Food Administrator, Mr. Neal Conrad, who has been called to Washington for a conference with the President of the United States," she said vibrantly, "I told him that I feared I might not be able to do so adequately. And since then something has happened which has made it—absolutely impossible for me to prepare the sort of address to which you are entitled to listen on such a great occasion as this. But in order that I might not seem to fail you entirely, when I should be glad to do anything for you that I could, I am going to try to tell you a—a sort of story."

Again there was an instant of silence so tense that the atmosphere seemed to throb.

"When I came here two years ago, I did not expect to stay very long," she continued. "I had lived in Hamstead when I was a little girl, and for years I had been hoping to come back for a visit—this had always seemed to me like the place where I really belonged. But my husband, Rudolf von Hohenlohe, had not been willing to have me leave him, or able to leave his own work and come here with me. So I was very much surprised when he suddenly consented to my wish. But after I reached here I began to understand why he had done so: it was because he knew there was going to be a great and terrible war, and he feared that soon there would be no part of Europe where I could be comfortable or happy or even safe. And so, because he loved me, he sent me away from him to this lovely peaceful valley, which is like the Valley of Avalon that you have read about with me, lying

'Deep-meadowed, happy, fair with orchard lawns,
And bowery hollows crowned with summer seas.'"

"Lord Almighty!" exclaimed Caleb Hawks hoarsely, leaning over and tapping the principal on the shoulder. "She's got 'em all spellbound—them hoodlums! Land, if I could get her to talk in a *campaign!* . . ."

"But of course we expected that when the war was over, he would come and take my little boy and me back to Germany," the clear voice went on. "We had even planned that we would take a long journey together, all the way around the world, stopping in beautiful countries which none of us had ever seen, on our way between my country and his. But now he has gone on a long journey to a strange country—all alone. And he has left me to go on a still longer journey—here among you. I want you to help me make my journey as bravely as I know he has made his. For his was the journey of death, which is very glorious and triumphant. But mine is the journey of life, which is very hard to make without purpose—and courage—and a singing heart."

"Spellbound!" whispered the principal leaning over toward Mr. Hawks. "She has them all crying—those tough foreigners! *Crying!* But how she could have come.—How she can stand up there and——"

"You don't know her same as I do," Caleb whispered back. "She'll stand up under *anything!* Listen! . . ."

"My husband went to the war, you see," Faith was saying. "He was appointed to serve on the Staff of the Crown Prince, under whose leadership the German army has been attacking the great French fortress of Verdun for months. The French have made watchword of their desperate cry for self-preservation. They have proclaimed that Germany should not pass. It has not passed. It will not pass. It—cannot pass. But while thousands of brave men have been giving their lives to defend this fortress, thousands of others, equally brave, have given theirs in the attempt to annihilate it. My husband was one of those men.

"Many years ago I told his mother, whom I love very dearly, that I felt as if there was something glistening about his spirit. It still seems this way to me. I feel as if I could see his spirit shining now—while I am talking to you! I feel as if I could see my husband as he looked to me when I first saw him—like a radiant Saint Michael! Driving away dragons! Bringing salvation and strength! Surrounded by All Angels!"

"Lord Almighty!" exclaimed Caleb Hawks again, passing the back of his hand over his eyes, "if she says anything more about angels I shall be crying myself. Her husband did look sort o' glorious, the first time I seen him. I know what she means. It's a mercy she can think of him that way, 'stead of like—carrion."

"We were very young then, and we—loved each other. Afterwards, after we were married, we misunderstood each other sometimes. I was an American, you see, and he was a German—it is often hard for Germans and Americans to interpret each other's thoughts and feelings and—standards. Besides, I believe in almost every marriage there must be misunderstandings, there must be divisions. But husbands and wives must not be discouraged by these—I am very much ashamed to remember now that sometimes I was, and I hope none of you will be ashamed for the same reason. Because these misunderstandings and divisions do not last, if there is respect, and confidence, and tenderness, to draw husbands and wives together again. It is like St. Paul's experience of seeing through a glass—first darkly and then face to face. In these last two years, Rudolf and I have understood each other perfectly and completely, and we have seemed close together, though he has been in the war and I have been here with you. But now I have lost him. I know he is near to his fellow angels, but I do not feel that he is near to me. And I am going to be very lonely. Unless—unless you will all go with me—on the journey Rudolf has left me to make without him. If you make me feel you need and want me here at school—that will give my journey purpose! If you promise me that from now on, whatever happens, your people shall be my people—that will give me courage for my journey! If you tell me that you trust and love me—that will give me back in time my singing heart! If you can do all this, tell me so to-day—and let us all start forward—onward—upward —on this journey of life together!"

Almost imperceptibly a subtle and portentous change had been taking place in the supercharged atmosphere. There was still a tense vibrancy in the air; but it was no longer the vibrancy of profound silence, but of pent-up emotion seeking release. As Faith finished speaking, she stretched out her arms, her head held high, her face illumined. And from her audience surged an answering cry that seemed torn from the hearts of every one of her listeners. They were on their feet, they were out of their seats, they were crowding the corridors, they were hurling themselves upon the platform, they were closing in around Faith. A lame ugly boy pushing his way painfully against the throbbing mass, slipped and stumbled his way until he had fought his way to the piano. His soiled powerful fingers closed down over the keys with a sound of crashing chords. Then resonantly he struck the first bars of a hymn that Faith had taught him and his classmates. The next instant the school was singing it in unison:

"The Son of God goes forth to war,
   A kingly crown to gain;
His blood-red banner streams afar:
   Who follows in his train?
Who best can drink his cup of woe,
   Triumphant over pain;
Who patient bears his cross below,
   He follows in his train.

. . . .

A noble army, men and boys,
   The matron and the maid,
Around the Saviour's throne rejoice,
   In robes of light arrayed.
They climbed the steep ascent of heaven
   Through peril, toil, and pain:
O God, to us may grace be given
   To follow in their train."

The song rose and swelled through the hall like a triumphant pæan. It had become a processional, for the students were marching now, marching with a verve and buoyancy that gave the effect of victorious troops gloriously returning to a city from which they had long before set forth to an unknown destiny. Someone had caught up the American flag and the school standards: the Stars and Stripes streamed away ahead of the class banners. But someone else—an undersized scrubby girl who could dart about unperceived—had shot out the door and down the street. Nobody saw her go. Nobody cared whether she went or not. Everyone was singing and marching. But when this scrubby girl came panting back into the hall again, she was bearing another flag—a flag bearing broad bands of red and white and black; and burrowing her way to Faith's side, she thrust it into her hands.

"This once!" she gasped. "This once, Faith, we must have Rudolf's flag too whatever happens afterwards! I got it out of Jacob Heine's saloon—I knew he had it in his back room with his own steins—he brought it with him when he came from Hamburg. You take 'em *both* —the 'Merican one and this one too—and lead us, see?—And we'll all come along after you!"

Faith's fingers closed swiftly around the German flag. She raised it, dipped it as if in salute, and raised it again. Then stretching forth her free hand for the other flag, which, just then, went floating past her, she took her place among the standard-bearers.

Caleb Hawks was still standing on the platform, passing first one hand and then the other surreptitiously across his eyes. He suddenly seized the principal's arm and pointed toward the advancing columns.

"Come on!" he said breathlessly. "Let's me and you get into this too! Lord Almighty! It's the biggest thing's ever happened in Hinsboro! But there's goin' to be bigger things happenin' from now on! Faith is goin' to keep on leadin' us, and the rest of us is goin' to follow!"

PART VIII

Sarah Atkinson

CHAPTER 38

Sarah Atkinson's standards had altered with passing years and changing conditions. She still wore taffeta dresses and did her full duty as she understood this. But the dresses were not quite so steely in color as they once had been, and they did not crackle quite so much; and she interpreted her obligations to God and her fellow men less rigidly than when she had left Salem as a bride. Her years of association with Sam had mellowed her nature and broadened her outlook. It was true that she had brought order and decorum to the helter-skelter studio apartment in the Latin Quarter when she took over its direction; but it was also true that she had gained as much as she had given. The constant ebb and flow of celebrities and strugglers, critics and promoters, wastrels and geniuses, through the spacious shabby rooms which she cleared of clutter and redeemed from dirt, and over which she learned to preside with grace as well as dignity, had left an unmistakable imprint upon her. She came to love her motley throng of visitors, to regard their shortcomings with indulgence, and to rejoice in all their triumphs as if these had been her own.

She had not been able to define the reason for the indefinite but persistent feeling that the time had come for her to wrench herself away from her familiar and congenial surroundings and return to the austerities of Salem, Massachusetts. It had not sprung from fear that the increasing helplessness with which she was so painfully handicapped by rheumatism, would make her a burden to him; Sam was wealthy, in spite of the prodigality with which he had shared his own earnings with fellow artists less fortunate than himself. And certainly it did not spring from discontent, for never had the creative vitality of the atmosphere in which she lived been more agreeable to her. Nevertheless, she instinctively knew that her days in Sam's studio were numbered, and had been determined to take her departure before this was mysteriously forced upon her. When Sam had brought her the intelligence of the murder at Sarajevo, she had instantly read in his face the response to her foreboding; and when David and Jacqueline had offered to give her safe conduct on her voyage across the Atlantic, she had seen the hand of fate in their opportune departure.

As she and Sam sat together before the long window of their *salon*, the evening before she sailed, looking silently down on the lights of Montmartre, flung out in the darkness like jeweled chains, she became aware that he was even more deeply troubled than he confessed. Not wishing to force his confidence, she waited tranquilly for him to unburden himself of his own accord; and when at last, almost overcome with pain and weariness, she was beginning to feel she could not endure the suspense of the charged silence any longer, he suddenly spoke with poignant vehemence.

"Cousin Sarah—I haven't known whether to say anything to you or not—but I am darned worried."

"About me, Sam? But I shall get along splendidly! I'm sure that David and Jacqueline will take the best of care of me. And after I reach home, I shall be among friends."

"No, not about you," he said almost brusquely. "I'll miss you a lot, but you'll be all right. I know that."

"Then you really think there is going to be a war?" she asked, searching for the next eventuality which might cause him distress.

"Yup. I guess so. Any day now. You'll be out of here in the nick of time."

The cheerfulness with which he said this was unmistakable. Again Sarah Atkinson waited.

"It's Faith," he burst out at last. "I'd like to know who the gentleman of color is among her firewood. I'm not so sure it's a *colored* gentleman at that.—Didn't you think, Cousin Sarah, there was something darned fishy about the way she lit out?"

"She had been longing to go home for years, Sam. And Rudolf's letter was perfectly clear and logical. I thought it was very thoughtful of him to write us as he did, explaining that Faith had not had time to do so herself, and that he——"

"Good God, Cousin Sarah, you're not such a damn fool as to believe Rudolf von Hohenlohe didn't write that letter with his tongue in his cheek! He's a gentleman—and a diplomat—and Faith's husband. If he hadn't been, he'd have sent me a missive that read something like this: 'Dear Sam: Sebastian de Cerreno has been in Denmark raising hell. He's raised good and plenty. Now there's been a show-down and Faith's got across the river before the ice cracked underneath her, but it's been pretty thin in places, and she's all in. So I've helped her make a quick getaway. It's just as well anyhow, because though *Gott ist mit uns* and all that, you never know, and maybe there'll be quite a war. If I should happen to be pushing up daisies in a year or two, Faith will be better off in the U. S. A. And in case S. de C. decides to leap lightly across the Atlantic in the meantime, I'd rather like to know that Don Juan would encounter a dueña. Thanking you for the same, I'm ever yours truly, R. von H.' "

"Sam! Really!"

"Well, that's the way things are, Cousin Sarah, and you're it."

"I'm what, Sam?"

"The dueña. Give up the idea of Salem, won't you? I always thought it was a damn poor idea anyway. Go and settle down on Faith, and sit tight till I can get there, like a good sport. I'll be along after a while, honest I will. But just for now—You could feature yourself in Hamstead, couldn't you?"

"My dear Sam——"

"Don't you think Rudolf has that much coming his way? He's had a tough break—mostly his own fault, I know, but he's had it. It seems to me——"

" 'Why don't you speak for yourself, John?' "

Sam, who had begun to pace up and down the room, stopped suddenly in his tracks.

"Why don't I—*Cousin Sarah!*"

"If we are going to speak without reserve, we might as well be thorough in the process," said Sarah Atkinson imperturbably. "But you know I shall be very glad to go to Hamstead—for Faith's sake as well as for Rudolf's. As for 'featuring' myself there, I shall be extremely happy. I will go and wait—for you to rejoin me."

. . . . .

She had not overestimated her prospective contentment in the quiet village. During the two years since she had gone there to live, she had not known a restless day. She found a deep and peaceful satisfaction in the performance of light household tasks, for she excelled in the homely arts, though she had never practised these since her girlhood; and as she went industriously about the paneled house in Hamstead, on the days when her rheumatism did not trouble her too much, she felt she was recapturing half-forgotten but treasured memories of her youth in Salem. Moreover, she adored Faith and Hansel, and she found all her neighbors congenial. The integrity and simplicity of Uncle Ephraim and Aunt Emmeline appealed to her strongly; she did not find it hard to be "sociable" with them; she found it agreeable. She was always pleased when the grim Miss Manning, or the gossipy Mrs. Elliot came to "pass the afternoon," bringing her sewing; and when Caleb Hawks, who was also a fairly frequent visitor, appeared, puffing and panting before her, the pleasure she took in his company was evident.

As he climbed ponderously upon the piazza, mopping his brow, one sultry afternoon in late August, she was instantly aware that he had not sought her out, this time, for the sole purpose of being "sociable." He "meant business" as he himself was wont to express it. And he came straight to the point.

"I want me and you should have a little talk together," he said. "Quiet."

"It is always quiet in Hamstead, isn't it, Mr. Hawks?" Sarah asked smilingly.

"Well, yes. In a manner of speakin'. But I don't want no interruptions. Where's Hansel? Down to the swimmin' hole?"

"Yes. I'm sure he won't be back a minute before suppertime.—Of course you'll stay for supper with us, Mr. Hawks?"

"Thank you kindly.—And where's Faith? Most generally, when I come over, I see her workin' in that garding of hers. She ain't took sick has she?"

"No, indeed! She's very well. In fact, though she isn't working in her garden, she's gone to a meeting of the Garden Club, at Mrs. Low's lovely place near Belford. You know Faith was invited to join the club last year—Mrs. Castle is one of the most prominent members and I believe it was she who suggested it. I think Faith has taken a great deal of pleasure in the meetings. Mrs. Conrad came for her early this morning. I imagine they'll be rather late getting back."

"Good!" said Mr. Hawks heartily. "What I mean is, I'm real pleased Faith is gettin' acquainted with these nice women all over the state, and that's a fact. Low and Conrad is runnin' about neck to neck politically these days—I look to see Low go faster and Conrad go further. M-mebbe I'm mistaken, but that's the way I figger it out.—I guess Cal Castle is pleased enough to be back in his shoe factory in Belford, 'stead of in Berlin these days, and he'll stage a come-back to public life when his party comes back into power again. I always thought his wife was a kinda hatchet-faced woman, but she's fond o' Faith and I don't deny she's ben real kind to her. I sorta think Faith mighter broke down if it hadn't ben for that fortnight she spent at the beach with the Castles right after graduation.—But Faith ain't got no airs and graces, no matter how stylish society she's took out in. She mingles considerable right here in the village, don't she?"

"Oh, yes! She and I have both joined the Daughters of the American Revolution and the Home Missionary Society, and we go to church regularly."

"You ain't got no suspicions Faith's got leanin's toward being a Catholic, have you?"

"Why, Mr. Hawks, I never thought of such a thing! Certainly she's never intimated.—What made you ask?"

"Well, I dunno. Now and again she goes off with the Perez. I never give the matter much thought 'til just lately. But my son-in-law, Ted

Jenkins, you know, that's manager of the factory, tells me he's heard some talk about her bein' seen in the Catholic Church real frequent. Odd times. Week days."

"It is probably because Faith is feeling the need—and the comfort—of prayer and meditation more urgently than ever before in her life," said Sarah Atkinson, with a candor which once would have been impossible to her. "When that sense of need overwhelms us, it doesn't always conveniently come at half-past ten on Sunday morning, Mr. Hawks. The Catholic Church realizes this, and no desperate soul yearning to enter it is ever turned away from locked doors."

"Well now, that's a thought," said Caleb Hawks looking relieved. "I guess I'll take it up with Mr. Sleeper, my pastor at the First Congregational. Mebbe we could keep our church open too. But be that as it may, I'm glad you don't think Faith's goin' to take any rash steps. I've got considerable respect for your judgment, ma'm. There's another matter, though, that's troublin' me that I think ought to be took up and took up quick."

"Yes," said Sarah encouragingly.

"I want Faith should be naturalized. Without waitin' a day."

"You want her to resume her American citizenship?"

"Yes, I do, Miss Atkinson, and that's a fact. An' I want she should do it before it's too late."

He spoke with extreme earnestness, leaning forward and pointing one large pudgy forefinger at Sarah Atkinson. She could see the carbuncle in his ring gleaming.

"It won't be many months now before the U. S. A. is drew into this damn war," he said with conviction. "And unless we can get them naturalization papers fixed before it is, Faith is going to be an enemy alien. Right here in her own home. Folks could make it pretty unpleasant for her. Some of 'em did the time the *Lusitania* wuz sank. But that warn't a circumstance to what it 'ud be now. Faith ain't rose the way she has in this community without makin' some enemies along with some friends. I want to spike the guns of them skunks that's aimin' to hurt her and me through her! I guess I can steal a march on 'em before they oust me outta office, like they think they're goin' to! That mayoralty ain't much in itself, but I aim to make it a pretty powerful lever!"

He paused for a moment, completely out of breath. Then he went on relentlessly.

"You talk to her," he said, "this very night. And listen—while you're talkin' to her about them papers—talk to her about her name too, will you?"

"Her name!"

"Any woman with your judgment can see that Faith can't call herself the Baroness von Hohenlohe," said Mr. Hawks, pronouncing the words slowly and painfully. "Not in a state like this, even if Germany and the U. S. A. warn't on the point of springin' at each other's throats, which they are. I called Rudolf Mr. Lowe myself when I met him, as a sort o' compromise for—Hohenlohe. An' them young hoodlums that feeds out o' Faith's hands at the High School and the Day Nursery, call her Mrs. Lowe for the same reason. It's a pretty good compromise, seein' as how 'lowe is the last part of her own name too! But now she's gettin' intimate with the wife of the Lieutenant Governor—over to her Belford place to-day you tell me!—and I don't want no confusion between Low and Lowe, not for the world. It's taken less than that to defeat a ticket a good many times, and that's a fact! I want she should come right out and call herself Faith Marlowe, and that fine kid of hers Christian Marlowe III. I tell you, if we're goin' to have the first Christian Marlowe spirit marchin' on—an' we are—his name's goin' to be a powerful help to us."

Sarah Atkinson hesitated. "I'm not sure that I follow you completely," she said at length. "But in any case, don't you think it is perhaps too soon—to bring up the question of changing Faith's name? She has a great deal of reverence for Rudolf's memory. And I think she reproaches herself—because her marriage was not altogether harmonious—more than she ought to, all things considered. I think she kept hoping against hope for a second chance to make it a success—after the war was over, you know. And now that she's been robbed of that hope—I think she's very sensitive—to anything she thinks might reflect on Rudolf."

Mr. Hawks rose restlessly, and began to lumber up and down the piazza.

"Well now, you know best," he said uneasily. "But if there wuz some ways we could manage, it 'ud take a load offen me, and that's a fact.—And there's another thing on my mind mebbe you can help with. It's about that nice hired girl o' yours. I took a likin' to her the minute she set foot in my kitchen, and so did Mrs. Mead and Myra, who ain't easy to please. I'd hate to think she's in trouble!"

"In trouble!" exclaimed Sarah Atkinson with displeased astonishment. "Why, Mr. Hawks, Hilda is not only respectable, she's much more than that. She——"

"I didn't mean what you think," said Mr. Hawks looking very red and confused. "'Course she's respectable—she's a real good girl and that's why I'm worried about her. I should hate like anythin' to have her get into trouble as a—spy."

"A spy!" said Sarah Atkinson, recoiling. "Hilda!"

Hilda's mild and humble face, illumined by honest blue eyes and framed with tightly wound flaxen braids, rose before Sarah's startled vision. It was almost fantastic to suppose that anyone could accuse so simple and sweet a soul with perfidy. Yet if Mr. Hawks dreaded this contingency, his fears must be well-grounded.

"I don't suppose we c'd coax her into bein' an American citizen, too," he said anxiously. "'Twouldn't be so easy in her case, to rush things through. I'm feelin' druv and worried, ma'm, and that's a fact. I guess I won't stay for supper to-night after all, if you'll excuse me. I ain't got no appetite. I could hardly swallow my dinner this noon, and Mrs. Mead's feelin's wuz hurt considerable. I guess I'll go back to my office and work for a spell. The Lord knows I got a sight o' things to do there. I guess I'll bid you good-evenin'. But I'm bankin' on your help, ma'm, more'n you know."

. . . . .

Mr. Hawks spent a troubled night. The more he dwelt upon the many complications in which he had become involved through his affection for Faith, and his belief in her destiny, the less he was able to rest. And he did his breakfast even less justice than he had done his dinner the day before. This time Mrs. Mead remonstrated with him, her mouth looking unusually grim, and her small nose quivering. But he escaped from her, pausing for a moment as he reached the stone deer, in an effort to decide whether he had better go first to the factory, as usual, or whether he should follow the impulse which seemed to propel him in the direction of City Hall instead. He finally decided upon the latter course; and as he opened the door of his outer office, he was amazed to find himself confronted by Faith, who greeted him affectionately.

"Well, well," he said, brightening at once. "Come right in, Faith, and set down. Did you have a nice time yesterday? I was real pleased to hear you went down to the Lows' place with Anne Conrad. It's downright handsome, as you might say, now ain't it?"

"It's a lovely place. And I had a beautiful time. I don't know just what there is about women who work in gardens that makes them appeal to me, but they always do. I suppose association with flowers puts a sort of fragrance into their lives."

"Well that's a sweet pretty thought, Faith. You have such thoughts frequent, don't you? And put 'em into words too, smart and quick. Lord Almighty I won't forget that talk you made to the school, not to my dyin' day. St. Michael! Surrounded by All Angels! Lord Al—"

"It was about Rudolf that I wanted to speak to you—that is indirectly," said Faith. "I have decided to build a memorial to him."

Caleb Hawks hitched around in his seat, and swallowed hard several times in swift succession. Considering his firm conviction that all Faith's affiliations with Germany and the Germans should be severed as soon as possible, and all traces of them removed, her suggestion was extremely distasteful to him.

"What kind of a memorial?" he said uneasily. "You mean a handsome monument, or the like of that, in the Hamstead cemetery? Sebastian Perez could help you with that, mebbe, better'n I could. He carves real natural-lookin' urns and wreaths an'——"

"Sebastian Perez is going to help me," said Faith. "I've been to see him already. But I need your help too.—No. I don't want to put up a monument to Rudolf in the Hamstead cemetery. Why should I? He isn't buried there. He's buried in France. I said a memorial, anyway, not a monument."

"Well?" said Caleb, still uneasily.

"As soon as the United States goes into the war, we're going to need more room at the Day Nursery," said Faith. "The factory hands and marblecutters will have to go off and fight, won't they? Well, that will mean that lots of women who aren't working now will have to begin. And they'll have to leave their children with us. I think you ought to have an architect draw plans for wings on either side of the present building—that could be the central unit in the new plant. I think you ought to get started on it right away too, before the price of construction goes up—you've land enough."

"Well I don't know but what I have," said Caleb. "I don't know but what it 'ud be a good idea, come to think of it. I dunno as women can chip up marble, but they can make pencils. I had orter of thought of that myself, Faith, without your remindin' me that I may be dependent upon 'em. They've all got parcels of young 'uns, and if their husbands gets drew into this war, same as you say, why they couldn't come and work in my factory unless they cud park them kids somewhere. And then what would happen to my factory, I'd like to know?"

An expression of alarm came into his bulging eyes, and he half rose, as if to start out in immediate search of an architect. Faith laid a detaining hand on his arm.

"Nothing is going to happen to your factory," she said soothingly. "Its output will probably be doubled and trebled—and possibly changed in character. Are your contracts for supplies in the most advantageous condition?"

Caleb Hawks' jaw suddenly dropped. He stared at Faith in amazement. As if oblivious of his looks, she went calmly on.

"So we must be prepared to meet the changed situation at the Nursery," she said. "And besides the new wings, which you will naturally wish to add yourself, we shall need a playground. Not just an open place on the street, bleak and bare, with a few swings and some sandboxes; but a secluded garden with plenty of room for the children to romp, and trees and grass and flowers too. So I came here to get your advice about buying the land back of the Nursery, where Mr. Emery has his garage and repair-shop, and where those tenements of his are. You know he is going to move his business into new quarters, because those he has aren't large enough any more; and of course you know too that the tenements have been condemned by the Board of Health, because you had a hand in that. So he is willing to sell me the property at a very fair price. At least it seems to me a very fair price. I talked it over with him Wednesday when I went to see him about turning in my Dodge for a Packard—the poor Dodge has taken an awful punishing on the roads between Hamstead and Hinsboro these two winters, and I need a larger car now anyway."

"Look here, Faith," gasped Caleb, "you're goin' ahead so fast I can't follow you. Emery has ben threatenin' to get me ousted from office, on account of them stinkin' tenements of his—beg pardon, that slipped out before I noticed—and now you have bought a new car, and made him an offer for his land and——"

"I think it will all work out very nicely," Faith said smoothly. "Especially if you should deed him some land in the suburbs for his new tenements—you have lots of it out there that isn't doing any particular good to anyone. Well, then we would have plenty of space back of *your* memorial for *my* memorial."

She came and sat down on the arm of his chair, picking up a pad and pencil that lay on his desk and beginning to sketch.

"It would be something like this," she said, "the swings and sandboxes would be over here, and a croquet ground and poles for volley ball; and this would be an open run for any kind of games. But here we would have gravel walks, with borders of flowers between them and the grass-plots; and we would have a lily pool here, and trellises with rambler roses here. And there would be a high brick wall around the entire enclosure, which would be covered with ivy by and by. And against this wall, in the center, a fountain——"

Caleb Hawks, following her fingers as they flew rapidly over the paper, nodded intently.

"A white marble fountain, with a bas-relief representing angels—multitudes of angels. And stepping out from among them, a full-sized figure of St. Michael. With his sword uplifted and his foot resting on a dragon. Sebastian Perez has made me a drawing of the model. I want you to look at it. Don't you think that is beautiful, Uncle Caleb?"

She drew a piece of heavy white paper from her handbag and held it out to him. Caleb swallowed hard.

"It's sweet pretty, an' that's a fact," he said rather huskily.

"Of course the whole garden will be a memorial to Rudolf, but this figure will—guard over it," Faith said simply. "You see, there will be an inscription on the base of the statue: just the letters and numerals—R. von H.—1880–1916—'*Dulce et Decorum Pro Patria Mori*': that is a Latin proverb which means, 'It is sweet and fitting to die for one's country.'"

Caleb blew his nose. "Well, I guess Rudolf thought it was," he said with visible emotion. "I dunno as you could do better than to put them words on that statue. An' I guess if there's anyone goin' to object to a memorial like this, he'd be a pretty mean skunk."

"No one is going to object to it," said Faith, in the same soothing voice that she had used before. "Uncle Caleb, after I got home last night, Cousin Sarah told me about your visit yesterday. I am sorry that you and she should have worried—about my naturalization, and my name, I mean. Because I had been on the point of talking to you on those two subjects myself."

Again Caleb's jaw dropped.

"You see," Faith said softly, "Rudolf thought of all that. He told me the night I went away that he had always been glad we named our son for both his grandfathers, because some time Hansel might want to choose—between his two names. So as soon as you can arrange for the necessary formalities—I will be Faith Marlowe again, and Hansel will be Christian Marlowe III. And we will both be American citizens."

Faith rose. It was evident that she considered the interview over and the question settled. Caleb rose too, and clapped her affectionately on the shoulder.

"Well, this is a big relief to me, an' that's a fact," he said heartily. "You sure have taken a pile o' worries off my chest, and give me some real smart ideas besides. Them raw materials! Them tenements! Them wings! That garding! I guess Will Emery's guns is spiked all right, and his crowd's too. I guess I won't hear no more gossip about not wantin' 'a pro-German mayor in Hinsboro.' I guess me and you is goin' to sail right along without any monkey wrenches being thrown into our works!" He paused, panting, and mopped his brow. "Well, I guess I can make out to eat some dinner after all. I guess Mrs. Mead's mind will be relieved. You'll stay and have a bite with me, won't you, Faith? Nothin' fancy of course."

Again he stopped, this time as if struck by a sudden thought. "Speakin' o' meals and such, Faith, reminds me of Hilda," he said anxiously. "The only thing's botherin' me now is what's goin' to become o' that poor girl, liable to arrest, like she is, as a German spy. It won't be so easy, takin' out naturalization papers for her. I guess we're stumped there."

For the first time since she had come into his office, Faith laughed. "I guess we're not," she said. "Hilda doesn't need any naturalization papers. After next Wednesday, she'll be an American citizen anyway."

For the third time that morning, Caleb Hawks' jaw dropped.

"What's that you're sayin'?" he gasped.

"Hilda and Perley Stubbs are going to be married," Faith said tranquilly. "At Marlowe Manor. Will you come to the wedding, Uncle Caleb?"

CHAPTER 39

On Thanksgiving Day a gala dinner was served in the new right wing of the Myra Higgs Hawks Memorial Day Nursery. This wing, like its twin, the left wing, was still incompletely equipped; but the families of the children who came to the Nursery regularly could easily be entertained there, and they and the numerous distinguished visitors who had come from various parts of the state were able to get a general impression of the improvements and innovations.

These impressions were highly favorable: even Mrs. Carolus Cavendish Castle, who was still prone to damning with faint praise everything she regarded through her clicking lorgnette, drew Sarah Atkinson aside with a purposeful gleam in her eye which certainly did not spring from disapproval.

"Suppose we sit down for a moment," she said impellingly. "I should like to have a quiet word with you. I am very much impressed with all this—really very much impressed. It occurs to me that it might be well for me to undertake the erection of a similar plant for my own employees in Belford—on a larger and more elaborate scale. If I did, do you think Faith would coöperate with me?"

"Faith is very busy," Sarah Atkinson said cautiously. "You know she has just taken over the management of the Marlowe Farm, with Perley Stubbs as foreman. Her Uncle Ephraim did not feel equal to the responsibility of it any longer—and there was no reason why he should have it, since Faith feels equal to anything! She has joined the Grange and the Holstein Friesian Association, and has spent every week-end lately going about looking at cattle. But it would do no harm, of course, to tell her what you have in mind and see what her reaction is. Here she is now, coming toward us. Will you excuse me, Mrs. Castle? I promised Mrs. Low to take her through the clinic, and I am afraid she is waiting for me."

Through her lorgnette, Mrs. Castle watched Sarah Atkinson's slow departure and Faith's rapid advance simultaneously. Her new victim had one arm linked through Hansel's, who had shot up unbelievingly during the last year, and the other through that of Angelico Mendoza's son, Serafino. She greeted Mrs. Castle gaily.

"Don't you want to come out to the garden with me and the boys, Aunt Annabelle?" she asked. "It is such a lovely warm day for November that lots of people are looking it over. When you consider that it is only three months since we began work there, I think you'll agree with me that we've made wonderful progress."

"Suppose Hansel and—his friend precede us," suggested Mrs. Castle, acknowledging the existence of Serafino reluctantly. "A little later we might rejoin them. But I should like to have a few words with you in private first, my dear, if I may."

"How fortunate! I was just wondering when I could wedge in a few words with *you!—Tante* Luise is sending me all my things, and I am expecting notice from the Port of New York any day saying that they are here. She went over to Copenhagen herself and supervised the packing, taking cases and cases from Schönplatz and Berlin to ship from Denmark with the rest of my possessions. I—I was very much moved. But it is exactly what I should have known she would do. Really, there is no one in the world like her. She and Father Hans have insisted that I should have not only everything that I—have acquired, but everything that was Rudolf's besides—his share of the heirlooms and all."

Mrs. Castle murmured something vaguely appreciative of such princely generosity.

"Of course most of it is Hansel's," Faith continued, "and he may wish to take it back to Germany sometime, since he may eventually inherit Schönplatz. All his cousins are at military training camps already." She shivered slightly, and looked out toward the garden where Hansel and Serafino were now vigorously attacking a volley ball and shouting at each other. "But at present it is better that all of it should be in the United States. And the part which is mine personally—some very beautiful Spanish things for instance, would never be sent back to Europe in any case. And I have no room for them in my house, even if they would be appropriate there. So I was just on the point of asking you if you wouldn't help me arrange for a loan exhibition at the Belford Museum of Fine Arts. We would call it a loan exhibition to protect Hansel's interest. But naturally much of it would be in the nature of a permanent contribution."

"My dear Faith! What a wonderful inspiration! We never could have acquired such masterpieces as you can offer us."

"I know," said Faith a little wearily. "There are paintings and tapestries and quantities of wrought silver and furniture. I might want to save out a few for myself or for—personal gifts. But not many. Most of them are really museum pieces. There is one of those gold beds, for instance, that is so very rare——"

"I should like to make quite an occasion of such an acquisition," said Mrs. Castle eagerly. "Before the exhibition is thrown open to the public we should have a pre-view sponsored by the Governor and Mrs. Warren and other public officials. Could I count on you to speak, Faith? You do it so remarkably well."

"Of course," said Faith almost listlessly. "Shall we go out to the garden now, Aunt Annabelle?"

Mrs. Castle rose, gathering her sables about her. She was already picturing herself presiding over the glittering gathering assembled in the Trustees' Room of the Belford Museum of Fine Arts. She had completely forgotten the Day Nursery which was to so far outshine the one she had come to Hinsboro to see.

. . . . .

Later on, she remembered it again. But for the moment her mind was agreeably and completely engrossed with the thought of the Loan Collection and Permanent Exhibit which she had persuaded Faith to give to the Belford Museum—for she was already convinced that the idea had been wholly hers, and was planning to present it as emanating from her resourceful brain when she next met the Trustees. She was so pleased that she graciously unbent and admired everything that had been accomplished in the Marlowe garden. And she was forced to admit that a great deal had been achieved in an unbelievably short time. Mr. Emery's garage and workshops and tenements had been razed; the ground had been leveled, resoiled and planted; the high wall of brick already shut out all unsightly surroundings; and from the center of the south side, the glistening statue of St. Michael shone white and splendid in the autumn sunshine against the background of angels.

Mrs. Castle moved toward it impressively, apparently oblivious of the groups clustered admiringly around it, though Faith was hailed by these with enthusiasm, and was soon conversing with them in a variety of tongues. Indeed she permitted herself to be detained so long and so often that Mrs. Castle finally felt forced to turn an impelling glance upon her. Faith gently detached herself from Mrs. Sokovitski and her baby, and rejoined the ex-Ambassadress.

"It is beautiful, isn't it?" she asked, with her eyes on the shining statue.

"It is really very creditable work. I was concerned when I heard you had entrusted it to an unknown marblecutter. I should have been delighted to approach some sculptor of real standing for you."

"But I didn't want a sculptor of standing to do it. I wanted Sebastian Perez. I went to him almost immediately after—after Rudolf was killed and told him about the memorial I had in mind. He worked on the figure secretly all summer. Otherwise it wouldn't have been ready for to-day, and I had my heart set on a Thanksgiving dedication."

"But there have been no dedication exercises!"

"Yes, there have," said Faith swiftly. "Everything that has happened to-day has been a part of them. You can have a dedication without prayers and programs, Aunt Annabelle."

Mrs. Castle glanced at Faith covertly, as if suspecting a veiled allusion to her own rapidly maturing plans for the opening of the Marlowe Permanent Collection and Loan Exhibit. But Faith's face was entirely bland, and Mrs. Castle decided it would be wiser not to charge her with thoughts that had possibly never entered her head.

"It is getting late," she said, rearranging her sables again. "I must find the Ambassador and go back to Belford. The last time I saw him he was sitting in a corner with that horrid Caleb Hawks, apparently telling ribald stories. And you call this a dedication!"

"Uncle Carolus tells funnier stories than any man I ever knew," Faith said enthusiastically. "That one about the plumber and his helper, for instance, is simply side-splitting."

"I'm surprised at you, Faith," said Mrs. Castle icily. "It verges on the obscene. I have repeatedly told the Ambassador that his stories will ruin his future and now when it is so important that he should reënter official life——"

"I think his stories are going to be almost as famous in this war as Lincoln's were in the Civil War," Faith said with conviction. "In drives, you know, and so on. If he thought up a really good slogan, he might even get into the next cabinet."

"I do not agree with you," said Mrs. Castle sharply. Nevertheless she looked at Faith covertly again, this time with redoubled attention. "Why not motor back to Belford with the Ambassador and myself for a late supper?" she asked. "I will send you home afterwards—unless you can spend the night, which would really be the better plan. Then we would have ample opportunity to discuss the Loan Collection."

"It is ever so kind of you, Aunt Annabelle, and I should love to. But I have promised to go and spend the evening with Señora Perez. She has not been at all well lately, and I am very troubled about her."

Mrs. Castle glanced carefully about her. None of the importunate and obnoxious groups was very close to her at the moment, although many of them were still lingering in the garden, far past the time, in her opinion, when they might reasonably have been expected to go home. She spoke to Faith in a metallic whisper.

"I don't often interfere in your affairs, Faith," she said in a tone that indicated she felt that she had been commendably forbearing. "But I really do feel I must speak to you about this Señora Perez, as she calls herself—of course that is equivalent to having an American woman call herself Smith or Jones or Brown. I really don't believe it is her name at all. I have only seen her once or twice, but I can't help feeling she isn't respectable. In fact—I dislike enormously to mention such a contingency, but we all have to face the facts of life occasionally, especially in connection with Europeans, though any woman of refinement shrinks from doing so—I can't help feeling that perhaps her son is—illegitimate. He has a great deal more talent than you would expect to find in an ordinary stone-cutter. And there is a certain distinction about his looks which is very arresting—I keep having the uneasy sensation of having seen him somewhere before. It makes me very uncomfortable to have you associate with him so much."

"Why?" asked Faith calmly. "Illegitimacy isn't contagious, is it?—Oh, Cousin Sarah! I was just going to look for you!"

Sarah Atkinson came forward with her usual slow and painful steps. She had on a new winter hat with a stiff turned-back brim, and a neat sealskin coat which nearly covered her gray taffeta dress, though the crackle of this could still be heard. Never had she seemed more completely the embodiment of all Puritan proprieties.

"Sebastian has had his Ford at the door for some time," she said without preamble. "So I think if Mrs. Castle will excuse you——"

"Of course she will! But what do you think she has been saying to me, Cousin Sarah? She has been telling me that she thinks Señora Perez is a lady with a past! Isn't that exciting? And that Sebastian Perez is a ba——"

"Faith!" exclaimed Mrs. Castle cuttingly.

"Well you did! That is you said you thought he was illegitimate. It means the same thing doesn't it? I always get mixed up on terms like that, because I have never heard them very often, except when silly little boys call to each other in the street, but I feel sure an illegitimate son is the same as a——"

"Faith!" exclaimed Mrs. Castle again still more cuttingly.

The corners of Sarah Atkinson's mouth suddenly twitched. She looked from Mrs. Castle to Faith with a gleam of curbed amusement in her fine faded eyes.

"Mrs. Castle is probably right, as usual," she said soberly. "But even if she is, we can hardly depend on the bar sinister to keep Sebastian warm, and he is sitting outside in the cold. Besides, I have the feeling that his mother wants to see you very much." She hesitated for a moment, and then laid her hand on Faith's arm. "I think she wants to talk to you confidentially," Sarah Atkinson added softly. "I know you will be very gentle with her, Faith, no matter what she tells you—very gentle and very sympathetic. And I really think you had better go to her as soon as possible."

"I am going," Faith said steadily, "and I will be very gentle with her, no matter what she tells me."

Mrs. Castle had moved majestically forward—she was preoccupied with a further arrangement of sables. Faith looked straight into Sarah Atkinson's eyes.

"And I shall not be surprised—or too much hurt, no matter what she tells me," she added unflinchingly. "Don't worry about me either, Cousin Sarah."

. . . . .

When Sebastian Perez had taken Faith to his mother, and placed a chair for her beside the great bed, draped with coarse spotless linen, he went quietly away. The bare whitewashed room was full of shadows. But as Faith looked down at the wasted figure lying motionless beneath the great crucifix, she knew, even though she saw the expression of the drawn gaunt face so dimly, that the dark silent woman who had kept her own counsel for nearly thirty years would indeed now unburden her heart.

"*Sea Usted bienvenida, Doña Fidelidad!*" she exclaimed almost joyfully, the smoldering light in her sunken eyes suddenly kindled. "You do me infinite honor in coming to see me—the one that I do not deserve."

"If it is an honor, I'm sure you do deserve it," Faith answered, trying to speak lightly. She had leaned over and kissed the sick woman on both cheeks, and as she did so, she had felt tears against her lips. Now, as she seated herself, Señora Perez clung to her hand as if she were grasping for salvation and strength.

"If I had known you were so ill I should have come in to see you every day," Faith went on. "Sebastian has excused himself for not telling me by saying he did not want to trouble me when I was busy with preparations for the dedication. But I am really very angry with him. I might have left Hinsboro without seeing you at all."

"The Baronesa is going away!" Señora Perez exclaimed with a note of questioning alarm.

"Only for a fortnight or so," Faith said soothingly. "Hansel and Mrs. Atkinson and Mr. Hawks and I are going to take a holiday trip to New York. We all want a change, for various reasons. So we are making an excuse of the fact that my mother-in-law has sent me a large shipment of household belongings. I think I really ought to see them through the customs myself, especially as I am planning to have most of them sent to the museum in Belford, and I must give orders for their direct dispatch. There are only a few pieces about which I have some special sentiment that I am reserving for myself." She hesitated for a moment, pierced with poignant pain. Then, conscious of the sense of deep mystic kinship which bound her to the prostrate woman before her, she added without betraying the effort the words cost her, "There are also a few that I should like to give to you, if you will let me."

"That you would like to give me!" Señora Perez echoed in stupefaction. "But why should you wish to do that, Doña Fidelidad?"

"Because they were given to me by Sebastian de Cerreno," Faith said steadily.

The invalid gasped and turned away her head, hiding her face. She did not loosen her grasp on Faith's fingers.

"Then you knew! You have known—all the time!"

"Yes, I have known all the time," Faith answered quietly, "from the moment that I saw—your son—and his. May I talk to you a little about him, and tell you how he happened to make me the gifts I wish to share with you? The first time I ever met him was in Madrid, at the home of his *Tia* Carlota, when I went there as a bride. He told me, rather satirically, that he supposed I would feel I was not really seeing Spain until I went to the Prado and stood in front of Murillo's 'Inmaculada' pretending to be spellbound. I was annoyed with him for jesting on such a subject, and I asked him if he would not take me to see it himself. He declined on the ground that he had an assignation with a little dancer named Felicidad. But afterwards he felt sorry he had hurt my feelings. So he sent me, with a very tender and delicate message, one of the sketches Murillo made while he was trying to put his vision of the Virgin in definite form. And from that time on, Don Sebastian made me many similar gifts. I think it is characteristic of him, Señora, that he is always sorry afterwards when he has been in the wrong, and has been eager to make atonement."

The Spaniard suddenly lifted her head. "It is true!" she said vibrantly. "He has the gift of repentance, as his brother has the gift of saintliness! He never guessed that I needed a protector! If he had, he would have given me protection."

"I know he would have," Faith said reassuringly.

"But he was only a young boy!" the woman cried impetuously. "A boy so beautiful that when he went along the streets of Granada every girl watched from her window or balcony till he had passed. He was an *hombre de amor,* even then, upon whom no woman of any age could look unmoved. But he was still so young himself that love was a mystery to him, and when it was offered him, he hardly knew what it was that he grasped for so hotly. He told me, Señora, that I was the first to—lie in his arms."

"If he told you so, you may be sure it is the truth," Faith said steadily.

"When I say I offered him my love, you must not think this was my practice, Señora," the sick woman went on imploringly. "He was my first and only lover—I swear it by the Holy Virgin! But from the moment I first saw him, I knew I could not live without him. I was a little older than he, and I made it very easy.—Can you understand what I'm trying to tell you, Señora?"

"Yes—yes—I understand," Faith said in a low voice.

"He gave me many presents, but he never offered me money—he had fine feeling, he knew that all he had had of me had been as freely given as it was freely taken. And then—when he had gone on his joyful careless way again, he would have come back—willingly—impetuously—if I had told him how it was with me. He might even have married me, for he was chivalrous as well as careless, Señora—he would not have looked prudently toward the future as a man of meaner spirit would have done. And I was tempted—greatly tempted. I loved him so that my heart pounded in my ears if I so much as heard his step, and I was carrying his child, his eldest son. And I was the daughter of an *hidalgo*, of a poor gentle family which would have been raised to glory and distinction by such a marriage.—Do you still understand, Doña Fidelidad?"

"Yes, I still understand. I—I shall understand everything you tell me. I have been even wondering if you would not tell me your real name, and whether you would not speak to me in English, which I know you must have learned at the convent to which you went as a girl."

"My name is Elena de la Barra, Señora," the Spaniard said slowly and distinctly.

"And what happened, Doña Elena, to deliver you from temptation?"

"I saw the child, Dolores de Romera, coming out of the Cathedral after her first communion," Elena de la Barra whispered. "She was all in white, and she carried lilies in her hand, and her face, beneath her veil and her garland, was the face of an angel. I knew that almost in her cradle she had been betrothed to Don Sebastian. And when I saw —what she could give him——"

"Many years later I saw her picture, taken on her wedding day," Faith whispered back. "Again she was all in white, carrying lilies in her hand, and her face was that of an angel. I know, Doña Elena, how you felt——"

"But afterwards—when tragedy came—I wondered whether I had done right. For Don Sebastian, who loves children as much as women love him, believed himself childless; and he was the father of my son. But how could I tell him the truth? I had fled from Granada, Doña Fidelidad, after seeing that vision at the church door. I took a ship in Malaga which brought me to New York, and then I found my way to Hinsboro, where an aunt and uncle now dead were then living. They befriended me. But they wrote my parents, when my baby was born, that we had died together. And then came the long years——"

"They must have been very long," Faith said slowly, gazing straight in front of her with unseeing eyes.

"They were endless! And through them all, I have been consumed with a burning flame. The fires of a woman's one passion are almost unquenchable."

"Yes," said Faith, still more slowly, "I know—that they are unquenchable."

"Even now, sometimes. . . . And added to the burden of loss has been this burden of futility. Since I have been so ill—it has seemed more than I could bear."

"If—if you knew that Don Sebastian was happy—after all—in the way that you had hoped to give him joy—would the burden be any lighter?"

"If I knew—*Sanctissima Maria,* what are you trying to tell me, Señora?"

Faith freed her hand gently, and walked slowly across the room. As she opened the door, Sebastian rose gravely from the deep chair in which he had been sunk, and looked at her hopefully.

"Have you any champagne in the house?" she asked surprisingly. "I think it would do your mother good to have some. Besides, I have learned to-day that I have a namesake, and it would make me very happy if you and the Señora would drink to her health with me."

"There is champagne, Doña Fidelidad. Sebastian will put a bottle on the ice at once. Will you tell us about the *niña* while it cools?"

Doña Elena's voice was breathless with excitement. She sat up in bed, her dark eyes glowing. Faith looked at her smilingly as she resumed her own seat.

"I used to hope that some day I would have a little girl of my own," she said. "But when my husband died, I thought I should have to wait until Hansel married, before I had a namesake. But now I have the good news of which I spoke. Shall I read you the letter which contains this? I have brought it with me."

"If that would be your pleasure, Doña Fidelidad."

Sebastian had come back into the room, carrying a cooler into which he had plunged a bottle of champagne. He sat down between Faith and his mother, his dark faoe glowing and expectant. As Faith opened her handbag, she noticed that the light in the shadowy room fell across his hair much as she had seen the light fall across the hair of a man sitting opposite her in a patio near Granada years before.

"My letter comes from Spain," she said, unfolding it, and spreading out the sheets covered with delicate handwriting, "from a very great and beautiful lady. Her name is Doña Dolores de Cerreno."

Sebastian gave a smothered exclamation, and half rose, glancing with distress toward his mother. She continued to gaze at Faith without moving, and Faith laid a restraining hand on Sebastian's arm.

"There is nothing in this letter that will cause any of us grief," she said reassuringly. "Listen! '*Excelentissima Señora:* Although I have never had the privilege of meeting you, I have long felt that you were my friend. My husband did not fail to tell me that had it not been for your firm faith in my recovery, our reunion could never have taken place, for he would not have permitted the great American surgeon to operate upon me. A year or more ago, when our son was born, my husband wrote to Dr. Noble, who in replying said, that he had shared the felicitous tidings with you; but now that he has left the peaceful valley of your habitation in order to extend his services to the suffering soldiers of France, I am venturing to communicate with you directly, to inform you that on All Saints' Day, I was safely and joyfully delivered of a daughter.'"

"*Madre de Dios!*" exclaimed Sebastian, half rising again. It was his mother who laid a detaining hand on his arm now.

"'When my husband entered my apartment to salute me after my *accouchement*,'" Faith went on reading, "'his first exclamation took the form of an impetuous question: Had I thought of a name for the child? My reply was immediate. "If it meets with thy pleasure, *alma de mi alma*, it is my wish that she should be called Fidelidad, since but for the lovely and courageous lady by that name, we could not have been accorded the bliss of bringing this precious infant into being."—"That was my thought also," my husband answered, in accents of unbounded happiness. We then embraced each other with ecstasy. . . .'"

The delicate sheets of paper fluttered in Faith's hands. Doña Elena leaned over and touched her.

"Doña Fidelidad!" she said imploringly.

"'We then embraced each other with ecstasy,'" repeated Faith more firmly, searching for the place where she had left off. "'And parted for the time being in order that I might maintain the tranquillity necessary for the welfare of my child. Owing to the injunction for early baptism laid upon us by our Holy Church, we were not able to defer this ceremony until after conferring with you, and therefore ventured to take your gracious consent to the name for granted; and on November the eighth our baby was baptized by Gabriel in the Capilla Real. To the name of Fidelidad was added that of Cristina, this being, as I believe you know, the name of my husband's sainted mother, who now rests with God. As if under the protection of her heavenly spirit and your beneficent influence, my daughter grows stronger and more beautiful every day; and it is my earnest hope that in the happy future you will do us the honor of coming to see her yourself. Meanwhile, I beg you to believe that I am, with expressions of the most exalted consideration, Dolores Antonio Maria de Cerreno y Romera.'"

"*Madre de Dios!*" exclaimed Sebastian de Perez once more.

This time neither Faith nor his mother sought to prevent him when he rose. They were gazing silently at each other, and he saw that the eyes of both were full of tears. And yet there was no grief in either woman's face. On one was an expression of infinite relief, as if from release from endless and unendurable strain; on the other was one of exaltation. It was Faith's voice which fell on the stillness like music.

"A secret shared is never so heavy a burden as one that is born in loneliness," she said. "May you and I not share ours, Señora? Shall we make a covenant together? I will reveal the hidden chambers of my heart to you, and you will do the same to me. Shall it be so?" She put her arms around Sebastian Perez' mother, and drew her closely to her breast. For a long moment they clasped each other. Then Faith turned and held out her hand to Sebastian Perez himself.

"We are going to drink to my namesake, are we not?" she asked, "to whom Don Sebastian gave my name because she is the child of my spirit, though I never bore him a child in the flesh. That great privilege has not been mine. But to a woman who has had it, I know it must have been the compensation for loneliness and exile and even shame, as the world, which understands so little, interprets shame.—Surely you will join with your mother and me, Sebastian, in our toast to your little sister!"

CHAPTER 40

FAITH was very tired. For two days after she reached New York, she did not get up at all, but lay listlessly in her brass bed at the Waldorf-Astoria, watching the comings and goings of the rest of the little group, in which, for the first time, she took only an inactive part. Sarah Atkinson went shopping while Hansel and Caleb stayed with Faith; then Caleb and Hansel went to the docks to make sure that the shipment from Denmark was all right while Sarah Atkinson stayed with her. When they came back with the report that it was, she was relieved, primarily for the reason that this meant she could stay in bed at least another day before she went down and looked it over herself.

"See here, Faith," Caleb said assertively, when for the third successive evening she dismissed the suggestion of getting dressed for dinner and going out to the theater with the brevity of complete exhaustion, "I'm going to get a doctor in to look at you if you ain't perked up by mornin'. You're plumb tuckered out. You need some good peppery tonic to build you up. I'm goin' to call the floor clerk and see——"

"Honestly, Uncle Caleb, I don't need a good peppery tonic! I was—rather exhausted, but I don't need anything except a good rest, and I'm having it. I'm enjoying it."

"Well, I've seen you when you looked to me as if you were enjoyin' yourself more," he said still doubtfully. "You ain't one of them women that favors layin' in bed. Some do. Now I seen one to-day that I bet my bottom dollar would delight in it. She was down to the dock pesterin' the officers there to tell her when some boat that's overdue would be in. She appeared to blame it upon them because there'd been a storm at sea. 'It's very inconvenient for me to keep comin' down here,' says she, lookin' as if she might burst right out cryin'. 'But I s'pose everyone would think I wuz heartless if I wasn't here when the boat come in, even if I froze to death waitin' for it.' And with that she turned to me and asked if *I* couldn't help her—in one o' them whinin' kind of voices. If there's anythin' I despise it's a woman that whines when she talks to you. Lord Almighty! As if I could tell her when the damned old boat would be in."

Caleb Hawks drew a large purple handkerchief from his pocket and blew his nose with a loud snort. Faith propped herself up on her pillows and looked at him with amusement.

"This woman seems to have annoyed you very much, Uncle Caleb," she remarked.

"Annoyed me! Say, Faith, she made me so mad I could of choked her. 'There isn't a soul in New York to help me,' she kept saying. 'It's pretty forlorn for a woman in my situation not to have someone to help her.'"

"Uncle Caleb, I believe she was trying to pick you up."

"Pick me up!" he roared indignantly. "Faith, you had otter seen her. Sixty years old if she wuz a day, and one of that type that's so skinny you can't tell whether they're comin' or goin' unless you look at them close. And stringy hair fallin' all around her face that didn't look like it had been combed in a week. And somethin' fishy about the eyes. Ugh! She give me the creeps!"

"Did she tell you whom she was waiting for, Uncle Caleb? Is it a long lost lover whom she hasn't seen since she was young and charming?"

"Now then, Faith, you quit your kiddin'—not but what I'm relieved to have you act a little more like yourself. Yes, she did. And that simply capped the climax. It's her son, her only son. 'He would go an' enlist in the French Army,' says she, 'though why he shouldda done such a crazy thing, I can't imagine. And now he's bein' sent back blind for me to take care of all the rest of his life. I'm not equal to it,' says she, 'what I need is someone to take care of me.'"

"Oh, Uncle Caleb, how—how horrible!"

"It wuz horrible, Faith, and that's a fact. Think o' that poor man bein' brought back blind and left at the mercy of a spineless specimen like that!"

As Caleb Hawks mentally reviewed this conversation during the night, he began to regret having told Faith about the episode. He had discovered that she had a way of regarding every case of perplexity and misery that came within the range of her observation as her personal responsibility. If she had not, she would never have stepped into the breach at the Hinsboro High School, or taken over the direction of the Day Nursery, or involved herself—as she evidently had—with the mysterious tragedy which had darkened the life of the Señora Perez. That he guessed, blindly but shrewdly, had somehow been the last straw—He had been anticipating her present collapse ever since Thanksgiving Day, when she had come into his house so silently, with that strange sacrificial look on her face, after leaving the Spaniards' house. She was carrying a self-assumed load of burdens too heavy for her strength. Yet he felt uneasily certain that in the morning, she would tentatively suggest the assumption of another.

He was not mistaken. She knocked at his door before he had finished shaving, and confronted him, completely dressed for the street, while he stood staring at her with tufts of lather dropping from his ruddy double chin.

"I am sorry to be so inopportune," she said apologetically. "But I was afraid you would escape me. I would like to have breakfast with you and afterwards I think we had better go down to the docks. It is really time those cases were cleared, and on their way to the Belford Museum."

It was not until they were bumping along over the cobblestones of lower New York that she said anything to cause him uneasiness, and he had begun to be hopeful that he had worried unnecessarily, when she slipped her hand quietly into his.

"I have been thinking over what you told me about that futile woman," she said. "If she is on the wharf again when we get there, I think I will talk to her a little. If she really isn't able to take care of her blind son, and doesn't know anyone who can do it for her, don't you think perhaps——"

"Now, Faith! I ben kickin' myself all night for tellin' you that. I don't see how I ever come to be so dumb. You gone way beyond your strength already, and the Lord knows I'm so druv I don't know what to do, with a war comin' on an' all——"

"I know. But we could manage somehow. I've been thinking of building a little cottage for Perley and Hilda anyway, and that would give me plenty of room——"

"Land sakes, Faith! You can't take this fellow into your house! He may be a regular scalawag for all you know. A man ain't moral just because he's blind."

"I don't like men that are too moral," retorted Faith. "No woman does, really. She only pretends she does, when she thinks she ought to. And I don't think I ought to."

"Faith, you'll get into trouble some day, the crazy things you say. And the crazy things you *do!*"

"I'm not going to get into trouble this time."

After they had spent nearly two hours on the wharf without seeing anything of a docking ship, or of the latest disturber of Caleb Hawks' peace of mind, he thankfully decided that this might be true. But as he and Faith were preparing to leave, after giving every necessary direction in regard to the shipment of her cases, he suddenly caught sight of the whining woman charging rapidly in his direction.

"It's just coming in!" she gasped. "The boat, I mean. It'll be tied up before noon, and the passengers let off. You were so sympathetic with me yesterday when I told you about my terrible trouble, that I couldn't help wondering whether you and your daughter wouldn't stay with me now and see me through my ordeal."

"I warn't at all sympathetic with you," Caleb said shortly. "An' my daughter ain't well. She's had a tirin' mornin'. I want she should go home and rest."

"Oh, but it would detain you such a short time, and I haven't anyone else to help me! Otherwise I wouldn't think of appealing to a stranger! —Won't *you* try to persuade your father?" the woman insisted, turning to Faith, who was looking at her with veiled aversion.

Certainly Caleb Hawks had not given her an exaggerated description of this obnoxious creature. She was all that he had said and more. Nevertheless, Faith answered her courteously.

"I'm really not tired at all. If you think we can help you, we shall be glad to stay. That must be the boat, just turning around now, isn't it?—I was distressed to hear that such a tragedy had overtaken your son."

"Yes," the woman said impatiently. "It is sad, but as far as he's concerned, of course it's his own fault. He didn't have to go to war. It wasn't as if he'd been French. Though he'd lived in France so long, he'd got into all sorts of loose ways." She lowered her voice, and drew Faith a little away from Caleb. "The last time he came home, almost ten years ago," she said querulously, "he shocked the people in my home town almost to death. He kept talking about men's mistresses and nude models and things like that just the way you'd talk about the weather. He'd refer to friends of his who were dope fiends and degenerates without any more shame than if they'd been clergymen and merchants. It'll be the same now—perfectly disgusting. I don't know how I'm going to put up with it, because this time, I won't be able to look forward to having him leave. There isn't a soul I can ask to help me with him. I'm a widow and he's my only son. He went away from me voluntarily when he was hardly more than a boy, and he's only been home two or three times since. I feel as if I scarcely know him. And I haven't got a lot of useful cousins and aunts, the way most women have. And think how helpless he's going to be!"

"Yes," said Faith slowly, "I am thinking—how helpless he's going to be. Are you sure you can't think of anyone who would take care of him?"

"Oh, I'm positive! I've tried to find someone—*anyone*—and I can't. I've cried all night long, every night, since I gave up hope of relief." She began to cry now, hysterically. Then, after a few moments of senseless sobbing, she dabbed at her eyes, rolled her handkerchief into a wet ball, and looked searchingly at Faith. "Haven't I met you somewhere before?" she asked curiously. "I can't remember that I have, but somehow you look familiar to me."

"No," said Faith still more slowly. "I don't think we've met before. I don't remember you, and yet I usually remember people very well—even people I haven't seen since I was a child. But it's strange—even though I can't remember seeing you, it seems as if I could remember hearing you cry. Do you—cry a good deal?"

"I guess you'd cry a good deal if you had as much to bear as I have!" the stranger sobbed plaintively, raising her handkerchief again.

"The boat's starting to swing in, ma'm," Caleb said brusquely. "Mebbe we better walk over to where they're puttin' the gangplank, if we're goin' to meet this son of yours. He won't be lookin' for you, the way things are."

"No, he won't be looking for me," the woman agreed, crying more violently than ever. "I'll have all the responsibility to bear. In fact I don't even know that he'll be able to walk off with someone leading him. He's been injured in other ways besides his eyes. He may be a permanent cripple. Oh, it's perfectly awful! You don't know how helpless I feel!"

Caleb, aware that Faith was trying to meet his eyes, looked uncomfortably away.

"Well, I guess we do at that," he said scornfully. "But if you go on cryin' like that, you'll strangle.—Not but what it would be much of a loss," he added under his breath. "I guess Faith's right as usual. I guess mebbe we'll have to look after this poor blind feller whether he's a scalawag or not. It 'ud be murder to leave him to the mercies of a woman like that. Why, she'd drown him, just cryin' over him.—If I could find you a glass of water somewheres, would you drink it?" he added aloud.

"Oh, I couldn't possibly swallow anything! Oh, I think the gangplank is going to be put down! Oh, I simply can't bear it!"

The usual crowd of porters and visitors had begun to collect. There was the confused sound of shouted greetings, creaking ropes, lowered boards, and rushing feet. A stream of people carrying small but multitudinous pieces of precious hand baggage, began to come down the gangplank, squirming and wedging their way along. The tumult of voices rose higher.

"Look, there's Mae! Hello there, Mae, it was great of you to come and meet us! . . . You just wait 'til you see what I brought home for you! It's the peachiest little. . . . Oh, any time now! All the Americans that could left Europe long ago. . . . How's mother, Jim? I said, *how's mother?* Gee, isn't it great to get home before Christmas after all? The worst storm in twenty years, the captain said. Yes, but this time he meant it. . . . There, there, for God's sake don't cry so. . . ."

Something suddenly snapped in Faith's subconscious mind. She seemed to be lying again, for the first time, in a narrow berth on an ocean liner, listening to the voices of men and women who had come to see their friends off, and the voices of men and women who were going away, as these resounded through the corridor outside the little cabin where she lay, lonely and frightened.

"Hello there, Tom! Are you with Jack and Mabel? No I haven't been able to locate them anywhere. . . . Well, I did mean to bring some flowers, but I couldn't seem to get around to buying any, and I thought oranges would taste pretty good, they're such a rarity at this time of year. . . . *For God's sake don't cry so, Helen, it isn't as though the boy were in his grave. Most mothers would be pretty proud to have their sons win a prize that would give them two years in Paris free——*"

Faith gave a quick gasp of horror. Then she put her hands on the sobbing woman's shoulders and shook her.

"Listen!" she said. "I think I remember where I heard you crying before! On a boat, the night your son started for France to study art. Do you live in Jonesville, Ohio? Is your name Helen Dudley?"

The woman gulped, dropping her handkerchief. Before she had time to reply, Faith had read her answer in her face, and had given an exclamation that cut through to Caleb's heart.

"You're Sam Dudley's mother!" she cried. "*Sam Dudley's mother!* And Sam—Sam is being brought home—*blind!*" She threw back her head, as if to shake away the tears which blurred her own vision. Then she held out her hands and rushed forward.

She was just in time. A stretcher, carried by four men, was being carefully borne down the gangplank, and on it was extended a motionless form, so emaciated that the blankets which enshrouded it were hardly lifted by its outline. Two transparent hands lay nervously over the coverings which concealed the long figure. Above these was a bandaged head, of which only the stubbly chin, the blue lips, and the shrunken nostrils were visible. Faith clove through the crowd, and flung herself down beside the stretcher as its bearers lowered it to the platform.

"Sam! My darling Sam!" she cried. "You're safe! You've come back to me! *Oh, thank God, I've got you anyhow!*"

PART IX

Sam

CHAPTER 41

"WELL sir, as I've been sayin' to my daughter Myra all winter, it was fortunate you come home just when you did. If you hadn't, Faith wouldda broke down. She was plumb tuckered out, and that's a fact."

"And since my return, of course she's had a complete rest," Sam answered rather dryly.

The two men were extended in easy chairs on the deep piazza overlooking the meadows and mountains at the rear of Marlowe Manor. Iced drinks, sandwiches, and smoking supplies were laid out on a small wicker table that stood between them; and at their feet lay a young police dog, which turned gleaming and watchful eyes on Sam every time he so much as shifted his position. Now and then Caleb refilled Sam's glass, measuring off whisky and ginger ale with the sure touch of one who is in no doubt of another's tastes; but Sam reached for his sandwiches and cigarettes himself, his long slim fingers closing quickly over them, without fumbling or hesitation. He smoked slowly, tilting his head back as if to watch the blue rings floating off into the quiet air; but he often lighted one cigarette from another, while Caleb, on the other hand, sat indefinitely chewing one huge black cigar, to which he apparently had no thought of applying a match.

For a long time an unembarrassed silence, permeated with comfort and congeniality, reigned undisturbed. Then Mr. Hawks broke in upon it with a continuation of his satisfied reminiscence.

"You couldda knocked me over with a feather," he said, though he now tipped the scales at two hundred and seventy-three pounds, "when Faith went down on her knees in front of that stretcher on the wharf. I certainly did think she had suddenly took leave of her senses. She'd ben lookin' pretty peaked for quite a spell, 'specially after Thanksgiving, when that sick Spaniard I told you about seemed to suck the strength right out of her—and I was considerable worried about her. But land! I never hope to see a woman act more level-headed than she did, after them first few minutes. I didn't know what had happened, hardly, before she had you to bed in Hansel's room, and a good doctor there, and everythin' runnin' on velvet as you might say. And she never once forgot to be civil to that lily-livered old bi–beg pardon, Sam. That slipped out before I noticed."

"Nice of you to speak for me, Caleb," Sam said reassuringly, waving the slim hand that held the cigarette, and taking another long drink from his highball.

"An' you settin' propped up on pillows, eatin' a real Christmas dinner a week later," Caleb went on, "when you looked as if you'd pass away any minute that morning we brung you up to the Waldorf. I know it don't depress you none to hear this, Sam, or I wouldn't tell you, but if I ever seen a livin' man appear like a corpse, you wuz it.– And Faith telegraphin' Sunnora Perez to find out would she take over Faith's Spanish classes for the rest of the year, and Sunnora Perez telegraphin' back that she *would!* An' Faith fixin' up her attic for you because an artist oughta feel more to home in an attic than anywhere else, and making it look downright handsome, as you might say–'course I don't care much for that gloomy picture you got over your bed, but that's a matter of taste. The rest is certainly fine. An' you helpin' to arrange that exhibit down to the Belford Museum, and sayin' just where everythin' ought to go, same as if you had your sight, so's 'twould be just right when 'twas finished. An' since then, fittin' into everythin' easy and natural, givin' talks to the Fine Arts Class at the High School, and tellin' that gang o' young hoodlums that calls themselves Boy Scouts all about the Foreign Legion, wearin' your uniform with that funny bunnit on your head, and explainin' to the Persian Panthers how it was that Russia come to fall——"

Mr. Hawks paused for breath, spat out some fragments of his cigar which he had reduced to mere shreds, and refilled his own glass. As he did so, he turned his carbuncle ring around so that he could enjoy the color of the stone as he proceeded.

"If you hadn't done all that," he said gratefully, "I think it might have been a mite awkward for Faith, when war was declared, between Germany and the U. S. A., 'spite of everythin' we could do. 'Course folks are crazy about her–that is, most folks–an' all that, but feelin' runs awful high in war time, especially at the beginnin'. It made all the difference in the world, Sam, when you come here, just in the nick o' time, because you'd fought with the Allies, right from the start, and was a wounded hero and all that. Your condition has ben a real godsend, and that's a fact."

Caleb Hawks rose and stretched himself. There was a slight, but ominous sound of ripping.

"Lord Almighty, I guess I've bust somethin' again," he said, feeling around uneasily. "Sometimes I'm afraid I may be gettin' a mite too fleshy. But, land! If we go in for all them meatless, wheatless, sweetless days, they're talkin' about, I guess I'll reduce whether I want to or not. I guess Faith has got the right idea with all this plantin' of hers, and say, them farmerettes o' hers is real cute. I never wouldda believed I'd live to see the day that Emmeline Marlowe would let a parcel of High School girls overrun that house o' hers, but there they are, spry as can be.—Well, I guess I better go along and have Hilda look me over to see where that rip was. I hope I ain't seatless as well as eatless. See you soon again, Sam."

"You betcha," Sam answered, laughing.

He lit another cigarette, and leaning back in his long chair, reached for the smooth ears of the dog lying beside him. He felt these prick under his touch, and then, after a brief responsive quiver of joy, relax with contentment. The dog, whose registered name was Cerberus, but who was familiarly known as Russie, had been Faith's first gift to him after his return. She had brought it into his room on Christmas morning, and folded his thin arms around the warm, squirming puppy body, as she bent over to kiss his forehead.

"Here's a present for you, Sam!" she had said buoyantly. "Its name is Cerberus, and it's going to guard the entrance of the infernal regions for you—I mean so that you can't get into them, when you're feeling blue. A dog is so satisfying, don't you think so? It's always there, no matter who else goes off and leaves you. You don't mind if he licks your face, do you, Sam?"

No, he had told her a little huskily, he didn't mind. He wondered how she had realized instantaneously that he had been hungrily longing for a dog. Cerberus had never left him since then, except reluctantly and briefly, to be fed and exercised. The puppy was friendly to Caleb and Sarah, and fond of Hansel and Faith; but it was Sam whom he worshipped with all the intensity of canine devotion. Now, blissful under the soothing caress of his master's hand, he sank into the watchful doze which was his nearest approach to sound slumber.

Sam continued to stroke his dog's head, as he waited, without impatience and without restlessness, for Faith to come home. She was devoting much of her time to the farm these days, going over to the Nursery only two or three times a week, unless her presence there was urgently required. School was over for the summer, and even before it closed, she had not resumed the intensive work there that she had done before Sam's arrival. Señora Perez had proved entirely adequate as a Spanish teacher, and Miss Wilkins, Faith's assistant in the Home Economics Department, had been promoted. The Arts Class had remained under Faith's supervision, but Sam had actually done most of the teaching in it for her, from the time he was on his feet.

The transformation of the attic had absorbed them both during the period of his convalescence. Faith had conferred with him about every detail of its adornment and equipment. It was natural enough for her to ask whether he would rather have a tub or a shower in the tiny bathroom that was being wedged in between the eaves, and whether he wouldn't like the fireplace unbricked, and whether he didn't think it wouldn't be airier with more dormer windows. But that she should consult him about colors and fabrics exactly as if he could see them showed a sensibility of which only Faith, among all the women Sam had ever known, would have been capable. She did even more than this: she spoke to him about the pictures and furnishings which were originally destined for the Belford Art Museum, and asked him if he would not like to live surrounded by some of these.

"Of course I would, Faith," Sam said gratefully. "What are there for pictures?"

"There is one tiny Dürer—wonderful!—and two rather good Holbeins in the German art collection—nothing else you'd care for. It was surfeited with baroque that Rudolf's grandfather bought on his first trip to Italy—Carlo Dolce, Guido Reni, Sassoferrato—you know, all that. Belford would simply gloat and gasp over it. Don't rob Mrs. Castle of her triumph."

"I won't," Sam said, laughing. Then added, "Nothing Spanish?"

"Oh, yes. The Goya must go to Belford—inevitably—like Carlo Dolce's simpering saints. And I've kept out two little Murillos—a Mater Dolorosa for Doña Elena, and an Inmaculada for myself. Then there is a St. Sebastian by El Greco, and a portrait of Cecilia de Cerreno by Velasquez, and a Crucifixion by Ribera."

"Belford can have St. Sebastian for all of me," Sam said grimly. "And Cecilia de Cerreno too, as far as that goes. But if you think the Crucifixion wouldn't be missed, Faith—good God—what a picture!"

"I'm not sure that's a polite way to talk about God," she said teasingly, quoting the old reproof of her childhood. "Of course Belford won't miss it. I'll hang it over your bed, shall I? There's just the bed for you—"

"Not that gilded cage you had in Copenhagen?"

"Certainly not. That is the chief treasure of the Belford collection. Mrs. Castle and all the other virtuous ladies in the state will go and look at it every now and then, and think how wonderful it would have been to be wicked."

"Is that what you used to think when you slept in it, Faith?"

"Not exactly. . . . Well, anyway, the bed I started to tell you about before you forced all this ribaldry on me, is Portuguese, with big twisted columns—a wonderful carved headboard—not that you deserve it after the way you have talked—"

As soon as Sam was strong enough, he and Cousin Sarah and Russie went to Washington, so that he could consult Dr. Wilmer about his eyes—there was just the hundredth chance, Faith insisted, that the case might not be hopeless, and until the great specialist said it was, she would not believe it. She did not go with the little devoted group—she wanted, she said, to finish her work in the attic without interference! And when Sam returned to Hamstead, their worst fears confirmed, she led him straight to his new quarters, where he could hear the fire crackling and feel the cheerful warmth of its glow; and having installed him in a deep luxurious chair, drawn up beside his own hearthstone, she sat down on the floor in front of him, her head resting against his knees.

How long it was before either of them moved again, Sam never knew. Faith did not speak a single word of commiseration. There were many things, she said, which she had been waiting for just the right chance to tell him about. Now that everyone else had gone to bed, would he care to listen? She reached caressingly for his hands, and drew them down until he clasped them around her neck, his arms resting on her shoulders. Then without reservation or explanation, she opened her heart to him. She was not seeking for pity, she was not anticipating censure; but she poured out her story as if silence had become intolerable to her, and as if she had found the one confessor in all the world who had the wisdom and the power to sustain and comfort her. Every latent misgiving with which Sam had been tortured lest his infirmity might be another load with which he had no right to burden her, every hideous fear lest he might be the one to crush and break her at last, was swept away as his consciousness of her need of him and of her dependence on him crystallized into conviction. What, after all, did his blindness matter, since, in spite of it, she still turned to him for sympathy and strength?

Unremittingly, unfalteringly, he kept assuring himself that it did not matter at all; and still the enormity of his deprivation rose relentlessly before him. He could never ask anything of Faith now beyond that which she gave him so freely, he reflected rebelliously, in the long nights that followed the salvaging revelation which merged his shattered destiny, with mystic fusion, into hers. There could be no reciprocity in their relationship, as there would have been if he had come back to her, whole and triumphant, at the end of the war. That, as Sarah Atkinson had so shrewdly divined, had been his hope and intention. He would have brought her understanding and companionship; but in return he would have claimed his reward for his years of undemanding devotion. If she had said to him then that she had shut love out of her life forever, he would have laughed at her—tenderly and comprehendingly, to be sure, but still he would have laughed; and eventually he would have taught her to laugh with him at the fantastic idea that a normal and beautiful woman could be through with love at twenty-five. Rudolf—he would have told her—had been a young girl's vision of a glittering saint, whose tarnished splendor had been brightened to new radiance by the delusive glory of death. And Sebastian had been a fairy prince waking a sleeping beauty, and then vanishing into an enchanted castle of his own, leaving her stirred but desolate. The portraits were not entirely accurate, but they would have served his purpose. And then he would have painted another picture: a picture of marriage as she had never visualized it before, lightened with laughter, brightened with congeniality, stabilized with sympathy, cemented with children—not one charming, lonely, supersensitive little boy, but half a dozen lusty youngsters, tumbling and tearing about. He would have convinced her, holding her firmly in his arms at last, that it was not love that she was done with; it was star-gazing, it was moon-reaching, it was glamour, it was high romance. But now he would show her, before it was too late, what strong healthy passion between men and women really was.

Prostrate in the perpetual darkness which engulfed him, and which during the terrible endless night was unassuaged by the manufactured activities of the day, he ground his teeth at the thought of the wastefulness as well as the cruelty of the fate which had deprived him of Faith. He did not underestimate the value and the beauty of the work she was doing; but how incomplete this chaste and consecrated life was! What freedom and fulfillment she should have found in a marriage of maturity! How fair and fruitful she would have been! Often the vision of this became so unendurable that Sam wondered if, after all, he would not be justified in making a mirage a reality. If, as Faith had sat at his feet in front of the fire, resting her head against his knees, he had suddenly leaned over and gathered her against his hammering heart, what would have happened? Why should he sit listening to her faltering confession that only an accident had prevented her from giving herself to another man, without telling her that there was no accident, not even blindness, which would prevent him from claiming her for his own? He knew that she would not have resisted him—her compassion for his mutilation, her own crying need for confidential communion, would have delivered her into his arms twice over. But what would he have gained by so treacherous a victory? If she yielded herself to him through pity and loneliness alone, he would grasp nothing but the shell of the spirit which he longed to possess as completely as he longed to possess the entirety of her lovely flesh. Rudolf had had such a shell, and what Rudolf had had was not enough for him; while the loyalty which Rudolf had accepted with such composure, would have been gall and wormwood to him. To know that he had fettered her forever to a worthless wreck, would have been to redouble the weight of his own heavy chain, which shackled him in the prison house of blindness.

. . . . .

It was already late, judging from the pleasant perfume of cooking wafted to him from the kitchen, before he heard Faith's footsteps. And when he did, they turned first toward the pantry, from which the clink of china and silver were coming. She had gone, evidently, to confer with Hilda; and since she did not lower her voice, which, for all its melody, carried much further than many which were harsher and higher, everything she said was audible to him.

"Mrs. Atkinson and Hansel are going to have supper with the Mannings, Hilda. Oh—I'm glad they didn't forget to tell you themselves. It's such a lovely evening, that I thought I would try to persuade Mr. Dudley to walk down the lane with me and have a picnic supper by the river, if it wouldn't be too much trouble for you to change everything around now. Oh, you are a jewel, Hilda!—Well, in about twenty minutes, I think."

The swinging door to the piazza opened and closed swiftly. There was the soft rustle of a dress. Then Faith sank down on the edge of the long chair where Sam lay extended, and reached for his hand, locking her fingers in his.

"I'm tired," she said without preamble. "I've been way up beyond Whitewater buying cows—I've bought ten. I think this farm can carry twice as many as we've got now, if we manage right. Anyway, I'm going to try, and this is the beginning of the trial. I may have to go over into New York State next week to look for more. I thought it might interest you to go along—we could all go. I feel like taking a trip—somehow when I'm driving a motor I forget for a few minutes, every now and then, about the war."

"Good God! Don't you ever forget about it except when you're driving a motor?"

"Well, sometimes—not often. But I thought I might try to, for a little while to-night. It's going to be a lovely evening—a sunset and a moonrise both together. Silver and rose. You know."

"Sure, I know. So then——"

"So then I thought we might take a hamper and go off. Just you and I. If you would like to, that is."

Sam disengaged his fingers and rose slowly. As he did so, Russie, roused from his torpor, hammered expectantly with his tail. Sam smiled.

"I wouldn't consider it for a minute," he said whimsically. "Not just you and I. It wouldn't do. The proprieties must be observed. What do you say we take Russie with us?"

CHAPTER 42

Pansy Perkins, who guarded the door to the inner office in the Mayor's suite in the Hinsboro City Hall, had a new bob and a new permanent, to both of which, as well as to the transfiguration of her complexion, she devoted careful and constant attention. But underneath the thatch of frizzled hair and behind the plucked eyebrows and powder-coated face, there was a good deal of solid gray matter; and with the first swift glance with which she looked up from her typewriter at the click of the entrance door, she intuitively knew whether it had been opened by some troublesome intruder who should be told that Mr. Hawks had gone to Belford for an indefinite period, or by some welcome guest for whose benefit drinks and cigars should immediately be forthcoming.

Besides the clerks, the manufacturers, and the politicians who were constantly coming and going, there were two women, both of whom Pansy Perkins liked, who smiled their greetings to her, and then went on, unhesitating and unimpeded, to the inner office. One of these was Mr. Hawks' daughter, Myra Jenkins, who with each passing year resembled her father more and more closely. In spite of an active life and agonizing, though spasmodic, attempts at dieting, she had two double chins, and a figure which even the amplest "stylish stouts" were too small to fit. But she was the soul of good nature, and she never forgot to ask after Pansy's boy friends or to send her an enormous box of chocolates on her birthday; and she chuckled with relish at all Pansy's small witticisms.

The other woman—well, she was a lady—was that wonderful Mrs. Marlowe from Hamstead. It was nearly six years now since Pansy had first admitted her to Mr. Hawks' sanctum, and she had changed a good deal. Of course she had always been a "looker" and always would be. But at first there had been something about her that, honest, made you feel as if you would burst right out crying if you noticed the expression in her eyes. And she was so thin and so pale, that made you feel bad too. Though, mercy, her eyes and hair just burnt you up! But now she had gained a little, just enough to take away that starved look, and there was lots of color in her face, which didn't come out of a box either, Pansy reflected regretfully, adding another touch to her own cheeks. And though her clothes were so plain, they had an air about them—Pansy would have liked to know where they came from, only she didn't quite dare ask. But she didn't believe it was from any store in Hinsboro.

The entrance door clicked open. As if her thoughts had conjured up a reality out of a vision, Pansy saw that Mrs. Marlowe had come into the office. It was early spring, and wherever the visitor had done her shopping, she had evidently just been doing it. Pansy laid down her lipstick, and permitted her gaze to rest upon the attractive figure before her.

"Good morning, Pansy, how is everything?"

"Just fine, Mrs. Marlowe. You're looking swell."

"I treated my son to a trip during his spring vacation, so I thought I better treat myself to a few clothes at the same time. I brought this little compact back for you—I do hope you'll like it.—Is Mr. Hawks here? May I go right in?"

"Oh *thanks*, Mrs. Marlowe, it's simply stunning, and *just* what I need. Yes, he's in. He'll be awfully glad to see you."

Pansy rose and held the door open to Mr. Hawks' retreat. It was not often that she did this for a visitor, but something always impelled her to do it for Mrs. Marlowe. She wished she had not had her mouth so full of gum when the visitor came in. But it couldn't be helped now.

. . . . .

As Pansy had predicted, Mr. Hawks was delighted to see Faith, even though she had come to beg, and also scolded him a little before stating the real object of her visit.

"Uncle Caleb, are the front stairs of this building ever cleaned?"

"Why of course, Faith. They're mopped up regular every day or two."

"I don't mean *mopped*, I mean *scrubbed*. Because they need it. They're simply filthy. Besides, you'd think with all the cuspidors around—do you have to have cuspidors, Uncle Caleb?"

"Why, yes," Caleb Hawks answered uneasily, taking his half-chewed cigar out of his mouth and laying it carefully down on the desk in front of him. "Yes, we do . . . Faith, I do hope you ain't gettin' too poison neat to let folks be comfortable, the way my poor wife was. Did you come here this sweet pretty spring mornin' just to tell me to have the stairs in City Hall scrubbed and to throw away the spittoons?"

"No," Faith answered with a little laugh. "I didn't. I wish it hadn't been for anything more serious than that, Uncle Caleb. I came to tell you that poor Feodor Sokovitsky has been put in jail again."

"That scalawag! I guess there ain't nothin' that'll ever learn him to run straight. And you with your 'poor'!"

"Well, he never had much chance in Russia, did he? Or much here, for that matter, until the harm was all done. Anyway, it isn't his wife's fault that he's a scalawag."

Caleb snorted, recaptured his cigar, and began to regard the carbuncle in his ring.

"The eldest girl's doing awfully well at school," Faith went on. "She's at the head of her class—it would be a crime to take her out and make a little drudge of her. Then there are two little boys who are smart as steel traps too. The younger girls—both perfect darlings—are at the Memorial, but Mrs. Sokovitsky still nurses the baby—not that I believe she'll be able to keep on. She's—she's hungry, and a woman who's hungry can't nurse a baby long, Uncle Caleb."

"I bet she warn't hungry when you left her stinkin' little house!" he barked. "Beg pardon, Faith, that slipped out 'fore I noticed it. But just the same, I bet there was a sizeable basket of provisions a settin' right on her dirty kitchen table! It beats me why you raise a hullabaloo about a few spittoons in City Hall and then put up with all these filthy furriners. I wouldn't even put it past Sunnora Perez to skimp on her sweepin' now and then, though I don't deny her house is sweet pretty, 'specially now it has all them elegant fittin's you give her in it.—But what I started to say is, you won't hev anythin' put by for your old age, the way you go on. You give beyond your means all the time."

"Well then, if you're worried about that, you ought to be willing to have the city help Mrs. Sokovitsky out. Because if it doesn't, I'll have to."

"All right, all right!" shouted Caleb, pounding on the table in front of him. "I knew I wuz licked, the minute you come inside that door. Ten dollars a week will be ample, I presume?"

"It won't be so very ample. But it will help. Thanks a lot, Uncle Caleb."

She rose and smiled at him with affection. He looked up at her indignantly.

"You ain't leavin', are you, Faith, now you got what you want offen me?" he asked.

"I didn't want to wear out my welcome, Uncle Caleb, that's all. I know you're awfully busy."

"I ain't so busy as all that. Locate, Faith, can't you? It makes me uneasy having you movin' 'round. I want to talk to you. I've got this and that and the other thing on my mind I want to say."

Faith reseated herself quietly. For a moment Caleb chewed his cigar and studied his carbuncle reflectively. Then, without apparent rhyme or reason, he made an unexpected remark.

"Women is goin' to be votin' this next fall, Faith," he said portentously.

"Why so they are! I'd almost forgotten. Well, I'm glad—for the sake of the suffragists, I mean. They've worked hard for it."

Caleb Hawks snorted again.

"Yes, and most of them think politics and suffrage is the same thing. The pore ignorant fools, I'm kinda sorry for 'em. But the harm's done now an' it ain't no use cryin' over spilt milk. What we got to look out for is to see that some woman who does know somethin' about politics gets shoved forward. If we don't, we're liable to have someone like that crazy sister of Neal Conrad's meddlin' around and stickin' her long snoopin' nose into everythin'. Well, I ben talkin' things over with some of the crowd, and we've kinda decided that it would be a good thing to have a woman appointed on the State Committee. Some's agin it, and I don't deny but what it's kinda a startlin' idea, but—Mercy, Faith, but it's gettin' hot already, ain't it? It ain't often we get weather like this in Hinsboro, not so early in the spring. I look to see it followed by a hard frost."

"Did you and your friends have some woman in mind, Uncle Caleb, for the appointment to the State Committee?"

"Well, yes, Faith, we did, and that's a fact. We thought if you would serve on that Committee——"

He was interrupted by an exclamation of such utter amazement that he himself was startled. He jumped in his seat.

"Land sakes, Faith, you give me a turn! I ain't never heard you let out a noise like that before!"

"But, Uncle Caleb, you gave *me* a turn! Of course you're joking, but you're too ridiculous! I haven't been interested in suffrage at all! That is, I've been interested in a general way, but I've been so busy with the Nursery, and the school, and the farm, and the family, and everything, I mean, that . . . Why I don't *know* anything about politics!"

She had risen again, and was staring at him in stupefaction. He shoved her gently back into her seat, and stood over her, pointing at her with his large pudgy forefinger.

"You listen here," he said authoritatively. "You know just about all there is to know, except a few details I can learn you easy. Why you was weaned on campaign whisky, as one may say. I don't mean that just literal, Faith, but it comes pretty near to bein' a fact. Before your mother ever lit out on your poor father, you knew more'n lots o' grown men ever learn. Smart like you are, it hadn't oughta be necessary I should point that out to you, but I guess even the smartest women's got a blind spot—that's why we don't want 'em around any blinder than we have to have them. You think you ain't dabbled any in politics, do you? Why you hadn't ben in this town twenty-four hours before you'd settled a strike! I'd call that a pretty good job as a starter, if anyone should ask me! An' then you took over a sickly institution an' all of a sudden it started growin', and now it's doin' the best kind o' work in this part of the country. An' who was the first to think that it 'ud need to be bigger when men wuz drafted and women had to take their place in factories—who wuz it figgered all that out, and acted according? You tell me that, Faith Marlowe, 'stead of sittin' there wringin' your hands!"

"I'm not wringing my hands," Faith protested, ceasing to lock and unlock her fingers. "I suppose I have some executive ability, but——"

"*Some!*" barked Caleb. "I'll say you got some when you can run a nursery, and teach school, and manage a farm, and take care of a blind man, all to oncet! Not to mention always havin' time to set down and read aloud to a kid for an hour every night. That's what we gotta have in politics, someone with executive ability, not just a parcel of women gettin' up on a platform and screechin' about the worthlessness of men folks. That ain't politics, Faith, that's slander! Not but what you can make speeches all right, when it comes to that, and now and agin it does, tho' speeches in politics is kinda like window-dressin' in a store —just bait, not the real goods. Land! I ain't never heard such a speech in my life as the one you made in the High School after you heard Rudolf had ben killed. First you had them young hoodlums cryin' like babies, and then you had them marchin' like soldiers, and that's the way you got to handle any kind of a crowd when you want to swing it. You got the gift of gab and you got the right kind o' voice, and then you're so downright handsome, Faith, as one might say, that it ain't easy to keep from lookin' at you, not for a man, anyways. And women has got to keep on caterin' to men for a while yet, in spite of them being depraved like the suffragists says."

"Well, I never said they were depraved," Faith interrupted. "I *like* men, Uncle Caleb, you know that, but——"

"And I'll say they like you too!" Caleb Hawks interrupted in his turn. "You got lowbrows like Sebastian Perez and his crowd, and you got highbrows, like Cal Castle and his crowd, all on the run. And all them young hoodlums you hypnotized at the High School with that first speech of yours is voting now. Besides you got women folks on your side strong as men folks, and that ain't usual or even natural, not when a woman's good-looking as you are. You couldn't a done it if you hadn't kinda a cute way with you, either, no matter how smart you wuz nor how handsome—it takes a cute way to get ahead in politics, an' you've got it. An' when it comes to bein' a joiner, you've shown a lot o' sense in the organizations you've picked. All that's goin' to come in mighty handy now. The next meetin' of the State Committee is goin' to be in Belford on the twentieth, and I want you should——"

"But, Uncle Caleb!" Faith exclaimed aghast. "You talk as if this were all settled. I can't decide to join the State Committee just because you snap your fingers at me! I've got to think it over! I've got to see what Cousin Sarah would——"

"This ain't goin' to be no surprise to your Cousin Sarah, Faith. She's known what I wuz hopin' for an' aimin' for since a long while back —ever since I talked to her that day about gettin' naturalized. I threw out some pretty broad hints about some other things then and she caught 'em all. She ain't a stupid woman, Sarah Atkinson ain't."

"Well then, if you and Cousin Sarah have been plotting behind my back all this time, you might at least give me a chance to talk to Sam."

"Sam!" chuckled Caleb Hawks. "Land sakes, Faith, you don't suppose I ain't talked to Sam too, do you? I don't know that there's a more level-headed man anywhere in the state, or one whose judgment I'd sooner rely on. It's peculiar, seein' that the poor fellow is an artist, that he should have so much sense, but he has, an' that's a fact. He looks to see you go far, Faith, same as I do. But all I want you should do to-day is to say I can bring up your name before the State Committee on the twentieth."

Faith rose. There was, Caleb observed, with anxiety, an air of determination about her that might mean almost anything. She walked over to the door with composure. Then she turned.

"In the course of all this surreptitious discussion," she asked, the corners of her mouth twitching a little, "have you asked Pansy Perkins what she thinks?"

Caleb Hawks' jaw dropped. So did his cigar.

"Of course I ain't!" he said almost irritably. "I wouldn't athought o' askin' Pansy Perkins any more'n I'd thought o' askin' one of Myra's young 'uns."

"Well, I'm going to ask her. And if she thinks it's a good idea I'll do it. There are lots more women in this state like Pansy Perkins than like Cousin Sarah. You ought to have thought of that yourself, Uncle Caleb."

Faith opened the door. Pansy Perkins sat with one hand fluffing up her back hair, and the other busily etching a carmine bow over her pink lips. She started guiltily to her feet.

"Don't get up, Pansy," Faith said pleasantly. "I don't want to interrupt your work, not really. I just want to ask your advice. Mr. Hawks thinks there ought to be a woman on the State Committee, now that women are going to vote, and he believes I could fill the position. What do you think?"

"What do I think?" gasped Pansy. *"Oh lady!"*

She had swallowed her gum. But her meaning was unmistakable.

CHAPTER 43

After Neal Conrad of Hinsboro, who had served with great distinction in the United States Senate for several years, was nominated President of the United States, there was hardly one delegate in a hundred, who did not seize his grip and rush for the first train home. The national convention had been deadlocked for nearly four weeks, and by the time a compromise candidate had been finally chosen and put over, the hoarse and frenzied gathering had reached such a high pitch of nervous fatigue that even the thought of further immediate effort was abhorrent. Its members dispersed, in various stages of collapse, to all parts of the country, to sleep off their exhaustion and recover their enthusiasm, before mapping out the most elementary of campaign plans.

There were, of course, a few exceptions to this general rule, and Caleb Hawks was one of the exceptions. Like Carolus Cavendish Castle, who was almost certain to be an outstanding figure in the next cabinet—the press of the country was practically unanimous in this opinion—he had remained on the scene to confer with the Presidential nominee on various pressing questions. Caleb Hawks was now National Committeeman for his state, and Faith Marlowe was National Committeewoman. As Town Representative from Hamstead to the State Legislature, she was doing extremely well, and Caleb had every reason to be satisfied with her progress; but as National Committeewoman, a position to which she had risen without much effort, she was doing still better. Caleb found her coöperation invaluable. There wasn't another National Committeeman in the country, he was fond of saying, who could count on such certain, steady and capable help from the Committeewoman working with him. Faith was a Marlowe all right, and she was a marvel too. The phrase tickled him. He used it constantly.

The conference which was to take place in Neal Conrad's suite, was set for six o'clock, and Faith was to go to it with Caleb. But he wanted to have a word or two with her alone first, so he called her up to ask when it would be convenient for her to see him. Pansy Perkins, who answered the telephone, said that Mrs. Marlowe was asleep, and that nothing would induce her, Pansy, to wake the poor tired lady—it was a shame the way she had been overworked all through the convention! But Pansy thought if Mr. Hawks would come around about five-thirty, Mrs. Marlowe would be getting up by that time anyway for the Conrad conference, so probably——

Mr. Hawks smiled as he hung up the receiver. He was constantly accusing Faith of having stolen Pansy from him, and insisting that the City Hall had never been the same since she left him. But actually it was he who had suggested that she should serve as Faith's secretary when it became inescapably obvious that Faith would be obliged to have one. He knew that Pansy would eat up work almost as comprehensively as Faith herself, and that her loyalty and devotion would be unswerving and incorruptible. Not that he distrusted secretaries in general; but when so much was at stake, it was impossible to be too careful.

Pansy opened the door for him when he presented himself at Faith's suite two hours later. He could not have told what had caused the subtle change in Pansy's appearance. He did not know, for instance, that she did not chew gum any longer, or that her fresh pleasant face was unpainted, or that her hair was not frizzed and fluffed, but parted softly away from her pretty forehead and gathered into a smooth knot at the nape of her neck. But he knew she looked different—different and better; and he knew that the change and improvement were both due to Faith.

Faith herself, seated in front of a big desk, signing letters, looked up with a quick smile as Caleb Hawks entered the room. The desk was piled high with papers and correspondence of all sorts; but these were arranged in such neat stacks that there was no sign of confusion or clutter. The blotting pad was spotless, the silver desk set was polished, and a slender crystal vase containing three exquisite roses stood near the inkwell.

"And if you will acknowledge these telegrams as I have just indicated on the margins," Faith said, affixing her signature to the last letter which Pansy laid down before her, "and telephone Mrs. James that I shall probably be late for the Committeewomen's dinner because of the Conrad conference, that will be all, Pansy, for the moment. . . . Yes, Uncle Caleb? What is it?"

She turned toward him briskly, the personification of competence. Never, he considered, had she looked cooler or prettier than she did on this sweltering night. And how she had kept her youth! She was nearly thirty-five now, if he wasn't mistaken, and there wasn't a line in her face or a gray hair in her head. Again, if he had been capable of analysis, he would have realized that a little of the softness, a little of the bloom, of her beauty, had gone. She had presence now, rather than gentleness; but in spite of all her crispness, she still emanated charm.

"I'm very pleased about the Vice-President, aren't you?" she went on, still crisply, as he did not answer immediately. "Of course it was essential that he should come from the South this time, and Harvey Hurlbut has made a splendid record as Governor, besides fulfilling all the geographical requisites. I was terrified for fear the convention would simply dissolve without nominating any Vice-President at all, let alone a suitable one, considering the state it was in after Neal was finally put over——"

"Neal's goin' to tell us, when we get to the conference, whether he's goin' to resign from the Senate or not," cut in Mr. Hawks, fumbling for a cigar.

"Yes?—Unless that's very important, Pansy, take the message please! —Sorry, Uncle Caleb, but this telephone is simply inescapable.—Well, there's precedent for whichever course he prefers. If he shouldn't be elected, it would be too bad if——"

"He's goin' to be elected," Caleb shouted. "And he's goin' to resign from the Senate. To-night. Me and Cal and Warren have talked it all over, and it's as good as done already. He can't afford not to. He's got to have your support, Faith, and——"

"But of course he'll have my support, Uncle Caleb!"

"You bet your bottom dollar he will!" bellowed Caleb Hawks. " 'Cause he's goin' to have you on the ticket with him, see? You make that clear to him from the minute you set foot in that parlor of his. I like Neal Conrad and always have, though I'm inclined to think in that family the gray mare's the better horse of the two. But he's a mite too cautious when it comes to his own interests, and if he thinks he can run with the hare and hunt with the hounds, he's mistaken. We're goin' to have a President *and* a Cabinet Officer *and* the first woman Senator from our state this year, and the rest of the country can like it or lump it. The mornin' papers is goin' to carry headlines a mile high—'CONRAD RESIGNS FROM SENATE, FAITH MARLOWE TO RUN FOR HIS SEAT.' There won't be a bigger story break, not in the whole campaign! This is the day I've waited for and schemed for and, God damn it all—beg pardon, Faith, that slipped out before I thought—prayed for too! You're goin' to take your father's place in the Senate the same day Neal Conrad's inaugurated President, or there won't be no inauguration, so help me God!"

He brought his fist down on her desk with a thundering crash. The neat piles of papers flew off, scattering in every direction, and Pansy, getting down on her knees, began to gather them up again. Caleb saw that her hands were trembling. But this was no moment to waste on Pansy. He faced Faith compellingly.

"Faith," he said almost beseechingly now, "you know I can't never hold no high office myself, and I know it too! Lord, *don't* I know it! I know I ain't never gone so far from the pore little mongrel cur I used to be, that I can't rekkernize him in me still, good an' plenty. An' I never *will* go so far I can't. But *you* will, with me behind you. I can put you in the seats of the mighty anyway. You're more to me than anyone else in the world, Faith, more'n my daughter even—it's the same as if you wuz myself, the way I'd a been, if I'd had a chance.—You ain't goin' to let me down, are you, Faith?"

"No!" she cried impetuously. "No, Uncle Caleb—never in the world!"

The desk was no longer between them. She had risen and going swiftly toward him, had laid her hands on his shoulders. He could see the tears in her eyes, and knew that there were tears in his own. But after her first reassuring cry, she answered him calmly and steadily. She even managed to smile a little.

"You didn't take me quite so much by surprise this time as you did four years ago," she said. "Really, I'm not half so much startled at the thought of being the first woman to run for the Senate as I was at the thought of serving on the State Committee—that's due to your training, Uncle Caleb! Of course I realized you were fitting me for something—but I didn't think of the Senate until Neal was nominated for the Presidency. Then I began to wonder—and still not believe it could be true. . . . 'Something no woman ever was before!'—So that was what the gypsy meant!"

"What's that you're sayin', Faith?"

He had worked himself up to such a supreme pitch of excitement and anxiety that he felt curiously let down. He had expected that Faith would be stupefied, and that she would offer objections against which he would have to struggle. Now that he found he had no fight on his hands, he was actually conscious of embarrassment, as a young lover who had feared to disclose his feelings to his sweetheart might have been if she had suddenly told him she would be glad to marry him. He looked at Faith almost shamefacedly, while he waited for her to explain her cryptic remark.

"Don't you remember, Uncle Caleb, the day we went to the Sacro Monte in Granada? And the pretty gypsy, Chiquita, who told fortunes said,——"

Caleb slapped her heartily on the shoulder. "That's so!" he exclaimed. "Lord Almighty, I hadn't thought of it for years! We went up that hill where the prickly pears was with that good-lookin' brother of the Bishop's, what wuz his name now——"

"It was Sebastian de Cerreno," Faith answered slowly.

"So it was, and that's a fact. I recall him well, now you speak of him. I took to him from the first, and it's real peculiar, but I remember thinkin' there wuz a look about him reminded me of Sebastian Perez. —Say, that's a break for you, Perez just bein' elected president of the Marblecutters' Union. You'll have the furrin vote of the state delivered to you on a silver platter, Faith."

"Yes, I suppose I will," she said, still very slowly. "But it was bought at a great price." She was not looking at him any more, and there was something in her voice vaguely disturbing to Caleb. He clapped her on the shoulder again.

"It warn't bought at all," he said indignantly—"you ain't never resorted to graft, an' you know it. But land sakes, we ain't got time to talk that over this afternoon," he said. "You better get your bunnit, Faith. Now don't you forget: you put your cards on the table and make Neal Conrad do the same. When he sees he's pressed, he'll give in.

Warren's back of you, and Castle's back of you, and I'm back of you. Brown may or may not help—him and Conrad ain't pulled any too well together in the Senate—it's just possible he'll throw his strength to you, and then again he may not. Fletcher, who ran against Conrad in the last campaign, will probably be your opponent on the other ticket. He's a mean skunk, he don't fight fair, I wouldn't put anythin' past 'im. I wish you didn't have the mud he'll sling to face, but it can't be helped. Now, you do like I told you, Faith, and——"

Pansy Perkins emerged from Faith's bedroom, carrying a wide sheer hat, some long white gloves, and a small handbag, all of which she handed to Faith.

"It's two minutes of six," she said, her voice as well as her hands trembling a little now. "I know you don't want to be late to the Conrad conference—Senator Marlowe."

. . . . .

Ex-Governor Warren had come to the convention in his private car, bringing a party of friends with him; and though the personnel of this group was the same going home as it had been going away, it was hard to realize this: Neal Conrad was no longer the Junior Senator from a small state; he was a Presidential nominee. Carolus Cavendish Castle was no longer a submerged private citizen; he was a presumptive Cabinet Officer. And Faith Marlowe was no longer one of forty-eight National Committeewomen; she was the first woman candidate for the Senate.

The car was decorated with streamers, flags, and banners; enormous bouquets of flowers, boxes of candy, and baskets of fruit, filled every rack and corner, and telegrams were constantly being delivered in stacks inches thick. A press delegation traveled in the next Pullman; "prominent citizens" from Belford and Hinsboro and outstanding politicians from all over the country augmented the original number of Governor Warren's original guests. Cheering and curious crowds thronged every station at which the train stopped, brass bands played, committees of welcome orated, and journalists and photographers darted about. Neal and Anne Conrad appeared on the back platform together, smiling and bowing, and the mob broke into yells. Faith consented to say, "just a few words," and the yells redoubled.

By the time Hinsboro had finally been reached, everyone was almost frantic with fatigue. But at Hinsboro was still to be faced the largest crowd of all, the noisiest band of all, the most enthusiastic delegation of welcome. The Conrads made their way to their house through streets so jammed that the motor in which Caleb and Faith rode with them could hardly wedge its way along; and when they arrived at their destination in the pouring rain, they found small boys swarming over the roof, a packed piazza, and a force of police belligerently endeavoring to maintain some show of order.

It was two o'clock in the morning when Faith resolutely struggled into the coat closet, drawing Hansel after her, and locked the door. He had taken his entrance examinations for Harvard that year, and when these were over, he had joined her at the national convention; but he had wearied of the endless days of balloting and had gone back to his books and music in Hamstead; and he had not left these again until he motored over to Hinsboro that night to meet her. He had shot up into a slim graceful boy, with a sensitive serious face, taller and paler than his mother, and with far less animation and endurance. She saw that there were dark circles under his eyes, and realized that he was wearied to the point of exhaustion.

"You're tired, aren't you, darling?" she said sympathetically, pressing his hand. "I am too—I feel as if I had had as much of this as I can stand for to-night. I wondered if we couldn't possibly slip out of the back door together without being noticed. I thought I'd steal a cap and raincoat from here for disguise, and keep my head down and run. Do you think we could manage it? How far away is the car?"

"Just in the next block. We could try it anyway. But won't Uncle Caleb be worried if you disappear like that?"

Hansel's intuitive sensitiveness to the feelings of others had become more and more intensified as he grew older. Faith sometimes found it necessary to brush this aside.

"He'll guess what's happened, and we'll telephone as soon as we get home. I'm desperate, Hansel—you don't know what it's been like these last few days."

"No, I suppose I don't, mother. Well, are you ready?"

Their dash for freedom was not unimpeded, but it was finally successful; and as the motor swung away from the crowds and shot out toward the country, Faith felt her taut nerves and muscles gradually relaxing. She slipped down comfortably in the seat, and laid her head against Hansel's shoulder.

"You haven't congratulated me yet, darling," she reminded him, looking up at him lovingly.

"I'm sorry. There hasn't been much time though, has there? Of course I do congratulate you, mother."

"You're pleased, aren't you, Hansel?"

"I'm very proud. And I'm glad for Uncle Caleb's sake—this means everything in the world to him. But I don't think I'm exactly pleased myself."

"Why Hansel!" she exclaimed, sitting upright again in her amazement. "I thought you'd be delighted! Why aren't you pleased?"

"Well, you know you promised to go to Germany with me this summer, and I've been looking forward to it a good deal. You see every spring you've said, *this* year you thought we could go, and then when summer came you've always been too busy. I'd sort of like to see my grandmother and grandfather von Hohenlohe; you know I haven't since I was seven years old. I've been thinking about them a lot lately. I'd like to see Schönplatz and Berlin and Bonn, and I'd like to go to the musical festivals at Munich, and Nuremburg and Bayreuth."

"But darling," interrupted Faith eagerly, "I couldn't take you to Germany while the war was going on, or until feeling had died down afterwards! And since then I *have* been too busy! But you can do all that some other summer—next summer! I promise! This summer I want you to give to me. I've got a wonderful plan I'm counting on you to help me with. I'm going to talk to Mr. Emery the first thing in the morning, and see if he can't find or build me a sort of glorified gypsy wagon to do my campaigning in. It would be almost like a little house on wheels. I thought you and I would go about in it together, and I'd make speeches from the back platform wherever we stopped, and you would play the piano for me, and we would take turns driving. Don't you think it would be fun, Hansel?"

"Yes, I guess so."

"Why Hansel, I thought you'd jump at the idea! I know you'll like it after we get started with it! And you'll be simply invaluable to me. There's nothing on earth the public likes to have held up to it more than family devotion. We'll have our pictures taken together, and I'll talk about the stories we've always read together, and—don't you see, Hansel?"

"Yes, mother, I see. All right. Of course I want to help you all I can." There was a subdued note of wistfulness in his voice that Faith could not help but notice. "You haven't asked whether I've heard from Harvard about my entrance examinations," he added hesitatingly. "I did yesterday. I got honors in everything. And Junior Conrad and I have decided to room together."

"Splendid!" Faith exclaimed. But she said it abstractedly, and she went on, "I suppose that means I'll have to part with you the end of September, and I hate to, because I really need you six weeks longer. Of course, Pansy can go with me in the caravan after you leave for college, but it won't be half so effective."

"No, I suppose not," Hansel answered. And his voice was so very tired that Faith did not try to talk to him any more.

The car purred in and out of the peacefully sleeping village of Hamstead, swung up the river road, and passed the Big House, shrouded in darkness. As Marlowe Manor came into view, Faith saw that it was lighted from garret to cellar.

"Why Hansel!" she said again. "What do you think has happened? It's after three o'clock! You don't suppose that Cousin Sarah——"

"Oh, she's all right!" Hansel said reassuringly. "I'd have told you if she hadn't been. But Sam said, right along, that you'd come home tonight. I guess he's having an illumination in your honor. I guess he's waiting up for you."

CHAPTER 44

NEVER, in the annals of American politics, had any candidate waged a more effective campaign than Faith Marlowe did in running for the United States Senate.

In the first place, Marlowe Manor, from which her grandfather and her father had both stepped into public life, was as nearly perfect a stage setting as any that could have been devised. The rotogravure sections of the Sunday papers throughout the country were adorned with pictures of Faith standing under the portrait of the Cabinet Officer which hung above her library mantel, and holding a miniature of the Senator. They were also adorned with Faith (a) working in her garden, (b) walking in her garden, (c) entertaining visiting celebrities in her garden. She was shown standing beside a prize bull, and scattering poultry feed to prize chickens. She was shown, as she had predicted, with her arm through Hansel's, and her face turned adoringly toward his. Naturally, she was also shown at her desk in the Hinsboro High School, among her antiques in the Marlowe Loan Collection, surrounded by the small dark children of the Myra Higgs Hawks Memorial Nursery, and in deep conference with Caleb Hawks and Neal Conrad. But it was the photographs taken in Hamstead that had the widest appeal. On the strength of one that was especially attractive and successful, a large motion picture concern wired offering her a contract, in case she were defeated for the Senate.

Journalistically, as well as pictorially, her background was ideal. The interviews she gave out were always first-page news; and she wrote an article herself about her activities in Hamstead and Hinsboro for a woman's magazine with a circulation of over two million. Reprints of it, in pamphlet form, were distributed from one end of the state to the other. Incidentally, the check she received as an "honorarium" for this article was almost large enough to pay for her caravan, which Will Emery let her have at cost. And of course the caravan capped the dramatic climax for which Faith was striving. Her nomination was opposed by an antagonist representing the more conservative elements of the party—a hotelkeeper from the western part of the state; but it was evident, almost from the beginning, that he did not have a "tinker's chance" against her. The voting public was enthralled by the novel and arresting spectacle of a candidate who traversed the countryside in a huge apple-green motor vehicle with white lace curtains looped back from tiny spotless windows, and a little open platform at the back. If she traveled alone in it, that would have been just a shade too daring —after all, she was a lovely-looking woman, even if she was not quite so young as she appeared. But she always had that fine boy of hers with her, driving the caravan for her, playing the piano at her out-of-door meetings, distributing campaign literature for her, mingling in the crowds with her. Yes, decidedly, Hansel added immeasurably to Faith's inescapable allure.

Hamstead, as soon as it had recovered from the staggering shock of her candidacy, had rallied around her excitedly. Marlowe Manor, in spite of its elasticity, could not begin to hold all the visiting celebrities who had to be entertained; but Aunt Emmeline, the Mannings, the Grays and the Nobles, all opened their doors hospitably. Indeed, Jacqueline went so far as to forestall many emergencies, by telling Faith, at the beginning of the summer, that she would undertake to look after representatives of the press at the Big House. Faith could dismiss every concern for their comfort from her mind, once and for all.

David, seconding his wife's invitation, turned the scrutinizing gaze which Faith had almost forgotten upon the Senatorial candidate. He had been very little in Hamstead in the course of the last eight years. During the war he had invented a new anæsthetic, which had brought him such international acclaim that he had found it impossible to maintain any longer the fiction—already shaken by his brain-surgery—that he was "just a family doctor." This summer he was taking a long and much-needed vacation; and as he asked Faith if he might walk home with her from the Big House, where she had been dining, he realized that he had not had a talk alone with her since he had brought her the news of the birth of Sebastian's eldest son. His mind reverted to the conversation as he strolled along beside her in the moonlight.

"You did find your solution, didn't you, Faith?" he asked admiringly. "In fact, almost more solutions than you had problems! There was just one problem, really—how to keep yourself from thinking too much about a man with whom you were in love and whom you couldn't marry. And how magnificently you've answered it! You're still 'the gallant lady,' Faith."

"Thank you," she said so quietly that he found her reticence provocative.

"So all your solutions have been the compensations 'that do not quite compensate,' have they?" he asked searchingly.

"Yes."

"You haven't forgotten—after all these years?"

"No. You told me I never would."

"I remember. But I hoped I might be mistaken."

"You weren't," she said, still more quietly than she had spoken before.

"Have you ever heard from him?"

"Never directly. I've played fair, David. It was a clean break. But I have had strange reminders of him—even here—that have—hurt a good deal. I can't talk about those even to you. And his wife wrote me when his little girl was born, and has occasionally since then. Probably you know that baby was named for me."

"Yes. I've seen her. She's a beautiful child. Jacqueline and I spent a month this last spring with the Cerrenos at the Castello Viejo. They're very happy. They have two younger boys now too, you know."

"Yes, I know. Sebastian has his 'heritage' trebly assured. It ought to be safe. I hope it is—I'm not the only woman who's crucified herself to make it so——"

"Faith," David said suddenly, "I hate to hear you talk this way—to know you feel this way. It couldn't have been different, could it? You wouldn't want it to be different if you reasoned it out. And don't forget that no woman ever rose to fame without tragedy for her stepping-stone."

"Exactly," Faith answered gravely.

But afterwards, she reflected that the next time she had a chance to talk confidentially to David, she would confess to him that though she had never forgotten Sebastian and never would, the thought of him did not dominate her any longer. She had gone through a burning fiery furnace to rescue Señora Perez from torment, but after she had recovered from the shock of this ordeal she discovered that, miraculously, her own anguish had become less unbearable. She would admit, with less bitterness than she had previously revealed, that she realized that the tragedy which had transfigured her life had also enabled her to fulfill her destiny, as David had foretold. Even if her compensations for the loss of Sebastian, "did not quite compensate," they crowded her horizon and proved her powers and stimulated her spirit. And it was exactly because this was true that she did not have another opportunity for an intimate conversation with him before she had emerged triumphantly from the test of the primaries, and was intensively preparing to face the far harder trial of the election. Fletcher, the millionaire owner of the largest newspaper in the state, who had given Neal Conrad the fight of his life when Neal had run for the Senate himself, was her opponent now; and in him she had a far more formidable antagonist than in the conservative hotelkeeper who had been crushed—figuratively speaking—underneath the wheels of her apple-green caravan. The caravan itself would lose some of its effectiveness, now that Hansel was about to start for college; and the best of the glorious autumn weather, which had made her modern gypsying so delightful, would soon be over. She must count up her other assets without losing sight of any of them, and make the most of every one; and at the same time she must count up her liabilities.

She considered all of these meticulously. She was allied with the Presidential candidate, and since many citizens voted the straight ticket—to save trouble, if for no more intelligent reason,—she might be swept in on that, especially as the state was thrilled at the thought of supplying the nation with a Chief Executive for the first time. But she could not reckon without the possibility that the "Conrad crowd might cut her"—it had more than once hinted to her that she was too spectacular, that she stole Neal's curtain calls. The state normally went for the party which she aspired to represent, and that was a great advantage. But it was possible that the conservative wing, which had supported the hotelkeeper in the primaries, might swing to Fletcher. He had made enemies among the foreign population by indiscreet and disparaging references to "Canucks," "Wops," and "Dagos" in the columns of his paper before he had aspired to public life, and these had not been forgotten. Moreover, the intolerance which was his substitute for religion had aligned the Catholic vote against him. But on the other hand, the bulk of the Anglo-Saxons shared his horror of the Papacy, and suspected, though could not prove, that Faith had leanings toward it. This disadvantage was partially offset by her strength with the agricultural element, and her inherited prestige—"Put another Marlowe in the Senate!"—was a powerful plea. But she was just beginning to gauge the ugliness and might of bigotry, and to recognize that it could not be underestimated. The small weekly newspapers were nearly all behind her. But their joint circulation was not much greater than that of Fletcher's *Clarion-Herald*, and publicity released once in seven days could hardly compete with daily propaganda. She could count on generous financial support from Caleb Hawks, from the Castles, and from the Nobles. But with the principal of the money she had inherited from her father tightly tied up, and the necessity of keeping Hansel's legacy intact, she had a comparatively modest sum of her own at her disposal; and Fletcher was the richest man in the state.

If Sam would have voluntarily come forward with a substantial sum, it would have helped her enormously. But Sam had made no such offer. Indeed, for the first time in his life, he had disappointed her. Aside from welcoming her home when she returned to Hamstead when she announced her candidacy, he had not made a single spontaneous gesture. He listened attentively enough when she talked to him; but she had no more leisure nowadays to talk to Sam than she had to talk to David. She was touring the state in her caravan the greater part of every week. And when she was at home, she dictated to Pansy half the night in order to keep abreast of the mountains of correspondence to which she could give no attention when she was traveling, or as long as the ceaseless stream of guests and reporters sat at her table and overflowed her house.

The day after Hansel's departure for Harvard, a sense of loneliness and loss which she could not shake off seemed to overwhelm her; and though she stuck resolutely to her dictation until nearly midnight, she at last put her hand to her throbbing forehead and pushed back her chair.

"It's no use, Pansy," she said despairingly, "my brain just doesn't seem to function any longer. We'll have to give it up."

"Just write your autograph on these little cards that are to be inclosed with handkerchiefs and dolls for church fairs," Pansy said soothingly. "There are only fifty of them, and you can do it almost automatically. And the galley for your *Delineator* article has to go off the first mail to-morrow. I'll proof-read it for you if you say so, but you told me there were one or two little changes you wanted to make yourself."

The fine type of her printed views on "Careers and Homemaking —Which or Both?" seemed to zig-zag back and forth before Faith's tired eyes, the long sheets of galley kept slipping from her weary fingers. But she persevered, and finally, with a few scribbled notes on the margins, she handed them wearily back to Pansy.

"Well, that's done. Now I'm going——"

"You promised to send a night letter to the Forestville Woman's Club saying definitely whether you would make that speech on 'Consecrated Motherhood and its Relation to Politics' on October fourteenth."

"Well, did you check up on that with Mr. Hawks? Did he think the group was large and influential enough to be worth the effort?"

"He said yes, it was. And Mrs. Trent, the President, hopes you'll come to Forestville in the caravan, because the last time you were there a good many of the club women didn't see it, and they'd like to look it over."

"All right. Send the night letter."

"And Mr. Conrad telephoned late this afternoon to say he feels you must prepare a statement for immediate release about your stand on prohibition. He says there's a feeling in some quarters that you're pussy-footing. He thinks, in a dry state like this——"

"A dry state like this! Now Pansy!"

"Well, you know it is dry, politically, except for the foreign element. He knows you're trying to keep that placated, but still——"

"Keep that placated! I'm trying not to be a self-confessed hypocrite."

"Just as you say of course, Mrs. Marlowe. I can call Miss Letts, Mr.

Conrad's secretary, the first thing in the morning, and say you feel you can't possibly——"

"No—no—I mustn't let you do that. It would be Senatorial suicide for me—it might even jeopardize the ticket in this state. Telephone Miss Letts, and say I'll have a statement ready for release this Saturday, and that I promise it will be satisfactory.—Now that is all, isn't it?"

"I think these bills must be okeyed, Mrs. Marlowe, so that I can get the checks out."

"How much can we draw on from the national fund?"

"Well, not *any* more, Mr. Castle said, before the first of the month."

Faith gave a nervous little laugh. "Pansy, that settles it! You'll have to let me go and talk to Mr. Dudley. You know as well as I do that I've just sixty-five dollars and thirty cents left in my personal account to last until the end of the month!"

She rose slowly, stretching her arms above her head with a gesture of complete weariness. Pansy thought, as she watched her go out of the room, that she had never seen her act so tired or so depressed. She hoped that Mr. Dudley, if he were still awake, would be able to cheer her up.

Mr. Dudley had retired for the night, he called to Faith through his door, in response to her knock. But if it were really imperative that she should invade his chaste seclusion, she might come in. She managed to smile a little at his never-failing whimsicality, and as he switched on the light at his elbow, she smiled again. Lying in his Portuguese bed under the somber Ribera which hung above it, his long fingers resting on Russie's sleek head, his dull-blue sleeping jacket open at the throat, there was a certain medieval splendor about his figure which never failed to give her pleasure. The extreme thinness, bordering on emaciation, which he had never lost since his long period of hospitalization, revealed the beautiful bones of his face which youthful flesh had obscured, and gave him an aspect of asceticism; his prematurely white hair crowned his head with a dignity which his shock of sandy locks had never possessed. He might have been the Abbot of some princely order, relaxing after the cares and austerities of the day.

"You are growing handsomer every minute, Sam, do you know it?" Faith asked with admiring tenderness, as she sat down on the edge of his bed.

"Sure I know it," he retorted instantly. "I wouldn't have a lovely lady stealing into my room at midnight if I wasn't, would I?—Or is it just that you have given in at last about that statement Conrad has been hounding you for, and you instinctively turn to the place where the best drinks in the house are kept to buck you up again?—That's sherry in the decanter, Faith, and the cheese sandwiches are good."

"I did give in," she said a little ruefully, as she poured the rich amber liquid into a wine glass and picked up a delicately cut square of bread. "What else could I do?—And I do feel the need of getting bucked up. —But what I really came for was to ask if you could let me have some money?"

She saw a swift flickering change in Sam's expression, almost like that which might have passed over the face of a hopeful boy who had suffered a sharp disappointment. But he answered instantly.

"Why yes, of course. How much?"

"I need five hundred dollars, Sam, to pay bills that must be met at once. And next month I may need more."

"All right. Shall we say two thousand? I'd suggest three, but I don't like to use principal, considering that I'll never earn anything more. And I need a little extra cash myself just now. Cousin Sarah and I have decided to take a short trip to Europe."

"A short trip to Europe!" echoed Faith in stupefaction.

"Sure. On a boat, you know. It's being done all the time."

"But you're not doing it all the time!" Faith protested vehemently. "You've never even suggested such a thing before. And now—in the middle of a campaign——"

"I thought perhaps *you'd* suggest it, if I waited long enough. But you didn't, and when this Senatorial racket came along, I knew you never would. But there isn't any reason why I should stay here. You don't need me—and you don't need Cousin Sarah as much as I do. She agrees with me about that. So she and Russie and I are off on the *France* next week. Russie is going to be a sea-dog, aren't you, Russie? Well, don't upset the lamp in your excitement—I'll promise there won't be any hitch. I'm sorry Hansel couldn't go with us, but of course you *did* need him as long as you could have him, and now college has opened so——"

"Sam, you're hurting my feelings terribly! How can you say I don't need you? I do need you! I can't bear to have you go off and leave me! Just because I haven't time, in this nightmare of a campaign, to sit around for hours talking with you. . . . Why, I don't have time to talk to *anyone*. I've tried for weeks to have a quiet talk with David——"

She attempted, unsuccessfully, to control the trembling in her voice. But Sam seemed unaware that it was trembling.

"Well, by the time 'this nightmare of a campaign' is over, I'll be back," he said unfeelingly. "I agree with you. It is a nightmare. But I don't see why I should keep on having bad dreams forever just because you—I won't have 'em in Paris. It's gorgeous there at this time of year!—Hold on, Faith, don't go off the handle like that! Good God, you are all shot to pieces!"

He thrust his hand out suddenly, intending to force her to sit down.

But she eluded him, and rushed out of the attic, overwhelmed with anger and resentment now as well as fatigue. She did not seek him out again, and she did not discuss the impending departure even with Sarah Atkinson, whom she treated with coolness. When the travelers left, the following week, she laid her cheek briefly against Sarah's, but she did not kiss Sam good-bye. She was stung to the quick by his desertion.

CHAPTER 45

FAITH'S thoughts were diverted from Sam's departure—on which she had dwelt far more intensively than she could afford, considering the number of other pressing matters demanding her attention—by the receipt of a letter which came in soon after he left, and which she perused with startled pleasure. It was years since she had seen the exquisite, yet virile, handwriting which covered the pages; but she knew instantly, without turning to the stately signature, who had written them.

"My dear Faith—" she read delightedly——

"Since the Eucharistic Congress, to which, as perhaps you know, I was a delegate, I have been making a tour of the old Spanish missions in the United States, accompanied by Father Constantino. (He is now a very old man, but still vigorous, and sends his best regards to you.) We are returning to Spain via Cuba on the *Manuel Calvo* in about a fortnight, but you have been much in my thoughts lately, and I am longing to see you. Would it be convenient and agreeable for you to receive me as a visitor, in the old homestead which you described so vividly to me the first time I ever met you? Or, if there is not room for Father Constantino and me there—I remember you told me the beloved house was small—perhaps we could stay with the Nobles, who are, I understand, neighbors of yours, and to whom my family is now bound with ties of everlasting gratitude. I am writing to them by this same mail. Let me know your pleasure concerning these tentative suggestions, and I will endeavor to conform my plans with yours. I know that in your brilliant new undertaking, which I am following through the press with pride and prayer, your days must be sadly overcrowded already. But I should like to give you my personal blessing once more, and it is now so long since you have come to Spain that I have begun to fear that you will never do so again. Therefore, my dear child, I feel that I must come to you.

"Remember me with affection to Doña Sarah and to the inspired artist, and believe me, *in corde Jesu*, ever faithfully and devotedly your kinsman, Gabriel de Cerreno, Cardinal Archbishop of Granada."

"Pansy!" Faith exclaimed, looking up with an expression of unalloyed pleasure, "who do you think is coming to see us? The Cardinal Archbishop of Granada! He is the most wonderful person in all the world! Get Mrs. Noble on the telephone right away, please! Do you think the Cardinal would rather stay here or at the Big House? Now that Mr. Dudley has gone away, just at the wrong moment, I have no host here, and I rather think that when a Cardinal is your guest, it is more suitable—Oh, Jacqueline! You *did*? Well, what do you think? Yes, I agree with you, but of course you will all come here to dinner with me. We'll both wire, shall we?"

For the next two days she was entirely preoccupied with arrangements for the reception and entertainment of Gabriel. She cancelled a speaking engagement in the western part of the state—the stronghold of the conservative wing of the party—giving illness as her excuse, though she was well aware that a political candidate, like an actor, should never indulge in the luxury of ill health even when this is real. She turned a deaf ear to Pansy's signaled suggestion that she should invite a prominent merchant and his wife who had come up from Belford to remain for luncheon; she even cut short a long distance call from Ex-Governor Warren. And when Caleb Hawks came bursting into her library, on his way back from the important meeting she had failed to address, her guilty conscience smote her as she met his indignant gaze. She was, however, totally unprepared for the accusation he hurled at her.

"Sick, are you?" he thundered in a voice she had never heard him use before. "You know as well as I do, Faith Marlowe, that even if you'da had bubonic plague, you'd otta had made that speech! What do you want to do, let Shaw and all his stinking outfit in for another four years? Or do you want the Pope of Rome moving into the White House instead of Neal Conrad? Or have you just suddenly gone crazy? God damn it all, I want you should tell me!"

He had not even remembered to say, "Beg pardon, that slipped out before I noticed." Faith, angry in her turn, and as puzzled as she was angry, retorted with an indignation that matched his own.

"If I wasn't sick before, I shall be, if you shout at me like that! And I have no idea what else you were talking about!"

"Well, it's true, ain't it, that you got a coupla Catholic priests coming here to stay? Have you seen the extra the *Clarion-Herald* got out at one P.M.? Just take a look at that, and tell me whether you ain't got no idea what I'm talking about!"

He flung the cheap flimsy sheet down in front of her. Heavy black headlines, four inches high swept ominously across it. Beneath them were staggering captions and under all two columns in large print:

"FAITH MARLOWE CONVERT TO ROME
"POPE'S EMISSARY HASTENING IN STATE TO HAMSTEAD
"SPANISH CARDINAL DUE TUESDAY
"DOOM OF WOMAN CANDIDATE'S SENATORIAL HOPES SEEN IN RASH MOVE

"Special to the *Clarion-Herald,* Oct. 2

"It was learned by reliable authority late this morning that Faith Marlowe's failure to keep her speaking engagement yesterday was not due, as recorded, to sudden indisposition, but to the formalities attendant upon the impending abandonment of the noble religion of her forefathers. Gabriel de Cerreno, Cardinal Archbishop of Granada, Spain, the cruel land of the Inquisition, is hastening from San Antonio to Hamstead on a specially chartered train. It is well known that this bigoted despot comes from the Vatican under sealed orders. Though it has been given out that his visit is purely personal in character, this attempt to throw dust in the eyes of a watchful public has been thwarted, and a confession has been wrung from Faith Marlowe which will be given to the press in the morning. A further attempt at duplicity was made by using Mrs. David Noble, the wife of a well known surgeon, as a blind in the plot of this Scarlet Woman. Mrs. Noble is to be commiserated upon having permitted herself to be used as a tool, and it is to be hoped that she herself will see her way clear to renouncing a dogma to which she owes only nominal allegiance. Astute politicians have no difficulty in discerning in this rash move the doom of——"

Faith suddenly crumpled the paper between her hands and flung it into the fire. Then she confronted Caleb with blazing eyes.

"You know as well as I do that this silly story is made out of the whole cloth!" she said hotly. "It is true that Gabriel de Cerreno is coming to visit me. But he's no more an emissary of the Pope than you are. He's a cousin of mine! You know he is, and you know he's a saint too! You said so yourself in Granada! And this is the way you repay his kindness to you! Slandering him! Slandering Jacqueline! Slandering me!"

"Look here, Faith, I don't print that paper. Fletcher prints it. I told you he'd fight dirty. Mebbe I wuz a little too hasty, the way I spoke. But you'll never make the voters of this state believe this is just a friendly visit of the Bishop's, never in the world. Most of 'em don't know you ever *wuz* in Spain. Lord Almighty, ain't we sweated blood, to make 'em *forget* how much time you spent in Europe! I've always ben a mite uneasy about your leanin's ever since I see you goin' to Mass with the Perez, and that's a fact. I spoke to Sarah Atkinson at the time, and——"

"Why, I never had any leanings! I went to church with the Perez just because it seemed natural! But there's a limit to what I can stand, and I'll ask Gabriel, the instant he gets here, what you *do* to join the

Catholic Church! And if it's possible, I *will* join it, right away! This is a country of religious freedom, isn't it? I suppose I can be a Catholic if I want to! And I think I *do* want to!"

She was weeping hysterically. Caleb, aghast at the imminent wreckage of all his hopes, was still staring at her helplessly, when Pansy Perkins, impassive, collected and tranquil, came silently into the room.

"San Antonio is calling you on the telephone, Mrs. Marlowe," she said imperturbably. "Will it be convenient for you to accept the call now, or would you rather have it repeated in an hour?"

Faith snatched up the receiver. "Yes!" she said, still hysterically. "*Yes*—YES—This is Mrs. Marlowe. Oh—oh—of course I will!" The tension in her voice snapped suddenly. The next words she pronounced were so different in tone that Caleb could hardly believe they were uttered by the same woman. A stream of musical liquid Spanish followed, and Caleb, staring openmouthed at her, saw that she was not crying any more, that she was drying her eyes with her free hand, that she was smiling a little. She hung up the receiver, and turned to him with composure.

"Gabriel's plans have been changed. He's going from San Antonio to Mexico," she said. "He isn't going to sail for Spain until just after Christmas. He asked if I usually spent that here, and I told him always. We will feel very close to Christ, having him with us then."

Her face had softened almost unbelievably. Caleb felt both smitten and touched; but he was immeasurably relieved. By Christmas time the election, for good or evil, would be a thing of the past.

"Incidentally, he suggested to me," Faith went on, her expression hardening again, "that I shouldn't take the trouble to deny Mr. Fletcher's announcement, reports of which had just come to him over the wire with a request for a statement. He has wired back that he was dumbfounded at the rumors which had reached him, as he was just leaving San Antonio to visit a cousin of his in Mexico—it's too funny, Uncle Caleb, these Cerrenos have cousins everywhere!—And much as he would feel honored to pay his respects to the first woman Senator, it would be impossible for him to do so. I should hate to be in Mr. Fletcher's shoes when he finds out that there isn't any Cardinal coming to Hamstead, that there isn't any conversion, that the Pope is still in Rome!"

She actually laughed out loud. Caleb, conscious that it was the "bigoted despot" who, in the course of three minutes' conversation, carried on at the distance of several thousand miles, had wrought this change in her, became increasingly bewildered.

"I won't let you down again," she promised. "I'll make all the speeches you say, even if I do have bubonic plague. But Uncle Caleb—if I'm ever awarded the Golden Rose, we won't let Fletcher have the scoop story, will we?"

"I ain't got no idea what you mean," Caleb said shortly. "But you snuck out of trouble by the skin of your teeth again, and I hope you can keep on doin' it six weeks more. But I ain't any too certain. Ned Fletcher ain't through with you yet, and that's a fact. The madder he gets the dirtier he'll fight. And he's going to be mad, good and plenty."

. . . . .

If there was one person in the state who was angrier than Mr. Edward Fletcher, it was David Noble. His adoration for his wife amounted almost to an obsession; and the slurs cast upon her made him see red with rage. Up to that time his interest in Faith's campaign had not been intensive. He secretly shared the regret which Sam and Hansel felt at her increasing absorption in political life; while as her physician he deplored the already apparent wreckage of the perfect nervous balance which she had built up so slowly. He would have resented the unfairness of Fletcher's attack upon her in any case; but if Jacqueline had not been drawn into it, he might have regarded it as a blessing in disguise, had it been instrumental in bringing about Faith's defeat. Considering the turn it had taken, however, his resentment swelled to vengeful fury; and from the day the scurrilous story made its appearance, he became a militant partisan to Faith's cause.

His latent power in the state, overlooked because of his long and frequent absences, and the fact that he had never taken any active part in politics, began to make itself felt. His own fortune, though not as large as his wife's, was substantial; and he had both the leisure and the means to go about putting in quiet but effective work. There was no part of the state in which his personality and his skill had not been leaving their stamp for nearly twenty years: he had grateful patients everywhere, many of them almost fanatically devoted to him; and they had been eagerly awaiting an opportunity to bear testimony to their thankfulness for the miracles of healing he had wrought. He needed to do no more than make a casual suggestion that it would be gratifying to him if they and their families could see their way clear to supporting Faith's candidacy, to have this support assured. Inside of a fortnight, the number of adherents upon whom Faith could absolutely rely, had been increased by hundreds.

She herself was only vaguely conscious of how much David was doing for her, and when he tried to tell her, in order to reassure her of the brightness of the political outlook, he was shocked to see how ravaged she looked. That the tell-tale evidences of fatigue and strain should be evident by now, was to be expected. She had been under pitiless pressure for more than three months. But that she should look haunted as well as exhausted was distressing to him.

"Don't worry any more about that fantastic story of Fletcher's, Faith," he said kindly. "I've got the snake pretty well scotched now I think."

"Scotched but not killed!" she quoted with a wan smile. "David—I keep waiting for something dreadful to happen, the way I did during the first part of the war. I'm sure Fletcher's going to get out another story. In fact, there was an item in the *Clarion-Herald* yesterday, stating that, 'Further startling revelations concerning the true character of the unwomanly aspirant for Senatorial honors will soon be released.'"

"Well, suppose there are more startling revelations? You know perfectly that there isn't anything that can be said any more convincing than that other story was. People are laughing at Fletcher everywhere for printing such a far-fetched yarn."

"He might print something about—about Sebastian and me. If he found out about that——"

"But good Lord, Faith, how could he find out about that?"

"I don't know. But I'm terrorized for fear that he may. And if he did, Uncle Caleb would be—stricken. His compromises don't extend to—sexual shortcomings."

"Well, if you're going in for hyperboles!" David exclaimed sharply. Then more gently he added, "Don't talk like that, Faith. You were never guilty of any sexual shortcomings, and you know it—or would, if you weren't letting yourself get morbid."

"And Hansel!" she went on, almost as if she had not heard him. "You know how a boy feels about his mother—when she is involved in anything like that!"

"Faith, you never were 'involved' in anything! Do look at all this sensibly. As a matter of fact, Hansel isn't thinking half so much about this campaign of yours as he is about his own little personal triumphs. He's done well to stick on the football squad as long as this, because he's underweight—if he gets his letter, it'll be a triumph of grit over sensitiveness. And the fact that he's already been taken into the Instrumental Club is a real recognition of some very real talent. Did you know he'd been working on the score of a musical pantomime for nearly a year, Faith?"

"No," acknowledged Faith in astonishment. "I wonder why he never told me?"

"You haven't had much time to devote to Hansel lately, have you, Faith?"

She admitted that she had not, but added that she was planning to give up a week-end entirely to him very soon. She did not realize, when she spoke, how soon this would be. Fletcher's second broadside was discharged the following Friday, and as Pansy brought in the paper and laid it down, with the calm manner and trembling lips characteristic, with her, of supreme emotion, Faith's desperate thoughts leaped forward to the frenzied certainty that the disclosure she had so long been dreading, had at last been made. Her conviction of this was so strong, that she did not once visualize the black headlines towering before her accurately. When she did, their unexpectedness staggered her as much as their calumny:

"DIABOLICAL MACHINATIONS REVEALED
"FAITH MARLOWE'S WAR RECORD DISCLOSED IN HIDDEN DOCUMENTS
"SERVED AS SPY THROUGHOUT WORLD WAR
"ATTILA THE HUN WALKS AGAIN IN HIS FOLLOWERS' FOOTSTEPS

"SHALL WE SEND A TRAITOR TO THE SENATE?

"Belford, Oct. 15.

"After painstaking research, carried on in spite of almost insuperable obstacles, the *Clarion-Herald* is able to give its readers the true story of the woman calling herself Faith Marlowe, whose name is actually Faith von Hohenlohe. As a young girl, renouncing her American heritage for a mess of red pottage, she married a Prussian officer; and she served as his confederate in casting the diabolically widespread net which later was to snare the fine flower of America to its doom. When the conflict for which Germany, the pariah nation, had set the stage with fiendish glee became imminent, Rudolf von Hohenlohe sent his wife to act as his agent in the United States. Trespassing on the sacred soil of the forefathers to whom she had played false, she sent him constant communications in code. The frequency with which cabled messages were received in Hamstead and sent from there is attested. How great a burden of responsibility for wholesale murder rests on the shoulders of this woman and her husband, it is still impossible to say, though later disclosures will doubtless reveal all. Far from repenting of her dastardly deeds, she has caused them to be perpetuated by erecting a statue to her partner in crime which commemorates his blood guiltiness. Thus the atrocities committed by men like Rudolf von Hohenlohe and women like his wife can never be forgotten by the people of this state."

"Mrs. Marlowe, don't—don't look like that! *No one* will believe this —The other was fantastic—but this is chimerical! Oh, I can't bear to have you feel so!"

Pansy was weeping so bitterly she could hardly speak. Faith, her face ashen, looked past her without seeming to see or hear her. So this ghoul had not even spared the great and honorable dead, slain for the Fatherland——

The telephone had begun to ring clamorously. Outside, someone was hammering importunately on the knocker. There was a sound of motors whirring up the driveway. As if oblivious of every sight and sound, Faith walked out of the library and up the stairs, and locking herself in the deserted attic, flung herself on her knees under the great Crucifixion.

When at last she stirred from her agonized lethargy, it was to realize that the one voice that she could not disregard was calling to her, and that frenzied hands were battering at the door. She drew herself up slowly by the heavy bedpost, and walked across the room with dragging feet. As she turned the latch, Hansel pitched forward against her.

"Why wouldn't you let me in?" he cried agonizingly. "Didn't you know I had to see you—had to—had to! When I came off the football field the newsboys were all screaming extra—and then I heard—I saw. . . . I jumped in my car and drove straight through here! Mother—do you see what you've given them a chance to say about my father, who died for his country? That he was a criminal, that his hands were stained with blood! *My father!*—I'll never forgive you, never as long as I live!"

He wrenched himself free from the hands with which she strove to clasp him. Then he fell at her feet in a dead faint.

. . . . .

"No, Faith, it isn't a concussion—that is I hope it isn't. But I *am* afraid of chill as well as shock. Be patient, and try to be as quiet as you can. For the boy's sake, my dear."

Hansel lay, still unconscious, on Sam's bed under the somber hovering picture. Faith sat on one side of him, her body shaken with sobs, her head hidden in her hands. On the other side David was standing, his dexterous fingers at Hansel's inert wrists, his searching eyes on the boy's pallid face. Pansy and Jacqueline were moving noiselessly about the room. Suddenly Faith looked up.

"Pansy," she said in a harsh whisper. "Go and get Mr. Hawks on the telephone. You know what you are to tell him."

"Just a minute," David interrupted impellingly. His gaze did not wander by a hair's breadth from the motionless form in front of him. But he spoke with such intensity that Faith suddenly looked up, swayed by the certainty that he was facing her, and that he was forcing her to face him.

"Listen to me," he commanded. "This isn't just your fight any more—just a case of pretending you're not beaten when you know you are. You've got to vindicate Rudolf's name now as well as your own, for the sake of your son—and his. This boy's. If he convicts you as a coward, you'll never lift your head again as long as you live."

CHAPTER 46

"Mother, Sam didn't ever tell you why he wanted to go to Europe, did he?"

"No, darling, never."

"Didn't you ask him?"

"I don't remember. No, I don't believe I did. Why? Does it matter?"

"I don't know. I just happened to wonder, because I thought, perhaps he hoped you would ask him, perhaps he hoped you'd be interested in knowing. Instead of just being interested in the campaign, I mean."

Faith, locking and unlocking her fingers, pressed her lips together to keep them from quivering. Hansel was sitting up in bed now, with a high pile of snowy pillows behind his shining head, and there was a faint color in the young face, which, during the last year, had rapidly been losing its childish softness. A mass of periodicals lay in front of him, and he was turning the pages of these with desultory attention. Decidedly, in the past day or two, he had gained with surprising rapidity. But there had been a hideous interval, of which Faith knew she would never be able to think without shuddering, when she had been almost certain that Hansel was slipping away from her, that the scope of the tragedy through which she had risen to fame had been widened to embrace her child as well as her lover.

In attacking Faith through her dead husband, Edward Fletcher had been guilty of an error in judgment even far more serious than that he had committed in charging Jacqueline Noble with complicity in a plot with Faith. In the first instance, he had indirectly rallied hundreds to Faith's support through David, whose power he had underestimated; in the second he had indirectly rallied hundreds of others to her support through Hansel, whose power he had entirely overlooked. The news of the boy's collapse and the cause of it had spread like wildfire among an indignant and outraged people. There was not a village in the state where Hansel's shy, charming smile, his pleasant appealing voice, and the unaggressive grace of his manner had not made a deep impression. Even the way he had always brought the green caravan to a stop, leaning nonchalantly forward to put on the brake and shut off the engine, and then glancing toward his mother, as if to be certain of her unspoken approval, before turning with his wide disarming smile of friendliness toward the crowd, had been an entering wedge toward cordial relations. The music that rippled from under his slim fingers was permeated with elfin magic; the greetings which he gave so naturally as he mingled unostentatiously with audiences after meetings and welcomed guests before gatherings, had a fascination which was the more inescapable because it was utterly innocent of self-consciousness and sophistication. There was an almost spiritual quality to it, which his youthfulness and his ingenuousness enhanced. When the word went out that his life and reason were hanging on a thread, Caleb Hawks' declaration that if the boy died, lynching would be too good for Edward Fletcher, found a response so universal that it echoed not only through the state but through the country. When the word went out that he was really better, people laughed and cried for joy when they met together.

Neal Conrad, taking an extra campaign burden upon his capable shoulders, made an announcement whenever he rose to speak which never failed to crystallize the attention and cement the sympathies of his audience. "I know that you were all hoping with me that my friend, Faith Marlowe, the first woman candidate for the United States Senate, would be on the platform with me to-night. Since I resigned from the Senate myself, in order to facilitate her candidacy, I do not need to tell you that she represents my own choice for this high position. In my opinion, she will reflect fresh honors on the name which has already stood for so much that is noble and great in the annals of our country. 'Let us have another Marlowe in the Senate,' should be more than a slogan. It should be a watchword." Here he always paused impressively, in response to a storm of applause. "Naturally, it was Mrs. Marlowe's intention to greet you herself on this auspicious occasion, and to present to you in her own words the policies of the great party to which we confidentially expect you will entrust the destinies of this nation. But she is prevented from being with you for a tragic reason: her only son, the namesake of his grandfather and his great-grandfather, Christian Marlowe III, is lying at death's door. He is the room-mate of my own son at college, and like many of you, I have known him well from childhood. I know you are hoping with me that he may be spared to the state and the nation—and to his mother." Here Neal paused again, with a break in his voice, while a tense silence gripped his audience. "A dastardly attack made upon the boy's dead father, a brave and gallant soldier, came as a terrific shock to this boy when he was not physically or mentally prepared to meet it. He rushed from the football field, and drove for hours through the bitter cold of a windy night to get to his mother, after a newsboy, with careless cruelty, had shouted the slanderous story in his ears. Shock and pneumonia were the result. Pray with me for his recovery—and to his distraught mother, watching at his bedside, give such comfort as lies in your power—the comfort of knowing that, in spirit, you are sharing her vigil, and that she may count on your loyalty to her during her ordeal!"

. . . . .

Even the indefatigable Pansy could not keep abreast of the avalanche of telegrams of sympathy under which Faith's desk lay buried; and the offerings of flowers, fruit and miscellaneous delicacies, which poured in upon Hansel would have supplied all the patients in a small hospital. But Faith, though she yielded to the importunities with which Caleb Hawks and Cavendish Castle reënforced David's stern admonition that she must not withdraw from her candidacy, steadfastly declined to take any further active part in the campaign. This was her compromise, she stated unequivocally; if an attempt were made to coerce her, she would retire altogether. Her attitude admitted of no doubt that she meant what she said; and aware that for the moment her very absence from the arena had its own peculiar and poignant appeal, the campaign managers allowed her to remain unmolested by Hansel's bedside, hopefully confident that by the time the last rousing rallies were being held, he would be well on the road to recovery, and that she would voluntarily emerge from seclusion.

As Hansel made his ingenuous reference to her preoccupation, Faith's heart contracted. She had missed Sam hideously in the ordeal through which she had been passing; and the ever-deepening feeling of bereavement which his absence gave her, intensified her conscience-stricken sense of having failed him. The inactivity and isolation of his life were largely unrelieved when she was not beside him; its darkness was unillumined. She was aware of this and still she had neglected him. While her need of him had been dominant, she had found it easy enough to spend endless hours with him, no matter how multitudinous the occupations which crowded in upon her had been; but when the urgency of her dependency on him had passed, she had disregarded, with cruel carelessness, the urgency of his dependence upon her.

"You see," Hansel went on after a moment's pause, "he did tell me why he was going. He told me the French Government was going to confer the Cross of the Legion of Honor upon him. I happened to think about it just now because there is an article on it in the number of *L'Illustration* which I have here."

Faith's heart contracted again. Sam had known that this great honor was to be bestowed upon him. And it was in Hansel, instead of in her, that he had confided. It was to Sarah, instead of to her, that he had turned for help.

She stretched out her hand, almost mechanically, to take the magazine and read the story of Sam's triumph. But Hansel, drawing back a little, held it tightly between the thumb and forefinger which marked the place where he had been reading.

"Perhaps I'd better tell you what the article says," he remarked hesitatingly. "It—it might be too much of a shock to you if you read it all by yourself. You see, it seems that when Sam was sure there was going to be a war, after he had seen Cousin Sarah safely off with Jacqueline and David, he shut himself up in his studio and painted and painted and painted. He began to work as soon as it was light in the morning, and worked until it grew dark at night. And of course, in Europe, the days are very long in the middle of the summer, aren't they? So it wasn't long before he finished his picture. And after he finished it, he locked it up in his studio, and went off and left it."

"Did he forget he had left it there, Hansel?"

"No, he didn't forget. He waited for the right time to go back and get it. I think he hoped that when he did you would go with him. He never gave up the studio. He paid rent on it every year—Cousin Sarah attended to that for him. But early this last summer there was a bad fire in the building, and when the firemen broke into the studio, they found the picture, and rescued it. And—and it was hailed immediately as a great masterpiece."

"What kind of a picture was it, Hansel?" Faith asked chokingly. But she knew.

"It was a picture of you, mother, a picture of 'Faith.'"

He still held the copy of *L'Illustration* firmly beyond her reach. But now he leaned toward her.

"Don't cry, mother," he said tenderly. "There's nothing to cry about. I'm going to tell you a lovely story, much lovelier and more wonderful really than any fairy story you ever told me. You see, the picture was put on exhibition, and thousands of people went to see it. They felt as if it was almost a—miraculous picture, because of the way it had been painted and hidden, and then found and saved and all. And because it—well, it represents so much. It isn't just a picture of a beautiful woman—it's a picture of a woman who is the incarnation of faith. She symbolizes what faith means to everyone in the world. No one has ever interpreted that before as marvelously as Sam has now."

"Hansel, you must let me see it."

"I'm going to, mother. But not until you've listened to me."

Through her tears, Faith looked at him in astonishment. He was speaking to her in a voice of authority, which was not his voice, as she recognized this, but a voice she had not heard in years—his father's voice. For the first time, as she faced him, she realized that she was not only confronted by her own son, but by the son of Rudolf von Hohenlohe. Though half of his heritage had been so long submerged, he was still essentially the child of a dual tradition, and now the part she had almost forgotten was clamoring for acknowledgment.

"When Sam comes home," Hansel went on, compellingly, "he'll bring this picture with him. It'll be put in the museum at Belford. I don't believe he'll give it to the museum, but he'll lend it. I think he wants to keep it himself, the way he kept the one he painted of you just before you and father were engaged—that was saved too. The French Government has offered him every inducement to part with 'Faith,' and he won't. I think probably he'll put it up in this attic by and by. You know how he feels about having things like that around, even though he can't see them. He told me once you'd been wonderful about realizing that. It seems strange to me, mother, when you guessed how Sam felt about being surrounded by beautiful things, that you shouldn't have guessed how much he wanted to have you with him. Cousin Sarah does all she can for him, I know, and he appreciates it. But of course he doesn't love Cousin Sarah the way he loves you."

"Hansel, you don't know what you're saying."

"Yes, I do. I know just what I'm saying. I know Sam has loved you ever since you were a little girl, and I know he doesn't dare let you see how much, because he thinks it wouldn't be fair, now that he is blind and you are famous. It isn't because of my father. He knows my father told you that he was thankful to feel you could count on Sam's devotion whatever happened, and that he hoped some day Sam would be rewarded."

"Hansel—Sam can't—can't possibly know that your father said that."

"But he does. I've heard father say it, and I told Sam so myself."

"Oh, Hansel! *You didn't!*"

"Yes, I did. I'm glad of it too. But I can't argue about that now. It's bothersome getting tired so easily——"

"Darling, I don't think you ought to talk any more anyway. Just let me see the picture, and then——"

"I'm going to let you see the picture in a minute. And I won't be half so tired if I tell you what I want to before I rest, as I will be if I lie here thinking that I haven't told you what I started out to say about the picture. Sam will be home with it next week and put it in the museum at Belford. And of course there will be copies of it in all the rotogravure sections and stories about it in all the newspapers. It is wonderful, isn't it, mother, that Sam should have painted it the way he did and that it should have been found the way it was and that it should mean so much to the people who look at it?—Of course that's because it meant so much to Sam, and because he has the genius to show how he feels. I think you're wonderful too, mother, but I can't prove it to the whole world the way Sam does."

He smiled suddenly, his illusive irresistible smile. As she had recognized Rudolf's voice in his for the first time, so Faith now recognized Victoria Luise's expression. She had always taken it for granted that Hansel looked exactly like her. Now she saw that except for his coloring, he looked very much as the Archduchess must have looked when she was seventeen.

"You understand, don't you, mother, that everyone who sees the picture and copies of it, and reads stories about it, will get the feeling that they didn't realize before how wonderful you were? Because of course a woman who is *very wonderful* would make a man feel that he had to paint a picture like that. I'm not saying this very well, because I'm getting sort of tired, but what I mean is, lots of people will be thinking about this pretty hard just about the first of November, and–and—"

He broke off, groping for words. Faith found that she was powerless to help him go on.

"You know those big rallies, in Hinsboro and Belford, the two nights before election, mother? Well, if you ask Sam, don't you think he'd go to them with you? And then you see, when you came out with Sam, on the platform, wearing a dress something like this in the picture, and started to speak, and–and everything–Oh, mother, won't you do it, just to please me? You see I'm so awfully sorry I said what I did to you about never forgiving you because people had slandered my father, of course I know it wasn't your fault at all, that you've always been loyal to father. It's marvelous for a boy to be able to feel that his mother's been so loyal to his father, only really, I don't want you to be *too* loyal, that is–But if you're not elected now, I'll feel it's my fault, because you've had to stay at home with me while I've been sick and everything, and if you do what I say at those rallies, I know you will be elected, and so, oh mother, won't you *please*? Won't you *promise*?"

The voice of authority had vanished, and with it the illusion of all that it represented. Faith saw only a fragile boy, exhausted by illness and emotion, leaning forward to clasp his arms around her neck, and hiding his face on her shoulder so that she would not see that he was crying. The magazine he had been holding slipped to the floor, falling open at a full-page picture. As she turned to look at it, Faith found herself gazing at a vision of such mystic splendor that she caught her breath. Unsullied and undefeated by the world wreckage which formed the shadowy background of the painting, the radiant figure of a woman emerged puissant and victorious from the carnage with which she was surrounded. She seemed to transcend sin and suffering, disaster and death. Her bearing was triumphant; her face was exalted. The golden scroll with which the picture was bound was illuminated, as a priceless missal might have been. Half-blinded with tears as she was, Faith knew that it was inscribed with the immortal words of the Apostle Paul, which Sam had first heard from her lips years before on a dark and stormy night at sea:

"Stand therefore . . . having on the breastplate of righteousness, and your feet shod with the preparation of the gospel of peace; above all, taking the *shield of faith*, wherewith ye shall be able to quench all the fiery darts of the wicked."

Faith, clasping her son in her arms, bent her head until it rested against his. Their tears mingled together. But when at last she spoke to him, her voice was strong and joyous.

"My precious treasure," she said vibrantly, "of course I will! Of course I promise!"

CHAPTER 47

THE President of the United States and Mrs. Conrad were saying good-bye to the guests who had lunched with them after the inauguration, pausing for a moment, as they made the round of the circle which had formed in the Red Room, for a personal word with each in turn.

"This is the same sort of a chain that the diplomats used to make at the Royal Receptions in Copenhagen, isn't it, mother?" Christian Marlowe III asked in an interested whisper, his attentive gaze shifting for a moment from the lovely lady in fawn-colored lace who was advancing toward them at the President's side, and resting, with even more admiration, on his mother.

"The circle is formed in something the same way; but everything else is different, and it seems to me much pleasanter!" Faith Marlowe whispered back.

Her own smiling glance wandered from the tall graceful boy beside her to the wood fire glowing under the white mantel banked with flowers, and the south window where the warm spring sunshine streamed generously into the room. The rich crimson walls and hangings, the austere Presidential portraits in their massive frames, the furniture, the decorations, even the guests, seemed transfigured in its mellow warmth. The apartment had all the dignity and elegance befitting the drawing-room in the residence of the Chief Executive of a great nation. But there was nothing forbiddingly formal about it. It emanated a festive friendliness.

"Junior tells me that you went on the Dean's List at midyear's, Christian, and that this means you can stay over for the inaugural ball tonight."

The lovely lady in fawn color and the distinguished-looking man with the firm chin and square shoulders had stopped in front of Hansel. They were both regarding him with cordiality and affection.

"Yes, Mr. President. I'm awfully pleased."

"We're pleased too—and we'll look for you there. And Christian, when you come to Washington for your Easter vacation, we shall expect you for dinner. The new moving-picture machine will be all ready for use then. If your mother can spare you, perhaps you'll stay overnight with Junior, just for the fun of sleeping in the White House."

"Thank you, Mrs. Conrad, you know I'd love to."

The Presidential pair had gone forward another step. Hansel watched them excitedly as they paused before his mother.

"Well, Senator Marlowe, I know I can count on your support in every one of the measures I'm hoping to put through in the extra session."

"Absolutely, Mr. President. I won't desert you for a day, even if the thermometer goes up to a hundred and fifty!"

"Aren't you too ceremonious, with your 'Senator Marlowe,' and your 'Mr. President'! I hope it's going to be Anne and Neal and Faith, just as it has been all the years we've been neighbors."

"Absolutely again! And we're still going to be neighbors! I have a surprise for you! I'll telephone to-morrow and find out when I may come and talk to you about it."

Anne Conrad had passed along beside her husband, her laces flowing about her. Hansel turned to his mother with enthusiasm.

"They haven't changed at all, have they, mother? Somehow, I couldn't help being afraid they would, after this morning—Can we go over to Sam and Cousin Sarah now?"

"In just a minute, darling. We must wait until the President and Mrs. Conrad have gone out of the room and upstairs—at White House parties, it's the host and hostess who leave first. But next time we come here, nothing will be so formal."

The folding doors leading into the great entrance hall opened and closed impressively. Immediately afterwards, the circle broke, and the guests, converging into small congenial groups, moved forward, talking with animation. Faith and Hansel, crossing the room quickly, joined Sam and Sarah Atkinson, who had stopped to congratulate Carolus Cavendish Castle on his appointment as Secretary of the Navy. Mrs. Castle, armored with satisfaction and importance, was competently appropriating these congratulations.

"You'll let us take you over to your hotel, won't you, Faith?" she asked, when she felt that enough had been said on this paramount question. "We have room for Mrs. Atkinson and Mr. Dudley, too. The new official car is very spacious."

"It's ever so kind of you. But after all, it's only a step to the Willard. And it's such a perfect afternoon, I thought we might walk around Lafayette Square, before we went back to the hotel. I think we can do it and still be in time for the parade."

"My dear Faith, *nobody* bothers with parades any more! And why should you want to walk around Lafayette Square?"

"To see the house where my grandfather and father lived—the house where I'm going to live too! I've bought it back.—And Hansel adores parades. All boys do. And so does Uncle Caleb. We're going to meet him."

Mrs. Castle gave an expression of horror. "But my dear Faith, you can't live on Lafayette Square! It's changed tremendously since your grandfather's day, even since your father's. There's actually a tea-shop on it, and I'm told that the club which has its headquarters in the old Randall House is communistic! You won't have any suitable neighbors."

"Well, after all, I'll have Neal and Anne. They're suitable. Don't feel so upset, Aunt Annabelle. It's all settled anyway. What I need to do now is to take my family to see the house, and get a consensus of views on remodeling. I want to get started on the work right away, especially as I'll have to be here all summer, now that Neal's going to call an extra session. Do you mind terribly if I go out of the door in front of you? I know it's contrary to all precedent—I may start a new controversy, Senate versus Cabinet, but I must get started!"

She laughed lightly, stopped to shake hands with Mr. Cooper, the head usher, who stood, formal and vigilant, near the front door, bowed, passed out of the portico. Hansel, placing his hand protectingly under her elbow as they went down the steps, began to talk excitedly.

"The moving-picture men will be just outside the gate, mother—don't you want Sam and me to walk on either side of you, so we can push right by them? And Pennsylvania Avenue is roped off for the parade—I'm afraid we can't get through. Why didn't you tell me before about the house? Have you bought it really?"

"Yes, really. I always said I was coming back to begin again where my father left off, and I wanted his house as well as his seat in the Senate—I didn't tell you about it because I was keeping it for a surprise—I think we can cross all right if we go up the Avenue a little further. And of course I want Sam and you beside me. I think we might almost walk four abreast, don't you? Then Cousin Sarah and I could be in the middle and you and Sam——"

In spite of their combined perseverance, their progress was slow. The barrage of cameras and moving-picture machines was almost impassable; and the crowd, already gathering for the parade, was surging through the streets. Faith finally appealed to a policeman.

"I'm Senator Marlowe," she said swiftly, "and I want very much to take my son and my—my cousins across the street to see my grandfather's house. We're going to live there ourselves. Do you think you could help us?"

She glanced from the policeman toward Sam, and the officer, following her look, saw what she had not wished to say. He was galvanized into immediate action.

"Stand back there!" he shouted belligerently, addressing the multitude. "Come right along, Senator Marlowe.—Now if you'll just take this gentleman's arm——"

"There!" Faith exclaimed five minutes later. "It wasn't hard after all, was it? We're almost opposite the house now, Sam. It *is* a gloomy gaunt old-looking structure. But I *wanted* it."

"Of course you did!" Sam agreed instantly. He had been rather silent through the inaugural exercises and the luncheon, but now he spoke with evident interest. "I suppose it will need a great deal of repairing and remodeling. But then, you enjoy that sort of thing."

"Yes, I do. And I knew I could count on you to help me. I thought I would have a basement entrance, to do away with the long flight of steps, and make more room on the first floor. The front and back parlors can be thrown into one long drawing-room, I think, with a large dining room behind. The library will still be on the floor above, just as my father and grandfather had it, and I'll have the small study and big bedroom in the rear that were theirs too. That still leaves two stories above with all kinds of space for the rest of you. Would you like the room that used to be mine, Hansel?—Cousin Sarah, you and Sam can have a private sitting-room, and I thought I'd see about putting in an elevator.—Of course the plumbing will all have to be done over—there used to be just *one* bathroom, with a huge funny tin tub enclosed in a rectangular wooden box—and the service quarters must have been terrible, though I don't remember them distinctly.—Oh, we're *here!* I think that black walnut front door is rather impressive-looking, don't you, Cousin Sarah, even if it is dark? I don't believe I'll change that! Shall we go in? Here's the key, Hansel, darling!"

There were tears in her eyes as she stepped inside the door, out of which she had been thrust so precipitously and acrimoniously a quarter of a century before. For a moment she stood still, almost expecting to hear Lily and Ella clattering about in the kitchen, or her mother's shrill voice rising above her father's unhappy protests in the library. Then she linked her arm through Sam's again, and spoke with attempted lightness.

"I'm superstitious about a house," she said. "I always feel as if the people who had lived in it had left their imprint on it, no matter how far away from it they've gone, no matter how long they've been dead. Shall we go upstairs? I want to see my father's library first of all—and then I'm going to look out of the rear windows and try to plan for a little back-yard garden. It'll be such a godsend during the summer. I'd like to build a very high wall, to shut out all the unsightly surroundings, and have trellises and a fountain and—can't you visualize just how it would look, Sam?"

"Yes, exactly. You'd have brick walks as well as brick walls, wouldn't you? And borders of pansies? Ramblers on the trellises, and perhaps a bush of old-fashioned yellow roses in the corner? That's the idea, isn't it?"

They all made helpful suggestions. As they went from room to room, Faith felt that their interest and enthusiasm had taken fire from her own; and it was not until they had all returned to the Willard that her sense of abundant joy was shadowed. They were to dine with the Nobles and Caleb Hawks, and go on to the charity ball afterwards. But meanwhile there was a welcome interval for rest and relaxation. And Faith, after slipping into a negligee and ordering tea came back into the pleasant parlor of her suite to find that Sarah, Sam, and Hansel had already gathered there. Sarah had spoken of lying down for a little while, and realizing that she was very tired, Faith was astonished to see that she had changed her mind. She was also astonished at the sudden hush that fell on the little group, almost as if some subject had been under discussion, a continuation of which her presence precluded. She looked from one to the other, smiling.

"What are you doing, plotting?" she asked gaily. And as no one answered immediately, she went on, "Really, you all act as if I had caught you conspiring against me!"

"Perhaps you might call it that, Faith," Sarah Atkinson said slowly.

"Why, what have I done to deserve such shabby treatment?"

"You have done nothing to deserve shabby treatment, my dear. And I hope you will not feel that any one of us is treating you shabbily. But now that you have surprised us by your fortunate purchase of your old home, we feel that perhaps we should speak to you about our own plans, before we allow you to proceed any further without knowing what these are. We were just considering the question in its various aspects when you came in."

"I see. I'm very sorry that I interrupted. Shall I go away again?"

She spoke with slight sarcasm. After all, this was the greatest day of her life, and instead of permitting her to enjoy it in unalloyed triumph, those who were nearest and dearest to her were apparently preparing to pour drops of bitter into her cup of sweet. She half turned toward her room. But as she did so, Hansel sprang to her side, and put his arm around her waist.

"Don't go, mother," he said imperatively. "Come and sit down beside me on the sofa, won't you? There's nothing we mind telling you, nothing at all. It's just that we hadn't planned to tell you *to-day*. But as Cousin Sarah says, if you're going to start fixing over the house immediately, we thought perhaps you'd do it a little differently, if you realized we wouldn't all be there with you."

Faith looked at him in consternation. The clear direct gaze with which he confronted her did not waver.

"Suppose you explain, Hansel," she said, trying to speak quietly.

"Well, mother, you know I was terribly disappointed that we didn't go to Germany last year. But I knew you couldn't, with the campaign and all, and I knew you needed me to help you. So when you promised, absolutely promised, that we should go this year instead, I tried to pretend it really didn't matter very much; and I've been counting off the days on my calendar all winter, and I got sailing schedules and found the *Deutschland* leaves the very day after college closes——"

"But Hansel, darling, be reasonable! When I made that promise I had no idea Neal would call an extra session! I've got to stay in Washington."

"Yes, mother, I know you've got to. But I haven't. So I think I'll start for Germany the day after college closes, even if you can't go with me."

There was a knock at the door, and a waiter entered noisily bearing tea. Sarah Atkinson rose, supervised the arrangement of the table with a vain attempt to prevent the rattle of dishes, bestowed a liberal tip, and murmured hasty assurances, designed to check a flow of volubility, to the effect that she would ring if more hot water were needed, and that she really didn't think that any of them cared for cinnamon toast. When she resumed her seat, without reference to the inopportune interruption, she saw that Sam's expression was inscrutable, and heard Hansel calmly continuing his declaration of independence.

"I want to see my grandfather and grandmother," he was saying with succinctness. "I want to spend at least a month with them at Schönplatz. I want to do that every summer from now on. I'm going to be the next Baron von Hohenlohe, and it's disgraceful that I shouldn't know anything about the management of the estate. It must be very sad for my grandparents, now that they are growing old, to keep thinking that all their sons were killed in the war, and that the only Hohenlohe grandson who wasn't killed too, hasn't even seen the place that will be his property some day, since he was seven years old. I should think it would make them wish they could give it to one of the von Mitwelds, one of Aunt Rita's children. But they can't. It's entailed. They have to give it to me."

"But Hansel," Faith said faintly, "I never thought of you as the next Baron von Hohenlohe. I've thought of you for nearly ten years, as Christian Marlowe III. Your father said he was perfectly willing you should choose——"

"I know he did, mother. And I have chosen. I like Hamstead, and I love you, and I'm very proud of the Marlowe tradition. But I don't feel, inside, like an American myself. I feel like a German. I am a German. I want to go home, just as much as you wanted to come home."

Faith gave a little cry of anguish. Sam, rising suddenly, walked over with uncanny directness, to the sofa where she and Hansel were, and sat down beside her.

"Let the boy go on, Faith," he said in a low voice. "All this has been bottled up inside of him for a long time."

"I want to go to Bonn," Hansel continued inexorably. "I want to find the rooms my father had when he was there at the University, and try to reserve them for myself. I'm willing to go through Harvard, if I can spend every summer vacation in Germany, but after I've graduated at Harvard, I want to take a post-graduate course at Bonn. I want to study music, too. I want to have a boat on the Rhine, and go camping in the Black Forest, and see the picture galleries in Munich and Dresden and go to the Musical Festivals at Bayreuth. Of course I'll be very pleased to have you come with me, mother, whenever you can, and stay with me as much as you can, and I'm sure grandfather and grandmother will too. They've always loved you dearly, you know that. But I'm going home this summer, even though you can't come with me, and by and by I'm going home to stay. This isn't any time for Germans to be living in some foreign country. They're needed in their own."

He put his arms around her again, and kissed her on her rigid cheek. "I'm sorry, mother," he said more gently. "Really, I didn't mean to tell you this to-day. But when you began talking about fixing up that room that used to be yours for me, I thought you'd feel much worse, if I let you go ahead and do it, and then told you, than——"

"You're altogether too young to make a decision like this," Faith exclaimed suddenly. "I shan't allow it. When you're twenty-one, if you still feel this way, I suppose I can't stop you from going to Germany. But I can now. I shan't let you go."

"Faith, you were just Hansel's age, when Rudolf first declined to let you come home," Sam cut in. "Have you forgotten how you felt?"

"That was different."

"It wasn't different. It was the same—essentially. If you don't let the boy go, Faith, you'll lose him—in the same way Rudolf lost you. If you do let him go, you may keep him."

The telephone jangled. Sarah Atkinson rose, and walking past the table where the tea still stood cooling, picked up the receiver.

"Yes, this is Senator Marlowe's apartment," she said crisply, "but the Senator is in conference. She cannot accept any calls this afternoon. No, not from anyone. When she is at leisure again, I will advise you."

Again she resumed her place in the easy chair beside the sofa, her gray taffeta dress rustling as she disposed it about her. Faith had not answered Sam, and the moment seemed to Sarah opportune for speaking herself.

"I think Sam is right, my dear," she said composedly, "and when you have reflected a little, I believe you will see that he is yourself. Perhaps it would be well not to try to cross too many bridges at once. But at least you can give your consent ungrudgingly to the trip this summer. If Congress should adjourn by August, which is quite possible, you could still join Hansel in Germany for a few weeks. And meanwhile you would have the satisfaction of knowing that instead of being cooped up in Washington, sweltering, he would be cool and comfortable at Schönplatz."

"He can always go to Hamstead, if it gets too hot here."

"Do you think Hansel would be contented in Hamstead, alone?"

"Of course not!" Faith said almost sharply. "I supposed, all the time, that through the worst of the heat you would prefer to be in the country, and so——"

"My dear, I dislike to disappoint you, if you were depending upon me. But I have been waiting for the proper moment to ask you whether you did not feel the time had come at last when I might suitably suggest that I should like to go to Salem."

"To Salem!" echoed Faith, more and more aghast.

"Why, yes. That was my plan, you know, when I first thought of coming back to the United States. I abandoned it temporarily, because Sam asked me if I would not go to Hamstead and wait there for him. It was six years ago in December, Faith, that Sam joined me, and I have tried to be very patient. But now that you have entered the Senate, now that the tenor of your life has changed entirely, I feel that you do not need me as much as you did. I feel I have a right to spend my declining years in my own home. I feel, as Hansel does, that before permitting you to remodel your house with a view to my needs, I should tell you that I shall be there only as an occasional guest. Naturally, my dear, I shall not leave you until it is convenient for you to have me do so. But when it is——"

Faith rose in her turn. "I think," she said slowly and scathingly, "that I had better go into my own room—before Sam begins to tell me what his plans are. I've heard the one woman who's stood by me ever since I was a deserted, frightened little girl, say she's going off to leave me, and I've heard my son—my only child—explain that he's not an American but a German. And though I don't see how I'm going to bear all this, I suppose I shall somehow. But I think I won't listen to any more."

She moved majestically away from them, and went into her room without looking back. But as she tried to turn the key in her latch, the door was flung wide open again and slammed shut; and Sam, with his back against it, stood before her.

"Look here, Faith Marlowe!" he exclaimed vehemently, "you have no right to speak about me that way and you know it! If you think you can walk out on me, like a tragedy queen, just because you are now the first woman member of the Senate, you have made a great mistake. One of your greatest. And you've made a good many. Good God, I——"

"Sam, will you please go out of my room? At once? I want to be alone."

"No," he said, still more vehemently. "I will not go out of your room. I won't go at once, and I don't know when I shall go. Perhaps not at all. You don't want to be alone. It's the last thing on earth you want. You're like most people who've climbed to the top of the world. You're appalled to find out what a solitary desolate place it is. But I don't intend that you should be any lonelier there than you have to be. Certainly, I don't intend to let you luxuriate in loneliness. If you deliberately choose to be deserted, perhaps I can't help it. But I think I can. Anyway, before you do choose, I'm going to be damn sure you know what you're doing."

He stepped suddenly forward, and before she could draw back, seized both her hands, holding her at arms' length, but still fettered. She struggled ineffectually to free herself.

"Let me go, Sam! How dare you! You must be out of your mind!"

"I must have *been* out of my mind, to let you get in a state like this before I nipped your heroics in the bud. Stand still, Faith, and stop trying to behave like Sarah Bernhardt, will you? You're a lot nicer when you behave like yourself. You can save your oratory for your maiden speech in the Senate. It'll make a lot bigger hit there than it will with me." Then, as he heard a dry convulsive sob, he added more gently, "And don't do that either. Not until you've listened to me. Isn't there a chair in here where we could sit down and talk?"

"A chair?"

"Yes. Sure. A great big one. They have them, even in hotels. Where I could hold you in my lap, the way I used to do in my messy old studio when you were a little girl. I'm positive, Faith, that there's a big chair somewhere in this room, and I think it's awfully unfair of you not to tell me, when—Don't, Faith, don't! I didn't mean to be cross, but you were so damn stagey! You've been playing to galleries so long that you've half forgotten—Faith—darling——"

Her ineffectual struggle against him had ended abruptly. She had ceased trying to wrench herself free, but now he could hear her weeping. He drew a deep breath, and releasing one of her hands, but still holding the other, he groped his way across the room. As his questing fingers closed over a high padded chair back, he stopped, swung it swiftly around, and drew her down into his arms.

"Now then," he said comfortingly, but compellingly, "what do you say we forget that you are famous and I am blind? What do you say we forget that your career is beginning and mine is over? What do you say we forget everything in the world, this next hour, except that I love you and what that means?"

"What—what does it mean?"

"It means that Cousin Sarah is going to Salem and Hans Christian is going to Schönplatz, but that I'm *staying*. With you."

"But Sam," Faith murmured in a muffled voice, "if you stayed, when Cousin Sarah and Hansel were both gone——"

"It would make a scandal in the Senate? Perish the thought! Whoever heard of such a thing? I'm afraid I shall be driven into making an honest woman of you, Faith. Do you suppose there is a parson in the hotel?"

"Sam! How can you—joke?"

"Faith! How can I be serious? You never let me."

"If—if I did let you—what would you do?"

"Just the same thing I should do if you didn't. I'd marry you. I don't mind in the least being called, 'Senator Marlowe's husband.' Not if I *am*."

She gave a little startled gasp. Sam tightened the clasp in which he held her.

"Listen, darling," he said, and there was no levity in his voice now, "I've stood back and let you go your own way for nearly thirty years. Part of the time I couldn't help it. Part of the time I thought I ought not to try to help it. But now I'm just as sure I ought to make you marry me as I was that I ought to save you from drowning. I know what lies ahead of you better than you do. You're thinking just of making good your childish pledge of coming back to Washington, of taking your father's place, of carrying on his work and his name. I believe you can. I believe you will. But if you try to do it all alone, it'll be a rough road. You saw a little of how rough, this last summer, during the campaign. But that wasn't a circumstance to what it will be later on. Wouldn't it comfort you, Faith, wouldn't it help you, if you knew you didn't have to go over that road alone, that I'd always be near you, making it just as smooth for you as I could?"

"You know it would," she answered softly, "but—"

"I know what all the buts are, darling, just as well as you do, and they don't frighten me, not even the biggest one of all—the but that you got married once without being in love with your husband, and that though you're ready to shut your eyes and jump, when it comes to anything else, you don't dare do that again. You got badly burnt, and you're afraid of fire. Aren't you?"

"Yes. Terribly."

He felt her wince as she said it. But he only drew her closer to him.

"I know how much you loved Sebastian," he said gently. "But you don't love him any more. You think you do, but you don't. He set his mark on you and it made a pretty deep wound—you'll carry the scar of it to your grave. But it doesn't hurt you any more. You're still thinking of Sebastian as a vital force that changed the current of your life, and he was. But you haven't thought of him as a man in a long time. You haven't thought of any man—in the sense I mean—for a long time. You made up your mind that you couldn't and that you wouldn't, because of Sebastian. But you could. You can. You're going to."

"Sam!" gasped Faith.

"It's a waste," Sam said cheerfully, "this craze of yours for celibacy.

You ought to have half a dozen children. Four anyway. If there ever was a modern woman who was meant to be a fruitful vine, like the one in the Bible, it's you. You were made for maternity. I hope you'll have a baby every year or so. You can have them when the other Senators are off on junkets—they're always ranging around, at government expense, to the Panama Canal and Hawaii and the Philippine Islands. Well, while they're doing that you can have babies. You needn't tell me they would interfere with your public activities, because any woman who can do as many different kinds of things at once as you have in the last few years, can more or less take babies in her stride. There's lots of space for them in that house on Lafayette Square. The big front room on the third floor, for instance, that you meant to give Cousin Sarah would make an ideal nursery. Let's see, this is March. Well, by next Christmas we will certainly have a big bouncing baby in that nursery. We will have a tree for him and Hansel will be crazy about him."

This time Faith was beyond gasping.

"You're all through treating me as if I were an elder brother, or a youngish uncle or someone like that," Sam went on serenely, "kissing me casually on the forehead, and perching on the side of my bed, and sitting in front of the fire with your head against my knees. I don't see why I ever let you get away with it. I'm not your elder brother or your youngish uncle, and I never felt as if I were. But that doesn't matter any more. We won't waste a minute discussing it. Because from now on, you're going to treat me like a man—a man who's head over heels in love with you and always has been. And pretty soon you're going to treat me like a man you're head over heels in love with yourself."

"But I never could be—head over heels in love again, Sam. I had to stamp—all that out of my life, or I'd have gone insane. It wouldn't be fair to you to——"

"It *hasn't* been fair to me," he amended quietly. "But it's going to be. And it hasn't been wholly fair to you either. I know you've tried to 'stamp all that out of your life,' Faith, and I know why you felt you ought to. But you oughtn't to any longer. You mustn't forget that a woman who cheats nature, pays the penalty for it. No matter how much she gains in other ways—and you've gained a good deal—she loses something too: Gentleness. Sweetness. Bloom. Fecundity. Almost everything we mean when we say femininity. She grows hard or she grows bitter; she grows defensive or she grows aggressive. I haven't seen you, Faith, in ten years, but I know how much you've changed. I know you're beautiful, and still I know that—I wouldn't want to paint you now if I could. Not because you're older—you ought to be magnificent in maturity! But because you press your lips together in a hard line, because the outline of your face is sharper, because the softness has gone from your eyes."

He lifted his hands, and with a lightness that had in it the quality of a caress, touched her hair, her features, her throat, her breast. Then, cupping her face between his fingers, he lifted it to his.

"I want to change all that," he whispered. "I want to as an artist—and I want to as a man. I want the Eve and the Lorelei I painted back again—and the Mary—and the Faith too! I want her for myself—and I want her for the world!"

As he spoke, he drew her face closer and closer to his own. When he finished, their lips were already touching. He pressed his against hers, so gently that instinctively she returned the pressure. Then, almost subconsciously, she realized that the gentleness had fused with urgency, that her head was thrown back and his bent forward, that the embrace in which he now held her locked was as passionate as it was tender. A swift stab of pain, fiery and exquisite, shot through her body. But as it pierced her, all her rigidity, all her resistance, seemed to stream away from her. When at last he lifted his head, her own sank down on his shoulder, and she nestled against him, almost as if she were afraid he might let her go, and that with her release, her new-found sense of ecstasy would be shattered. He put his arms around her again.

"You see," he said exultantly. "But suppose I kiss you again, Faith—just to make sure!"

THE END

Pine Grove Farm, North Haverhill, New Hampshire, 1930.
La Fortaleza, San Juan, Puerto Rico, 1931.
American Hospital, Beirut, Syria, 1931.
Washington, D. C., 1932.
Pine Grove Farm, North Haverhill, New Hampshire, 1932.
Alexandria, Va., 1933.

The Great Tradition

TO MY SON

JOHN PARKINSON KEYES

WHO BOTH DIRECTLY AND INDIRECTLY
IS RESPONSIBLE FOR LARGE PORTIONS OF THIS BOOK

CONTENTS

FOREWORD

IT IS DIFFICULT for an author to gage the importance of a foreword. In the English edition of my novel *The Safe Bridge*, my publishers omitted one which had appeared in the American edition, carrying a statement to the effect that the book contained neither characters nor incidents which were fictitious. British reviewers promptly leapt forward to declare the former fantastic and the latter unimaginable and I greatly deplored the absence of my explanation concerning these. On the other hand, in my novel *Parts Unknown*, meticulous care was taken with credits and explanations. Yet hundreds of letters came in asking questions which had already been answered, and I decided that no one ever read a foreword anyway!

Under these circumstances it is difficult to know just how much to say about the sources of *The Great Tradition*. However, it is perhaps proper to explain that while the characters are all fictitious with the exception of Horst Wessel, the major incidents, and many of the minor ones, are founded on fact, and the settings are as authentic as lifelong acquaintance with them has made it possible to present them. I have lived in Germany during the Empire, during the Republic and during the Third Reich. I have traveled from one end of it to the other; I have visited in countless German homes, and in assembling reference material to supplement my own observations and experiences, I have consulted hundreds of responsible German authorities, representing every shade of opinion, and read with care every recommended document.

I may perhaps add that I have also spent considerable time in Spain and that I have a profound affection for it and for its people. I have had friends fighting on both sides in the recent conflict. My son John, to whom this book is dedicated, was there throughout the Revolution of 1931, and the notes which he took at that time have been invaluable to me. So have certain family letters and informal articles written during the same period by Mary Eleanor Peters, Instructor of Spanish at the Junior College of San Mateo in California; she has kindly permitted me to consult and adapt these. Miss Irene Wright, who lived in Spain for sixteen years, becoming Dean of Investigators at the Archives of the Indies in Seville, and receiving the Alphonso XII Decoration for Contribution to Culture, is another person to whom I am deeply indebted for co-operation. She is now an official in the Division of Cultural Relations at the State Department in Washington, and has permitted me to confer with her frequently and fully. Eleanor Carroll, Professor in the School of Journalism at Columbia University, and Charlotte Barbour, long a member of the firm of Barbour & McKeogh, Literary Agents, who both read the manuscript while it was under construction, helped me enormously by their wise and thorough editorial comments.

The retort attributed to Bautista Ramirez on page 576 of this book is based on one made by Miguel Maura, First Minister of Justice under the Spanish Republic, to the ex-Dictator Berenquer. The statement made by Sebastian de Cerreno on page 588 is based on one made by an unnamed Spanish grandee and printed on the first page of *La Voz*, April 21, 1931. The comments made by Sebastian to Beatrice on page 665 are based on a quotation contained in an article by Anne O'Hare McCormick published in the *New York Times*, June 12, 1939. Mrs. McCormick has most graciously given her consent to this adaptation.

Some slight historical liberties have been taken. For instance, the bombing of Madrid did not begin as early in the Civil War as indicated in Chapter 29, and the Insterburg and Königsberg episodes outlined on page 499 were reported in 1932 instead of 1930. The disastrous events described as taking place near Granada are all based on incidents which did occur in Andalusia, but some of them happened farther from Granada itself than the Cerreno *caseria* appears to have been located. The events specifically described as occurring in Santa Fe and Atarfe did take place there, and are presented in only slightly fictionized form.

F. P. K.

PART I

1924

Captain's Table

CHAPTER 1

"WHAT A beautiful day we've had for sailing! The skyline clear as a celestial city's——"

"Nonsense, Edith, you can't possibly be *yet!* Why we're hardly out of the harbor and it's as smooth as a mill pond——"

"I'll take hors d'oeuvres first and then some chicken soup and a small piece of fish. I might as well order from the grill now too, the service on this boat is so slow. Let me see . . . I really don't care much for mutton chops, but there doesn't seem to be much choice. Now on the Italian liners—— Oh! Would you care to see the menu too? Excuse me!"

The belligerent lady, wearing a severe toque which revealed neatly frizzed hair beneath it, closed her lorgnette with a snap. She had managed to disregard the sentimental cleric, who had remarked to the group at large that New York looked like a celestial city, and the beetle-browed man who was storming at his miserable though bejeweled companion. But something impelled her to bend her gaze upon the handsome boy beside her. He was almost too arresting a type, she instantly decided, and far too young—apparently still in his teens—to be honored with a seat at the Captain's table. However, at least he appeared to be well bred, which was more than could be said for the girl sitting opposite. She was really rather pretty, with lovely pink cheeks, big blue eyes, and a bush of curly brown hair. But she was flashily dressed in a red and black sports suit and she had on at least a dozen bracelets, one of them strung with silly little charms that tinkled every time she moved her hands. Petunia-colored nail polish glittered on her finger tips as she did this, and her mouth was petunia colored too. Her one conversational contribution had been addressed to the dumpy, frumpy woman with an anxious air who was seated beside her.

"Mumma, did you know I had eight corsages, besides all my other flowers? The steward was still bringing in boxes when I came down to lunch. Jimmie Nelson and Ted Sloane both sent orchids—I knew I could bank on that. But Harry Page, the tightwad, only came across with a dozen carnations. When I get home again, I'll tell him just what I think of him and his penny pinching."

Having delivered herself of this direful threat, the girl lapsed into silence, and the corners of her pretty painted mouth drooped. She had begun to smoke before the soup course was served, and she continued to do so, flicking away ashes indiscriminately and permitting them to fall on the tablecloth and the carpet. Obviously she had no manners at all.

Making a determined effort to ignore this lack, the lady with the lorgnette forced herself to smile, her comprehensive condescension taking in all her objectionable companions at once.

"As we are apparently to be fellow guests at the Captain's table this next week," she said, "it will be much easier and pleasanter for us all, will it not, if we know each others' names at the outset? Mine is Mrs. Armistead Carruthers."

She paused, but nobody seemed to be at all impressed. The simpering clergyman and the handsome boy bowed, but the girl with the petunia-colored fingernails, extinguishing the scarlet-stained butt of her fourth cigarette, stared and then snickered. The charms on her bracelet tinkled more provokingly than ever as she silently began to spread a large piece of French bread liberally with butter. She was not at all interested in Mrs. Armistead Carruthers and she did not care who knew it. Instead, she was intent upon unobtrusively studying the boy who sat opposite her and who had attracted her attention also, though with a different effect from that produced on Mrs. Carruthers; she thought he was just too smooth for anything, and she wished she could make him look at her. This wish absorbed her completely. Her mother, however, responded cordially to the imposing dowager's overtures.

"Can't say I ever heard your name before," she remarked with heartiness. "But then I'm not acquainted much in the East, and you're from the East, I guess, aren't you? Boston, maybe?"

"New York," said Mrs. Armistead Carruthers stiffly. "My ancestors were among the original settlers of New Amsterdam in 1640 and——"

"Well, is that a fact! I'm Mrs. Rufus Rhodes of Rhodesville, Kansas, and this is my little daughter Trixie. My husband publishes Rufus Rhodes' farm journals—*Contented Cows, The Kansas Rural Clarion, Rhodes' Guide to Poultry Raising*—and so on. He's prospered and he's a regular party man. But we never dreamed he'd get a political appointment, never. Not even if he did give thirty thousand dollars to the campaign fund. We were just dumbfounded when the President wrote and asked if he wouldn't like to be Minister to Holland. Rufus was tickled almost to death, and he took the next boat. I couldn't go with him, because I had the house to close and all that—any woman knows how it is. And of course Trixie wanted to buy some clothes before we started. She didn't know just how the stores in Europe would suit her, so she thought she better be on the safe side and do her shopping in Kansas. But here we are on our way at last!"

Mrs. Rhodes beamed beneficently all around her. Mrs. Armistead Carruthers shuddered slightly. However, before she could frame a suitable reply, the clergyman spoke suavely.

"Let me congratulate you on your husband's well-deserved appointment, Mrs. Rhodes," he said. "I have often observed the periodicals which he publishes in the homes which I have occasion to visit throughout my diocese. I know how great a force for integrity and progress they are. Perhaps I might be permitted to introduce myself also. I am Father Hastings, Suffragan Bishop of Pennsylvania."

"Catholic, I presume?" inquired Mrs. Rhodes, her cordial voice slightly tinged with anxiety, and yet with the air of one determined to face the worst and make the best of it.

"Not *Roman* Catholic, my dear lady—Anglo Catholic. It is a matter of deep regret to me that the word 'Protestant' has ever been used in connection with the Episcopal Church in the United States. She is a true daughter of the English Church, and has never fallen into the error of using that objectionable word. I am on my way to a great conference in London, where I hope official action may be taken to clarify much regrettable confusion in regard to the word 'Catholic.' I——"

"I'm awfully sorry. Really, I am. But I'm afraid I'll have to ask to be excused."

The pallid lady wearing the magnificent necklace and rings had turned almost the color of one of her own emeralds. She rose, hastily and apologetically, and plunging down the length of the dining room with an air of desperation, vanished from view.

Her husband made no move either to assist her or to follow her. He had been dismembering a broiled live lobster as his wife prepared for flight, and now he began to break the claws with gusto.

"My wife's a very poor sailor," he said contemptuously, picking up the cracker. "Imagination mostly. That's all seasickness is, in my opinion. Though I don't know as a cloud of cigarette smoke helps out a sinking feeling any." He glared at Trixie, who did not even notice his ferocious glance, for she was covertly studying the striking boy as she tilted back her head and inhaled slowly. "Well, Bishop, I feel in a way I know you already," the speaker continued with a slight snort. "You keep a pretty good account at our bank—the Fifth National, Wide Street, Philadelphia. I'm Elbert Fuller, the First Vice President."

"Of course, Mr. Fuller, of course! I'm glad to meet you personally. How delightful that you happen to be taking a crossing just at this time! I hope you're off on a well-deserved vacation?"

"Well, a short one. I've no patience with people who go to Europe and stay for months on end. A few weeks is all *I* need to see everything there is worth taking in over there. Restaurants are what interest me chiefly. Then I hope to get in some bridge on the voyage. That's one of the reasons I've taken a slow boat. You don't play by any chance, do you, Bishop?"

"Well, just a friendly game. Never for money, of course. I don't mind taking a hand to make up a fourth if I'm needed, just to oblige, but——"

Mr. Fuller gave another slight snort. "That wasn't exactly what I had in mind. That's the kind of bridge my wife plays—ladylike and dumb. No offense, I hope, Bishop. I go in for tournaments and stiff stakes. But it doesn't matter. I'll find three other businessmen and we'll make up a table. The Lord knows I need some relaxation. It's been a bad year for bankers. Before this administration gets through with inquiries and reforms we'll be sunk."

"Oh, but the President is such a *kind* man! He has such a nice smile! I'm sure he wouldn't do anything to hurt the banks for the world!"

Mrs. Rhodes spoke with acute distress. Mr. Fuller regarded her with the venomous eye of one who does not suffer fools gladly, but before he could frame a sufficiently scathing answer, her daughter addressed her pettishly.

"Mumma, where's the Captain? Is that him standing over there by that post?"

"That is the Chief Steward," interposed Mrs. Carruthers icily, as she observed Mrs. Rhodes looking about her in bewilderment. "It will interest you, I am sure, to learn to recognize the different ship's officers by the insignia they wear on their sleeves. The Captain has four gold stripes. He sits at the head of this table where he has so graciously invited us to join him. But not, of course, until the ship is well out at sea. Up to that time he naturally remains on the bridge."

Trixie Rhodes seemed unaware that she was being snubbed. Without responding in any way to Mrs. Carruthers' informatory remarks, she lighted another cigarette.

"I wonder if there aren't any young people on this boat," she said in a voice which, though curiously flat and immature, was designed to be devastating in its effect. "I can't seem to see any. I bet it's going to be an awfully dead crossing. I shall simply go bugs if it is."

For the first time, she looked provocatively at the boy across the table as she spoke. However, it was Mrs. Rhodes, assuming that the remark had been addressed to her, who answered.

"There, Trixie, I'm sure it'll be all right as soon as you get acquainted," she said reassuringly. "I see two real nice-looking girls sitting over at that little table in the corner. Mercy! I shouldn't wonder if they were twins!"

"I don't see anything wonderful about them just because they happen to be twins," retorted Trixie still more pettishly. "I saw them before anyway. I bet they're college girls or something like that, reading books all the time and planning to go and see cathedrals and picture galleries. You know I didn't mean girls anyway."

"That little slut's mother is afraid of her," said Mrs. Carruthers to herself with scorn. Aloud she remarked freezingly, "I happen to know that young Richard Eustis, who graduated from Harvard last year, is on board with his mother. They would, of course, have been placed at the Captain's table if it had not been for their mourning—Senator Eustis died less than six months ago, and Mrs. Eustis has been simply shattered. She is going abroad on the advice of her physician. I have known Richard ever since he was a small child. He is very attractive. If you like, I will present him to you."

"Well, I don't know," remarked Trixie unenthusiastically. Her covert glance had already included Richard Eustis, and she had decided that he would do in a pinch, though he did not begin to intrigue her to the same degree as the silent young stranger at the Captain's table. "He's probably glum himself, if his mother's taking on so," she continued aloud. "I heard that Terry O'Shaughnessy, the middleweight champion, was going to take this ship, but I guess that's too good to be true. Anyhow, he trains all the time with Carlotta Carew, and I don't suppose he'd look at me. She's simply my ideal. I thought she was marvelous in 'The Double Bed.' If I could pry him loose from her, that *would* be thrilling!"

"I suppose I'm too young to fill the bill. But I'd be very glad if I could help out at all."

Mrs. Carruthers started slightly in her chair. She had had a vague impression that the boy sitting beside her had murmured a name when she had mentioned her own, but he had not spoken since, and she had almost forgotten him, so complete had been her preoccupation with the bishop, the banker, and the mother and daughter who had been catapulted into diplomatic life. Now she saw that he was leaning forward and smiling very charmingly.

"I am Chris Marlowe, from Hamstead, Vermont," he said agreeably. Although he imparted this unremarkable information to the table as a whole, it was quite evidently designed primarily for Trixie Rhodes, and the manner in which she responded to it was electrifying. This was the moment for which she had been waiting. Her look of blankness vanished, her big blue eyes brightened suddenly, and her painted lips parted over her pearly teeth in a way which was really entrancing. Her bracelets tinkled as she clasped her dimpled hands together ecstatically.

"I'm awfully pleased to meet you, Chris," she said sweetly. "I've finished lunch, haven't you? Let's go and give this tub the once-over together. Shall we?"

"If the others will be kind enough to excuse us," he said deferentially, rising and sliding his chair back into place before an attentive steward could spring forward to do this for him.

He led the way out of the dining saloon, threading between the closely ringed tables without the slightest awkwardness, and lifting his hand to greet the leader as they passed the little balcony where the orchestra was playing—a salute which was beamingly returned. As they stopped beside the lift in the corridor beyond, a diminutive blond bellboy instantly sprang to attention. Chris Marlowe turned to his companion.

"Where would you like to go? There's a veranda café, beyond the social hall, that's very pleasant. I sat out on it for an hour or so this morning while the ship was leaving the harbor. We might have coffee there first. Afterwards we could shoot in the gallery on the sports deck, or play tennis. Just as you prefer."

"I'd simply adore it!"

"Which?"

"Why, all of it, of course!"

Chris gave a brief order, and the small lift began a slow ascent. When it came to a stop, the blond boy opened the door solemnly and bowed with a jerk after the manner of a toy soldier manipulated with a string.

"*Bitte*," he said, speaking as mechanically as he moved.

"He's weird, isn't he?" Trixie remarked to Chris, as the lift started down again.

"Oh, no! He's been trained to act that way."

"Why? And why does he say bitter?"

"*Bitte* means please, in German."

"But why should he say please to us, when he runs the elevator?"

"It's the custom, in Germany, to express pleasure in service. It's symbolic of the German spirit."

"I think it's weird, myself," Trixie persisted. Then, for no apparent reason, she giggled. The sound of her laugh was not unlike the sound of her bracelets. It tinkled as she linked her arm through Chris Marlowe's and skipped down the corridor beside him. Although he appeared to walk without haste, he took long steps and she had to scramble to keep up with him. She was quite breathless by the time they reached the open-air veranda. But such breathlessness was as of the elixir of life to Trixie. She settled herself firmly in the wicker chair which Chris drew out for her, rested her elbows on the small table which separated her from him, and leaned forward.

"It was swell of you to ask me to come out here with you. I really did think I'd go bugs if I had to sit at that table any longer."

"I'm sorry. But what made you feel that way? I enjoyed watching our table companions immensely. I thought they were interesting."

"Interesting! Why, they were all older people and horrid besides. I'll bet that grim-looking woman with the Queen Mary hat is a Tartar."

"But Tartars are awfully interesting. That is, in their own way. Don't you think so?"

"No, I don't," replied Trixie, her voice slightly sulky. She opened her bag, extracted a case and a lighter, and for several moments puffed away at the cigarette Chris lighted for her. She had been struck with admiration by the ease with which he found his way about and the casual manner in which he gave orders; but the fear that he might be a "high-brow" had begun to consume her. None of the fellows she knew in Rhodesville pulled out chairs for their lady friends and she was sure that none of them spoke smilingly to stewards in German. She might have known there would be a catch somewhere, that this was too good to be true. Because Chris was the best-looking thing—she had thought his hair was brown at first; but now that the sun was shining on it, she could see that it was full of copper-colored lights. It stood out crisply from his head and she felt sure that it would have curled if it had not been cut so close. His eyes were sparkling blue; but when he was not smiling, a dreamy look kept coming into them, which Trixie thought was even more fascinating than their sparkle. His skin was the sort that usually went with red hair, very white at the neck and forehead but almost scarlet over the cheekbones; she felt as if she would like to put out her finger and touch it, as if it would be smooth as satin under her hand. She wondered how long he had been shaving. He had said himself that perhaps he was too young to fill the bill for her; there was something awfully fresh looking about his face, like a young boy's, and he was slim as a reed. Still he was reassuringly tall, and he wore his well-tailored clothes as if they had grown on him. Besides, he did act grown-up—almost too grown-up; that was what worried her, more than his actual age——

"How do you happen to speak German and know all about everything the way you do?" she finally inquired, in a tone of voice that was defiant rather than baffled.

"I lived abroad when I was a little boy. My father was a German. He was killed in the World War. I'm on my way to see his parents now. They live in East Prussia."

"Is that near Holland, where I'm going?"

"No, it's on the Baltic, beyond the Polish Corridor."

"What's that?"

"It's the narrow strip of land that was sliced off the German Empire when President Wilson visualized Poland as a 'united, independent and autonomous state' requiring a seaport. He made his vision into a point—one of fourteen—and it found its way into the Versailles Treaty."

A slight note of irony had crept into Chris Marlowe's voice. But though this was entirely lost on Trixie, she realized that if she encouraged Chris to continue in this strain, she would soon be out beyond her depth, conversationally speaking. She decided to retreat to firmer territory.

"You said your father was killed in the World War," she remarked, applying a fresh coat of white powder to her nose. "He didn't fight on the German side, did he?"

"Of course. Didn't your father fight on the American side?"

"He didn't fight at all. He got exemption because he was married and had a wife and child to support."

"I see. Well, in Germany men fought anyway. They lost, but they fought to the last ditch." Then, as if unconscious of any tension in the atmosphere, or any reason for it, Chris continued amicably, "Those shrubs banked along the side of the veranda are beautiful, aren't they? Germans are so fond of flowers that they raise them everywhere, even on board ships."

"I adore flowers myself," said Trixie, brightening a little. She had not previously noticed the shrubs banking the sides of the veranda, and she gave them only a passing glance now; but the thought of the eight corsages reposing in her stateroom, and the intelligible masculine devotion which they represented, was extremely cheering to her. For she was increasingly puzzled by Chris. He did not seem like a sissy in spite of his dreamy expression and gorgeous skin. But he certainly had a queer line. She decided to redouble her efforts at drawing him out.

"How do you happen to live in Vermont if your father was a German?"

"Oh, my mother is an American. We've lived in the United States ever since my father died."

"Is Hamstead a big place?"

"No, just a little village. My ancestors settled it. The countryside's lovely there."

"Are there many young people in Hamstead?"

"Not many. But we have good times. And we're not far from Belford. That's a fair-sized town."

"Do you go to high school in Belford?"

"I did, before I went to Harvard."

Harvard! Well, that might account for a good deal. Trixie had not heard Harvard very highly commended among her boy friends who attended the State University. Just the same, she knew that some people thought it was tops, of its kind.

"Do you do anything special at Harvard?" she inquired with genuine eagerness.

"Nothing very special. I've managed to keep on the Dean's List so far. And I wrote a little operetta last winter that——"

"You don't play football or anything like that, do you?"

"Oh, yes, I play football. But I like to play the piano better."

Chris was apparently inclined to dismiss football without further comment. But Trixie's cheeks had already flushed with excitement under their rouge at the magic word.

"Would you take me to a Harvard-Yale game sometime?"

"If you'd like to go, I'd be very pleased to see that you get there. I can't go with you if I am still on the squad. But I'll have eight tickets and any number of willing friends."

He spoke as casually as if he had acquiesced to a request for a banana split. Trixie, more and more intrigued, regarded him with mounting curiosity, her blue eyes growing rounder and rounder.

"Who's with you on this trip?" she demanded, an unwelcome suspicion that there might be competition for Chris Marlowe's attention permeating her mind.

"I'm alone. My mother couldn't leave her work to come abroad this summer."

"What kind of work does she do?"

"She's a senator."

"A *senator!* I thought senators were men!"

"Well, all the others are. Ninety-five of them."

"*Goodness!* Does your mother go to Washington, and see the President, and things like that?"

"Oh, yes! Mother has a nice house in Washington. It's the same house her father and grandfather lived in when they were in the Senate, very near the White House. She can run over to see the Conrads any time. But, of course, Hamstead is her real home."

"Do—you go to see the President too?"

"Oh, yes!" Chris said again. He rose as he spoke, indicating to the reluctant Trixie that he considered the first part of their date at an end. "The President has always been very kind to me, though he doesn't altogether approve of everything I do. I room with his son at Harvard. I've known him all my life. So, naturally— Would you care to go and have a little shooting now? I'm afraid later on the gallery may be crowded."

He drew out Trixie's wicker chair as punctiliously as he had pushed it in. Then he began to assemble the various knickknacks which had strewn themselves over the table when she opened her handbag to delve for cigarettes and make-up, and which she had shown no disposition to recapture from the places where they were scattered. These knickknacks included a bunch of small keys, a package of chewing gum, a rabbit's foot set with blue beads, some theatre ticket stubs, a rumpled handkerchief daubed with rouge, a scent bottle, and several dog-eared letters scrawled over with collegiate handwriting. He had just gathered these into a tidy pile and was offering them to Trixie one by one, so that she might stow them away again, when a ship's officer, looking very sleek and spruce, approached them politely, clicked his heels together as he bowed to Trixie, and then spoke to Chris in rapid, deferential German.

"What is it? What does he want?" Trixie inquired, as the officer, having spoken his precise little piece, bowed himself away again. Instinctively she sensed an attempted interference with the monopoly of Chris, which she was now determined, at all costs, to achieve and maintain. It was a sure thing that if the officer's remarks had included her, he would have talked English. Her petunia-colored mouth drooped fretfully at the corners, and again she linked her arm through Chris Marlowe's, less playfully and more clingingly than when they had started for the veranda.

"Nothing that will interfere with our shooting," Chris said reassuringly. Trixie was struck afresh with the nice way he had of speaking and the shining look in his eyes when he smiled.

"The Captain of this ship used to know my father," Chris explained. "So he sent me an invitation to come to tea with him at five. It is natural, under the circumstances, that he should wish to see me alone first. But the mate was careful to say that tomorrow, or possibly the day after, the Captain will begin giving a series of small parties in his quarters, and, of course, you will be invited to one of those. Besides, you will soon be seeing him regularly at lunch and dinner, all the time."

"I don't care anything at all about seeing the Captain! He's probably red nosed and pigheaded, with a wrinkle of fat at the back of his neck, like most Germans!"

"I'm sure he is nothing of the sort, any more than I am."

"But you aren't a German!"

"Oh, yes I am," said Chris Marlowe calmly. Trixie saw that he was not smiling any longer, and that a different look had come into his face —a look that frightened her a little, and at the same time made her feel like crying, though she could not in the least understand why. "Perhaps I should have told you that in the first place," he went on. "But I thought you were rather bored and lonely, and that it would be more fun for you to feel that you were going out with an American than a German. That is why I introduced myself to you as Chris Marlowe."

"Isn't that your name?"

"It isn't my whole name. I was named for both my grandfathers; my father told my mother, before he died, that he was glad I was, because both were men of great traditions, and that when I was old enough, I could choose which tradition I wanted to follow. My mother doesn't think I'm old enough yet to know my own mind. But I do know it. I am eighteen years old, and she was only eighteen when I was born. I am going to Germany just for the summer now, but I hope that someday I am going there to live. And my whole name is Hans Christian Marlowe von Hohenlohe."

CHAPTER 2

After twenty-four hours, during the course of which she had not "guessed wrong," Mrs. Rhodes' spirits had begun to rise.

Her first mistake had been in tipping the stewardess before she had been aboard ship for an hour. She had been assured on every side that all continentals had perpetually outstretched palms. To her chagrin, she had found the hand of the stewardess limp and unreceptive, and afterwards she had learned that ships formed the exception which proved the rule, that nobody tipped until the voyage was over. Her second had been in asking Mrs. Carruthers, as they left the luncheon table, whether the evening would be formal. Mrs. Carruthers had crushingly replied that life on shipboard was never formal. So the budding ambassadress had appeared at dinner in a brown print of the type usually known as "serviceable," Trixie charging along beside her in baby-blue taffeta ruffles. Mrs. Rhodes' consternation was great when she found that Mrs. Carruthers was wearing silver tissue, which enhanced the severe elegance of her carriage and manner; and that Mrs. Fuller, ashen but exquisite, was in molded white satin, her neck and arms bare except for the necklace and bracelets of superb aquamarines with which these were clasped.

"There, I *am* sorry not to appear more suitable," Mrs. Rhodes had said with genuine distress, as she sat down heavily, the brown print bunching about her. "I certainly understood you to say this wasn't going to be a formal evening."

"A formal evening? Oh! You meant to ask me whether you should dress for dinner? I am sorry that I did not understand you. In New York, we don't use the expression as you did. Of course, I took it for granted you knew that on shipboard, as elsewhere, it is customary to appear at dinner dressed for dinner."

While Mrs. Carruthers was speaking, Mrs. Rhodes glanced about her towards the surrounding tables in the hope of finding someone else who had made a mistake. But even Mrs. Eustis' sheer somber draperies were parted in a deep V at her throat, and her long flowing sleeves fell away from her slender arms. Even the twins' homemade pink chiffon dresses had round necks.

Mrs. Rhodes was so obviously chagrined that even Mrs. Carruthers feared she might have gone a little too far in her attempt to show this uncultured person just how uncultured she was. But she herself had a grievance: She had sent some of her own flowers to the dining saloon—some fragile white lilacs and fragrant Ascension lilies—and instead of placing them in a graceful vase on the Captain's table, the steward had thrust them into a pitcher on the sideboard, feeling that they were too funereal of aspect to adorn a festive board. In their place rose a flamboyant gilt basket crammed with crimson roses, which some crude youth had undoubtedly sent to Trixie Rhodes—indeed, the oversized card with which they had been dispatched was still fastened to them. "Trixie, please affix me," was scrawled across it in a straggling handwriting. "And don't you fall, for Dutch at all. Stan."

Mrs. Carruthers felt that persons who permitted such vulgarities should be made to feel their inferiority, and she had certainly succeeded in creating this feeling.

But there was nothing the matter with her dress tonight, Mrs. Rhodes felt sure of that—a nice green lace; and Trixie's red velvet had come from the most expensive shop in Topeka. The shade was just like the tint in her cheeks, and Mrs. Rhodes had read in a fashion magazine once that you should "match the color of your clothes to your make-up." Trixie had certainly done that, nails, slippers and all; and Mrs. Rhodes was puffed with pride as she addressed the bishop.

"Well, Bishop, we've missed you, and that's a fact. It's just a shame that you should've been seasick, such lovely weather, too."

She was dismayed to find that he seemed to take her cordial greeting amiss. "But my dear Mrs. Rhodes! I assure you that I have not been seasick, not for a single minute. I had a slight cold when I came aboard, and I thought it prudent to take precautions before this became worse. Besides, I have had a great deal of work to do—in preparation for the Anglo-Catholic Conference, you know. I have been toiling away in my cabin, deprived of the pleasant company that I could have enjoyed if duty had not kept me there. But the work of the Lord, you know—a man may not serve two masters!"

The bishop paused rather abruptly. He was conscious that Trixie Rhodes was looking at him, her large blue eyes half veiled by the long black lashes that drooped over them, her small crimson mouth relaxed, a cigarette hanging from the side of it. But there was something contemptuous in her expression. He suddenly remembered that he had seen the Rhodes' name neatly placarded on the door of the suite beside his stateroom, and was uncomfortably fearful that this insolent girl might have heard certain repulsive sounds, not usually associated with slight colds or the service of the Lord, issuing from it. He had been vomiting violently all the day before; and moreover, several times, in his anguish, he had spoken to his steward in a manner unbefitting his cloth. He decided that possibly it might be best to divert the attention of the table to someone else.

"I'm sorry to see that Mrs. Fuller is missing from our congenial little circle," he said brightly, turning to the banker. "Perhaps she really is sick?"

"Sick as a dog," her husband answered impatiently. "Lord! Sometimes I think if she just looked at a picture of a clipper ship hanging on the wall she'd retch. I beg pardon! But it does get on my nerves. They're not in very good shape just now anyway."

"It must be tedious for her, lying in her cabin all day," Mrs. Rhodes said kindly. "If you think she'd like company, don't hesitate to tell me. I could go in and see her any time."

"You don't need to bother," Mr. Fuller said tersely. "She hasn't spirit enough to be bored. When she feels like doing anything at all, she amuses herself with her jewelry. She's got a lot of it, and she likes to fool with it, taking it out of the box, you know, and spreading it over the sheets. It's sort of childish of her, but the jewelry's all well insured, so there's no danger in case of loss, and I'm glad she appreciates it. There aren't many men who've made the effort I have to give their wives handsome jewelry. Did you happen to notice her pearls?" he inquired abruptly, addressing himself to Mrs. Carruthers.

"Yes, Mr. Fuller, I noticed them."

"Used to belong to a member of the Russian Imperial family," said Mr. Fuller with satisfaction. "She's got a tiara and a pair of earrings too—diamonds and rubies—that came from the same collection. How about that, Baron? Got anything to beat it in your family?"

The exciting facts regarding the identity of "Chris Marlowe" had spread like wildfire about the ship. Overnight, he had become the chief topic of conversation on deck, in the bar, and at every table in the dining room. Hans Christian himself appeared to be entirely oblivious of the furore which he had aroused. Now, at Mr. Fuller's brusque question, he drained the glass of Rüdesheimer that he was drinking, and set it down carefully before he answered.

"My mother has never cared much about jewelry," he said. "For years she's never worn any at all, except her engagement ring and a beautiful old Spanish cross. Probably my grandmother von Hohenlohe, whom I'm going to visit, has more. I was with her a good deal when I was a little boy, and I seem to remember that she looked rather glittering when she went to a Court ball."

"Of course, the Archduchess Victoria Luise was known as one of the most regal women of her time, throughout Europe," remarked Mrs. Carruthers, in an explanatory voice.

"Is your grandmother a Russian?" avidly inquired Mr. Fuller, who had missed some of the details concerning Hans Christian's family, turning to the boy again.

"No. She's an Austrian by birth, and her first husband was an Austrian too. But she's lived in Germany ever since she married my grandfather."

"Well now, I have understood the Hapsburgs had about as much jewelry before the war as the Romanoffs, and that they are parting with it about as fast now."

"As far as I know, my grandmother's been able to hang on to hers," Hans Christian remarked, still quietly.

"But there's no telling when this inflation is going to stop, is there? I understand people are getting harder and harder pressed in Germany all the time. If anything should arise——"

"If I find it would be worth your while to come to Schönplatz, Mr. Fuller, I will let you know. But since your time is so short, I shouldn't advise you to change any of your present plans on the chance of it." Hans Christian's glass had been refilled by an assiduous steward, and raising it, the boy took another slow sip of Rüdesheimer. Then he turned to Mrs. Carruthers. "Are you planning a longer visit abroad than Mr. and Mrs. Fuller?" he inquired conversationally.

"I shall be in Europe for several months at least," said Mrs. Carruthers, with an expression which Mr. Fuller realized was aimed at him. "But I shall not rush madly about from one country to another. I am disembarking at Cherbourg to visit some cousins who have a chateau in Normandy, which fortunately has not been overrun by tourists like the Loire Valley. Later I think I may motor with my friend, the Duchess of Ducheyne, to the Dalmatian Coast. I shall probably sail for home from Trieste. The Italian boats are so much the best in every respect."

"Mrs. Carruthers—it rejoices me to find that you with us cross again, that you do not us altogether desert for the Italians. *Aber, gnädige Frau,* permit that I have my so small joke! Mrs. Rhodes—to you my congratulations on your husband's appointment, and to us, congratulations that you so honor a German ship by your presence—*gnädiges Fräulein,* there is nothing that brings such fine luck to the table of a Captain as the presence of one charming young lady—unless, Father Hastings, it might be the benediction of an eminent divine. Mr. Fuller, it makes me grief that your lady should not well be. I take the liberty to her some Henckel Trocken to send with my compliments—*Also,* Hansel, *mein lieber Junge, wie geht's?*"

A tall man, solidly but not heavily built, with clear color, dark eyes, and black hair gone gray at the temples, kissed Mrs. Carruthers' hand,

and appeared to sense Mrs. Rhodes' distress lest he might kiss hers also. Placing an arm affectionately around Hans Christian's shoulder, he bowed to her instead, and then to each of the other persons whom he addressed in turn. Afterwards he seated himself, with unhurried dignity, at the head of the table. In spite of the cordiality of his manner, there was a hint of reserve in it; he was not bluff. And though his being seemed to be permeated with salt air, it had been tempered by careful grooming. The blue of his uniform was lustrous; the gold stripes and gold stars on his sleeves, the double row of gold buttons on his jacket, the medals on his chest, were all glistening; his linen was so white that it seemed to sparkle. On one hand he wore a massive carved ring with a huge dark stone sunk deeply into its setting. The stone glittered as he picked up the "Card of Suggestions" attached to the menu.

"Crême Nelusco," he read. "I shall an understanding with the chef need to have not to use these French names. They confuse me. What do you suppose a Crême Nelusco might be, *gnädiges Fräulein?*"

"It's a thick carroty soup," Trixie answered, emerging, as if by magic, from the silence which had enveloped her ever since the meal began. "It's real pretty and it's real good."

"Since you commend it so highly I shall some have to try. *Also*, Crême Nelusco, steward. If it is so excellent, like you say, we must some send to Mrs. Fuller. I hope you impress on her, Mr. Fuller, that for seasickness it is always necessary that one should eat."

"Well, I've tried," said Mr. Fuller, briefly, with the air of implying that it was a hopeless task to endeavor to impress much of anything on his wife. "But I finally gave it up. She won't do anything but lie with her eyes shut and moan. She won't even fool with her rings. It gets on my nerves. So I've spent most of my time in the smoking room. Last night I ran into a man I know there—Ferris of the Chicago Loan and Trust—and I knew he played a good hand of bridge. So I asked him how about it, and he said 'Fine!' if we could get up a foursome. We gave the place the once-over, and saw a man and his wife who were sitting sort of vacant eyed, as if they hadn't much to do with themselves. They said they'd be pleased to have a game. We played until about three o'clock this morning and then ended up with a snifter. The Hunts—that's the name of this pair, Mr. and Mrs. Harris Hunt from Macon, Georgia—know their cards and they put up a stiff fight, but they weren't any match for Ferris and myself in the end. We cleaned them out of nearly a hundred dollars. But the Hunts took it in good part."

"It pleases me that for you everything has so well worked out," said the Captain cordially. Then he turned from Mr. Fuller to Trixie, who was snapping her enameled lighter in a vain attempt to make it work.

"Please to mine accept, *gnädiges Fräulein,*" he said courteously. "The steward will see to it that yours shall be fixed. That is better, is it not so? This is your first trip abroad, *ja?* I hope you enjoy yourself."

"Yes, it's my first trip," Trixie replied, with another dimpling smile. "I was sort of sorry to leave Rhodesville—there's going to be quite a lot going on there this winter. And the ship seemed dead as a doornail to me at first. Nothing much going on. I guess most of the young people were seasick. Besides, I can't see much sense in shuffleboard and deck tennis, and those were all I could find doing at first, except that I passed Carlotta Carew and Terry O'Shaughnessy walking up and down the deck together. The way they were looking into each other's eyes was just divine! I did get a thrill out of that. But they went off somewheres and I didn't see them again, so it didn't last long. I've danced quite a lot of evenings, though. I simply adore to dance. I'd rather do it than anything else in the world. And I like those little wooden horses you have races with. The deck steward said I can shake the dice tomorrow afternoon. I won three times this afternoon. Chris helped me make my bets. He's been simply sweet to me. I guess I'd have passed right out if it hadn't been for him."

She shifted her smile to the opposite side of the table. Hans Christian returned it pleasantly, lifting his glass.

"Prosit!" he said gravely. Then, looking from the girl to the Captain, he added, "The best thing I've done has been to present 'Card' Eustis to Trixie, *Herr Kapitän.* He knows more about amusing girls than I do."

"So, the Senator's son," said the Captain, glancing quickly in the direction of the Eustis' table. "You knew him before, then, did you, Hansel?"

"Yes, *Herr Kapitän.* He was a senior at Harvard when I went there. But we both play football and belong to the same Club."

"That is then most fortunate for the present pleasure of all— And those two young ladies in the corner— Have you met them, *gnädiges Fräulein?*"

"They were in swimming this afternoon," Trixie answered rather reluctantly. "They seem to be just crazy about sports—sports and Shakespeare. They're college girls. They talk about all sorts of things I never heard of in my life. Mostly just to each other though. I guess nobody else wants to listen. Anyway, they don't seem to know many people. I guess no one ever showed them a really tall time."

"Ach so!" exclaimed the Captain again. "We shall have that to remedy. Could you not show one of those poor underprivileged young ladies a tall time, Hansel?"

Hans Christian smiled.

"I've been trying already," he answered. "I was dancing with one of them last evening and making some progress with light conversation when Card cut in. So I went off to smoke a cigarette and collect my thoughts for further persiflage. When I went back to the Social Hall I cut in on Card. Then I began my light conversation where I had left off. The young lady looked at me coldly and asked if I wasn't rather fresh—starting out with a line like that. And I burst into a cold perspiration! I had made a mistake! I was dancing with the other twin, whom I hadn't met at all!"

The Captain laughed outright, Mrs. Rhodes and Mr. Fuller echoed him heartily. Trixie, her face gone blank again, took a lipstick and a powder puff out of her small beaded handbag and began to apply these vehemently to her already dazzling complexion. It was evident that she had not welcomed the intrusion of the twins upon the scene, either conversationally or otherwise. The bishop looked grave. Mrs. Carruthers, her expression severe, addressed the company at large.

"I cannot sufficiently deplore this custom of cutting in," she said. "When I was young there was still such a thing as good society left in America. Father Hastings can doubtless remember this also."

"Yes indeed, my dear lady, yes indeed! Those were the halcyon days, though it has now become customary to deride them. At present our unfortunate nation seems to have fallen into an abyss of vulgarity as well as an abyss of crime."

"Goodness!" exclaimed Mrs. Rhodes nervously. "I hadn't the least idea it was as bad as all that! Perhaps it's different in the East. In Rhodesville there's as nice a crowd of young people as you'd ever wish to see. Nice, clean, upstanding young men. Nice, quiet, modest girls. All Trixie's friends——"

"Oh, Mumma, don't be such a fool!"

Trixie had pushed back her plate and now sat furiously smoking one cigarette after another, flicking the ashes to the floor with her crimson fingernails as she did so.

There was a moment of electrified silence. Mrs. Carruthers and Father Hastings exchanged glances. Mrs. Rhodes reddened uncomfortably, her kind ingenuous face suddenly looking like a crushed and wilted peony. The Captain rose.

"I think we have all our dinner finished," he said evenly. "It is pleasant coffee to take in the smoking room, is it not? And if to the rest of you it is agreeable I shall also these so bewildering twins ask if they will not give us the honor of their society. It seems to me a shame that they should be so much alone, as *Fräulein* Trixie says, and that Hansel should not the opportunity have of learning to tell them apart."

He certainly must have known them apart before the end of the evening, Trixie decided. He danced first with one and then with the other, not unconsciously, as he had done before, but purposely; and there was every indication that he was not only giving them a "tall time," but having one himself, primarily with the twins. He did ask Trixie for one waltz, but she could not waltz nearly as well as she could fox trot, and she found herself tangled up in her attempt to follow his intricate lead. Under these circumstances, the performance became one of watchful technique on his part and enraged effort on hers; it was impersonal and unstimulating. Trixie was actually relieved when the encore was over, and she was quickly claimed again by Richard Eustis.

"Chris really does act like a German when he dances," Card observed, swinging her easily into a one-step. The remark was meant to placate Trixie, but as she made no immediate response to this overture, either conversationally or physically, he went rambling on along the same line, hoping for better results. "Usually you don't notice it—when he's around with other fellows, I mean. But he's behaved badly to his mother. So I hear, anyway. And that's another typically Teutonic trait."

"What do you mean, behaved badly?"

"Oh, she didn't want him to strike off like this, all by himself. She wanted him to stay with her. Just the way my mother likes to have me hang around."

Trixie did not fail to notice the comparison between Chris as an erring son and Card as a dutiful one, but somehow the picture did not seem convincing.

"Germans are great on keeping women in their place, you know," Card went on, persistently. "And they think the place is beside a kitchen stove or hanging over a cradle. I believe even the Kaiser said something to that effect. Chris didn't raise a rumpus when his mother went into politics. In fact he acted the part she wanted him to play damned well. But he hated it— Gosh, how he hated it! And I suppose eventually she found this out and then they began to get on each other's nerves."

"Maybe his feelings were hurt first. Maybe she struck off and left *him* alone when this political bee stung her. Maybe he was lonely when he was just a kid. Maybe they sort of grew away from each other then, and he thought she wouldn't care if he came away and left her. You don't actually know that he's on bad terms with her, do you?"

"No, I can't swear to it. But everybody thinks so. You see, the general impression was, that when Rudolf von Hohenlohe told his wife he didn't care what tradition their son followed, he was making it easy for her to bring him up in the *American* tradition. That's what she thought herself. She never dreamed of anything else. And then Chris suddenly sprung this *Junker* idea on her. He stirred up an awful lot of talk in Washington and Cambridge when he came away. Almost as much as he has on this boat."

"Well, we might talk about someone else for a change."

Card was quite willing. Indeed, what he really wanted was to talk about Trixie and himself. It was only because he did not dare rush his fences, as his fox-hunting Southern relatives called it, that he had diverged at all from this topic. For the rest of the evening he stuck to it assiduously. The results were less satisfactory than he had hoped, however. Trixie danced with him readily and repeatedly enough. But eventually an awful truth dawned on him. She was not listening to his line. She was mastering the mysteries of the waltz.

CHAPTER 3

Trixie Rhodes sat at her dressing table scrutinizing her face with a magnifying glass, and taking appropriate steps to transform it. She was a great believer in preparedness. Although she had chosen a sheltered spot for her date with Card Eustis—the most sheltered, indeed, which she had discovered on the ship—she had agreed to meet him first in the brilliantly lighted bar, where a large majority of the passengers habitually forgathered, and where Carlotta Carew and Terry O'Shaughnessy regularly got drunk in each other's stimulating company. Half the thrill of having a date with a fellow like Card Eustis lay in bearing him off to cover with the consciousness that you were followed by envious eyes, and she had reason to believe that even Carlotta, when sufficiently sober, coveted Card. Besides, you never knew: of course everyone else had been in bed when she and Card had finally parted the night before—or rather, this same morning around three. But possibly tonight someone would still be up at that hour. It was even conceivable that Chris Marlowe might be mooning around on deck all alone, looking at stars or sea foam or something of the sort. He was quite capable of such eccentricities.

At the irritating thought, Trixie attacked her paint pots with a certain savageness. Her original estimate that there was a dearth of young people on the ship had quickly been proven fallacious. After a day or two they seemed to spring up from every side, and many of the male contingent promptly "fell" for Trixie. The twins, Nancy and Nora Lindsay, also annexed admirers without effort, and the resemblance which had led Chris astray on the first evening out resulted in countless other baffling episodes. The character of the "crowd" thus created, at no time standoffish, quickly grew uproarious. The movies in the Social Hall were subject to disrespectful interruptions in the form of snickering and catcalls. A peaceful *Bier Abend* in the smoking room developed the characteristics of a riot, as paper hats were hurled through the air and the sound of wooden whistles mounted to pandemonium. When the featured entertainment of the evening was over, the unruly youngsters devised other amusements for themselves; some of these took a form which caused both Father Hastings and Mrs. Carruthers to complain to the Captain, in addition to airing their views on the subject to other censorious travelers who lent a willing ear to tales of depravity as they comfortably consumed their morning bouillon.

At first the Captain listened to the complaints of his star passengers courteously but noncommittally, and commented casually upon them to Hans Christian, the next time the boy came to his quarters, in a manner which indicated that he took little stock in such criticism. Within three days, however, the ship's discipline was so openly flouted that he called several of the ringleaders together and spoke to them with a certain show of severity.

"Well it is that young company should on a ship find itself *lustig*," he remarked in an admonishing tone, "but to be *lustig* is it then needful that the boat deck should still be cluttered with couples after all lights are out and it is the moment that the proper work of cleaning should begin? *Nein, nein,* that does not do itself, *meine jungen Freunde!* The night watchman, making his rounds, must on no such scenes stumble that he will blush when he his report to me makes. He must on nothing at all stumble, a leg perhaps to break. And the sailors must room and time to holystone have. This is no French *paquebot* lightly to be brushed off once or twice a year, and encouraging indiscretions. Such are not the standards of the German Merchant Marine, and our guests must by our standards abide." He came to an impressive pause, and added still more somberly, "If again anyone on deck after hours is found, he shall straight to our lock-up be marched. It is a nice clean place, but bare. And all visitors are *verboten. So!* We will no more about the matter say."

The culprits disbanded, overlooking the slight twinkle in the Captain's eye as he dismissed them, and for the most part in a somewhat shamefaced manner. But it took far more than a threat or a lecture to embarrass Trixie.

"Phooey!" she had said, linking her arm through Card's as they went down the companionway together. "Just feature getting off that line about the blushing watchman! I don't believe even Terry O'Shaughnessy and Carlotta Carew could get a rise out of him, and I've caught them in some pretty close clinches. If the watchman never sees anything worse after dark than the little light necking our crowd has been doing, I'll say he's missing a good deal. Look at the color of his face anyway—raw beefsteak wouldn't match it. How are you going to tell whether a man with a mug like that is blushing or having a fainting spell? And I wish he would break his leg."

Card made no immediate answer to her persiflage. They were walking aft, and his eyes were thoughtfully fixed on two hooded ventilators which towered over the swimming pool like giant caterpillars.

"How far would you say it was, at a guess, from the top railing around the pool to the inside of one of those hoods?" he inquired.

Trixie followed the direction of his glance without excitement. "Oh, I don't know," she said idly. "Four or five feet maybe. Why?"

"There's a piece of wire netting stretched across the funnel inside the hood. I happened to see it this afternoon when I climbed up to take a high dive. We could lay a rug across that netting and sit on it. I could climb up first and pull you up after me. I guess the night watchman wouldn't look for us there, or break a leg stumbling over us."

"Card, I do think you are the cutest thing! We could try it out to-night, couldn't we?"

All this had happened early in the week, and since then they had been trying out the convenient ventilator with great success. The only trouble was, that as she sat secluded under its shelter, cuddled up to Card, Trixie kept thinking all the time how much more fun it would have been to sit there cuddled up to Chris.

She had tried pretending that she was, but it didn't do any good. Card had a grand line, one you could hang clothes on; he was simply swell. But there was no use talking, he didn't have the same class that Chris did. There was more of a thrill just looking at Chris than in necking with Card. She kept saying to herself that she was a sissy and a softy, that a date was a date, that one Senator's son was as much of a catch as another's. And still it was Chris that she wanted. Still it was Chris that she was determined to get——

She must have filed her nails down too far. The sharply pointed white pencil had gone straight to the quick that time. Furiously she flung it across the toilet table, pulled her dress down once more over the hips, and rose to regard herself in the mirror.

She had begun to think that ruffles were a mistake, now that she had attentively looked over a couple of New York girls whose abode conversation had revealed as Park Avenue, and whose evening wraps, draped negligently over chair backs, had revealed Hattie Carnegie's labels. So she had chosen something different to wear this time—something very slinky and sophisticated in green satin, with accessories of costume jewelry which, as far as she could see, were every bit as good looking as all that junk of Mrs. Fuller's that everyone was making such a fuss about. The green satin was a little too tight; it pulled in places. And it was pretty low. Not just behind, of course it had no back at all, and that didn't count. But perhaps in front— She had an idea that Chris——

However, it was too late now to change. She had sat forever at the dinner table while Mr. Fuller talked about debts and reparations and how much money he had lost at bridge, and Mrs. Carruthers had kept saying that she knew General Dawes personally and was sure he would prove the salvation of Germany, and Father Hastings had murmured that they should not forget true salvation came from only One Source, and that they must pray that the Prince of Peace would soon rule all the world. Then the stupid steward, who looked so skillful when he was serving the Captain or Chris, had spilled macaroon ice cream on her gold lamé and that had been the last straw. Of course, he had pretended to be terribly upset about it, and she *had* reached for a cigarette just as he started to serve her. But this did not alter the fact that the lamé was a mess and that she could not possibly wear it on her date with Card. The green satin was the next best thing, and she had an idea Card would like it. She had better not keep forgetting that after all he was the person to be pleased, at the moment, anyway.

Card was waiting for her in the bar. He was sitting at a little table with Chris and one of the twins when she went in. They had big mugs of beer in front of them and a huge platter of sandwiches between them, and apparently they were having a grand time, for they were laughing and talking like anything. There was a place saved at the table for Trixie, and for an instant she had a feeling that it would be sort of cozy to stay right there in the bar and not climb up into the ventilator at all. Then Chris made a remark that queered everything.

"The Captain seems to have cheered up since you and Card stopped giving him so much trouble, Trixie. He's having a party himself tonight—aft, in that open space on B deck. He's planning music and a midnight supper and all that. He said the air was so soft and the moonlight so pleasant, he thought the ladies would enjoy it."

"What ladies?" inquired Trixie, instantly alert.

"Oh, your mother and Card's and Mrs. Schuyler and Mrs. Fuller. And a few others, I believe. Of course, he's asked a corresponding number of men."

"He hasn't asked you and Nora, has he?" Trixie inquired suspiciously.

"I'm Nancy. Nora is over there in the corner," interposed the twin who was seated beside Chris, nodding—darned smugly Trixie thought—in the direction of a table where a duplicate girl was playing bridge with three personable young men.

"He said if we had no other plans," Chris remarked, with apparent unconcern. "It was all arranged very quickly. Your mother tried to find you and tell you about it before she went into the Social Hall to see the movie. But she couldn't. So she told the Captain that she thought you and Card *did* have other plans."

"Well, we have. Haven't we, Card?" retorted Trixie, rising immediately. "Who cares about the Captain's stuffy old party anyway?"

"If you don't care, I don't see why you get all hot and bothered about it," remarked Nancy calmly, helping herself to another sandwich.

Trixie shot a glance of venom in Nancy's direction. As usual, the twins' appearance was unarresting. This evening they were wearing embroidered muslin dresses, of the type which Trixie recognized as coming in "patterns," boxed and partially made up. Neither the initial nor the final stages of this development revealed much knowledge of the art of dressmaking, and the white design, against a pale blue background, had about as much character as cambric tea. The gold beads around Nancy's neck and the turquoise bracelet encircling her right wrist were equally schoolgirlish. But it was also undeniable that she never seemed to be at a loss for words, and that her hair, which she had not had the sense to cut off, was a gorgeous color.

"I'm not hot and bothered. I'm in a hurry to get out of this stuffy room, that's all," snapped Trixie.

"Well, I hope you'll find it nice and cool under the hood in the ventilator," observed Nancy, beginning to blow bubbles from the froth on her beer.

Trixie stalked out of the bar without deigning to answer, Card close at her heels. She was very angry. It was one thing to show off her conquest. It was quite another to leave a victorious and mocking rival in the field. Previously she had had no idea that anyone had found out about her hideaway, and she was beyond measure upset that this knowledge should have come to the ears of Chris. Nothing that Card could say or do had the effect of appeasing her. Instead, she drew as far away from him as their limited quarters would permit, sitting stiff and sulky in her own corner.

"What's the grand idea? You didn't come up here to ponder, did you?"

"I don't know what I came up here for."

"Well, I do. What's eating you anyway, Trixie? You came up here because you've got a crush on me."

"Don't flatter yourself."

"Well, I've got a crush on you anyway. Gosh, but you looked swell when you came into the bar tonight! That's a grand dress you've got on."

As if to further indicate his appreciation of it, Card's hand slid upward an inch or two from her waistline and came to rest, caressingly, on Trixie's bare back. As she made no resistance to this overture, or, indeed, showed the slightest sign of response to it, he concluded that he might venture on bolder tactics. Abruptly, he drew her closer to him and tried to bury his face in the hollow between her breasts.

The effect of this action was immediate. Hampered as she was by lack of space, Trixie managed to get hold of his head and tug vigorously at his hair. Simultaneously she began to voice her opinion of him in no uncertain terms, and this opinion was far from flattering.

"Let go of me, you filthy cad! Take your dirty hands off me this instant! If you don't sit up and behave yourself, I'll start to yell!"

"For Chris to come and rescue you? When he didn't ask you to step out with him himself?" mumbled Card, without raising his head. "I don't think anyone but him and Nancy knows where we are so far. Do you want to tell the whole ship?"

"I don't care who knows where I am as long as I get out. I'm going to jump."

"Into the swimming pool? With a big splash? And come out looking like a drowned rat?"

Trixie wasted no further words. She was past caring where she came out or what she looked like, as long as she could make good her escape. Shame, such as she had never known before, was surging through her. Card's strong fingers digging into her bare back, his hot face pressed against her bare breast, had outraged all the latent modesty of which she had hitherto been unaware, and kindled a flame of feeling hitherto unaroused. She began to writhe in his embrace, certain that eventually she could get clear of the netting; even if she could not wrench herself free, she would drag him with her when she jumped, and once they were in the air or the water he would instinctively release her. But she had hardly begun to put this plan into precipitate action when she was seized with another sensation of horror.

The ventilator was moving. Something had happened to shake its stability, and it was turning, slowly but relentlessly. As it revolved, the swimming pool, which had been so reassuringly close below it, disappeared entirely. For a terrific moment, the ventilator's panic-stricken occupants found themselves swinging out over the ocean. Another revolution brought it to rest again. But not in the position from which it had originally started. On the contrary, its hooded form now faced the stern of the ship, jutting out beyond the short upper deck where the swimming pool was located.

"Christ!" ejaculated Card Eustis fervently. He was still gripping Trixie tightly by the waist. But he had raised his head, unconsciously, when the uncanny movement of the ventilator had indicated that something abnormal was happening; and now, as he gazed down towards the distant deck, he gave a short nervous laugh.

"We'd better kiss and make up, Trixie," he said, his voice shaking in spite of its defiance. "If we try to jump at this stage—or if you try to jump and drag me with you—we'll go from the deep sea to the devil, instead of the other way around, as it usually is. And I don't mean maybe, either. Just take a good long look and see what's underneath us."

Still seething, and far more shaken than he was, Trixie followed his glance with forced fascination. At first she could see almost nothing. The light was lovely, as Chris had said. But it was the light which came from a young moon, already rocking away toward the horizon; it was not brilliant. It was some moments before she was able to hear the strains of soft music, to discern, on the distant lower deck over which they were suspended, a group of persons clustered around a table which had been convivially spread in the open.

"I don't know what you mean, but if you think I'm going to make up, not to mention kissing, you've got another guess coming. Well, what *is* it, Card? I can't tell from here. It might be almost anything. Oh, my God—*the Captain's party!*"

There was no blinking the actualities of the situation. She would either have to stay where she was, under conditions which now seemed to her abhorrent, or take a leap in the dark, in a very real sense of the word. Either alternative was intolerable. But while Trixie was trying to figure some way to fight her way clear, the ventilator began to revolve again.

For one wild moment, the thought of drowning crossed her distracted mind without aversion. If she disappeared into the engulfing sea, everyone would be sorry, including Chris. Her mother would cry quarts; the Captain would read the burial service in a solemn voice; perhaps white flowers would be scattered on the waves. The picture was hardly complete, however, when she saw that it was no longer over the ocean that she was swinging; she was safely back above the swimming pool again. But beside it two sailors with flashlights in their hands were standing, and between them a solidly built officer, whom she recognized with a sinking heart as the Chief Engineer.

"*Ach, du lieber Gott!*" he ejaculated, reaching brusquely up into the recesses of the ventilator. His stocky arms closed quickly around Trixie, the braided bands on his sleeves scratching her bare back. Having pulled her out, he set her on her feet and stood for an instant staring at her, indignant exclamations rising in a growl to his lips as he did so. Before he could make another lunge into the depths, Card had swung himself down to the edge of the swimming pool, dragging the shawl after him. But not in time to effect an escape. The brawny arm shot out a second time, gripping Card by the shoulder.

"*Was macht das denn?*" demanded the Chief Engineer, his voice shaking with rage. "For two nights now, the air in the engine room, she does not move at all. And this night she is hot, so hot the men cannot breathe. So my assistant, he come to trouble me while I take a little ease at the *Gesellschaft* which the *Kapitän* he assemble. And I say, 'Turn you then the ventilator around. It is possible that he do not the wind catch.' Then the ventilator they turn him around, and still in the boiler room it is hotter than hell. And the men howl, and my second, he come to me again, when I am on deck so pleasantly assembled with distinguished ladies, and he tell me, if the wind he does not blow now all shall suffocate, so shall then I not myself come, and find out why the wind she does not blow. And I come and find my netting covered with a thick rug and upon it two numskulls sitting, so that honest workers cannot get their breath. *Ach, du lieber Gott!*"

"Oh, Mr. Loeffler, we're terribly sorry! We never thought about the men in the boiler room and that they needed air. Honestly we didn't. Don't tell the Captain! Don't make us go down there!"

"Not to tell the Captain! Not to make you go down there! Ach, du lieber Gott!"

"Miss Rhodes is right, sir. It was very careless of us, but we didn't mean to do any harm, and if you can see your way clear——"

The Chief Engineer was not even listening. Relentlessly he dragged his two victims along, still muttering furiously under his breath, still followed by the sailors with flashlights, who bore up like a bodyguard in the rear. He did not so much as pause until he had reached the midst of the startled *Gesellschaft*. Then still clutching both Trixie and Card so tightly as to preclude any possibility of evasion on their part, he poured out the tale of his grievances to the assembled company.

It was terrible, too terrible for any mortal words. The Captain gave Trixie one withering glance, which left her feeling as if her last shred of clothing had been stripped off. Then he ignored her completely, and began to talk to Card in a tone of controlled courtesy which revealed far more formidable anger than the fulminations of the Chief Engineer.

"If you did not others consider at all, what then do you suppose would have happened to you and *Fräulein* Rhodes if that so light netting had happened to break?"

"Well, sir, I suppose it would have been quite a long fall to the engine room. But I didn't think of that at the time I planned to sit on the netting."

What a nitwit Card was, what an absolute idiot, not to know you couldn't be fresh and get away with it, no matter whose son you were, no matter to whom you were talking, at a time like this, Trixie thought desperately. There was Mrs. Carruthers looking at her as if she was the scum of the earth, and Mrs. Eustis, too, for that matter, though it was Mrs. Eustis' son who had got her into this mess, and if he were such a paragon as his mother seemed to think, he would have got her out of it, too. Her own mother was sobbing into her handkerchief, and between gulps wiping her nose, which was getting redder and shinier every moment. And that Fuller woman sat swinging a pendant as big as a hen's egg and looking at her overbearing husband to give her the signal whether to laugh or frown. Women were cats, all of them, unless they were fools, and there was no way of getting even with them, ever, except by walking off with the men they wanted, and these women were all so old that probably——

"Would you care to dance for a little? If the *Herr Kapitän* would excuse us——"

It simply couldn't be true, and still it was. Chris was standing beside her, speaking to her in his nice quiet way as if nothing at all had happened, as if nothing were likely to happen. She gazed up at him with agonized eyes, unable, for the moment, to speak.

"Nancy has a headache. She went to bed early," Chris continued conversationally. "That leaves me rather at loose ends for the rest of the evening. Unless, of course, you'll come to my rescue."

The *Gesellschaft* seemed to have melted away. Trixie did not know how or when, but then that did not matter. All that mattered was that she was alone in the stern with Chris, that they were leaning over the rail looking at the foam, in the way that had seemed to her so silly a day or two before, when she had seen other couples doing it, and that now seemed so natural and lovely. And she was saying whatever came into her head and Chris understood everything that she tried to say.

"I'll never get over this as long as I live. I'd like to kill Card Eustis."

"Oh yes you will. Oh no you wouldn't. What is there to get over anyway? I think it's all a huge joke, and so does the Captain, really. He'll be telling his guests about it—without mentioning any names, of course—for years to come, amid chortles of glee, in which he will lead. To my mind you're a benefactor, considering all the dull moments there are at a Captain's table, and all the long pauses that need filling in. And Card is an awfully good sort, when you get right down to it. You'll find that out someday too. His technique has flaws in it, that's all."

"Flaws! It's got gaps in it as big as a crater! And did you see the awful look that snooty Mrs. Carruthers gave me? She'll waylay me the first chance she gets and tell me exactly what she thinks of me."

"What do you care if she does? Or what she thinks? Her thoughts belong to about the same period as her hairdressing."

"Oh, Chris, you're just trying to cheer me up! You don't mean a word you say!"

"Of course I do. And I meant what I said when I asked you to dance. Come along."

"I can't go into the Social Hall looking like this. I'm a mess."

"Well, I can wait for you here, if you want to powder up. It wouldn't take long, would it?"

"I don't want just to put on fresh make-up. I feel dirty. I want to take a bath and change everything I have on."

"Well, that wouldn't take long either, would it? I shouldn't suppose so, to look at you."

He was laughing at her, but he was laughing so lightly and whimsically that it did not hurt at all. It almost made her want to laugh too, though a few moments earlier she had decided that she would never be able to laugh again as long as she lived.

"No, it wouldn't take long. Will you really wait for me?"

"Cross my heart and hope to die." Apparently intent upon the foam again, he lighted a cigarette and leaned out over the ocean, his attitude seeming to imply that his patience was as boundless as the sea.

"All right. I'll be as quick as I can."

She sped down the corridor towards her cabin, mentally reviewing her resources as she ran. Her wardrobe had seemed voluminous in Topeka. But now there was nothing just right, nothing quite good enough for this date with Chris. She was still undecided, still dissatisfied, as she stripped off the green satin and dropped it loathingly into the scrap basket. But when she emerged, tingling, from the shower, she had made up her mind.

She had a white crepe dress that she had not admired very much at first. In fact, the only reason she had bought it was because it was so expensive, and because the saleslady who had waited on her had so enthusiastically told her that it was an original model, straight from Paris. It had a full flowing skirt and flat bands over the shoulders. The bands crossed in the front and the back of the bodice, but there was no trimming on the dress at all. It was just white and simple. Now, as Trixie slipped into it for the first time, she saw that it was lovely looking, that she was lovely looking in it. She thought, shyly, that perhaps Chris would think so too, that he might even tell her so. She was so eager to have him that she decided not to stop to put on any make-up. She wanted to get back to him the very first moment she could. But for the second time that evening, she found herself gripped by a force she did not understand, a force that was stronger than she was. She could not start right away. There was something else she had to do first.

She tried her cabin door to make sure that it was locked. Then she knelt down beside her narrow bed and hid her face in the counterpane.

"Please, God," she whispered, "let me have him. Please, *please*, PLEASE!"

CHAPTER 4

HANS CHRISTIAN stood on the bridge watching the shifting scene with fascinated eyes, as the ship made its way slowly up the Elbe River. The Captain's invitation had not included the rest of the "crowd," so he was quite alone, except for the officers on duty. He was glad that this was so. Any other presence would have seemed to him like an intrusion at the time.

He had been on the bridge before, for the Captain had been conspicuously cordial to him throughout the voyage. But he was not mechanically minded. The machinations of the electrical steering device, the engine revolution counter, the fire detector, direction finder and emergency alarm switch, though these had been thoroughly and painstakingly explained to him, still remained so mysterious as to be slightly irritating. The fathometer, the chronometers and the sextant were slightly less baffling; but it was only in the charts, over which he had pored for hours, that he had taken genuine pleasure. Even in midocean these had proved fascinating to him; now that the ship was approaching its destination and he saw landmarks and water depths indicated on a large scale, he was beyond measure intrigued.

The final days aboard ship had seemed superb. He had been wakened very early the morning before by the cessation of the engines' movement; springing up to look out of his porthole, he had seen the lush emerald-colored shores of Ireland shimmering in the opalescent light which overspreads the earth immediately before dawn. Dressing hurriedly, he had gone on deck to find a few passengers disembarking at Cobh, and a still smaller number taking passage. But there was little bustle and confusion, and without difficulty he had discovered a quiet corner where he could watch the quickening of the dormant harbor and the transfiguration of the heavens. Apparently it had not occurred to any of his fellow travelers that these might be worth seeing, and none of the officers or crew had penetrated to the place where he stood. For two hours he was entirely undisturbed.

He went down to breakfast ravenously hungry, but returned to his hide-out for the passage of the English Channel. The weather was superb, and the white cliffs of Dover sparkled like glittering palisades of snow. The next day at noon the ship sped past Heligoland, near enough for Hans Christian to see the rust red of its gaunt, grim coast line, and the bare rock called "The Monk," standing like a sentinel before the island. Dusk was descending when the Kiel Canal was reached; and by the time Blankenese came into view, little lights were twinkling along the shores and on the dredges and tug boats and freighters crowding the Elbe River. Music kept rising unexpectedly from these: the tinkle of a guitar, the blare of brass, the lusty melody that pours spontaneously from German throats. Hans Christian, watching and listening, began to sing softly himself.

It was at Blankenese that the Captain sent for him, clearing his throat slightly as he put his hand on the boy's shoulder.

"*Also, mein lieber Junge,* the voyage is at an end. But I hope, should a happy chance bring you ever to Hamburg when my ship is in port, that you will to see me come. We could have an evening's outing together, perhaps, and to the Zillertal go."

"I'd like to very much, sir— What is the Zillertal?"

The Captain raised his hands in mock horror. "A German who does not know what is the Hamburg Zillertal!" he exclaimed. "Why, every man, from seaman to sovereign, goes sooner or later, and often both early and late, to the Zillertal to seek amusement. It is the most famous beer garden in the Sankt Pauli district, where at midnight all the guests on small tables mount, to sway and sing in unison with the band. The music it is excellent, and the musicians wear Bavarian costumes and sit upon a small stage while they play their merry tunes and carol in so strange dialects. *Ja!* I am sure you will the Zillertal greatly enjoy, and greatly shall I enjoy to take you there. A tour of the Hamburg harbor in some small speed boat we must also make, that there you may see the ships of every nation gathered in our great port—Russian and Roumanian, Spanish and Swedish and dozens of others. And among them many-masted sailing vessels, not as numerous as heretofore, but still enough to show a doubting world that once they ruled the sea, and, if need, could do so again."

"It's very good of you, sir— And you must come to see us too, when you can, in Berlin and at Schönplatz."

The Captain regarded Hans Christian thoughtfully, and, after a moment of obvious hesitation, spoke as if he were weighing his words. "That also would me much pleasure give," he said. "But, *mein lieber Junge*, may I one word of warning to you say? This Germany to which you are making your homecoming—you think of it, you speak of it, as if it were a magic land. It is, on the contrary, a crushed and conquered country, smarting under defeat, writhing under insult, seeking, though so far vainly, the means and the man to strike back at its foes and effect its revenge. There are bright spots in Germany still, we have our cheerful beer gardens and our mighty harbors yet intact, and much besides and beyond these. I trust it may be only such *Gemütlichkeit* and power that you may see."

"But *Herr Kapitän*——"

"I think I have already too much said. But I loved your father, though I was not blind to his faults, of which he had many and of which you seem unaware. You idolize his memory, Hansel, that I know, and it is well that a son should so think of one who has died a hero's death for his country. But your mother, she is a fine woman too, brave and loyal. Do not forget her or neglect her altogether, now that you have come to your *Heimat*."

"I shan't, *Herr Kapitän*. But she doesn't need me, and——"

"I love your father's son too," remarked the Captain with a smile, putting his hand around Hansel's shoulder again. "I can that he is an idealist observe, and of such we have need in Germany even more than of avengers. *Nun, mein Junge!* I have no time further to talk to you. See, we shall to Altona soon come, the haven—and the heaven—of retired sea captains. We will mark them this evening, sitting on their trim little porches, watching the ships that come and go, and sighing perhaps, as they puff away at their pipes, because such ships no longer under their orders sail. Someday you will come to visit me when I live in such a neat little house behind such a trim little porch. And we will talk of this voyage we have together made, while I was still in command of a fine ship—and of many other things. But that is still a long way off, Hansel—still a long way off."

The Captain moved away, and an instant later Hans Christian heard him giving an order in a voice unusually peremptory for him; evidently he was seeking, in command, the vent for some emotion which he had suppressed. For a few moments the boy followed his forceful figure with troubled eyes; the Captain had slightly shaken his serenity. But this uneasiness was ephemeral. As the spell of the evening's beauty closed in upon him again, he took up his interrupted song where he had left off with it.

He was glad to have this time to himself, before he met his grandparents. Until he had managed to conceal himself at Cobh, the inroads upon the tranquillity which he enjoyed had been increasingly numerous. The "crowd" insisted on regarding him as its ringleader, in spite of his disinclination for such a role. He had won the first prize at the costume dance, at which he had appeared in a dress parade uniform worn by one of his ancestors, Kurt von Hohenlohe, at the Court of Frederick the Great; and at the *Weisse Rössel* dinner, the small silver horse—symbol of the ancient hostelry for which the festival was named—had been found imbedded in his ice cream. To be sure, he had not kept it long; Trixie, whose own sherbet cup had contained only the specialized sweet of the evening, had been so obviously disappointed that he had tossed the little token across the table to her; it was already firmly attached to her charm bracelet, which now tinkled more provocatively than ever. But it had been his in the first place, and this had not passed unremarked.

The atmosphere of the Captain's table, unharmonious from the outset, had been supercharged with animosity ever since Trixie's "experiment with ventilation," as Hans Christian insisted on calling her escapade. Neither Father Hastings nor Mrs. Schuyler would speak to her; indeed, they went so far as to avert their eyes from the place where she sat, as if fearful of contamination. Mr. Fuller, who had regarded the episode as a huge joke and hailed its denouement with guffaws of laughter, had for a time bridged over the gap caused by their icy silence. As long as this buffoonery was good natured, it had a more or less beneficent effect; but when he suddenly appeared on the scene in a towering rage, an electrical storm would have been mild in comparison with the explosion.

He had been gypped, he had been fleeced, he had been done in. Mr. and Mrs. Harris Hunt, the nice quiet couple from Macon, Georgia, whom he and his friend Ferris, of the Chicago Loan and Trust, had persuaded to make up a pleasant little foursome of bridge with them, had skinned him out of two thousand dollars at a single sitting! They were professional gamblers, there was not the slightest doubt of it, plying their nefarious trade under a mask of meekness! He would have the law on them yet, he would see them penalized and jailed. What was more, he would take steps to see that he was reimbursed himself and that none of his influential friends traveled by a ship which permitted such nefarious practices. As soon as it arrived in Hamburg, he proposed to call both on the President of the Line and the American Consul General. Between them, they would cause justice to be done.

Mrs. Rhodes, who had not fully recovered from the discovery of Trixie's indiscretions, trembled and twisted her handkerchief into fresh knots as she listened to Mr. Fuller's fulminations, which the Captain heard civilly but unresponsively. It was not until the banker's vehement voice rose to a bellow and his words became actually insulting in character, that the Commander made any rejoinder, and this was brief and pointed.

"It is the first time since I go to sea that a case of this kind has to my attention been brought," he remarked cogently. "It is well known that on shipboard gamblers there are, as on land. But inexperienced players they seldom attack, since too obvious would their advantage be; and experienced players themselves are well on their guard and can for themselves fend, without calling upon maritime law and the American Government to protect them. Is it possible, *Herr* Fuller, that this is the exception which the rule proves, that you are yourself then a novice, both at this so skillful game of chance and mischance, and in the ways of the travel-wise?"

Mr. Fuller sprang from his seat and stalked out of the dining room, swearing as he went. But in ten minutes he was back again, blind with rage.

"I tell you there's monkey business going on!" he shouted. "My wife planned to have her dinner on deck, and then, seeing that she was feeling better than usual, she went down to dress. When she opened her jewel box to get out her jade necklace, it was gone. Clean gone! It's been stolen straight out of the stateroom, I'd have you know!"

This time the Captain rose. "This is very serious," he said gravely. "I will myself with you come, the catastrophe to investigate. Steps shall at once be taken this so costly necklace to trace. Though valuables, of course, should with the purser be placed. That also you must know, Mr. Fuller."

"But damn it, my wife always keeps her jewelry with her! I've told you, she plays with it, just as a kid plays with dolls. Why shouldn't she? It's all insured——"

"For that, at least, we must thankful be. What would you say the value of this necklace might come to, Mr. Fuller?"

The banker's answer had been inaudible at the Captain's table; he and the Commander were already on their way out of the dining room when he made it. Nevertheless, Hans Christian, turning to Trixie as if nothing had happened, and asking her how about a little ping-pong, had seemed to hear a small insidious voice whispering in his ear. "The necklace is very well insured. It is worth a great deal. At least two thousand dollars. At least. At least."

He seemed to be hearing the same small sound now, as the ship continued to nose its way up the river. The necklace had not been found, in spite of the thorough search that had been made for it and the ample reward that had been offered for it; and the Fullers had appeared no more at the Captain's table. But Mr. Fuller had sought Hans Christian out, as the boy stood watching the coast of Heligoland, and had spoken to him brusquely and pointedly.

"Mrs. Fuller's all upset over this terrible affair," he remarked. "I've got to do something to make up to her for it. So I've been thinking– You know we spoke once at the table about your grandmother's jewelry, and you said you thought it was all intact. Well, if you should find it was, and that circumstances had changed any, so that now——"

"Mr. Fuller, I told you before——"

"Yes, I know what you told me. There's no need to get mad about it either. But circumstances change sometimes. You might do me a good turn and I might do you one. Suppose you'd let me know if they should."

The banker departed as abruptly as he had come. It was fortunate that he did, Hans Christian thought. The boy had never before wanted so much to hit a man in the face. He hoped he never would again——

He wondered if his grandmother would be wearing any of her jewelry when she came to meet him, and if Mr. Fuller's covetous eye would light upon it. He thought again of the way she used to look, when he visited her, as a little boy in Berlin, and she came in to bid him good night before going out in the evening. He had failed to describe her adequately in saying that she looked "rather glittering" in Court apparel. She had been gorgeous, simply gorgeous, from the top of her small regal head to the soles of her tiny, arched feet. But her coronet of gems had been no more beautiful than the wreathed braids of her hair, her sparkling necklace less lovely than her slim white throat, her radiant rings mere accessories to her rosy-tipped fingers. It was her husband's boast that he could encircle her waist with his two hands, and Hansel had tried to do the same, sometimes, when she stood in all her panoply of splendor before him; he could still remember the stiffness of the brocade that was laced so close to her supple figure. She had laughed, in those days, and said that she must be losing her shape, when his small hands would not stretch as far as his grandfather's. And then she had caught him up against her breast, and kissed him, and he had smelled the sweet scent that clung to her garments and felt the softness of her delicate skin——

The mental vision which he had conjured up was so vivid that he scarcely noticed that the ship was actually nearing the wharf at last. The dock was crowded, but no arresting figures detached themselves from the general throng to attract his attention. When Hans Christian finally began to look about, he could not see any strikingly beautiful woman or any tall, soldierly man of noticeable distinction, gazing searchingly towards the deck. One elderly lady, in dark, nondescript clothing, had managed to advance a little beyond the other patient waiters, who consented, with typical German obedience, to be kept within well-defined limits. There was a certain grace about her movements, and she was speaking eloquently with one of the guards, arguing perhaps, or pleading; at all events, he seemed disposed to permit her to press forward. She was quick to realize that he was moved, and to take advantage of his leniency. When the gangplank was lowered, she was the first person to set foot upon it, and she came swiftly up it, her progress now quite unimpeded. As she stepped from it to the deck, she came unerringly to the place where Hans Christian was standing, and put both her hands on his shoulders.

"Hansel—mein Schatz—kennst du mich denn nicht?"

It was terrible, but it was true. He had not for one moment recognized, in this shabby, persistent old lady, the glorious creature his grandmother once had been. She was slender and erect still, to be sure; her dark eyes had retained some of their sparkle; her skin, though colorless and lightly wrinkled, was still soft and delicate. But her mouth had lost its merriment, her throat its lovely curves; the hair which escaped from under the battered bonnet was wholly white, the hands, encased in the worn gloves, quivering. The elegance, the glamour, the strength, which her very presence had once emanated, were gone completely; only her dignity and graciousness had remained imperishable.

"Why, grandmother!" he stammered. "Of course I know you. But I was looking for you in the opposite direction. And I didn't expect to see you alone. Where's grandfather?" he asked, kissing her belatedly.

"He is not very well just now, Hansel. Nothing serious. But it seemed better for him not to attempt the trip from Schönplatz to Hamburg. The railway service in East Prussia is very inadequate. We must first take a small local train to Allenstein, and then change for Berlin, crossing the Corridor, which is tedious and trying. And in Berlin we must change again."

"Couldn't you have come more easily in your car?"

"Well—you had written me, darling, that you were bringing your own little runabout with you, and I thought we could return to Schönplatz together in that. It would be in the nature of a real lark, would it not, Hansel?"

"Yes—I suppose that since grandfather couldn't come with you we won't be stopping off in Berlin, will we? I'd been looking forward, rather, to going there— It was always such fun, visiting you when I was a kid. But of course, as things are, I'd rather go straight to the country."

"Yes, dear, it will be best. In any case. You see we do not have our house on the Tiergarten Strasse any more."

"You don't have it! Who does have it?"

"It has been bought by a very rich industrialist. It was an expense no longer justified, for your grandfather and myself, all alone as we have been so long now, to keep it. If we could have been sure that you would one day return to us, Hansel—though, no, not even then, as things have been these last years."

"But, grandmother, I don't understand. Do you mean that you and grandfather have been in trouble, real trouble, and haven't let mother and me know?"

The Archduchess slipped her arm lightly through his, and drew him forward.

"My dear boy, I fear we are blocking the passage of travelers who wish to disembark," she said gently. "And we should be getting off ourselves too, *nicht wahr?* We will talk over all these things later on, as we ride across country. Or even tonight. I knew you would be landing too late for us to start our journey this evening; so I have taken rooms for us at a small, clean hotel. Of course, it is not like the excellent *Vier Jahreszeiten* facing the beautiful Alster. But we shall be quite comfortable there. And tomorrow morning, if you like, we can have a *Rundreise*, which costs only a few pfennigs, so that you may see the lake and its swans, so famous all over Germany. And even linger for lunch at the *Bürgerhaus* if you would like to stay so long, and are feeling enough in funds to give an old lady a great treat."

She smiled as she spoke, and as she did so, Hans Christian caught a glimmer of the bygone charm which had once so illumined her face. They had already reached the foot of the gangplank, and the tall officer who had permitted the Archduchess to pass through the lines now saluted respectfully as she came by. She stopped and spoke to him.

"Let me thank you again for your kindness," she said. "This is the young man of whom I told you—my grandson, whom I had not seen in ten years. I am sure that now you will understand my eagerness."

"It was an honor to serve your Serene Highness— *Herr Baron, wenn ich bitten darf*——"

The lines had been lifted again, they were advancing quickly towards the customs. These would be only a formality, the Archduchess explained. If Hansel did not care to claim his car until morning, they could be on their way almost at once. On the other hand, if he wished to get it now, she was quite willing to wait. She had made no engagement for the evening, because she had felt sure he would share her wish that they might spend it quietly and alone.

"Then if you haven't any plans, I do think I'd better get it off now. So that we can start tomorrow as soon as we care to. Though I'd enjoy the *Rundreise* and lunch at the *Bürgerhaus*, too, of course," he added quickly, seeing the slight shadow that crossed the face of the Archduchess, and loath to have her feel that any project of hers might seem unimportant to him.

"I will wait for you here then. Indeed, by the time you return, I think I can promise that your baggage will be cleared, and we can drive off immediately in your own runabout, instead of taking a creaky old taxi."

Her pleasure in his presence was contagious. She already had almost succeeded in making him forget her shabby clothes and saddened face, through the magnetism of her manner. It *would* be a lark, driving her about and giving her a good time again, though the knowledge that good times were to have no center in the stately old house facing the Tiergarten was still a bitter blow. Hans Christian tried to escape from under its impact as he busied himself with the car. There was a certain amount of red tape about having it cleared, rather more than he had expected, from the way his grandmother had spoken; and apparently it hastened matters in the end if the port officers were allowed to take their own time, to read documents meticulously, to demand signatures authoritatively, and put stamps here and seals there. But the process was smooth, even though it was not speedy, and Hans Christian was treated with formal courtesy throughout. When at last he seated himself at the wheel and swung around a designated circuit, he had not been moved to irritation or impatience.

As she had predicted, his grandmother was already awaiting him, and by her side was a ruddy and beaming porter, who had possessed himself of Hans Christian's bags, and who now began to stow these comfortably into the rumble seat. The trunks, it appeared, had already been dispatched to their destination. There was no cause for further delay.

"We're off then, are we?" Hans Christian inquired gaily, slipping several coins into the hand of the gratified porter, and helping the Archduchess into the car. "Which way do we go, grandmother?"

"Straight ahead first. I shall tell you when to turn."

He shut the door carefully, walked around to the other side of the car, and got in himself. He had already released the brake and reached for the gearshift when he heard someone calling him.

"Chris! *Chris!* You aren't going away, are you?"

"Who is that, my dear?" inquired his grandmother, her gentle voice betraying slight astonishment.

"I think it must be Trixie Rhodes, one of the girls I met on the boat. I'm afraid that in the excitement of meeting you I forgot to say good-by to her."

Hans Christian's voice had suddenly gone flat. There was no enthusiasm left in it.

"That was rather thoughtless, was it not? Of course you must go back at once," the Archduchess urged, still gently.

"I think she's coming here."

It was perfectly true. Trixie, still panting from the wild rush she had made, was already abreast of the car. Before Hans Christian could get out of it again, she had wrenched open the door and catapulted herself down on the seat beside him.

"Oh, Chris, how *could* you?" she exclaimed.

"I'm terribly sorry. But I expected to see you again on deck. And then I had a pleasant surprise which drove everything else out of my alleged mind. Trixie, this is my grandmother, the Archduchess Victoria Luise."

"I'm very pleased to meet you," Trixie informed the Archduchess.

PART II

1924

A Great House

CHAPTER 5

THE FIRST sight of the East Prussian countryside was destined to make an indelible impression on the receptive mind of Hans Christian: The straight road, lined with spaced trees, which clove its way alternately through stretches of dark forest and wide expanses of undulating field, so free and open that only the sky and the horizon seemed to limit them. The great herds of Holsteins, huge and impassive, reclining in lush pastures or moving rhythmically towards the corners of white fences where they met their milkers, and stood calmly awaiting the coming of sturdy peasant women who approached with small stools in one hand and large pails in the other. The horses, far less heavy of build than the cattle, attached in twos and fours to a single team, and dominating the highway as well as the hillsides, for neither trucks nor tractors had preempted their place. The flocks of black-faced sheep in the meadows, with here and there two or three storks, comic and pompous, among them. The ducks diving beneath the placid waters of small pools without rippling their surface, and rising again to glide across the water as if it had been made of green glass. The snow-white geese, with golden bills and feet, waddling across the cobblestones, negligent of their fate. The tiny cottages and big barns, alike bright with window boxes and wreathed with flower gardens. The spires of village churches ascending above churchyards where all the graves were blanketed with bloom——

"Do you remember that scene in Maeterlinck's *Bluebird*," Hansel asked his grandmother, "where the two children are alone in the cemetery at midnight and the poor little girl is so frightened? Then suddenly there comes a sound of music, and light after darkness, and every mound is transformed with blossoms, and the little boy cries out to his sister, 'There are no dead!' "

"Yes, I remember it— Did the churchyard we just passed make you think of this scene? I am glad, very glad if it did, my dear boy. But alas! There are many dead in Germany. There is an old saying in my family that to every human being comes the sorrow of losing three, each one of whom means the most to him at the moment of loss. But many times three would not cover the losses which I have endured—"

"You believe in resurrection, though, don't you, grandmother?"

Victoria Luise looked at him searchingly before she answered. "Immortality is one of the tenets of my faith," she said at last, "and I have always been a practicing Catholic. Do you believe in it yourself, Hansel?"

"Of course. It seems as natural as springtime to me."

He pronounced the words with finality as well as conviction. They had already left another village behind them, and Hansel's gaze kept wandering from the wheel towards the fields. Apparently he was not inclined to pursue the subject of immortality, and Victoria Luise gradually recovered from the astonishment which he had caused her. His next remark was as practical as his last one had been visionary.

"You can feed yourselves and all your neighbors here in East Prussia, can't you, grandmother? Your national neighbors, I mean."

"Yes, if we are so inclined."

"But why shouldn't you be so inclined? I shouldn't think two and a half million people could begin to consume all the butter and cheese that must be produced here, or all the milk and meat. Isn't it profitable to sell it? Isn't it wise to encourage trade?"

"We send butter to Berlin, and elsewhere."

"Elsewhere in Germany you mean?"

"Yes, elsewhere in Germany— See, *mein Schatz,* there ahead of us is the beginning of our own land."

The questing look in Hansel's eyes kindled quickly. The landscape through which they were passing was much the same as it had been already; but somehow it seemed suddenly to have become still more verdant, still more fresh and flowing than before. He spoke, shyly and excitedly, under his breath.

"I never had such a sense of space," he said, "and of freedom—and beauty. Do you suppose I can put it into music, grandmother?"

"I hope you will put it into something, my dear boy," she said gravely. And he saw that there were tears in her eyes.

They were entering another small village, saved from squalor by the quaintness of its architecture and the brilliance of its flowers. Secreted somewhere beyond it, Hansel supposed, Schönplatz itself must lie, deep in the woods or at the end of a long avenue. But they had hardly reached the outskirts when a high wall appeared, flanked with luxuriant trees, and blank except for an unpretentious iron gate at one end. It was here that they should turn, Victoria Luise signified, in answer to Hansel's unspoken question. The next instant the *Herrenhaus* itself loomed up before them, its wide façade terminating in two towers, its tiled roof intersected with chimneys and dormers, its deep doors open to the summer sunshine.

The boy's first sensation, as he looked at it, was one of amazed relief. He had expected a monumental pile, moated and buttressed, suggestive of sieges, torture chambers and incarceration. Instead he saw walls of rose-red brick, almost completely covered with glossy green vines, and set in the midst of a green lawn studded with shrubs and shaded with chestnut trees. The shape of the house was sturdy and symmetrical; its size was not overpowering; there was nothing grim and gloomy, nothing chilly or forbidding about it. On the contrary, it seemed to emanate not only security, but a warmth which antiquity had made the more mellow.

"Oh, grandmother, it's great!" he exclaimed, lapsing into an American colloquialism for the first time that day.

"Yes, Hansel, it is great. It has been great for nearly seven hundred years. We are counting on you to keep it so," his grandmother answered.

It appeared that the General was resting, that he would not be able to see his grandson until teatime. One of the menservants who took their bags out of the car busied himself with the possessions of the Archduchess. The other had already put Hansel's meticulously into place, by the time he and his grandmother had mounted the massive stairway leading from the vast hall into which the entrance led directly. In spite of the sunshine outside, the light in the house was dim; Hansel could see hardly more than the outlines of great carved chests, of tawny tapestries and somber family portraits, as he climbed the two flights of steps so steep and winding that he marveled at the ease with which his grandmother went over them. But she showed no sign of breathlessness when she finally lifted the heavy latch of a paneled door on the third story.

"This was your father's room, when he was a boy, Hansel," she said in her grave, controlled way. "I thought you would like to have it. Nothing has ever been changed in it. But if you do not find what you need to make you comfortable, of course you must let me know. I am not coming in with you. I have not been over this threshold in ten years now. I had lost three sons before your father, you know—perhaps you yourself can remember when your Uncle Hans was killed at the Battle of the Marne and your Uncle Heinrich died of wounds received at Ypres— My eldest son, their half brother, had died a violent death years earlier," she went on in an altered voice, "and finally when Rudolf fell at Verdun—well, I suppose there are always limits to our weak human endurance. You must forgive me, Hansel, and try to understand, not only why I cannot enter this room, but why I feel there are so many dead in our country."

"I do understand, grandmother. I wouldn't have come to you, would I, if I hadn't?"

He was not sorry to be left alone. Beyond the paneled door he found that the light was still dim, for the room was very deep, with windows only on one side, and these deeply recessed, many paned, and overhung with vines; such sunshine as filtered through them did not reach more than halfway across the wide-planked floor, nor rise to the broad-beamed ceiling. Nevertheless, as Hansel's eyes became accustomed to the duskiness, he did not find the room depressing. The walls were covered with rose-colored plaster, much the same shade as the exterior of the house, and the whitewashed beams were also rose edged. A tall green porcelain stove reared itself impressively at one side of the room, while the round center table, and a chest of drawers standing between an immense wardrobe and a cheval glass which stretched from floor to ceiling, were covered with green moire antique. The rest of the color scheme was haphazard: a divan was spread with a Paisley shawl; a davenport was upholstered in brown tapestry; a chaise longue was covered with figured crimson velvet, while similar varieties of decoration characterized all the chairs. Near one of the windows stood a commodious desk; in one of the corners an equally commodious washstand. Both were surmounted with family portraits of bygone von Hohenlohes, primly presented in pairs.

"I wonder how I see to shave," Hansel murmured practically, as he glanced from the mottled marble stand, in which two large basins were imbedded, to the belaced and beribboned couple who looked down at him from the place where he had expected to find a mirror and a light. Inadvertently, his hand touched a copper pitcher, covered with a crested linen towel, which stood between the big basins. It was surprisingly hot, and he drew his fingers away quickly. Then, one by one, he took up the smaller objects on the washstand, wondering what useful purpose they might serve—two little white bowls, a narrow china tray, and an empty carafe with a glass turned upside down over it.

"I shall have to learn to wash all over again," he said to himself rather whimsically, and, by way of a beginning, poured some of the hot water into one of the big basins. But there was no soap in evidence, and after a brief search for some, he sat down in one of the puffy armchairs, which proved surprisingly comfortable, and continued to look around him.

He was not depressed, but he was disappointed. He had never said that he wanted to occupy his father's room. But he had vaguely hoped that it might be given to him. Now that it was, he could find no trace of his father in it, neither of the Rudolf von Hohenlohe whom he had known as a child, and whom he vividly remembered, nor of the boy that Rudolf von Hohenlohe once had been. He had vaguely imagined that there would be a boy's books in the room, a gun or two, perhaps a collection of minerals or some stuffed birds. He had visualized it as small and Spartan, but revealing. Instead it was immense, luxurious and impersonal. He would rather have been confronted with his father's ghost than with such nonentity.

A light tap on the door roused him from his reverie. He sprang to open it, then stood blinking, wondering if in the dusk his eyes were playing him altogether false. The girl who stood there did not look real. Framed in the dark embrasure of the door, she gave the effect of an idealized genre picture. Her flaxen hair curled around her face and was wreathed in thick braids over her small head. She was pleasantly plump and her eyes were blue and beseeching. She was clad in a white blouse and apron interwoven with bright colors, a black bodice fastened with amber buttons and blue skirt banded with velvet ribbon. In response to Hansel's startled exclamation, she dropped a quick curtsey which seemed indicative of fright.

"Der Herr General ist jetzt im Garten!" she breathed, and scurried down a dim corridor like a terrified rabbit.

Hansel's next shock came at the sight of his grandfather, whom he remembered—vividly, in the same way that he remembered his father—as erect, ruddy and dictatorial. Nothing had prepared him to see a shrunken man, sitting in a wheel chair with a rug over his knees. Only the bristling white mustache and the white hair rising stiffly from a high forehead, were as he recalled them. Even the General's eyes, which had once shone with a glacierlike glitter, were changed. They were less direct in their gaze, less clear and brilliant. As Hansel bent over the old man, he saw that his grandfather was simply staring at him, that there was no joyful recognition in his look.

"Here is Hansel, your namesake, come to see you, Hans," the Archduchess said gently. "Rudolf's son."

The staring eyes flickered, and the transparent hands, extended unclasped over the folded rug, twitched a little.

"Rudolf," the old man said in a thick voice.

"No, my dear, Rudolf's son. Think a minute. You have greatly looked forward to his homecoming. He is going to spend the summer with us."

A sudden smile illumined the blank countenance, giving it charm and dignity again. One of the twitching hands began to move slowly upwards.

"He knows you. He wants to touch your cheek, perhaps to kiss you," the Archduchess whispered to Hansel. But as the boy put his face against his grandfather's, the old man began to sob bitterly.

"Wait. This attack will pass," the Archduchess said, whispering again. Hansel stood still, bracing his own body against the paroxysm which shook his grandfather, appalled lest he might involuntarily reveal the revulsion with which his pity was tinged. When his grandfather finally kissed him, he managed to return the caress. But as the old man sought to wipe away, with his shaking hand, the tears which had been shed, and which had fallen on both faces the boy felt tears welling up in his own eyes.

"Talk to him. He understands more than he can express. He has really recognized you, and you must take advantage of this lucidity, before it passes."

"We are going to have good times together this summer, aren't we, grandfather?" Hansel asked, resentful of his own inadequacy.

"Yes. Good times. Riding every day."

"You'll teach me to ride? I've never learned, you know. But every Prussian can ride, can't he? And I'm going to be a Prussian now, like you."

"Yes, yes. A Prussian like me. We shall ride every morning before breakfast on our beautiful white horses."

"Shall Fritz bring the horses around now, my dear, so that Hansel may see them?"

The General did not answer. He was staring into space again, his vacant gaze turned towards the dim corner of the park. Eventually he raised one of his quivering hands and pointed.

"The Russians!" he muttered hoarsely. "The Russians are attempting a new attack. They are upon us already! I can see them over there."

"No, Hans, you are mistaken! There are no Russians in our peaceful park."

"Sh-sh-sh—!" the General said warningly, painfully putting a shaking finger to his lips. "They will hear you, Luise, and then all will be lost."

"The Field Marshal himself has assured me that they are all gone."

"Sh-sh-sh— Hindenburg won at Tannenberg. But he is not infallible. This time he is mistaken. They are upon us again."

"Shall I send Rudolf to the park to drive them away?"

"Send Heinrich. Send Heinrich. Rudolf is not the soldier that Heinrich is. Heinrich will force them back."

Victoria Luise signaled to Hansel. He rose and went quickly down the gravel walk, between the formal flower beds and moss-grown statues. His grandmother's voice, sweet and soothing, followed him as he went. "There, there," he could hear her saying. "Heinrich has gone, my dear, as you wished, to drive back the Russians. They will not trouble you any more. Heinrich is the best soldier among our sons. Though they have all been good boys, have they not?"

The General's feeble answer did not reach Hans Christian, perhaps because he felt himself fleeing from him. Involuntarily he had quickened his pace. He had crossed the great garden and entered the park which overlooked the lake. Green trees surrounded him, sparkling water lay before him. But now he had none of that sense of space and beauty which had filled him with such joy that morning. He scarcely saw his surroundings. The pitiful wreck of a strong man obsessed his mind and formed his only vision.

He could not blame his grandmother for having failed to warn him of her husband's condition. He realized that it must be so heart-rending to her that she could not bring herself to mention it. Probably she did not permit herself to fully face it, and surely she should be forgiven if this were the case. She was an aging woman, bereft of almost everybody and everything that had made life glorious, as far as she was concerned. Her husband held the last links in the slender chain which still united her with an imperial past. When these links were severed, what would she have left? Nothing, Hans Christian knew, nothing at all that mattered. Unless, through some miracle, he himself——

A settee and some armchairs of elaborately wrought iron, painted white, were drawn up around a small table near the place where he was standing. He sat down and began to try to think things out. In coming to Germany to see his ancestral home, he had not possessed the faintest inkling that it would be like this. He knew in a general way that the country had suffered from the blockade and the inflation; but the details of this suffering had remained comfortably vague in his mind. He had not realized that it was intense or widespread; it had never occurred to him that his own people and his own possessions could be affected by it. His desire to return to his native land, sincere and intense as it was, had been largely due—he now realized for the first time—to his own loneliness and restlessness in the face of his mother's self-sufficiency, rather than to any strong inner conviction that his grandparents needed him.

But now that he had come, what—in the face of existing conditions—should he do? What *could* he do? His mother had kept his own small patrimony intact for him—the legacy which his father had originally inherited from the unmarried uncle for whom Rudolf von Hohenlohe had been named. But it was a modest one, entirely inadequate to clear up the wreckage which Hans Christian already saw around him. How much more there was still to discover, he could not even conjecture. In any case, he would not come into unsupervised use of his small fortune for three years yet. It had been only with the greatest difficulty that he had persuaded his mother to let him cut into his capital for travel funds. It was inconceivable that she would allow him to use it towards the reclamation of a vast estate and the rehabilitation of a fallen fortune. And even if she had been willing that he should apply it to these ends, to what would it amount? A drop in a bucket of water cast over a torrential dam.

He could not then hope to help. But, on the other hand, having come, how could he turn back? His pride would not permit him to confess to his mother that his quest for contentment had been a failure; his pity would not permit him to desert his grandmother in her hour of need. For the present, at least, he must stay where he was, and mark time. And with the decision that this was what he ought to do, came also the renascence of the conviction that it was what he wanted to do. This was his *Heimat,* his Fatherland; America had been only an adopted country for him at best. These were his people; his mother with her complete preoccupation in American affairs had long been alien to his understanding.

But even though this were true, in the larger sense, would there be any immediate escape for him from the nostalgia which had so long obsessed him, in spite of his collegiate success? If his mother, who was still young and strong and beautiful, had proven inadequate as a companion, for what sort of satisfying communion could he look with a tragic, broken woman and a paralytic old man? Obviously for none. He must seek for it somewhere beyond the limits of Schönplatz.

Involuntarily, the thought of the buoyant group on the boat entered his mind, and with the thought an undefined longing for its zestful comradeship. The breezy brightness of the twins, the gay impudence of Card Eustis, had been tonic in their effect. Even Trixie Rhodes, petty and provincial as she seemed, emanated superabundant vitality. He visualized her again as she had looked when the paint had been washed off her face and the ruffles clipped from her shoulders. She had lovely lips, so lovely that neither the scarlet with which they were generally smeared nor the sulky line into which they so often drooped, could altogether obscure their soft natural curves. It was easy to understand why Card had lost no time in reaching the stage of "petting." If ever there was a girl whose mouth was meant to be kissed, Trixie was that girl, and Hans Christian felt resentful of his own lack of importunity, as far as she was concerned. Her eyes were beautiful too—dark blue, like a sapphire; when she laughed, they had a sapphire's sparkle. And on the rare occasions when she was thoughtful, their clarity was shot through with a shrewd gleam. Hans Christian had not forgotten the look she had turned on Father Hastings, when the bishop had spoken of being confined to his cabin by the service of the Lord. Buried somewhere beneath her apparent triviality, there was real intelligence. She was not a blonde baby doll with a baby doll's eyes, like the apparition that had appeared at the dark door of his bedroom that afternoon——

He felt a light hand on his shoulder, and sprang up to see his grandmother standing beside him. She had come so quietly across the grass and through the trees that he had not been aware of her until she touched him. Slightly startled, he blurted out an unstudied question.

"Who was the messenger that you sent for me this afternoon, grandmother?"

"The messenger? The butler sent one of the maids. I don't know which. Why?"

"This one looked like a doll. She had flaxen hair, china blue eyes and chubby pink cheeks. And she was wearing a dress that I suppose is the local costume—a *Tracht* you call it, don't you?"

"All the maids in the house wear the village *Tracht*. I insist upon this. It makes a very satisfactory uniform." Was his grandmother's charming voice rather cold and formal as she said this, or did he merely imagine that it was, Hans Christian wondered. "As for the flaxen hair and baby-doll stare and the chubby cheeks—you may as well get used to seeing hundreds of those, without excitement, wherever you turn. They are almost inescapable among the lower classes in Germany. I really have no idea which of our empty-headed little peasants it was who called you. But if she was almost noticeably half-witted, it was probably the second underchambermaid, Trudchen."

CHAPTER 6

Hans Christian dined with his grandmother, sitting opposite her at an immense round table in an apartment which she designated as the "small dining room," though it was at least thirty feet square. Its white expanse, covered with a darned damask cloth into which the family coat of arms was woven, seemed to stretch out endlessly between them; its smooth surface was unbroken except for a ponderous silver epergne which stood in the center, and the coroneted knives and forks at each place. The menservants, who had officiated at their arrival, and to whose shabby uniforms threadbare white gloves had now been added, served the substantial but unimaginative dinner. The drinking water was lukewarm and the wine sour. There was no butter, and the bread, disclosed when the large smooth napkins were unfolded, was coarse and black; but the roast goose was excellent, and Hans Christian had already begun to take boiled potatoes as a matter of course, and to dispense philosophically with a variety of vegetables. When strawberries had been offered on fruit plates realistically painted, the Archduchess rolled her napkin neatly inside a silver ring and led the way through a succession of drawing rooms, gliding across the glittering parquet flooring with no suggestion of slipping. When she had reached the fourth one, she signified that they would pause at this point and sip their coffee.

"Would you care to light the fire, Hansel?" she asked, nodding towards a corner mantle of hooded stone, under which logs had been laid upright above a foundation of light branches. "The evenings are nearly always cool in East Prussia, even in midsummer, and you may find the climate trying at first– There is a good deal of rain, and there are many dark days. . . . I am so glad that your grandfather knew you. I am sure he had real pleasure in seeing you. He was tired afterwards, but not overmuch. He was sleeping quietly when I came out to dinner."

Apparently she intended to make no reference to her failure to inform Hans Christian of the General's actual condition, before their arrival at Schönplatz. The boy, having lighted the fire and accepted the cup of coffee which his grandmother herself served from an enameled service, decided that it would be wiser for him not to refer to this either.

"Do my cousins come here often?" he inquired instead. "I've been looking forward to seeing them again." It was amazingly light, considering how late they had dined, and, holding his coffee cup in his hand, he walked over to one of the great windows and looked out past the garden to the park and lake, the same unaccustomed desire for young and zestful company, which he had felt that afternoon, welling up irrepressibly again. "Not that I remember them very clearly, or that we've written each other much of any," he went on. "But, you know– Aunt Rita's eldest son is just a little younger than I am, isn't he? Karl? It would be fun if he and I could get together. And there are seven of them in all, aren't there?"

"There were. But two of them have died. And one is a cripple, as a result of uncorrected rickets. Your Aunt Rita has had a very sad life. Her husband, Friedrich von Mitweld, has never been able to reconcile himself to the abdication of the Kaiser. In fact, he seizes on every possible pretext to go to Doorn as often as he can, and to stay there as long as possible each time. I think he would like nothing better than to head a Restoration Movement, which would, of course, represent an entirely forlorn hope. Karl, on the contrary, has embraced many of those communistic ideas which are such a menace to Germany just now. So the household is torn with internal strife, that is very hard for Rita, with her peace-loving nature, to endure. She hides herself at home, and I do not see her for months at a time. In any case, it is a long expensive journey from here to Bavaria."

"And my Aunt Elsa? Don't you see her either?"

"She is a nun, you know, in Cologne, and that is as hard and as costly to reach as Munich. Besides, the rules of her Order are extremely strict. Family visits are not encouraged; and, to tell the truth, I have never found them very satisfactory, when they must be carried forward on either side of a veiled grill."

"I shouldn't think they would be. But I should think you'd like to have your grandchildren come to see you."

"There is one grandchild, at least, whom I am very happy to see," said the Archduchess, with her disarming smile, as she poured herself a second cup of coffee and motioned to Hansel to stop pacing about and seat himself beside her. "And Luischen, my namesake, was here for a time in the spring. But she is a wild girl, already bent on making a most unsuitable marriage, though she is far too young to be thinking of such a thing; her visits are too much of a strain, now that we have a semi-invalid in the house." Victoria Luise paused, and added, "I hope, Hansel, that when your fancies turn to thoughts of love, it will not be either too lightly or too wilfully."

"I don't think they'll turn in that direction at all, at least for a long time."

"Of course they will. That is inevitable. But it will mean everything to me, my dear boy, if you will try not to be headstrong when it comes to affairs of the heart."

"I'll try not to be headstrong about anything, as far as that goes. Don't worry."

"I do not worry, I think, unduly. But a suitable alliance for you is a matter of paramount importance."

"You haven't anyone special in mind, already, have you, grandmother?"

"Well—not to any point of insistence, you may be sure of that. But sometime, before too long, I hope it may be possible for you to take a trip to Spain. I should like to have you meet our kinsfolk there. They are not closely related to us, by blood; but, on the other hand, the ties which do unite us have always meant a great deal. I refer especially to the Cerreno family, of which I am sure you have often heard your mother speak."

"Why, no!" Hansel answered candidly. "She never speaks of them at all. But I remember Sebastian de Cerreno perfectly, myself. He came to Copenhagen once on a special mission—a Centennial, or something of the sort—when father was German Minister there. He brought me a splendid set of Spanish soldiers—museum pieces really, though I used them as toys—that I have still. I keep them set up in a part of the attic that used to be my play room, in our Hamstead house. I thought he was a wonderful person. But his children are just kids, aren't they? He didn't have any until he had been married for a long time."

"Yes. They are just kids, as you have put it. But you are not markedly middle-aged yourself, Hansel, you know. Sebastian has two boys, Gabriel and Estaban, and two girls, Cristina and Cecilia. Their mother is a very beautiful woman, and Sebastian himself has always been known as one of the most fascinating men in Europe. Their daughters can hardly fail to be entrancing."

"Well, maybe. Ten years from now," Hansel replied without enthusiasm. "But, really, grandmother, I'm not interested in girls."

"All the better. And all the more chance that you will be, ten years from now. In the meantime, I shall try to help you ward off young ladies from the Middle West, as importunate as the one who hurled herself into your car the night of your arrival in Hamburg."

His grandmother had previously made no reference to Trixie's rash behavior, and Hansel, who had been silent on the subject himself, had secretly dreaded the moment when she might. Now she spoke with such delicate archness that it was impossible to be angry. Nevertheless, Hans Christian found himself instantly on the defensive.

"I hope you didn't get a wrong impression of Trixie, grandmother. There are lots of nice things about her."

"Perhaps. But what an awful name, to begin with! And what strange manners!"

"Her name is really Beatrice, of course, and that isn't awful, is it? I think it's rather pretty—just as pretty as Cristina or Cecilia!" he said, speaking mischievously in his turn. "And I think her manners will probably improve, among the polite Dutch. I don't believe I told you, her father has just been appointed American Minister to the Netherlands. She and her mother have invited me, very cordially, to come and visit them."

"I have not the slightest doubt of their cordiality, my dear boy. Nevertheless, I should much rather see you go to Spain than to Holland when you have the opportunity and the inclination to travel."

"Mr. Rhodes is what's called a solid citizen. He's made a great deal of money, all himself, in a very praiseworthy way," persisted Hansel, reddening at the mocking reference to cordiality. "And Trixie's adaptable, like most American girls. She'll probably learn to do things very well, in the end."

"The Cerrenos also have a great deal of money. And none of them need to learn to do things well. They have been doing them well for centuries," the Archduchess retorted quietly. "Would you care to have a game of chess with me, my dear boy? If you do not know how to play, this might be a good time to begin learning. I am sure, when your grandfather is better, that he will wish to engage you in contests very frequently."

That was a fiction which must be kept up, Hansel recognized, as the evening wore interminably on; not even tacitly would his grandmother admit that her husband would not eventually regain his normal health and resume his normal pursuits. She referred to him several times, intermittently, in the course of their play; and when she had won three games of chess, and the board had been folded up and put away, her talk reverted constantly to him. Hansel tried to keep up his end of the conversation courteously, and he was careful to avoid any further appearance of argument. But he was very tired; the warm fire made him feel sleepy after his long day in the open air; and the varied experiences through which he had passed had been emotionally exhausting. He was thankful when at last his grandmother rose to retire.

"I hope you will sleep well, my darling. You will let me know if you are not perfectly comfortable, will you not?"

"I am sure I shall be. Thank you, grandmother. But I wonder if I might take something to read upstairs with me? A newspaper or a book? There didn't seem to be any in my room."

The Archduchess looked at him in surprise. "I am afraid it is true that there are no newspapers there," she said. "Wait, I will ring– There must be one in the house, and hereafter I will see that you receive it regularly. But there are quantities of books in your room, Hansel, which belonged to your father–the Danzig chests are full of them, and of his various collections–medals and coins and so on. I suppose you thought, because you saw no open cases——" She glided across the parquetry again, and beckoned Hansel into still another room, which he had not previously seen, and in which the walls were covered with inlaid panels. "This is the library," she said. "There are shelves upon shelves of books behind every one of those doors. Feel free to browse among them as much as you like, tomorrow, and after that. Meanwhile, here is today's *Berliner Tageblatt,*" she added, handing him the paper which a servant had brought in response to her summons. "I am afraid I have hardly glanced at it myself, there is so little about current events which I care to read. Besides, any good *Hausfrau* has a great deal to do when she has been absent from home for a few days, and I pride myself on my attention to detail."

Hansel took the paper and glanced casually over the unfamiliar layout, slightly baffled by the lack of headlines and by the strange script to which he had not yet had time to fully reaccustom himself. There seemed to be nothing of great moment worthy of passing on to his grandmother at such an hour of the night, especially when she had just said that current events did not interest her. But as certain half-forgotten items from the American press filtered through to the forefront of his mind, he made an idle comment and asked a casual question, his hand already on the knob of the drawing-room door.

"We've been hearing quite a little lately at college about a man named Adolf Hitler. What are people saying about him in Germany?"

"A man named Adolf Hitler? I cannot recall anything at all. Who is he, and what has he done?"

"He's an Austrian by birth, like yourself. He was a sergeant in the World War, and afterwards–or before, I'm not quite sure which–he was a paper hanger and sold picture post cards on the side. I can't make out that he ever did anything much. But he's tried to start some sort of Reactionary Movement in Germany. And he seemed to emerge a sort of special hero after a *Bloody Putsch* in Munich."

"An Austrian, *like myself!* I do not believe he can bear much resemblance to me, Hansel, even though he was born an Austrian, if he was the hero of something so unpleasant as a *Bloody Putsch!* When did this disagreeable event take place?"

"Oh, sometime last winter. He and a few friends of his tried to buck the Government, and most of the friends got killed. Didn't Aunt Rita write you anything about it? This all happened in Munich!"

"She wrote that there had been some kind of disgraceful street brawl in which Karl had been hurt. No details—I supposed because she was ashamed of his quarrelsome propensities. Did anything of importance happen afterwards?"

"I suppose it depends on what you call important. Hitler himself was clapped into prison, and people said it would be the last that was ever heard of him and his so-called Movement. But I happened to see a little item about him in this paper. That's what made me think of it. He's going to be let out after awhile, and, meantime, he's writing a book."

"Writing a book? An ignorant man like that?"

"Yes—Bunyan wrote a book in prison, didn't he? A book that made quite a stir, called *Pilgrim's Progress.*"

For the first time the Archduchess looked at her grandson rather coldly. "My dear Hansel," she observed, "you certainly do make some extraordinary remarks. Several times this morning—and now— What caused you to think of a comparison of that sort?"

"I don't know, I'm sure. I just happened to, that's all. I haven't offended you, have I, grandmother?"

He looked so earnest, he seemed so genuinely upset by her displeasure, that she melted instantly. "No, my dear boy, you have not offended me," she said with tenderness. "You will never do that, I know. But I hope you will never forget, either, that you are a *Junker* and a von Hohenlohe, and act and think accordingly, in family matters, as I have said before. And in national matters also. Be true to your own class and you will be true to your own country. It is inconceivable that in the regeneration of Germany, which I hope you are to be helpful in bringing about, that there could be any time or any place for an imprisoned paper hanger named Adolf Hitler."

CHAPTER 7

HANS CHRISTIAN passed a restless night. When he first went up to his room, tired and sleepy as he was, he could not resist the temptation of opening the Danzig chests, so great was his relief at finding that there were, after all, some personal relics of his father's boyhood in existence; but he burrowed through them vainly, as far as finding anything interesting in itself was concerned. He had left the dining room still thirsty, and now his attempts at exploration made him doubly conscious of this discomfort; but the carafe with the glass upturned over it was still empty, and the tepid water in the two pitchers had a light coating of dust over it, as if it had been there for several days already. He turned from it with aversion and got into bed, pulling the mountainous eiderdown with which it was covered firmly around his chin; as the Archduchess had said, it was cold, even though it was midsummer. The truth of the statement was brought home to him with double force when he felt his feet protruding below the eiderdown. He rose, pulled it back, and tried to tuck it in at the bottom without much success, for it kept puffing up around his hands wherever he touched it. Moreover, he found, when he climbed back into bed, that his chest and shoulders were now completely exposed; the eiderdown was so short that it could not be stretched to cover his entire person at once; and eventually he got up a second time and hunted for his overcoat in the dark, the electric switch by the door, which was the only one in the room, having eluded his search. With the Burberry for a blanket, he decided that he could manage, and, as a matter of fact, he did fall almost instantly asleep. But his dreams were troubled and fantastic, and he found no repose in them.

He seemed to be sitting in the ventilator beside Trixie. But she did not look natural. She had a mantilla draped over a high comb on her head and a glittering painted fan in her hand. She had turned from an American into a Spaniard, at least so far as her outer attributes were concerned. He decided to try calling her Cristina, which he thought would please his grandmother, and when that did not work, he called her Cecilia instead. But she only sat and sulked, and he saw that he had made a mistake, that it was Trixie all the time. So then he decided not to talk to her at all, but to caress her instead. She made no resistance. Her smooth shoulders were soft in his embrace, her red mouth sweet under his kiss. At last he released her and looked at her again. To his horror, he saw that it was not Trixie whom he was holding now, but Trudchen——

The loud clamor of a bell came clanging across his distressed somnolence, rousing him abruptly. He leapt out of bed, still shivering with shame, and convinced that a calamity of some sort must have befallen the household. Could there be a fire? Was this a toll for the dead? But he could smell no smoke, he could hear no hurrying footsteps. Surely if anything were vitally wrong, there would be some further indication of it.

He went to the window and looked out, his attention arrested by a strange sound of scraping. Far below him he could discern the figures of women with implements of some sort in their hands. As his eyes grew accustomed to the dimness and the distance, he could see that these women were raking the gravel walk in the garden, at the meticulous order of which he had marveled the day before. Completely reassured, he turned away; they could hardly be pursuing so superfluous an occupation in the midst of disaster. As he crossed the room, however, a nearer noise distracted him, such as wood might make against wood, though slightly muffled. He flung open the door of his bedroom, and in the somber hall outside saw a girl leaning against a long pole to which a heavy block covered with felt was attached, and which she was laboriously pushing across a hardwood floor, polishing the parquetry as she moved. With a contracting heart, he realized that the girl was Trudchen.

She had looked up instantly, at the raising of the iron latch. But this time she had not scurried away. Instead, after dropping another quick curtsey, she had stood as if transfixed, gazing at him with melting eyes.

"What are you doing here at this hour?" Hans Christian asked sharply, snatching at the bathrobe which hung on the rack near the door and wrapping it firmly around him.

"But, *Herr Baron,* I am always here at this hour. The great bell, summoning us all to work, sounded ten minutes ago. I was even a little late. If Her Serene Highness knew this, she would be much displeased, she might threaten to send me away. I beg the *Herr Baron* to intercede for me if she should. I need money so much."

"Don't be absurd," said Hans Christian, still sharply. "Of course she won't send you away— So that was the seven o'clock whistle I heard, was it?"

A baffled expression overspread Trudchen's rosy face. "I do not understand the *Herr Baron,*" she faltered. "That was not a whistle, it was a bell. And it is not seven, it is only five."

"Five? And what time do you get through at night?"

"Sometimes at nine, sometimes at ten. Now that there are not many guests at the castle, it is often a little earlier. The work is not hard. It would be easy for me to do more." Up to this point she had continued to look at him meltingly, her breast rising and falling quickly. Now curtseying again, she bent her head, her shoulders drooping. "Has the *Herr Baron* need of me in any way?" she asked submissively.

It had never before been brought home to Hans Christian that the relation between a dream and a reality might be so close. He was appalled at the revelation.

"Certainly not," he said, even more brusquely than before. Then, seeing how utterly crushed the girl looked, he added, "That is, you might tell me if I can get a bath in this house, and, if so, where."

"*Aber natürlich,* the *Herr Baron* may have a bath whenever he pleases. I shall prepare it for him. In the little room at the end of the corridor."

"You won't do anything of the sort. I don't need to have my bath prepared for me by anyone. I do that myself."

"But, *Herr Baron,* I always prepare the baths. Her Serene Highness would be very angry with me if I neglected my duty."

"I can't help it. I'll make her understand that I don't like the idea of having a girl prepare my bath. But I'll tell you what you can do, since you're the chambermaid. When you make up my bed this morning, you can put a couple of blankets on it, and tuck them in at the bottom. And you can keep a pitcher of ice water in my room all the time."

"Yes, *Herr Baron,* both shall be done. I shall not fail in anything that you ask me to do."

Again he saw all implications of her docility. She was almost asking for seduction. He knew that he had only to stretch out his hand to take her; and with the realization, a hot gust of desire swept through him. But beneath it ran the dark thought that such subservience could not be spontaneous, that it must have its source, at least partly, in the fear that a lack of compliance might mean a lack of food. He wondered how often the girls in the village had yielded to the lords of the manor, their hearts taut with terror, while their bodies lay limp. No matter how many times this had happened before, he was resolved that it should never happen again.

"Then run along, Trudchen, and get the ice water, like a good girl," he said, cheerfully and casually. "I'm thirsty enough to drink a well dry."

The day to which he eventually descended differed, in no essential detail, from dozens of others which followed it. He spent hours at the piano and hours in the library; he wrote conscientiously to his mother, and, from time to time, briefly answered the letters with which Trixie showered him. He did not defer his riding lessons. His grandmother had told him that there was not a boy in the village who, before he was five years old, had not gone out in the pasture alone with a halter in his hand, and planting his great toe on the neck of a grazing horse, swung himself up into a seat unaided, and ridden proudly home. In spite of the nonchalance with which the Archduchess had told this story, Hans Christian had interpreted it, and rightly, as a challenge. He was in the saddle every morning by seven, returning at nine to the bath, which, in spite of his protests, Trudchen always prepared for him, and the hearty breakfast spread out in the "small" dining room, where his grandmother awaited him.

In a way, it seemed futile to rise so early when after breakfast there was nothing pressing to do. He had offered to help with the accounts, to take over as much of the management of the estate as his grandmother would permit. But he had coupled these offers with some questions about wages and some comments on the length of working hours which the Archduchess seemed to resent. The result of this tactlessness had been to close all avenues of responsibility to him. There would be time enough, later on, she assured him, for him to bother with matters like that; any day now, his grandfather would be expecting to take up the reins again; it was hardly worth while for dear Hansel to begin a task which he would not be expected to continue. She was accustomed to figures, she could manage quite well by herself until her husband was in the mood to relieve her.

Some of the young men in the neighborhood came to see him. They were all well born and well bred, and they were extremely courteous to him in a formal, precise sort of way. He was made welcome, when he called upon them in return, at the various *Herrenhäuser* that they inhabited, many of which were far more imposing than Schönplatz; and he enjoyed many aspects of the East Prussian country life that these contacts revealed to him. He was especially intrigued when he found that falconry, which he regarded as a mediaeval pastime, was still considered a contemporary sport; and for a time the hooded bird which he learned to hold on his wrist, and which swooped and circled towards its prey when he released it, had a fascination for him. But, basically, the whole principle of hunting for pleasure revolted him. It made him feel sick and faint to see a harmless and defenseless bird or animal, at one moment free and joyous and vital, transformed, in a twinkling, to a mangled mass of inert flesh. His squeamishness was regarded as strange; it detracted from the popularity which he might otherwise have enjoyed. Even his excellent game of tennis and his skill as a swimmer did not wholly atone, it was soon plain, for the lack of hardihood with which his tenderheartedness stamped him.

He might have had more success with the young girls whom he met than with the young men, had his own indifference to them not been insurmountable. Dances were fairly frequent, and he was duly invited to all those which occurred in the vicinity. But he could find nothing alluring in the sight of an insipid girl, who appeared at a party with a tweed coat slung carelessly over a dowdy dress, who ducked and kissed her hostess's hand, like an automaton, and who expected to be returned to a chaperon's side between the dances through which she stepped with complete mental and physical detachment. All of these girls bore venerable names, all of them lived in historic houses; and some of them might have been very pretty if they had been properly dressed, or even if they had shown more animation. Hans Christian remembered that the twins, whose dowdiness Trixie had decried, had nevertheless been excellent company. But these highly born Prussian maidens, with their flat figures and faint smiles, were wholly unstimulating to him.

The countryside continued to beguile him, and he went for long walks, usually quite alone, and for long motor rides, on which his grandmother sometimes accompanied him; a *Schwester* had now been put in charge of the General, by a doctor's orders, and the physician also insisted that the Archduchess must have occasional respite from the strain of watching beside her husband. Hans Christian was enthralled by the beauty of the Masurian Lakes, which he and Victoria Luise visited together, lunching upon *Moräne,*[1] in the open air at Nickolaien, and taking a speedboat to Radjanyi afterwards. Every day he found some fresh phase of the landscape which charmed him. He loved to watch the windmills turning slowly in the breeze; to come, unexpectedly, upon some village festival; to see the goose girls sitting motionless in the midst of their flocks. These girls seemed to him the epitome of tranquillity; and he found grace and purpose in the gait of the older women who went, at sundown, with white kerchiefs tied firmly around their heads, to milk the cows forgathered in the pastures, near the picket fences. Only when he saw some ancient crone staggering under the heavy weight of a wooden yoke laid heavily across her shoulders, did he feel his heart contract; it was senseless, it was sinful, that any human creature should be so overburdened. More than once he stopped and tried to take away the water pails depending from these yokes, and carry them himself. Always he met with a blank stare or a bitter protest when he strove to give relief.

Once, he succeeded in overriding the objections so querulously voiced, and walked triumphantly beside the aged woman whose load he had assumed, as far as her home. When he entered it, he was amazed to find how cheerless it was. The flowers which bloomed brightly in its garden, its quaint shape and thatched roof, had given it, from without, a false effect of coziness. Inside it was dark and dingy, and pervaded with a stale smell. But the old woman's daughter, a not uncomely matron, with half a dozen children clutching at her skirts, welcomed him politely, and thanked him, with obvious sincerity, for his kindness.

"Our Trudchen has already told us of the *Herr Baron's* never failing goodness," she said, with feeling. "And now we can see for ourselves how great it is. The *Herr Baron* does us too much honor."

"Is Trudchen yours too?" he asked in surprise, looking up from the small, blond heads which he had been impartially patting, as one by

[1] A fish peculiar to the region, similar to smelt.

one the children left their mother and came shyly clustering around him.

"Yes, *Herr Baron.* She is my eldest *Mädel.* And such a good girl! I do not know what I should do without her, now that I have lost my *Mann* and that I myself must stay at home with all these others," the woman said, amiably but anxiously.

"Could I help in any way? I should be so glad if I could," Hans Christian said eagerly.

"The *Herr Baron* does us too much honor," Trudchen's mother repeated. "But there is nothing, as long as my *Mädel* has work and does it faithfully. She brings her wages home. She is not scatterbrained or silly. She does not run about, Heaven knows where, at all hours of the night, like the daughters of many of my neighbors. She comes straight home from the castle, where I know she is safe, and goes soberly to bed. I have much to be thankful for."

Hansel walked back to the castle in an unusually thoughtful mood. The hall was empty as he entered it, and crossing it, he looked out into the garden to see if his grandfather might be there, in his wheel chair. But the garden, like the hall, was deserted, and a light tap on Victoria Luise's door elicited no response. Apparently both his grandparents were resting. Solitude still pervaded the stairs, as he mounted to the second story. But as he approached his own room, he saw Trudchen standing on the threshold in the same place she had stood when he had first seen her.

It was almost as if she had been waiting for him. Her early terror of him had left her completely; so had the fixed idea that any kindness he showed her must have an ulterior motive; and as if her trust in him had restored her hope in a harsh and harrowing world, she held herself more confidently now. Her pretty little figure was erect, her blue eyes unafraid. She did not even curtsey as he approached her. Instead she looked straight at him and smiled in a way that went to his heart.

"Come into my room a minute. I want to speak to you," he said abruptly.

She followed him without hesitation. When he had closed the door, he went up to her and put his hands on her shoulders.

"Listen to me, Trudchen," he said impellingly.

"I am listening, *Herr Baron.*"

"This afternoon, as I came through the village, I saw an old woman carrying two pails of water on a heavy yoke. It is a sight which always makes me very unhappy. I took the pails away from her, and went home with her. When I reached the house, I found it was your house too. I saw your mother and she told me."

"Yes, *Herr Baron.*"

"She also told me that you were a very good girl, that you bring all your wages home to her, that you help take care of your younger brothers and sisters. Well, I do not know how much your wages are, because Her Serene Highness does not like to tell me about such things. But I know they must be very small, and I know you must need more. So I am going to give it to you. I have a little money of my own, so I can. But you must never tell. You must not tell Her Serene Highness, because she would be very angry at the idea that I was meddling with her servants; and you must not tell your mother because she might misunderstand. You must only let your mother know that from now on you will have more to give her, and she will naturally suppose that the Archduchess has raised your wages. Is that clear?"

"Yes, *Herr Baron,* it is clear."

"Very well. Here are fifty marks to begin with. I shall try to give you fifty marks every month. Now run along, and keep on being a good girl."

"Fifty marks! Fifty marks every month! *Aber, Herr Baron, ich verstehe nicht! Aber, Herr Baron, das kann nicht sein.*"

Before he could stop her, before he so much as realized her intention, she was on her knees before him. She had seized both his hands and was covering them with warm kisses and grateful tears. Terribly embarrassed, he strove to draw them away.

"Look here, you mustn't do that. Listen, Trudchen, I don't like to have you kneel to me, I don't want you to kiss my hands. Stand up this minute and behave yourself."

She paid no attention to what he was saying. When at last he did succeed in lifting his hands, he lifted her with them, because she would not let go. She flung herself against his breast, still crying happily, still murmuring her gratitude. Her soft rosy face looked up into his with infinite devotion. It was so close that his own touched it. The next instant, they were in each other's arms.

CHAPTER 8

It was Hans Christian's habit to sit with his grandfather for an hour every morning and two hours every afternoon. The Archduchess had feared that the boy might cease to do this, when the General's increasing weakness necessitated the abandonment of the wheel chair. She realized that the atmosphere of a sickroom was more trying than that of a garden, and that the sight of a helpless man, stretched stiffly out upon his bed, was far more gruesome in its suggestion than that of a quasi-convalescent, seated, apparently at ease, among pleasant surroundings. She was therefore touched when she found that Hansel, instead of finding pretexts to neglect the tiresome tribute, became more and more solicitously attentive. She realized that he was genuinely distressed at the sadness of a situation which was now admittedly hopeless.

She had not, at first, been inclined to regard his tenderheartedness as an asset. She shared the scorn of the neighborhood concerning his aversion to hunting; and his inopportune questions about wages and working hours irritated her all the more because she detected in them a possible desire to tamper with established custom, in an impracticable manner, rather than because she dreaded to have him discover how hollow was the structure of their house, how essential it was to stretch every resource to the last limit, in order to prop up the tottering frame. When she learned that he had taken Gertraud's water pails away from her and carried them to the old woman's cottage, she had been so much shaken that she had spoken to him without any of her characteristic suaveness; and on their occasional excursions together, when he ceased to regard the countryside with admiration and concerned himself critically with the people instead, she never failed to resent the change.

Once they had driven out from Königsberg to the *Kurische Nehrung* and had spent a happy afternoon there, hunting for amber and wandering over the dunes. The Archduchess was secretly flattered that Hansel should consider her an adequate companion for such outings, though she lamented that they could not extend this one as far as Memel, to the loss of which she was still unreconciled. She was still an excellent walker, and could climb and stoop without effort; but she knew that few boys of her grandson's age would have given her credit for possessing such prowess or the chance to prove it. There was color in her cheeks, as well as laughter in her eyes, for the first time in many a long day when they started on their homeward drive along the isthmus. Then a series of episodes occurred which robbed her of all the pleasure she had felt in her adventure.

A doe emerged from the forest and sprang fearlessly across their path, with twin fawns gamboling in its wake. Hansel stopped the motor abruptly, and gazed at them with delighted eyes. Then, as they disappeared into the leafy depths again, he turned to her eagerly.

"Wasn't that a lovely sight? Do you wonder now that I like to see them leaping like that, instead of lying maimed and bleeding at my feet?"

The Archduchess stiffened instantly. "I thought we had agreed not to bring up that subject again, Hansel," she said in a reserved tone of voice.

"Then you really don't see my point at all?"

"No, I really don't see your point at all. I want you to emulate in every way the men in the class from which you have come. They have all excelled in manly sports. They have all been good shots and great soldiers."

"Don't you think the *Junkers* have any faults at all, grandmother? I believe it's generally conceded that most individuals and most groups have the weakness correlative to their strength, and the vices correlative to their virtues."

"You sound as if you were talking out of a textbook, my dear boy. I am afraid that Harvard is becoming extremely modernistic in its manner of teaching. No—I have never discovered weakness among the *Junkers*, Hansel. They are a race of mighty warriors."

"They lost the World War. There must have been a flaw in the system somewhere. You know, grandmother, I always thought it was strange— The Prussian officers were a gorgeous *looking* lot of men, when I was a kid— I have never forgotten their bright helmets and their long sabres and their flowing cloaks. The first time we went to France, I thought the soldiers there were a slouchy, slovenly lot in comparison. But it was the French who had the more shining spirit, after all, wasn't it?"

"Hansel! I beg of you never to speak in this disloyal manner again! Remember that your father and his brothers, who died gloriously for their country, were all Prussian officers!"

The boy pressed his lips together and put the car into quicker motion. As he did so, he became aware of a magnificent stag, its great antlers towering above its superb head, standing motionless at the edge of the woods. Instantly he slowed down again and looked intently at the stag. The Archduchess could see that his mouth, rigid as he tried to keep it, was quivering, that there were actually tears on his lashes. But he said nothing, and, after a moment or two, he went on again. As they neared the next village, he spoke quietly and conversationally.

"I think we could get some beer or tea here, grandmother, if you'd care for it. There seems to be a little inn facing the *Haff*. Perhaps it would refresh you to get out."

"I should enjoy it very much," she answered formally.

They sat down at a small tin table, one of several placed in the open before the *Gasthaus*. It was very pleasant and peaceful. There were small sailing vessels in the harbor, and the sun, shining over the water, gave a soft reflection. It was not until Hansel happened to notice a plume of smoke rising from an adjacent promontory, that anything happened to mar the restored harmony of their relations.

"Do you see that smudge over there, grandmother? What do you suppose it is?"

"I imagine that someone is smoking fish. It's done in this locality, by putting flounder in a pit with fire underneath it, and covering the hole with heavy canvas. Of course it all has to be watched very carefully."

"I'd like to look at it, wouldn't you? Let's walk over there. Shall we? That is, if you've finished."

The Archduchess rose reluctantly. It was one thing to take a walk over beautiful, clean, sweeping dunes, quite another to pick one's way across rough, dirty ground, strewn with a variety of rubbish and offal. But she did not like to refuse. She went warily beside Hansel to the place where the mound of blackened canvas covered the earth.

A wretched old woman was bending over the mound. She was dressed in voluminous garments, dingy and dilapidated, the remnants of a black knitted shawl knotted closely around her head. Her chapped hands and weather-beaten face were reddened by the wind, her eyes bleary with smoke. She hardly seemed to notice the approach of the strangers. She was too intent upon the painful task with which she was occupied.

Hansel touched her on the arm. "Would you let me look at your fish?" he asked courteously. "I've never seen them drying, like this."

The old woman nodded, apathetically. Then, giving a vigorous tug, she lifted a corner of the canvas. Hansel bent over to help her, but drew back abruptly, blinded by the smoke. It was some moments before his smarting eyes grew accustomed to the vapors and he was able to discern the lines of flounders, suspended in neat rows over the fire underneath. He had hardly been able to take a good look at them, when a gust of wind, scooping under the lines, caused the flames to soar dangerously. The next instant the canvas was on fire.

He sprang up and helped the old woman to stamp it out. It was hard work, and for a few breathless moments, he feared that his curiosity, which had endangered the entire contents of the pit, might actually have destroyed it. But the old woman did not seem to share his concern. She expressed neither alarm nor reproach; and when the fire had finally been put out, she apologized for the trouble she had caused him. He left her staring stolidly after his retreating figure, clutching, with fumbling fingers, at the coins which he had slipped into her hand.

"How long does it take to dry a batch of fish like that?" Hansel asked his grandmother, when they were in the car again.

"I don't know exactly. Four or five hours, I believe."

"And that poor old creature, or some other woman like her, has to stoop over the mound all the time to watch it, with the smoke in her eyes and the wind blowing all around her!"

"Of course. The fish represents her livelihood next winter. She's thankful to have the chance to watch it. It was quite unnecessary for you to give her money— I do not wonder that your mother declines to let you control your own patrimony, considering how you throw coins around."

"Well, I don't throw around many on cards or races."

"I shouldn't mind in the least if you did. That would be quite in keeping——"

"With the traditions of my class? But I mustn't give a wretched old woman a mark or two to make up for the worry and trouble I've caused her?"

The Archduchess had never heard Hansel speak sarcastically before. The tone of her own voice rebuked him.

"You are not going to make an issue out of this episode, are you, Hansel, as you did with Gertraud's water pails?"

"Oh, no. I am not going to make an issue out of anything. And as far as Gertraud herself is concerned, I shan't try to carry her water pails through the village again, if that's any comfort to you."

"It's a great comfort to me. If only you will not do something else equally absurd."

"Don't worry, grandmother. As far as the peasants in the village are concerned, I think I am fast learning to follow in the footsteps of my forefathers."

His smile, usually so pleasant and open, had been ironical and enigmatic as he spoke. This, and the bitterness with which he had made the last remark, still troubled the Archduchess when she thought of them. But this was very seldom nowadays. She was far too preoccupied with her husband's condition to waste worry on a few wretched villagers; and she was too much moved by Hansel's constant kindness to his grandfather to harbor resentment for his occasional failure to conform to caste in either thought or deed.

It was evident that the end could not be distant now, that the General's days, vacant of coherent thought or natural motion, could not be much further prolonged. At last she brought herself to speak of this one night to Hansel, as they left the sick man in the deep drugged sleep which represented the one surcease from his mental and physical wretchedness, and went from his bedchamber into her own.

"We must begin to think of the funeral, Hansel. It is terrible to do so beforehand, but we must."

"Yes, of course. That is, I do not know much about funerals, but I suppose we must. Tell me how I can help you the most, grandmother. I want to help, in every way I can, but I am not sure what I ought to do."

"If you knew of any way in which I could get hold of some money, that would be very helpful to me, Hansel. Funerals cost a great deal of money—especially state funerals, such as we must provide for your grandfather. At the moment, I have no idea where I could raise any— Everything I have is sold or pledged already. Except my jewels. I still have those. If I could find a purchaser——"

"You'd sell your Austrian Imperial jewels?"

"But, my dear boy, the von Hohenlohe jewels were all sold long ago. It is only the Austrian jewels that I have left. And those would have gone too, of course, if I could have found anyone in Germany rich enough to buy them."

She sat down at her dressing table and unlocked a deep drawer. There was a small safe inside, which she drew out and set down among her toilet articles. Then, one by one, she opened its compartments and lifted out their contents: a coronet, two tiaras, necklaces, earrings, bracelets, brooches and rings. There were great pear-shaped pearls among them, emeralds that flashed green fire, rubies that shone like newly spilled blood, diamonds that sparkled with a glacial glitter. For a few moments she fingered them thoughtfully, as if recalling all the vanished glory for which they stood. Then she pushed them back into place, and closed the safe again, her blue-veined fingers trembling as she did so.

"Grandmother, I have a little money. Mother did let me cut into my capital for travel funds, and I'm still well supplied. If a thousand dollars would help at all——"

"A thousand dollars! I must have at least ten times that, immediately, and more very soon. There is not only the funeral to consider. There are other obligations which I must meet. If I do not, I may lose my husband and the only home I have left at the same time! Besides, if you gave me all you have, what would you do then yourself?"

"I don't need much, for the moment. We can go into that later on. I really spend awfully little, and mother would send me more, for an emergency, if I cabled. Besides, my return passage is paid already."

"Your return passage! Yes, of course— In a few weeks now you will be going back to America. And then I shall be entirely alone!"

"Your Serene Highness, I regret to disturb you. But I feel that you and the *Herr Baron* should return to the General's room at once. I have sent Fritz for the doctor. A sudden change seems to have taken place——"

The *Schwester* in charge of the case, usually a placid person, had spoken urgently. The Archduchess rose, and with Hansel followed her back to the sickroom and sat down beside the General's great carved bed, shadowed with heavy draperies. His face had become livid, his breathing stertorous. Occasionally he choked, and seemed to struggle. Then the paroxysm passed, only to renew itself again with increased violence. Victoria Luise turned to the *Schwester* with a cry of anguish.

"This is too terrible! It mustn't go on! Surely there is some way to prevent it!"

"The *Herr General* is unconscious, your Serene Highness. This is far more dreadful for you than it is for him. Nevertheless, when the doctor arrives, he may think it wise to administer further opiates, to insure complete hypnosis."

"I cannot believe that he feels nothing. Every time he gasps, it seems as if he were calling for succor! And still we are giving him none!"

"Grandmother, you must believe what the *Schwester* says. I am sure that it cannot be as bad as it seems. You are right, that would be too terrible."

He put one arm around his grandmother, and with his free hand touched the fingers that lay inert on the counterpane. Hans Christian had never seen death, or its approach, before; as its dread presence came closer and closer, he found that it was in the feeling of those strange fingers that it revealed itself first. All warmth went from them, and all color; they lay like wax in his grasp. As he lifted his fascinated eyes from them to his grandfather's face, he saw that this, too, had slowly changed; the lividness had gone, a beautiful translucency had taken its place. The gasping had ceased too. Breath came more and more gently now, like a series of soft sighs. Then it seemed to cease altogether.

"Hans! My dear husband! Don't go— Don't leave me! You can't— You mustn't! I have no one else in the world!"

Almost as if he had heard his wife, the General drew a deeper breath, and the soft sighs began again. But each one came more faintly than the one before it. At last there was one which seemed to have no end, even as it had no beginning. The *Schwester* met Hansel's questioning gaze, and bent her head.

"Grandmother, grandmother dear, it's all over. He isn't suffering now, he never will any more. You can find some consolation in that, can't you?"

Hans Christian knew that she would want to be alone with her dead, in those last moments before strangers came into the house and laid their alien hands on the lifeless body, to prepare it for burial. The time was so short before the acts which—inevitable though they were—must seem to her like a sacrilege, should be performed, that he had no right to intrude upon it. The only kindness he could show her, the only consolation he could give her, would be in safeguarding her solitude.

He walked out into the garden, to find it steeped in stillness. The very skies were somber, for there were no stars in the heavens; and when he had sat beneath them for an hour or so, he found he could no longer bear the sadness that seemed to sink from them. He rose and went up the dim stairway to his own room.

Unconsciously he paused on the threshold, half dreading, half hoping to see Trudchen standing there, waiting for him. He knew then that as he had mounted the stairs he had unconsciously listened, wondering if he would hear her sobbing with grief because she knew that he was sad. But for once she was absent. The same stillness which had engulfed the garden enveloped the house. There was not a step, there was not a sound, anywhere. He did not have even Trudchen with him at this zero hour.

He switched on the light, and hesitated as he crossed the room. Then he sat down at his desk, opened the inkwell, and drew his pen and paper towards him. When once he had begun to write, he did not stop.

"My dear Mr. Fuller:

You told me, before we left the boat, that if circumstances should ever change, so that my grandmother might consider parting with her jewels, you hoped I would let you know.

Conditions are now such that she would like to do so. If you and Mrs. Fuller would care to come to Schönplatz, my grandmother and I would be glad to have you. If this would not be convenient for you, and you are still interested, I will meet you in Berlin, or in any other place you care to designate.

Very sincerely yours,
Hans Christian Marlowe von Hohenlohe"

He read the letter through, placed it in an envelope, and addressed it. Then he reached for another sheet of paper.

"Dear Mother:

It is very hard for me to write you as I am about to, but I do not see any way to help it, and I hope you will understand.

My grandfather has just died, tonight. He has been sick for a long time, and it has all been hideous to my grandmother. Now she is entirely alone, except for me.

I know our agreement was, that if you would let me come to Germany, I should stay only for the summer, and then return to college. But I hope you will release me from this promise because I firmly believe I ought to stay here.

I feel this way not only because my grandfather has died, though, if he had not, I would have come back, at least for the present. But I feel this way for other reasons too, which seem to me important, and which I will try to explain to you someday, if you are interested.

Of course Schönplatz belongs to me now, and a great many responsibilities go with the ownership. I shall try to meet these as well as I can, though some have arisen that I did not foresee. For one thing, I find that there is almost no money to keep up the place with, and if you would let me have my own, after all, before I am twenty-one, I should be very grateful to you.

Please believe that I am not wilfully disobedient or unreliable or grasping, and that it makes me very unhappy to think that perhaps it will seem to you that I am. But whatever you think, I know that I have to stay.

Always your loving son,
Hansel"

PART III

1924

"The Hedge of the Count"

CHAPTER 9

THE BAROQUE splendor of his hotel at The Hague had a depressing effect upon the American Minister to the Netherlands. From the moment that he entered it, and hastened past the head porter's lair, his discomfort increased apace. He did not like the large lounge, where stolid people sat perpetually around little tables in big chairs, consuming unlimited quantities of liquid refreshment. He did not like the circular dining room, with its rococo white and gold carvings, its glacial mirrors and stiff draperies. He did not like the formal bedrooms, with their inadequate wardrobes and their inevitable center tables, their curtains controlled by complicated pulleys. But when he complained about any or all of it, his wife laughed good-naturedly and told him what he really meant was that he didn't like hotels on general principles, that he found just as much fault with them at home as in Holland; he wanted to get her out into one of those great gloomy houses with damp dripping grounds in the Zorgvliet, where it would take her hours to get into the center of things, and where she would be compelled to have a dozen Dutch servants, who couldn't understand her and whom she couldn't understand, to keep the place running. She had kept house for nearly twenty years, and she had tried hard never to shirk. But now she really thought the time had come——

"What you mean is, Trixie thinks the time has come," the Minister answered, laughing good-naturedly. "Well, maybe it has. A hotel's all right when you're traveling, and I don't know but what this is as good as any. I guess I've got to admit it's better than most. But just the same, now that we know we're going to be staying here at The Hague for the next few years, I do think it would be kind of nice to get settled more permanently. If you don't like the Zorgvliet, there are some handsome houses here on the Lange Voorhout, right in the heart of the city."

"They're big, and they look substantial, same as the people do, if that's what you mean. But when you get into the center of the town, naturally there isn't much garden space. I don't know how good the heating system is in those houses either. I wouldn't call this country hot, exactly, even in summertime, and I think we better take a look around come December, before we sign any leases on the dotted line. Just locate for awhile, Rufus, if you can. It isn't like you to be in such a hurry."

The Minister insisted that he was henpecked, and said that soon he wouldn't be able to call his soul his own; but there was a twinkle in his eye when he did so, and he patted his wife affectionately on the shoulder. If his days had been otherwise more strenuous and stimulating, he might have settled down with better grace to the inertia of hotel life; but after fifty years of uninterrupted activity, he was finding time hanging rather heavily on his hands. This capital city, this "Hedge of the Count," was unstimulating to him. The Court left him cold. His other official contacts were equally disappointing. He would have enjoyed getting out into the country to see the fine herds and fertile farms, but he assumed that he should stick closely to the capital, though he did not seem to be of much use there. The Legation staff was experienced and competent; there was nothing he could do himself at the Chancery which the members of his staff could not do as well, or better, without him. They were extremely polite to him; but he was aware that their courtesy was tinged with condescension. He was the only self-made man among them and the only political appointee; the others were "career diplomats." The Second Secretary, Winthrop Ayer, especially, was a thorn in the Minister's flesh; the more so because, without even the semblance of a struggle, this apparently unsusceptible snob had "taken a tumble" for the Minister's daughter, and Mr. Rhodes did not feel at all sure what the outcome of the infatuation would be.

He had never found Trixie bewildering before. But ever since her arrival in Holland she had baffled him. Not because she preferred the publicity of a hotel to the seclusion of a suburban villa. Not because she scattered a good deal of money around. Not because she would not conform to the prim pattern of The Hague. But because, with dogged determination, she was systematically sight-seeing and studying during the intervals between her escapades. She was going, apparently without enjoyment but with unswerving fidelity, to monuments and museums, and her lack of enthusiasm for these expeditions did not deter her from continuing to pursue them. She was taking lessons in French and German from the only hungry-looking man the Minister had seen in Holland, and practicing for an hour every day on a rented piano, her progress supervised by a corpulent old lady who came rolling into the state suite at the hotel twice a week. Eventually she also suggested that she would like to take a course in Fine Arts at the University. It was at this point that her astonished parent betrayed his increasing amazement.

"A Fine Arts course at the University!" he exclaimed. "Why, Trixie, what's come over you? It was all I could do, at home, to get you to finish high school! And now you want to learn every language in Europe all at once, and hammer away at piano pieces that haven't any tune to them, and pace through picture galleries for hours on end. I can't make head nor tail of it."

"You ought to have made me study harder when I was a little girl. You ought to have told me how important it is to be well educated."

As she spoke, Trixie selected a bonbon from the ornate basket of chocolates, which, together with an even larger basket filled with showy flowers, occupied a place of honor on the center table in the drawing room of the state suite. Winthrop Ayer kept her well supplied with offerings of this sort and she seemed appreciative of them without being cheered by them. Her face was earnest, even slightly troubled, while she munched away at one piece of candy after another. Her father's mood was rapidly becoming more serious still.

"I ought—listen, Trixie, I couldn't have made you study hard when you were a little girl, not if I'd stood over you with a club. I couldn't have made you listen while I talked to you about being well educated, not if I'd tied you to a chair while I did it. You know you could have gone to the University of Kansas if you'd wanted to. You know your mother and I would both have been tickled to death to have you."

"I didn't want to. I'm not sorry now I didn't go, either. But I wish you'd sent me to Farmington or Foxcroft or some other school in the East, or maybe to Lausanne when I was small and later on to the Sacré Cœur in Paris, so that my French would have been good. If I'd gone to college at all I wish I'd started in at Vassar. That's where those twins I met on the boat went. But I think hordes and hordes of girls are depressing, especially as they're all so awfully jolly in a systematic sort of way, as if they were trying hard to make up for not having any men around. So I think instead of going to college I'd rather have gone around the world."

Her father stared at her speechlessly.

"Of course it isn't too late for that even now," she went on. "In fact, I think you ought to make a point of getting to Java while you're Minister to the Netherlands. Someone was saying at the Waroong Djava just yesterday—the new Swedish Attaché I think it was—that no one could completely understand the Dutch people without seeing the East Indies. I'm sure you'd agree with him, Daddy, if you would just go out to the Waroong Djava yourself instead of hanging around that stupid old Haagsche Club all the time. The Javanese waiters wear the cutest things on their heads you ever saw—pieces of batik wound into turbans and finished off with knots that look like rabbits' ears. And the Reistaafel is simply marvelous. I could sit for hours mixing peanuts and cocoanut and chutney and chopped egg and curry into mounds of rice and chicken. And just think how much better it would taste in Batavia than in Scheveningen! Do let's go there, Daddy! Afterwards we could come back by way of Hawaii. It would be simply grand."

"You don't think we ought to take in the Straits of Magellan and Rio de Janeiro before we come back to The Hague by any chance, do you, Trixie?"

"No, because we'd be specializing in Insulinde on this trip. But I do think we ought to get to South America sometime. It's the coming continent."

Decidedly, Winthrop Ayer must have been putting ideas into Trixie's head. The Minister felt sure she had never heard of Farmington or the Sacré Cœur—as indeed he never had himself—before arriving in Holland, much less of international points of view and coming continents. Winthrop Ayer was exactly the sort of person who might be expected to overemphasize the importance of these, since he had grown up in a rarefied atmosphere where they were freely discussed. But when Mr. Rhodes tried to sound out his daughter, he could find no indication that she took Winthrop Ayer's stilted opinions too greatly to heart. She devoured his Krul chocolates and wore his Van Houweningen flowers and accepted his invitations to drink cocktails and eat seafood with him at the Haack Restaurant; but she seemed impervious to his attempts to establish a more intimate footing. Since her emotional indifference to him was apparently so complete, her father could not believe that she would be unduly moved by him as a cultural mentor.

Even though Mr. Rhodes' deductions were not wholly correct, they served to soothe him. But as other suitors began to clutter the scene, the distracted Minister sought elsewhere for a plausible explanation of Trixie's extraordinary behavior. For a time he thought he had found it. A personable youth named Richard Eustis arrived in The Hague, accompanied by his mother, the widow of an outstanding Senator, and herself a woman of great elegance and distinction. They had visited Holland several times and had numerous friends there; so they were not in need of the tourist information perfunctorily handed out at the Legation, nor were they bent upon closer contacts with a quaint country and its cleanly people, like the serious students who occasionally upset the Chancery's well-ordered routine with their importunities. In fact, the Chancery, which suffered from chronic fear that this might happen, made a rather unfortunate mistake as far as Richard Eustis was concerned, upon the occasion of his first call.

He presented his card to the Dutch doorman, with the casual remark that he had come to pay his respects to the Minister, and walking into the outer office, seated himself in a large leather chair, lighted a cigarette, and picked up a dog-eared copy of the *Foreign Service Journal.* The outer office was otherwise empty, and for half an hour no one else entered it. At length, however, a native clerk appeared with Richard's card in his hand, and inquired at which hotel he was staying.

"I'm not at a hotel. I'm with friends on the Violenweg," Richard replied, lighting his fourth cigarette and shifting to a Sunday supplement of the *New York Times,* three weeks old.

Another half hour passed tranquilly by. At the end of that time, Winthrop Ayer opened the door of the outer office and looked Richard over with extreme coolness.

"Well?" he said, when he had completed his inspection.

"Well, what?" inquired Richard.

Winthrop Ayer had been unprepared for such a retort. He was extremely pained by it.

"Just what did you want?" he asked freezingly.

"I didn't want anything. I just came to pay my respects to the Minister. I told the doorman that in the beginning."

"The Minister is extremely busy. And I'm afraid I couldn't interrupt him at present."

"I'm not in any particular hurry. I've waited here an hour already. As long as I get some lunch, sooner or later, I don't especially mind how long I wait."

"The Minister will not be at leisure to receive you at any time this morning, Mr.—er—Mr. Eustis. He has a great many official appointments. They're crowded unusually close together, because he's on the point of leaving town to attend the dedication of a monument to the Founders of the van Rensselaer family, in North Holland. This is an occasion of great international significance, and naturally——"

"Perhaps you think I better come back after lunch?"

For the second time, Winthrop Ayer appeared to study Richard's card before he replied. He finally said with great detachment, "I don't think I should encourage you to do that either, Mr.—er—Mr. Eustis."

"Perhaps you think I better not come back at all?"

"Well, of course, if there is something very urgent, you might tell me what it is. Unless the trouble is financial. I must advise you that there are no provisions which enable us to assist stranded tourists. But——"

"No, the trouble isn't financial. In fact, there isn't any trouble at all. As I've said twice before, I just came in to pay my respects. If not now, whenever it would be convenient for the Minister to see me. But it doesn't matter in the least. I'm immensely intrigued to hear that he's so busy. I'm sure the Secretary of State will be too. He rather had the idea things were quiet here just now, stagnating in fact. But apparently business is booming. Uncle Gilbert will be simply delighted. He—"

"Winthrop, maybe this is one time when I could manage things a little better than you can. I know that doesn't happen often, but suppose I take a try?"

Both young men had been too preoccupied and too angry to observe that the door of the outer office had opened and shut again, and that Rufus Rhodes was standing behind them. For once, this gentle and genial man was angry also. He took Richard's card out of Winthrop Ayer's hand with scant ceremony and glanced quickly at the superscription.

"I'm very sorry you've been kept waiting so long, Mr. Eustis," he said as formally as if he were addressing a contemporary. "Especially as I've been doing crossword puzzles all the morning, hoping and praying that someone would come in to break the monotony. There was one word I couldn't get, and it rode me, so that at last I decided to give up and go home. You can't think of a four-letter epithet common among the Egyptians and ever since, used to express contempt, can you? Well, neither can I, but never mind. I was just passing along the hall when I happened to overhear your conversation with my secretary. It was the first I knew of your being here. Unaccountably your card seems to have been delayed, somewhere between the front door and my own quarters. I apologize. A really good executive always has efficient subordinates. I'm on my way out now, but I'd be delighted if you'd come along with me. I know my wife and daughter would be pleased, too, if you'd drop in on them. How long are you planning to be with us, here at The Hague?"

They went down the Chancery steps together, leaving Winthrop looking after them with venom in his eyes. Within an hour, Mrs. Eustis and the friends she was visiting had been persuaded to join the Rhodes and her son informally at luncheon. It soon transpired that the Eustis' sole purpose in coming had been to renew a pleasant shipboard acquaintance, and if agreeable to the Rhodes family, to further it. With no signs of haste or impatience, they settled down at The Hague in pursuit of this purpose.

Mr. Rhodes did not need his wife's assurance, though this was swift in coming, that she was pleased and flattered by the turn things had taken. Indeed, he was inclined to be pleased and flattered himself. Mrs. Eustis was the most charming woman he had ever met, and her son had inherited many of her most attractive qualities. It was with increasing bewilderment therefore, that the Minister found his daughter disposed to give short shift to Richard Eustis. Instead of placing the flowers and confectionery he sent her on the center table, as she did those from Winthrop Ayer, she tossed them into the scrap basket; he himself rescued a large box of Haagsche Hopjes, the famous coffee candy of The Hague, under the impression that it had been thrown away by mistake, only to find that Trixie had disposed of it on purpose; so he refrained from rescuing dahlias and gladioli from a similar fate. He refrained also from comment when she declined to go swimming with Richard Eustis at Scheveningen, on the ground that the water was too cold, though she had disported herself in it nearly every day all summer, or dancing with him at the House of Lords, on the ground that it was too crowded, though she had been consistently helping to swell that crowd for some months herself. But when she flatly refused to spend the week end at a beautiful estate near Doorn, which belonged to friends of the Eustises who had kindly included the Rhodes in their comprehensive invitation for a visit, he ventured to give tongue to his astonishment, though he tried to do so tactfully.

"I think you'd enjoy those people, Trixie. I hear they have one of the finest places in the Netherlands, that they've fixed it up to look like one they had in Java, spacious and green and open and all that. It seems that lots of the estates around Doorn are owned by families who have spent a good deal of time in the East Indies and brought back a considerable feeling for the exotic, as your friend Winthrop Ayer would say. They run their lives and plant their grounds to give 'an impression of leisure and luxuriance.' It ought to be very pleasant, staying with them. Besides, you might get some pointers on that world trip you want to take."

"I'd like to go to Doorn all right. But I'd rather go sometime when Richard Eustis isn't around."

"Well now, if it hadn't been for the Eustises you wouldn't have been invited there at all."

"Not yet. But maybe later on I will. I'll take a chance on it anyway."

There was no doubt about it, Trixie was patiently and persistently building towards some goal which she not only hoped but expected to achieve. Her father wished she would tell him what it was. But though their relations had always been cordial, they had never been close. He could not force her confidence beyond a certain point. However, he felt impelled to ask one rather leading question.

"You don't seem to care much for Richard Eustis. Have you got anything special against him?"

"Yes. He's fresh."

The Minister was completely taken aback by this rejoinder, not only by the immediacy and candor of the announcement, but by its unexpected implications. He had never unloaded prudish advice upon his daughter, or asked her prying questions; but though he shrank slightly from admitting it, even to himself, he would not have supposed that she would take what her mother called "liberties" too seriously. He knew that the "crowd" with which she had grown up took a certain amount of "petting" for granted; and Trixie's type almost automatically provoked it, in any time and place. Any young man would be likely to find his arm stealing around her waist or his hand straying over her shoulder, before he was aware of it. That was to be expected. The unexpected lay in the disclosure that Trixie so deeply resented the idea of any such overture.

"Well, Trixie—of course I don't know how you young people run things nowadays. But in my time when a young fellow wanted to marry a girl, she didn't think he was being fresh, as you call it, if he sort of showed her how he felt."

"What did she think if he showed her how he felt, as *you* call it, first, and then asked her to marry him three or four months later, after he found out that she wasn't such an easy necker as he supposed? I don't know what she thought, but I think it's disgusting."

"Now, Trixie, I believe you're a little hard on Richard Eustis, I really do. I believe he's very fond of you and that he'd make you a good husband. I believe——"

"Daddy, I don't want to marry Richard Eustis or anyone else who just cares about—well, you know. I want him to think I'm wonderful, *every way,* just as I think he's wonderful every way. I mean, the way I would, if I—if there were anybody—so I've got to learn things, don't you see, just in case—because the way I am now no one would love me, really and truly, no one that mattered."

She leapt up, and left the room hurriedly, slamming the door after her. The Minister was not sure, but he thought her voice had trembled a little as she spoke. So she was troubled, seriously troubled, and she was taking Winthrop Ayer in earnest after all, because she thought he could help point the way to the paths which she desired to tread. The Minister, who would gladly have given his right hand to supply his only daughter with every possible "advantage" himself, felt humbled and disheartened at the idea that he had failed her. Even the knowledge that he had done so inadvertently did not comfort him much. He had never heard the phrase *ad astra per aspera;* but if he had he would still have said that if Trixie were going star snatching, he would like to smooth her ascent to the heavens.

During the next few days he pondered the situation in solemn silence, and rather reluctantly he told his wife he thought they had better decline the invitation to Doorn. Shortly afterwards, the Eustises took their departure from the Netherlands. Mr. Rhodes had the impression they were puzzled also, that mother and son alike had assumed that the eventual success of Richard's suit was practically assured before they had come to The Hague at all, that only details regarding it remained to be settled. His resentment at finding that Trixie had unconcernedly led two families into a blind alley and with the same unconcern left them there, was assuaged only by the discovery that his daughter had been greatly influenced by Mrs. Eustis, even though she declined to accept her as a mother-in-law. It was due to Mrs. Eustis, in no small measure, that Trixie's sight-seeing ceased to be stereotyped. She began to find beauty beyond the museums and monuments which had imprisoned her at first. It was with Mrs. Eustis, for instance, that she first went to the butter market in Middleburg, bringing home the costume that started a collection of these, and a great deal of correlative study into the subject. It was also with Mrs. Eustis that she first went out to see the fishing fleet starting off for Iceland, its sails as red as the sunset into which it was steering. And a week or so later, she asked her father enthusiastically if he would not enjoy seeing it too.

"It's wonderful, Daddy, up there on the coast, with the colored nets and the silvery-looking catch spread out to dry, and the fishermen's families all standing around waiting to see them go out on Sunday nights, or clumping along as fast as their wooden shoes will take them to welcome the fleet back the next Saturday. There are nearly a thousand boats, all with their own numbers painted on them and all so perky. I like boats to be perky, don't you?"

"Well, Trixie, that's another of those things I hadn't thought much about, before I came to Holland. But now that you speak of it, I guess I do. They need to be perky, nosing their way up into the North, like they have to. It's cold and rough up there. And the men on them have to be pretty plucky. They lead a hard life."

"They get what they go out after," Trixie remarked cryptically.

She meant more than she said, very often nowadays, her father reflected, and her voice had taken on a different tone, no matter in what language she was speaking. She also appeared to enter and leave a room in a manner more studied and less spontaneous, and the arts of dress and dining had taken on a new meaning for her. Most of these metamorphoses could be laid, directly or indirectly, at Mrs. Eustis' door. The most welcome form of all which Trixie's appreciation of this lady's example and precepts took, however, lay in her change of attitude about a residence. Mr. Rhodes gathered it was largely due to Mrs. Eustis that his daughter gleaned the fact that no hotel, however smart, could indefinitely serve as a suitable setting for a dignified diplomat of assured standing. Once convinced of this, she began house hunting with zeal, dragging her still hesitant mother along with her, and finally announced she had found exactly what they needed: a tall house on the Javastraat, with the dining room and service quarters on the ground floor, double drawing rooms and a library above them, and the bedrooms higher still. Her mother was afraid the servants would "mind the stairs," and could not understand the blank looks with which the first applicants for positions turned upon her, when she asked them, through an interpreter, if they objected to this feature. Trixie's father teased her, telling her that it was only the name of the street which had decided her. But as a matter of fact, he and his wife were supremely satisfied with the comfort of the commodious quarters in which they were presently installed.

The winter began agreeably. Contrary to Mrs. Rhodes' expectations, the Dutch servants proved uncomplaining and the heating system adequate. They were all very comfortable in the big house on the Javastraat, and the social contacts which had been unsatisfying at first, were more agreeable now that they were less strange. The Rhodes called meticulously on all their fellow guests within twenty-four hours of each dinner to which they were invited, and they began to entertain themselves, finding a ready response to their hospitality. The Minister's days were not empty any longer. He had begun to establish a sense of fellowship with the Dutch, to find friends in all sorts of unexpected quarters. One of these friends was a retired priest, Father Maartens, who had spent the active years of his life in Wichita, and who now lived, with his two aged sisters, in a small house in the heart of Haarlem. Another was a highly successful businessman possessing relatives in Topeka whom he had visited from time to time. Mynheer Kool was entirely self-made; and the monstrosity of concrete and glass which he had built for himself bore no shadow of a resemblance to Father Maartens' cozy and artistic quarters.

Trixie, whose conception of the artistic was undergoing transition, insisted that this house gave her the creeps, especially the staircase made of strawberry and chocolate colored marble; the piano lamps shaded with Spanish shawls, and the ruby-tinted door surmounting the courtyard. But she did not deny that Mynheer Kool and his buxom wife were themselves very likable, and that the "snowballs" which they served during the evenings devoted to table football at their house were the most glorified sort of doughnut which she had ever tasted. She also had a word of passing praise for the red wine cooked with spices, brought into the fantastic drawing room in a big kettle, and drunk hot; but since she was even more fully and agreeably occupied than her parents, she did not often go to the Kools with them. She had begun to make her own friends among the Dutch, and had several pink-cheeked young Netherlanders among her followers now. One of these, Kleijyn van Boltzelaer, lived in Doorn, and had a sister Sophia, conveniently near Trixie's age; the girl's confident assertion that she would not long be dependent upon Richard Eustis for opportunities to enjoy the transplanted magnificence of Insulinde was quickly fulfilled. The van Boltzelaer family owned a tea plantation near Buitenzorg, and

Trixie returned to The Hague after her first stay on their Dutch estate prepared to press still further upon her parents the desirability of a trip to Java. Surely they must agree with her that life on a tea plantation would be too romantic for words, that they ought not to miss such a wonderful chance to see what it was like. She had found turbaned Malay servants and copious Reistaafels even more intriguing in a private house than in a restaurant; cold coffee essence served with hot milk, early in the morning, and steaming tea sheltered by a padded cosy, late in the afternoon, had proved added attractions to the scheme of life; while initiation into the mysterious rites of Javanese dancing had been most alluring of all.

"So the van Boltzelaers have asked you to visit them on their tea plantation too, have they?" Rufus Rhodes asked his daughter, his shrewd eyes twinkling. "You're sure they included your father and mother in the invitation, are you? And you're sure it was just a visit that was suggested by the entire family, not a permanent residence, by Kleijyn? When you begin to talk about the romantic aspects of the situation, Trixie, I can't help wondering."

"Don't be silly, Daddy," Trixie said rather sharply. It was so seldom she spoke sharply nowadays, that she aroused her father's suspicions. It occurred to him, with an anxious pang, that Kleijyn van Boltzelaer was an even better match, in his way, than Richard Eustis, and that in this case it was unthinkable that Trixie could object to a suitor as "fresh." Kleijyn's love-making would certainly be circumspect and deferential; on the other hand, it might be persistent; and these stubborn Netherlanders had a faculty for getting their way in the end. It was no part of Rufus Rhodes' plan that his only child should be separated from him by half the world, and he did not like the sound of the word "romantic" in connection with the tea plantation. But after a moment or two, Trixie began to rattle on about something else: It appeared that she had been invited, with the van Boltzelaers, to lunch at Doorn Haus, by the ex-Kaiser and his second wife, the Princess Hermine, who were on very friendly terms with the neighboring gentry. Trixie was quite as excited over this actual experience as she was over the remote prospect of Buitenzorg. She described the gardens and drawing rooms at Doorn Haus minutely, the clambering roses, the guarded moat, the mellow tapestries, the multitudinous *objets d'art.* She thought the Princess Hermine, whom everybody called "Your Majesty," just as if she had been really an Empress and not the wife of an abdicated Emperor, was "just as nice as she could be"; and she thought the Kaiser himself was "too cute for anything."

"He isn't ferocious at all," she said enthusiastically. "He's a friendly, white-haired old gentleman, very spruce and sprightly. When he came out into the hall to meet us, his eyes were twinkling, and he had a bouquet of sweet peas in each hand—pink for me and lavender for Sophia. He had raised them himself and he seemed pleased as punch about it all. I'm glad mine were the pink ones. I pressed some of them in my diary. Did I tell you, Daddy, that I've begun to keep a diary? Well, anyway, I have— The Emperor talked to Sophia and me both in the nicest way, as if we were grown up, I mean, and important. He was dignified but he wasn't a bit distant. I felt as if I'd known him all my life, in no time at all. He gave me his picture, autographed, when we came away, and so did the Empress. She sent mother a tea cosy too, like the ones the van Boltzelaers use, only bigger and more elaborate. She made it herself, out of puffy yellow silk covered with white embroidery, and worked an 'H' with a crown on top of it in one corner. If mother doesn't want to use it, I'd like to put it away in my hope chest. I've decided to have a hope chest, didn't I tell you that either?"

"No, Trixie, you certainly didn't. I should think there would be time enough for that when——"

"It's a form of preparedness," Trixie flashed back. Then changing the subject before he could comment again, she rattled on. "You don't suppose people at home were mistaken, do you, in heaping quite so much war guilt on the Kaiser's head? There was a man visiting at Doorn named Colonel von Mitweld, who thinks the sun simply rises and sets on the old gentleman's head. The van Boltzelaers told me he spent most of his time at Doorn Haus, that he would like to head a Restoration Movement. And what do you suppose? I got to talking with this Colonel, and I found out he was the uncle of a boy I'd met on the boat coming over. He'd told me about the Kaiser too. His mother used to know him when she was a young girl, and he was awfully nice to *her*. She used to go to the Palace a lot, in Berlin, to balls and things, and she remembers how the six young Princes used to look when they came clattering out of the cobbled courtyard on horseback with their little sister beside them——"

"I'm not sure that I quite follow you, Trixie. I don't understand exactly who it is you're talking about now."

"Oh, it doesn't matter! But I hope you and mother will go to Doorn Haus too someday, Daddy. The Emperor and Empress both said that they'd be very pleased if you would. And we could all stay in the Orangerie, that's what they call the guest house, and have rooms with oil paintings hanging over big double washstands, and sleep under feather beds made of lace and red satin."

"Is that the latest thing, Trixie, in household decoration?"

"You know it isn't, Daddy. But it looks comfortable even if it does sound queer, and I like it."

There were more visits to Doorn, as the autumn advanced, and in due course Rufus Rhodes shared in the manifold advantages of these without too much concern as to where they might be leading. Kleijyn van Boltzelaer had not been summarily dismissed, like Richard Eustis, nor did Trixie accept him quite as diffidently as she did Winthrop Ayer. But she had many other preoccupations which distracted her. The Fine Arts course had become a reality, and she went on with her music and French. She learned to skate too, patronizing the Haagsche Isclub with as much zeal and far more enjoyment than she put into her studies. She always returned from the rink with her eyes shining and her cheeks glowing. Secretly, her father said to himself, she was getting prettier every day of her life.

He had never been more convinced of this than he was one evening in early December, when, contrary to her custom, she came home alone. Her father was sitting by the fire in the big paneled library when she entered it, a glass of hot, spiced wine and a cheese platter on the table beside him, contentedly turning the pages of his latest "find" from Martinus Nijhoff, the bookseller on the Lange Verhoot whose steady customer he had become. The sense of general well-being that comes from warmth and food and drink pervaded him, and as he glanced up at his daughter, he felt this sense deepen and take on tenderness. She had never looked lovelier. A small gray fur cap rested jauntily on her brown hair, and her trimly belted burgundy-colored coat was buttoned close to her throat under a collar of the same soft fur. She tossed the muff and gloves she was carrying lightly down on the sofa, and crossed the room to kiss him. Her cold cheek, pressed against his own, was as fresh and fragrant as a winter flower, and warm as her lips were, there was a crystalline quality to her caress. The sparkle of snow seemed to encompass her.

"Why look who's here!" he said affectionately, laying aside his book and drawing her down to the arm of his chair. "I didn't expect you back for hours yet. I supposed you were skating down the Molenvliet through the meadows to Leyden in the moonlight. Didn't I hear something to that effect?"

"The rest of the crowd went. At the last moment I decided I wouldn't. I thought there might be some mail here for me."

"You didn't give up a skating party for a letter, did you?"

"Yes. Because I hoped it might be a very special sort of letter."

She rose from the arm of his chair, took off her hat, and began to unbutton her coat. Underneath it she was sheathed in close-fitting red silk, cut in a V at the neckline, which accentuated the curves of her young figure and the whiteness of her throat. Released from her wrappings, she nestled down beside him again.

"Daddy, do you mind if I talk to you confidentially?"

"Trixie, my—my dear little daughter——"

"I hoped you wouldn't. Because, you see, I'm in love. I have been, ever since last summer. I've wanted to tell you about it, only I haven't dared. But tonight, sort of, I feel as if I could."

Rufus Rhodes cleared his throat. "Who is this boy you're in love with, Trixie?" he inquired, striving to speak casually. "Anyone I know?"

"Well, not exactly. I've talked to you about him sometimes—without ever saying I was in love with him, I mean. But you never seemed to be much interested or take much notice. Mother knows him though. She likes him too. No one could help liking him."

For several months now Trixie had been referring to Mrs. Rhodes as mother instead of mumma and until now the Minister had never failed to twit her about it. At the moment, however, he did not even notice.

"You don't mean someone else you met on the boat? There seems to be no end of the people you met on that boat! We've already had that Carruthers woman who had even Winthrop Ayer frozen with fear when she turned up, and the banker's wife who looked as if she'd just helped herself to Cartier's window dressing, not to mention the looks of the banker! You're not talking about that German boy—are you? Hans von Hohenlohe, if that's his name?"

"Yes, Daddy. Only I don't ever think of him as Hans von Hohenlohe. I think of him as Christian Marlowe."

"Wasn't his father a German? Hasn't he gone back to Germany to stay? Doesn't he live there now?"

"Yes, Daddy. And I know you don't like Germans much. That's why I've dreaded to tell you. But his mother's an American. She's a Senator. That makes her very American, doesn't it? It was she who used to know the Kaiser when she was a young girl. Don't you remember I told you, the first time I came back from Doorn, that there was someone? Well, anyway, you're bound to like her, and I'm sure you'll like Chris too, just as mother does, just as everyone does."

"You're sure I'll like him! How am I going to know whether I like him or not without meeting him?"

"Well, you see, Daddy, I hope you're going to meet him. If he should happen to come to Holland, for instance, at Christmastime, of course you would be likely to meet him. Because——"

"If he should happen to come to Holland at Christmastime! But why should he? It's a time most people spend with their own families. And Prussia's a long way from The Hague!"

"Yes, I know. But I wrote and asked him if he and his grandmother wouldn't come and spend Christmas with us. I thought it would be terribly lonely for them on that big place in East Prussia. You know his grandfather has died and I think Christmas must be hard to live through, don't you, when there's been a death in the family that same year? You must keep remembering——"

"But look here, Trixie— Have you told your mother what you've done? Does she know about this?"

"No, but she won't mind. That is, if you don't. And I thought I'd better tell you about it, without waiting any longer, because Chris has had time to answer my letter by now. I expect I'll find one from him waiting for me in my room, saying he's coming."

Her voice, which had been unnaturally shy, suddenly became unnaturally joyous. As she leaned over and kissed him again, Rufus Rhodes felt the full significance both of her shyness and of her joy. So here was the explanation at last of her determination to "improve," of her indifference to Winthrop Ayer and her resentment towards Richard Eustis, and her procrastination regarding Kleijyn van Boltzelaer. She wanted to be worthy of Hans von Hohenlohe, she wanted to find favor in his eyes. Steadily, for months now, she had been laboring towards that end. Secretly she had held that hope to her heart.

Her father did not know what to say to her. He was deeply moved, tremendously touched; but he was troubled too. It was true that he did not like Germans on general principles; though he had never known many of them personally, he had shared the opinion, common in Kansas, that they had been bullies before the War and whiners after it; instinctively he recoiled from the possibility, so suddenly presented to him, of acquiring one for a son-in-law. But his anxiety went deeper than that. A fear for the future, such as he had never known before, seemed to strike suddenly into the depths of his being, with the poignancy of a sharp pain. How could this beloved child of his find happiness and peace amid the alien corn which seemed so fair and fruitful to her inexperienced eyes? Yet if she had set her heart upon this stranger, who would be able to persuade her that she should give him up? She had the same tenacity of purpose, the same singleness of heart, which had taken her father all the way from a poverty-stricken farm laid desolate by drouth, to a luxurious Legation in one of the world's proudest and pleasantest cities——

"I'm going upstairs now to get my letter," Trixie said, still joyously.

The confidence with which she spoke only seemed to strengthen her father's misgivings. He watched her silently as she picked up first her muff and gloves, then her hat and coat. She did so slowly, as if she were waiting for him to speak to her. And still he found nothing to say, though he did manage a smiling salute. She left the room, and when she had gone, it seemed hushed and dark. The fire had sunk to a faint glow; there was no longer any sound of licking flames and crackling wood; and the dark paneling had absorbed the light as a sponge soaks up water. The Minister picked up the glass at his side, but the wine was stale and tepid; the warmth and aroma had gone from it, and the drink had ceased to be stimulating. He had lost the place where he had been reading, and his book had slipped to the floor. All the comfort, all the cheer of the evening seemed to have vanished. He drifted back to the anxious questions which seemed so unanswerable.

He was still sitting there, half an hour later, when Mrs. Rhodes came bustling into the room. She was already dressed for dinner, with some resplendency. She had found a very good shop called Kuhne's, on the Plaats, that kept French models, and she had bought a number of dresses there. The one which she was wearing now was made of noisy green silk, and it was cut more daringly than any she had ever owned before. She had half feared and half hoped that her husband would make some comment on it. But from the way he looked at her, she might have been wearing any old thing, bought back in Rhodesville.

"For mercy's sake, Rufus!" she exclaimed with unaccustomed sharpness. "Aren't you dressed yet? You don't mean to sit there and tell me you've forgotten we're having dinner with the Foreign Minister, do you?"

"I'm sorry, Julia. To tell you the truth, I'm afraid I had. But I'll hurry. I'll be ready in just a minute. Is Trixie going with us?"

"Why no! You seem to have forgotten everything tonight, Rufus! She's gone skating, down the canal to Leyden, with a group of young people."

It was on the tip of his tongue to say that Trixie had changed her plans for the evening as completely as he had forgotten his. But something silenced him. If Trixie had not told her mother, herself, that she was in the house, he would not do so either. But in spite of his haste, he knocked on the door of his daughter's room on his way to his own.

"Come in," she said tonelessly.

Trixie had made her room very charming, with furniture painted in pastel shades, and pale blue silk draperies embroidered with birds and flowers. Genre pictures hung on the tinted walls and a little gilt clock ticked cheerily on the mantelpiece between the amorous porcelain shepherd that stood on one side of it and the coy porcelain shepherdess that stood on the other. The clock was striking eight as the Minister went in, which should have served as a further warning to him that he was late, but which failed to do so. He knew from the way Trixie spoke that something had happened, already, to make her unhappy. The shyness had gone from her voice and so had the joy.

She was standing at the window between the pretty blue curtains, looking down at the street. She was not crying. But she did not seem to be seeing anything either.

"Didn't you get your letter, Trixie?" her father asked gently.

"Yes. I got it."

Rufus Rhodes waited, and the strange poignant pain darted through his body again.

"Chris isn't coming."

"Why, Trixie, I'm sorry, I'm very sorry. I know you're disappointed. If there's anything——"

"Of course, I'm disappointed. But I wouldn't have minded that so much if he had wanted to come and couldn't. His letter's very polite. You can see it, if you like. But I can tell from the way it's written that he could have come and that he didn't want to. There isn't anything you could give me or do for me that can make up for that."

She had managed to speak steadily, and to hold her head high while she spoke. But as she finished what she had to say, her lips quivered and a little gasping sob came through them. The next instant she had hidden her face on her father's broad shoulder and was crying as if her heart would break.

He found his own voice at last. "There," he said cheerfully, "there. Listen, Trixie– I've been thinking things over, about that trip to Java you mentioned, and I believe you've got a good idea. I believe I'll go down to the steamboat office in the morning and see about tickets. I believe——"

"If you believe taking me to Java or anywhere else will make me forget Chris Marlowe or give him up, you're mistaken!" Trixie announced with startling clarity.

She had raised her face again, and she was already resolutely wiping her eyes with a small crumpled handkerchief as she spoke. Then she gave her father a slight shove.

"If you don't go and get dressed, the Foreign Minister will probably skin you, or whatever else they do to delinquent diplomats," she said firmly. "Don't you worry about me either. I don't need to go to Java or anywhere else, just now. I'm going to stay right on the spot, like General So and So, and fight this out along these lines if it takes all summer."

PART IV

1926

"The Beautiful White Horses"

CHAPTER 10

HANS CHRISTIAN sat in the small office at the right of the latticed entrance to the *Gestudsekretariat,* painstakingly trying to balance the Schönplatz stud books. It was a tedious task, for he had always hated figures. Involuntarily, his eyes kept wandering to the weathervane, in the form of a prancing horse, which surmounted the tower of the granary across the cobbled courtyard and which had always fascinated him. His thoughts wandered much farther afield.

He had been at Schönplatz for two years now—two years of unmarked monotony. His mother had not declined to send him his patrimony; indeed, she had not so much as bargained with him for its undisputed possession. She had shown herself generous as well as just, though it would have been a simple matter for her to stipulate that the price of his independence must be the completion of his college course. She had not even referred to his failure to keep the promise upon which her consent to his temporary absence had been based; her letters had contained neither recriminations nor reproaches. On the other hand, they had been increasingly impersonal, increasingly aloof. He scanned them in vain for signs of sympathy and terms of tenderness. Instead she wrote in a way which indicated that her life was crowded and complete without him, and it did not occur to him that she did this defensively, because she was wounded to the quick by his desertion. She did not respond to his repeated suggestions that she should come to Schönplatz during the summer, when the Senate was not in session. The Washington scene, on which she had quickly attained a prominent place, seemed all-absorbing to her. She moved proudly and powerfully from one triumph to another, her beauty undiminished, her security unassailable. Although she was the imagined figure on his horizon, and his grandmother the visible one, she was far the more vivid and vital of the two.

For Victoria Luise was also more and more withdrawn from him, and in her self-imposed isolation, which meant isolation for Hans Christian also, she sat so surrounded with the shadows of the past that at times her own form seemed indistinguishable from these. She never discarded the heavy crepe in which she had emerged from her chamber on the night of the General's death; apparently it had been in complete readiness to assume at any moment, and to Hans Christian there was something ghoulish in this anticipation of her widow's weeds. She had directed, with a skillful hand, the details of the state funeral which had been a superb spectacle, somber only in its implications; and she had shown herself completely composed during the calls of condolence made upon her by the local gentry. But though she had returned these, she had not encouraged their repetition. She had not even invited her daughter and son-in-law, Rita and Friedrich von Mitweld, and their children to come back to Schönplatz a second time after the General's death; and she had not left there herself, either to visit them in Bavaria or to go anywhere else in Germany. The sale of her jewelry had been accomplished without her personal supervision; Hans Christian had spared her the ordeal of an actual meeting with Mr. and Mrs. Fuller. Afterwards the direction of the estate had been turned over to him as the male heir without protest or interference on her part. But if she appreciated the sacrifice which he had made to stand by her, or recognized how trying the unrelieved tedium of the form of existence which she had forced upon him must be to a normal youth, she had never given any sign that this was so.

Hans Christian had not expected effusive expressions of gratitude; but he missed the awaited sign of its existence; and he longed, unutterably, for some stir in the sequence of days which brought him no stimulation, no variety, and no sense of progress. He had moments of feeling that the horse on the weathervane moved in a larger orbit than he did, and with more animation.

Resolutely he turned back to the balance sheets and tried to focus his thoughts no less than his gaze upon them. In themselves they were not disheartening. The year before they had shown a deficit which he could ill afford. Not only had his inexperience been against him; there had been a series of "bad breaks" for which he had in nowise been to blame: he had found that much of the stable flooring was rotten, and he had been obliged to replace crumbling wood with fresh planks; an unseasonable storm had destroyed a large part of the crops just as they were ready to harvest; and Otto, the "apple boy," had proven unworthy of his trust, and had failed to make the daily rounds with his wicker basket at foaling time when cleanliness in the stalls was essential to the welfare of the young colts. Hans Christian had not immediately grasped the character of Otto's calling, for he had not unnaturally assumed that an "apple boy" gathered up fruit rather than dung; and later he had had several clashes with the youngster, finding him surly and slovenly as well as negligent. He had been disposed towards mercy, upon discovering that Otto's weekly wage came to less than two marks, and had tried to reform him by reminders of "apple boys" who had risen to the rank of keepers and even stud masters. But this had been to no avail and Otto had been relegated to the scullery, under threat of still severer discipline and with no chance of advancement. But this was not until his carelessness had been disastrous.

So all in all it had been a bad year. But this year Hans Christian seemed in a fair way to do better. Though many repairs on the buildings were indicated, none had been essential; there had been a bumper crop and he had been able to sell produce besides stocking his own storehouses; and Max, Otto's successor, did his current duty meticulously and appeared to have his eyes fixed upon future advancement which would be well deserved. To be sure, Hans Christian was paying him three marks a week, which was economically unsound, considering the modest dimensions of the total budget for the stud. But after all, Hans Christian had been told that the beautiful white horses, whose origin merged into so lovely a legend, would never represent solid revenue. That came from the sheep, in whose substantial presence there had never been anything mystic, anything symbolic. The first of the flock had been bought by Kurt von Hohenlohe, who had returned to Schönplatz after the Napoleonic Wars to find ruin and desolation reigning there. In his extremity he had appealed to the *Oberpräsident* of East Prussia for co-operation, only to be brusquely informed that it was not consistent with the honor and station of a nobleman, whatever his straits, to ask or accept help from the State. Stung by this rebuff, Kurt had ridden savagely through the woods, his distracted thoughts revolving: Where could he turn? What could he do? When his mind ceased to operate in circles, he had come to an abrupt decision and taken a desperate step. Walking into the bare cold study of the village pastor, he had demanded the immediate overturn of three hundred taler from the meagre Church funds. The bewildered Divine, too dumbfounded to refuse, had yanked open the small strongbox, which contained the contributions which his flock had made to his salary, and had poured the taler into the Count's outstretched hands without query or complaint. Kurt had stalked out and bought sheep.

From the first they had multiplied and prospered. They took prizes and they made money. Their wool was sought for the manufacture of beaver hats; their lambs were bespoken by breeders everywhere; their flesh furnished unlimited food. Kurt, the incipient bankrupt, had quickly become a man of means and had bequeathed a legacy to his descendants which had continued to expand up to the time of the World War. Indeed, it had survived even that, albeit in a shrunken state. In spite of his revolt against unqualified ancestor worship, Hans Christian felt considerable admiration for Kurt's resourcefulness, though he doubted if this lusty landowner had ever been troubled with scruples as to whether his conduct in holding up his pastor for Church funds had been more in keeping with the "station and honor of a nobleman" than squeezing something from the State coffers would have been. After all, there was nothing in Kurt's record to show that he had ever been a squeamish man. The Great Frederick himself, in promoting him to the rank of General, had remarked, "I am giving you the High Command because you are a rough and ready man. The lily-livered creature who cannot show himself coarse upon necessity does not create and keep order among the Brigadiers."

The saving grace of coarseness, if such it were, had certainly manifested itself more than once, not only in Kurt von Hohenlohe, but in his antecedents and his progeny as well. True, there had been scholars and scientists and occasionally a conscientious skeptic among them; one had been a disciple of Kant, another had prepared a pamphlet against *Ausgedehnten Gottesdienst und krasses Gesangbuch.*[1] But for the most part they had been men of brawn rather than of brain, buccaneers and breeders rather than students and celibates. Rather surprisingly, they had married wisely and well, on the whole. They were a sensual lot, but they had brought no undowered brides and none with tarnished reputations to Schönplatz; not a few of the girls who had come there had carried culture and consecration to the castle, and had shown themselves pious even in their pleasures. The ancestral portraits, neatly paired, which hung in Hans Christian's room, did not reveal a single female form or face which was lacking in grace and refinement. On the distaff side, the family tree was fair as well as fruitful.

Hans Christian sighed as he picked up the balance sheets which he had laid down again to gaze out of the window at the weathervane, while considering the subject of the sheep, and all that their acquisition by Kurt implied. He would not have been averse to imitating this ancestor's highhanded methods, if he could have done so, instead of plodding along month after month trying vainly to make both ends meet. But the occasion to show similar resourcefulness never seemed to arise. Perhaps because the World War had not left the same sort of an aftermath as the Napoleonic Wars. Perhaps because there were no more pliant pastors left whose strongboxes could be commandeered. Perhaps because he himself was lacking in those essential qualities

[1] Long-drawn-out Church Services and Vulgar Hymn Books.

which had made Kurt's boldness irresistible. He did not know. It was all a problem, all a puzzle, like everything else.

For times had certainly changed. It was no longer considered inconsistent with the "station and honor of a nobleman" to have help from the State. There was hardly a *Herrenhaus* in East Prussia, as far as Hans Christian knew, which did not take *Osthilfe* as dole; it had come to be regarded as a *Junker* prerogative. Some of his neighbors squandered the sums they received at expensive hotels in Berlin during the winter season, or on the balmy Riviera; others, more conscientiously inclined, spent it on the upkeep of estates which without it would have been close to disintegration. The Countess, whose immense property adjoined Schönplatz, spent all her share on her roofs, which covered acres, and which for years had been in a crumbling condition. Chris accepted what he could get, which was little enough considering his needs, along with the others. At first he had done so reluctantly and shamefacedly; but now he had come to take it all as a matter of course, though he tried to avoid thinking about it, aware that searching reflection would result in a smirching sense of degradation. And elsewhere in Germany, he knew, there were murmurings, less and less hushed all the time, against the so-called "corrupt distribution of public funds in East Prussia." At any moment these murmurings—far more bitter and menacing than any he had ever heard in America—might become protests; at any moment an open secret might become an open scandal. To avert this, it was rumored that there was a plan to take over the large estates which could not be made to pay, and distribute them among small peasant holders like the parents of Otto and Max. If this plan were put into effect, Schönplatz might be among the first of the great places to suffer dismemberment. There had never been greater need for prompt and efficient action on the part of the landed gentry than now.

"Bitte, Herr Baron, Sie haben Gäste."

Hans Christian roused himself from his troubled reverie, pushed aside the disregarded balance sheets, and took the card which Fritz extended to him on a crested salver. The superscription was astonishing:

RUFUS RHODES
Envoy Extraordinary and Minister Plenipotentiary of the
United States of America

"Where is His Excellency?" Hans Christian inquired without eagerness. Much as he had longed for diversion, he would not have chosen to have it take this form.

"He is in the Great Hall. He awaits the *Herr Baron's* convenience. It appears that he is motoring through the countryside, and comes to pay his humble respects."

In spite of himself, Hans Christian smiled. It was evident that Fritz had been extremely ingenious in adapting the envoy's phraseology to conform to the standards which he himself considered suitable in addressing his master.

"Is he alone?" Hans Christian went on to ask.

"No, he has a chauffeur with him, dressed in fine English cloth. And the car is great and glistening. I could not see the interior from the door when I admitted His Excellency to the Great Hall. Therefore I do not know whether there are other *Herrschaften* with him or not."

"There are sure to be," said Hans Christian rather cryptically. "Say to His Excellency that I will come at once. And tell Her Serene Highness that we have guests who will certainly be here for tea, and possibly for overnight."

He had never considered, analytically, what sort of a person Trixie's father might be. Now, as he crossed the succession of courtyards leading from the stable enclosures to the open park, he tried to do so, without success. He only knew that if he were asked to hazard a guess, the answer would not be enthusiastic. Therefore he received something of a shock when he entered the Great Hall. From the first glance, it was evident that the man who was awaiting him there was the embodiment of kindliness. His beaming eyes, his genial expression, his hearty handclasp, all bespoke sincere and intrinsic goodwill. But there was nothing breezy or boisterous about him. Hans Christian could not conceive him as the hero of a backslapping campaign, or the professional promoter of the homespun. He was solidly, but not heavily built, and he carried himself well; his manner had dignity as well as assurance. Moreover, though there was complete friendliness in the glance that he turned on his host, it was a surprisingly shrewd and searching glance for all that.

"Well, Chris Marlowe!" he exclaimed with obvious pleasure. "I am sure you'll forgive me if I call you that, instead of Baron von Hohenlohe. It seems to come more naturally. You see, Mrs. Rhodes and Trixie always speak of you as Chris, and I've formed the habit myself. You certainly were kind to them on shipboard. They've never forgotten it. And I appreciate it enormously myself. When I found that I was in your neighborhood, I couldn't resist the temptation of dropping in to see you, so that I could thank you in person."

"It's tremendously kind of you, Sir. I hope Mrs. Rhodes and Trixie are with you?"

"No—no—I'm all by myself this time. A man feels, once in awhile, that he likes to get off by himself, doesn't he now? I had a little vacation coming to me, and I thought I'd like to slip over to East Prussia and see some of this fine farming land of yours I've heard so much about. Sometimes I think I'd have done better to stick to farming myself. Not but what I've enjoyed publishing too. And now I'm enjoying diplomacy, if you can call my brand of action that. Holland is certainly a nice tidy little country and I like the Dutch. They have good habits and sound ideas, and they can give us cards and spades when it comes to making farming on a small scale pleasant and profitable. But just the same I hope someday I can go back to my own farm. Trixie tells me you felt the same way about this place. And now that I've come here I don't wonder, I certainly don't."

The sincere admiration evoked by Schönplatz in the breast of Mr. Rhodes was evident. Hans Christian felt himself warming to his guest's praise as well as to his personality.

"I'm glad you came to see it. We'll take a look around it after tea. Of course you'll give my grandmother and myself the pleasure of staying a few days with us."

"Well now, I'm afraid I couldn't do that, much as I'd like to. And it's very nice of you to ask me, Chris, very nice indeed. But I have just a short time free, and I'd like to cover as much territory as I can. I will take a look around the place with you though. That is, if you wouldn't be interrupting anything important you were doing, to show me."

"I'm only too glad to be interrupted, Sir. Especially as I was trying to balance my stud books when you arrived. The result wasn't too encouraging."

Hans Christian laughed, a little ruefully. The alert ears of Rufus Rhodes were quick to catch the lack of real merriment in the boy's tone, though his answer gave no real indication of this.

"Your stud books, eh? You raise horses then? Wait a minute! Of course you do! I've been hearing all along the line about 'the beautiful white horses of Schönplatz.' So those are yours!"

"Yes. Those are ours. I'll take you out to see them. But first my grandmother will wish to tell you all about them. She does that much better than I do."

There was nothing forced in Hans Christian's smile now. The look he turned towards the Archduchess, as she came towards them, was tenderness itself, and Rufus Rhodes caught the quality of this also. His own voice was gentle as he acknowledged the greeting of the woman who wore her mourning like a regal garment and whose white hair wreathed her head like a crown. It was a grave greeting, extended with no glow; but if there was reluctance as well as reserve in her welcome, nothing which she said or did revealed this. And when tea had been served on the terrace, and her visitor reverted to the subject of the horses again, she did not decline to tell the story.

"I cannot guarantee how much is fact and how much is fancy, Excellency. I am an Austrian myself, not a Prussian; I do not know the

Märchen of this region as well as I know those of the Tyrol. But the tale is told of a circus caravan, which stopped long ago at the gates of Schönplatz, in dire distress. The beautiful dapple gray which was its pride and joy had succumbed to some obscure sickness, and it seemed about to die, for no shelter or succor had been found for it along the road. So the circus leader turned to the owner of Schönplatz 'as one sportsman to another' to save the steed. Of course the appeal was not vainly made. The caravan came in and camped upon the grounds. It must have been a sight worth seeing, the tents and wagons and cages spread all over the park, and the circus people, in their bright clothes, coming and going through the garden and sitting at night around their fires, singing and telling fortunes and throwing dice."

"You make me see this sight, too, Highness. What happened next?"

"A veterinary was summoned at once and it was soon plain that the plight of the dapple gray was not hopeless. But it was critical, it required care and watching. The case could not be hurried. So long before the horse was finally healed, the circus had gone on its way towards Königsberg."

"Leaving the dapple gray behind?"

"Yes. There was no choice, since it could not travel and the circus could not wait. But the leader left with the promise of a return and a reclamation."

"And then?"

"And then these never came to pass. The caravan vanished as suddenly and as strangely as it had come. And forever."

"But the horse?"

"The horse remained and never sought to stray. Eventually it became the sire of countless colts—all pure white! Even when the mares to which the dapple was bred were coal black. Their descendants are white as snow to this day. The strain has never shown pollution yet."

"I think Mr. Rhodes would like to hear the complete story, grandmother."

"I believe that the complete story has never yet been told, Excellency, because the end has not come yet. But Hansel means, I think, that our peasants are very superstitious about these white horses. The mystery which surrounds them is interwoven, in the popular mind, with magic. Some simple people insist that if a colored colt is born at Schönplatz, it will be a bad omen, that it will show the beginning of weakness in the strain not only of the stud but of the family."

"Grandmother, it isn't only the peasants that feel the force of something strange about the horses. You know yourself——"

"Yes, I know myself—or think I do. And my husband, in his last illness——" Victoria Luise paused and looked away towards the glen which they were facing, almost as if she expected to see something swift and snowy emerge. Then, with less reserve than she had shown before, she turned back to her guest. "I am sure Your Excellency does not wish to dwell on local legends all the afternoon," she said. "And I, for my part, should like to hear something of your Dutch impressions. I used to visit The Hague frequently myself, when a cousin of mine, the Archduke Stefan, was stationed there as Austrian Minister. But it is many years now since I have been there. I hope you have found it a pleasant post? And that your wife and daughter also have enjoyed it?"

"Yes—yes—we've had a very good time there. As I was telling Chris when I first came, I like the Dutch and I like Holland. And I've learned a good deal about the things I'm interested in myself. I've tried not to neglect the social side. I realize an American Minister has a certain position to keep up, that this and that are expected of him, and properly. But I've managed to get out of the city a good deal too. I've looked into the Netherlanders' methods of making butter and cheese and marketing farm products. They're good, very good. Mrs. Rhodes has enjoyed seeing them too. She's been happy going around with me. She and the women she's met in the country understand each other, if you know what I mean. Not that she talks any Dutch. Trixie's done better at learning that. She's studied hard and it's come natural to her. She speaks it like a native. And she's taken up French and German too, and isn't doing a bit badly in them either."

Mr. Rhodes paused, his genial face revealing the satisfaction of a proud parent.

"When Trixie came to The Hague," he said, "the good people there were inclined to look at her a little askance. She drives her own car and it's a pretty powerful roadster. It was something of a shock for some to see a diplomat's daughter tearing around bareheaded in an open motor; and I expected every day to hear she'd been arrested. But since then she's made friends with every cop in the city. They're a queer looking lot, those Dutch cops. They're all stoop-shouldered, and they all wear great long clanking swords, which you'd think would trip them up in a minute if they had to get into quick action. Of course, mostly they just wander around looking pompous. But they certainly have taken a shine to Trixie— And she's made no end of other friends too. The Legation just swarms with young people, tumbling in and out of Trixie's car at all hours of the day and night. That is, if they haven't bulldozed their families into giving them cars of their own, along the same lines as Trixie's."

Mr. Rhodes' smile became increasingly expansive as he dwelt on his daughter's popularity. He needed no urging to continue speaking on such a congenial subject.

"There was some talk too because she went around so much with young men. To Scheveningen and the Haack Bar and the Restaurant

Royale, for instance, without a chaperon. Well, we don't go in much for chaperons in Kansas, beyond a certain point, I mean, and I can't see that the results are any different than they are anywhere else. So I didn't like to start drawing the line too close in The Hague either. Trixie's the sort of girl that finds her own feet, sooner or later, and the more I see of that sort, the more I believe in driving them with a loose rein. Now the talk has all died down, and Trixie isn't so much interested in restaurants anyway, because she's invited to so many nice houses. She's made mighty welcome everywhere. Folks have got her sized up right and they like her. They like her very much."

"I don't see how they could help liking her," Hans Christian remarked, tactfully taking advantage of the Minister's first noticeable pause. "She's a grand girl. I wish you'd brought her along with you to East Prussia."

Victoria Luise and Rufus Rhodes both regarded Hans Christian attentively as he made this statement. But before the Minister could frame a gratified reply, the Archduchess spoke suavely.

"Naturally Hansel and I are much disappointed that Mrs. Rhodes and your daughter did not accompany you on your trip," she said. "But I hope you can encourage us to believe that at some future time we may have the pleasure of welcoming them at Schönplatz."

"Thank you," Mr. Rhodes said, heartily. "Thank you very much." He paused again, this time as if something portentous were on his mind which he hesitated to divulge, although desiring to do so. "I believe they will come here with me sometime," he continued. "Since you're so kind as to suggest it. Because I expect we'll be spending most of our time, the next few years, in Germany, and of course we'll want to identify ourselves with all parts of it, the same as we've done in Holland. You see, I'm expecting to be transferred before long. The appointment hasn't been made public yet. But the President's been good enough to name me as the next American Ambassador to Germany."

CHAPTER 11

Without much difficulty, Mr. Rhodes was persuaded to change his plan of "pushing on" to Königsberg at once. It would be simple enough, the Archduchess explained, to take a side trip the following day or the day after, for the purpose of visiting the *Ostmesse;* but it was unthinkable that the Minister should undertake to make the rounds of the exhibits when dusk was already setting in.

"It takes several hours nearly to walk through the Fair Grounds, without pausing to inspect any of the cattle and sheep or attending the daily horse shows," she said. "And besides, you have not reached there yet. I know, Excellency, that you make light of distances in your great Middle West; but Königsberg is really a considerable drive from here. Moreover, we have a rule at Schönplatz, which we try to enforce, that every guest who comes to us must stay long enough to sleep under our roof. We shall be desolated if you force us to break this."

"Well now, I never did believe in using force. There are so many pleasanter means to almost any given end."

"I am so glad that we see eye to eye on this question, Excellency. It leads me to believe that we shall agree on many others also, and find mutual pleasure in this harmony. Fritz will take your bags at once to the Königszimmer in the State Suite where all the kings of Prussia have slept when they visited Schönplatz. And, of course, we shall see that your chauffeur has suitable accommodations also. Dinner is at eight-thirty, if that hour is agreeable to you, and I am sure some of our neighbors will join us for the evening, when they hear how fortunate we are in having you with us. Meantime, while I spread the good news that you are here, what can Hansel show you about the place that will give you the most pleasure?"

It was evident that the Archduchess had immediately "taken a liking" to the Minister, as he himself would have said, though Hansel had feared she might look upon his visit as an intrusion. The vibrancy in her voice, which had so long been toneless, was even more telling than her warm words; and her suggestion of giving a dinner at Schönplatz, for the first time since her husband's death, was more significant still. In spite of the short notice, a sizeable and distinguished company had forgathered by half past eight in the baronial banqueting room which led from the Great Hall: The *Oberpräsident* of East Prussia, a Senior Senator from Danzig, and two Generals, all with their wives; Counts and Colonels, Barons and Burgraves, likewise suitably accompanied. Orders and Decorations were greatly in evidence; so was ancestral jewelry of the more massive type. Tall candles flickered in the candelabra rising from the long table and from the sconces fastened to the frescoed walls. Mounds of fruit and clusters of flowers curved alternately above the silver epergnes surmounting the gleaming damask. Plates of rare porcelain and goblets of chased crystal, both heavily encrusted with gold, were set at every place; and the maids who supplemented the services of the butler and houseman wore the festival dresses and amber ornaments reserved for the most important occasions.

"This certainly is a handsome sight," Mr. Rhodes told the Archduchess, his observant eyes taking in every detail of the scene with appreciative thoroughness. "I wish more than ever that I had my family with me. They would have enjoyed this dinner, they surely would. Those soup plates now, with the pictures of all the European queens on them—Mrs. Rhodes would certainly have been taken with those.

She used to do some china painting herself when she was a girl. But after we were married, and Trixie was born, she had her hands so full with the housework and the baby and all that, she didn't have time to go on with it. She's never lost her taste for it though, and I'm sort of hoping, as things are easier for her these days, she'll take it up again. Trixie doesn't care so much for things of the kind. But I'm afraid we'd have had hard work to keep her from getting right up and asking one of those pretty waitresses of yours to change clothes with her. She's bought several costumes in Holland lately to wear at fancy dress parties. But they don't any of them compare with the ones those girls of yours have on. And as long as I know she's got her eye peeled for some more——"

"The *Trachten* of our village are all made there," Victoria Luise informed him. "The women weave and spin still, throughout the long winter evenings, just as they have for hundreds of years. The older ones keep only enough clothing going to supply their current needs. And those are almost unbelievably restricted. But the young girls try to put something aside each year for their trousseaux, so they generally have a few extra garments on hand that have never been worn. I believe I could easily assemble a complete costume, almost overnight, by getting a blouse here and a bodice there and so on. I should be delighted to do this, if you will permit me, and send it to your daughter as a little token of my interest in her, and my hope that she will soon come and see for herself the place where these costumes are made and worn."

"Well now, that is kind and thoughtful of you, Highness, very kind and thoughtful indeed! I know Trixie'll be delighted to have it, and I'll be delighted to take it to her. I don't know when I've seen anything so nice looking as those colored bands, matched up on the white sleeves and the white aprons. And I shouldn't be a bit surprised if you'd go first of all for supplies to that pretty girl who just passed us the jelly we're eating with this fine venison. I've never tasted any to equal it, if you'll let me say so. Now tell me—did I guess right?"

Victoria Luise did not even look up from the plate upon which her eyes were fixed as she delicately dissected a morsel of the venison which Mr. Rhodes had so highly praised. "I agree with you that the girl is pretty," she said smoothly. "But it happens that she is unusually stupid, even for a peasant, and few peasants are overburdened with brains—which after all is just as well! Nevertheless, a certain modicum is necessary and Trudchen falls so far short of possessing this, that so far as I know, she has never had a serious suitor. I should be pleased to hear that she did—if for no better reason than that it would mean the kind of trouble her type almost automatically invites might then be averted. To tell you the truth, I have always been afraid that someday I would have a sudden call to send swaddling clothes to Trudchen's house; but I should never think of looking there for a trousseau. Now—I mustn't monopolize you! I can see that Frau von Edelblut, who is on your other side, is eager to talk with you in her turn."

Mr. Rhodes found Frau von Edelblut a rather ponderous person. She was a heavy woman, and the brown grosgrain silk and cameo jewelry she was wearing did nothing to detract from her size. Her face was full and ruddy and framed with frizzed hair, arranged to escape slightly in front from a knotted net, though otherwise closely confined. Her English was excellent, but her voice was deep and she had a lisp. This childish defect, in combination with her bulky appearance, had a ludicrous effect.

"I thee you are intrigued with our hothteth-eth thtorieth," she boomed. "But I can tell you thtorieth too, about ghotht-th! We have ghotht-th galore at Erntht-thtein, my cathtle. Jutht fanthy! The thide of my drething room fell down latht Thaturday, and a long lock of flaxthen hair thlipped out of it, jutht like a thnake. I thcreamed when I thaw it thliding around on the thlippery floor. There wath not anything elthe with it—no thkeleton, no dreth, no thoeth, no thign of what it may mean. But I think that maketh it all the more thtrange and thinithter, don't you?"

Mr. Rhodes agreed that it was very strange and sinister, and strove to change the subject. He was beginning to feel slightly surfeited with the supernatural. The story about the white horses really had intrigued him and had sharpened his enjoyment of the stock and stables, the paddocks and riding rings, which Hans Christian had taken him to look over after tea. He had seen the snowy descendants of the dappled gray circus stallion for himself, and needed no urging to believe in their beauty or admit their actuality. But incarcerated curls were something else again. When the company had left the banqueting room and gathered around the immense fireplace in the Great Hall for coffee and liqueurs, his eyes followed Trudchen with renewed attention, as she circulated about, carrying a heavy silver tray. The Archduchess, beside whom he was still sitting, and whose glance was quite as penetrating as his own, did not fail to observe his preoccupation.

"Trudchen," she said suavely. The girl stopped short and looked at the Archduchess with frightened eyes, as she tried to balance her tray in her shaking hands. "His Excellency has been kind enough to concern himself in your behalf," Victoria Luise went on, in the same even voice, as if she had not noticed the little peasant's terror, "and to inquire about your possible prospects. I told him I did not think you had ever had a serious suitor. I am right, am I not?"

The unexpectedness of the attack was calamitous. The confusion which such a question would have caused the girl in any case was intensified a hundredfold by the suddenness with which it was asked, and the surroundings in which she stood. For one desperate moment she continued her vain attempt to keep her tray on an even keel, as she stammered something unintelligible under her breath. Then it pitched forward and fell on the floor, carrying crashing china with it, and sending a stream of coffee gushing over the carpet in the direction of Frau von Edelblut. This noble lady gave a little shriek and clasped her pudgy fingers dramatically together.

"How thocking!" she exclaimed. "Jutht thee how that thmall thtream ith thpreading and thinking into your thplendid Thirith rug, Victoria! I thympathithe with you, I thertainly do! Thervent-th are thurely getting more and more careleth day by day!"

The Archduchess had risen majestically, drawing her silken skirts away from the spreading pool of liquid at her feet. The faithful Fritz was already on his knees beside her, picking up fragments of porcelain and mopping with a large damask napkin at the mess which the coffee had made. Hans Christian, who had taken the wife of the *Oberpräsident* into dinner, was pouring out a glass of *Danziger Goldwasser* for her when the crash came, with his back to the scene of disaster, and did not turn around. The guests, almost without exception, looked with elaborate unconcern in every direction except the one where the accident had occurred and redoubled their efforts, already somewhat self-conscious, at casual conversation.

Mr. Rhodes was one of the few who did not seem to feel it incumbent upon him to ignore the accident. Having assured himself that Fritz was dealing competently with one sort of salvage, he hastened to undertake another. Though he had no idea of the direction which the terrified Trudchen had taken in the flight which followed the fall, he found his way to the obscure corner where she was hiding, and put his hand protectingly on her shoulder, patting this as he did so.

"There, there," he said in a soothing voice. "You mustn't cry. You mustn't feel bad either. Why all of us have accidents! I've had dozens of them myself. When I was about your age, I fed some mash to the hogs so hot that it killed them. And they weren't my hogs. They belonged to the man I was working for, and he was a grim old miser, if there ever was one. I had to pay him back for every one of those hogs in work before I got another cent of wages. And I'd been saving up my money for two years, hoping to get to the State University, for a term anyway. So I never did get there. I grieved over it considerable. But it doesn't do any good to cry over broken china or burnt hogs any more than it does over spilt milk."

Mr. Rhodes had spoken in English and consequently Trudchen did not understand a word he was saying. Nevertheless the kindness of his manner was unmistakable. Her sobs began to subside, and between them she managed to form a few broken phrases, which Mr. Rhodes, in spite of his imperfect knowledge of German, managed, in his turn, to piece together.

"Bin kein böses Mädchen—aber kann mich nicht verheiraten und nichts sagen—wenn Herr Baron wüsste, wäre alles los."

"There, there," said Mr. Rhodes again. Slowly and painstakingly he began to speak in German himself. "Of course you're not a bad girl," he said reassuringly. "The Archduchess doesn't think that! Nobody thinks that. And why shouldn't you get married, if you want to? Or say anything about it for that matter? If I were you, I'd go to the Archduchess and make a clean breast of things."

"Nein, nein! Das ist nicht möglich."

"Well then, go to Chris—to the *Herr Baron,* I mean. He's got a very kind heart. It hasn't taken me long to find that out. Go to him and ask him if he can't fix it so you and your young man can get married right away."

"Den Herr Baron sprechen! Ach, du lieber Gott!"

Trudchen began to sob again, with redoubled force. Mr. Rhodes cleared his throat.

"Yes," he said slowly. "Yes, I think that's what you better do. You speak to the *Herr Baron* the first moment you can. You tell him all this has got to be cleared up. After you've had a talk with him, I may say a few words to him myself. We'll see. I'll have to think that over. But it'll probably be best, at that."

The clear mind of Mr. Rhodes was confused and his kindly heart troubled as he finally climbed into the immense *Himmelbett,* curtained in burgundy brocade, where so many celebrities had slumbered, most of them, he feared, more comfortably than chastely. Indeed, at the last moment before he parted from his hostess for the night, she had observed that it might interest him to inspect the draperies of the *Himmelbett:* It seemed that long ago a veiled lady had come to the castle one evening at dusk, when the family was absent in Königsberg, asking to be allowed to visit the State Suite alone. Perhaps she had bribed the guardian, or perhaps he had merely been touched by her tears. As to that, nobody knew. But her mournful request had been granted. The next day the sad discovery was made that a great square had been cut, presumably as a souvenir, from the brocade curtains which enclosed the bed and made it so secret a scene of voluptuous delight.

Mr. Rhodes had enjoyed this story even less than those about the ghosts; but his mind kept reverting to it as he tossed from side to side in the *Himmelbett,* unable to go to sleep. The radiance of the room was eerie. The moonlight streamed in through the windows, for the only way to exclude this was to close the heavy wooden shutters, which would likewise have excluded all air; and Mr. Rhodes was a man who liked to have a fresh breeze, reminiscent of the prairies, flowing about him at night. So the bed draperies and window hangings, the massive Danzig chests and polished parquetry, and the painted ceiling, representing a starry heaven surrounded by sturdy trees, were all transfigured with a silvery translucence, unlike any which Mr. Rhodes had ever beheld on land or sea before. But this uncanny lambency, disturbing as it was, could not wholly account for Mr. Rhodes' uneasiness. There was more than a quality of color involved. There was something sensual in the atmosphere, for the episode which the Archduchess had related so casually was apparently characteristic of the sort of thing which constantly happened at Schönplatz. Was he to understand that privileged men "took advantage" of youth and innocence as a matter of course? Or worse still, that women not only succumbed to seduction without a struggle there, but treasured the memory of their subjugation? Had he been rash in suggesting to Trudchen that she should seek out Hans Christian "the first moment she could" without qualifying his statement in any way? Was it possible that she might interpret this advice to mean that very night instead of the following morning? It did not seem so, and yet, the more Mr. Rhodes thought of it, the more firmly convinced he became that it was probable. If he were right, what then? What would happen to her? What had happened to her already that she should seem so terrified? It was inconceivable that Hans Christian—sensitive, tenderhearted, high-principled—should stoop to a dishonorable deed, no matter how ruthless and sensuous a lot his ancestors had shown themselves to be. It was inconceivable and yet—the boy was horribly lonely, inescapably harassed, almost at the end of his tether.

Rufus Rhodes was moved by the thought. But his pity for Hans Christian did not detract from his anxiety for Trudchen. At last he could bear inaction no longer. He descended, not without difficulty, from the crimson heights of the *Himmelbett*, and groping for his serviceable bathrobe, wrapped it securely around his substantial form. The parquet flooring creaked under his bare feet, and he was ashamed to feel cold shivers running down his spine as he stooped for his slippers. When he reached the next room, still another sound startled him, for this contained a glass cabinet filled with priceless porcelains and lovely lacquerware, which rattled as the floor shook slightly under his weight. His fingers were chilly as he placed them on the knob of the door leading from the antechamber of the State Suite to the upper hall. Before he had actually grasped the knob, the door swung open of its own accord.

Beyond its enclosure, only emptiness and silence confronted him. The light from the waning moon did not strike this side of the castle; there was no murmur of voices, no patter of passing feet. He thought of what Hans Christian had said, desperation in his voice, as they had followed a little fir-bordered walk from one set of outbuildings to another late that afternoon. "Pretty soon it will be dark. I think the darkness is blacker here, and the stillness heavier, than anywhere else in the world." Rufus Rhodes knew now what the boy had meant. The blackness and the heaviness were upon him now, impenetrable and crushing. He could not prevail against them. He could do no possible good and he might do great harm if he persisted in a quixotic quest which he realized had been ridiculous to undertake. He had no idea where Hans Christian's room was, and in searching for it he might well stumble into that of the Archduchess instead. He could only return to the sinister shelter of the *Himmelbett*. But though he had not heard them and could not see them, he was sure, beyond any shadow of a doubt, that somewhere, beyond the blackness and the heaviness, Hans Christian and Trudchen were together——

He closed the door of the antechamber firmly, trying, as he did so, to lock it this time. But the heavy iron key was rusty; it would not turn; the big bolt was broken in two. There was nothing to do but leave it as it was, hoping that this time it would stay shut. Rufus Rhodes did not care at all for doors which swung open by themselves, any more than he cared for china which clattered as he walked past it, or flooring which creaked under his feet. In fact he did not care for any kind of unaccountable noises occurring in the dead of night. When the sound of soft but persistent knocking also came to his ears, he swore under his breath.

He could not instantly make up his mind to go and open the door. Yet he recoiled from the thought that it might swing open of its own accord again, or that the mysterious suppliant on his threshold might enter uninvited. Gritting his teeth, he retraced his footsteps, thankful that in the course of his progress he had inadvertently touched a switch and that there was now a pale gleam of electricity in the room. Feeble as it was, it enhanced his sense of security. He threw open the door with a show of boldness and Trudchen slipped inside it.

She was not crying any longer. Even in the dim light, Rufus Rhodes could see that her round rosy little face was now wreathed in smiles. She ducked and kissed his hand, but having done so, she instantly straightened up again and faced him beamingly. Then she began to talk in a way which he had no difficulty in understanding.

"I saw Your Excellency open the door just after I had come out of the *Herr Baron's* room, so I knew Your Excellency was awake. I was watching and waiting to make sure no one was in the hall before crossing it, as the *Herr Baron* has taught me to do. I hope I do not intrude upon Your Excellency. But I am so happy, all because of Your Excellency's great wisdom and goodness that I wanted to say so at once. If it had not been for such sage advice, I should never have dared to tell the *Herr Baron* the truth."

"Has he ever been unkind to you?" Rufus Rhodes heard himself asking, incomprehensibly.

"Oh, no, Your Excellency! Always he has been most gentle, most tender. He has never been rough, even in his speech. He has never used violence against me in any way, or shamed me by coming to my house and locking the door of my room in my mother's face. He has safeguarded me as if I had been a lady, and we have never met except secretly. Still I feared he might be angry at learning that I was sought in marriage and that I wished to accept my suitor. Especially since Hermann's younger brother Otto is in disgrace at the castle—he was formerly the *Apfeljunge* and now he is in the scullery. Besides, I feared he might tell Hermann how it had been between us, and then Hermann would not marry me after all. He is insanely jealous. How should I know that the *Herr Baron* would not be jealous also, that he would be willing to let me go? A peasant girl cannot take that for granted, Excellency, when she has found favor with a *Grossgrundbesitzer*. But the *Herr Baron* has been more than generous. He has told me that I shall not lose my place, as long as I wish to keep it, and that I shall come and go about the castle unmolested. Also that my mother will continue to receive the extra money he has given me for her each month."

The orderly mind of Rufus Rhodes was reeling. Before him in the treacherous light was standing the pretty little peasant who had aroused his sympathies, her pink face guileless as a baby's. That much was certainly true. Yet he could hardly bring himself to believe a single word that issued from her prim pink mouth. Surely he could not have understood her correctly, surely his imperfect knowledge of German must be causing his comprehension to play tricks upon him! No decent girl would babble blandly along in this wise to a man she had never seen before that night about an illicit love affair and a smug betrothal in one and the same breath. It was all a riddle which would have been ridiculous if it had not been revolting. But out of it emerged a scrap of salvage at which Rufus Rhodes grasped.

"Perhaps the *Herr Baron* is pleased to have you marry," he said. "Perhaps he has felt for sometime that it was unwise for you to come to him secretly, besides being wrong, which he has known it to be from the beginning, even if you did not. Perhaps he hesitated to tell you he would be pleased for fear of hurting your feelings, or perhaps he tried to tell you so and could not make you understand." All this was true, and yet Rufus Rhodes knew also that Hans Christian's pride must have been cut to the quick at the disclosure that the girl whom he had treated so tenderly voluntarily was turning from him to the coarse caresses of the refractory *Apfeljunge's* brother. "I know the *Herr Baron* must have felt a great responsibility, as far as you were concerned," Mr. Rhodes went on, trying to close his consciousness to the corroding thought which had just crossed it. "Having been led into this, he did not see how he could withdraw from it. He will be happier and better off now that you have made the withdrawal easy. Though you are hardly fair to Hermann, are you, in letting him marry you under false pretenses?"

Rufus Rhodes was aware that his German was faltering, that he did not sound like himself when he tried to talk in this language. Perhaps that accounted for the fact that Trudchen was now beginning to look bewildered in her turn. She shook her head stupidly.

"I do not understand Your Excellency," she muttered. "But I am sure that I have nothing to fear. The *Herr Baron* will never betray me to Hermann, any more than he has ever betrayed me to others. He has told me that the banns may be published at once, if I like. I showed him the ring which Hermann has given me—a real gold ring engraved with an arrow, to show that the heart has been pierced. I have been keeping it in my pocket. I did not even dare hang it on a chain around my neck, for fear that it might be found. But now I shall wear it quite openly. Her Serene Highness will be astonished, and perhaps she will not be pleased. She never admits she is in the wrong about anything, and since she has said before other *Herrschaften* that I have never had a serious suitor, she will be chagrined to learn that this is not the case. But the *Herr Baron* will protect me from her anger. I have nothing to fear in that quarter either."

It seemed to Rufus Rhodes that Trudchen actually shrugged her shoulders. He realized that if she could do this, she had indeed left intimidation far behind.

"Well, now that you feel sure that everything has turned out so well for you," he remarked dryly, "don't you think it would be a good plan if you went home and got to bed?"

Trudchen curtsied and kissed his hand again. But this time the gesture was more lingering than when she had come in. She continued to kneel at his feet as she went on speaking.

"I am most grateful for Your Excellency's kindness. If there is anything I can do to serve Your Excellency——" she murmured—and waited.

Rufus Rhodes was not a squeamish man and he had not known what it was to blush since boyhood. But when he had slammed the door behind Trudchen's scurrying figure, he strode across the floor unmindful of the clattering china and wiped the sweat from his brow as he delivered himself of a biting oath coupled with a brief epithet which he had never applied to a woman before.

"And the sooner I get that poor trapped youngster out of this old hell hole and away from that young hell cat," he concluded, as he climbed back into the *Himmelbett,* "the better deed I'll have done in the sight of the Almighty."

CHAPTER 12

Mr. Rhodes was not himself much of a horseman. Nevertheless, figuratively speaking, he knew better than to "rush his fences." For the next three days he suffered himself to be led around the countryside, and docilely accepted every suggestion which the Archduchess made to him. He went with her to the woodland cemetery where General von Hohenlohe lay entombed in monumental black granite, surrounded by his three sons, whose graves were marked with elaborate iron crosses. Mr. Rhodes stood with bowed head while Victoria Luise knelt in prayer, arranged cascades of flowers, and described similar cemeteries which she proposed to show him in the near future. He went with her to Ernstein, and listened, patiently and politely, while Frau von Edelblut told him "thtorieth" about the eventful past of this classic pile. It had originally been a plain, substantial *Herrenhaus,* but it had been remodeled, according to the ideas of an ancestor of hers who had spent a *Wanderjahr* in Greece, and who, in spite of having contracted malignant fever and other ailments there, had conceived a consuming passion for it. He had returned to his native land, bent on adorning the park with group after group of substantial sculpture, setting up pilasters with gilded Corinthian capitals in the *Festsaal,* and placing alabaster tables between marble busts in every corridor of the castle.

"Hith father wath not at all pleathed," Frau von Edelblut explained. "Ethpethially when he inthithted in building a pavilion in Doric thtyle whith he thaid wath a temple, and could not be uthed or made thuitable for hortheth. Hith father wanted to thtable them there, you thee."

"I see," Rufus Rhodes replied gravely. Secretly he sympathized somewhat with the outraged parent, for the chaste and chilly marble surrounding him scarcely seemed adapted to the lusty life of a typical East Prussian *Grossgrundbesitzer.* But he gathered that Frau von Edelblut herself was a champion of the son, so he held his peace. The result of his forbearance was that his appreciative attitude was admired, and he was taken off to see another castle, where a careful cult of Goethe had been maintained for more than a century, and "Werther" was enacted every spring in a sylvan theatre, by various members of the family. This cult, Mr. Rhodes learned, had its origin in the friendship which a wandering daughter of the house had formed in her youth with the great poet, and which had remained a romantic memory for her after she had been unwillingly dragged away from the delightful laxness of glowing Weimar to the stern simplicity of patrician Prussia.

"It is so easy to go from place to place in these days," Victoria Luise remarked, leaning against the comfortable upholstery of Mr. Rhodes' limousine as it glided over the smooth highway again. "In the days when the roads were full of ruts, and the *Junkers* went lumbering about in great coaches—unless they rode horseback—it was not such a simple matter to visit back and forth. Though some of the state equipages were very beautiful. We have several still, in the old carriage house. One is made of green lacquer. I must remind Hansel to show it to you. I am sorry that he was not inclined to come with us today. The habit of solitude seems to have fastened itself upon him. When he first came to Schönplatz, I sometimes feared that he would not be able to endure its loneliness. But lately he has shrunk from society quite as much as I have myself. I might even say more so! For I have been delighted to accompany you while you made the acquaintance of our countryside and our country life, though he has persisted in staying shut up in the *Studsekretariat*, poring over pedigree sheets and balancing books!"

The Archduchess spoke lightly, as was her habit, but her suavity was edged with sarcasm, which Rufus Rhodes had discovered was not unusual with her either. He decided that the time had come to make the plunge which he had hesitated to attempt too soon.

"Perhaps a different sort of company would suit Chris better," he suggested. "Just for a change, I mean. Of course, I can't imagine anything pleasanter than the sort of life you lead here—everyone more or less related to everyone else, everyone interested in the same sort of sports, everyone owning a fine place, just right for having lots of company. But along with it all, there is a good deal of stress laid on the past, now isn't there? Ancestors and history and all that sort of thing, I mean. After all, the present's pretty exciting too. I should think Chris would enjoy taking some kind of an active part in this new Youth Movement that's beginning to sweep through Germany like wildfire. I'm not sure yet whether it's a good thing or a bad one, but anyway, it's alive! It isn't embalmed, if you know what I mean. Chris might help his country considerably. Germany's in a bad way just now; it needs young fellows like him to give it a hand up. But my main point is that it might help him considerably if he got out more with boys his own age."

"There is no lack of boys Hansel's age among our neighbors, Mr. Rhodes. And they did their best to make him welcome among them. But unfortunately he did not respond to their hospitality in any way at all."

"Well, perhaps he didn't find much in common with them. Perhaps his tastes and theirs weren't congenial."

"That is all too true. But I should regret to see my grandson identifying himself with a group of hoodlums and fanatics, and thus tacitly acknowledging his failure to adapt himself to the views and ways of his own class."

"It seems to me that you're just a little prejudiced in your views, if you'll allow me to say so, Highness. The boys in this new movement aren't all hoodlums and fanatics by any means. There's good material among them, and they've got a mighty shrewd, able leader—Grueber, his name is. I believe Chris might go a good ways in an organization like that. I think you're a little hard on him too, if I may say *that*. He was an American boy, to all intents and purposes, when he came here. He's had quite a lot of adapting to do. I think he's tried hard to do it. In fact, I'd go so far as to say I know he has. But his views and ways weren't *Junker* views and ways when he left Hamstead and Harvard. You'd hardly expect they would be, right off the bat, now would you?"

"He came of his own free will. He desired to leave Hamstead and Harvard, to take up his father's heritage, to become a German."

"Ye-es, theoretically. But he hadn't a very clear idea, had he, what it really meant to become a German, to take up his father's heritage?"

"He knew when he decided to stay. The original plan had been that he should remain only for the summer, that he should return to the United States in the autumn. He was free to do that also."

"In a way, yes. But I believe he felt bound, don't you? That is, there had been a death in the family. He seems to have a very kind heart and——"

"I have never made my own bereavement a pretext to hold him, Mr. Rhodes."

"Of course not. Of course not. He stayed of his own free will, as you say. But now that he *has* stayed, for more than two years, don't you think it would do him good to get away for awhile? To Berlin, for instance. Most boys of his age would get a lot of pleasure out of a city like Berlin."

"It had been my husband's hope, and my own, that Hansel would find Berlin a congenial center. Not that we would have encouraged him to spend too much time there. The Prussians are not absentee landlords, Mr. Rhodes. They live on their own property, year in and year out, century in and century out——"

"That's just what I'm saying. I think it might be a good thing if they didn't stick to it quite so closely. It's rather far from the beaten track. In Berlin, people refer to it as the 'Far East.' The Corridor has cut it off considerably from the capital."

"It certainly has. But remember that the Corridor was created over the dead bodies of our heroes, not through the free will of a free people. What could be more cruel than to make a jest of the isolation it has imposed? Nothing in my experience! Besides owing to the unfortunate economic situation which exists in Germany just now, we have been obliged to part with some of our property. We no longer own our house on the *Tiergartenstrasse*."

"But you could take a little furnished apartment somewhere, couldn't you, for the winter months? Just big enough for you and Chris? Or if you didn't care to leave Schönplatz, he could strike off alone and dig himself into lodgings."

The Archduchess drew away slightly, as if she were trying to create of her own corner a stronghold for herself. "I am still afraid that you do not fully grasp the situation, Mr. Rhodes," she said, "though I appreciate your interest and your cordiality. We have an old Prussian hunting slogan in which we believe implicitly, and it runs, 'The pack must stay together.' There is a very great feeling of family unity and class unity, among Germans. It is true that Hansel has not fully absorbed these feelings yet. But it is also true, as you have pointed out, that he is trying to do so, and that in a certain measure, he is succeeding in his attempt. I am sure that having progressed so far, he would not do anything so contrary to custom as to leave his home, and his nearest relative, and 'strike off alone,' as you suggest. Believe me, he will be far more contented in the end if he remains where he is, prevailing over his own diffidence and discontent. Both will disappear, in any case, I believe, as soon as he is suitably married."

"I beg your pardon. Did you speak of yourself as his nearest relative? Isn't his mother living?"

"Yes, his mother is living. But he and she have never been very close together, since he was a child, and now they are almost completely estranged. She is a beautiful woman, but a wilful and selfish one. She has no sort of hold upon him."

Rufus Rhodes privately thought that there was more than one selfish and wilful woman involved in the case, and it was on the tip of his tongue to remark that such an estrangement did not speak well for the sense of family unity which he had just heard so highly vaunted. However, he wisely held his peace on that score, and asked another question.

"He's still rather young, isn't he, to think seriously of settling down? Most boys need a chance to have some sort of fling before they are married."

"If Hansel feels the need of 'some sort of fling,' no doubt he will manage to have it, even at Schönplatz," the Archduchess said in the smooth tone which Mr. Rhodes was beginning to dislike so intensely. "I assure you I should not interfere with anything of that sort. I should not even give it false importance by appearing to notice it. But it is never too soon for the heir of a great estate to think of marrying suitably. In this instance, I may tell you in confidence, since you have been kind enough to concern yourself about Hansel, that the complication is not caused by his youth, but by the fact that the bride I have in mind for him is much younger still."

"*You've* selected a bride for Chris? Already?"

"I should not go so far as to say that I had selected her. He will do that for himself, of course, under proper guidance, at the proper time. But I should be extremely pleased to see him married to one of the daughters of our distant kinsman Sebastian de Cerreno."

"*One* of the daughters? *Any* one?"

"There are only two, Cristina and Cecilia. They are both still little girls. Otherwise I might be tempted to leave Schönplatz for a time after all, and spend a winter in Spain. But I do not want my plans to miscarry because of prematurity."

The Archduchess smiled charmingly, and glanced out of the window. "How fast time flies, when one is in congenial company!" she said. "See, we are almost home! Or do you not recognize our local landmarks yet? I think we shall have time for an hour in the library before dinner. You have hardly seen that at all, and it contains many volumes which I am sure you would enjoy. For instance, we have a complete collection of sixteenth century madrigal music. Also the manuscript of an opera, composed by a member of my husband's family and performed in honor of Queen Luise and King Wilhelm Friedrich when they made the first of their many visits to Schönplatz. But after all, the greatest treasures are a Württemberg Bible bound in pigskin, and a copy of Kant which is unique. There is a story about that which I must not fail to tell you."

For the first time Rufus Rhodes found a pretext for not falling in with her plans. Possibly she would be good enough to show him the collection and tell him the story at some other time, he suggested. He had eaten such a hearty lunch and such an enormous tea—in spite of the chilling effect of the classical surroundings on both occasions—that he felt an overpowering need for exercise before attacking the equally prodigious dinner which he knew was still ahead of him. He thought he would walk out over the fields, cross country. A five-mile hike would do him no end of good. Besides, the sky was beautiful just at this time of the evening, a queer pale color, streaked with green and purple and orange light. He had never seen its equal anywhere else. Or birches that could compare with the long rows edging the lake. In a way, he liked them even better than the pine groves, much better than the alleys of lindens. He wanted to have a look at them, with all those flame-colored clouds streaming out behind them. He didn't suppose he could persuade the Archduchess to come with him, part of the way anyhow?

He hoped he was safe in extending the invitation. The Archduchess had been a fine figure on horseback, in her day; but she had seldom strayed beyond the park and garden, or the sylvan glades immediately surrounding these. Rufus Rhodes swung off unimpeded. But as a matter of fact, he had no intention of taking a solitary walk. He was firmly resolved to seek out Hans Christian, and talk with him, now that he was in the mood, as man to man.

He did not have to seek far. He had not gone beyond the first cobbled courtyard, when he saw the boy, dressed in riding clothes and holding a crop, standing with his hands behind his back and staring up at an empty nest, perched above a large chimney. He was so absorbed that he did not notice his guest's approach until Mr. Rhodes came up and stood beside him, following his gaze.

"What are you looking at, Chris?" the Minister asked. He could see the empty nest for himself, of course. But there was nothing about it, in his eyes, to rivet attention.

The boy turned, blinking a little. "I'm sorry, Sir, that I didn't see you come up. I just noticed that the storks are gone."

"The storks are gone? But that doesn't bother you, does it? They'll come back, won't they?"

"Oh, yes! They'll come back! In East Prussia the storks bring the *Fohlenkinder* as well as all the other babies—we couldn't have our little white colts at Schönplatz without the help of the storks." Hans Christian smiled, and Rufus Rhodes found something touching and irresistible in his expression, just as Trixie had from the beginning. He made an attractive figure as he stood there in his whipcord breeches, polished boots, and soft shirt. The clothes became him, and he wore them easily; no one would have guessed that two years earlier they had been strange and unfamiliar to him. "But at that, the storks are the last of all the birds to return," he went on. "The village children have a song that they sing about that. They go through the streets chanting,

Alle Vögel sind schon da,
Blos noch nicht der Adelbar.

And they're not only the last to come back. They're the first to leave. When I looked up and saw that the storks had gone——"

"You knew that presently you'd be picking the last rose of summer? Is that it?"

"Yes, that's it."

"And you didn't relish the prospect?"

"Well, the winters are pretty long here. Napoleon said that East Prussia was a country where there were nine months of winter and three that you couldn't call summer."

"Chris, didn't it ever occur to you that it might be a good plan to stop dwelling for awhile on what Napoleon said and Frederick the Great did and Queen Luise thought and give a little attention instead to what this man Hitler is thinking and saying and doing?"

"Yes, it's occurred to me. But it hasn't occurred to my grandmother yet."

"You might call her attention to it."

"I have. At least, I've tried. But she doesn't listen."

"She'll have to listen, someday, unless I'm very much mistaken. It might be a good plan for you to begin a serious attempt to make her."

"Oh, I've begun. But I haven't got very far."

"Chris, you had guts enough to break away from Hamstead and Harvard. You ought to have guts enough to break away from here."

The boy began to trace lines around the cobblestones with his crop, apparently as intent upon the futile gesture as he had been on the stork's nest a few minutes earlier. When he finally looked up, Rufus Rhodes saw that his face was quivering.

"Do you think it would take more guts to break away than it does to stay?" he asked vehemently.

For an instant, Rufus Rhodes was nonplussed. He had not been prepared for this form of counterattack. But he rallied quickly.

"Yes. In a way I do. You're lonely here, and discouraged. You feel you don't fit in, and that's all the harder for you, because you expected to, because you didn't fit in at Harvard either, and you thought this would be different. But though you've made up your mind to stick it out this time, and believe that's what you're doing, what you're really doing is to follow the line of least resistance. You're letting your grandmother suck your strength and plan your life, because it's easier for you to do that than to oppose her."

"You're wrong, Mr. Rhodes. None of it's a question of what's easy. As far as my grandmother's concerned, it's a question of what's kind. I can't be cruel to her."

"She can be cruel to you. She doesn't intend that you shall stir from her side. She proposes that you shall stay here, shut up with spooks and stories, for the rest of your natural life. She doesn't even intend to let you choose your own wife. She has you as good as married to some silly little Spaniard already, instead of giving you a chance to see something of a sensible modern girl your own age."

"Mr. Rhodes, I don't wish to be rude to a guest. But I can't permit anyone to speak that way about my grandmother. She's a very wonderful person, and she's suffered a great deal."

"I know she's a wonderful person, and I know she's suffered a great deal. But the same thing is true of your mother, and you went off and left her. I'm not even suggesting that you should leave your grandmother. Take her with you, if you must. But get out of this place, before it gets you."

"My mother has her own interests, Sir, if you'll excuse me for saying so. My grandmother has no one but me. And just now, I've no one but her. And nothing but Schönplatz. I don't believe I could make you understand how I feel about 'this place,' as you call it. It's true, I have been lonely and discouraged here. But just the same, I love it. Everything about it, even its spooks and stories. They're real to me, and precious. But quite aside from that, Schönplatz represents my only means of making a living. I haven't been very successful in that direction yet, I know. But I've got to keep on trying. I can't go away from here in the winter. That's the foaling season. Our foals are all born between November and April. And you see those 'beautiful white horses' are a potential source of income. So far, as I told you, it's the sheep that have been most profitable. But I believe the horses will be profitable too, sometime. I'm superstitious about them in my own way, just as the peasants are in theirs. Only I have a different theory about omens."

"Well, what's your theory?"

"I believe a colored colt would bring us good luck instead of bad. I want a dapple gray, like the original stallion. I'm hoping to get this. I believe it's time for a new strain, or a return to the original strain, just as you look at it. But anyway, a strong strain, not a weak one. I'm experimenting. I've made some dreadful mistakes, but I'm going straight on."

He paused for a moment, and then brought his crop, with a snap, up over his shoulder. "I haven't bred my dappled gray colt yet," he said with a smile. "I haven't sired my own son, either. When I do, nobody but me is going to choose his mother. Not any woman living. And not any man either."

PART V

1929–1931

"Banners High"

CHAPTER 13

The interior of the Restaurant zum Nussbaum in Alt-Berlin was dark and dingy. The cartoons and chromos tacked on the walls gave it a tattered look, rather than a picturesque one; amid these, the steel engraving of a prim Victorian couple struck an incongruous note. The settees were stained, the tables marred by the hieroglyphics hacked into them. The air was thick with smoke and the stale smell that comes from underairing and overcrowding. The place was filled, for the most part, by rather drab individuals. There were a few roisterers among them, but the majority talked in low guttural voices, or sat staring stolidly into space. Here and there a face that was sinister stood out among several that were merely sullen. One shabby man, who sat alone in a corner with the collar of his coat turned up and his hands thrust deep into his frayed pockets, glanced towards the door at the arrival of each newcomer with an expression that was searchingly sardonic.

Beer was brought in by a fat, frowsy woman who slopped it over when she set it down. But the beer itself was excellent. Trixie Rhodes bent over her mug and blew the foam lightly to one side before she took a long sip.

"My, that's good!" she exclaimed, as she raised her head. "I was terribly thirsty too. Weren't you, Chris?"

"You have some foam on the end of your nose," he remarked irrelevantly. Then as she brushed it off without concern, and buried her face in her beer a second time, he added, "Yes, I was. But I would have been willing to wait until we could get to Kroll's, or some such place, for a drink, instead of coming here."

"Oh, but I simply had to come to the Nussbaum! My sight-seeing wouldn't have been complete if I hadn't seen the oldest restaurant in Berlin. You know it wouldn't."

"Well, I hope it's complete now. I'll be going back to Schönplatz on a stretcher if I let you drag me around much longer."

"But you haven't any idea of going back to Schönplatz yet!"

"I didn't have. But I may need to, in self-defense. You set a pretty strenuous pace, Trixie."

His tone was bantering, but his smile was sunny, and Trixie's heart warmed to it. She had been a long time in getting him to Berlin, for he had stuck grimly to his self-imposed task at Schönplatz. But finally he had received his reward, though no one besides himself knew what this had cost him in determination and self-denial. The balance sheets which had caused him so much concern at last began to give him gratification instead. The reliable sheep continued to do their share, and the stud slowly evolved from a liability to an asset. The day came when he sent a wire to the American Embassy in Berlin which caused the Ambassador to break into a roar of hearty approbation as he tossed the telegram across the table to his daughter.

"Well, the youngster surely has guts! I never thought he'd see it through. I wouldn't put anything past him now."

"I don't know what you mean. And I don't know what this telegram means either—except the last part of it."

"*'The strong strain is started. I have bred my dappled gray foal and she is a beauty,'*" Rufus Rhodes read aloud, recapturing his dispatch. "*'Delighted to come to Berlin now, if you still want to have me.'* Well, Trixie, Chris had a notion— But I'll tell you about that afterwards. The main thing is to get an answer right off telling him to take the next train. Isn't it?"

Hans Christian had not taken the next train, or indeed any train, for the railroad service across East Prussia and the Polish Corridor still left much to be desired. Nevertheless he had appeared promptly, driving the same car which he had brought with him from the United States five years earlier, and wearing the same clothes. He made no apology and apparently felt no embarrassment for either, and he proved, from the first, a delightful guest. Mrs. Rhodes was completely captivated by him; he adapted himself so pleasantly to the ways of her household and was such an addition to it that she felt she would like to have him there indefinitely. Mr. Rhodes reveled openly in his presence, with the pathetic satisfaction of a man who has always starved for the vigorous young male companionship which he would have found in a son. And Trixie, quite as candid as her parents in her joy over his visit, dashed gayly about with him from one end of Berlin to the other, and paraded her prize before the envious eyes of all her friends.

At first, it was to the Ambassador that Hans Christian responded most freely. Rufus Rhodes had been to Schönplatz himself; consequently he was in a position to understand the progress which had been made there; and Hans Christian, after his long lack of listeners, was eager to talk about this. He had brought with him sketches of the structural changes which he had made, or was hoping to make, in the stables, and snapshots of the dappled gray foal; he spread these forth on a long table and pointed out their best features in detail. He spoke of building improvements with sober pride, after the manner of a man who has planned them with frugality and care and has executed them with skill; but when he talked about the little foal, his face lighted up and his voice rang with happiness.

"I had her by Isolde out of Schönplatzstolz," he explained. "She was Isolde's first foal. Now I don't see why that mare shouldn't have more dappled gray foals, do you, if they were sired by the same stallion? Of course that is what I'm going to try for first. But if I don't get results that way, I shan't be discouraged; I'll wait patiently until the little filly is old enough to be bred herself. I know she'll set up the strain."

"I shouldn't be surprised, Chris, but what you're right."

"Naturally I wouldn't have come away, even now," Chris went on, picking up one of the snapshots and looking at it lovingly, "if I hadn't left her in the best possible hands. I haven't had a chance to tell you yet— This isn't the first time I've been away from Schönplatz. I took a trip through Bavaria and the Rhineland last fall. I couldn't persuade my grandmother to go with me. She hasn't left Schönplatz at all yet, and she didn't approve of my going either. But I decided it was about time I saw my German relatives again—the von Mitwelds, you know, who live in Munich, and my Aunt Elsa, who is a Carmelite nun in Cologne."

"I think you had a good idea there, Chris, very good."

"I think so too. I didn't get much out of my visit to the convent, and at first the outlook in Munich was pretty discouraging. The von Mitwelds certainly have a queer household. My uncle was away at Doorn, as usual, and my Cousin Karl kept trying to pick a political quarrel with me. He's an out-and-out Communist, and would like to see everything the *Junkers* stand for scrapped tomorrow. There's nothing I could do for the poor little cripple, or my Aunt Rita either; but I took a great shine to the youngest girl, Luischen, my grandmother's namesake. There's something so sincere about her looks—straight dark brows, rather heavy—level eyes, clear color. Well, I can't describe it, but the quality is there. She's been in love for years with a nice fellow her family thought was 'beneath her' and who was out of a job—like most of the other nice young fellows I met."

"Yes, I want to talk to you sometime about this unemployment situation, Chris. It's serious, very serious."

"It certainly is— Well, when I found out this suitor of Luischen's, Ernst Behrend, was a trained studmaster, I had a brainstorm. I asked him if he wouldn't like to come to Schönplatz to be my *Landstallmeister*. I could just see him in the *Gestudsekretariat*, keeping the account books, and out in the paddocks, watching over the little foals. I asked Luischen if she wouldn't marry him and come along. I could see her, too, letting sunshine into the house and filling vases with flowers. They both seemed so cheerful, in spite of all their troubles and disappointments, and so competent— They jumped at the chance I gave them, and when I went home they went with me. Aunt Rita was furious, and so was grandmother. But they'll get over it. There's going to be a baby pretty soon now, and they won't be able to resist that, no matter what they think beforehand. And having Luischen and Ernst at Schönplatz has been a godsend to me. It's as if a fresh breeze had begun to blow through a musty place, if you know what I mean."

"I think I do, Chris, I think I do. I'm glad everything seems to be coming along so nicely for you. Now that you've got this trustworthy man, you won't be tied down so closely; and with a nice young woman and a cunning baby in the house, that'll be considerably pleasanter for you too. When a lady gets to be your grandmother's age, she doesn't always remember how much sunshine and flowers mean to young folks, especially if she's seen a lot of sorrow in her own life. But I know how it is——"

"Yes, you seem to. But what I wish is, that I could think up a way of solving our national problems as well as my personal ones have been solved. I've got the foundation laid for prosperity and progress at Schönplatz now, I feel sure of that. But East Prussia generally—and Germany as a whole— We're not getting anywhere, Mr. Rhodes, the way we're going now. There's wretchedness on every side, and desperation—even under the surface smoothness of Berlin's most fashionable quarters. I turn a corner—hardly more than that—and see starvation. I turn another and find depravity. I don't think Trixie's conscious of it. The spring is so beautiful, the tulips are so bright, the trees are so green—those are the only things she sees, and I'm glad of it. But more than once I've had to hurry her past a place where I was afraid she'd see more—gruesome sights, obscene sights. There must be some way out of all this, someone who could lead us out."

"Well, let's hope there is. I'd like to talk to you about that too, sometime. But I mustn't keep you any longer just now. I ought to be off to the Chancery, and I know Trixie's waiting for you. I think she wants you to go with her to some picture gallery or other."

"No, Sir, it isn't a picture gallery today. We did that yesterday. I think I must be the first victim Trixie's found that she can sacrifice to her craze for sight-seeing, she's making such a thorough job of it. But it's quite all right with me. I go to museums and monuments with her in the daytime and she goes to concerts and operas with me in the evening. It's a mutually satisfactory bargain. We're off now to the Palace in Charlottenburg and afterwards to an East End restaurant, the 'Nut Tree.' Tonight we're going to *Götterdämmerung*."

"The 'Nut Tree'?"

"Yes, Sir. The Nussbaum in Alt-Berlin. It's the oldest restaurant in the city. That's why she wants to see it. She's read about it in a guidebook. But the guidebook apparently didn't mention the fact that nowadays it's a pet place for Communists. I don't know just what sort of a crowd we'll run into there. But I'll look after her."

"I know you will, Chris. Well, have a good time, both of you."

They had a very good time, though neither the Palace nor the Nussbaum had quite come up to Trixie's expectations. But it was a beautiful day and they were both feeling carefree and content. The avenues in the park at Charlottenburg were feathery with fresh green, and everywhere the tulip beds were bright. Trixie said that it gave her a lift just to look at them, and Hans Christian began to sing little tunes under his breath. Even the restaurant was partially redeemed from squalor by the red geraniums in the window boxes under its gables, and the verdant boughs of the ancient tree which stood in front of it. Besides, the beer was certainly very good and they were undeniably thirsty after their long tramp through the state apartments and among those endless alleys winding around the blue-domed mausoleum. They sat relaxed and sipped unhurriedly, smoking cigarettes and badgering each other with great good humor.

"About that stretcher, Trixie. I think I better call up the Elizabeth *Krankenhaus* and make arrangements for it when we get back to the Embassy."

"Nonsense! We can improvise one for you ourselves, if you really want it. And I'll go along with you to Schönplatz as your nurse. You don't need one of those demure little deaconesses."

"What do you know about nursing, Trixie?"

"It doesn't take much knowledge to sit beside a bed and smooth a sheet. Any girl would be glad to do it—that is, if there was someone in the bed who had what it takes. I could put on a cap and apron, if you think that would help out, of course. I'm sure I'd have a very soothing effect upon you."

"Are you? I'm not so certain."

His tone had lost none of its lightness. Momentarily, the basic depression which he had revealed to Rufus Rhodes had been lifted. His release from long loneliness, the stimulating society into which he had suddenly been thrown, the heady atmosphere of spring and sunshine —all these had been intoxicating in their effect. He was in the mood for merrymaking, almost in the mood for love-making. From the beginning, he had enjoyed Trixie immensely as a companion; now he began to visualize her vaguely as a sweetheart. Although he did not deeply desire her, he recognized all her desirable qualities. He knew it would take very little to ignite a spark between them, and he saw no reason for refraining from playing with such pleasant fire. Moreover, the typical male aversion to trespass upon any possible preserves of his own had begun to possess him. Trixie seemed to have a good many suitors, and he did not know how seriously she might take any one of these at any moment. He asked a casual question, which was actually less inconsequential than it sounded.

"Do you ever hear from Card Eustis nowadays?"

"Oh, yes. He turns up regularly every summer."

"Do you drag him through picture galleries too?"

"No. That isn't Card's idea of a good time."

"It isn't mine, either."

"Well, I'm afraid I'm not very successful at pleasing either of you. Card keeps complaining too. You know what his idea of having a good time with a girl is just as well as I do."

"And what's your own idea, Trixie? About having a good time with a man, I mean?"

"It depends an awful lot on the man. For instance, I'm having a good time with you this minute. But if I were here with Card instead of you, I don't believe I'd think the old Nussbaum was so hot."

She smiled engagingly, and her blue eyes sparkled as she spoke. But as if forestalling any special response to her candid declaration of enjoyment, she picked up her gloves and handbag and got to her feet.

"Just the same, no matter how good a time I'm having, I suppose we ought to be cruising along, if we're going to the *Götterdämmerung*. Talk about your endurance tests! I'd say an opera that lasts five hours and doesn't have a single tune in it from beginning to end was enough to lay anyone out! But you don't hear me whining about stretchers and strenuous paces."

Hans Christian laughed in his turn, paid their infinitesimal *Rechnung*, and followed her out into the street. The man with the sinister face, his hands still buried in the pockets of his shabby overcoat, looked up at them as they passed. But he did not speak to them or try to stop them. The other patrons of the restaurant appeared to be as oblivious of their departure as they had been of their presence. Unalterably drab, they continued to talk in low guttural voices, to carve their initials in the benches, and to drink the excellent beer which the slatternly *Stubenmädchen* slopped over as she set it down in front of them.

Outside, the sky was still bright and beautiful and a fresh breeze gave a quality of stimulation to the soft air. It blew in fitful gusts down the narrow street, between the tall blank houses lining this on either side. But the sunshine overhead did not stretch to the sidewalks; it was swallowed up in the gloomy recesses of the colorless thoroughfare. Except for a few slinking and scuttling figures, Fischerstrasse was empty. There were no children playing exuberantly on the pavements, no groups of laborers swinging home from work, no crowds pushing good-naturedly into little open shops. The normal bustle of business and pleasure was completely lacking. A solitary whistle, undefinable of origin, and mysteriously echoed, vibrated through the air. Then everything was silent again. The vacancy and stillness were eerie in their effect.

"I'm afraid we ought to have come in my car after all," Hans Christian said. A queer little quiver was forking its way through his body, and he looked searchingly up and down the street. "But since neither of us knew our way around the East End— We might at least have kept our taxi. I was a fool not to realize that it might be hard to pick up another."

"Don't worry. I'm sure one'll be along in a minute. We might walk on down towards the canal. There's probably more traffic there."

"*More* traffic! I don't get the comparison, Trixie."

"You ought not to mind emptiness, after East Prussia."

"The country never seems empty to me. But a city street with no one in it is weird. That whistle was queer too. Don't you think so?"

"Sort of. But I'm not going to let it get me."

As she spoke, a sharp spitting sound crackled through the air. She jumped back, instinctively clutching at Hans Christian's arm.

"What's that, Chris?"

"I can't imagine. I don't see a soul anywhere."

"It sounded like a shot to me."

"How could it be? There's no one around to do any shooting."

"It must have come from one of those houses."

"But they look empty too."

"Well, I guess they're not."

As if in confirmation of her remark, several windows were suddenly flung open, and an uproar arose from within them. At the same moment, a second report rang out. It was louder than the first, and longer, and was followed by an ugly snarling outcry.

"Es muss etwas geschehen! So geht es nicht weiter! Nieder mit den Nazis! Nieder mit der S. A.! Nieder mit dem Horst Wessel!"

Tightening his hold on Trixie's arm, Hans Christian quickened his pace. "This is a bad quarter," he said under his breath. "Some kind of trouble's up. We've got to get out of it, if we can."

"Yes, I know. I can run, Chris, if you think we better. But I'm not afraid."

They could hear tumultuous shouting now, and the sound of rushing feet. Before another shot had rung out, the empty sidewalks were swarming, so suddenly that they could not see whence the crowd came. They were hemmed in on every side by a mob that had apparently gone mad. Escape was completely cut off. Ducking down, and dragging Trixie along with him, Hans Christian fought his way through the rioters towards a doorway. Twice he was knocked down, falling over her as he fell himself. Someone stamped on him before he could get to his feet again, and when he had dragged himself halfway up, someone else kicked him over; but he could still feel her clinging confidently to him. When at last he reached the doorway, he managed to push her behind him and crouched in front of her, warding off hit or miss blows with his arm. Most of the men around them were fighting with their fists. But some of them had rubber clubs, and a few revolvers. He was sick with fear lest a stray shot should whiz past him. The next time the crackling started, there was no telling where it might end.

"I'm all right, Chris. I'm not frightened. Please don't worry."

Somehow, above the din, she made him hear her. But he could not answer her. The mob was milling towards the doorway now. At any moment they might be crushed by it. Unless it receded, unless it scattered and disappeared as quickly as it had come. A moment before, he had been cursing his own folly for bringing Trixie into this hotbed of violence, but from cursing he went to prayer. Let me get her out, don't let any harm come to her because I've been such a bloody fool, keep her from being hurt——

"Really, I'm all right, Chris. I think it's going to be over in a minute anyway."

Something snapped. The impact of struggling bodies against them slackened. The blows, the crackling, the shouts and stamping abated. The electrified air began to clear. The rioters were surging forward now, instead of pressing backwards; then they separated, charging in different directions and calling out as they went. Hans Christian, still bent defensively over, heard Trixie speaking to him a third time.

"Someone is trying to talk to you, Chris. I think he means to be friendly."

Hans Christian slowly straightened himself up. A young man dressed in brown twill—hardly more than a boy—was standing over him, looking down at him fixedly. His blue eyes were keen, but they were not hostile. He was breathing hard and perspiration was streaming from his face; his clothes were badly disheveled. In spite of these evidences of conflict, however, his manner was completely controlled.

"Also," he said peremptorily. *"Was ist denn los? Warum sind Sie hier?"*

"You may be very sure it isn't from choice," Hans Christian retorted.

He was still greatly shaken; it was more than a matter of moment to regain his self-control. "This lady and I were walking quietly down the street when a mob appeared from nowhere. We got hemmed in by it," he added by way of brief explanation. Then he turned to Trixie. "How much hurt are you?" he asked anxiously in English.

"Sind Sie Engländer?" inquired the young German, regarding them with still greater attention.

"We're Americans," Trixie interposed quickly. Her German was faulty, but fluent, and she had no more trouble now than Chris in shifting swiftly from one language to another. "I'm not hurt, except that someone seems to have given me a sock on the jaw. My cheek's bleeding a little."

She had been dabbing at her face with a small square of cambric. Hans Christian, accustomed to her constant manipulation of make-up, had hardly noticed the unobtrusive gesture. Now he saw that the handkerchief was soaked with blood.

"I should think it was! Is there a Red Cross station or an apothecary shop anywhere around here?"

"I am afraid there is not. But my own quarters are in this house. If the *gnädiges Fräulein* would be so good as to step inside, I think I can stop the bleeding myself. I know the principles of first aid. *So, wenn ich bitten darf*——"

The young German twisted an iron ring hanging from the great studded door against which they had been leaning, and it opened creakingly down the middle. Beyond it there was a dim courtyard, where a dark carved stairway curved upwards amid hanging vines. It was beautiful, but battered, and a noisome smell rose from the dank ground about it. Everything connected with the place bespoke bygone splendor sunk to decadence.

Their host produced a latchkey and unlocked a door at the right of the entrance. Then, with grave politeness, he ushered them into a room lined with ancient paneling and sketchily equipped with cheap modern furniture. Offering the one armchair to Hans Christian, he told Trixie to lie down on the couch while he fetched cold water and clean cotton from the kitchen; and briefly disappearing into an adjacent room, he returned with a small tin basin and other supplies and capably began to bathe her bruised cheek.

"We are very much indebted to you for your hospitality and help. But perhaps you'll also explain to us what this fracas was about," Hans Christian remarked. He had not taken the proffered armchair, but stood beside the couch, watching the proceedings with anxious interest. He still spoke rather curtly, and his host, without betraying any resentment of his manner, answered with slightly satirical stiffness himself.

"It was nothing serious. Only a group of the K. P. D. carrying out orders from Karl Liebknecht Haus: '*Schlagt die Faschisten wo ihr sie trefft!*' A comrade of mine, who lives with me here at the Bomb Palast, was coming peacefully home when he was set upon. He was alone for the moment, so the opportunity was favorable. But other comrades managed to join him, and fortunately he was not hurt at all. I saw him pursuing the last of the aggressors just before I spoke to you. He will probably be along in a few minutes. In fact I do not think any of us were killed this time."

"You're not one of those wicked S. A. men they talk about, are you?" inquired Trixie, excitedly, sitting bolt upright.

"Yes, *gnädiges Fräulein.* Oskar Kraus, at your service. It goes better now, *nicht?* But I think it would be well if you would lie still for a few moments yet, until I can be sure that the bleeding is entirely stopped."

"It's practically stopped now— Why do you call this house the Bomb Palast?"

"It is only a nickname we give it, *gnädiges Fräulein,* because the Communists have sought so many times to destroy it with bombs since my comrade and I have been living here. It was formerly the residence of a great prince. Now, as you see, it is only a tenement. But it is the best we can do at the moment."

"Do you mean to say you live here in these dirty slums on purpose? When you don't have to? With bombs going off over your head all the time? And that you go around shooting up the streets and think nothing of it?"

"Your pardon, *gnädiges Fräulein.* It is not the S. A. who 'shoot up the streets,' as you say. It is the K. P. D. We only defend ourselves from them, as best we can. And I must beg of you to lie down again, as I said before."

"But what does all this street brawling *prove?*"

"Trixie, please stop talking and do what *Herr* Kraus tells you. This isn't any time for argument."

"I shall be delighted to explain our party principles to the *gnädiges Fräulein* later, if she is really interested. And for that matter to you also, *Herr*——?"

"My name is Beatrice Rhodes," Trixie announced, bounding up again before Hans Christian could answer. "And this is my friend Chris Marlowe."

"Miss Rhodes is the daughter of the American Ambassador to Germany," Hans Christian remarked dryly. "I certainly hope, for everyone's sake, that she isn't much hurt."

"It is my sincere hope also. But only because I should regret that she should suffer. I am sure the American Ambassador, whom we hold in high esteem, would not make an incident out of an accident."

"Do you know my father?" inquired Trixie, still more excitedly.

"I have not had the privilege of meeting him personally. But he has done us the honor of coming to one or two of our meetings—unofficially, of course—as an onlooker. He did not make himself known to anyone. But he was recognized, and with gratitude. It is not often that a foreign envoy takes the trouble to observe what is really going on about him—You would also be most welcome if you would care to attend a gathering of ours, *Herr* Marlowe."

"I'd like to, sometime. And perhaps I can come back here someday, and hear about your party principles, as you suggest. But now, if you think Miss Rhodes is all right, I'd like to try to get her home as quickly as possible."

With the assuagement of his anxiety, and his recovery from the shock of assault, Hans Christian's natural courtesy had begun to reassert itself. He was already secretly ashamed of his incivility in the face of the young Nazi's considerate kindness. His change of manner met with immediate response.

"Of course. I am afraid there are no taxicabs near here. But as soon as my comrade comes back, he will get one. I would go myself, were it not for leaving you alone here in my Bomb Palast. Not that I think there is any real danger. But sometimes, after an encounter like the one we have just been through, there are slight reprisals."

For the first time, Oskar Kraus smiled. Then, tentatively, he touched Trixie's cheek with his fingers. The bleeding had stopped entirely. He opened a small jar of salve and applied the ointment meticulously to the bruise. Then he picked up his bottles and basin and the wet cotton and stained towels, which he had discarded, and carried them carefully back into the kitchen again.

"May I help you? I seem to be awfully useless! Or I could go out and find a taxi myself, couldn't I, and leave Miss Rhodes with you?"

"Thank you. There is nothing more to do. And I think it would be better that you should not go out, *Herr* Marlowe. I see that your German is excellent, but after all you do not know your way around this quarter, and as you have seen, it is apt to be disorderly. However, I am sure it will not be long now before my comrade comes. And meanwhile you are most welcome. Perhaps I could offer you and *Fräulein* Rhodes some slight refreshment. My larder is rather bare, because I have not yet bought my provisions for supper. But such as I have——"

He was interrupted by the sound of knocking. It came firmly though not aggressively, in a succession of swift strokes against the door, repeated like signals. Oskar Kraus turned quickly.

"That cannot be my comrade. He has his key. But do not be alarmed. I know the knock. It must come from some other member of our troop, arrived to assure himself that all goes well with us."

He opened the door cautiously, saying something that sounded like a watchword as he did so. This was instantly repeated, and it was followed by a murmured greeting and one or two quick questions and answers. Then another fair slim boy stepped into the room. He looked even younger than Oskar Kraus. Indeed, his face still had the ingenuous aspect of adolescence. But he carried himself with assurance, notwithstanding the slightness of his build, and there was an indefinable air of authority about him. He clicked his heels together and bowed to Trixie.

"I am sorry you have had so poor a welcome to Alt-Berlin, *gnädiges Fräulein*. But happily you have come to no real harm. And now that I am here, Comrade Kraus will go at once for a taxi, and at the same time telephone the American Embassy so that there may be no anxiety about you." He bowed a second time, looked searchingly at Hans Christian for a moment, and held out his hand. "I am sorry too that you should have come to us first in such a way," he said. "But it is better that you should have come to us thus than not at all. May I present myself? I am Horst Wessel, Storm Leader of Troop Number Five. It is a privilege to greet you—*Freiherr* von Hohenlohe."

CHAPTER 14

"Für Deutschland das Leben zu wagen,
Wo andre greifen vergeblich an,
Da zieht man den fünften Sturm heran!"

"GOOD, COMRADES! That time it went better—much better! Next troop night it must be snappier still! In the meantime you will be practicing in your separate groups. You know how to do it: One song at the beginning—for instance, *Kameraden, lasst erschallen*. A second after intermission—*Wer will mit uns zum Kampfe ziehen?* At the end—*Hoch die Fahne*.

"No smoking! This isn't a social club! Troop night means service night! Later on everyone may smoke as much as he likes, and of course if anyone wants a drink— But now, every man on his toes. Chests out, heads high! Why, there's not a paunch among the lot of you. It's plain you're not with the Communists any more. When you went to their meetings you sat this way, with your head propped on your elbows, and your hands on your cheeks, and your mouths wide open!"

The speaker paused long enough to slump into a slouch. Momentarily his alert face assumed a vacant expression. Then echoing the roar of merriment with which his byplay was greeted, he sprang to his feet again.

"Beginning with our next meeting, I'm going to take a quarter of an hour each evening to talk to you about politics. It's true that we're not a debating society, any more than we're a social club. But a Storm Trooper must be able to stand up for his side. He can't convince Marxists by mouthing phrases; what he says has got to have meat in it. We're going to put it there. But for tonight we'll let that slide. We'll talk about the subject that means the most to us—the *Sturm Abteilung*. What does it mean—S. A.? What does it mean to be an S. A. man?"

The *Lokal Zur Möve* in the Grosse Frankfurter Strasse was packed with people. Most of them were Storm Troopers; but there were also a number of onlookers. The meetings were not secret and outsiders were welcomed, for among them many recruits were made. Within the last month seventy had been added to the ranks, and the question of a meeting place had become something of a problem. It was not too easy to find an accommodating host in Friedrichshain, and *Heinrichs Festsaal*, where Horst Wessel had directed his first troop night, had long since overflowed with his followers. But finally a landlord had been discovered who was not afraid of what the Karl Liebknecht Haus might do to him, and Troop Five had forgathered in his largest hall.

"Loyalty. Obedience. Self-control. Reliability. Honorable conduct in the service and out of it. *Kameradschaft*—these are the qualities demanded of an S. A. man," the speaker went on. "The leader of my old *Standarte*—most of you know him—never tired of hammering these fundamental principles into his troop members and especially into the leaders he had under him. I am going to take time this evening to explain these fundamental principles which underlie the training of an S. A. man.

"LOYALTY is the greatest S. A. virtue. The S. A. man is loyal when he stands by the vow he made as he gripped his leader's hand. Along with loyalty to his leader goes loyalty to his comrades. A man is a faithless coward who leaves his comrades in the lurch at times of need, who fails to rush to his comrades' need when alarm is sounded."

"It is said of Horst Wessel's father that he was not only a good pastor but a great preacher," Oskar Kraus whispered to Hans Christian. "You see that his son has inherited his talents. In all Berlin, there is no one more in demand as a speaker. I know of fifty speeches which he has made within the last three months. Listen!"

"Next after loyalty comes obedience," Horst Wessel was saying, "and obedience always calls for self-control. Together these two constitute discipline. DISCIPLINE is the foundation on which co-operation between the S. A. man and the S. A. leader rests. A person may be a fine orator and a great organizer, a political authority and a trained athlete, with courage, energy and presence of mind. But if he does not know how to obey, he has not the marks of merit. In spite of his brown shirt, his cap, his *Koppel*, his shoulder straps and his party insignia, he is no true S. A. man. A troop may have imposing strength, it may be commanded by a capable leader. But without discipline it is still nothing but a heterogeneous group.

"The S. A. man who is impressed with these truths shows his leaders the respect which he owes them because of their position. Deportment is always the expression of an inner attitude. Therefore the S. A. man, like the soldier, salutes his leader when he greets him, standing erect and facing him squarely. But he bows his head only before the majesty of God and the majesty of death."

He was only twenty-two and he looked younger still. But as he spoke, the men around him, many of them old enough to be his father, paid him the tribute of their deference. There was something Biblical in the simplicity of his language and the composure of his bearing; but there was force behind both. This force made itself felt, like an electric current.

"Let me sum up what I have said so far: If loyalty is the most outstanding of the S. A. virtues, discipline is their most important attribute. Without forgetting this, we must not forget the great quality of trustworthiness—the quality which makes a man 'faithful unto death'—or the great requisite of honorable defense. But among comrades questions of honor are not settled by fighting. Remember this, when you are confused and angry. Never strike a comrade, for in doing so you break the bonds of *Kameradschaft*. As my last point, shall I speak to you on this subject? I should do so if it were a problem in the S. A., but thank God such is not the case. The brown battalions may have lacked every other great quality of which I have been speaking. But *Kameradschaft* is the one which has been theirs from the beginning.

"The feeling that in a world full of hate and infamy we are bound together for better or worse, in life and in death—this feeling has always inspired us every one, the leaders and the led. That spirit of *Kameradschaft,* based upon valor and discipline, that spirit which gave to millions at the front the strength to serve and to sacrifice, must also animate the S. A. For it is now in the hands of the S. A. that the future of Germany lies!

"*Sturm* Five— Attention! Quiet! I declare this meeting adjourned."

"Raise high the flags! Stand rank on rank together,
Storm troopers march with steady quiet tread. . . ."

It was over. The ranks were breaking, the men were leaving the hall or gathering together in little groups at the doorway. They were lighting cigarettes now, as they laughed and chatted. But Hans Christian continued to stand as if he had been transfixed. Oskar Kraus touched him lightly on the arm.

"Would you like a glass of beer? Is anything the matter?"

"No— But I have the strangest feeling. As if I could hear thousands singing that song, not just this small assembly."

"There's a lilt to it. It's easy to sing. I imagine it will take on."

"I don't mean just that— I can't explain— Do you suppose I could talk to Horst Wessel myself?"

"Tonight?"

"Yes, now."

"I don't know. He's generally very busy. He's got a lot on his mind. But we can find out."

They went on to the back of the hall. Horst was still standing there, talking earnestly in a low voice with two or three others. Kraus approached them and saluted.

"*Mein Führer, Freiherr* von Hohenlohe is here. The man you met in my quarters with the young American lady."

"Yes, I remember. He is very welcome."

"He says he would like to have a talk with you."

"He would be welcome to do that also. I will tell him so."

Horst Wessel, himself, saluted. Then he turned and looked cordially towards Hans Christian. When he smiled, he seemed younger than ever. And the smile was irresistible. Hans Christian was drawn to him as if by a magnet.

"Good evening. I'm so glad you came to our meeting. I hoped you'd come to one, sometime, after I saw you the other night. Did you enjoy it?"

"Yes, very much. That is— I want to talk to you."

"So Comrade Kraus tells me. Would you care to come to my quarters? I live with my family on the Judenstrasse, near the Rathaus and the Nicolai Kirche—my father's church. I'd like to have you meet them sometime—my mother, my brother Werner, who's in Troop Four, and my sister Ingeborg. You'd admire her, she's very talented. But I have some small diggings of my own, besides, close by here in the Grosse Frankfurter Strasse. If what you want is a quiet conversation, we could go there. That's why I keep it—for just such conferences, I mean. I have a good many."

He smiled again. If there was any element of irony in the remark, Hans Christian did not catch it. He grasped eagerly at the opportunity which had been offered him.

"Thanks a lot. Shall I wait till you're through here?"

"I'm through now. We can walk along together."

There was rain in the air when they went out. Horst Wessel lifted his head as if he welcomed the freshness of it on his face.

"I love weather like this. In my part of the country, we call it '*ein richtiger, erbärmlicher Landregen.*' Do you have the same expression in East Prussia? *So!*— Sometimes I wish my grandfather had never come to the city. I like the land. While I was still in Standard Four, my brother Werner's troop, I used to get out there once a fortnight at least, over the week ends. Now I'm too busy. But there's a farm not far out, owned by a man who's friendly. He always lets the S. A. come there. He has a big barn, three hundred can sleep in it. I've often acted as sentry there. Sometimes the nights seemed pretty long, if I'd been doing guard duty and drilling all the week. But there was something about it—the stars and the silence. Or on evenings like this, the haze and the mystery. I could feel their beauty as if it had been alive. And I was never tired the next morning. Perhaps because of all this somber splendor. Or perhaps because a sense of responsibility is always a stimulation. Or perhaps just because cold water out of a pump, dashed over your head at five in the morning, and coffee made in a field kitchen, are even better ones!"

He laughed, pleasantly. Hans Christian laughed too, but he asked an earnest question.

"Could I go out into the country with the troop too, as well as come to the meetings?"

"But of course! Werner would be delighted to take you if I cannot. And in August you should come to Nuremberg with us, you should see the great celebration of our *Parteitag*. I promise you it is worth it!—Well, here we are at my lodging. You must tell me whether you like it as well as the Bomb Palast."

Horst Wessel unlocked the door of a bleak house, stale-smelling after the fresh misty air they had been breathing, and Hans Christian followed him up two flights of steep slippery stairs covered with brown linoleum. At the top of these Horst ushered him into a small dormer room overlooking the street and furnished in nondescript fashion. Magnetized as it was, its furnishings did not matter.

"May I offer you some refreshment? No? Then tell me what it is you have on your mind."

"I want to tell you first of all that I didn't intentionally conceal my identity from Oskar Kraus that night at the Bomb Palast. I'm tremendously proud of being a German—in fact, I'm one by choice. I'll tell you about that too. But *Fräulein* Rhodes was terribly overwrought, and she was injured. Every time I tried to say anything, she interrupted me. She's obsessed with the idea that I'm essentially American. I didn't want to seem to argue with her before a stranger or do anything to make her worse."

"Of course. I understood perfectly. And so did Kraus, afterwards. At first, since he didn't know who you were, it didn't matter anyway. But it is my business to be informed on such matters. Any prominent guest whom the American Ambassador might have for a prolonged period—

May I ask if his daughter, the pretty young lady I saw, is your *Braut*? On this particular point I am not informed!"

"No, she is only a friend. But a very good friend. I'm extremely fond of her—of the whole family."

"It appears that they have made a very favorable impression in Berlin. That is fortunate. We have not always been so pleased with the officials which the United States has seen fit to send us and it is better this way. We need something to counteract the trouble made by this cursed Young Plan. What Dawes did was bad enough. It never could have worked, a substitute had to be found. But what is this substitute? A policy of humiliation, a plan for bondage! The Reichspräsident is defending it and the Reichstag will accept it—but to their own cost as well as Germany's!"

He spoke with mounting fervor, and for the first time Hans Christian was conscious that there might be a strain of vindictiveness in his valor. But there was cause enough for vindictiveness in German hearts; even the most lofty natures could hardly escape it. And Hans Christian was eager to speak of Germany's wrongs himself.

"I'm glad you mentioned politics. I especially wanted to talk to you about these, since you didn't mention them in your speech. Things are in a bad way in East Prussia."

"You could do a great deal to make them better, if you cared to."

"I? I've succeeded as a horse breeder, but for all the prestige I have, I might as well be the *Landstallmeister* in my own *Herrenhaus*. All my neighbors look down on me! They think I haven't got the true *Junker* spirit."

"Then show them that you have the true German spirit—the spirit of the new Germany, the resurrected country! Who could be so supremely suited to do so as yourself? A man who has voluntarily left luxury and leisure behind him in America to cast his lot with our hard one, to perpetuate a proud name and revive an ancient house!"

His praise was stimulating. Hans Christian felt his self-assurance returning. But his mind was still in a state of upheaval. Reluctantly but resolutely he steered the conversation back into the political field, and Horst Wessel followed his lead with enthusiasm. Hans Christian could not imagine how so young a man could have mastered so much or how he could impart what he had learned with such skill. He embarked fluently on the subjects of unemployment and reparations as if he were intimately acquainted with them. He spoke with assurance of the characteristics of Stresemann, Streicher, Hanfstängl, Hess. From policies and personalities he passed easily on to the discussion of principles.

"Have you read *Mein Kampf*? It's so expensive most of my men can't do so. I pick up a copy here and there as I can, to lend to leaders; and I read aloud, key sentences, at most meetings. By and by there'll be a popular edition, that will help a great deal. But probably you haven't needed to wait for that."

"No, I've read the book. Some of it's very moving. But other portions are almost revolting."

"Isn't that a rather strong expression? Are you sure you understand the parts that trouble you? Some are factual, some are merely symbolic. I'd be glad to go over them with you, a page at a time, if you feel that would be helpful. Occasionally two heads are better than one, you know, in cases of this kind."

"You're probably right. I may have read into it meanings that don't exist, partly because I've had such a guilty feeling about owning it at all. My grandmother was bound there shouldn't be a copy of it in the house. But I bootlegged it and since then I've hidden it."

"Your grandmother? *Ach ja,* the Austrian Archduchess who stands in so well with the Church– You have no Catholic leanings of any kind yourself, I suppose?"

"No– My grandfather von Hohenlohe was a Lutheran. His sons were baptized Catholics, like the children of all mixed marriages, but when my father was old enough to choose for himself, he became a Lutheran too. I was raised as a Protestant from the beginning. But probably you know most of this already."

"Yes, but it is gratifying to have your confirmation of the facts. Your grandfather was a great general. I hope you may follow in his footsteps, as far as leadership is concerned."

"That was my own hope when I came to Germany. But so far I've done nothing."

"I should say you had done a great deal and that you will do much more. In regard to the Austrian question, for instance. It is a ticklish one, and you must be in a position to know a good deal about some forms of feeling concerning it. We will talk that over sometime also. I have spent six months in Vienna myself and I think you would enjoy going there, which would be a natural thing for you to do, considering all your connections– A pity the first *Anschluss* movement was a failure. But after all, these adjustments do take time. We must not be impatient or allow ourselves to become discouraged– So your grandmother does not approve of our Party. That is very interesting. And your mother, what about her? What do they think about Nazis in America?"

"I haven't been back there in five years. But my mother sends me some clippings. I gather they think the club foot and cleft foot are pretty close together—not to mention the affiliation between dope fiends and perverts."

"*Ach,* that freedom of the press of which Americans are so proud!

What a channel for chicanery it can become! When you meet the men who have been so slandered, your gorge will rise with indignation."

"Do you think I'm likely to meet them?"

"Of course, if you wish. Nothing could be easier. Unless your own time is fully filled with functions—or unless, lacking a *Braut,* you have a sweetheart."

"No, I haven't a sweetheart yet."

"Well, they do sometimes lead to complications! On the other hand they add to the zest of life. In any case, since your time is so free, I must help you to fill it. Shall we arrange for another meeting?"

It was not a dismissal, it was an invitation. Nevertheless, as he accepted it, Hans Christian rose to leave. Horst Wessel straightened his shoulder straps and reached for his own cap.

"I'll walk with you a few blocks."

"But then you would have to come home alone!"

Horst Wessel laughed again.

"And quite right that I should. Right and entirely safe. Nothing'll happen to me. Other comrades are occupying our friends the Communists just now. I know the orders that have gone out from Karl Liebknecht Haus. '*Den Horst Wessel den lasst zunächst mal in Ruhe. Das besorgen wir schon. Der kommt auch noch ran.*'"

"But then any time——"

"No, not any time. Not for a long while yet."

A strange shiver passed through Hans Christian. Again, as in the *Lokal,* he seemed to hear multitudes singing Horst Wessel's song and the tramp of millions of marching feet. But the dark street was still as they went into it, and they went down it together in silence. At the canal Horst Wessel stopped.

"Now I know you will be unmolested as you go on your way. I thank you for your visit. Remember your promise to repeat it."

"Indeed I shall. *Auf Wiedersehen.*"

Horst Wessel saluted. "Since we are now friends, suppose we part in the modern fashion. In the new Germany we do not say either '*Grüss Gott*' or '*Auf Wiedersehen.*' We say 'Heil Hitler!'"

It was a long way to the Tiergarten Strasse; but something impelled Hans Christian to go on walking. The spell that had been cast over him during the meeting had deepened while he had been talking in the quiet room. He could not bear to break it now; he wanted it to close more and more tightly in around him. The electric currents which had been unleashed were still coursing through his body; he wanted to go on feeling their mounting magnetism, their invincible power. Cold caution and rigid reason were both quiescent within him, lulled or drugged —he did not ask which—by wonderful words and matchless fervor. He had never felt so much. He had never reflected so little. His high mood sustained him as he swept on through the night, sure that he had seen with his own eyes and touched with his own hand the force which was to save Germany.

CHAPTER 15

Hans Christian had fitted easily and well into the Embassy set. He was made instantly welcome in the circles where the Rhodes moved, and was soon accepted as a permanent part of these. But after a fortnight's visit, he announced that he was moving into a bachelor flat; he had been fortunate in finding one furnished which he could take over temporarily from a young diplomat who was going home on leave. He did not wish to trespass too long on her hospitality, he told Mrs. Rhodes; he must look up some more of his German relatives, and his father's and grandfather's old friends, he explained to the Ambassador; he was encountering so many black looks at tea dances that he was afraid of what the suitors whose style he cramped might do to him, he said to Trixie. They all protested vigorously. Nevertheless, at the time he himself had appointed, he drove buoyantly away in his battered car. After that, though he dropped into the Embassy frequently at all sorts of odd hours, he declined to return to it on the still more intimate footing of a house guest.

The spring continued to be balmy and beautiful, and as the season advanced, every week end witnessed an enormous outpouring of pleasure seekers from Berlin. Camping, tramping, bicycling, swimming, racing, tennis tournaments—these and kindred diversions lured the youth of the capital out into the suburbs and the country, to lakesides and mountaintops. Sometimes they went in gay, heterogeneous groups; sometimes in sober, purposeful bands; sometimes in amorous, isolated couples. Hans Christian, once he was ensconced in his own flat, occasionally disappeared entirely from Saturday to Monday, without giving any very definite explanation of his absence afterwards. He was sorry he had not been accessible by telephone, he had been dashing about here and there, he had wanted to get off entirely by himself, some friends who were rather retiring had invited him to join their quiet outing— These were the unsatisfactory explanations which were all that Trixie could get out of him. His elusiveness irritated her intensely, but her attempts to overcome it were vain; the more she teased him, the less he told her. Repeatedly, she declared she would never ask him anything again, only to break her vow the next time she saw him. Repeatedly, she declared she would never invite him to go out with her again, only to urge him eagerly to do so at her first opportunity. For the most part he accepted her invitations with sufficient show of pleasure to salve her piqued feelings. His periods of withdrawal were the exception and not the rule.

One Sunday morning, as they went down the steps of the Embassy together, Trixie noticed a girl wearing an elaborate costume and carrying a baby covered with a long lace veil, who was parading slowly up and down the avenue opposite. With the rich green of the Tiergarten as a background, she was an arresting figure. Trixie touched Hans Christian's arm.

"Look, Chris! What sort of fancy dress do you suppose that is?"

"It's the Spreewald *Tracht*," he said smilingly. "When I was a little boy, the Tiergarten used to be dotted with them. The Spreewald nurses were supposed to be tops, as you put it. In fact, I should probably have had one myself, if my own mother hadn't proved so adequate. Now you hardly ever see those costumes—except in the Spreewald itself, of course. Babies are fed with formulas, aren't they, out of bottles, when there isn't any natural source of supply? Not that I know much about it——"

"Chris, you do put things the craziest way! Where is the Spreewald, and *what* is it?"

"Dear, dear! Haven't you picked up any information at all since you've been in Berlin, Trixie? You must have crossed the Spree thousands of times. It's the selfsame stream that flows through this very city. About sixty miles from here it divides into natural canals and intersects a forest. That's the Spreewald. There are a few villages in the region, and clearings of farmland, too, along some of the canals, which the people use for streets. They speak a queer dialect of their own, called Wendish, and the women still wear costumes like those you just saw, with a special *Tracht* for christenings, and another for communion, and so on. The *Spreewäldlerinnen* are very religious. But apparently they're clothes conscious too. As soon as a girl leaves school and begins to make money herself, she starts buying all these different outfits and putting them away in a big chest, so that when she's married, she'll have a complete assortment. Her husband never has to replenish it. Not such a bad idea at that."

"There you go, crazy again! Why didn't you ever take me to see this Spreewald, instead of talking to me about it as if you had just studied a geography lesson? You know how wild I am about costumes."

"Well, you hadn't told me before that you wanted to go there. You've wanted to go everywhere else—to all the museums and monuments and shows and races and music halls and beer gardens. But you never——"

"How could I ask you to take me there when I'd never heard of it? But I'm asking you now——"

"Very well, there's no reason, as far as I know, why we shouldn't start for the Spreewald this minute instead of going to Karlshorst or Hoppegarten."

Trixie hesitated. She had not expected to be taken quite so literally, and she adored the excitement of Hoppegarten, as Hans Christian was well aware. But after all, he had called her bluff, as he had such an uncomfortable way of doing. If she were to save her own face, she really had very little choice.

"All right. Shall we go in your car or mine?"

"Oh, I think we'd better go in yours. It's speedy as well as resplendent, and mine is such a forlorn old derelict. If we broke down we'd have a very dull day. The towns between Berlin and Lübbenau are all pretty dreary."

"Are we going to Lübbenau?"

"Well, it's the usual starting point for excursions through the canals. But I think we might go to Burg first. That's where the most stylish show is staged, at church. We may be in time to see it, if you step on the gas."

"Are you expecting me to drive?"

"Of course. I'm not in your class, Trixie, when it comes to speed—or in anything else, for that matter."

He opened the door of the car and offered her his hand, looking at her in the whimsical way which she had always found so winning. For the first time it angered her; behind the smiling surface of his face, she sensed a slight sarcasm. To be sure, she had often done so. But never before had this ironical element been so disturbing. She sprang into her seat unaided and pressed her foot down savagely. The car leapt forward, lurching as it turned a quick corner.

"What you really mean is that I'm not in *your* class at all," she said vehemently. "Why don't you tell me so, Chris?"

"I've never had the least idea of telling you so."

"No, but you've always thought so. I'd rather you came right out with it, like that snooty Carruthers woman we met on the boat, than to have you keep hinting."

"So Mrs. Carruthers did speak to you about your little experiment with the ventilating system! What did she say?"

This was the last question which Trixie would have chosen to have Hans Christian ask. Her rage mounted at the consciousness of the trap she had set for herself.

"She said everything you think."

"The conversation must have been fulsome and lengthy. Just how did she embark on it?"

"Spitefully. Just as you're doing now."

"Trixie dear, you're not going to spoil this beautiful day by quarreling with me at the very beginning, are you?"

Trixie's heart missed a beat. Hans Christian had never before spoken to her in that tender tone; he had never before called her "dear." Instantly her anger evaporated. Her pulses still pounded, but not with rage. The electrified atmosphere was transformed. It was all she could do to keep her eyes on the stream of traffic pouring out past the airport towards the country. Yet one grievance still persisted. Why had he chosen such a moment to give the first sign that he was not utterly indifferent to her, that he did not inwardly deride and despise her? If he had only waited until they reached that strange forest of which he had told her, she might have been in his arms by now. While as it was——

"We'll have to go into all this more thoroughly later," Hans Christian remarked. His voice was whimsical again, as if he had read her thoughts and were gently teasing her. But now his banter did not seem to hurt—not with the sound of "dear" still ringing in her ears. "Meanwhile I wouldn't run down that group of bicyclists if I were you. The consequences of that might be even worse than a quarrel," he concluded, still jestingly.

"They're a highway menace," observed Trixie, dodging the pedaling youths expertly, with no slackening of speed.

"*That*, from a young lady traveling at a hundred and twenty kilometers an hour? People in glass houses, Trixie——"

"I'm in a hurry. I want to get to this Spreewald of yours."

"You're always in a hurry. You always want to get somewhere."

"Yes, and I do too! I got from Kansas to The Hague and from The Hague to Berlin, didn't I?"

"You certainly did. Where are you bound from Berlin?"

"I told you, to the Spreewald."

"You may find it a step in the wrong direction."

"I don't expect to."

Hans Christian had been right, as usual. The towns through which they were passing were certainly dreary. There was a famous church in one of them; a famous man had been born in another. But Trixie shook her head when Hans Christian asked if she would like to stop anywhere for sight-seeing.

"You said yourself we had barely time to get to Burg before church let out."

"You're right. I did. Drive on, MacDuff!"

He settled more comfortably in his seat. As he did so, however, one of his arms strayed, as if by accident, across the back of it, and presently it slid easily down over Trixie's shoulder. After that she ceased to notice the dreariness of the towns. Electric currents seemed to flow from the fingers that rested so lightly on her sleeve. She could count all five of them, coursing in different directions through her body. Hopefully, eagerly, she wondered if the delight were mutual, if Chris were conscious of her ardent response to the magnetic forces he was releasing. But if he were, he gave no sign of it.

"Oh—you should have turned left there," he said suddenly. "This is Vetschau. You'll begin to see women in costume any minute now."

He had scarcely spoken when two girls on bicycles wheeled past their backing car, both equipped with umbrellas tucked expertly under their arms, and both wearing the huge triangular headdresses, gay aprons, and voluminous skirts of the Spreewald. Closely in their wake a child came trudging along, her small face encircled with wide-spreading silk and lace, her small feet emerging from under bright bands. Encumbered though she was with her petticoats, she was evidently hurrying; presently they saw that she was trying to catch up with her mother, a solidly built woman whose *Tracht* was made of unrelieved black.

"Oh, Chris, I think they're too quaint for anything! This is going to be good!"

"I hope so. Look out! There's another sharp turn here and the road's awfully narrow."

The bicyclists were rapidly increasing in number, and all the women Hansel and Trixie saw were in costume now. They went clattering over the cobblestones of another small village and across another stretch of pleasant countryside. Then again they approached small clustering houses and an open square flanked on one side by two taverns and on the other by a red brick church. The place was crowded with people coming and going, with large carts and small shabby motorcars standing side by side. There was a sound of music in the distance, and in the foreground, the jovial noise arising from a jesting, jostling crowd.

"This is Burg," Hans Christian said, somewhat superfluously. "Look, Trixie! Do you see that little procession going into the church? I believe it's a christening party! Let's hurry and catch up with it."

They parked the car quickly, disregarding the admonitions of a grumbling guardian, who tried to indicate exactly where they should place it, and went rapidly across the park. Trixie had not declined Hans Christian's proffered help this time; and they were still hand in hand when they went into the church, which was gayly decorated with tissue paper festoons. Apparently the regular services were already over; only the first rows of pews were occupied; at the left of the altar a group of costumed women were facing a grave young pastor who wore the long black robes and white-tabbed collar of the Evangelical Church. One of the women was carrying the white bundle which had first attracted Hans Christian's attention outside; and as layers of embroidered net and thin silk were gradually lifted from this, a small pink face and swaddled form were at length disclosed. A faint protest had risen at intervals from the wrappings; but as the pastor began to pray, these outcries were stilled. The sturdy arms upholding the baby swayed gently back and forth, soothing it. Except for the pastor's voice, the little church was hushed.

The sponsors began to recite the Lord's Prayer, slowly, with the pastor. They all together advanced toward the small font, surmounted by a brass ewer and basin, which stood midway between the altar and nave. The swaddled bundle was held over it, the name "Margarethe Martha" pronounced to the sound of trickling water. Music issued from an unseen organ. The layers of silk net were carefully replaced. Smiling, the procession went down the aisle and out of the church.

"It was sort of sweet, wasn't it, Chris? I wonder why there were no men in the group around the altar though, don't you? I should think the baby's father——"

"I don't know why, but perhaps we can find out. Let's go across to the *Gasthaus* and get some coffee and pound cake— It's hours since breakfast! Besides, the christening party may be taking place there. But even if it isn't, probably the landlady can tell us something about local customs."

The tavern was as crowded as the square. In the room at the left of the front door, men were gathered around the bar, and seated with their families at small tin tables, drinking early beer and morning coffee. In the room on the right, two christening parties were assembled, with the young pastor, looking less grave now, but still bearing himself with dignity, standing impartially between them; apparently the ceremony which Chris and Trixie had witnessed was the second to be performed that day. One of the babies was lying on a pillow in the center of the table around which its admiring relatives were gathered; they were sharing their creamed coffee with it. The other baby—Margarethe Martha—was now reclining in an elaborately decorated carriage, a rubber pacifier in her mouth. As wine began to circulate, her mother removed the pacifier, dipped it in her own glass, and restored it to the baby, who sucked at it with renewed relish.

"I guess those formulas you were talking about haven't got to Burg yet," Trixie observed, lighting a cigarette. As she sipped the hot coffee Hans Christian had ordered, she continued to watch the babies, while he talked with the landlady, who had answered cordially when they asked her if they might sit in the *Festsaal.* Trixie could understand German very well now; indeed, if Chris had not been with her, she would have talked to the landlady herself. She knew that she still made a great many mistakes, but usually she did not hesitate on this account. Now she felt suddenly shy, listening to his flawless flow of ready idiomatic language. It was one thing to have other people hear her horrible grammar; quite another to have Hans Christian do so. Especially since—

Once more she seemed to feel the pressure of his fingers against her shoulder, their warmth and strength penetrating the stuff of her sleeve.

The landlady was explaining that it was usual for fathers to remain at home on the day of a christening, to oversee the preparations for the feast. It appeared that the drinks which were now being circulated were only by way of preliminary, that the real celebration came later. Chris was listening to her with absorption; but Trixie's interest was beginning to wander. She had taken in the situation with characteristic swiftness. Now she wanted to move on, to see more. Above all, she wanted to feel Hans Christian's fingers locked in her own again, or pressing against her shoulder.

"I liked the sound of that music we heard before we came in here, didn't you, Chris?" she asked. "Let's go and see where it comes from."

He nodded, but he finished his cake and coffee and went on talking with the landlady as he counted out coins. Trixie could have risen, of course, at once, and gone to the door without him, to make her impatience plain. Once she would have done so. Now she knew better, knew that Chris did not like to be hurried about anything, that she must let him take his time if she were to get good results, whatever they were doing together: even on the day when he had first made a gesture which could be interpreted as a caress and had called her "dear" for the first time.

Her restraint was rewarded. As they finally went out of the tavern door, Chris took her hand and tucked it into the crook of his arm. All the other fellows who were out with their girls were walking that way, he said gayly; she had only to look around her and she would see. She had seen already, and the rite lost some of its significance because it seemed to be so generally observed. But not all of it. Nothing could rob her of the sense of comfort and security which it gave her to walk like this with Hans Christian. Nothing could render his touch so casual that it did not thrill her.

The cobblestone street was lined with booths, at which all sorts of Spreewald souvenirs were sold. As Chris and Trixie passed the third one, a small black puppy lying beneath the counter wriggled out and wagged its tail in friendly fashion. Hans Christian paused.

"I really think we ought to buy something to assure future dog biscuits for that puppy, don't you? What about one of those costume dolls? You could name it Margarethe Martha after the baby we saw baptized—or a miniature Spreewald boat? See how the settees stand on two bars, with nothing at all to hold them down, apparently! Well, I seem to be rambling on— Perhaps you think it would look too touristy to go around carrying little packages?"

"I don't at all. I'd love to have you get me a doll and a boat."

"'Damned white of you!' I promise I won't take advantage of your mood to sit down and dash off a few fond messages to absent friends on post cards."

"I wouldn't care if you did that either."

It was perfectly true. Chris had never given her a present before, had never suggested that he might. She knew that until lately he had been terribly hard up, and she had not expected anything from him, both because he was so pressed for money and because he was so indifferent to her. That is, because he had seemed so indifferent. He couldn't be any longer, or he wouldn't be carefully counting out those coins into the thin hand which the vendor extended with such pathetic eagerness. The large doll and the small boat were nothing much in themselves. But as symbols they had vast importance.

"If you like, we can leave the packages here, and get them later on, after we have seen the *Heimatsfest.*"

"No, I want to take them with me— What is a *Heimatsfest?* I heard the vendor say there was one, but I didn't know what it meant."

"It's the German version of Old Home Week. We're in great luck to have got here for it."

They were passing a big open-air pavilion now, which, like the tavern, was crowded with guests seated at little tables. Beyond it was a band, the source of the hitherto unexplained music; beyond the band stood a series of wide wooden platforms, where country dances were in progress. The girls' dresses were gayer here than any that Trixie and Chris had seen before, their aprons made of pleated lace, their headdresses embroidered, their white stockings spotless. As they whirled about, snowy lace-edged petticoats were revealed beneath their bright skirts. Trixie gazed at them entranced.

"Could— Do you think we could dance too?"

"Those are all special steps, harder to do than you'd think. And I wouldn't like to intrude, to give them the idea that we were trying to crash their party. After all it *is* their party. Don't you think we'd better just watch for awhile and then go back to the pavilion for lunch? We must have eels with Spreewald sauce, and white beer with raspberry syrup floating on top of it, in big goblets that look like champagne glasses run riot, that hold about a quart."

"Chris, I couldn't eat an eel, even to please you!"

"Nonsense! Pretend you're a German *Mädel* today, out with her *Schatz.* You'd eat whatever he suggested, if you were. You'd lap it up immediately, gloating over it."

"Yes, but I am not a German *Mädel.* And you're not my *Schatz.*"

"Couldn't you pretend that I was?"

There was nothing which Trixie would have been so glad to pretend. In her intermittent pursuit of the German language, she had learned that the literal translation of *Schatz* as treasure was entirely inadequate.

She knew that the word was also used to designate a very special sort of sweetheart. There was a quality of entreaty in the look she turned on Hans Christian.

"Yes, I could. But that wouldn't make it true."

She was deeply chagrined, so deeply that she was almost angry again. Her voice trembled as she spoke. She hadn't been able to keep it under control. Now large unwelcome tears came welling into her eyes, and she turned aside, furiously, to hide them.

"Aber Liebchen! Was tust du denn? Du weinst—heute? Unser fröhlicher Tag?"

It *had* been a happy day. But it had also been a day of startling surprises. One had followed so closely upon another that Trixie, for all her vaunted swiftness of thought and action, had not been able to keep apace with them, either figuratively or literally. Now two supreme shocks had come together: Hans Christian had spoken to her instinctively in his mother tongue, instead of in English, which showed her that he was deeply moved himself. And not only that. He had used the familiar form of speech—the *du* reserved for intimate relationships. He had addressed her as *Liebchen,* a lovely term of endearment which had no exact equivalent in any other language, but which came under the same general classification as *Schatz.*

The sequence of events after that was never quite clear to Trixie when she tried to disentangle these from the maze of mysteries in which she had been caught. She did remember, however, that entirely without self-consciousness, Hans Christian had wiped her eyes with a large handkerchief and kissed her gently on both cheeks. Then he asked her to wait for him a minute—as if she would not have waited endlessly!—and had gone over and spoken to one of the couples standing near them. There was a lull in the dancing just then, so it was easy for him to do this. The Spreewälder looked at him as if they were surprised too, but they were very cordial to Chris, and when he came back to Trixie, he told her that it would be quite all right for them to dance after all, even if they didn't know all the steps, that they would be very welcome. So they had joined the revellers on one of the wooden platforms and had been taken into a figure, and danced for a long time. It was not hard to catch on, after all; it was easy. And it was the greatest fun of anything that Trixie had ever done in her life.

Finally she and Chris realized that they were tired and hungry, so they went back to the pavilion with some of the other dancers, and had their dinner. They did have Berlin white beer in big goblets, with raspberry sauce floating on top of it, just as Chris had told her that they would; but they did not have eels at all. Instead they had some nice little white fish called *Schlei,* which looked and tasted something like smelts, though they were boiled instead of fried; and the Spreewald sauce was a good deal like any other kind of cream sauce, except that it had more butter swimming on top of it. They also had quantities of boiled potatoes, and afterwards some flat pasty little cakes, with pale cherries embedded in them. And coffee, and then more coffee, because they had had lunch so late that before they had finished it was really time for afternoon refreshments. And finally when they could not swallow another drop or consume another morsel, Chris said they could take one of the funny boats at Burg just as well as at Lübbenau, if Trixie would like to—the "harbor" wasn't quite so big, that was really the only difference. And when she said she would like to, very much, he went off to see about getting one, tactfully remarking that she might like to powder her nose or something while he was gone, which was unlike the usual German.

Presently they were gliding along over a smooth dark canal, sitting side by side on one of the queer settees, while the boatman poled in the stern. They passed a few picturesque little cottages, which all seemed to have small private canals leading up to them: houses with brightly scalloped window frames and latticed window boxes, and clean lace curtains draped inside the glass. They saw scarred targets fastened to the sides of the houses, and ducks swimming primly in rows up and down the private canals. They heard dogs barking and cows mooing. At a sudden bend, they came across a man seated alone in a boat drawn up at the water's brink, playing an accordion, and tossed him some coins, as they saw the passengers doing in another boat, coming from the opposite direction. After that they did not pass any more boats. It was growing late, and besides, they were leaving the main arteries now. As the boat slid under one little arched bridge after another, the farmlands began to disappear. There were fewer fields and more swamps beyond the banks. And finally the forest closed in around them, the curving branches of the trees reflected in the polished water below.

"Trixie, I want to tell you something."

He had not spoken to her in a long time. Like her, he seemed to have fallen into the spell of their surroundings. Now, at the sound of his voice, her heart contracted again.

"It's something that means a great deal to me. I didn't mean to tell you so soon, but we've had such a happy day together, you've seemed so close to me, that I can't wait any longer— I've joined Horst Wessel's Troop. I'm an S. A. man."

The rhythmic motion of the boat had ceased. The beautiful green forest had turned black. Trixie spoke in a smothered scream.

"Chris, you're joking, you're teasing me again. You don't mean that. It isn't what you started to say."

"Of course it is. Why should I start to say one thing and end up by saying another? I haven't told anyone else. I wanted you to be the first to know."

Far off in the distance, Trixie could hear soft singing. Passionately, she rebelled against the intrusion of song upon her anguish.

"Chris, you *can't* mean it. You've got too much good sense to let that slick agitator hypnotize you with his gift of gab!"

She shouldn't have said that, no one should say anything against a man another man revered. It was almost as bad as insulting his mother, or his religion. Chris would be terribly angry with her and he would have a right to be. But now that she had started, she could not help going on. The words came rushing to her lips of themselves.

"He's never taken my father in, not for one minute. I don't see how he can take you in, either. He's supposed to be a 'student,' isn't he? Why doesn't he ever go to classes at the University? Why hasn't he any friends there? Why does he spend all his time in the slums? What does he live on? What did he live on all the time he was in Vienna? Why did he go there? *Who sent him?* I can't see that the Nazis are any different from the Communists, except that they're cleaner and better looking and better drilled. They're both stirring up trouble, they're both bent on destruction and despotism, they're both ready to go to any lengths to gain their ends!"

"Trixie, you don't know what you're saying. Horst Wessel is a great leader, a great idealist. Someday he'll be regarded as a great hero. He's not destroying, he's creating. I want to help him if I can. By and by you'll understand what he's tried to do, what he's done already. I thought you'd understand now, if I talked to you about it. That's what I meant to do, what I looked forward to doing. I thought it was something we could share. And if we could share that— I'm sorry I made such a mistake."

"Oh, Chris, don't—don't speak to me like that. You know how much it means to me to have your confidence! You know how much I care! Only——"

It was a cry straight from the soul. Startled, the boatman ceased to paddle, and sat motionless in the stern, permitting the current to sweep his craft farther and farther down the stream. He had been out many times with lovers, and often he did not understand the words which they spoke. But he understood their dreams and their desires. The fragrant forest might shelter them in its depths and screen them from his eyes; but it could not shield them from his knowledge of their urgent need for each other. Never had he heard this need more poignantly expressed. After that cry, he must not look, he must not listen. . . .

A hand was resting firmly on his shoulder. Startled afresh, he sprang to his feet, rocking the boat. The young *Herr* who had hired him and who was now standing over him, helped him to steady it.

"I think we will not go any farther," the stranger said quietly. There was not a trace of passion in his voice; it was merely civil and toneless. "Please start back to Burg as soon as you can turn the boat around. The *gnädiges Fräulein* is very tired. We shall not go walking in the woods after all. Of course I will pay you the same as if you had waited while we did so."

CHAPTER 16

AFTER HANS CHRISTIAN was shot in the shoulder, there were endless hours when he lay wakeful and rigid, reliving the series of episodes which linked his new life and his old one together.

The break with Trixie had been a greater blow than he had realized at the moment. Afterwards he remembered how casually he had accepted her companionship on the boat, only to long for it later, amid the silences of Schönplatz. This was a similar experience, but one which meant much more. He had been horrified at her reception of his tremendous tidings. That she should have denounced his allegiance to a compelling creed and insulted the prime prophet of the New Nationalism seemed to him nothing short of a sacrilege. That she had spurned his tender of the confidential relations which he had assumed she was eager to establish humiliated him so deeply that he could conceive of no compensation which would assuage his hurt pride.

He could see her as she looked throughout the dreadful drive home, defensive and defiant, with her shoulders straight and her head held high. He remembered now that her cheeks had been unnaturally red, her eyes unnaturally bright; but that he had not seen at the time. For the sake of surface civility, he had tried, at infrequent intervals, to bridge the uncomfortable stillness between them with trite remarks; but her monosyllabic replies had rendered this effort futile. They had covered the last part of the way back to Berlin in stony silence. By the time they reached the Embassy, he was past caring for any conventional gesture; and when Trixie brought the car to a sudden standstill and made a precipitate appeal to him, it required no will power to steel himself against it.

"Chris— Please— Please don't do this awful thing!"

"If by this 'awful thing' you mean joining the National Socialist Party, I've done it already. It can't be undone now."

"Are you sure?"

"Certainly I'm sure. In any case I don't want to undo it. I believe this movement will be the salvation of Germany. And God knows it needs saving."

"Well— If you feel that way absolutely, so that nothing could change your mind, couldn't we just agree that we wouldn't ever speak of it? I mean, couldn't we be friends, the way we have been, but avoid certain subjects? Like Horst Wessel and Party politics and——"

"I don't see how it's possible to be intimate and guarded at the same time. You can't talk freely to a person if you keep saying to yourself, 'There, I almost mentioned something that wouldn't be pleasing, something that might be misinterpreted.' There has to be mutual confidence and respect, between real friends."

"But, Chris, I am your friend, I think the world of you. I——"

"I thought you did. But as I said once before tonight, I realize now that I made a mistake. I'm sorry. Good night, Trixie."

He did not see her again for a long time, not until after he had been shot, not until he no longer remembered clearly how they had quarreled. But he saw the Ambassador. Mr. Rhodes sent for him to come to the Chancery and gave explicit orders that they were not to be disturbed. He settled himself securely in a deep leather chair and motioned to Hans Christian to take one also.

"Chris, I'm sorry to gather that you and Trixie have had a kind of falling out. It does seem to me as if something could be done to patch it up. Especially since, as far as I can make out, it wasn't in the least personal, it was all about politics."

"But politics are the most personal thing in my life right now, Mr. Rhodes."

"Well—I can understand that, in a way. But you can't expect a girl like Trixie will. She wants a young man to take a personal interest in *her*."

"I did take a personal interest in Trixie, Mr. Rhodes. You knew that. I wasn't in love with her but I was very fond of her. I'm very fond of you and Mrs. Rhodes too, if you don't mind my saying so. But I can't keep on caring for Trixie now that she's denounced a great cause and slandered a great man. I feel dreadfully about it myself. But it just isn't possible."

"Now Chris, I wish you wouldn't take what Trixie said quite so hard. I think myself she was a little too harsh in her judgment. I can see some mighty fine things about this New Movement. It's a good thing to take young people into consideration as a political factor. Most of the energy and selflessness and idealism in the world are concentrated in young people, and stodgy old statesmen usually forget that. This man Hitler doesn't— It's also a good thing to teach the doctrine that every kind of work is worth while, as long as it's well done, to make a day laborer feel just as proud of what he's accomplished as a student, say. The world hasn't got very far along those lines, and in most places it hasn't even seriously tried to. In this part of the world a man is trying. And he's trying to give a feeling of unity to a lot of different groups that can't any of them get anywhere because they're all pulling in different directions."

"I'm awfully glad you can see all that, Sir. Now if Trixie had only seen it——"

"Maybe she will, maybe she will, if you give her a chance. But there are a lot of other things she sees too, and that I see, and that you don't seem to, Chris. This attitude towards religion, for instance— Not that Trixie's especially religious, but she does like to see fair play. How can you swallow this fanaticism, hook, bait and sinker? Here you grew up in New England, which never would have existed, if freedom to worship God according to their consciences hadn't meant more to a forlorn little sect than safety or comfort or anything else in the world! You're a descendant of those Pilgrims yourself, on your mother's side. You've seen what came out of their courage and their convictions. I don't see how you can shut your eyes to intolerance long. Pretty soon the Catholics will be in for the same kind of treatment, more or less, that the Jews are having now. Next the Protestants will begin to get it in the neck. Then you'll feel differently about it—after it's too late for the way you feel to make any difference."

For an instant, something seemed to click in the back of Hans Christian's brain, something that came as a warning. He remembered that there had been a note akin to veiled satire in Horst Wessel's voice when he had spoken of the Austrian Grand Duchess "who stood in so well with the Church," a light warning in the question "You've never had any Catholic leanings yourself, have you?" But the alarm was stilled, almost as soon as it was sounded, by other arguments that came crowding in.

"I don't mean to seem disrespectful to you, Sir, but what you're saying is absurd. Why Germany's a third Catholic— No leader would ever buck one-third of a country's population, much less the other two-thirds! Besides, Protestant or Catholic, it takes its religion pretty seriously—much more so than we do—than Americans do, I mean. The pastor is a power among his people as well as the priest. I see that all around me, in East Prussia."

"Exactly. And when a man's after power, Chris, he likes to keep it pretty well in his own hands. He doesn't like interference with it. He——"

"After *power!* You think our leaders are after power! Why they're after unity, as you said yourself, after vigor and decency, after national self-respect and national salvation."

"I guess there are several thousand boys in this country today, Chris, who feel just the way you do, who believe that with all their hearts and souls. I guess in a few years there'll be several million of them—

It looks that way to me, anyhow, from the way things are going, more's the pity!"

"More's the *pity!*"

"Yes, because things aren't going that way just of their own accord. They're going by force. You're tenderhearted, Chris, unusually so. You're sensitive to suffering of every kind. Why even falcons and fawns get you down, and if you think a woman's overworked, you're so crazy to lighten her labors that you're easy prey yourself. I don't believe you'll be able to take it when it comes to seeing men brutalized and abused. It's going to be hard for you not to look the other way when acts of violence are committed, so hard that I don't know but what you'll do it, but what you'll try hard not to see everything that's going on around you. I think maybe you'll try to close your mind as well as your eyes. And I don't know how long or how well you'll succeed. And when it comes to committing acts of violence yourself, I don't know how you'll ever bring yourself to that."

"I shan't see men brutalized and abused. I'll see them trained and hardened. I'll be trained and hardened myself. You're quite right, I need it. I've been a pretty soft specimen."

"Now, Chris, I didn't say that. I said——"

"I know what you said and I know what you meant. Anyhow, I can assure you that I won't be easy prey for any woman again, whether she's overworked or underdisciplined, and I'll never try to take another completely into my confidence."

The Ambassador opened his lips and closed them again, pressing them firmly together. There was a long pause. The drab curtains at the window flapped, the leather chairs creaked slightly. At last Mr. Rhodes cleared his throat.

"Well, I guess there isn't anything more we can say to each other, Chris. I guess maybe you're right, that we can't be friends any more. And I'm sorry. Let's not try to talk any more about this now. Only someday, when you're in the mood, I want you to explain something to me—not to argue with me about it, you understand, just explain it. How it comes that a horse breeder like you, who spent years trying to introduce a new strain into old stock to make it stronger— Well, we won't go into that right now. I'll say good-by to you, Chris, much as I hate to do it. I think a lot of you. I think there's fine stuff in you, as fine as in any young fellow I ever knew. Someday it'll all come out. I hope I live to see that day, Chris."

Hans Christian had never gone back to the Chancery again. In the memories which preoccupied him, as he lay on his hard hospital bed, there were none of Trixie or of Rufus Rhodes that reached further forward than that tragic trip to the Spreewald, or to that futile discussion in the Chancery, when he and Mr. Rhodes had sat in the deep leather chairs with an ugly wooden table stretching out beside them, and dark window shades flapping on the curtainless casements behind them.

As the image of Trixie receded, other images began to take its place. Very few of them were feminine. To be sure, there was Agathe, that girl he had met in Nuremberg, where he had gone in the early fall, as Horst Wessel had suggested, for the celebration of the *Parteitag*. He had heartily enjoyed the tramp down with his troop. They had gone to a fair in Leipzig and a music festival in Bayreuth, on their way south, both of which had delighted him; so had the verdant countryside through which they passed, at the zenith of its late luxuriance. Most of all, he had revelled in the exhilaration of good companionship and strenuous exercise, of songs sung in the march and snacks devoured by the roadside. He had told the truth when he said to Mr. Rhodes that he would be trained and hardened himself. His easy mastery of horsemanship at Schönplatz, his unsupervised hours in the saddle and the *Studsekretariat*, had been in no way comparable to the discipline of the planned program which he was forced to follow now. He was no longer his own master, and occasionally his mind and his muscles both revolted. At first he was so stiff and sore by night that he could not relax, and he had to bite back retorts and smother argumentative answers. But gradually his body responded to the treatment it was undergoing; it took on new vigor, new elasticity; at the same time, his mental processes became more tractable. Evening found him ready to drop in his tracks without self-analysis or inner rebellion and sleep wherever he could bunk. In the morning he waked refreshed, eager for the effort which lay ahead of him, ready to accept command unquestioningly.

When he reached Nuremberg, the sight of the mediaeval city with its gables and towers, its grim fortresses and tall façades all decorated with floating banners, had a still more animating result. He had not realized that these flags would be so red in their general effect. The black swastika on the white circle which formed their center was obscured when they fell in folds; but their scarlet streamed from the housetops, and—except for that accidental encounter with Agathe—gave him the greatest thrill he experienced. The speeches were long and dull; the Party chiefs preoccupied; the clashes with Communists much the same as in Berlin. Even the great parade, in which he participated, and the presence of sixty thousand men, impressive from the numerical viewpoint, did not provide the uplift he had expected, nor the same excitement as the march. Reaction seemed to set in, and he realized that he was still smarting from the aftereffects of Trixie's rebuff. Then, going into a crowded beer garden above the bluffs to snatch a hasty bite, he had slid into the last vacant place at a long wooden table, and found himself face to face with a pretty girl, in a Red Cross uniform, sitting opposite him, wedged between two laughing groups of kindred spirits, but herself quite alone.

It had been natural enough to speak to her, after the friendly fashion of any continental café. And when it evolved that she had been separated from her friends in the crowd and did not know where to find them, it had also been natural enough to linger along, chatting with her. Hans Christian's duty for the day was done. So, it appeared, was hers. Eventually he asked her if he might not return with her to her lodging. He did not leave it until it was time for him to report again to his troop. And after that, there were several intervals when he found it possible to return to her. They were both lonely, having missed something of the holiday spirit which others were so amply enjoying. They were both young, eager and ardent. There was enough, in these attributes, to draw them forcefully to each other, and neither made any attempt to withstand the attraction. They packed an extraordinary amount of robust pleasure into a few broken days and nights.

Hans Christian looked back upon this affair without either regret or repentance. He had neither seduced the girl nor bribed her. She had known how to look out for herself, and she was not mercenary; she was simply overflowing with lust for life, and she had stimulated and strengthened his. During his moments of rebellion against the helplessness and incapacity imposed upon him after he was wounded, he thought hungrily of Agathe. He did not recoil from her image with disgust, as he did from Trudchen's, and he bore her no deep-seated grudge, as he did Trixie. Though he had never tried to see her again, while he was still up and around, he was inclined to feel that perhaps he had made a mistake. If he had gone back to Nuremberg, he could probably have persuaded her to come to Berlin. As Horst Wessel had said, a sweetheart might create complications. On the other hand, a girl like Agathe, who was strong limbed and light hearted, could contribute an immense amount of good cheer and good feeling to a bachelor's existence.

In spite of this normal viewpoint, the episode of Agathe had been an isolated one. For the most part, Hans Christian had been wholly absorbed in his novitiate as a Storm Trooper, and most of his memories centered around this. A few of them still made him wince. He never had reconciled himself to all of Horst Wessel's orders. For instance, he had never been able to bring himself to act as an informer on a friend in spite of the admonition that a man who failed to do so was an offense to the Party, that loyalty to its leader transcended loyalty to a comrade. He had never been able to accept the theory that "sensitivity was not in order," that a harsh element was not an obnoxious one, or to view cruelty in the light of vigor. But he tried to dismiss these disturbing principles from his mind, to keep his memories unmarred.

He loved to dwell, for instance, on the thought of that abnormally cold day, when he had first taken part in a drill himself. It was in the Neuern Markt at seven o'clock on a Sunday morning. Only a few windows in the houses roundabout had shown signs of life, for on Sunday people slept later than on other days. A streetcar, just coming around the corner, was almost empty. The motorman and the conductor had a long way to go; they did not concern themselves with what was immediately before their eyes. They were still drowsy, and after all, it was no unfamiliar picture that confronted them here: Two hundred and fifty S. A. men, formed in two ranks. Five *Stürme* altogether. At intervals on the right wing the *Sturm* flag. One flag-bearer and two men. Three steps ahead of the flag-bearer the *Sturm* leader, distinguishable by his three stars and the black and white braid on his collar and around his cap.

A police lieutenant, in company with several sergeants, was observing the formation of the *Stürme* more attentively than the motorman and the conductor, though without seeming to do so. Hans Christian thought that he was probably full of private approbation for what he was witnessing. It would be easy for him on duty today. There was not a sign of disturbance anywhere. It was not as if he had a later watch or a longer beat. He knew that these S. A. men would make no trouble for him, and he on his part would make none for them either. He was doubtless saying to himself that he would make no search for arms today, that there would be no point to that. After all, this was just a drill. The youngsters had discipline in their bones—Hans Christian felt sure this was what the policeman, whom he had been observing with interest, was saying to himself when the order to fall in came.

"Close ranks— Line up with the man ahead— Dress ranks!"

Everything was done silently, each man looking at the leader of his standard at the front with his adjutant.

"S. A.—'Tention!"

The command came like the crack of a whip. The men sprang to obey it. They loved this voice of authority, a clear, ringing voice, dispelling weariness, warming the heart, stirring the soul: The voice of Horst Wessel.

"Standard Five — Left wheel — In step — March — Sing — 'Banners High!'"

After the drill was over, Hans Christian had started for the Bomb Palast to have a chat with Oskar Kraus and his comrade Max Müller, with whom he had become very friendly. As he walked briskly along, something familiar in the face and figure of a man slouching behind him arrested his attention. He slackened his pace, looked at the shabby individual more closely, and stopped short.

"Karl! What on earth are you doing here?"

His cousin came forward, disregarding his outstretched hand, and spoke in a surly voice.

"Why should it be any stranger that I should leave Bavaria than that you should leave East Prussia? I thought you went in for nothing but breeding—horse breeding, I mean. It seems you're taking another sort seriously too."

There was no mistaking his sneer, but Hans Christian tried to disregard it, though this was doubly hard in view of the similar comment from Mr. Rhodes. Karl certainly looked down at the heel, he must have run into hard luck.

"I don't devote all my time to it anyway. I'd like to see something of you. Can't we get together?"

"I'm afraid not. We seem to be on opposite sides of the fence."

"You don't mean to say you're under orders from Karl Liebknecht Haus?"

"Not too strictly. We leave strict orders to you Nazis." Karl laughed unpleasantly. "But I'm voluntarily associated with it and I take helpful hints from it. This morning it was suggested that I might see what you were up to."

Hans Christian could not believe his ears. He spoke his stupefaction.

"A von Hohenlohe—a von Mitweld—throwing away his birthright! Conspiring against his own flesh and blood!"

"Those funny little vons don't mean as much as they used to, Hansel. You know that yourself. Your own doctrine teaches you to pour all men into the same mold, to put princes on a par with paupers. Why should you quarrel with me if I do the same thing? I don't call myself von Mitweld any more, by the way. I'm more consistent than you are. Karl Welder, your humble follower. Very humble and very much your follower."

"But, Karl, your mother must be broken hearted!"

"Well, what about your own mother? I suppose you've been a source of unmitigated joy and comfort to her these last five years! The United States Government is looking at National Socialism with its tongue in its cheek, I can tell you that! And when a high Government official thinks of her only son fraternizing with panderers and prostitutes——"

Hans Christian had never knocked down a man in his life. But he did so now. Karl fell so swiftly to the sidewalk that he did not know what had struck him until afterwards. Hans Christian left him lying where he was, and went on to the Bomb Palast, seething with such rage that he neither knew nor cared what the consequences of his rash act might be. Afterwards he realized how much he must have changed already that he could have done such a thing; also that from that day he himself had been a marked man.

When the young diplomat whose apartment he had temporarily taken over returned to Berlin, Hans Christian rather hesitantly asked Oskar Kraus whether he and Max Müller could make room for a third person in their quarters. They hailed the suggestion with enthusiasm, and Hans Christian moved without more ado from the select surroundings which he had enjoyed in the Margarethe Strasse to the dubious shelter of the Bomb Palast. The transition was surprisingly easy for him. He was genuinely attached to both Oskar and Max, and he was far less lonely bunking with them than he had been living all by himself. Besides, since the break with the Embassy set had come, he preferred that it should be a clean one. He cared nothing about hanging on the fringes of a milieu into which he felt he no longer fitted. Indeed, as far as he was himself concerned, he would have been willing to postpone his return to Schönplatz indefinitely. He could not get up and walk away from his grandmother if she grieved or angered him. He could not turn on her and berate her either, and certainly he could not convert her. But he knew that his present course would be as obnoxious to her as it was to Trixie. He dreaded the rebukes and recriminations with which he foresaw the stately old house would ring. Yet there was a point of delay beyond which he could not go. When it came, he braced himself for his encounter with the Archduchess in much the same spirit that he would have met a major operation.

As a matter of fact his grandmother rather reminded him of an officiating surgeon. She did not so much rebuke him as dissect him, and she used no merciful anesthetics meanwhile. The process was painful throughout, and in the moments when she spoke scathingly of birds that fouled their own nests, she made it clear that she considered him no less a traitor to his class than Karl. Indeed, she coupled their names in referring to what she called dishonor. There had been mutual recriminations. She had asked him how he could justify the assault upon the station agent at Insterburg, who, according to reliable report, had been set upon by Nazis and taken to their *Heim*, where he had been stripped and beaten with riding whips until he had collapsed: Was that the sort of sport in which the cavaliers forgathering for their annual contests now specialized? He had retorted by asking her if she had heard about the Nazi who had been stabbed in the neck by a Communist, and who had died as a result of a severed artery, in Königsberg the day before the Insterburg incident. There had been a heated argument over the ensuing episodes, which included attacks upon a Communistic councilor, shot in his bed, upon the editor-in-chief of a Democratic paper, and upon a former *Regierungpräsident*. Reverting once more to proverbs, Victoria Luise had spoken of the old adage about the pot which called the kettle black, and had made the caustic comment that perhaps now the pot was brown and the kettle red. He left her presence writhing, and wretchedly aware that much of her condemnation was deserved. But Luischen, whom he had dreaded to see almost as much, was far kinder, far more tolerant and understanding.

"I don't know whether you will want Ernst and me to stay here any longer, Hansel, after the stand Karl has taken."

"Of course I want you to stay. I wouldn't be free to go on with my work in Berlin if you weren't here to look after my grandmother, if Ernst weren't in charge of the stud."

"I know you trust us. And we're doing our best for you, our very best. We—we love you, Hansel, and we're grateful to you. But after all, Karl is my brother. I love him too. I think he's misguided and mistaken, but I love him."

"Do you think I'm misguided and mistaken also?"

"Ernst doesn't. Ernst thinks you're right about everything. He thinks you're marvelous. He says, when the time comes, when you say the word, he'll help you all he can in East Prussia. He thinks there's a fertile field for the New Movement. I don't know anything about politics myself, I don't care anything about them. But when I listen to Ernst I want to agree with him. Isn't that a natural way for a married woman to feel, Hansel?"

"Of course it is. It's the natural way and the right way, the way that will make Ernst happy, that will keep him close to you. Every woman who's alienated me has done it because she meddled in politics of some kind, in some way. First my mother, now my grandmother. And in between——"

"I'm sorry there was someone in between, Hansel. I was afraid there might have been."

"Don't let's talk about it, Luischen. It didn't amount to anything, really. I wasn't in love. When I marry it will be a girl like you, a girl who will leave public questions to her husband's judgment, who'll keep house for him and look after his children."

"When you marry it will be someone much more beautiful than I am, Hansel, and much more wonderful. And she'll adore you. You'll be very happy, you'll forget this hard period you've been through. It will all be over by that time."

She had comforted him and encouraged him. He still remembered her loving kindness with gratitude as he lay wounded in the hospital. But when she asked him to go out to the paddocks with her and see the dappled gray colt, he shook his head. The words which Karl and Rufus Rhodes had spoken were still rankling in his heart. Whatever joy might lie ahead of him in his stable, he had lost all sense of it now. He did not even visit it, during his short stay at Schönplatz.

There was reason enough, quite aside from his personal grievance, for him to hurry back to Berlin. Things were in a bad way in the Friedrichshain district. The Communists seemed to be gaining strength. A Storm Trooper, walking alone, was brutally attacked; after twenty-four hours had gone by, he was still lying unconscious, battling with death. Then another surprise attack occurred. Again a solitary man was assaulted and knifed. His injuries were not as serious as the other's; it seemed unlikely that he would lose his life; still the matter was serious. The following week there was a third assault, and after that a fourth. There was system in this, that was plain. The question was how the malefactors were to be stopped.

Hans Christian knew that Horst was pondering this, then that he had formed a resolution, finally how it was to be carried out. There were great doings in the beer shop where the Communists generally held forth. A representative had been sent from headquarters in Moscow to express to his Red comrades in Friedrichshain the appreciation of the Bolshevist leaders. All the revellers were in high spirits. Otherwise they might have been somewhat distrustful of two young workmen who stood beside the counter, taking no part in the general jubilation. They had come in quietly, ordered a beer apiece, and lighted their cigarettes. Then they did nothing further. They did not even bother to say *Prosit* as they lifted their glasses and buried their noses in them. Those who were conscious of them at all concluded that they must have further plans for the evening, for one of them kept looking at the watch fastened to his left wrist with a broad leather strap, as if he were watching the time. The landlord, who alone troubled to closely observe them, noticed that they were powerful fellows, decided that any Nazi they got by the neck would have a hard time. But having reached this point, he did not continue his reflections. At that moment the door of the *Stube* was thrown forcefully open and twenty men burst into the room with Horst Wessel at their head.

The Reds were completely surrounded with such suddenness that none could escape. Only one, alert in emergency, managed to bound towards the telephone, intent on giving the signal of alarm for an attack. He reached it at the same time as the landlord, but the booth was already blocked—by the two young workmen who had been so stolidly drinking beer: Hans Christian and Oskar Kraus.

Horst made short shift of what he had come to say. His clear voice was not heart-warming tonight; it was death-dealing. There was more than a threat in it; there was a sentence: From that day on, for every S. A. man assaulted, two Communists would fall. It was as trenchant as that and as final. He added a single word of warning: "I believe that my meaning is clear. You pay double for all that you take. And there is no escape. If you crawl into holes in the earth, we shall still know how to find you. Remember this, for it is the last notice I shall give you!"

He was gone as he had come, suddenly, stormily, surrounded by his troopers. Weeks passed without further assaults. The proud boast that the "streets would be free for the Brown Battalions" seemed fulfilled. There were still threats, there was vile abuse, there were fist fights now and then. But there was fear, and with it something like respect. Men from the Red Front who had been in the beer *Stube* at the time of the strange apparition came to apply for membership in the Troop. There were other signs too that the tide had turned. Christmas would have been joyful for them all, if great personal sorrow had not come to Horst: Werner, his brother, who was in Troop Four, went on a holiday excursion to the Riesengebirge and was lost in a snowstorm. When he was found, he was dead. There was a funeral instead of a festival, and in the general mourning that followed, the Communists were temporarily forgotten by most of the Wessels' friends. Hans Christian was one of the few who did not succeed in dismissing them from his mind. This was not because he feared them. It was because he was still secretly smarting from the charge, made first by Trixie and later by his grandmother, that ethically there was little to choose between Communism and National Socialism. He had not yet succeeded in triumphantly refuting this, and he knew he would never rest until he had.

His own resurgent sense of fairness and logic was his greatest handicap. He was no longer convinced that all the men who had fought a losing fight to save Germany from the first postwar chaos were traitors, or that all those who now succeeded them were heroes. The first thrill of his participation in the New Movement was gone, the first blindness concerning its principles beginning to clear. When he was under the spell of Horst's oratory or swayed by the excitement of vigorous action, the *Hakenkreuz* seemed to emanate radiance. But when he was alone, or when he tried to give form to his faith, he groped towards a glow which eluded him. False notes seemed to have crept into the melodious gospel of progress, unity and austerity which had first been preached. He heard threats about heads that should roll and others that should be placed on pikes, after the Party came into power. In spite of reiterated assurances that the Movement was legal, that nothing should be done unconstitutionally, he knew now that vengeance and violence were an integral part of its plan. He heard hints about the absorption of Austria, the reclamation of the Sudeten, the abolition of the Polish Corridor; he learned that acts of aggression and repudiated promises were not considered inconsistent with the new code of honor. He tried to quiet the "still small voice" that spoke to him of all this; sometimes he succeeded, reminding himself that the means justified the end and that no pattern was perfect. But there were other moments when he wondered, wildly, if the miracle which he had seen as saving Germany were after all to prove a mirage.

Most of Hans Christian's periods of reflection and rebellion, strangely enough, were associated with the humblest tasks which he was called upon to fulfill. He had more natural culinary skill than either Oskar or Max, and he had unconsciously learned a good deal about making simple fare appetizing as well as wholesome during his New England boyhood. When he suggested that he might take over the domestic direction of the tenement in the Bomb Palast, his offer had been hailed. From that time on he was chief cook, though his comrades always helped as bottle washers. While his hands were busied at the stove and sink, his thoughts flew far afield. It was at such times as this that he found them hardest to control.

While he was getting supper one cold night in January, he analyzed the new "Ten Commandments" of National Socialism. Some he could wholeheartedly follow—"Your Fatherland is called Germany, love it above all and more through action than through words!"—"Be proud of Germany; you ought to be proud of a Fatherland for which millions sacrificed their lives!"—"Make your actions such that you need not blush when the new Germany is mentioned!"—"Believe in the future; only then can you be a victor!" But then there were others—"Germany's enemies are your enemies; hate them with your whole heart!"—"Strike a rogue more than once! When one takes away your good rights, remember that you can only fight against him physically!" Would hate not breed further hate, bloodshed further bloodshed?

As he asked himself these troubled questions, he heard Oskar tearing into the courtyard and pounding on the door of their lodging, without waiting to use his latchkey. Hansel dropped the skillet he was holding and rushed forward.

"Hansel, you must come at once. The worst has happened."

"The worst——"

"Horst has been attacked!"

Horror that he could ever have questioned Horst's commands swept through Hans Christian. A sense of traitorous guilt engulfed him.

"You mean——"

"No, he isn't dead. Not—not yet. But he's dying——"

"Where?"

"He was in his own room on the Grosse Frankfurter Strasse when he was shot—through the half-open door!"

Oskar strangled as he spoke. Then he went on chokingly. "He's been taken to the hospital—the *Krankenhaus am Friedrichshain.* We can't see him, of course. But we can go there."

They could always go there. The hospital authorities were kind, from Dr. Braun, the director, to the humblest orderly. But the small pavilion where Horst had been taken was not large enough to hold them all at once. Only a few could take shelter there at the same time, in the corridor between the small room where Horst lay and the general ward. The others milled around in the little park that separated the pavilion from the larger units of the plant encircling it. Occasionally some of them stamped their feet or swung their arms in an effort to stave off the biting cold; but for the most part, they tried to march, in orderly formation. That was the way Horst himself would have wished it. ("Now every man on his toes—chests out, heads high! Why there's not a paunch among the lot of you!"—"Close ranks—Line up with the man ahead—Dress ranks—S. A. Halt!"—"*Sturm* Five—Attention! Quiet!") Marching men, as many as the park would hold, from the very first; and yet, miraculously, it seemed to hold more and more all the time. Waiting men, standing guard. The death watch of a hero.

They could always go there. And finally the day came when they could see him. He himself had asked for them, and the doctor had told them that they might go in, that it would not matter any more—Still, they tried to be quiet. As they entered the pavilion, they sat down on the bench in the corridor and pulled off their heavy shoes. They prepared to enter Horst's room in their stocking feet, not because anyone had told them to do so, but because they themselves did not want to make any noise, they did not want to disturb him.

His room, at the right of the entrance as you went in, was small and very white. The walls were white, and the narrow bed, and the dress of the *Schwester* who stood behind this, and Horst's face, upheld by the wide pillow. Whitest of all, that uplifted face. From time to time his eyes closed quietly, as if he were too tired to hold them open any longer. But for the most part, he looked at his men as they passed, recognizing each one, cherishing each one. Occasionally his lips moved, he murmured their names: "Heinrich—Oskar—Ludwig—Max—Gustav—Hansel!" Then he fell silent again.

His men went through in single file, stopping just long enough to salute. And Horst saluted them. Even when his eyes were closed, even when his lips ceased to move, his right arm rose rhythmically from the snowy spread, rose and fell, and rose again. The men, coming out of the narrow room, saluted each other, with tears streaming down their cheeks. Then they went back to the bench, and sat down, and pulled on their boots, which were stacked up beside it, and went outdoors again, to make room for other men who had not yet seen Horst and saluted him.

Every man who was in the garden that night saw Horst and saluted him. But the last that went in he did not see, he did not salute.

Horst himself had told them that a trooper bowed his head only before the majesty of death and the majesty of God. The troopers in the garden bent their heads now.

On the day after Horst Wessel's death, Hans Christian heard Joseph Goebbels speak. He had never before been able to overcome a certain instinctive aversion to the "Little Doctor"; the man's grotesque appearance, and the malignancy of mind which seemed to complement his deformity of body had always roused Hansel to repugnance. Now, as he listened to the moving words which poured from the Minister's lips, he forgot everything except his thankfulness that Horst's eulogy should have been so proclaimed.

"Horst Wessel has gone to the Great Beyond. After storm and stress, the mortal part of him lies here, mute and motionless. But I feel, almost as though assured by the evidences of the senses, that his risen soul reaches down towards us all. He himself believed that this would be so. He bore witness to his belief when he said he would march on in spirit within our ranks.

"In coming years when in a Germany redeemed workers and students march together, they will sing his song, and he will be among them. Already they are singing it everywhere, the soldiers in brown. Ten years from now the children in the schools, the workmen in the factories, the soldiers along the highways will be singing it.

"In spirit I see columns of marching men, endless—endless. A nation once humbled rises up and sets itself in motion. Behind the standards he marches with us, keeping step.

"The banners wave, the drums roll, the fifes announce the jubilee, and from a million throats rises the song of the German Revolution: 'Banners High!' "

So that was the meaning of the vision Hans Christian himself had seen, of the sounds he himself had seemed to hear, the first time he saw Horst Wessel. Now that Horst was dead, nothing would stop the spread of his song, nothing would halt the march of his men. If, as an individual, he had possessed human failings, these were already forgotten. As a leader, he had been peerless. As a martyr, he became invincible.

It did not matter that two months after Horst's death the Reichstag accepted the Young Plan, which Horst had held in abhorrence; the acceptance was bound to be short-lived. It did not matter that Bruening, the pale-faced, thin-lipped leader of the Center Party, against which Horst had fought, became Chancellor of Germany; he would not be Chancellor long. These facts Hans Christian accepted as certain, and his faith was justified: In the September elections, the Nazis polled six and a half million votes. Two years earlier, they had managed to muster twelve deputies. Now they had nearly ten times that many. A startled world suddenly became Nazi conscious and a powerful English publisher printed a statement that set forth the tenets of Hansel's own belief:

> *These young Germans have discovered—that it is no good trusting to the old politicians. Accordingly they have formed a parliamentary party of their own— We must change our conception of Germany——*
>
> *If we examine this transfer of political influence in Germany to the National Socialists, we shall find that it has many advantages for the rest of Europe. It sets up an additional rampart against Bolshevism. It eliminates the grave danger that the Soviet campaign against civilization might penetrate to Germany, thus winning an impregnable position in the strategical center of Europe——*
>
> *Were it not for the new direction given to the energies and ambitions of a youthful Germany by the National Socialists there was a grave likelihood that the cause of Communism might have made a sensational advance and even become—who knows—the first party in the state— I repeat that the dramatic success which the German Party of Youth and Nationalism have just won should receive the closest possible attention——*

Hans Christian, poring over these words, paused in his reading long enough to buy extra copies of Viscount Rothermere's paper which had contained them, and to send these, marked, to both his mother and his grandmother. But after all, words were cold and lifeless things. It was actions that counted, and there was plenty of action for him in those days. He was a troop leader himself now, organizing, directing, planning, perfecting. His physical world had shrunk to the East Side of Berlin, where his duties lay; his only companions were the comrades working with him and under him. But his mental world embraced all of Germany, and he saw himself surrounded, on every side, by the legions of liberated German youths. He no longer shrank from any means that might serve this end and his purpose had never been so pressing as the night he himself was shot down as he left the Cemetery of St. Nicolai, where he had gone to spend a few moments of restful silence in the sanctuary enclosing Horst Wessel's grave.

He was alone when the assault occurred, and he told Oskar and Max and the others who questioned him closely afterwards that he never saw his assailant, that he could not swear who had shot him. This was true enough. And he was suffering so greatly, he was so exhausted from loss of blood, that his comrades did not press him. They knew he must have complete quiet, complete rest, if the same thing were not to happen again that had happened to Horst Wessel and so many others. They did not need the warnings of the grave surgeon and the grim *Schwester* to cause them to leave Hans Christian in peace. But for all that, they knew he was sure, in his heart, that it was his cousin who had done the deed, and they meant, when the time came, to deal with Karl Welder themselves. But not now, not when Hans Christian might ask them awkward questions, when anything they said or evaded saying might upset him. They were too overcome by his anguish to add to it in any way. However cruel they might be to outsiders, they were still kind to their own.

It was a long time before they could keep their anxiety out of their eyes when they came to see him, and therefore they did not look straight at him as they sat in his room although he was their leader now, although both duty and discipline bade them face him. But he did not seem to care. He lay still and white, as Horst had lain before him, in the same hospital, in the same pavilion. They could not help thinking the same thoughts, as they looked at him, that they had thought before. They could not help dreading the same end. Often they did not stay very long, because it did not seem bearable to go all through this a second time.

Late one afternoon, when Oskar was tiptoeing out of Hans Christian's room, leaving him seemingly asleep, he saw that a young lady was standing at the door, with flowers in her hand. He did not recognize her, he only observed that she was very pretty and beautifully dressed in rich furs that enveloped her slim figure and framed her rosy face. To his surprise, she stepped forward and held out her hand, smiling although her face was sad.

"Don't you remember me, *Herr* Kraus? I came to the Bomb Palast once with Hans Christian, about a year and a half ago. I think it was the first time he went there himself. My name is Beatrice Rhodes."

"*Aber ja, gnädiges Fräulein!* You were Hansel's great friend! But then you never came to see him after he lived at the Bomb Palast himself."

"I would have been glad to come, but he didn't care to have me. Because we had quarreled. You see, I don't believe in all your Party principles. But when I heard he had been hurt, I had to come, at least to inquire. I hope I may see him now."

Oskar had stiffened slightly. He resented the reference to disagreement with Party principles. But the young lady disregarded his change of attitude.

"You'll see a very sad sight."

"I'm not afraid of sad sights."

"And he is very weak. He is not allowed to talk."

"I won't talk to him. I'll just go in and sit beside him for a few minutes. The *Schwester* at the desk told me I might do that, after you came out."

"Then of course it must be all right. The *Schwester* is very careful. She has to be."

"I'll be very careful too, *Herr* Kraus."

He watched her enter, with eyes that were more anxious than ever. He saw her seat herself very quietly, and he caught her expression as she looked towards Hans Christian. Momentarily he could not harbor resentment against her and he went away. Because he knew she had not meant that anyone else should see this look.

When he came back the next day, Hans Christian was better, and the flowers that *Fräulein* Rhodes had brought were attractively arranged in a vase which stood by his bedside. A week later, he heard them talking earnestly together when he came in, and he knew that peace had been made between them, probably without any words of explanation, since Hans Christian was still too weak. But surely if Hansel had seen the same look that Oskar himself had seen on *Fräulein* Rhodes' face, he would have known that no explanations were necessary. However that might have been, it was only a few days afterwards that they greeted him laughingly, and Hans Christian said *Fräulein* Rhodes had been asking why he did not treat himself to a trip to Spain when he was able to travel, and that he himself was inclined to think it was a very good idea.

Oskar Kraus thought so too. He knew now that there would not be another black cortege winding its way to the St. Nicolai Cemetery, another black polished stone marking a new grave. He knew that instead of dying, Hans Christian was going to get well, and Oskar was very grateful to the lovely young lady who, in some mysterious way, had helped where all the rest of them had failed. He admired her very much, and at the same time he felt sorry for her. He could not imagine why, since she was so pretty and so pleasant and since she and Hans Christian were obviously such good friends again.

PART VI

1931

"This Is the Day"

CHAPTER 17

"YOU ARE sure I can be of no further service, *Señor?* Anything at all that I can do——"

"It's more than kind of you. But I'm quite sure. And there'll be someone at the station to meet me, I know."

Hans Christian's smile was reassuring and his voice confident. Nevertheless, the stocky Spaniard who had shared his compartment from Irún to Madrid, continued to regard his traveling companion with troubled eyes. He knew that the delicacy of skin and slenderness of build which characterized the young stranger often gave a false effect of fragility, that actually persons of this type sometimes had great resilience; but this boy was half helpless as well as woefully weak. It was incomprehensible that he should have been permitted to travel at all, much less that he should have undertaken a long journey alone.

"Please don't be so concerned. My grandmother felt just the same way that you do about having me strike off by myself. But I told her I knew I should meet a good Samaritan along the way. And you see I did. I met you!"

There was no doubt about it, this youth was *muy simpatico*. The Spaniard found himself regretting the imminence of their arrival in Madrid, not only because of solicitude, but because of attraction.

"If your friends should not meet you——" he began again.

"If they shouldn't, I'll be immensely grateful if you'll let me come home with you—long enough to telephone and find out what the hitch is anyway. And maybe to have a cup of coffee. Coffee always tastes extra good after a night in a train, doesn't it?"

"You are right, *Señor!* Because I am of that opinion myself, there is always an extra supply prepared for me when I have been absent. And if the absence has entailed a sojourn in France, where, so save us, coffee in the true sense does not exist, the supply is tripled instead of doubled, as in the case of ordinary journeys! So there will be enough for you also, and to spare. My house is yours. And permit me to offer you my card. If you do not come home with me now, it is my hope that you will seek out my address at some future time."

Hans Christian accepted the small white square, glanced at the superscription, and nodded.

"Thanks again, *Señor* Ramirez. I'm afraid I can't reach my own card-case, but if you've got a scrap of paper in your pocket, maybe you'll scribble my name down on it yourself. Von Hohenlohe, Hans Christian von Hohenlohe. I'm on my way to visit some Spanish kinsfolk of mine, the Cerrenos. Perhaps you know them?"

The pause before the stocky Spaniard answered was almost imperceptible. Hans Christian barely caught it—that and the slight stiffness that crept swiftly into the courteous voice, to be as swiftly suppressed again.

"All Spain knows the Cerrenos, *Señor*. If you are to be their guest, there is indeed nothing I can do for you. But I shall still hope that someday you will be mine."

There was no time for further conversation. The train had already begun to slow down while they were talking. Now it had come to a standstill. Hans Christian, leaning his sound shoulder against the window casing, saw that this framed a face and figure which he recognized instantly, though he had not seen them in over fifteen years. He tapped on the glass and called out.

"I'm here, Sebastian. Right in front of you."

"So I see. *Se bien venido!* And stay where you are; I'm coming in to help you out myself."

Sebastian de Cerreno had pulled down the window as he spoke, and instantly Hans Christian felt the man's magnetism flow out to meet him, like a sparkling stream. Remembering the tragic disillusionment of his reunion with his grandmother, he had shrunk from the possibility of a second such experience, as far as this distant kinsman was concerned. When he was a little boy, he had idolized Don Sebastian, who had come to Copenhagen as a Special Envoy of the King of Spain and who had been frequently at the German Legation; he had feared that now he might find his idol's feet were clay. His father, he dimly remembered, had always been cool and constrained in manner towards Sebastian; his mother had been constrained too, though in a different way. He had never understood why or sought to do so at the time. His own sense of admiration had acted as an anodyne to anxiety on the subject. But afterwards he had remembered the strain. If there were not some flaw in Sebastian's seeming perfection, would his parents have acted towards him as they did? The question had often risen out of the past to trouble him. Even more than his grandmother's insistence that he should go, it had deterred him from coming to Spain. Now that he was here, it was instantly submerged. The feeling that flooded his being as he looked at Sebastian was still closely akin to hero worship. In the extremity of it, he entirely forgot his traveling companion for the moment. When he remembered *Señor* Ramirez again, and turned from the window to say good-by to him, the stocky Spaniard had vanished.

Hans Christian felt a genuine pang of disappointment. The rather coarse-looking man had gone out of his way to be kind, helping him to undress and to dress, even rising more than once in the night and descending from the upper berth to see that Hans Christian was well covered and that his pillows were comfortably arranged. And now he had been swallowed up by space, before any adequate words of appreciation had been spoken. Well, Hansel could always write—that is, as soon as he had the use of his writing hand again. And meanwhile he would ask Sebastian to telephone. Sebastian, who was himself the personification of courtesy, would, of course, be only too glad to undertake such an office. Though now that he thought of it, there had certainly been something very strange in the look that had gone over *Señor* Ramirez' face, the minute the name of Cerreno had been mentioned. Had he unaccountably hit upon constraint again, as far as Sebastian was concerned?

For the time being, he had no chance to give the matter more than a passing thought. Sebastian supported him from the *wagon-lit* so casually that it seemed as if they were walking arm in arm merely for the mutual pleasure in so doing; then he had been eased into a wheel chair that stood just outside and they had chatted gayly together as this wove its way along the station platform between the unhurried passengers and the laden porters and the pushcarts where luscious fruits and fluttering periodicals were being pleasantly offered for sale.

"The train connections between here and the South are deplorable. But I have a glorified gypsy wagon waiting for you outside. If it appeals to you, we might push along to Granada in it at once."

"A glorified gypsy wagon! You mean a motor caravan?"

"Yes. It's my latest toy. Do you dislike the idea?"

"No—no. But I couldn't help thinking it was strange you should have one too."

"Too?"

"Yes. My mother thought of the same thing, the first time she ran for the Senate. She even called it the same thing that you did, a glorified gypsy wagon. I used to travel all around with her, in hers. It was a great drawing card, and really helped her to win the election. Since then, lots of people have taken to using what they call 'trailers' in the United States—a supplementary cart with living quarters in it, that can be attached to an ordinary motorcar and towed, instead of being all in one piece, like a truck, as hers was. But when my mother got her green caravan it was such a novelty that it created a sensation."

"Yes? A curious coincidence, as you say, that she and I should have had the same idea. But mine has never taken definite form till now. Well, you can see how you like it. There is no reason at all why we should not stay in Madrid, if you prefer. The Azucena Palace here is open and fully staffed. But I have a feeling that our Andalusian sunshine——"

He broke off, his smile seeming to complete the sentence which his words had left unfinished. In repose, Sebastian de Cerreno's face would have been somber, had it not been for a certain bladelike quality which gave it luminescence as well as keenness. But when he smiled, it was transfigured. For the first time, it crossed Hans Christian's mind that this smile of Don Sebastian's must have made him almost irresistible to women, when he was younger, in spite of the disfiguring scar across his left cheek. When he was younger? Was there, after all, any occasion to place his fascination in the past? His hair had turned iron-gray at the temples, but that had only enhanced his general air of distinction. There were a few lines lightly etched around his eyes; but Sebastian's eyes, Hans Christian remembered, had always "crinkled when he smiled." Recalling his own childish phrase, Hans Christian smiled himself.

"Here we are, *amigo*. Tell me what you think of my glorified gypsy wagon?"

It stood backed up against the curb, its small rear platform half concealed with bright potted plants. Beyond them, through an open door, Hans Christian could see a narrow bed at one side, its snowy sheets turned down invitingly. Beside this two easy chairs were drawn up near a little table, set with a silver service. The scent of coffee mingled with the perfume of flowers. Two men in spotless linen suits stood at the foot of the descending steps, their dark lean faces anxiously attentive. Sebastian de Cerreno motioned towards them.

"Leopoldo and Leonardo have come with me from Granada to greet you," he explained. "They used to drive for your mother, so I thought you might like to have them drive for you. We will have breakfast here in any case. I am sure you must be starving. Then you can decide whether we shall push on to Granada or whether we shall stay in Madrid."

"I've decided already," Hans Christian answered. "In fact, there's only one thing that isn't quite clear in my mind. I can't understand why I've been such a stubborn fool not to do what my grandmother advised, why I didn't come to Spain years ago!"

"What man wants to take his grandmother's advice? None that has red blood in his veins! You have lost more of that than is good for you lately; but I am sure you still have plenty left! To me, the surprise is not so much that you have come tardily as that you have come at all."

Leopoldo and Leonardo had helped Hans Christian expertly from the wheel chair to the platform. As he sank down, gratefully, into one of the cushioned seats, Sebastian took the other, lighted a cigarette, and went on talking as if there had been no interruption.

"But I am gladder to see you than I can say. And to relieve your mind at once on a certain score, may I tell you that my two little daughters are not at home, that they are both safely installed in an excellent convent school, where the rules about receiving young male visitors, even under close supervision, are exceedingly strict? I doubt whether you will catch so much as a glimpse of them. Which is just as well. Were it not for their absence, I might have hesitated to introduce so appealing an invalid as yourself into my peaceful home! Though one of these children has already decided more or less that she wishes to become a nun, a plan which harmonizes admirably with her mother's wishes, something might happen to disrupt this. You never know."

Sebastian de Cerreno's voice was still merry, but a note of light mockery had crept into it. Hans Christian felt himself flushing.

"Oh, but I'd be terribly disappointed——"

"Nonsense! You are terribly relieved and you know it. Well—we do not really need to dwell on that subject, do we, now that I have clarified it for you. So you think that you are going to like Spain?"

In the face of Sebastian's perfect ease, it was impossible to remain long embarrassed. Hans Christian answered enthusiastically, his flush fading.

"I've been here about fifteen minutes, and I feel already as if I'd lived here all my life, up to now, and as if I wouldn't mind if I lived here the rest of it. Do you know, Sebastian—if I hadn't been a German, I think I should have rather liked to be a Spaniard?"

"'Every man has two countries, his own and Italy,'" Sebastian quoted gravely. "There are many who paraphrase that statement, and say 'his own and Spain' instead. I hope and believe it may be so with you. Make yourself at home in the caravan, *querido*. It is all yours."

Hans Christian woke to the pleasant consciousness that he had been asleep for a long time, and that if he so desired, he could turn over and sleep indefinitely again. He lay still, enjoying the soothing sensation that this gave him. His bed was very comfortable, the handwoven sheets cool and coarse, the mattress soft and springy; Leopoldo had helped him to bathe and shave before he settled down, and the refreshment this had given him still prevailed. The movement of the "glorified gypsy wagon," which had been Sebastian's tactful substitute for an ambulance, was rhythmic and quiet, causing neither disturbance nor pain. Rather, it seemed to invite complete relaxation, prolonged slumber. There was no sound beyond the muffled one made by its wheels. He had almost drifted off again when the instinctive feeling that he was being watched caused him to open his eyes, so suddenly that Don Sebastian, whose gaze had been riveted on him, did not have time to glance away before the boy had caught sight of the strange look of tenderness suffusing the bladelike face.

As usual, however, Don Sebastian did not betray the slightest embarrassment. "*Que tal?*" he said. "You have had a long sleep—so long, in fact, that you slept straight through the luncheon period and it is now late in the afternoon. Will you have some tea? Or will you join me in a glass of red wine, with bread and ham and olives, which is what old-fashioned Andalusians like myself still prefer to take at this hour?"

"I'd like it too then. And I'd like to know, if it isn't awfully rude to ask, what you were thinking about, just as I opened my eyes?"

"I am glad to have you ask me anything you wish, *querido*. I was thinking how uncannily you look like your mother, when your face is in repose, as it was then. When you are speaking, there is occasionally something in your manner and expression which reminds me of your father's family. But caught off your guard, so to speak, you are essentially American."

"Essentially American!"

"Perhaps I should say essentially Marlowe. Would you like that better?"

"I'm afraid I shouldn't. You see——"

"Oh, I know how you have spent the last seven years. Sacrificially, which is much to your credit. Successfully too, on the surface. But I have a feeling—I might almost say a hope—that your Prussian attributes are only skin deep. After all, why should you wish to obliterate that Puritan heritage of yours so completely? It is a good one—or at least your mother thought it was. She has patterned her whole life after it."

"Yes. Perhaps that's why."

"Why you revolted from it, as in the case of your grandmother's advice? But that was natural, whereas this— You are inconsistent, *amigo*. Your father was Prussian to the marrow of his bones, so you determined to pattern yourself after him, or rather after what you imagined him to have been. Your mother is a Puritan, so you determined to shatter the New England mold if you may. I warn you that I do not believe it can be done. And certainly I do not see the logic in your course of action."

Don Sebastian rose, not restlessly or irritably, but as if bringing an amiable argument to an easy end. He pulled back the soft orange-colored curtains from the window facing Hans Christian's bed, so that the caravan, which had been in darkness while the boy was sleeping, might be flooded with mellow evening light. Raising himself on his pillows, Hans Christian could see the landscape through which they were gliding. Save for the dazzling sky above, it bore no resemblance to the arid plain, rough and rock-strewn, which had met his eyes when he wakened that morning near Madrid. Golden wheat fields and silvery olive groves sloped all around him. He noticed that plowing and planting and harvesting were all taking place simultaneously and resolved to question Sebastian about this later on; for the moment he was too entranced for curiosity. Long lines of oxen, sleek and shining, were plodding away towards the sunset; there were mules in evidence too, with gay tassels on their bridles and bells around their necks, driven two abreast; and here and there a clustering flock of goats. Occasionally they passed a cloaked horseman, who swept off his hat with a flourish, or a peasant driving a small laden donkey, to which he talked volubly, and which twitched its ears in response; and though there were no signs of human habitation except a few scattered farm houses, placed far apart, the fields were full of laborers. Hans Christian had begun to wonder where all these workers turned for food and shelter at the end of the day, when without warning the caravan dove into a tight little town and wove its way through a narrow cobblestoned street with brown-roofed white houses on either side. They were out of it almost as quickly as they had entered it; and when the hills which had concealed it parted on either side of it, Hans Christian saw that it was crowned with a stronghold of tawny stone.

"So castles in Spain are real, are they?" he said to Sebastian, who was still standing by the window.

"Certainly. You may have one of them, for the asking, whenever it suits your fancy."

He walked forward and gave an order to Leopoldo, who was seated beside his brother at the wheel. Then he returned to his lounging position again.

"I want to talk to you about your mother very soon," he remarked, picking up the thread of conversation where he himself had broken it off. "Though I gather you have seen almost nothing of her during these last few years. That is correct, is it not? For the moment, however, I want you to talk to me about yourself, if you feel rested enough now to do so. You have had a rather bad time, I gather from your grandmother's letters. So you got a shot in the shoulder?"

"Yes, from a Communist sniper on the Fischerstrasse. The Berlin streets are full of them, you know. Of course the bandages were taken off long ago and the wound seemed to heal well. But the nerves must have been severed, for my arm is still pretty painful. That's why I still keep it in a sling most of the time. And I don't seem to have made a very quick convalescence generally. So grandmother was determined that I should come South, and the surgeon backed her up. I had no trouble at all in getting indefinite leave."

"Your grandmother was quite right, of course. As for your surgeon and your superiors, naturally the sooner you are in shape to do some shooting yourself again, the better they will be pleased. Perhaps you were not in the best possible condition nervously, even before you had this accident?"

"Would you expect a fellow to be in the best condition nervously who keeps seeing his comrades killed before his face and eyes? There have been fifteen of us so far, besides all the wounded. Of course, much the greatest loss and the hardest to bear, was Horst Wessel's death."

"You cared greatly for him then?"

"Cared greatly for him! Why, Sebastian, there was no one like him! He was the greatest leader, the greatest organizer we had, among the Youth Groups, and the most beloved. And the way he could talk! It was like that phrase in the Bible, don't you remember, about the 'tongues of men and of angels'?"

"So there is a little of the Puritan still left in you after all, Hansel? You haven't forgotten that your mother taught you to read out of the Bible."

Again Hans Christian felt himself flushing at the light mockery in Don Sebastian's voice, and again the older man went on as if oblivious of his confusion.

"I should like to have you tell me everything you will, Hansel, about the Youth Groups in Germany and about Horst Wessel himself. You are convinced, are you not, that National Socialism is a good thing? You think that Wessel himself was really a patriot and a martyr? Some stories have filtered through——"

"Those dirty Communistic lies smearing his memory! Don't tell me you've listened to those, Sebastian?"

"Oh, yes, I have listened. When you get to be as old as I am, you will know that it is generally a very good thing to listen. One learns a surprising amount that way, both of what is true and of what is false, and how to distinguish one from another. I did not mean to infer that I believed anything to Horst Wessel's discredit. Though as a matter of fact, a young hero would be no less a hero in my eyes because he knew a pretty girl when he saw one. Would he in yours?"

"It isn't a case of saying he knew a pretty girl when he saw one! It's a case of saying he was killed in a quarrel over a light-of-love, instead of saying that he was treacherously shot from behind when he sat quietly studying alone in his room!"

"I know that is what he was supposed to be doing, according to the Minister of Propaganda, who has used the episode to magnificent advantage. But sometimes I find the 'Little Doctor' almost too clever to be convincing. Since you were not present at the time, how do you know Horst Wessel was studying alone in his room?"

"I know his habits! I know his ideals!"

"It is the habit of most young men, idealistic or otherwise, to fall from grace now and then. Have you not found that out for yourself, Hansel? Never mind, do not look so upset. I was not asking for a confession. Only for the admission that this young leader of yours was a creature of flesh and blood and not a plaster image molded by a cunning hand to suit the need of the moment. Ah—here is Leopoldo with our so-called tea. Now you will have a chance to tell me how you like this, Spanish style."

Hans Christian had been hungry, he had been looking forward to this strange repast with eagerness. Now his hand shook as he extended it to take the bread and olives which Leopoldo offered him, and he could feel tears stinging beneath the surface of his lids. When he tried to sip his wine, it choked him. He did not want to talk to Don Sebastian any more. The sense of communion which had seemed to bring them so close together was shattered. Only pride prevented him from bursting out crying, like a baby. When the caravan came to a quick, lurching stop, he was thankful for the excuse it gave to ask a commonplace, steadying question, unconnected with controversy.

"Is something the matter? Have we had an accident?"

"I do not think so. But I will go and see. Lie still, I shall be back in a moment."

Hans Christian was glad to be alone, and even in his resentful state, he realized it was probable that Sebastian, with his uncanny intuition, had divined that this would be the case, and had purposely left him, instead of quietly waiting himself to be told what had happened. When he reappeared, Hansel had pulled himself together again.

"There is nothing the matter," Sebastian said reassuringly. "We were hailed by the driver of another caravan going in the opposite direction. He has run out of gas, and has asked us to lend him some. As a matter of fact, he probably has no money to buy any more, and simply went as far as he could on what he had—then swung across the road to block it, so he could hold up the next passer-by for more. Leonardo is going to syphon a fresh supply out for him. I want you to catch a glimpse of this outfit, if you can. It is not drawn by one large white horse, as your mother used to insist all real gypsy wagons should be. But it is typical, for all that—perhaps more so because it moves—when it does move—by engine power. Even gypsies must keep abreast of the times! Here, let me help you up so you can look out of the doorway."

It was impossible to withstand Don Sebastian's persuasiveness. Hans Christian suffered himself to be wrapped in a dressing gown and supported to the entrance. From the small platform, the vehicle which had blocked their progress came into view—a queer cartlike structure with a top not unlike that of the Western covered wagon. From under its shelter, a dark, shawled woman with gold hoops in her ears and a gay cloth on her flowing hair looked rather anxiously out. She had a baby at her breast, and beside her nestled a chubby child with large liquid eyes and a seraphic expression. The woman's face brightened as she caught sight of Hansel, and rousing the sleepy baby she held it up for him to see, while the man who had accomplished the holdup came forward to say thank you, his white teeth gleaming, his shabby cap in his hand. Then he climbed up on the seat and they started on their way again, waving bright handkerchiefs and shouting *Adios!* as they disappeared in a cloud of smoke and dust.

"The ideal way to travel," commented Sebastian, "with the highwayman's spirit and a pretty woman beside you. Ours is a dull journey compared to theirs."

"It doesn't seem dull to me. I'm finding a fresh thrill in it every minute," Hans Christian protested. He spoke sincerely. Nevertheless, Sebastian's suggestion proved provocative. Left to himself, it would not have occurred to Hansel that a nomadic existence could be attractive, or that feminine companionship would enhance the charm which it might have in any case. Now he began to consider the question; and surprisingly, when he did so, the image of Trixie rose buoyantly before him, as it had during his first desperate days at Schönplatz. Against his will, he visualized an open road enlivened by her gayety, in the same way that he had seen her reanimate the dying embers of his ancestral hearth. He could almost hear the tinkle of her bracelets in the breeze and feel the fluff of her hair blown across his face. Gold loops in her ears and a gay cloth on her head would become her——

He drifted off to sleep again, and when he woke, found he could not distinguish fact from fancy. For a time he lay still, striving towards clarity. Finally he gave it up and appealed to Sebastian, who was still sitting quietly beside him.

"Did those gypsies really exist or did I dream them?"

"Oh, they really existed! You can see plenty more of them, on the Sacro Monte, near Granada, any time you choose. I will take you there to have your fortune read, as I did your mother." Don Sebastian looked musingly out at the landscape for a moment, then turned back to Hans Christian. "Why not eat our interrupted meal out here, on the platform?" he inquired. "The air is very pleasant at this time, and it will rest you to have a change of position." And as Hans Christian acquiesced eagerly, he went on, "I cannot help reflecting how history repeats itself. I met your mother when she first came to Madrid, on the *train de luxe* from Irún, just as you did. She felt instantly as if she had always lived in Spain, or would like to, as you did. And shortly afterwards, when she came South to Andalusia, the place put a spell on her, just as it has already on you."

"She was married then, wasn't she? I must have known, but I have forgotten."

"She was just married. She came to Spain on her wedding journey."

"And you—you were married too, weren't you?"

"Yes. I had already been married a number of years. But my wife was an invalid, living in isolation among the Pyrenees. In fact, it was not until long afterwards that she was restored to health, and during those years of her retirement, the march of progress passed her by. She is still a lady of the old school, completely absorbed by her Church and her children. Her recovery is largely due to your mother. It was she who persuaded me to permit an American doctor, an old friend of hers, to operate on *Doña* Dolores. The result was an almost miraculous cure."

"It was David Noble who operated, wasn't it? Of course, it must have been! He's a great surgeon—and a grand person besides."

"Yes, that is very true. I do not underestimate the part he played. But still, the major part of the credit is due your mother. As David said of her himself, she is a very gallant lady." Don Sebastian looked out over the *vega* again, and then added inconsequentially, "By the way, your Spanish is very good. I noticed it at once, when you spoke to Leopoldo, and again when you were talking with the gypsies. Did your mother teach you that?"

"Yes. That is, she taught all the children in the local school after my father was killed and she went back to Hamstead to live, you know. I think you're right. I think she must have been very gallant. Anti-German feeling was pretty strong then, in New England. But she never let it touch me or mar my father's memory. Children can be awfully cruel, you know, to other children, and I suppose she must have had to shield me from a good deal. She was terribly busy too, teaching, and managing a day nursery, and running a farm, but somehow she always contrived to have a free hour just before supper. She read aloud to me every night. And I slept beside her, in an old-fashioned trundle. So if I were frightened or wakeful or sick, I could always climb into her big bed. And lots of times I did."

He paused, reminiscently. They were approaching another small compact village, and from the tower of a near-by church, the Angelus sounded softly. As the music melted away into the encircling stillness, Don Sebastian laid his hand on Hans Christian's arm.

"I am tremendously interested in everything you are telling me, Hansel. It is a long time since I have heard anything about your mother."

"There is a lot more I could say, of course. She seemed to have time for everything and everybody. She used to mean the world and all to me, too. I think it was politics, in the first place, that caused the estrangement between mother and me, Don Sebastian. She became so absorbed in them that after awhile she forgot everything else. Well, she didn't forget exactly, but everything else seemed to fade from the forefront of her mind. Do you know what I mean? She was so efficient and executive and successful it didn't seem human or—or womanly. I wouldn't have minded half so much if she'd married again. In fact, I hoped she would. For a little while I thought she was going to. But she never has. I know now she never will. Her life's complete just as it is."

"*Querido,* I wish I thought you were right. But I am afraid you are mistaken. I am afraid her life is very, very empty. That is why she had permitted politics to absorb her. To take the place of all she hoped would fill it and which has not."

Again Hans Christian was conscious of the pressure of Don Sebastian's hand on his own and of the tenderness of his touch.

"You have told me much I did not guess at all before, and much that I had only half guessed. As I said, I know I owe a great deal to your mother. But I am beginning to believe that the debt is even greater than I thought. However, you will see the harmony of the family life which is due her, as soon as you get to the *caseria*."

"The place where my parents spent their honeymoon?"

"Yes, close to Granada. It is very old and primitive. Ordinarily I do not spend much time there—more often I am at Ventosilla, near Toledo, which is much more of an estate. But just now I am at the *caseria* so that I may be near my brother Gabriel, the Archbishop of Granada. He is not well and he is much older than I am, old enough to be my father—which makes him a veritable patriarch, does it not? Well—I am glad, as things have turned out, that it is to the *caseria* you are coming, and not to Ventosilla. Your mother used to call it 'a magic house,' so I believe you yourself may find happiness and healing there. And Gabriel will be glad of a chance to welcome you—as we all are— Ah, we seem to be stopping again. But this time I think it is only the *consumista,* who must assure himself that we are not carrying contraband provisions from one locality into another—you were asleep the last time we went through the local customs. This time you should take a look at our smart *Guardia Civil.*"

Hansel glanced admiringly at the natty uniforms and upturned black hats and raised his own hand in response to the salute of "Go with God." But he was growing very drowsy again, and after saying to Sebastian, rather shyly, that he felt as if they were doing just that, he did not try to talk any more. He had been reflecting with a happy glow around his heart that everyone did indeed seem very glad to see him, that even the man on the train had gone out of his way to be courteous and considerate. He had meant to speak to Don Sebastian about his traveling companion, to ask if he knew anyone named Bautista Ramirez. But somehow he had never asked the question because the conversation had been switched into other channels, and he had rambled on, without asking any questions at all, because it was so easy to confide in Don Sebastian, who sometimes mocked him and sometimes made him angry, but to whom he was drawn as he never had been to an older man before. Then he realized that he was not rambling now but dreaming. He was dreaming that the setting sun had changed into a great crimson bowl from which liquid color was being dipped to spread out over the *vega,* and that the stars which had come out were not like the stars at Schönplatz, small and cold and distant, but big and warm, and so close that he could reach up and touch them. He did so, and found that he could not only touch them, he could gather them, as if they had been sparkling flowers, and make them into a garland. But after the garland was made, he did not know what to do with it. After all, you could not give a starry garland to anybody. Only to an angel——

"*Querido,* I am sorry to waken you. I think your dreams must be very pleasant. But you can dream again soon, as long as you like, in your own room. We have come to the end of our journey."

Hans Christian rubbed his eyes and sat up. The caravan had stopped in front of a tall blank wall, intersected only by one immense iron-hinged door. As this swung open from within to admit them, the caravan rolled slowly into a large outer patio, containing hedges and flowers and trees, and stopped a second time before a grilled gate.

"We shall have to walk now. But I do not think you will find it too hard. The inner patio is paved and the *galeria* which surrounds it leads straight to your room. Lean on me, *amigo.* It will be but a minute."

There was a fountain in the paved patio. Hans Christian could hear the water flowing over the form of a small stone cherub in the center of it and dripping down to the stone cockleshell on which the statue stood. The sound it made was sweet and soothing, and the scent of the flowers surrounding the fountain seemed subtly mingled with this sound. Overhead was a sapphire sky, star spangled like the one in his dream, and almost as close at hand; it seemed to form a dome over the patio, mysteriously enfolding it.

"Is it real like the gypsies? Or am I dreaming this time? I was, just now, as you guessed. I dreamed I gathered stars and then I grieved because there was no one to whom I could give them. I wanted to offer them to an angel——"

Certainly he had heard no other sound in the patio than that of the flowing fountain, no footfall, no opening or closing of a door. Yet suddenly he saw that he and Sebastian were not alone there. A white form was gliding among the shadows of the *galeria,* its nebulous movements only half detached from the encircling gloom. As Hans Christian watched it, fascinated yet frightened, his heart seemed to stand still. The apparition had come closer, and the outlines of a young figure were visible under its flowing draperies; the moon shone full on a flowerlike face, framed by dark hair smoothly parted over a pure brow and falling in long plaits across a budding breast.

"That is not a ghost, Hansel. It is a girl," he heard Don Sebastian saying reassuringly. "How she escaped from school I do not know, but I suppose she will tell us all in good time. Apparently bolts and bars slip sometimes, even on convent doors—and I have never been able to cure her of a childish habit of stealing out to meet me when she is at home, no matter at what hour I come in myself. Perhaps I have not tried as hard as I should." He stepped forward and kissed the girl's white forehead. Then with one arm still around Hansel, he put the other about her. "*Querida,* this is the young kinsman of whom I told you," he said. "He has been very ill and needs good care. You must help your mother and me to see that he gets it. —Hansel, as you have probably guessed by now, this is my daughter Cristina."

CHAPTER 18

THE WHITEWASHED walls of Hans Christian's room were high and blank. The tiled floor was bare. One large metal lamp hung suspended from the distant ceiling. The great carved bed in which he lay was set into a shallow recess with a long narrow window across the top. It faced the double doors leading into the *galeria.* In addition to the bed the room contained, for furniture, a *bagueno,* a chest, two tables and two chairs, also exquisitely carved. There was a *prie-dieu* surmounted by a crucifix beside the bed, and in the niches on either side of the doors leading into the *galeria,* small wooden statues with silver crowns on their heads. The brocade coverlet and window curtains were gold colored; so were the top-heavy, full-blown roses which stood in a silver vase on the *bagueno.*

How quiet it was, he thought contentedly, how cool and restful and spacious! He tried conscientiously to make no mental comparisons between its superb simplicity and the inharmonious clutter of his room at

Schönplatz. He tried to argue with himself that the latter was comfortable, even though it was hideous. He was unsuccessful. He knew, down deep in his heart, that he had never, in all the years he had spent in East Prussia, found as much comfort as he had already experienced in this beautiful bare Andalusian chamber.

There was an old-fashioned bellpull by his bed, and at length, idly, he tugged at it. The answer was not instantaneous. Apparently there was no spurred service here. But presently he heard firm footsteps padding across the patio, and the sound of panting and puffing in the *galeria.* Then the square of sunlight made by the doorway was blocked out, and a beaming peasant woman of prodigious size entered the room.

She was carrying a breakfast tray, which she set down on the bedside table with a flourish, before she leaned over to possess herself of Hans Christian's pillows, propped them up behind him, and lifted him bodily higher in the bed. All of this she did without the slightest effort. Afterwards she folded her arms and stood staring at him, her smile becoming wider and wider as she broke into voluble and excited speech.

"Anywhere I should have known the *Señor* Baron, anywhere!" she exclaimed. "His eyes—his hair—his skin—in all of them do I see again our beloved *Baronesita.* Have I not watched over her again and again in this very room? For as the *Señor* Baron must know, it was here that his lady mother came as a bride. I can see her still as she lay where he lies now, *la preciosissima,* so little and so lovely that she looked like a rosy child. But that was only at first. Her roses faded fast enough. She had her husband to thank for that, if the *Señor* Baron will forgive me for saying so of his father, who, I understand, now rests with God. It was little enough he rested then, or let his young wife rest either. Bridegrooms are much the same when it comes to that, so I mean no disrespect to nature, but this man was like one possessed." The peasant woman paused to cross herself and draw breath before she rattled on again. "He sapped strength away from your mother, so that when she began to make her baby, she was very sick. Remembering all this, how could I but dread the outcome, *Señor* Baron? I feared that some mark of your mother's suffering might have been made upon you. But now beholding you, I know that all is well!" She turned towards the *galeria* and called lustily. "Felipe! Come at once! The *Señor* Baron is awake and has need to be served, and still you see fit to tarry, indolent creature that you are!"

"Be still, Catalina! Felipe has gone out to gather pomegranates. I am coming in to see the *Señor* Baron myself. If you have brought him everything he needs for the moment, you may go."

The square of sunlight by the door was obscured again, but only partially this time. Radiance still streamed in on either side of the lady now approaching, for her slim figure did not suffice to block it out completely, as Catalina's substantial bulk had done. She was wearing black silk, made with a fitted bodice and full skirt and finished with flat bands of lace at the neck and wrists; though exquisitely fashioned and finished, as if it had been made by a master hand, the dress had the old-time effect of one painted in an ancestral portrait, and it was fastened at the throat with a jeweled cross of antique design. A bunch of silver keys fell on a ribbon from the lady's small waist, tinkling lightly as she walked, and her long earrings tinkled too, though with an even softer sound. A sprinkling of white showed in the shining black of her abundant hair, which she wore parted in the middle and drawn down over her delicate ears to form a large knot behind; but her face was still as smooth as a girl's. It had the serenity of a woman, temperamentally calm, whose life has always been sheltered and softened, and the same sort of pure beauty which Hans Christian had seen so startlingly revealed in her daughter's the night before. She came over to the bed and held out a white hand which was cool against Hansel's lips as he kissed the long tapering fingers.

"*Se bien venido,* Christian," she said, seating herself in one of the large carved chairs. Her voice was cool and pleasant too, and the smile which parted her perfect lips, though a little grave, was gracious. "Pray drink your coffee while it is still hot—I see you have hardly begun on it. No, no, if you do not continue, I shall be obliged to leave you until you have finished your breakfast. I am glad that you have been able to sleep so late—the house is not as quiet as usual when my daughters are at home. Not that Cristina makes any noise—my husband tells me that she actually startled you, she came into the patio so quietly last night. But Cecilia makes enough for two—more than either of her brothers! She has gone into town this morning with her father to see her uncle, the Archbishop. When she gets back you will hear her singing and romping from one end of the *caseria* to the other."

Doña Dolores took a scrap of net from a small silken bag which had been hidden by her keys while she was standing, and which, like them, hung suspended from her waist. "Perhaps Sebastian told you that our sons are at school in England," she said, drawing a fine thread through the gossamerlike fabric. "We agreed that they should be educated there, as he was, in the modern manner, but that our daughters, on the other hand, should go to the old convent where I went myself. It seemed a well-balanced arrangement, and it has been satisfactory to everyone. Indeed, it is so satisfactory to Cristina that I doubt whether she will ever wish to leave the convent. I believe she has a true vocation."

"Isn't it too soon for her to be sure?"

"Vocation is a matter of instinct, not of age," *Doña* Dolores replied. "As all the world knows, the little Saint Theresa was so sure of hers that as a mere child she obtained special permission to enter the Carmel of Lisieux when she was only fifteen."

"But you wouldn't be willing to have Cristina do such a thing, would you?"

"I should rejoice to have her become the bride of Christ. It is very evident that Cecilia will never be suited for a cloistered existence. And it has always been my prayer that one of my daughters might devote her life to worship, in order that through her, my own prayers of thanksgiving would rise the more effectively to the Throne of Grace. God has shown his divine mercy in giving me four beautiful children, after all hope for them had been lost, and my husband seemed destined to be the last of his line. Can I do less than give one back to Him?"

Hans Christian could see that *Doña* Dolores was supremely sincere in what she was saying, that she earnestly believed such a sacrifice should be made. Respect for her piety prevented him from arguing with her further, though her logic seemed to him as unsound as her faith was great. He could not understand why anyone should feel that the incarceration of a beautiful young girl should be pleasing to God, or why a daughter should be doomed to celibacy because her mother had proved fruitful. Besides, he had heard horrible tales about convents. He recoiled from the thought of fasting and flagellation in connection with the radiant vision he had seen the night before. Cristina's mother, he could see, was thinking of her as she would look in the candlelight at a glorious festival, veiled with white lace for her investiture; he seemed to behold her instead, kneeling on bare stones, with a knotted cord in her hands——

"Well, I am very glad she is here now, anyway," he managed to say at length, hoping that his voice would not betray overmuch earnestness. "I hope I shall see a great deal of her."

"Inevitably, you will see her," *Doña* Dolores replied. Her manner had become more reserved, and it seemed to Hans Christian that there was actually a note of regret in it. "Unfortunately, several cases of severe illness have occurred in the school, and the Mother Superior decided that it was best to send the pupils to their homes and keep them there until all danger of further contagion is past. But I shall make arrangements to have my daughters study regularly here, of course. And you will require a great deal of rest, for the present. Do you not think, on the whole, that it would be prudent for you to remain in bed today?"

Nothing could have been less appealing to Hans Christian than such a suggestion. He had slept long and heavily, but now he felt restless—the more so because so many of the remarks to which he had been listening were disquieting to him. Of course Catalina was only an ignorant, coarse-mouthed peasant; he had no idea of taking her seriously.

Still, it was upsetting to learn that the very servants at the *caseria* had failed to respect his father and had thought his mother ill-treated— And of course, *Doña* Dolores would not forcibly induce Cristina to become a nun; the girl would be allowed to follow her own mind in the matter. But it was disturbing to wonder whether she would have a chance to know her own mind.

He was eager to be up and about, to rid himself of such troublesome ideas; and when *Doña* Dolores saw that he was uneasy, she did not insist that he should remain in bed. She rose, refolding her embroidery and placing it in the small silk bag again, and said she would summon Leonardo to serve him, since she understood from her husband that the man had been satisfactory to him the day before. Then she left the room in a rustle of silk, remarking that she would see Hansel at lunchtime and adding again that he was very welcome, as if she feared he might have misinterpreted her growing reserve. A large tin tub which in due time was filled from buckets with tepid rain water was brought into the room, and Hans Christian bathed and dressed with comparatively little help. His shoulder pained him less, his right hand and arm were not so stiff. He felt much stronger, much less listless. He penetrated to the patio without undue exertion, and there the sound of dripping water, which had been so soothing the night before, seemed stimulating now; so was the song of the birds fluttering among the yews and myrtles. The perfume of the flowers had a pungent quality; there were spicy geraniums among the scented roses. And he had never seen such sunshine. It gilded the very stones with its luster and penetrated to the innermost depths of his being with its warmth. In the full flood of it, all his apathy, all depression was suddenly submerged.

He was hesitating whether to linger beside the fountain or to wander about in the extraordinary sunshine, when he saw that the patio was not empty. A table, heaped with roses, was drawn into the shade of the *galeria;* and Cristina, with Catalina beside her, was sitting behind it. The girl's small feet, encased in black kid slippers trimmed with stiff little bows, were crossed demurely in front of her; but her fingers, fluttering among the flowers, were as swift as they were sure: unerringly she selected the loveliest of these, freed them of thorns and foliage, and added them to a garland which had already taken fragrant form. Her dark head was bent over her task, in which she seemed wholly absorbed; and Hans Christian could see, more clearly than the night before, the sheen of her black hair with the white part running through it, and the fluid grace of her young figure. She did not look up, and he felt uncertain whether he ought to stop and speak to her. But Catalina, meeting his eye, smiled broadly and gave a hearty exclamation of welcome.

"*Señorita!* Here is the *Señor* Baron come to help you with your labor of love! Wait but a little minute, I will fetch another chair."

"If I won't disturb you, I should like immensely to stay for a little while," Hans Christian answered, seizing upon so pleasant a solution for his indecision.

"You will not disturb me, but will you not find it rather dull? If we were making a *nacimiento,* we could all work on it together, assembling and arranging the different figures. But garlands are different. Two persons cannot very well twine the same one. Though perhaps you would like to start another yourself?"

"I'm afraid I'd be very clumsy at twining. But possibly I could hand you the roses," Hans Christian answered, suiting his action to his words. He had no illusions about his helpfulness, but it occurred to him that in the course of handing roses to Cristina, their fingers would almost inevitably meet, and the idea seemed to him singularly pleasant. He also hoped that she might look him full in the face; while her eyes were downcast, he could not determine their color, and he was consumed with curiosity concerning them. Logically, he should expect them to be brown; but he had an instinctive feeling that they might be gray instead.

"What is a *nacimiento?*" he inquired, conversationally, as Cristina, though accepting his rose, neither touched his hand nor met his gaze in doing so. "Is it the Spanish equivalent of our German *Krippe?*"

"I have never been to Germany, you know. But I think it must be. We are generally in Madrid at Christmastime, and we all go together to the old market on the Plaza de la Santa Cruz to choose the figurines for the *nacimiento.* My little sister, Cecilia, especially enjoys doing this; but the entire family takes pleasure in it."

"Tell me more about it," Hans Christian said encouragingly, holding up another rose.

"There really is not much to tell. There are booths and stalls all around the Plaza, and in the middle of it too; and each stall has its own specialty for sale. For instance, there are drums decorated with paper flowers and long streamers, and there are tambourines and *zambombas.*"

"*Zambombas?*"

"Yes. They are musical instruments also, made of pottery jars with parchment stretched across the top. A straw of wheat or barley is inserted in the parchment, and the musicians who play on the *zambombas* wet their hands and rub them up and down the straws. They really produce quite a variety of tone. After the midnight mass—the *Misa del Gallo,* the Cockcrow Mass, we call it—the *zambomba* and tambourine players go through the streets singing *villancicos,* which I believe you call carols. They represent shepherds searching for the Christ Child, and since Spanish shepherds use just such instruments as these, what could be more fitting?"

Cristina asked the question artlessly. Hans Christian, though his thoughts had not been diverted from his original purpose in helping her to weave garlands, was genuinely touched by the simplicity with which she spoke and eager to have her continue her recital.

"And what else can be bought at the Christmas fair besides *zambombas?*"

"Let me see— Well, there are some stalls which specialize in tiny three-branch candelabra with pink candles. I have never understood exactly why the candles must always be pink, but they are very pretty in that color. Then of course there are the figures for the *nacimiento,* the Blessed Virgin and the Holy Child and St. Joseph and the shepherd. Also the animals that are appropriate to go with them. And the houses and stables to fill out a village scene. And a windmill."

"A windmill?"

"Why yes. No Spanish *nacimiento* could be complete without dear old Don Quixote and his windmill, could it?"

Hans Christian put back his head and laughed, spontaneously and joyously, as he had not laughed in a long time. The idea of Don Quixote in connection with the Nativity seemed to him irresistibly amusing. But though he heard Catalina echoing his merriment, he was aware that Cristina had not. He checked himself swiftly and glanced towards her, so quickly that she did not have time to avert her eyes, which she had lifted at last. With a triumphant thrill, Hans Christian saw that they really were gray, large and limpid and fringed with long black lashes.

"Why are you making fun of me?" inquired Cristina. She continued to look at Hans Christian, and in spite of her slightly puzzled expression, her gaze was one of clarity and candor. More and more moved, Hansel hastened to reassure her.

"I wasn't making fun of you, Cristina. I wouldn't for the world. I was amused—in a pleasant way, I mean—at something you said, that was all. I couldn't quite picture Don Quixote at the Nativity, in the beginning. But as you explained, it was a Spanish village scene you were creating, so of course he would have to be there to make it complete and typical. Just as the carollers had to play the *zambomba.* I can see that now."

"I am very glad," Cristina answered gravely. But she bent over her flowers and seemed disinclined to talk any more. Hansel, cursing himself for his maladroitness in silencing her, was wondering how on earth he could make amends for it, when Catalina came to his rescue.

"*Señorita,* you have not told the *Señor* Baron that you yourself can play the tambourine, as well as the guitar, that you and *Señorita* Cecilia also sing Christmas carols. You have not told him how I choose the *turron* and the turkey for the *Noche Buena* dinner, at the same time that you are selecting all the pretty figures, and how I oversee the preparation of the feast while you and the little *señorita* are arranging the *nacimiento.* He will like to hear about that too."

"Indeed I shall. Please tell me, Cristina."

"I do not wish to tell you too much, all at one time. You would end by thinking I was a bore or a chatterbox. Besides, I am not getting ahead very fast with my wreath."

She looked up again, and for the first time she smiled. There was the slightest suggestion of archness in her look. Hans Christian's heart bounded again.

"I do not think you are a bore or a chatterbox. I think you are a darling," he said fervently. Then as Cristina became quickly preoccupied with her flowers again, and Catalina's broad grin developed into a chuckle, he decided that the time was hardly opportune to continue in such a vein. Instead, he asked, with an attempt at nonchalance which he was very far from feeling, "And when do you have your presents?"

"Our presents? Why, on Three Kings' Day, of course!"

"You don't have any presents at all on Christmas Eve? Or any tree?"

"No, we have our dinner—a special feast, with turkey and *turron,* as Catalina has told you, and many other good things besides—and then we go to the *Misa del Gallo.* Of course we have all made our Christmas confessions, so we take Holy Communion, and then, after the benediction, we go again to the altar rail and kiss the foot of the image of the Christ Child which has been placed on a table just behind it. By that time it is very late—or very early, just as you choose to say!—and we are glad to have a long sleep and a quiet Christmas Day. We do not have any merrymaking until Innocents' Day, on the twenty-ninth, when we play all sorts of pranks on each other. Then on New Year's Eve we each take twelve grapes and go out to the Puerta del Sol, which is not far from our *Palacio,* to eat them as fast as we can while we watch the big clock and listen to it strike the hour of the New Year. And finally on January fifth, after we have been to see the procession of the Three Kings parade through the streets, we come home and open our presents."

"It seems to be a long time to wait for them. You must come to Schönplatz next year and have them on Christmas Eve, as we do! And a special tree, festooned with stars and lighted with candles, which I shall decorate myself, on purpose for you!"

"Cristina, I have been waiting for you in the library nearly half an hour! Have you forgotten that we were to read *L'Histoire d'une Ame* together at eleven? Never have I known you to be so slow in making a wreath!"

Cristina and Hans Christian sprang to their feet simultaneously. Catalina had disappeared with a speed surprising in one of her size, and *Doña* Dolores was standing directly behind them. Even when she did not seem to be moving, her black silk dress rustled slightly, and it was inconceivable how she could have come into the patio unheard and unobserved. But somehow she had managed to do so, perhaps because the trio at the table had been so deeply absorbed in each other that they had been unreceptive to any other presence. Her beautiful face was still characteristically calm, her cultured voice still characteristically controlled; but the annoyance that she evidently felt, though actually invisible and unexpressed, was nevertheless unmistakable. Hansel hastened to apologize and to explain.

"I'm afraid it is all my fault, *Doña* Dolores. I saw Cristina sitting here when I came into the patio, and I asked if I could not help her with her garland. But I have hindered her instead. I dreamed last night that I was making one myself, out of stars; but in reality I do not seem to be able to make one out of flowers! I do hope you will forgive me for being such a nuisance! Because I have enjoyed myself so much and have learned so much. Cristina has been telling me about all sorts of Spanish customs."

"And you have suggested showing her some old German ones in return? It is very kind of you. But as I believe Cristina has told you, we generally spend Christmas in Madrid—and possibly by next Christmas, she will not be leaving the convent at all. Be that as it may, I think possibly I had better help her finish her garland, if we are to get in our French lesson. Since you are interested in stars, you might like to visit the Astronomical Department of the University of Granada, when you are stronger, or even to take some courses there. It is considered one of the best in the world. Meanwhile, I am sure that instead of staying all the morning in the shade, you should get out into the sunshine. It is very beneficial, after an illness. We will excuse you while you explore our garden, which we think is a pleasant one."

For the second time that morning, Hans Christian's freedom of choice had been taken from him. He knew that he was definitely dismissed, and he feared that in the future, Catalina's supervision might not be considered sufficiently rigid for Cristina. Nevertheless, he could not manage to feel completely crushed. He had just been handing Cristina another rose when *Doña* Dolores had revealed her presence; and in their start of mutual surprise, their fingers had met. Both the wishes he had made, in seating himself beside Cristina, had been fulfilled: He had looked into her eyes and found them full of clarity; he had touched her hand, and found it soft against his own. Since so much had happened in one morning, why should he despair as to what another day would bring forth?

Uplifted by this thought, he sauntered out between the fragrant box and graceful pomegranate trees. Though unconcerned at the prospect of solitude, he was almost instantly hailed. Don Sebastian was coming towards him, dressed in tweeds. He always wore his clothes casually, after the manner of a man who can afford to be indifferent to what he wears, both because he has the means and the taste to secure the best, and the face and figure to set this off. But Hans Christian was aware of a subtle difference in his appearance; the day before he had been debonair and detached, almost adventurous of aspect; now he looked the part of the important and responsible landowner bound by family ties. At his side a little girl, who was obviously his younger daughter, tripped along. Her only resemblance to her mother and her elder sister lay in the fact that she too was dark and beautiful. Her hair was not smoothly parted, as theirs was, but hung in a full fluffy bang across her brow, like a page boy's; her face, instead of being pale and oval, was round and rosy. Her rather old-fashioned white dress was demurely cut, but she wore it with undefinable dash, and she had on a red sash and a coral necklace. Hans Christian had a feeling that *Doña* Dolores had undoubtedly chosen the dress and insisted that it should be worn, but that the vivacious child had added the sash and the necklace, after a successful struggle for self-assertion, in which she had perhaps been surreptitiously aided and abetted by her father. Just now she was swinging a large hat by its ribbons, and she managed to make this simple action seem like a defiant gesture as well as a gay one. She had a small, neat box tucked under one plump arm, and she was humming happily beneath her breath. If her father had not caught her back, she would have sprung ahead of him and run up to Hans Christian alone.

"*Momentito*," he said, laughing, as he looked down at her restrainingly. "Our guest is not going to escape, *querida*, if you do not succeed in reaching his side in one bound— *Que tal*, Hansel? I am happy to hear you had such a good night. Permit me to present you to the firebrand of the family. You saw the flower of it last night."

"I should say you had two flowers in your family—one white rose and one red one."

"Very pretty. It would be more correct, however, to say that we had a Madonna lily and a blossoming thorn."

The little girl paid no attention to her father's bantering remarks. She gave a quick, quaint curtsey, and then, smiling contagiously, offered the box she had been carrying to Hans Christian.

"I have brought you some *mazapan*," she said. "It comes from Toledo, and it is very good. If you would open the box now, we could all have some."

"A very good idea. Thank you, Cecilia. I have always been very fond of *mazapan* and it has been a long time since I have had any. Besides, I was just beginning to get hungry. Weren't you, Sebastian?"

"*Mazapan* does not happen to be among my many weaknesses. However, I will have a piece—if for no better reason than to reduce the amount on which my daughter will gorge herself— And now, Celita, since you have had the meeting with Hans Christian that you have been plaguing me all the morning to arrange, suppose you go and find out what your sister is doing."

"I know what she is doing without going to find out. She is making a wreath for the Virgin."

"Then suppose you help her."

"Oh, *padre mio*, you know that I hate to make wreaths, and I see so much of Virgins in the convent. I would much rather see a young man for a change."

In spite of himself, Sebastian joined in Hans Christian's laugh. Almost instantly, however, his face grew grave.

"No doubt. But your mother will be waiting for news of your uncle. Run and tell her that we found him better today than I have seen him in a long while. Then if she has no task for you before lunchtime, you may come back."

"*Por favor!* She always has a task for me, unless you are with me. So let me stay with you, *padrito*. You are always saying that no news is good news, when mother tries to make you write letters and you are seeking for an excuse. So she is sure to guess that nothing is wrong with *Tio* Gabriel. . . . He asked after you," the pretty child went on, addressing herself more directly to Hans Christian again, "and said he hoped you would come to see him soon. He was very fond of your mother. Everyone in Spain was very fond of her, because she was so gay."

"What nonsense are you talking now, Celita? People were not fond of *Doña* Fidelidad because she was gay, but because she was good."

"I do not believe it," the little girl objected, skipping forward again. "Catalina has talked to me a great deal about *Doña* Fidelidad, but it was her gayety Catalina admired, not her piety. She thought you admired it too. She said she used to enjoy hearing you and *Doña* Fidelidad laughing together in the patio, after her horrid German husband had gone away. Do you really believe, *padre mio*, that ladies are ever loved just because they are good? I know *madrecita* says so, when you can get her to talk about love at all, which of course the nuns never will, no matter how hard you try to make them. But somehow she swallows her words. Is that the reason why you married *madrecita*, that she was good?"

"Of course."

"And the way she looked had nothing to do with it at all? You know,

I have seen the pictures taken of her when she made her First Communion and when she was a bride, and she was very pretty. You mean you would have wanted her just as much if she had had buck teeth and squinty eyes, just so long as she was good?"

Sebastian laughed again. "You are absurd, Celita. If you do not do as I tell you, and go to your mother now, I shall be really angry with you." Then as the little girl tossed her head and went laggingly away, looking backward with almost every step she took and still swinging her hat and chewing *mazapan*, he asked, "Well, what do you think of her, Hansel? She is a little baggage, isn't she?"

"She's bewitching. I'm so glad scarlet fever, or whatever it was, broke out in the convent."

"I wouldn't put it past Cecilia to scatter germs herself, if she only knew how, in order to get out. She is in a state of constant rebellion at all restraint. Sometimes I think a different sort of school– But my wife and I had an agreement——"

"Yes, she told me. But couldn't you overpersuade her? If you really felt it would be better for your daughters, I mean?"

"I didn't say my daughters. I said Cecilia. I think Cristina is perfectly placed where she is. Suppose we sit down for a few moments. Perhaps it would be just as well if I tried to tell you, at the very start of your stay here, how men feel about women in Spain."

"Is it so different from the way men feel about women in other parts of the world?"

"In a sense, I think it is. Seclusion of every kind has almost passed out of the picture elsewhere, and naturally the seclusion of women has been part and parcel of this disappearance. Theoretically we have kept up with the march of so-called progress too. For instance, institutions of higher education have been open to women in Spain longer than they have in the United States. But as a matter of fact, very few men of our class have encouraged their daughters to seek the freedom of university life and all that goes with it, and very few well-born and well-bred young girls have tried to take matters into their own hands in this or any other respect. Though questions of the sort are never discussed in their hearing, they subconsciously associate liberation with laxity, and the wall between the Spanish lady and the Spanish light-of-love is impregnable. In republican and radical circles, of course, there is much more feminine emancipation, and some individuals, like Concha Espina, the writer, and Isabel de Palencia, the feminist, are respected both for their talents and their integrity. I must also admit that the young barrister, Victoria Kent, was very adroit in her defense of certain notorious revolutionists at their recent dramatic trials. It is unfortunate that her cause was unworthy of her talents. Even if it had been, however, most gentlewomen look upon all such evidence of emancipation askance and the viewpoint of their husbands and fathers is the same. Very often Spaniards do not even admit the existence of change. Have you never heard the classic story of Fray Luis de Leon, who was dragged away from the University at Salamanca by the Inquisition?"

"No, never. What happened?"

"After four years' imprisonment he was permitted to return to his school. He walked into his former classroom, where students had continued to forgather, and remarked calmly, 'As I was saying yesterday, gentlemen——' "

Hans Christian laughed. Sebastian's charming smile flashed momentarily across his face. But he continued seriously.

"I thought you would consider that amusing. As a matter of fact, it is typical of our immobility. We cling, in a closed circle, to the ancient customs inherited from the Moors as well as the Christians. It is not wholly a matter of religion. The patio, surrounded on all sides, is almost as remote as the cloister."

"But not as futile."

"I cannot argue that point with you, because I am a Latin and a Catholic, and you are a Nordic and a Protestant, and we could never agree, or come close to agreeing. All I am trying to make you understand is that for centuries, in Spain, well-born women have lived in voluntary seclusion, and well-born men, in both civil and clerical life, have safeguarded this seclusion for them. Such a career as your mother's would be inconceivable in Spain, and since we did agree, yesterday, that this has not been without its disadvantages, both for herself and for you, perhaps you can bring yourself to believe that our system has its merits after all."

"In spite of everything you've just said, I can't see much merit in a system based on the assumption that a girl can't be happily married!"

"But there is no such assumption."

"Isn't that what you said, to begin with, before you got started on the general theme of seclusion?"

"I was speaking only of Cristina at the moment. Girls for whom marriage is the manifest destiny are entirely different. Indeed, *Doña* Dolores and I will select a suitable husband for Cecilia in a very short time now, for obviously she should marry early. But Cristina is very different. Marriage would be a martyrdom for her unless she were treated with supreme tact and tenderness."

"But she might be."

"Not by any man I can visualize."

"Isn't it possible you're lacking in vision?"

"I think not. I know a good deal about men."

"In other words, though the wall between the Spanish lady and the

Spanish light-of-love is so impregnable, the *caballero* feels free to take his fun where he finds it—provided he can scale the wall?"

"Yes, and in spite of the other differences I mentioned, in this respect the Spanish *caballero* is no different from the German *Junker*, as you know very well! Except that the *Junker* is more brutal in his methods!"

Hans Christian had spoken satirically, almost insolently, considering that he was addressing a man old enough to be his father; Sebastian de Cerreno answered with a degree of intensity that had in it elements of fury as well as scorn. The boy felt himself flushing painfully, as if every act of impetuous folly which he himself had committed had been laid bare before Sebastian's searing glance; the barb with which he had been struck also seemed to dart through him into the past. The memory of what Catalina and Cecilia had said concerning his father forced itself again to the forefront of his mind. It was on the tip of his tongue to ask a question which he would instantly have regretted; only his embarrassment and confusion halted him; and fortunately Sebastian spoke again before he had found any words in which to form a retort.

"Forgive me, my dear boy," he said gently. "I had no right to speak to you like that. But neither—if you will pardon me for saying so—had you any right to goad me into it. Let us stick to safer subjects—though if you will permit me the last word on this one I might add dispassionately that I not only know a great deal about men, little of which is reassuring when I consider them as suitors, but also that I know a great deal about women. Unfortunately most of that knowledge is more to my discredit than theirs. So perhaps you may think that it is the voice of the guilty conscience that has been speaking rather than the voice of wisdom. And alas! you would not be far wrong. But one thing I am glad to be able to say with some certainty: I have safeguarded my wife, according to the old Spanish custom of which I spoke, and in spite of many departures from grace, that would cause her anguish if she knew of them, which pray Heaven she never may! And I mean to safeguard my daughters also. That is all—I believe we understand each other now and need never quarrel again— Shall we go up to the house and have some *refrescos* after this very serious discussion? I am sure it must be almost lunchtime. And I can hear Cristina playing her guitar in the patio."

CHAPTER 19

At the end of three weeks, Hans Christian was convinced that a deliberate conspiracy existed to keep him from being alone with Cristina.

He saw her constantly, of course: at luncheon and dinner in the patio, at tea on the terrace which led from the turreted library at the top of the house, in the garden where the box and pomegranates grew. When callers came, he was always summoned to see them, with the family, in the *salita* containing the dark screens painted with flowers and the great crimson velvet chests studded with metal. He sat in a tall gold and black chair, and sipped pale sherry, and conversed civilly with these visitors, trying to keep his eyes and his thoughts off Cristina. She also sat in a tall black and gold chair, her dark head bent, her white hands clasped, her small slippered feet crossed in front of her; and she was invariably separated from him by the length of the room, just as she was always separated from him by the breadth of the family board and the depth of the patio pool.

Not that these visitors bored him, or that he felt the same antagonism and contempt for them that he had for many of his neighbors at Schönplatz. On the contrary, they greatly intrigued him, and if Cristina had not fascinated him even more, he would have been charmed by them. Their manners were suave and sophisticated. The men were well turned out in English country clothes or natty uniforms which they set off to advantage by their svelte figures and their rich coloring. The women, who fanned themselves incessantly, opening and shutting their fans with a swift little click, invariably wore dark silk dresses and black mantillas drawn across their creamy brows. They were beautiful in a smouldering distant way, and gradually Hans Christian began to feel the force of what Sebastian had told him about their voluntary seclusion. They had elements of unreality about them, and he could not reconcile their remoteness to the easy affability of their husbands. Yet he recognized that these men and women were closely linked together by powerful ties. Their lives might seem strange, but they were not without splendor.

Some of these callers came in sleek Hispano Suizas or *nuevo modelo* Fords; but for the most part they arrived in red-wheeled open victorias, very spruce and smart, and emblazoned with coats of arms to proclaim their noble ownership. Occasionally they actually swung into sight in a coach-and-four, flying a ducal flag, the men on the box wearing bright cockades and dashing livery. Andalusia and East Prussia had at least one point in common: The horse had not been driven out of his kingdom in either place, though the uses to which he was put were not the same. As a connoisseur and a breeder, Hans Christian revelled in the beauty of the satiny creatures that came prancing into the outer patio. He thought how much he would like to see Cristina seated on one, and he finally asked her one day at luncheon if she never rode. Her mother answered for her.

"Certainly Cristina knows how to ride," she said evenly. "When we are in the Pyrenees, we all ride together, a great deal."

"*Mamecita* and Cristina and I wear red bodices and long white skirts and *padrito* wears a scarlet coat," interposed Cecilia. "We dress up exactly as if it were carnival time, or as if we were going to a masquerade."

"Not at all. We merely keep up the customs of our ancestors, in the style of our riding habits as in other respects," *Doña* Dolores said with a touch of asperity. "There is nothing fantastic about that. It shows that we do not feel obliged to slavishly follow every new fashion. But that is vacation time, as it is when we go to Biarritz for the bathing. This is not. Merely because the school schedule has been interrupted by a catastrophe, there is no reason for taking a holiday, especially during Lent. Cristina and Cecilia both go to Mass with me every morning, Hansel, while you are still asleep, and begin their studies before you are up and dressed. By the time they have finished these, for the morning, it is too warm for them to dash about in the sun; it is better for them to sit quietly over their needlework. After luncheon, of course, comes the siesta period, and then, if we have no visitors and are not driving out ourselves, I like to have them resume their studies for a time, and set apart an hour for evening devotions. Thus the day is very full, without further diversions."

"But riding is such good exercise," objected Hans Christian.

"I rather agree with Hansel," Sebastian remarked, uninsistently. "Perhaps by the time his arm is better, so that he could join us, we might do some riding here, Dolores, in the early morning. It would do no great harm if you and the girls skipped a Mass occasionally, or even if they missed a few study periods."

"*Padrito*, you always have such nice ideas!" exclaimed Cecilia. "And if we missed the needlework, too, I do not see that it would make much difference either. And you know you promised me that I should have a horse this year. My poor pony is so fat and wheezy. I want a spirited steed. Don't you think I should have a spirited steed, Hans Christian?"

"Yes, and I think Cristina should have a gentle palfrey," he answered, rather absently. His thoughts were preoccupied with a mental picture of Cristina, dressed in a close-fitting red bodice and a flowing white skirt, coming on horseback down the steep incline from a moated castle. The mediaeval vision fascinated him.

"Ah—I fear that when Hans Christian's arm is well again, he will find the quiet of the *caseria* irksome," *Doña* Dolores said, addressing her husband and disregarding the others entirely. "There is really so little for an athlete to do here. Even you complain that you cannot keep occupied, Sebastian, and say you would much rather be in

Madrid or Toledo. How can you imagine that a young man would fail to be restless? Besides, I believe the girls will soon be able to return to the convent. I had a note from the Mother Superior this morning, saying that no more cases of illness had broken out, that the epidemic was certainly subsiding."

The manner of *Doña* Dolores was characterized by its customary graciousness, but Hans Christian was not slow to catch the inference in her words. She had already remarked that he should get away from the *caseria* as soon as he felt able, that he must not leave Andalusia without seeing something of the countryside. She had also urged him to accept an invitation for a visit which had reached him from Don Jaime de los Rios.

"You will find Malaga a delightful city and Don Jaime a charming host," she had said persuasively. "Perhaps you remember him? He was the Spanish Minister in Copenhagen when your father was stationed there. They were very good friends."

"Oh, yes, I remember him. He was at the German Legation a good deal," Hans Christian answered rather shortly. His curtness was based partly on the fact that while he did remember Don Jaime perfectly, he also recalled that it was his mother's society, rather than his father's, that the Spanish Minister had seemed to enjoy, and that he was tiring of reminders concerning his parents' comparative popularity. But he also could not help wondering whether this recent invitation from Don Jaime had been wholly spontaneous, whether the elderly diplomat had not extended it because the Cerrenos, or more specifically the Duquesa de Cerreno, had intimated that it would be to the benefit of all concerned if such hospitality were suggested. He had experienced similar misgivings every time he had seen Sebastian's brother Gabriel, the Archbishop of Granada. The gentle, white-haired old man, whose dark eyes were so kindly and yet so piercing, had repeatedly told Hans Christian that he would be more than welcome to stay at the Episcopal Palace; and his invitations became increasingly urgent after Hans Christian had escorted Cristina there, to see the Holy Week processions from one of the Archbishop's wrought iron balconies.

They had, of course, been amply accompanied. Don Sebastian had declined to leave his library; but *Doña* Dolores had gone with them, and so had Cecilia. However, it was Hans Christian who had precipitated the expeditions, in the same persuasive way that he had spoken of riding horseback; and there had been little in his manner to suggest that he was primarily interested in sight-seeing, or that he was much moved by religious ceremonies. On the contrary, his attitude from the beginning had been that of a gallant, and as the week wore on, it became more and more definitely that of a suitor. After the ladies and the prelate were seated on the balcony, he invariably turned his own chair in such a way that he could see Cristina much better than he could see the procession; and though *Doña* Dolores kept icily recalling his attention to superb floats preceded by military escorts and followed by hooded *penitentes,* his errant glance quickly strayed from the wooden figures in the street to the warm figure of the girl at his side. True, he asked her to tell him what all the richly robed images represented, and listened to her explanations with the same eagerness that he had shown when she talked about *zambombas* and *nacimientos.* But when she fell silent, his own interest waned. A bejewelled Virgin, a bleeding Christ, a galaxy of saints in stiff brocades—none of these thrilled him except when he saw them through Cristina's admiring and awestruck eyes. The sound of shuffling feet, made by the bearers concealed beneath the draperies of their burdens, intrigued him momentarily. But when he saw the men set down their loads and emerge from hiding to wipe the sweat from their swarthy faces and turn their task over to another shift, while they went rollicking off to drink beer, he was perilously close to laughter. What was far worse, he made Cecilia laugh more than once. He kept upsetting the solemnity of the occasion. It required a grave word from the Archbishop to remind him that what he was seeing was traditionally sacred.

He had not been deliberately sacrilegious, and he genuinely regretted his apparent lack of respect. At the same time, he was now past keeping either his eyes or his thoughts off Cristina. She looked enchanting in a mantilla; and every now and then, when her mother was momentarily preoccupied, she spoke to him with the same suggestion of archness that had charmed him when she had been weaving her wreath. She dropped her fan, and though he stooped to retrieve it, he did not forestall her own quick motion. Their fingers met again, and this time he managed to press hers as he placed the fan in them. It was after this fell to the floor the second time on the same day that the Archbishop's invitations to Hans Christian took on a new tone, and shortly they became actually urgent. Apparently the importunate guest's adroit but complete removal from the scene was under general contemplation.

He was irritated beyond measure that this should be the case. He had not come to Spain on his own initiative: Both his grandmother and Sebastian de Cerreno himself had been urging such a step for years; and he had finally succumbed to their importunities because he had been weak and ill, and not because he had any idea of paying court to Sebastian's elder daughter. It was unjust to suspect him of any such intention—or so he hotly asserted to himself. Yet, at the very moment of doing so, his own essential fairness compelled him to admit that while he had indeed been possessed of no such intention in the beginning, he was now. He had fallen in love with her at first sight, on the night of his arrival at the *caseria,* when he had dreamed about offering a garland of stars to an angel, and she had come gliding out from the shadows of the *galeria* to meet her father.

He argued that it must be madness to want to marry a girl with whom he had never even spoken alone, and yet instinctively he knew that it was not, except in so far as that all lovers are obsessed with madness. The sound of her guitar, tinkling in the patio, was in itself enough to stir him. He did not need to talk to her alone to know that her face was beautiful, that her voice was sweet, that her heart was guileless. All this he saw and heard every time he was in her presence, no matter how many other persons were gathered around her. In fact, he had gradually acquired the faculty of ignoring alien elements which crowded in upon them, of pretending that he and she were alone, of imagining what communion with her could become. He knew it would mean more to him to put his hand on her hair, or to feel her fingers clasped in his, than to take largesse from anyone else. The memory of Trudchen's easy subjugation was horrible to him now; the thought of a mercenary marriage with a self-willed heiress scarcely less loathsome. He wanted nothing, for the moment, except Cristina's gentle companionship. He was confident that in time her tenderness would blossom into love.

It would have meant much to him if he could have said all this, frankly and freely, to Sebastian; but a barrier seemed to be rising between him and his Spanish kinsman almost as insuperable as the one that divided him from Cristina. It had not existed at first. Sebastian had really been glad to see him, he felt sure of that; the older man had been kindly and understanding in his attitude, he had treated his guest as a kindred spirit, expansively and sympathetically. But from the moment of Cristina's unexpected appearance, he had changed. He had continued to be courteous and considerate, but he had become defensive. Hans Christian would not have put it past him to clap her into a convent at the first intimation that his guest was seriously interested in her.

Under the circumstances, Hans Christian did not know what to do. Obviously he could not linger on indefinitely in a house where he was made welcome as an individual but considered superfluous as a suitor. On the other hand, he could not accept defeat on the terms which were being dictated. Later, after Cristina had taken the veil and was lost to him forever, Sebastian would be quite capable of illogically taunting him with having left the firing line before the battle had half begun, and asking him what he expected to have happen, in that case? He did not know what he expected to have happen. His thoughts went round and round, in a vicious circle. At last he decided upon a course which seemed to him ingenious. He determined to go and talk to Gabriel.

No one made the slightest objection when he asked if it would be convenient to send him into Granada. Sebastian assured him that Leonardo would be at his disposal at any hour he would like to start out. *Doña* Dolores told him that he should be sure to see the Capilla Real and the Virgin of the Angustias. Cecilia said he would have much more fun if he went up on the Sacro Monte, where the gypsies were, and had his fortune told, and intimated that she would like to go with him. Cristina, addressing him spontaneously for almost the first time, asked him if it would be convenient for him to stop at the Palace for a moment, as she would like to send a little note to her uncle——

Relieved to find everything made so easy for him, he answered them all gayly. He would really like to try driving himself, if Sebastian did not mind—he could not manage a motor, but surely by now he ought to be able to amble along behind Cecilia's fat wheezy pony without straining his arm— And for the very reason that he was in such an unsociable mood, he wouldn't advise her to take him on as an escort, though he hoped some other time both she and her father would go with him to see the gypsies. He hardly thought he would get as far as the Sacro Monte that afternoon— In fact he would rather wait until they could all go together. But he would certainly plan to see the Capilla Real and the Virgin of the Angustias and possibly part of the Alhambra as well. He would also be glad to take a note to the Palace— It would give him an excuse to say *Que tal?* to Gabriel himself——

He set off in an old pony cart, his spirits actually higher than they had been at any time since his arrival. Leonardo, in handing over the reins to him, had told him proudly about certain points of interest for which he should watch on his way into town; and he found so many of these along the dusty road that the turrets and domes of Granada came into sight almost too soon to suit him. Conscious that he would be questioned about his movements on his return, he asked his way to the Capilla Real. Then, after a hasty glance at the tombs of the "Catholic Kings," he left the pony cart in charge of a willing street urchin and mounted the incline towards the "door of justice" leading to the Alhambra gardens. When he reached the plaza overlooking the *Albaicen,* he sat down to rest for a few moments on a bench beside a blind man who was tinkling away at a guitar, and watched some *seminaristas,* in black and scarlet, walking slowly up and down; then, succumbing to the importunities of a garrulous guide, he suffered himself to be led past the baroque monstrosity built under Charles V, into the courts and courtyards of matchless beauty lying immediately beyond this. A quarter of an hour later, he astonished his conductor by giving the man a liberal tip and asking to be led out of the Alhambra again, before he had seen a fraction of it or listened to any details about dates and dimensions; and fifteen minutes later still, having enriched the waiting street urchin with even greater liberality, he presented himself at the Palace gate and asked to see the Archbishop.

He was instantly admitted and conducted to Gabriel's study, where the prelate was alone, occupied with a collection of medallions on which he spent much of his leisure time. The old man laid down the one he had been fingering, and held out his hand cordially to his caller.

"This must be mental telepathy," he said, smiling, as Hans Christian kissed his ring and straightened up again, "or perhaps, since I am a Churchman, I should say instead, it must be an answer to prayer. I was just thinking about you, and wishing I could have a talk with you."

"Cristina asked me to give you this note," Hans Christian said, producing a small white envelope from his pocket.

"Ah— Well, I am always glad to hear from Cristina. She is a great favorite of mine. I will see what she has to say, if you will excuse me." The Archbishop opened the envelope, extracted with care the small sheet of paper which it contained, and glanced over it, a pleasant expression hovering around his mouth as he did so. Then he laid it down on the desk beside the medallions he had been arranging when Hans Christian entered. "This is a very interesting letter," he said, still smiling. "I am extremely grateful to you for bringing it to me. But I hope, now that you have done so, you are not going to run away immediately. It would give me great pleasure if you would stay and dine with me."

"I'd like to, if you still want me after you hear what I've come to say."

"So you had a special reason for coming? Aside from acting as messenger for Cristina?"

"Yes. I came especially to tell you that I've fallen in love with her, and to ask you what you would do about it, if you were in my place."

"I am very much touched at your confidence. And when it comes to a matter of good counsel, I should certainly advise you to do what is most natural and fitting under the circumstances. In other words, if I were you, I should ask Cristina to marry me, with the hope and expectation that she would accept me, and then I should hasten back here to urge the cleric of the family to perform the wedding ceremony without delay."

"You'd ask her to marry you! When you'd never had a chance to get a word in with her edgewise! And you'd expect to be accepted, when so far she had hardly glanced in your direction!"

"Why, yes. The situation seems complicated, I know. But perhaps it is simpler than it looks. Sit down, my dear boy, and let us talk this matter over quietly. It makes me uneasy to have you stand there, as if you might disappear at any moment." Then as Hans Christian seated himself on the edge of a chair, the Archbishop shook his head. "No, I did not mean like that," he remonstrated, "I meant that I wanted you to really settle yourself. What about a cigarette and a glass of sherry? Or perhaps you are tired of sherry by this time? I can give you *Lacrima Cristi* or *Bastardo* instead, if your taste runs in either of those directions."

"I'd like very much to smoke, if you'll let me. But I don't care about anything to drink," Hans Christian answered, somewhat astonished at the Archbishop's light satire, but deciding to disregard it.

"Please follow your own inclination—and now for my little homily. Part of the trouble, my dear boy, lies in the fact that you have been rather a laggard in love."

"A *laggard!* Why it is only three weeks since I came!"

"Yes. But you were a long time coming. And you made it quite clear to your grandmother why you did not wish to come. She passed this information along and Dolores was piqued."

"So you think if I'd come sooner——"

"I think your delay has made matters much worse for you, primarily for the reason I have just mentioned. It is always better for a young man to ingratiate himself with a girl's mother than to antagonize her. You have made precisely this mistake. And in the second place, if you had come before Cristina's thoughts began to turn towards a cloistral life, such contemplation might have been avoided altogether. It is part of the normal picture for a Spanish girl, who is naturally devout, and who is beginning to be conscious of emotion without understanding it, to feel she will find her best outlet for this in religion, that she has a vocation to become a nun. Sometimes she is right, of course. Only time can tell. There are exceptions to every rule, as in the case of the Little Saint Theresa, which I believe Dolores cited to you. Under usual circumstances, however, I should say that no girl should be prevented from taking vows if she still wishes to do so when she is twenty-five, but that no girl should be encouraged to do so before she is twenty-one. As the Archbishop of this Diocese, I should certainly do everything in my power to prevent Cristina from taking such a step earlier than that."

"You would!"

"Yes. I do not feel at all sure that she has a vocation. Her mother and I disagree about that, as we have on many other points, though we are devoted to each other. On this one I feel very strongly. It is far more likely that Cecilia might follow such a course triumphantly. She has nearly all the qualifications for a successful abbess."

"Cecilia!"

"Yes—vitality, determination, endurance and intelligence. I think we may take her faith for granted—she takes it for granted herself, without dwelling on it overmuch, as her mother is inclined to do. However, you did not come here to discuss Cecilia, but Cristina. Well, as I was saying, it is unfortunate you did not come sooner, for several reasons. But I do not think your delay has necessarily been fatal to your hopes. Especially since Cristina herself does not seem to have been as much piqued by it as her parents."

"What difference does it make whether she was piqued or not, if she's so determined to become a nun?"

"I'm not sure she is so determined. In fact I am very doubtful of it. Her mother is determined, which is quite a different matter."

"But you said——"

"I must beg you to listen to me more carefully, Hansel. I said, to begin with, that you had unnecessarily antagonized Dolores by your procrastination, and that this same procrastination had been unfortunate as far as Cristina was concerned. If she had met you for the first time two years ago, she probably never would have thought about becoming a nun, because almost certainly your image would have filled her thoughts instead. Consequently she would never have mentioned such a plan, on her own initiative, to her parents. Of course, they might have taken the initiative in mentioning it to her. Dolores is excessively pious. I have no doubt that she honestly believes her attitude is prompted entirely by piety in this instance, instead of partly by pique. And Sebastian is fearful, with reason, of the extremes to which passion can carry a man. But in the end I do not think their determination can prevail against yours and mine, if Cristina is on our side."

"But how can we hope that she is?"

"Well, she came in to see me the other afternoon, accompanied by Catalina, who remained in the kitchen while she was in my study. The ostensible purpose of her visit was, I believe, to inquire for my health. But after telling me that she had greatly enjoyed your company while she was making a garland, she continued to talk about you the rest of the afternoon. Since then she has been back here twice, and the subject of my health has not even been mentioned. And now she has written me a letter saying she is in the deepest despair because she never has a chance to see you alone, and asking if there is not something I can do to help her out of her difficulties. You may read the letter if you like."

Without waiting for a repetition of this suggestion, Hansel seized upon the small piece of paper which the Archbishop shoved gently in his direction. The very sight of the script, flowing lightly across the crested sheet, sent a thrill through him. But as he read the unbelievable words, the handwriting in which they were formed faded into complete insignificance. For a moment he was too much moved to speak.

Then, still holding the precious paper, he looked across at the Archbishop.

"What—what shall I do?" he asked, striving in vain to keep his voice steady.

"In the end you will do what I advised in the beginning: You will ask Cristina to marry you and you will invite me to perform the ceremony. We will both accept. But I am afraid there must be a few preliminaries. First of all you must talk to Sebastian."

"I wanted to do that anyway. But I was afraid he wouldn't listen. I'm still afraid he won't."

"Possibly you are right. No one can ever foretell what Sebastian will do. But if he should decline to listen to you, he will come rushing in here, greatly enraged, and eventually he will be obliged to listen to me. I can prevent him from clapping Cristina into a convent, and I can advise him to let her marry you. I shall certainly do both."

"I can see how you might make it impossible for Cristina to become a nun. But I don't see how you can make it possible for her to marry me, if her father won't consent."

"Suppose we face one difficulty at a time. As long as she does not become a nun, there is no insuperable barrier to her marriage. I admit it may take patience to win Sebastian over. But Cristina is still very young. I myself think it would be just as well if she did not marry for several years yet."

"You want me to wait *several years!*"

"Yes—partly on general principles and partly because Sebastian has an aversion to early marriages. In this regard, I should consider you bound to respect his viewpoint. There are tragic reasons for it."

The Archbishop sighed softly and looked away. Hans Christian, who would ordinarily have been curious as to the causes for Sebastian's viewpoint, was far too preoccupied with his own pressing problems to give it a thought.

"There is another aspect of the case which I think I should mention," the Archbishop went on, after a moment. "That is the question of your nationality. All things being equal, I think Sebastian would have been glad to have an American for a son-in-law. He admires Americans very much. But he has never cared greatly for Germans—again on general principles. He insists he has never known one who would admit he was wrong about anything or who had a sense of humor. And his natural antipathy for them was intensified, a number of years ago, by several unfortunate circumstances. I know it was a great shock to him when you decided to remain in East Prussia."

"But why should my decision to stay in East Prussia have made any difference to him? I should think it would have been just the opposite! After all, I'm related to him through my father, not through my mother."

"You are related to him through your Austrian grandmother. She and his own mother, whom he adored, were both originally Hapsburgs. You do not need to be reminded how long, or how closely, the Hapsburgs have been allied to Spain. But the *Junkers* have not. There are no binding ties there. Quite the contrary."

"Are you trying to tell me that Sebastian disliked my father?"

"I have tried not to tell you. I have hoped against hope that it might never be necessary for you to know that. But I am afraid, as things have turned out, that it is. He disliked your father intensely. In fact, he hated him. And he is obsessed with the fear that you may come to resemble him. You look like your mother—the resemblance is very striking. But you are molding yourself after the Prussian pattern which is so obnoxious to Sebastian. Your course of action makes him think of you as a wolf in sheep's clothing."

"But why should he put it that way? Why shouldn't I want to follow in my father's footsteps, even if I do happen to look like my mother? They were glorious! He died a hero's death! Why should everyone here hate him so?"

The question, so long suppressed, came surging out to his lips. Gabriel looked at him with pity.

"My dear boy, everyone here did not hate him. I did not, for instance, if that is any comfort to you. I was infinitely sorry for him. I regret that some servant's gossip or childish prattle has disturbed you. I know how Catalina and Cecilia are apt to run on."

"Yes, they do run on, and I've tried not to listen to them. But how can I help being disturbed by things they hint, by things they let slip? If nothing they say matters, why did Sebastian hate my father, why were you sorry for him?" Before Gabriel could answer, Hans Christian had sprung to his feet and confronted the Archbishop with blazing eyes. "You were sorry for him because you knew another man was making love to his wife!" he cried. "And Sebastian hated him because he wanted my mother himself! That's why he won't trust his daughter to any man—because *he* wasn't to be trusted! And besides, he means to have his revenge—that's why he won't let me marry Cristina! Not because of anything I've done or haven't done!"

The Archbishop rose in his turn, and laid his hand on the boy's shoulder. Frail as he looked, his fingers were like steel. He forced Hans Christian back into a seat, swung his own chair around, and faced the boy imperiously.

"Listen to me," he said sternly. "I am going to tell you the whole truth, because nothing on earth is so deadly as a half-truth, and that is what you are battling. Sebastian did love your mother—they loved each other. But they were both already married when they met. They had been married so young that they did not know their own minds.

Perhaps you will begin to understand why Sebastian is opposed to early marriages when you hear the history. His own was arranged by his family and his bride's. He saw that Dolores was beautiful, he sensed that she was docile and devout. He thought nothing else mattered. Like many other men, he was prepared not to take his marriage vows too seriously. He did not dream, at twenty, that he would hunger and thirst for a mind to match his own, for a radiance that would dazzle him, for a courage he would find invincible—in short, for all the qualities he found in your mother. He thought that Dolores de Romera would adorn his house and bear his children and that he would continue to find light diversion wherever he looked for it. He was mistaken on both scores. Within a few months of her wedding, Dolores began to act strangely; within two years she was violently insane. She tried to kill her husband and she very nearly succeeded. That scar on his cheek was made by a dagger she threw at him. After that she was shut up in the Castello Viejo under guard. She remained there for years, a raving maniac. And meanwhile Sebastian drank his cup of dissipation to the dregs and found it bitter brew."

"Good God—what a ghastly story!"

"It is a ghastly story. But it would have been ghastlier still if it had not been for your mother. It was she who declined to make Dolores' condition a pretext for escape—escape for Sebastian or for herself. Though she was very unhappy. At sixteen, she visualized your father as a sort of shining St. Michael, just as you do. She married him with that illusion and it was cruelly shattered. She was sensitive, idealistic and immature. Instead of acting towards her with gentleness and loving kindness, your father treated her with ruthless selfishness. That is why I was sorry for him—because I saw him destroying the innocent trustfulness of a young girl, and knew that for such a sin as this, there can be no forgiveness either on earth or in heaven. And that is why Sebastian hated him. He could not endure the spectacle, or the thought, of your mother's persecution. But she endured it. She is one of the bravest women I have ever known."

"Yes," Hans Christian said in a choked voice. "I have always known she was brave. But of course I did not know any of this. Only that it was she who insisted that David Noble should operate on *Doña* Dolores."

"If the malignant tumor which was pressing on Dolores' brain had not been successfully removed, she would never have been restored to sanity. She never could have lived a normal married life. She never could have achieved maternity. She owes all this to your mother—who could so easily have stolen her husband instead of restoring him to her. Dolores is not blessed with keen intellect or great vision, but in her limited way she realizes this and is grateful. I believe I can make her see that this gratitude should express itself in a changed attitude towards you. But it will take time and tact."

"And—and Sebastian?"

"Ah, Sebastian—I suppose you would not consider saying, when you talk to him, that you might go back to America after all?"

"And leave Germany?"

"Your father is dead, Hansel, and all that he personified has gone too. But your mother is still alive, and what she stands for is vital also. Go back to her. Go back to America."

"And abandon the Fatherland when it needs every one of its sons?"

"I believe your mother needs you too. I believe you are needed in America. A terrific collapse has taken place there this last year. Perhaps you have been too preoccupied to give it much thought."

"A stock market crash! What does that amount to, compared to the rebirth of a crushed country?"

"It amounts to a good deal more than a stock market crash, my dear boy. However, I am not trying to persuade you against your will to do something you do not feel is right. I am only trying to ease your path, if I can."

The Archbishop leaned back in his chair. The tenseness of the hour had passed and he was very tired. He hoped that Hans Christian would not argue with him any more at present, that the boy would go tranquilly away and ponder on what had been said already, before attacking any more problems. He was unprepared for the almost irrelevant remark, coming quietly after the outburst that had preceded it, with which Hansel broke in upon his reverie.

"Even if my father is dead and everything that he stood for is gone, my grandmother is still living. I mustn't forget about her. She's all alone in the world except for me. My mother at least has her career. Even though I see now that it doesn't mean to her what I thought it did, it represents some sort of fulfillment."

With a great effort, the Archbishop roused himself once more. "Your grandmother!" he said musingly. "No, of course you must not forget your grandmother. I have never forgotten her, for a single moment— You have listened to so much ancient history tonight, Hansel, that perhaps you could bear it if I told you a little more. You know that I was the eldest of a large family and Sebastian the youngest—all our brothers and sisters died long ago, leaving this gulf of age between us, for I am old enough to be his father. Consequently your grandmother and I are about the same age. I met her shortly after I had taken Orders —I had delayed doing so for a long time, until after Sebastian's marriage in fact, when I thought our heritage would be secured. But I had many bitter moments of wondering whether I had delayed long enough, after all. Partly because of the dreadful debacle of Sebastian's marriage and partly because if I had not forced myself with anguish to be mindful of my irrevocable vows, I should have been sorely tempted to break them, for the sake of your grandmother."

As he spoke, Gabriel bent his head and clasped his hands in front of him. His attitude might have been one of fervent prayer, or merely of overwhelming exhaustion. As a matter of fact, it was both. Hans Christian, still mindful of the great ring glittering on the Archbishop's finger, of the richness of his robes and the splendor of his room, saw him for the first time as a sad and sacrificial figure. He slid from his own seat and knelt beside his kinsman, bowing his own head. The old man placed a hand gently on his hair.

"So you see," he whispered, "that through two generations already there has been sorrow in surrender to the will of God. I pray it may be part of His plan that in this generation there may be joy instead. We are told that like as a father pitieth his children, so the Lord pitieth them that fear Him. I hope he may show pity on you and on Cristina. Go in peace, my son. We are all in His keeping."

CHAPTER 20

Hans Christian went down the Palace steps in a state of tumult. The astonishing revelation of Cristina's tenderness towards him dominated his distracted mind. But underneath the beatific assurance this gave him, surged doubt and dread in a hundred forms. Now that he knew his love was returned, how could he await fulfillment of it for years? The mere suggestion of such a delay was unreasonable and intolerable. On the other hand, unless he accepted every condition with which Sebastian chose to hinder and harass him, how could he dare to hope that he would ever win Cristina at all?

When weariness overcame him, the Archbishop had evidently forgotten his invitation to dinner, for it had not been renewed; and unaware of the enervating aftereffects of an upheaval such as he had just experienced, Hans Christian was surprised, and slightly ashamed, to find that he was hungry and thirsty. The street urchin to whom he had entrusted the pony cart outside the Alhambra had pursued him to the Palace, and insisted upon mounting guard over it there; and telling him to continue his vigil, Hansel crossed the street and sought out a sidewalk café.

He did not have to look far. There were several within the next block, and he sat down at a small tin table and asked for beer. The thin Spanish brew which was brought to him was a poor substitute for the rich foaming *Brau* he got at home; but he could think of nothing else to order; and at the moment he did not even notice that it was sweet and tepid. He drank it down uncomplainingly and motioned for more, grateful for the tempered refreshment it gave him.

The café was crowded and people pressed all around him, though none of them bothered him. Many were alone, as he was; they sat staring into space as they rolled their cigarettes and sipped their sherry, neither moving nor speaking. He had the feeling that they had been there the day before, and that they would be there the next day. A small shabby man, with a mild bearded face, seated at the table next to his, seemed especially quiet and detached. Other men, in convivial couples, exchanged innocuous remarks about the passers-by, and gesticulated as they conversed volubly with each other. Hans Christian himself was too abstracted to pay any attention to what they were saying. So Sebastian and his mother had been in love, and before them, Gabriel and his grandmother! And *Doña* Dolores had not always been pious and precise, but had hurled daggers and inflicted deadly wounds! It was all unbelievable and unreal, and yet, now that he knew it was true, many mysteries were clarified for him. With clearer vision, he would be able to act more tolerantly and intelligently. If only there were not that aversion to Prussia and all that was connected with it to combat! If only Sebastian would not make the renunciation of these a condition! If only he would not harp on an American note which to Hansel himself was inharmonious——

A soldier with his arm around a pretty girl, his blue chin close to her glossy head, sauntered past, oblivious of the café and its occupants. A water vendor loitered by, calling in a singsong voice as he went, "*Agua, agua quien se quiere refrescar?*" No one paid any attention to him, and he did not have the air of expecting trade or notice. A photographer and a flower woman stopped at the sidewalk with ingratiating smiles; but though they seemed a little wistful, they were not intrusive, and presently they too went quietly along the street. At their heels came a newsboy, who threaded his way among the tin tables, and the occupants of some of these bought the paper which he rather diffidently offered. Among them was the small bearded man sitting beside Hansel; and mechanically, the boy's eyes followed the black headlines that were so close to him. There were some items about the elections which had been held the day before: The Republicans had made a surprisingly strong showing in most of the major cities. The Government was withholding comment for the moment. But Zamora, and the other leaders who had been imprisoned with him the previous December, were all ahead by large majorities. Hans Christian, who had been far too preoccupied in Berlin to pay intensive attention to anything that had happened in Madrid, did not know whether this was significant or not. He did not suppose it was. What was even more to the point, he did not care.

A peculiar rustling finally caused him to look at the paper with attention. He saw that the hands of the small bearded man were trembling, and that the reason the paper was making such a strange noise was because it was so unsteadily held. There was something fascinating to Hans Christian about the sight and sound. For the first time since leaving the Palace, he ceased to isolate himself with his own thoughts. As if aware of being under observation, the small bearded man lowered his paper, folded it with fingers which still quivered, and returned Hansel's look with a solemn gaze.

"This is the day," he said, portentously and without preamble.

"I am afraid I do not follow you, *Señor*. What day?"

"The day for which we have been working and waiting. The day for the great change."

"The great change? What change?"

The mild-looking man raised his shoulders, after the customary manner of Spaniards wishing to emphasize what is being said, and to imply more than the spoken word actually indicates. His voice betrayed greater and greater exaltation.

"I am not sure. It is still too early— If you will excuse me, *Señor*, I will return to my home and read this paper to my father. He cannot read himself, and he will be anxiously awaiting me. He also hoped this would be the day."

Hans Christian returned the queer little man's polite bow, asked for his bill, and after a moment's hesitation, left the café himself. No one else seemed disposed to speak to him or to share a paper with him, and as the newsboy had disappeared, he could not buy one himself. For the second time, he tipped the street urchin who had stood guard over the pony cart and drove carefully out of the city, his mind reverting to his impending conference with Sebastian.

Hans Christian heard no more gossip and felt no further stir of excitement. He stopped to dine at a *ventorillo* set high up on a hill, and built in a succession of arbors, overhung with purple morning-glories. The place was almost empty, for it was very late; and the *patron*, though courteous, was uncommunicative. But the food was excellent and abundant, and Hans Christian rose from his rustic table soothed and refreshed, and took to the road again in a tranquil mood. When he reached the outer patio of the *caseria*, he found Leonardo waiting for him with a lantern, scanning the landscape anxiously.

"We were becoming anxious about the *Señor* Baron," the faithful servant said, with unconcealed relief in his voice, giving a poke at the pony's well-covered ribs. "Not that this fiery animal would have run away! But that something else untoward might have happened. Has Your Excellency dined?"

"Yes, and very well."

"Ah— Catalina has continued to keep food hot. There was a fine suckling pig for dinner tonight, *Señor* Baron."

"I had some too. It was very good."

"It is always very good, but this is the best season of any for it," Leonardo remarked with a certain importance. Then he yawned behind his hand. "Has the *Señor* Baron further need of me?"

"No, thank you. And thank Catalina for keeping the roast hot too, but tell her I could not swallow another morsel tonight."

Leonardo closed the grilled gate leading to the inner patio carefully behind him. The *galeria* and the rooms surrounding it were all in darkness. But in the turret a light was still burning. Hans Christian hesitated for an instant. Then following an impulse, he mounted the stairs leading to the terraced library.

He immediately saw that he had been right in obeying his instinct. The library door stood invitingly open, and Sebastian was alone there. He sat reading in a large chair drawn up beside an old-fashioned student lamp. The light which streamed from under its green glass shade made a single circle of radiance in the shadowy room. As Hans Christian approached, he looked up from his book with a smile.

"*Que tal?*" he said, in his usual agreeable way. "I was beginning to wonder what had become of you."

"Leonardo said you had been anxious. I'm very sorry. I'm afraid you sat up on purpose for me."

"Yes. But I was glad to do so."

"I did not realize it was so late, and of course I had no way of sending you a message. I did some sight-seeing and then I had a long talk with *Tio* Gabriel. Afterwards I went to a café and stayed longer than I intended. There seemed to be more or less excitement there, and I was intrigued. Have you seen today's paper, by any chance?"

"No. Haven't you discovered that Monday in Spain is always a day without newspapers until evening, in compliment to the principle of the *descanso dominical*, the Sunday rest? Is there some special news tonight?"

"The men sitting around me at the café seemed to attach a good deal of importance to the result of yesterday's elections. One of them, a pale, bearded little man, kept saying 'This is the day!' in a very solemn manner. It seems the Republicans have won by a very substantial majority."

Sebastian shrugged his shoulders. "I am not sure that the King was wise in permitting these municipal elections to take place," he remarked. "There have been none since 1922, and there was no sound reason why there should have been any now. You may have noticed that I did not take any part in them myself. This is the main reason why I suggested that we should all go off on a picnic yesterday. It gave me a valid excuse not to vote. I was not among those who advised Alfonso to have the elections held. Personally, he is very liberal minded. I see no reason why he should pay the penalty at this time for the suffocation of popular expression which Primo de Rivera enforced years ago."

"The King permitted that too, didn't he?"

"Yes. And I fear he was ill advised then also."

"Are you worried—about what may happen now?"

Sebastian closed his book and laid it down on the table beside him. "No," he said slowly. "I am not really worried. Yesterday's elections do not obligate the King to inaugurate a republic. As matters stand now, parliamentary elections will not be held until next month and senatorial elections not until June. There will probably be time enough to worry then, for those who are bent on doing so. Personally I have ceased to worry very much about anything. When I was younger, I went about beating my head against stone walls and raging because I could not batter them down. I no longer do so. I accept the fact that they are there. Sometimes they crumble of their own accord. Sometimes they prove even more impregnable than I supposed. In either case, they do not infuriate me."

Hans Christian, to whom this declaration of fatalism was more significant than it would have been twenty-four hours earlier, considered it without replying to it. Sebastian went on talking of his own accord.

"Almost anything may happen to Alfonso. Almost everything has, already. He is immensely popular. People call him *El Rey Valiente* and he merits the title. Besides being valiant, he is debonair, tactful and extremely able. He is an excellent scholar and a fine sportsman. I really must arrange to have you meet him. You would be captivated by him. Everyone who comes in contact with him is affected by his magnetism, and even to those who do not know him, he is fascinating as a figure and a symbol. Yet he has bitter enemies also, and he has always been the victim of murderous attacks. Sometime when you are in Madrid you must go to the room at the Royal Palace which has been converted into a museum for the weapons, or what is left of them, that have been used against him. One of them is a milk bottle with which an attempt was made to poison him when he was a baby. So you see the attacks began early. Even on his wedding day he did not escape. Twenty-seven persons were killed in a blast which he mercifully survived. But he and his bride were bombed in their carriage. He turned to her quite calmly and helped her to wipe the blood from her lace veil, with the remark that he regretted she should have been subjected to an 'accident of his trade.'"

"So Spaniards are not always able to safeguard their wives after all? Not even the King of Spain?"

Sebastian laughed. "*Touché!*" he said humorously. "I knew that conversation of ours would rankle in your mind and that someday you would have the last word in it after all. Your retort is exactly the sort of thing your mother used to say, and still does, I hope. You are really extraordinarily like her, as I have told you before."

"Does that predispose me a little in your favor?"

"It has always predisposed you in my favor. I thought you knew that. But why do you ask?"

"Because I want to ask you something else. I want to ask you to let me marry Cristina."

The words which he had supposed would be so hard to say, and which he had meant to string into so many formal phrases, had come tumbling out haphazardly of themselves. He drew a deep breath, and waited for the impact of the volley with which he felt sure they would be returned, determined not to flinch or falter under it. By the time he was fully braced against it, he incredulously realized that no volcanic explosion was taking place. Sebastian said nothing at all for a moment. Then he rose, and put his arm around Hans Christian's shoulder, in the same friendly way that had marked his manner at the beginning of the boy's visit.

"I am very happy that you should have spoken to me in this way, at this time, *querido,*" he said kindly. "I knew of course that you had fallen in love with Cristina. But I hardly dared to hope you would come and tell me so, quietly, of your own accord, before you spoke to anyone else on the subject. I was afraid you would rush in upon Cristina someday, when she was quite unprepared, and try to tell her exactly how you felt."

"I never wanted to do it that way. I wanted all along to speak to you first. But I didn't dare. I thought you had taken a dislike to me. As a matter of fact, though, I didn't speak to you first. I spoke to *Tio* Gabriel first. And he encouraged me. He told me that through two generations already there had been sorrow in surrender to the will of God. He said he prayed that in this generation there might be joy instead. I thought possibly you might feel the same way about it, if you could come to look at it fairly. So when I saw the light in the library, I came straight up. I hoped I'd find you here."

"The hope was quite mutual," Sebastian said, still kindly. "I did not suppose that your conversation with Gabriel was political, no matter what you discussed in the café. I thought you had probably gone to talk with him about the matter nearest your heart. It is the way of many persons in perplexity, and it is a good one. I have often gone to him myself, under circumstances somewhat similar to these. Personally I have never known him to be quite so candid as he was with you. But since he has seen fit to confide in you, that brings us all closer together, does it not? Besides, when I said I was glad you came to me before anyone else, I was not thinking of Gabriel. I was thinking of Cristina—and of her mother."

"Well, now that I have spoken to you, can't I speak to Cristina? And won't you speak to her mother?"

"I shall certainly speak to her mother. And I am sure she will appreciate your attitude. But you know her plans for Cristina. She will not be easily persuaded to change them."

"But you could persuade her, couldn't you? I should think you could persuade almost anyone to do almost anything!"

Hans Christian's voice rang with sincerity. Sebastian smiled, but he shook his head.

"I have not always been so successful at persuasion as you seem to imagine. Besides, you also know that I have shared my wife's viewpoint regarding Cristina's vocation. It was because you became so vehement on that subject that you and I nearly quarreled. Not because I disliked you. I could never do that."

There was something so tender in Sebastian's tone that Hans Christian was deeply touched. The poignancy of the moment, instead of silencing him, gave him courage to go on.

"Then if you don't dislike me, couldn't you consider me as a son-in-law? Couldn't you change your viewpoint about Cristina's vocation? Especially if you found out she had changed hers?"

"*Querido*, I found that out some time ago. Perhaps before she was aware of it herself—certainly before she went to Gabriel about it. I am right in assuming she has also been consulting Gabriel, am I not? You see it is quite the family custom. *Bueno!* It is possible I might change my viewpoint about Cristina's vocation. It is even possible I might consider you as a son-in-law. But that is not equivalent to saying I am ready to have the banns published next Sunday, or even that I am willing to have you propose, unconditionally, to Cristina. There are more complications to the situation than you realize. Suppose we go outside on the terrace and talk them over. It is very cool and pleasant there, and I always think a sense of space and darkness is helpful at such moments as these."

Sebastian moved away from the circle made by the student lamp and walked towards the double doors leading to the terrace. They stood wide open, and arm in arm, he and Hans Christian went through them together. The groves and gardens, the wide plains and distant mountains were all dimly visible in the starlight. But there was no moon, and the night had a mystic quality. Slowly approaching the parapet, the two men leaned over it in silence.

"I had a double purpose in asking you to come out here," Sebastian said at last. "I want to talk to you not only about Cristina but about your grandmother. I had a letter from her today, after you had gone in town. I am afraid, from what she writes, that she is not at all well. And it is evident that she misses you very much, that she is extremely dependent on you. I really feel you should return to Germany immediately. I hesitate to say this to you, because I am afraid you will think I am using her illness as a pretext to send you away at this time. But that is not so."

"What do you mean by 'immediately'?"

"I mean exactly that. I have had your bags packed. There is a train leaving early in the morning. If you feel well enough yourself, I think you ought to take it."

"Without seeing Cristina at all?"

Sebastian did not answer at once. When he did so, he spoke as if he were weighing his words carefully.

"Since you have had a long talk with Gabriel, I see no reason why you and I should talk at length. You probably know by this time that I do not approve of early marriages, and why. You probably also know that I like Americans much better than I do Germans—and why. You cannot leave your grandmother just now, I can see that. But if your grandmother, who is already a very old lady, should die—what then? Would you go home then?"

"Germany is my home, Sebastian."

"Are you sure? Remember I have told you that you seemed to me essentially American."

"Yes, I do remember. But I'm very sure."

"You wouldn't leave it—not even to pay your mother a visit? You wouldn't go there—on a wedding trip, for instance?"

Hansel caught his breath and clutched hard at the parapet. He tried to answer quietly.

"Yes. I'd go there to visit my mother. If there were no misunderstanding about it. That it was just for a visit, I mean. And of course I'd go there—on a wedding trip."

"Very well. I want you to promise me that if your grandmother should die, you will go to see your mother—at once. And whether she dies or not, I promise you that you may take Cristina there on her wedding trip, two years from now."

"*Two years!*"

"Yes. It is a long time, I know. But do you realize how young Cristina is? I do not believe you do, because Spanish girls seem so much older than Germans or Americans at the same age. She will be still under twenty, Hansel, two years from now. That is early enough for any girl to marry. After all, what are two years? They will be gone before you know it, the passage of time is so swift! And meantime, of course you may see Cristina. You may see her now for that matter. I am perfectly sure that she is not asleep. I am certain she is lying awake, wondering what you and I are saying to each other."

Sebastian leaned over the parapet and gave a low whistle, which penetrated the air between the soft notes of a nightingale's song. He waited for a moment, and then repeated it. Almost instantly there was an answering call.

"We have had that signal ever since Cristina was a little girl," Sebastian said. "She will be here in a minute. You had better think fast. Because when she comes, I'm going to speak to her myself on the subject we have been discussing. So it will be necessary for me to know whether you are willing to meet my conditions. Ah—here she is now."

Hans Christian turned sharply from the parapet. Cristina was coming through the doorway and across the terrace, dressed in white, with her long braids hanging over her breast, as she had been the night he first saw her. Sebastian went to meet her and took her hand.

"*Alma de mi alma,*" he said fondly, "Hans Christian and I have been having a long talk together. I have been obliged to tell him the sad news that his grandmother is ill, that I think he should go to her at once. Therefore, he is leaving very early in the morning, and you may not see him again in some time. But he has told me something too, something that has caused me to send for you, since I felt you should hear of it before he goes. He says that he loves you, and has asked my permission to tell you so himself. Do you feel you would be happy in accepting him as a suitor?"

"Yes," answered Cristina without hesitation.

Hans Christian gave a quick movement. Sebastian spoke warningly.

"Just a moment," he said. Then he turned to Cristina again. "You know it has been your mother's hope, and mine, that you would become a nun, *querida*. We understood that it was yours also. In fact you have repeatedly said so yourself. Have you changed your mind?"

"Yes," said Cristina again.

"I have told Hans Christian that I am not willing you should be married for two years. If you do not stay in the convent, you will inevitably have many other suitors. But if you give him a promise tonight, you should be prepared to keep it. You must not change your mind about this too. Do you feel sure you can be loyal to him, so that his long wait will not be in vain?"

"Yes," said Cristina a third time.

Sebastian was still clasping her fingers. But with his free hand, he reached out, and taking Hans Christian's, placed Cristina's in it.

"Are you ready now to accept my conditions, Hansel?" he asked. "If you are, I will leave you to talk to Cristina for a few moments yourself. Do not keep her too long. It is very late. But I will go into the library and wait for you there. And while I am waiting I will repeat Gabriel's prayer that in this generation there may be joy instead of sorrow in surrender to the will of God."

CHAPTER 21

Cristina did not withdraw her hand from Hansel's. Instead, after a moment, he felt her fingers flutter lightly against his palm. Then she interlaced them with his.

"Shall we sit down?" she asked softly. "We are free to say anything we wish to each other now, you know."

He nodded, and moved with her towards a stone bench. But still he did not speak. The miracle had come to pass so swiftly that he could not believe, even though he beheld. It was Cristina who went on talking, after they had sat down side by side.

"I have kept trying to be calm. I have kept saying to myself, 'Something will happen. Something will make it possible for us to be together, after all.' And I was right. You see that it has."

"Yes," said Hansel hoarsely. "I—I see that it has."

He was powerless, for the moment, to go on. But Cristina, who had been gazing lovingly towards him, continued to regard him with large trustful eyes, undisturbed because his emotion did not take articulate form. Exultantly, he became aware that in spite of her youth and inexperience, she had divined the reasons for his restraint, and that since this was so, there would never have been any need of explanations between them. The joyous conviction that they would always understand each other had a steadying effect. He leaned towards her, speaking more naturally.

"I want to hear you say that you love me!"

"But *querido*, that is something you must say first! And so far you have said nothing at all!"

"Only because I was so stunned that I couldn't. You know that!"

"Yes, I know that. But now, you seem to be recovering from the shock of finding out that my father is not an ogre after all and that I—"

"That you—"

"That I am just like any other young girl, *querido*."

"But you're not! There isn't anyone like you in the whole world."

"I am glad you think so, even if it is not true. But what I meant was, I am just like any other young girl when it comes to falling in love."

"And I was so sure you wanted to be a nun!"

"You mean, you were so credulous when *mamecita* told you so. You never talked to me about it. If you had, I should have told you at once that I stopped wanting to be a nun the morning that we wove garlands together."

"If I had guessed anything of that sort, of course I would have done so long ago. I would have found a way somehow. But I am not going to do so now. I am going to talk to you about being a bride instead of a nun. Oh Cristina— Cristina—since I know you love me, how can I wait for you two years?"

"But how unreasonable you are, *mi corazon!* Will it not be much easier to wait for me, knowing that I love you, than wondering whether I did or not? And after all, what are two years?"

Unconsciously she had repeated her father's question. Then she began to count off the calendar on her fingers, which were still interlaced with Hansel's. "This is 1931," she said with a light tap. "One year will be up in 1932. Then comes '33! That is all that there will be to our waiting. It will be over just like that!"

She blew into the air and tossed her head slightly, dismissing time as a trifle. One of her long glossy braids, which Hansel had so desired to feel, brushed against his cheek. He took hold of it, and of its twin, and drew her closer to him by her own plaits.

"And then we shall be married," he said, as she came nearer and nearer, "and live happily ever after!"

"Yes. Then we'll be married—and live happily ever after!"

He had sworn that he would always treat her with that tact and tenderness of which her father believed no German capable, and he meant to keep his vow. Indeed, he might have left her with no caress beyond their long handclasp, if she had not raised her lips to him as trustfully as she had raised her eyes. Then he kissed her, gently, without taking her in his arms, and she did not turn her head away until she had kissed him in return.

"I must go back to my room," she said with a little sigh, which was half sadness and half ecstasy. Then after a moment, she added, "And you must talk to my father in the library. Come! We will walk across the terrace together, and then we will part—for the present. But someday there will be no more partings between us. Do not forget that, *vida de mi vida.*"

They had reached the steps leading into the library, and once more she raised her lips. "Go with God," she said softly. "And come again—to me."

Had he made a mistake in claiming no embrace, he asked himself repeatedly the next day, as the slow train jolted northward? He did not think so, though he had longed for it so unutterably. He knew now that Cristina would not have shrunk away if he had attempted it. But he himself shrank from the thought of mere acquiescence, in connection with Cristina. Having beheld her eyes lighted with love and felt her lips warm beneath his own, he wanted more than ever to see her arms spontaneously outstretched before they were passionately pinioned. And she herself had not indicated that she was ready for an embrace. Perhaps the next time he saw her—oh certainly the next time——

He had tried to persuade Sebastian to set a date for this, when they said good-by to each other. But on this point Sebastian had been somewhat evasive, and Hans Christian had decided that it was wiser not to press it, especially in view of the fact that otherwise Sebastian had been very liberal. He had promised to speak to both *Doña* Dolores and Gabriel the next day; he had raised no objection to correspondence; it was evident that he recognized the existence of a definite, though informal betrothal. Indeed, he raised one question of his own accord which had not once entered Hans Christian's mind.

"You have said nothing at all about a dowry. Did you have any special sum in mind?"

"A dowry? *Money?*"

"Why yes. Of course Cristina will have a very substantial dowry. You have seen us living so simply here, perhaps you have forgotten that this is not our usual mode of existence, that we have a palace in Madrid, and several castles besides the one in the Pyrenees and the one near Toledo. Had it slipped your mind that Gabriel and I are sole heirs to one of the greatest fortunes in Spain, and that Gabriel has no children?"

"Yes. That is, I never thought about it at all. I'd rather not think about it now, if you don't mind."

"But my dear boy——"

"Yes, I remember it's customary, now that you speak of it. But I've thought of heiresses—differently. You see, I know another. And sometimes I've thought—for the sake of Schönplatz——"

"Oh, so you know another heiress, do you?"

"Yes, a very rich American. She's a nice girl too. But I don't love her. And I do love Cristina. I can take care of her, Sebastian. Not lavishly, but suitably. If you'll only trust me——"

"Strangely enough I have considerable confidence in you," Sebastian remarked, rather dryly. "Well, we will let the matter of a dowry rest for the moment. Though I hope very much you will not object if I give Cristina the *caseria* for a wedding present. It was originally built by one of my ancestors, as a bower for the lady he loved. It seems to me appropriate that you and Cristina should have it, since you have met and been happy here. I shall not need it when there is no reason why I should stay close to Gabriel. And I am afraid there will be none very much longer." He broke off abruptly, and after a moment went on in a changed voice, "There is still another reason why I should like you to stay from time to time at the *caseria*, Hansel. I—once offered it to your mother as a gift, and she declined to accept it. Not because she felt she could never take presents from me. I am glad to say she did so honor me from time to time. She declined it because she felt, if she owned it, she might come to regard it as her home, and she wanted Hamstead to be her only home. Since you do not share that feeling, perhaps you—"

"I'd like to have you give the *caseria* to Cristina and me, Sebastian. And—thank you for telling me about the other too."

Yes, Sebastian had been surprisingly generous, all things considered, and Hans Christian had so much cause for contentment that he knew it should be possible for him to possess his soul in patience, as far as seeing Cristina again was concerned. For the moment his yearning for her was mercifully numbed by fatigue. The day before had been supercharged, in every sense of the word. He had exerted himself far more than at any time since his accident; and he had experienced doubt, despair, reassurance, and joy within the space of a few short hours. He was both physically and emotionally exhausted, and he might even have gone to sleep, sitting bolt upright on the hard seat of the compartment, if it had not been for the conversation of the two men who were sharing it with him.

They had both greeted him courteously when he had entered, and both had offered him a share from a laden lunch basket, a gesture which he had duly returned. They had also made a conscientious effort to draw him into their talk, and it was only after he had indicated that he was a stranger in Spain, and knew next to nothing about its internal affairs, that this conversation became a dialogue.

It was wholly political in character, but at no moment did it become heated. The two Spaniards did not lose their tempers, as Hans Christian had repeatedly seen both Americans and Germans lose theirs, in the discussion of similar subjects. Indeed it did not seem to occur to them that there was any reason for doing so. They were absorbed, not angry. In their possession were newspapers, printed later than those Hans Christian had seen in the café the afternoon before, and these they spread out, reading aloud to each other, and commenting on the news items therein contained. The march of events had apparently been very swift. There had been an emergency meeting of the cabinet the night before, and the possibility of setting up a military dictatorship had been considered. Now it was already announced that the cabinet was about to resign, in the face of a Republican threat to use force to make the King heed the Republican victory, and the word "heed" was being interpreted in terms of abdication. Moreover, the Labor Party was prepared to paralyze public utilities if any attempt were made to resort to force. The Civil Guard had already killed two persons. A few agitators had been shot in Madrid and Seville, and many other persons hurt in the course of unbridled revelry. On the whole, however, the demonstrations, though riotous, had been harmless.

"But it is impossible! The King will never abdicate!"

"It may be impossible, but it is true. See, *Señor,* he is quoted as saying he knows he has lost the love of his people, that therefore he is prepared to resign in favor of the Infanta Juan."

"Yes, he is so quoted in one paper. But in the other he states that he has no intention of renouncing the throne, and asks that this assertion be published. What then can one believe?"

"I believe, *Señor,* that the King is sincere in saying he knows the country is angry with him. Has it not been angry ever since the fiasco in Morocco? He is right about that. But he is wrong when he says the people are monarchistic at heart."

"And I believe, *Señor,* he is right in this also, and that the throne may yet be saved. The King has acted in strict accordance with the Constitution. If a new cabinet is now formed, conservative-monarchistic in character, with Cieva at the head, it will be empowered to use military forces to quell a revolution and a general strike."

"*Empowered!* What power could such a cabinet have in the face of everything else that has happened? The Republican Committee has been in session all night, and when Maura left the meeting at dawn, he remarked, 'There is no news now, but there will be, after Aznar visits the Palace today!' And Aznar himself, on being asked whether a crisis existed, replied, 'When a monarchistic country turns Republican within twenty-four hours, that is crisis enough for anyone!'"

"And I still say it has not so turned! When did the election of a few aldermen ever change the political complexion of a country? Listen to this dispatch from Barcelona: 'All the Captains General in Spain have been ordered to Madrid. This was interpreted as indicating the Government's implicit faith in the Army.'"

"It may be so interpreted. The loyalty of an Army numbering eighty thousand, where one man in ten is a general, may perhaps be taken for granted. The Army, like the Church, is well subsidized. But how shall it prevail against the nation as a whole? How could it even prevail against Catalonia alone, now that you speak of Barcelona and bring that issue to my mind?"

"There, *Señor,* I see we are agreed. Those cursed Catalans! One never knows what they may do! Francisco Cambo has left for Madrid as well as the Captains General. That also may portend almost anything!"

The dialogue went on and on. Even the siesta hour was forgotten in the intensity of it. Hansel only half heard it. Recalling the prevailing air of apathy in the café the day before, and Sebastian's philosophic attitude, it caused him no alarm, though it roused his interest intermittently. He was actually much more concerned because it had tardily occurred to him that nothing had been said about a ring for Cristina the night before. He should have found out what she would like, he should have asked Sebastian for permission to present her with one immediately. He was comforted with the conviction that Cristina would not be offended at his oversight—the complete harmony of her spirit with his would cause her to understand that he had not been wilfully neglectful, that he had overlooked a minor point because he had been occupied with a major issue. Yet would she consider the question of her betrothal ring a mere detail, as he did? He knew the feminine penchant for jewelry, he had never forgotten Mrs. Fuller's passion for gems, or his grandmother's prostration over the loss of them. And Cristina had reminded him, playfully, that she was just like any other girl!— Well, amid the wreckage, there must be still one ancestral ring of the von Hohenlohes' that he could offer her. And yet, after all, he thought he would rather give her one he had planned and purchased himself. He did not think that massive designs or flamboyant stones would be suitable for her. Pearls, lightly set in platinum, and perhaps surrounded with small diamonds, would be far more fitting. And a pearl cross, set like the ring and hung on a long flexible chain, would be lovely for her to wear with it. He hoped he could afford to get her both. Yet someone had told him there was a superstition that pearls were unlucky for brides. He wondered if Cristina shared this——

The train slowed down at a station, and one of Hans Christian's fellow passengers got out, after bowing gravely to the other occupants of the compartment, and expressing the hope that they would continue to have a pleasant journey. The second man succeeded in securing an afternoon paper from a vendor who was besieged for them, as he rolled his pushcart down the platform; and by this time, Hansel was eager to listen to the news. It appeared that excitement unparalleled in fifty years was reigning in Madrid. Upon a report that the King had abdicated, a mob had surged through the Puerta del Sol, shouting *"Viva la Republica!"* Shots had been fired into the air as the cabinet change was cheered. Benches had been smashed, streets closed, traffic paralyzed. Meanwhile the King had remained secluded with his family in the Palace, reputedly seeing a moving picture show. But the Socialists, after a meeting of the "Directive Committee," had "given him only until night to make up his mind——"

"I thought the King was greatly beloved. I'm very much confused."

"*Señor*, we are living in a confused world, and as yet we have seen only the beginning of its confusion."

"If the Church and the Army and the aristocracy all stand by the King, doesn't that still give him the balance of power?"

"No, *Señor*. For when you say the Church, you can count only on the Cardinals and the Bishops. You will find many simple priests with Republican leanings. And when you say the Army it is the same. It is topheavy with monarchistic generals and colonels and captains, as our Lord knows. Even so, there are some sixty odd thousand enlisted men and noncommissioned officers, and many of these are Republican also. As for the aristocracy—well, it is true enough that there are a thousand grandees in Spain, that the gentry owns more than ninety per cent of the land—as it did in Russia, *Señor,* before 1918. God grant that what happened there may not also happen here!"

At the word "Russia," a small quivering fork of fear darted through Hansel's body for the first time. He found that he dreaded the answer to his next question.

"These Spanish Republicans—they're not Communistic, are they?"

"Heaven save us, no, *Señor!* But there are Communists and Socialists in Spain as well as Republicans—not to mention Carlists, and Separatists and Catalans and all the other groups. In a crisis like this, it is hard to tell which will prevail. Politics makes strange bedfellows."

The Spaniard picked up the paper again and began to read aloud from it. " 'Nobody who is not wilfully blind or crazy would deny that these elections are the most important political act in our history. The national will has been expressed, and since we want peace and order, we hope everyone will make the necessary sacrifice to reach a peaceful solution.'— I am a lawyer, *Señor,* as well as a patriot, and I concur in that hope. I rejoice that the will of Spain has been expressed within the law— 'We ask the King, who frequently has shown his patriotism, and to whom we offer our respects, not to demur about taking the action which his conscience as a good Spaniard must inspire——' "[1]

"But how can his conscience as a good Spaniard inspire him to do something so unpatriotic as to leave his country? I thought you called him your *'Rey Valiente.'* "

"A thousand pardons, *Señor.* I see you are still very young. When you are older, perhaps you will feel, as I do, that sometimes it takes more courage to retreat than to advance, to disappear from a scene rather than to dominate it— I wish it were possible to continue this conversation with you, by which I have greatly profited. But we seem to be approaching my own station. *Feliz viaje, Señor! Vaya con Dios!*"

He was gone, his flowing cape wrapped around him, his soft black hat still held in one hand. He had insisted on leaving his lunch basket behind him, lest Hansel's own supply should not be adequate for his needs until he reached Madrid. Dusk was creeping over the landscape, and the small dingy globe in the ceiling of the compartment emanated little light; since he could no longer see to read, Hansel tried to eat.

[1] *Informaciones,* April 14, 1931.

But he found he could not choke down the food. He was angry with himself now because he had not listened more attentively during the earlier part of the day, because he had not scanned every line in an effort to understand what was happening. He was angrier still because he had left Granada at all, because he had not stayed with the Cerrenos in this crisis. What would happen to Gabriel, who was so frail and aged, if there were a forcible separation of Church and State? What would happen to Sebastian, who was so charming and so nonchalant, if the aristocracy were dispossessed of its lands? What would happen to Cristina, if—if—if— At one moment he resolved to take the next train he could catch back to Granada. At the next he was convinced that he should go on to his grandmother. His reason told him that Sebastian would resent his return. His heart prompted him to speed to Cristina's side.

Tardily, as he thought of a ring for Cristina, he wondered why he had not asked to have his engagement to her formally announced at once. From every point of view, this seemed to him desirable. His grandmother would be immensely pleased; in her complacency over the turn things had taken, she would doubtless gloat over him a little. Well, he was willing enough she should remind him that she had been right all along, if this would give her satisfaction. There was little enough joy in her life— On the other hand, there were persons who would be less pleased, but to whom he owed candor on such a subject. He could not imagine why the thought of Trixie should give his heart a queer twist just then; but it did. Illogically his conscience smote him at the idea of telling her that he was in love with another girl. He could see exactly how she would look when he did so—slightly startled, slightly defiant, her cheeks redder than usual, her eyes momentarily bewildered but her head held higher than ever, as she had on the drive back from the Spreewald. As darkness descended, the image became increasingly vivid.

When the train finally jerked into the Madrid station, he was appalled at the abnormal quiet of this. There were no pushcart vendors on the platform, and no porters; the absence of their cheerful importunities left a strange void. With some difficulty, Hansel shouldered his own bags and stepped out of the compartment, striving to suppress his sense of the uncanny, which increased as he walked through the vacant waiting room and passed the blank ticket windows. His arm still hurt him if he put much strain upon it. But he felt he should at least be able to reach a cab unaided. To his increasing dismay, he found no taxis outside. The station plaza was as empty as the station itself. Shifting the position of his heavier suitcase, and gripping the smaller one more firmly, he set out across the vacant space on foot, incredulously searching for a trolley or a subway. Neither was anywhere in sight.

He was overwhelmed with a feeling of unreality before he came upon a few scattered pedestrians. As one after another hurried past him, he strove to stop them, to ask his way to a hotel where he could spend the night. No one regarded him with animosity, but no one offered to help him, and no one gave him any information.

"Ah, *Señor!*" one man paused long enough to exclaim, "to think that you should have to carry bags on such a night as this!"

"It is a rather disagreeable thing to be doing," Hans Christian replied. "But unless——"

"No gentleman should ever carry anything!"

Again Hansel agreed, asking the way to a hotel with the same futile result.

"No one will have to work any more."

"That will be a happy state of affairs. How will it be arranged?"

"The new government will arrange it. The new government will arrange everything."

The man scurried on again, as if regretful of having wasted so much time in explanation. The *new government!* So that was it! There was a new government already! As Hansel went blindly on, still undirected and still without sense of location, he came upon clustering groups which slowly thickened into a milling mass. Flags were fluttering all around him, from the staffs of big buildings, from the iron balconies of houses, in the hands of the pressing people. Nearly all were crudely put together, as if they had been made hastily or surreptitiously. Most of these flags were striped, purple, yellow and red; but there were a few black ones also, carried aloft between pictures of "martyred" patriots, and many which were wholly red. Indeed, a weird note of red was repeated in different forms on every side. Automobiles flaunting red posters, inscribed with the words *Republican Socialistic Union,* were coursing through the crowds, unmolested by police wearing red arm bands. Taxicabs flying red flags seemed to be spreading some kind of news, and excited throngs, gesticulating, gathered in their wake. Above the entrances of shops, workmen were hurriedly covering the royal coat of arms with red paper. Hansel saw that little boys were wearing red bow ties, little girls red hair ribbons, that men had long red caps on their heads and that women were carrying red roses. One stepped out of her red petticoat and waved it over her head, crying aloud as she did so, "The petticoat of the Queen!" The noise, like the crowding, was overpowering. Amid the shouts of "Long Live the Republic!" and "Death of Alfonso!" rose the strains of the *Marseillaise* and the *Internationale.*

Hansel had long since ceased trying to find out where he was going, or saving himself from being swept along in the general direction of the mob. He could see plenty of streetcars now. But they seemed to be going around in circles, almost like merry-go-rounds, for the purpose of pleasing revellers, rather than of taking passengers to any fixed destination. Their small platforms were packed, and even their roofs surmounted with teeming humanity. The advertisements on their sides were completely covered with moving arms and legs, heads and bodies. Every now and then a man who had been riding inside, swung himself out through a window and was quickly hauled upwards by helpful hands. As he climbed, he continued to sing, and to wave the flag which he still managed to hold tightly clutched.

There was no possible point in trying to board any such demoralized streetcar, provided it could be reached at all, which was doubtful. As Hansel approached a great archway which he supposed must be the Puerta del Sol, the throng became denser than ever. His shoulder was becoming increasingly painful, his exhaustion annihilating. But if he could do nothing else, he decided, he might be able to take shelter in some doorway, as he had in his first Berlin street brawl. Many of these had deep embrasures, and the crowd, pushing ahead, shouting and singing as it went, was not pausing in any event. When his vague idea had become a fixed purpose, Hansel found a way of carrying it out. By forcing his way slowly farther and farther from the curb, and nearer and nearer the blocks of buildings, he reached the sort of indentation he was seeking. He struggled into it, and the mob roared past, leaving him behind.

He set down his bags and leaned against the wall, thankful for its support. For a moment, he slumped; then he took out his handkerchief and wiped his streaming face. As he put it back into his pocket, his eye lit upon a row of neatly lettered plates, placed one above the other, near the bell inside the inner doorway. Reading these mechanically, something stopped him before he reached the last one. It occurred to him that he was looking at a name which he had seen or heard before.

With increasing bewilderment he tried to remember where and when this could have been. At last, surprisingly, he did so. He put his hand back into his pocket and drew out his wallet. When he had opened this, he saw, still slipped into its depths, the card of the man he had met a month earlier, on his way to Spain.

CHAPTER 22

Hans Christian had very little hope that his tug at the bell would be answered. The porter's cubbyhole, inside the vestibule, was empty. He was almost certain that the quarters above would be vacant also.

Judging from the size of the mob outside, it looked as if every habitation in the city must have disgorged its occupants. But since another miracle had happened to him, he would not disregard the significance of this. He seized the iron handle attached to the end of a long-jointed metal bellpull, and drew it down with all his might.

There was no answering click to the latch, no sign of a slight swing setting the door ajar. But after a moment he heard steps descending the stairs, not with a sudden rush of feet, but with a slow cautious tread. Apparently whoever was coming had been almost at the top of the house, for the sound continued for some time before Hansel saw anyone. Then a man's figure, blurred by the obscurity, appeared around the bend of the mottled marble staircase. He came to the door and opened it a crack.

"Good evening, *Señor,*" he said. "Were you seeking somebody?"

His manner was neither surly nor suspicious. He merely showed the hesitation that any sensible householder might display at finding a total stranger on his threshold at midnight.

"I was looking for *Señor* Ramirez. I see he is listed as living here."

"Then Bautista Ramirez is a friend of yours, *Señor?*"

"I can't say that exactly. But he has certainly been very friendly. We shared a compartment on the Paris Express a month ago and he told me I would be welcome at his home any time. At the moment I am feeling very badly in need of a welcome."

Hans Christian extended the card he was holding for the stranger's inspection. The man barely glanced at it.

"If that is the case, I am sure that he will wish to see you now. I gather that you yourself are not a Spaniard, *Señor?*"

"No, I'm a German. But I have Spanish kinsfolk whom I've been visiting in Andalusia, while recovering from a bad wound. Now I've had word that my grandmother is very ill, and I'm on my way back to East Prussia to see her."

"Ah—I am afraid you may find the trains to the frontier full to overflowing. But in the morning we must see what we can do for you, since such an emergency exists. In the meantime, I know my friend Ramirez will wish you to consider his apartment yours for the night. You are correct in assuming that he lives here. A little meeting is taking place in his quarters, which I happen to be attending. But you will not disturb us, if we do not disturb you. Follow me, *Señor,* that I may show you the way. The stairs are dark and rather winding. Pardon me, but I see you are burdened with baggage. Permit me to relieve you of part of it."

The stairway had the cold stale smell which Hans Christian had often noticed in continental apartment houses, and the pale bulbs of electricity, which cast an intermittent glimmer on it, were few and far between. He mounted slowly and painfully, still carrying his smaller suitcase. From time to time his guide paused and spoke to him encouragingly.

"I'm afraid you will find this a long climb, *Señor,* since you have been ill and are now very tired besides. We still have no lifts in our old houses, as you see—in Germany I believe everything is much more modern— Did I understand you to say you had come from Seville today?"

"No, from Granada."

"Granada! Everything is quite quiet there, is it not?"

"It was, yesterday. But a good deal seems to have happened since yesterday."

"You are right. Much has happened since yesterday, and much more will happen tomorrow— We are almost at the end of our ascent, *Señor.* Before we reach our destination, permit me to tell you my name. It is Pedro Valeza."

"And mine is Hans von Hohenlohe, *Señor.*"

Valeza had stopped, and knocked on a dark door. It was opened after an almost imperceptible delay, and in the narrow corridor beyond, Hans Christian saw the man who had befriended him on the train.

"An old acquaintance has done you the honor of coming to see you, Bautista," Pedro Valeza said immediately. "*Señor* de Hohenlohe tells me he met you last month, when you were returning from Paris."

"Of course! We compared notes on French coffee and I invited him to come and try mine at any time. And felicitously a fresh pot has been brought to me at this very moment. Come in, *Señor.* Come in! *Esta es su casa!*"

The man's manner was completely cordial. Hansel had been drawn inside the door, and this had been closed again, before he himself had been given a chance to speak.

"I must apologize for intruding on you like this, *Señor,*" he managed to say at last. "I was afraid you wouldn't even remember me. And apparently I've come at a rather disturbed time. But I'd been looking for shelter over an hour before I found your name in the doorway."

"*Lastima!* But I am glad you saw it at last! Let me lead you to a little room where I hope you will sleep well tonight. Then when you have arranged your belongings, you must come into the *salita* and meet the friends who are holding a conference with me."

"You're sure I won't be in the way?"

"But how should that be possible, *Señor?* A guest—in the way?"

Hansel was far too exhausted to protest. His host led the way into a tiny bedroom, barely big enough to contain a ponderous wooden bed of the Isabelline period, and a marble-topped night table, washstand, and chest of drawers to match. In order to set down the baggage, it was necessary to shove two small chairs around. The rest of the massive furniture loomed large and dark against the drably papered walls, enhancing the general air of gloom.

"I am going to bring your first cup of coffee in here," Ramirez said kindly. "You can drink it while you're getting oriented." He disappeared, to return almost instantly with a steaming drink. But short as his absence had been, Hansel had already sunk down on the big bed before his return, his shoulders bowed, his body sagging with fatigue. He looked up to acknowledge his host's thoughtfulness, and Ramirez saw that his face was pallid.

"Why not go to bed at once?" the man suggested solicitously. "It will be time enough to meet my friends tomorrow. They will be in and out all day. I will explain all that has happened to you then also. I suppose you are eager for news? But it can wait."

"Not all of it— Is it true that the King has abdicated?"

"Yes. He left Madrid secretly this afternoon. He is now speeding along through the night to some undisclosed destination, probably Cartagena. It would not have been safe for him to attempt to reach Portugal or pass through Northern Spain."

"Not safe! Has his life been endangered?"

Ramirez hesitated, but only for a moment. "Not in Madrid, since he did not delay. But elsewhere there has been more disturbance than here."

"More disturbance than here!"

Ramirez smiled. "I can understand that you should feel, after your experience, that there has been considerable disturbance here. But nothing serious has happened in Madrid. Yesterday there were a few clashes between the students and the police. The latter did some disciplining with the flats of their swords, and the youngsters finally retreated, rather vociferously, to the subway. But they were not pursued there, and no one was really hurt. Today the atmosphere has actually been characteristic of a fiesta rather than of a revolution. A flowing stream of joy and light and music is rippling over the city of Madrid. Her people are intoxicated with its splendor. If you were not so tired, I would suggest that you should go out again later on and join in the jubilation yourself. But you can do that tomorrow instead."

"Tomorrow! Tomorrow I must be on my way back to Granada—or off to Germany."

"I doubt whether you should attempt either. There is such an exodus of Spanish nobility that northbound travel is completely choked. When I went out to get your coffee, Valeza told me that he had tried to explain this to you already. As to returning South— You know best, of course, but are you sure it is wise, all things considered? Would it not be better to wait over a day, and see what develops? Since your grandmother has need of you, I assure you we will bend every effort to getting you on the first train where there is an inch of space."

"You don't understand—any better than I do. I'm almost beside myself with anxiety. I don't know what I ought to do, I don't know who needs me most!"

Hans Christian had struggled to his feet. Ramirez took his coffee cup from him and put it quietly down on the night table. Then he laid a restraining hand on the boy's arm.

"You mean you're almost beside yourself with fatigue and emotion," he said. "There is no cause for anxiety—unless your grandmother's condition is critical, which I doubt. I have observed that elderly ladies are apt to summon their young relatives to their bedsides long before there is any question that these may become deathbeds! I will explain everything you wish to understand tomorrow, and you shall explain to me whatever you wish me to understand—no less and no more. Meanwhile, I can assure you that as far as the Cerrenos are concerned, they are wholly unmolested."

"You can assure me! But how can you be sure?"

Ramirez smiled again. "Because I am very thoroughly informed," he remarked. "It is my business to be. Come, perhaps I had better tell you. If you have seen the papers today, you have perhaps read that several exiled Republicans are on their way back from France— Indalecio Prieto, who will probably be the next Minister of Finance, and Ramon Franco, the famous flyer, among them. Well, I have been in exile also, but I succeeded in getting back sooner than some of my fellow Republicans. I was just returning when I had the honor of meeting you before. Since then I have been extremely busy, as you will understand, *Señor*. But your comment that you were on your way to visit the Cerrenos interested me so much that I have kept a watchful eye on that family, in spite of my preoccupations. I shall continue to do so. They may find themselves, by tomorrow, with fewer titles than they had yesterday—than they have had for centuries, as far as that goes. And eventually Sebastian de Cerreno may find himself with somewhat less land. One of the first problems of the new government will be how to best break up the great estates, though property rights will have such respect as they merit."

"You are a Communist—*you!*"

The friendly expression of Ramirez' face did not change. "I understand that Communists are not popular in Berlin at present," he said gravely. "However, they are not always characterized by horns and a tail, or even by bloodthirsty behavior and churlish manners. As far as I am concerned, however, you do not need to be in the least alarmed, *Señor*. I am not a Communist, and neither are any of my immediate associates. Of course there are Socialists in Spain, as elsewhere, and no doubt those who held radical views and who nevertheless merged their votes with ours on Sunday will demand some recognition in the new government. But that does not mean it will turn red overnight."

"Perhaps not overnight, but sooner or later! I know the breed! I know the way they work!"

He was so close to tears that he could not control his voice. A terrible sob choked him and a great wave of nausea swept over him. He sank back on the bed again, drowned in dizziness. The last thing he saw before he fainted was the face of Bautista Ramirez, the kindliness of its expression transfigured by its solicitude.

It was also the first thing he saw when he came to himself again. At first he was not sure where he was, and the thought flickered across his mind that his stay in Spain was ending, as it had begun, with strange and fitful sleep, that he should never be able to disentangle truth from trance when he thought about it afterwards. The crowded little room was still engulfed in obscurity, for its one window was closely muffled by drab woolen curtains, tightly drawn over Venetian blinds. However, Hans Christian had a feeling that it was day again, and as his eyes became accustomed to the dim light, he could see the outlines of the ponderous furniture and the objects with which this was ornamented, most of them ludicrously fragile by contrast—brittle bric-a-brac, unfurled paper fans, family photographs framed in hand-painted silk and velvet. He noticed, with passing surprise, that there was no crucifix beside the bed, and no pictures of religious character on the walls; but the fact struck him as curious rather than portentous. And after all, it was not half so curious as the fact that a self-confessed revolutionist who was a complete stranger to him should have given him comforting shelter.

He fixed his gaze more firmly on the seated figure beside the bed, and again he was struck, as he had been on the train, by the kindliness of this swarthy, stocky man. Something about his thoughts was apparently telepathic in its effect. Before long, his host, who had been staring into space as if completely absorbed in his own weighty reflections, turned his head without moving his bulky body, in an evident attempt to avoid making the slightest sound which might disturb a sleeper. Then seeing that Hansel's eyes were open, he rose creakingly and lumbered over towards the bed.

"*Que tal?*" he asked, not after the casually charming fashion of Sebastian, but with real concern in his voice. "You gave me a bad turn last night, *amigo,* with your fainting fit! Fortunately there was a physician among my comrades who were conferring with me in the *salita* and he brought you out of it. Then he gave you a good strong sedative before you could do any more worrying or ask any more troublesome questions. Now you have had a fine sleep, and all will be well with you again—if you do not immediately attempt another long journey, or try to drag heavy baggage for miles through a mob! I am sorry my city seemed to give you so indifferent a welcome— Shall we let some sunshine into the room? And what about coffee? I am sure you would like a cup at once!"

He manipulated the cords controlling the heavy curtains, and rolled up the blind. Then he departed, to come back carrying a tray laden with coffee, hot milk, and soft sugary rolls.

"I am a widower, *Señor,*" he remarked, as he set down the tray and plumped up Hansel's pillows with a capable hand. "I live alone, except for an old servant, whose name is Antonina. She is a good woman and a good cook, which perhaps is even more to the point, under the circumstances. You will find her glad to be of service, and you will see her when you get up, for such plumbing as there is in my apartment is behind the kitchen. But I hope you will not be too greatly inconvenienced. She would have brought in your tray had I not preferred to serve you myself for the moment, so that we could talk undisturbed."

He reseated himself, making the same creaking sound as when he had risen, and drew a telegram from his vest pocket.

"I took the liberty of wiring your grandmother last night. I also took the liberty of opening her reply, so that I might know whether it was necessary to arouse you. I am sure you will be relieved at the good news this telegram contains."

He handed the flimsy piece of paper to his guest: RESTING COMFORTABLY AFTER RECENT HEART ATTACK—Hans Christian read eagerly—DESIRE BUT DO NOT REQUIRE YOUR IMMEDIATE PRESENCE. V. L. VON HOHENLOHE.

"How did you know the address?" he asked in astonishment, looking up from the dispatch.

"But, *amigo,* I naturally keep an *Almanac de Gotha* on hand for easy reference! My library is unpretentious, but that volume is indispensable to me. If I had not possessed it, I should naturally have telephoned the German Embassy. I am rather glad, however, that this was not necessary, since Germany has not yet recognized our new government. A statement to the effect that she has will doubtless come in at any moment, but it has not come yet."

Hans Christian, who was still torn between revulsion and gratitude, took refuge, for the moment, in silence on this subject, though he found his admiration for his host's ready resourcefulness mounting rapidly.

"Nevertheless, I have telephoned to Granada," Bautista Ramirez went on, "and I have learned that everything at the Episcopal Palace is quite as usual. His Eminence, the Archbishop, has stood the shock of recent events remarkably well for a man of his age and convictions, and he has not seen fit to ask the government to permit him to move his residence, as it is rumored his colleague, the Archbishop of Seville, has done."

"*Tio* Gabriel would die first!" Hansel exclaimed heartily.

"I do not doubt it. But let us hope no such calamity will occur. I have always had great admiration for Gabriel de Cerreno. If all Churchmen of rank were like him, the present situation would be considerably simpler. However, there will be no complications as far as he is concerned, as I tried to tell you last night."

"But the rest of the family——" began Hans Christian.

"As you know, there is no telephone at the country place where Sebastian de Cerreno is staying with his wife and daughters. However, I have asked for a report on them at once. Merely to ease your mind. Let me assure you again that they will be quite unmolested. But it might be interesting to know whether they will join the general exodus. I understand that no fewer than thirty-six families are leaving today with the Queen and I could not tell you how many have gone already."

"*Today* with the Queen! Didn't she go yesterday with the King?"

"No—no. He went by motor, accompanied only by the Duke of Miranda and two Civil Guards. He has always been a rapid driver, but I understand that this time he broke all speed records in reaching Cartagena. Now he has embarked on the cruiser *Principe Alfonso,* presumably for Marseilles."

"He left the Queen behind him when he fled? And that poor sick son of his, suffering with haemophilia? *El Rey Valiente!*"

"Drink your *cafe con leche, amigo,* before it becomes completely cold. If you will pardon me for saying so, you should learn to take life more philosophically. You must not let the crash of your illusions overwhelm you so, when they are shattered; otherwise you will end by being shattered yourself— Doubtless the King realized that the Queen would be entirely safe with the good Republican guard which was placed all around the Palace to watch over her. As for the suffering of the Prince, that may be laid to Victoria's door, not Alfonso's. The bleeding sickness was not among the diseases which are part of the Hapsburg legacy, though those are not pleasant ones either."

Hans Christian flushed angrily. "My grandmother is a Hapsburg," he said curtly. "And therefore I am part Hapsburg myself. Those stories about Hapsburg diseases are all slanders."

"Your pardon, *Señor.* We will let them pass as such. And since I spoke unwittingly of your own family, let us return to a discussion of the Cerrenos. I understand they are kinsmen of yours at least, if not near relatives."

"They are much more than that now. I'm engaged to Cristina, Sebastian's elder daughter. He's stipulated that we shouldn't be married for two years. But that's all got to be changed. That's why I want to go back to Granada at once."

"Again your pardon, *Señor*. Of course I did not guess anything of that sort. As you said, there was much I did not understand. But I am beginning to understand better now."

Ramirez removed the tray from Hansel's knees and carried it carefully over to the bureau. When he turned back again his face was troubled.

"If you would prefer to move at once to the German Embassy, *Señor,*" he said slowly, "I shall take no offense. I will send you in a motorcar as soon as you are dressed, and you can make all arrangements for your future movements from there. Of course the Ambassador and his staff would be delighted to receive you— Or I will send you to the Azucena Palace. The family servants are in residence; they could look after you; and of course the place is properly guarded. Not that it would be harmed in any case. It will be respected, in the same measure that the Royal Palace has been. Perhaps you would consider the Azucena Palace even more suitable than the German Embassy under the circumstances."

"I'd like to go and see it. Not that I doubt your word. But I'd like to see it for myself."

"Of course, *Señor*. As soon as you like."

"But I wouldn't want to stay there unless Sebastian invited me. You see, it was he who thought I ought to go away. He has consented to my engagement, he's been very fair, but he's not enthusiastic about it. And it doesn't seem possible, but it was only night before last——"

Again Hans Christian felt himself flushing, not with anger this time but with remembered ecstasy. Bautista Ramirez continued to regard him gravely.

"In that case, *Señor*, perhaps I might go on with what I was about to say when you told me of your betrothal, on which please accept my congratulations. I asked my comrade in Granada with whom I spoke on the telephone to inform both the Archbishop and *Señor* de Cerreno——"

"Señor de Cerreno!"

"The decree has already been issued, *Señor*, abolishing titles of nobility—to inform them both, as I was saying, where you are, in order that they might communicate with you rapidly, should they wish to do so. If you feel you can be contented and comfortable with me, I should be honored to have you remain here until some message comes through. If you do not, I will send you wherever you may specify, and dispatch a message after you with as little delay as possible."

"Of course I can be comfortable, and of course I'd rather wait for the message here so that no time will be lost. You've done everything in the world for me, *Señor*. I can't ever thank you enough. But how can I be content—anywhere?"

"That is a question of character, *amigo*, not of conditions. I hope that someday you may achieve contentment. And for my part, of course, I cannot see why you should be more contented in Germany than in Spain."

"I could have been contented enough in Germany if there had been no Versailles Treaty and no communistic consequences!"

"Someone has said there are no ifs in history, *Señor*. Be that as it may, I have been doing what I could to facilitate your return to Germany, for I know you feel your duty lies there, even though I now understand that your heart does not. I think I may promise you that you can leave by plane, either tomorrow or the day after, just as you prefer. In that way you will arrive as quickly as if you had gone by train today."

"As I said before, I can't begin to thank you——"

"Pray do not try, *Señor*. I will leave you now, while you dress, if you feel able to do so. Afterwards perhaps you would enjoy sitting in the *salita* and listening to the radio. It has done much to clarify the issues of this election, for the proclamation of the Republic was broadcast and the voices of our leaders have been heard by all the people. They have not been obliged to depend wholly on rumor, or on an unreliable press, as heretofore. How I wish you might have heard Zamora's great speech last night, in which he said, 'The Republic does not represent happiness, but it shall be my endeavor to have it represent law and order!'"

"Zamora is already elected President?"

"He is our provisional President, *Señor*. He will serve until elections can constitutionally be held."

"And meanwhile, how is the country to be governed?"

"By decree. All official orders will be issued by decree."

"Then isn't Zamora a dictator, just like Primo de Rivera?"

"No, *Señor*, for he will act only with the advice and consent of his cabinet, and not without the advice and consent of anyone." The Spaniard still spoke with the utmost politeness, but a slight note of forced patience had crept into his voice, as if he were speaking to a child who either could not understand or would not try to do so. "You will find the morning papers as well as the radio in the *salita*," he went on. "On the whole, they have been fair and accurate. Stay to lunch with me in any case. And afterwards, if you feel able, go out and see the city, while it is still in holiday mood. Tomorrow it will be back at work again, as if nothing had happened. By evening you will probably have had a message from *Señor* de Cerreno. If not, you can decide for yourself what you had better do. I must leave you for a time now, to go out myself. But I will see you a little later. *Hasta luego!*"

Ramirez smiled and left the room, closing the door quietly after him. Hans Christian, pushing back the heavy linen sheets and hand-woven blankets, swung out of bed and rummaged in his suitcase for his dressing gown. Then, toilet articles in hand, he set out to find "such plumbing as there was." It did not take him long to find it, for the apartment was tiny. A second bedroom, similar to his own, opened from the other side of the *salita,* which apparently served as both living room and dining room. The inevitable center table was now covered with a dark woolen cloth and strewn with papers. The radio, which was in action, stood in the center of it. The curtains at the windows were thick and clumsy, and the chairs were finished off with antimacassars. Directly behind was the kitchen, where an elderly woman of formidable proportions was standing over an old-fashioned range, intersected on top with openings in which there were live coals. Her back was towards Hans Christian as he entered, and it was quite evident that she did not hear him, for she was engaged in singing the *Marseillaise* at the top of her lungs. Even so, she was not wholly successful in drowning out the notes of the national anthem of Royal Spain, which rang forth with equal vigor, from an adjacent apartment. It was evident that the maids of the two establishments were engaged in a vocal duel designed to announce to the world their sympathies with the political views of their employers!

The plumbing was certainly archaic, and without the personal service which had been a satisfactory substitute for modern conveniences at the *caseria,* Hans Christian felt that his toilet was rather sketchy. But in spite of himself he was intrigued by his surroundings, and after he was dressed he followed the suggestion of his host, and settled down in the *salita* with the radio and the newspapers. He searched in vain for a statement from the fugitive King, justifying his position; there was only a brief announcement with an indirect quotation outlining the inevitability of his course. On the other hand, Zamora's radio address, to which Ramirez had referred, was given in full, and Hans Christian learned that the first decree signed by the new government had been one granting complete amnesty to all political prisoners. He also noticed, with some surprise, that the provisional President had sent special greetings to America "as the leader of democracy in the world." It had never occurred to Hansel that the historic revolt of the Colonies against the Crown could possibly have set any precedent for the sort of uprising he had just witnessed; and as he laid down his paper, he tried to recollect fragmentary episodes in the American Revolution. Later, when he picked it up again, he happened to see, tucked in an inconspicuous corner, a brief dispatch from Berlin, stating that the Blücher Palace, bought by the United States for an Embassy at the cost of two million dollars, but never yet occupied as such, had been gouged out by fire.

He knew how greatly Trixie had looked forward to living in this prodigious establishment on Unter den Linden, even more pretentious than the French Embassy on the other side of the broad street. She had told him some of her plans for the renovation and decoration of her own quarters. Her experiments at The Hague, though these had been carried out on a small scale compared to what she now had in mind, had whetted her appetite for that sort of thing. She had planned accommodations for private parties of her own, to take place while large official functions were going on in the great gilded drawing rooms; she had even gone so far as to ask Hansel to help her with a housewarming. Well, she would be disappointed, and he was sorry. She strove so sincerely to give other people a good time that it seemed too bad she should ever be thwarted in plans for a good time herself. But after all, Trixie's personal disappointment was an infinitesimal matter, in the midst of the cataclysm of world events. He forgot it almost as quickly as he had thought of it——

Antonina came in from the kitchen, placed the radio on a side table, cast most of the papers on a sofa in the corner, and laid a white linen cloth, which was evidently not being used for the first time, over the dingy dark one. She spoke to Hans Christian with the unembarrassed goodwill which seemed to be such a characteristic of Spanish servants and which was so different from the menial subservience to which he was accustomed in East Prussia. She was afraid the patron might be late, she told him. If he himself would like something to eat or drink, she would bring him a snack at any time. He assured her that he felt as if he had hardly finished breakfast; but still she seemed to feel uneasy about him. Presently she brought him some variegated hors d'oeuvres, a long loaf of bread and a bottle of sherry, and set them down in front of him with a triumphant flourish.

It was nearly three o'clock before Ramirez returned. He apologized for having kept Hans Christian waiting, and after briefly brushing his hair before the long glass in the bedroom which led from the *salita*, joined his guest at table. The meal which Antonina set before them was elaborate as well as excellent; Hans Christian did not see how she could possibly have prepared it, with only the primitive equipment which he had seen in passing through the kitchen; but her hand was evidently as light as her tread was heavy. There was a well-flavored omelet, followed by fried fish, veal cutlets surrounded by vegetables, roast chicken served with green salad, fruit, cheese and her justly famous coffee. The wine that went with the meal was sweet and sound. When Hans Christian praised her efforts, she lifted her great hands in a deprecating gesture.

"It is nothing, *Señor*, nothing! I was taking part in the carnival most of the night, and this morning I have been too drowsy to do myself justice. But after the siesta I shall be refreshed. I shall prepare small white eels and a suckling pig. Will those please the *Señor*?"

"I haven't eaten any small white eels yet, in Spain, Antonina, but I'll take your word for it that they are good—as good as the big black ones we have in Germany! And I know I shall like the suckling pig—it was wonderful, in Granada."

"It is always better in Madrid," remarked Antonina, giving another triumphant flourish and closing the door of the *salita* after her with a skillful thrust of an immense foot. A moment later the strains of the *Marseillaise* floated vociferously through the air again.

"If Antonina was drowsy this morning, I think she will be deafening this afternoon," Hans Christian said with a laugh. "She sang all the forenoon—apparently in keen competition with a neighbor. If she starts in again, after she is 'refreshed,' we shall have to put on ear muffs."

Ramirez smiled in his turn. "She's a good creature, as I told you," he said, lighting a big black cigar. "You notice she spoke of going to the 'carnival' last night. That is the way she and most of her kind think of this—episode. The ill feeling is remarkably short-lived. By the way, the Queen has gone. She left the Palace quietly by the Puerto Campo Moro, and was rushed out to the Escorial, where she took the train for France. I understand that she went first to the Mausoleum, and knelt in prayer before the tomb of her mother-in-law. Now there, *Señor*, was a woman for whom it was impossible not to feel respect."

"Another Hapsburg!"

"Yes, another Hapsburg. There are flowers in every family, *Señor*—Well, we must not get into another disoussion. Would it interest you to go out to the Cuartro Vientos Airport with me this afternoon? Ramon Franco is expected to arrive by plane from Paris, and there will be a great demonstration."

"If you don't mind, I'd rather stay in the house. I saw enough demonstration last night to last me for a long time! And I can still see a good deal, just by looking out the window. Besides, if I'm here, I'll get the message from Granada the minute it arrives. Then I'll know better what to do next."

"You are right, *Señor*. And I am more happy than I can tell you that you have decided to stay with me. I myself must go out again. But I shall be in, if all is well, for an early dinner, not later than ten o'clock."

He departed, leaving Hans Christian to his own devices again. Surprisingly, considering the boy's impatience to hear from Cristina, the afternoon did not drag. He took a siesta himself, when the cessation of Antonina's song indicated that she was beginning hers. Later he carried a chair out on the small iron balcony and watched the crowd. It was still shouting, still singing, still milling about, as it had been the night before. Hans Christian felt it had not once stopped; he could not bring himself to believe Ramirez' quiet assertion that the next day everyone would have gone back to work. Such ill-feeling as the mob continued to harbor was apparently vented now on royal statues. Hansel had already seen the crown unscrewed from the head of one of these; now he saw another pulled from its place and hammered to pieces. Here and there a miniature guillotine appeared high above the head of some reveller, who held it as if he were showing off a toy. Aside from such grim exhibitions, the prevalent note was still one of hilarity rather than bloodthirstiness.

Antonina came out on the balcony to offer him some *refrescos,* and her glance followed his as he watched the mutilation of the royal statue. There was no venom in her gaze, but it was evident that she was intensely interested. Having set down his drink, she leaned back against the wall of the house and volunteered various items of information.

"My brother told me a week ago that I should see such sights as these, *Señor.* I laughed at him then, but now I perceive that he was right. Therefore I do not doubt that he is right about other matters also."

"What other matters, Antonina?"

"About the matter of the churches. These will have the next attention of the people."

"What kind of attention?"

"The people will take from them what is rightfully theirs, *Señor.* They will strip the altars of their pretty dolls and gilded flowers and take these home to their children. Other things they will burn."

"Burn! Beautiful old statues and paintings! Surely they wouldn't destroy treasures like those! Especially if they feel such things are their own property. They'd preserve and respect them, just as they have the Royal Palace."

"Perhaps, *Señor.* I only know what my brother has told me. He says he already has a list of ten churches which the people are planning to enter very soon now. And that the police will look the other way when they do so. The police will not interfere with anything the people want to do. All the people are going to be happy and rich and free in Spain, now that we have a new government. So my brother says."

She picked up her little tray and disappeared into her own regions beyond the *salita,* her manner still confident and calm. Hansel, striving for calmness himself, tried to keep his mind fixed on the scene before him, without looking too far into the future.

The sunset was extremely beautiful. The sky changed color, as if its brilliant blue were a mere overlay to the fiery rose behind this; then it seemed to glow like a great opal. Against it, a huge square tower, looming solidly above its lesser surroundings, shone as if it had been made of black onyx. Lights began to appear in the blank windows above the heads of the populace, which went on exulting in its frenzy of sound. The noise that it made rose to the housetops; it drowned out the radio, which continued to function in the *salita,* and the song which Antonina had resumed in the kitchen. But at last, above its din, Hans Christian thought he could hear someone knocking at the door. Sure that the awaited message had come at last, he leapt up, overturning his chair as he did so, and rushed to open it himself. When he flung it wide, he saw Sebastian standing on the threshold.

CHAPTER 23

For a moment he stared at his kinsman speechlessly. Before he could recover himself, Sebastian stepped inside, and spoke with concentrated fury.

"This is the last place on earth I should have expected to find you!"

"It's the last place on earth where I would have expected to find myself. But if you've wandered around lost for two hours, carrying two heavy suitcases in the midst of a mob, and see a familiar name on a strange door, you're pretty apt to take shelter."

He was amazed at his own coolness. Sebastian, on the contrary, seemed to be still further infuriated by it.

"With a Communist! After you've seen your own country nearly wrecked by them! After your best friend's been killed by them and you've nearly lost your own life by one of their bullets! If you have no respect for Alfonso as King of Spain, have you forgotten that he's also an Archduke of Austria? A kinsman of yours no less than I am? Is blood so much thinner than water as far as you're concerned?"

"I haven't forgotten anything, and there's nothing the matter with my blood. Besides, when I rang Ramirez' doorbell, I didn't know anything about his politics. I only knew he'd been kind to me on the train, which was the one place I'd ever seen him before. I thought he might be again. I was right. He has been."

"And you were willing to put yourself under obligations to a man like that! If you had told me you'd met him on the train, I could have given you a *dossier* that would have left no doubt about him in your mind. Why didn't you speak to me about him?"

"I meant to, but to tell you the truth, I forgot. He disappeared as soon as we got into the station, and I was absorbed with you right away, and then afterwards with Cristina. I suppose if a man falls in love at first sight, he forgets a good many things. I've never done it before so I don't know. But I even forgot to write and thank Ramirez for looking after me so well between Paris and Madrid."

"When he was on his way back to the country he'd been plotting abroad to betray! I can well understand that he might have found it convenient to vanish, especially if you told him who was coming to meet you! How much real difference do you suppose there is between a so-called Republican and a self-confessed radical? Moscow and Madrid are a good deal nearer together than you imagine!"

"I can imagine that in some respects they aren't far apart. But Sebastian, what could I do? I couldn't get out of Madrid today. And I had to wait somewhere for word from you. I thought I would get it quicker here than anywhere else. And apparently I was right. Though of course I never dreamed you'd come yourself. How did you do it?"

"I understand that Alfonso's enemies are already saying that he broke all time records in trying to escape. Well, I have broken some records too, though not for that reason. If anyone else has ever covered the ground between Granada and Madrid in less time than I have, I should be interested to know it."

"You drove!"

"Yes, I drove. I started almost immediately after I got your message—or rather the message from that man Ramirez! Though as a matter of fact I meant to come in any case. I was not thinking primarily of you. I wanted to see the King! And I got here too late! Because first of all I had to put my wife and daughters in a place of safety before I could leave them."

"What do you call a place of safety?"

"They are all at the Convent of Our Lady of Perpetual Sorrows. Cristina and Cecilia have returned there as pupils and Dolores is installed as a guest. I suppose a convent is safe, even in the midst of anarchy."

"Well, let us hope so— Sebastian, please come in and sit down. I want to hear all about Cristina, how she is, how she's taken all this. And about *Tio* Gabriel. I've been worried about him too."

"You have reason to be. I shall be surprised if the shock of this revolution does not kill him. We hear about freedom of worship, just as we hear about freedom of the press, and then comes an announcement that all government officials will be forbidden to go to church. What kind of freedom is that?"

"It's a pretty poor kind. I think the new government is just groping its way along. Ramirez told me at lunchtime that Miguel Maura walked into the Ministry of the Interior and said, 'There is no precedent for what I am going to do, so I shall merely say that I am taking control of this office.' Other leaders are floundering instead of grabbing. I think most of them really want to provide for some kind of arrangement like that existing in France, for instance, where there's separation of Church and State, but where most of the people are Catholic. But before they get it formulated there are bound to be disturbances. I don't even feel as confident as you do that convents are going to be perfectly safe. That's one of the things I want to speak to you about. I'm all alone here— Ramirez has gone out to the airport. So we can talk quite freely. By and by I'll go with you to the Azucena Palace or wherever else you say. But I can't run off a second time without thanking Ramirez for what he's done."

"Thanking him for what he has done! Inciting rebellion and treachery! Did you know that the Socialists have issued a manifesto saying that they have a hundred thousand armed men ready for action? You may depend upon it, Ramirez has had a hand in this preparation!"

"I mean, thanking him for what he's done for me. And honestly, he's very sincere. He doesn't think he's a traitor, he thinks he's a patriot. And he's quite likable. You'll see for yourself— Anyway, we can't stand here forever in this dark little hall. If you won't come into the *salita,* you can come into my bedroom while I pack."

"*Your* bedroom! Oh, my God!"

Nothing that had happened to Hans Christian so far had given him so completely the feeling that the world had been suddenly turned upside down as it did to see Sebastian in such a state. His very appearance was an anomaly in his bourgeois surroundings. His beautifully cut clothes, the easy grace with which he wore them, his elegance of figure and refinement of feature—all these were incongruously out of place in the drab little flat. His lack of self-control was even more bewildering. Hansel had never visualized his kinsman otherwise than charming, suave, and wholly master of any situation in which he might be found. That Sebastian should have lost his assurance was quite as incredible as that a king should have lost his crown. In the face of such a phenomenon an appeal to reason seemed fantastic, yet Hans Christian decided to attempt it.

"Sebastian, it's only two days since you told me you had stopped beating your head against stone walls, that you accepted them, knowing they'd either crumble of their own accord or prove impregnable. Isn't this a good time to put that theory into practice?"

"I'm not a German. I can't philosophize in the face of a cataclysm, any more than I can try to stop one by brute force."

"Well, in a way it's a relief for me to know your philosophy isn't impregnable after all," Hans Christian retorted. "On the other hand, if you simply stand there reviling me, instead of telling me more about what's happened, from your point of view, how am I ever going to get the other side of the picture? And I've got to, haven't I, somehow? I've got to know how best to stand by you. That's what I've been trying to find out, right along!"

"Are you sure you want to stand by me? This is a day of desertions, not of loyalties!"

"Sebastian, you know better than to ask me such a question or to say a thing like that to me—or you would, if you weren't beside yourself."

Everything in their respective positions seemed suddenly to have been reversed. It was Hans Christian this time who put a steadying arm around Sebastian, propelled him gently towards the small bedroom, and drew forth the two straight-backed chairs. Sebastian sat down mechanically in one of them. The first impact of his rage against Hans Christian had spent itself. But he went on talking frantically.

"Have you heard what happened at the Palace? All the grandees who were in Madrid, or who could get here, gathered in the Throne Room to bid their Sovereign farewell. Many of them were white-bearded old men, who had known him ever since he was a baby—as my father did—he was in the Palace the night the King was born! They stood in a row, and embraced him, with tears running down their cheeks! And I was not there among them—neither I nor my sons! And now the Palace is empty, except for poor old Aylar, the Intendente, who is packing up the King's belongings! The approaches are deserted, and all the glittering guards are gone! One soldier, dressed in a field uniform, is at the only open gate! And exhausted revellers are lying asleep on the walls!"

"Well, at least the Palace hasn't been looted, at least the King's right to his personal property isn't questioned. And he'll be made very welcome in England. Remember, he's regarded as a member of the British Royal Family too. Besides, his exile may not be permanent. Perhaps he'll come back eventually, and everything will be as it was before."

"Nothing will ever be as it was before. If you were older and wiser, you'd know that."

"You are older, and you weren't wise enough to see this coming. You felt sure it wouldn't."

"You remind me of that at such a time as this!"

"Only because I think that if you were mistaken in one way, you might be in another. Only because I'm so desperately sorry for you, Sebastian!"

Hans Christian drew his chair nearer Sebastian's and laid his hand on the older man's knee. He could feel it quivering under his touch.

"Have you seen the King's manifesto?" Sebastian went on, drawing a piece of paper out of his pocket. "No, I suppose not, since it hasn't been publicly printed—the people don't even know that their Monarch has honored them by his confidence! But I have a copy of the statement here—read it for yourself and tell me if you do not think it is one of the most touching documents you have ever seen."

"'*The elections which took place Sunday have clearly shown me that*

I have lost the affection of my people,'" Hans Christian read, accepting the small slip from Sebastian. "'*In my conscience I am certain this disaffection will not be definitive, because I have always done my utmost to serve Spain— I am King of all Spaniards and I am myself a Spaniard. I could have employed divers means to maintain the royal prerogatives and effectively to combat my enemies, but I wish resolutely to step aside from anything that might throw any of my countrymen against others in fratricidal war. I do not renounce any of my rights because they are more than mine—they are the accumulated store of history and I shall one day have to make a rigorous account of their conservation . . . I am deliberately leaving Spain, recognizing in this way that she is the sole mistress of her destinies. Once more today I believe I am doing a duty which is dictated to me by my love of country. I ask God that all Spaniards shall understand their duty as deeply as I do mine.*'

"I think it is beautifully worded," Hans Christian said guardedly, as he handed the paper back. "But just the same, Sebastian, I am surprised that Alfonso left. I don't believe you would have left under the same circumstances. You are not planning to leave as it is, are you?"

"Certainly not."

"I wish you would, of course. If the King's possessions can be sent to Bohemia for safekeeping, yours could be sent to Prussia. And I wish you would come to Germany with me. I've waited here on purpose to tell you that, Sebastian. And to tell you too that I want to marry Cristina at once. I don't want her to go back to the convent, even as a pupil. I'm afraid of it."

"You have no reason to be. It's the proper place for her at present."

"I don't agree with you."

"It makes no difference to me whether you do or not. I am her father. I must decide what is best for her without interference."

"But you can't. Because I'm going to interfere."

"You will never marry her if you talk to me like that."

"I shall certainly marry her, and I talk to you like that only because you force me into it."

He leaned forward again, and put his hand on Sebastian's knee a second time. "Listen, Sebastian," he said urgently. "I'm fonder of you than anyone in the whole world except Cristina. I admire you more than any man I ever knew. I'm proud that you are going to be my father-in-law. I'd have been proud if—if you'd been my father. I want to do everything I can to follow out your wishes. I think I've proved that to you already. I agreed to every condition you made about Cristina and me. I'll agree to anything now in reason. But it isn't reasonable any more for you to expect me to wait for her two years. It isn't reasonable to expect me to go back to Germany and leave her behind. When I agreed to do that, I didn't know that Spain was on the verge of a revolution. You didn't know it yourself. In fact you kept assuring me that it wasn't."

Sebastian did not answer.

"You told me that castles in Spain were real, that I could have one for the asking, any time I liked. I'm afraid I can't. I'm afraid the castles in Spain are crumbling, Sebastian; I'm afraid the convents may crumble too. But my love for Cristina won't. That's enduring. Don't try to interfere with that because everything else is rocking around our feet. There's all the more reason for us to cling to that because love is about all there is that can survive a real revolution."

Sebastian still did not answer. Hans Christian, feeling that his plea had failed, changed his tactics abruptly.

"What are you going to do next? This afternoon, I mean? When you leave here?"

"I'm going to my own house to spend the night. As far as I know, that hasn't been taken over by the government yet."

"Of course it hasn't. I don't believe it will be. Well, I'm coming with you. And in the morning we can motor back to Granada together. Or I'll stay here as long as it suits you. I've had a wire from my grandmother. The heart attack has passed. Her condition isn't critical at all."

"It may be again, at any moment."

"Well the condition here is critical right now. I'm not going away, Sebastian, as long as it is. If you won't let me stay with you, I'll stay with *Tio* Gabriel or—or somewhere."

"I suppose you will tell me in a minute that you will soon storm the Convent of Our Lady of Perpetual Sorrows in the dead of night, and carry Cristina away with you?"

It was the first flicker of Sebastian's old spirit that Hans Christian had seen. He retorted almost gayly.

"I'd thought of it. But I decided I wouldn't tell you about that part. I was afraid if I did you'd spirit her off to some other convent, and I wouldn't be any better off than I was before."

"Of course I should—and of course you wouldn't. I must admit that you have basically sound sense, *querido*. And since that is the case, you must see that it is impossible for you to marry Cristina now. If she were even a year older, I might consider it—conditions, as you say, have changed greatly. But I have already reminded you——"

"Then at least bring her to Germany, where she will be safe!"

"And what makes you think that Germany is so supremely safe, Hansel? Are your reasons any sounder than mine were when I said the traditions of Spain were inviolable?"

"If they aren't, there's no security left anywhere."

"Certainly there is. It still exists in America."

"Then take Cristina to America! Take her to my mother!"

Hans Christian had sprung to his feet. From the room beyond, the rumble of the radio continued to come persistently to his ears, and from the street below, the roar of the populace still rose raucously. He was ready to defy them both, and all that they represented, to pour out a plan which had suddenly sprung, full-grown, from his brain, when he caught a warning look on Sebastian's face, and swung swiftly around to see what had caused it.

He had heard Sebastian's knock, but he had not heard Bautista's latchkey. Now he saw that Ramirez had come in, that the man who had befriended him was standing at the entrance of his room as unexpectedly as Sebastian had appeared at the entrance of the flat an hour earlier. Then he saw a gleam of enmity, vital as a living thing, flash quickly between his host and his kinsman before the two men bowed formally to each other.

"*Señor* de Cerreno does me too much honor," Ramirez said slowly, "in coming to my poor abode."

It was the first time that Hans Christian had ever known the customary salutation, "*Esta es su casa,*" to be left out. He knew that its absence constituted a deliberate omission. He wondered how this would be taken.

"Your pardon, *Señor*. It was not so much to do you honor that I came here as in the hope that you might be able to satisfy my curiosity, which has been piqued. I have been wondering why I was not arrested."

"As to that, I can tell you easily, *Señor*. First, because the prosecuting attorney has not yet fully formulated his charges against you. Second, because your offenses did not take place under the jurisdiction of the present Minister of Justice. And third, because we knew all the time where you were if we wanted you."

"I thank you, *Señor*. I am glad to have that point settled. It only remains for me to add that incidentally I also came here to reclaim my erring kinsman, who has apparently strayed."

"That can easily be explained also, *Señor*. If I am not misinformed, you had invited *Señor* de Hohenlohe to leave the shelter of your home. I invited him to accept the shelter of mine. That illustrates, I think, the difference of our respective methods. But I should say that our guest himself had been equally blameless, in both cases."

Ramirez bowed to Sebastian a second time, and turned to Hans Christian. "Have you now decided what you would like to do next, *Señor*?" he asked.

"I should like to return to Andalusia tomorrow with *Señor* de Cerreno. But he does not seem to think that is desirable. Therefore I have no choice but to accept your offer of a seat in a northbound plane."

"It has been my pleasure to secure one for you, *Señor*. A special plane will leave at ten tomorrow morning, and your ticket will be held for you at the Cuartro Vientos Airport. If you will excuse me, I will go at once to make the final arrangements. Lest I should not find you here on my return, let me thank you again for doing me the honor of being my guest, and wish you a pleasant journey. Let me also add that I hope to see you in Spain again sometime. You will always find a pot of coffee on the stove here, and a warm welcome, if you care to accept it."

He shook Hansel cordially by the hand and bowed to Sebastian a third time. As the door of the apartment closed after him, Hans Christian spoke eagerly, his words coming in a rush.

"Don't you think I've had a good idea, Sebastian? Your sons are both safe in England. Leave *Doña* Dolores at the Convent of Our Lady of Perpetual Sorrows, if that's where she wants to stay. She'll be near *Tio* Gabriel there, she can keep in close touch with him and go to him if he needs her. Leave Cecilia with her. Cecilia is sure to be all right anywhere! But don't try to keep Cristina there! And don't stay at the *caseria*—or the *Palacio* either—all by yourself! Don't you think it would be wonderful to take Cristina to my mother?"

The words were hardly spoken before he realized their double implication. The scar on Sebastian's face had grown livid, the corners of his mouth worked painfully. He turned his head away as if conscious that his face betrayed the fact that Hans Christian had put into words a yearning he had long held in leash, and which the revolution at last gave him a pretext for fulfilling. There was an interminable silence, and Hans Christian knew that when it was finally broken, the threads of many interwoven lives would be severed too—or else knotted more closely together than ever before. But, though dimly, he knew also it would not be in this hour that he would clearly see the ultimate handiwork of fate.

"Yes," Sebastian said at last, clearly and steadily. "It will be wonderful for you to take her, by and by. But not for me to take her now. I am a Spaniard, and I must live in Spain. All of my duty lies here, even if all of my heart does not. When Isabella the Second fled, some of her nobles met in France, thinking thus to show their loyalty. But when she saw them, she said, 'It was not here, I wanted to meet you again.' I must run no risk that my Sovereign will ever say that to me. Besides, it should be remembered that a grandee of Spain does not go through a door ahead of his King, even to escape."

CHAPTER 24

Convent of Our Lady of Perpetual Sorrows
Cerca Granada
May 2, 1931

Vida de mi vida:

Your dear letter has been a long time in reaching me. But now I have it and I have read it over and over again. Every line is precious to me. First, because it tells me all is well with you and with your grandmother, that you were in no peril on your journey and that your homecoming was happy. Second, because it tells me that I have your whole heart, as you have mine.

When my father returned from Madrid, he came at once to see us, and urged my mother to go back to the caseria, since he is now there to protect her. But she has preferred to remain here, at present, for meditation and prayer. I am sorry, because this leaves him so much alone. I am certain that after you and I are married, querido, I shall never willingly be absent from your side, for I am most loath to be separated from you even now.

But Tio Gabriel tells me I must be patient under this affliction. He has come twice to the convent since you went away and has talked at great length with my mother. I think he too has urged her to return to my father, and I believe he has spoken to her about our marriage. But she does not speak about it herself. I know she is displeased because I have decided not to become a nun. This displeasure would weigh heavily upon me if it were not that my joy in being betrothed to you is so much greater than any sorrow which she can cause me.

Cecilia and I have resumed all our lessons. I wish that I might study German, and learn to speak to you in your own tongue. But after all, there is no need for words between us, nor are there words in any language which would tell you adequately of my love.

Besides being busy with our lessons, we are preparing for Ascension Day. It is one of our greatest feasts, and all must be in readiness to do honor to Our Lord. Reverend Mother has told me that had I wished, I might have begun my novitiate at this time. I have asked that instead I may begin to embroider my bridal linen.

The Sister who supervises my singing also supervises my correspondence. But she is young and she has a kind face. It is my hope that she will let me send this letter exactly as I have written it. It goes to you with my fondest greetings mingled with my most fervent prayers for your happiness now and for our happiness together in the future.

Maria Cristina Fidelidad de Cerreno y Romero

Convent of Our Lady of Perpetual Sorrows
Cerca Granada
May 12, 1931

Mi Corazon:

This is a Day of Rogation and only by special permission am I allowed to write you. This permission comes from the Sister with the kind face, of whom I told you.

I write because I am afraid you may be worried. Rumors have reached us that there have been sad happenings in Madrid and elsewhere, and possibly these same rumors may reach Germany. I wish you to know that in the sanctuary of Our Lady of Perpetual Sorrows tranquillity still reigns.

Pupils at the convent are not allowed to read newspapers and it is a habit my mother has never had. But that does not matter, for my father and Tio Gabriel, who read them searchingly, say that all news has been suppressed or censored. The rumors of which I speak have all come by word of mouth, from travelers on the roads and on the trains. My father has seen some of these travelers, and after talking with them, he has come again to the convent, this time urging my mother not only to return to the caseria herself, but to bring Cecilia and me with her. Again she has refused, saying that only by force can he compel her to do so, and naturally he will never use force against my mother. I think she believes that if she remains here, and talks to me daily on the subject, she can still persuade me to become a nun. She is mistaken.

The sad happenings of which we have heard concern churches and convents. It is said that ten structures in Madrid alone have suffered. Among these are the Jesuit College and the Church of the Carmelite Fathers. A convent in Cordova has been stoned and two in Cadiz have been destroyed. The Episcopal Palaces in Alicante and Malaga have been burned. Of course Malaga is not far from here. Still we feel safe. We are sure that if there should be an attack it would be frustrated by the police, as it was in Saragossa. Tio Gabriel tells us that a very slight outbreak in Granada itself caused great popular indignation, that it failed instantly and completely. A single guard stood at the door of the Cathedral and every time the mob approached, he shook his head and quietly said, 'Not here.' Then the mob retreated again and finally it dispersed altogether. So you see there is nothing to fear.

Nobody has been killed or badly hurt. The nuns and priests who have lost their schools and churches and cloisters, have all been given homes by friendly families. We know that there are only small irresponsible elements that seek to cause trouble. Most of them are very young people. They will learn better. The crowds have shown respect to the cloth. I am sure they always will in Spain. And among the officials of the new government there are many believers. The President and the Minister of Justice are both practicing Catholics. They do not agree with the sectarian advances of their Socialist colleagues. We hear that the President confessed and received Communion on the very day the Republic was proclaimed; he was aware that it might be the last of his life and he did not wish to die unshriven. Señor Maura, like his father, Don Antonio, has a private chapel connected with his home, and has never concealed his devotion to the Church. The new Minister of Education has long been a highly respected professor at the University of Granada; we have all met him, we have all liked him. Even Señorita Victoria Kent, the strange woman who has become Director of Prisons, has announced that nuns who customarily supplied prisoners' wants on a concession basis, would be allowed a month in which to clear their accounts and turn their commissariats over to the officials who work under her. It seems sad that the nuns should lose their concessions. Still I believe that Señorita Kent means to be fair.

So far I have said nothing about love. That is because my heart has been heavy with the thought of the sorrows which others have endured. But when I think of our joy it becomes light again. And so it is that I bid you farewell happily and not sadly.

Adios, mi Corazon.

Maria Cristina Fidelidad de Cerreno y Romero

Caseria Cecilia
Ascension Day

Alma de mi alma:

You see that I am at home again. And I am safe. We are all safe.

Just after I had written you on Tuesday, the great bell of the convent began to toll. I was still in the schoolroom when I heard it, and then I heard a crashing sound, and saw stones come hurling through the windows. One of them struck me, but it did not hurt me. The other girls had left the schoolroom already, so none of them was hurt either. I had stayed behind to write your letter.

I ran out into the corridor, and the other girls were there, running too. But the nuns were not running. They were walking quietly along, telling the girls not to be frightened, not to lose their self-control and their faith in God. They made the girls stop running and march in an orderly way. Cecilia and I marched with the others. Cecilia is very brave, she did not cry at all. Some of the other girls did cry, at first, but they stopped, after the nuns had comforted and encouraged them.

I did not see my mother with the nuns or among the girls, so I asked our Reverend Mother if I might go back and look for her. She had a little room to herself, on the second floor, between the girls' dormitory and the nuns' cloister. Reverend Mother hesitated a moment and then she said yes, I might go. She told me not to alarm my mother, but to give her a message that she was to come at once to the courtyard, no matter what she might be doing.

I found my mother in prayer before a statue of Our Lady of Perpetual Sorrows. She had not heard the bell or seen the stones, she did not want to come with me. But I told her I had brought her a command. So finally she came. When we got to the courtyard everyone had gone out of it, except the Reverend Mother, who was waiting for us. The great doors leading into the street had been butted in, and flames were leaping all around them. We were scorched a little, because we were so late in getting through. But none of the others who went before us was burnt.

The mob which had come inside the courtyard had built a big bonfire in the middle of it. When we went out we could see men throwing the beautiful old books from the library and the statues from the chapel and the vestments from the sacristy into it. Every time they cast something onto the flames and saw these leap higher and higher, they howled. They also jeered at the Reverend Mother as she went past, and one of them jerked at her veil. But outside the crowd was very quiet. Hardly anyone spoke at all. Except that as each nun went by someone came forward and said to her in a low voice, "Have you any place to go?" If she said yes, the throng stood aside to let her pass through it. If she said no, the person who had spoken to her took her home. It was the same way with the girls. If their own homes were not near by, other persons' homes were open to them. The Reverend Mother and the religious with the kind face of whom I told you, whose name is Sister Josefa, and four of my schoolmates, have come home with us.

Reverend Mother told us not to look back as we went along so that we would not see the destruction of the convent. But we could hear the licking sound the flames made and the howling of the mob. They were dreadful noises and we felt very sad, but we obeyed our Reverend Mother and did not look back.

It is a long walk from the convent to the caseria and we saw other sad sights along the way. We heard weeping in some rushes bordering a dry stream near the roadside, and when we went to see what it might mean, we found several nuns and a number of little orphan girls huddled together in a cleft on the bank. They told us that early that morning they had been expelled from their convent. So they had made their way somehow to a large country house which was empty except for a caretaker. He gave them some milk and told them he was willing to shelter them if his landlord would give him permission. But presently the Communists came there also, and set fire to this house. So then the nuns and the orphans wandered down the dry riverbed until they were so exhausted that they could go no farther. We had no food with us that we could give them, and no water, which they needed even more. We told them that we would send help back to them, if we could find any, and then we went on in search of it.

When we got to Santa Fe, we found that the convent there had also been burned that morning. The Alcalde had telephoned to Atarfe and had told the authorities to lie in ambush for the destructionists as they came through. It was a well-meant warning, but it resulted in bloodshed. When a motorcar came into Atarfe at high speed, the authorities ordered it to stop, because they thought it contained fleeing Communists. The driver in his turn thought that the order came from Communists and drove faster than ever. The authorities fired and then the occupants of the car fired too. One person in the car was killed and several in the crowd.

I know you will be especially grieved to hear this, because the man in the car who was killed was Leopoldo. My father had heard about the destruction of our convent and had started out to seek us, taking Leopoldo and Leonardo with him. Of course he would not have stopped for anybody just then. But he is terribly unhappy, because Leopoldo had served our family ever since he was a little boy, and now he is dead and nothing will ever bring him back to life. We are afraid that Leonardo may die too, of grief for his twin, though his wounds are not serious in themselves.

We stopped in Atarfe until the authorities were satisfied that this had all been a sad accident, and then my father and Leonardo were released, and finally we came home. Of course we could not all come at once, because there was not room in one car, and we could not get another. So first my father took away the body of Leopoldo in order that it might be prepared for burial, and Leonardo because he was wounded, and the Reverend Mother because she did not shrink from the sight of blood. The rest of us waited in Atarfe until my father could return for us and some of the good people there who saw that mother and I had been scorched gave us salve for our hands and faces and did what they could to make us comfortable until my father could get back. Cecilia went to sleep with her head against Sister Josefa's shoulder, and the other little girls slept also, on the floor.

Today Leopoldo has been buried. Tio Gabriel conducted the services and we all went to them except Leonardo, who is delirious with his wound. It is the saddest Ascension Day I have ever known.

Sister Josefa has been talking to me. She has reminded me that nobody will talk to me any more about becoming a nun, because this will be impossible. It will be a long time before there can be new nuns in Spain. Once I might have rejoiced in knowing that this was so. But now, because I know the reason for it, I am sorrowful. We have never been able to find the nuns who had taken refuge in the rushes with the poor little orphans again.

Alma de mi alma, I have written you a long letter, the longest letter I have ever written in my life, and this time I have not spoken to you of love at all. You seem so far away. Is it possible that I was mistaken, that we are not to have happiness together after all? God grant that this may not be so! Somewhere in the world, outside of Spain, there must still be joy.

But whether in joy or in sorrow, I am completely your own

Cristina

Author's note: Hans Christian Marlowe von Hohenlohe did not receive this letter until long after it was written. Upon getting the one dated May 12th, but considerably delayed in transit, he at once started back to Spain, flying from Berlin to Paris and from Paris to Madrid. He reached Granada by car the morning of May 22nd. The following day he and Cristina de Cerreno were married by the Archbishop of Granada in the private chapel of the Episcopal Palace.

PART VII

1931–1934

"The Night of Long Knives"

CHAPTER 25

THE ONLY hours that mattered to Cristina von Hohenlohe were those she spent with her husband.

She was not fretful or restless when they were separated. She could sit indefinitely in the garden or by the fireside, occupied, composed and contented, as she played her guitar, studied German or bent over her needlework. But these were merely periods of preparation and anticipation for her. They had no definite meaning of their own.

She arranged the flowers at Schönplatz, because her touch with these was lighter than Luischen's, and Luischen had been the first to recognize this, and to urge that the bride should take over the pleasant task. Cristina also had a way of giving loveliness to linen. The snowy sheets stacked in the Danzig chests, the bath towels big as bedspreads, the crested cloths and damask napkins had never lain in such even piles, they had never been so smooth and sweet-scented as after she took charge of them. But when the flowers were fixed and the linen in order, her household labors were over for the day. When they were done, she wrote long affectionate letters to each member of her family in turn, taking one a day, and wishing it were as easy to express herself to her mother as to her father. After that, she sat and waited for Hans Christian.

He never left her for long, except when he was obliged to go to Berlin on Party business. He knew that it did not seem natural to her, as it did to Luischen, to range about the place alone, to visit the kennels and stables unattended, or to jump casually on a horse and gallop across the field. So he took her himself to see the foals and puppies, he walked or rode with her at some time every day that he was at Schönplatz. She never knew beforehand exactly when this would be. Hence there was all the more reason to be ready and waiting when he came for her.

She studied German because she knew her mastery of this would please him, though he never harassed her about her progress in it. She realized, too, that as his wife it was fitting she should be competent to converse with his friends and direct his servants; it was not hard for her to advance in it, partly because she proved to have a natural aptitude for such learning, and partly because she had such a powerful incentive for proficiency in it. She played her guitar and sang to its accompaniment, because music was a natural expression of emotion for her. But she preferred to sew, because while her fingers flew over the fine fabrics, her thoughts were free to fly back over all the hours she had spent with Hans Christian.

First of all they flew back to the May morning when he had come, unheralded and unhoped for, to the *caseria*. She had been sitting sadly in the patio, unmindful that birds still sang and flowers still bloomed there. Leonardo had died of his wounds as well as Leopoldo; and the Reverend Mother's burns were causing her great suffering. She did not refer to this or to the destruction of her convent and the loss of her school; but every day something more went out of her face which had been there before. *Doña* Dolores locked herself in her room, presumably to pray, and Don Sebastian stayed in the turret, turning over the leaves of books with unseeing eyes, or pacing the terrace which looked out on the land which at any moment might cease to be his. Even Cecilia no longer laughed. She studied, with unnatural industry. But when she had learned her lessons, no one would hear them.

And then Hans Christian had come. Cristina had heard the door of the outer patio open and close, and footsteps coming swiftly through the garden. His footsteps. She had recognized them at once, and she had leapt up and run out to greet him, the sad world suddenly a different place. She had met him just as he reached the inner entrance, and he had caught her quickly in his arms and held her as if he would never let her go. It was a long time before he spoke to her at all. And when he did, he still held her in his arms.

"I've come back for you, Cristina. I never should have left you. I'll never leave you again."

"What are you going to do?"

"I am going to marry you at once. Before any more sacrileges occur. I started back from Berlin the minute I learned of the destruction in Madrid. I ought to have known it was coming. I'd heard about the ten churches before, but I thought it was only ignorant prattle; I couldn't conceive that horrible arson could take place in a civilized country. Cristina, can you ever forgive me? I went to look for you at your convent first. I've seen what happened— Darling, tell me how much you are hurt, how much you were frightened! No, never mind, don't talk about it yet— You can tell me about it later on, but not now. I'll talk to you. I'll swear to you that you shall never be hurt or frightened again, if I can help it, never as long as you live."

After that he began to cover her face with kisses. He sat down on the tiled seat beside the patio and drew her on his knees and held her so close to him that she could feel his heart beating against hers. When he finally put her on her feet, it was to ask her, almost abruptly, where he could find her father. He had seen her uncle, he said, already. He had gone straight from the ruins of the convent to the Episcopal Palace, he had spoken with *Tio* Gabriel. He had made it clear that all this talk about two years must stop. It had been folly from the beginning; now it was flying in the face of Providence. The Archbishop's duty lay in Granada, that was true; he owed it to his church and to his people to stay with them, even though this cost him his life. And if Don Sebastian felt the same about his loyalty and his land, Hans Christian would not argue with him again. But nothing that either of them could say or do should keep Cristina in Spain another week. She must be married, and go to her husband's home, where she would be safe.

It was pitiful, Cristina realized then, to see how little either her uncle or her father tried to do to keep her in Spain. It was only a few short weeks since they had bargained with Hans Christian, since they had told him what he could and could not do. Now they listened while he talked to them. Even *Doña* Dolores listened. Secretly, she herself had already made a dress which she had hoped Cristina would wear on the day when her daughter became a nun. Now she took it from the fine linen in which it had been swathed and dressed her in it on the day when she became a bride. Cristina went to the altar robed in dazzling white, carrying long lilies in her arms.

She and her husband reached Ventosilla that same night, for Hans Christian drove steadily and fast. He had bought a car within an hour of the time that he had landed at the Cuartro Vientos Airport in Madrid, on his journey South; it was in this city that he had come on, at breakneck speed, to Granada, and it was in this that he bore away his bride. A message had been sent to the servants at the old castle, which Cristina, like her father, loved better than any other they possessed; and though messages often went astray in these days, this one had not, and everything was in readiness to welcome the bride and groom. When they reached the ramparts, they saw that hundreds of flickering lanterns had been placed there, and inside the *castello* the vast arched halls were illumined with torches. Supper had been spread in the banquet hall where for hundreds of years wedding feasts had been held; and in the vaulted chamber above, the bridal brocades, ivory with age, had been draped above the great golden bed.

Cristina had been in this chamber before, since it formed part of the state suite which was shown to visitors. But she had never seen it used, for she was the first bride of her generation. The myriad lights were missing here. There was only one large lamp, swinging like a censer above the bed, and small candles standing in the dim corners. She had thought beforehand that it would seem strange to see Hans Christian moving about her room, acting as if it were his also; now she was thankful to hear his firm footsteps echoing across the dark stretches, to hear his happy voice ringing through the distances that divided them. He had ordered her belongings placed in the alcove, his own in the antechamber; and when they had come up from dinner, he had said he knew she must be very tired, that of course she would wish to get undressed at once.

"May I help you? I want to if you will let me. It would be like lifting your veil, to kiss you, as I did this morning after *Tio* Gabriel had married us. But if you would rather be alone——"

"I think I should rather be alone, for a few minutes."

He had said no more about it. He had put his arm around her and walked with her to the alcove, and then he had kissed her lovingly, and left her there. Afterwards she was sorry she had sent him away. Her fingers trembled as she took off one garment after another, and when she slipped her nightgown over her head, she was shivering all over. If he had stayed with her, he would somehow have saved her from this frightful fear. He would have made her feel, as he himself had said, that he was only lifting another veil, like the one he had lifted that morning, and not that he was affronting her modesty. He would have encompassed her with compassion, he would have comforted her. As it was, panic overcame her. She thought of coarse jests she had heard Catalina make, from which she had instinctively recoiled, though she could not grasp their full meaning. She thought of *Doña* Dolores saying in cold, measured tones that since she had spurned the vocation of a virgin, she must accept the suffering of subjection. She thought of her father telling her he would trust her to remember that her first duty lay in obedience to her husband and her second in the conception of children.

As she thought of all this, she became more and more bewildered, more and more terrified. She no longer saw Hans Christian as her savior and her lover; she saw him as her persecutor and possessor. She knew that now there was no escape from him; but there was always a refuge from every trouble in prayer. She knotted her dressing gown around her and thrust her feet into her slippers. Then, resolutely, she crossed the dark empty space again and knelt down at the *prie-dieu* beside the bed. There was a tiny vigil light there, which she had not noticed before, burning under a small silver statue. She lifted her eyes to this, and prayed.

When she rose from her knees, she saw that Hans Christian was beside her, looking at her with infinite loving kindness, as if he had seen into all the secret places of her heart. He put his arm around her gently, and spoke to her gently too.

"Cristina, I want to talk to you. Are you too tired? Would you rather have me leave you again, and let you sleep?"

"I would rather never have you leave me again. I was wrong to ask you to do so before. And I know I shall never wish to sleep if you want to talk to me."

Although she spoke with an effort, she felt that what she was saying was true. And she did not shrink away from him when he seated himself on the edge of the great bed, drawing her down beside him and looking into her eyes.

"My darling, has anyone ever told you what marriage means?"

"No. Only that a wife should submit to her husband's will, even under compulsion. But this was mysterious to me. I could not understand why there should be either submission or compulsion where there is love. But it does not matter. For now I know it would always be my will to yield to yours."

"I don't want you to yield to my will, Cristina. I want you to trust to my tenderness. Can you do that?"

"Yes— Oh, yes!"

"Then nothing will be hard. Do you remember when I first held your hand, Cristina? And when I first kissed you? You knew that these caresses were acts of love. You were happy when you felt your fingers resting in mine, you were happier still when you felt my lips pressed against yours. Isn't that so?"

"Yes, that is so."

"I shall never tell you anything that is not true, my darling. The closer caresses are, the more joy they bring. The greatest act of love merges two beings into one. That is what marriage means."

She remembered the joy that had suffused her soul when he had embraced her in the patio, and all her formless fears melted away. She yearned to feel his heart beating against hers again, and as if he knew this, Hans Christian drew her nearer to him.

"I want to achieve this supreme state, Cristina. I want to take you in my arms and hold you fast until I have made you mine. Can you look into my eyes and say, 'I am ready for your love, I am not afraid of fulfillment, I can give myself utterly into your keeping'?"

"I am ready, I am not afraid, I can give myself utterly——"

Hans Christian rose and extinguished the brazen lamp above the great golden bed. Only the vigil light remained, under the silver statue, and soon that also flickered out. In the profound darkness, which now formed so kindly a cloak, Cristina could feel his arms encircling her again, his heart beating once more against hers, as she had longed to have it. She could hear him murmuring words of endearment and encouragement as his mouth closed down on hers. Adoration for him filled her being, and deep within her something suddenly stirred, demanding his dominance. She passed unflinchingly beyond resistance into realms of rapture. Then his passion poured through her in a rush of glory.

Eager as he was to be gone from Spain, Hans Christian did not suggest that they should leave Ventosilla the next day. They spent it languorously, without marking the flight of its golden moments; and when evening again enveloped them, they welcomed its advent together. The consummation of their marriage had released them both: It was no longer needful that he should strive to save her from shock; he could rejoice, without restraint, in his every prerogative. She was no longer bewildered by mysteries and bound by barriers; she could anticipate, with perfect pliancy, his every desire. The last veil had indeed been lifted, the last depth penetrated.

In her first flush of abandon Cristina was conscious of nothing except the flood tides of love. It was only long afterwards, when she could reason again, that she recognized how unerring Hans Christian's instincts had been in all that concerned her. If he had precipitated their union, without preparing her for it, she could never again have given herself to him with such confident self-surrender; there would always have been lurking fear underneath her submission instead of rapturous response. On the other hand, if he had retarded his conquest, some vital element would have been lacking. He had seen that her spirit could soar to meet his own, and had swept her along in the surge of his own passion.

They went from Ventosilla to Saragossa and from there to Carcassonne, lingering for some days above its matchless parapets. Theirs was no longer a flight from revolution, Hans Christian told Cristina; it was an excursion into high romance. They stopped in Nîmes and Arles and Avignon, Grenoble and Chamonix, beside the Swiss lakes among the Tyrolean Mountains. Then they went to Vienna, where they stayed for some time, and where Cristina gradually became accustomed to having Hans Christian leave her from time to time, for he explained to her that he had work to do here, though he never told her exactly what it was and she never asked him. It was late summer when they finally reached East Prussia. And there they found a feudal welcome waiting for them, and Cristina stepped proudly into her predestined place as the young chatelaine of an ancient house.

They had been married for many months and were already well settled at Schönplatz before Cristina asked Hans Christian a question which she had been considering for some time. He was resting peacefully beside her, desire already drowned in sleep, when he became aware that she was still wide eyed and wakeful in the darkness. He instantly turned to her again.

"Is something the matter, darling? Aren't you feeling well?"

"Nothing is the matter, and I am feeling quite well. But I have been wondering— When two people love each other as we do, doesn't that mean that by and by there will be a child?"

"Perhaps. Probably— You would not be afraid if you found you were to have a child, would you, Cristina?"

"Why should I be afraid?"

"Because childbirth brings suffering with it, my darling. I could not save you from that no matter how hard I tried."

"You know that I am not afraid of suffering. I am only afraid— Would I know by now if I were going to have a child?"

"Yes, if it were the child of our first love. But it might not come until later."

"There is no chance, is there, that I might never have one?"

"Of course not. Of course you will have one. You have put it beautifully, darling— When two persons love each other as we do, they are certain to have a child. It is the natural result of their love. But often they cannot tell when this result will come about."

"Would you be glad to have a child, *querido?*"

"Yes. But I shall be just as glad if we do not have one too soon. I do not want to share you with anyone for a long while. I want you all to myself. I want you unutterably."

Desire was no longer drowned in sleep. It was sweeping through him like a flame, threatening to consume him altogether. For the first time he forgot Cristina, except as the chalice for his passion, and thought only of himself, of his own craving and his own need. And, for the first time, she forgot him, though it was not of herself that she thought, as she lay in his arms throughout the long night. Later he remembered the words she had spoken, when at last he released her.

"I hope that now there will be a child."

But more than two years had gone by since their marriage, and this hope was still unfulfilled. Hans Christian had been sincere in saying that he wanted Cristina all to himself; his first feeling had been that a child would interfere with the closeness of their communion. But as time went on, the primeval yearning for a son asserted itself, and he began to be conscious of frustration, even of slight shame. When his grandmother finally spoke to him on the subject of Cristina's childlessness, he flared up defensively.

"I really think you should take her with you to Berlin, Hansel, the next time you go, to see a doctor."

"I won't have her mauled around by some surgeon who treats her as if she had no more feeling than a machine. She's sensitive and high strung. It would be a terrible ordeal for her."

"It's a great cross to her to go on like this. I know, though she has never spoken about it to me except once. But I shall never forget the night when Luischen's boy was born. You know that there were complications, in spite of the fact that both the little girls had come so normally into the world before that. There were several hours when the doctor was much concerned, when Luischen suffered horribly. Cristina was sitting in the next room with me, because we had been told we might be needed, that the doctor and nurse might not be able to manage alone. We could hear Luischen's cries quite clearly; I was afraid such sounds of suffering would unnerve Cristina. But when I looked at her to see how she was standing it then, she returned my glance calmly, though there were tears in her eyes. All she said was, 'I wish I were in Luischen's place.'"

"She ought never to have been in the next room to Luischen at such a time. I would have forbidden it, if I'd been here."

"Ah— But you see you were not, Hansel. You were away at one of your Nazi meetings, as you so often are."

The Archduchess had never reconciled herself to his participation in the New Movement. While public meetings were still forbidden in East Prussia, Hans Christian had conceived the idea of holding private ones on his own grounds, since the authorities had not reached a point where they were ready to interfere with gatherings around a *Herrenhaus;* and there he had installed loud-speakers so that all the neighborhood could not help hearing what was said in the course of the speeches. Finding himself unmolested, he had next gone a step further; he had caused loud-speakers to be attached to his automobile, and had gone boldly about in it, making speeches in various villages and towns himself. His ingenuity had resulted in many converts; now that the ban on meetings had been lifted, he already had a large nucleus on which to work. The doctrine of National Socialism was sweeping over East Prussia like wildfire.

Hans Christian's work took him away from home a good deal. That was his one regret, as far as it was concerned. Cristina meant more to him than any cause or creed, and he could not bear to be separated from her. But he believed it was his duty to go, and she never tried to hold him back. She took it for granted that whatever he did was right and necessary—even when he told her that he thought he should spend six months at a Labor Camp.

CHAPTER 26

HE WAS not forced to do so, he explained. Such service was entirely voluntary, he could get excused from it. Only men who intended to become teachers, or who wished to establish their eligibility for government positions, were actually required to undertake it. The unemployed, of course, were only too thankful for the chance to get free board and lodging. As far as he was concerned, it was largely a question of good example. If he went, other *Junkers* might be moved to do the same, and great strides towards equality of both fact and feeling would be made. That was the way the matter had been put to him in the letter he received from those in high quarters. Personally, he felt the experience would be invaluable to him. He would never have been able to serve the Party so well if he had not left his comfortable quarters in the Margarethe Strasse and gone to live in the Bomb Palast tenement. A six months' sojourn in a Labor Camp would certainly enable him to serve it much better.

Cristina had never missed the revelation of details in regard to his work, but now she was touched that he should have told her all this, and her pride because he had done so helped her to hold her head high and to shed no tears until after he had gone. Then she went quietly to her room and locked the door. But when her grandmother-in-law tapped two hours later, she opened it with her customary composure.

She was greatly attached to the Archduchess. There had never been any friction between Victoria Luise and herself, or between herself and Luischen. Harmony reigned at the *Herrenhaus*, and it did not seem to any one of the women there that either of the others infringed on her prerogatives. Besides, Cristina adored Luischen's children. In them she found an added occupation and an added joy. But she had always been careful not to separate them from their mother, and she had never said to Luischen what she had said to Victoria Luise on the night the baby boy was born and what she said again in substance now.

"I am so glad you have come to me. I was wondering whether I should come to you, but I thought perhaps you would prefer to be alone. I did, for a time. And as I sat here, I could not help thinking that if I had a child, this would not be so hard to bear."

"Then our thoughts were much the same," the Archduchess replied, embracing her fondly. "Indeed, I have come to speak to you on that very subject. I think you should see a doctor, a specialist. I think you should go to Berlin for that purpose. I told Hansel so, months ago, but he declined to discuss the matter. He said he would not have you maltreated."

"Maltreated?"

"Doctors sometimes seem harsh in their methods. Modesty, as we understand it, means nothing to them. The more eminent they are, the more occupied they are, and they do not always take time to be gentle. I must admit that a visit to a gynecologist's office is not a pleasant experience. They ask searching questions about the most delicate matters. They subject their patients to painful examinations. The click of their instruments makes a nerve-racking sound, even if these are not used, and of course often they are. It is from all this that Hansel has insisted on sparing you. Mistakenly, in my opinion. For such a visit might reveal the cause of your childlessness and indicate steps which could correct it. Why not take advantage of his absence to find out whether this is the case?"

"You know how hard it is for me to believe that he can be mistaken about anything. But if you really think that secretly he would like to have me go to a doctor, that his hesitation has been based on a wish to spare me——"

"I am sure of that, Cristina. So now that he is away, I feel you should act. I do not need to tell you that this great and ancient house should not be left without an heir."

"No, you do not need to tell me– Do you think I should start for Berlin at once? Would you be willing to go with me?"

"If you would like to have me, my dear child. I am pleased that you should wish me to do so."

Financial conditions at Schönplatz were much better than they had been. Hans Christian's self-sacrifice and initiative and Ernst's skillful service had both helped to put them on a better basis; and Don Sebastian had been determined that whatever his personal reverses might be, Cristina should not be the first bride to go undowered to the *Herrenhaus*. By sacrificing some of his foreign investments, on which he could realize money quickly, he had managed to send her a very substantial sum. It had never occurred to her to keep this for herself; she had turned it over at once to Hans Christian to use as he thought best. Now that in his absence Ernst was administering the estate, she went to him and asked for enough money to take the Archduchess and herself to Berlin, telling him candidly the reason why she wished to make the journey.

He gave her the cash without demur. Indeed, he encouraged her to feel that since she was going there in any case, she might as well stay for a few days and derive some pleasure from the trip. A little outing would do both herself and the Archduchess good. He was only sorry that he and Luischen could not come with them, but obviously they should not all leave Schönplatz at once. Besides, there were the children— He smiled as he placed the necessary bank notes in Cristina's hand.

"You'll know how that is yourself sometime, Cristina."

"Oh, Ernst, I hope so! Thank you for being so helpful—"

The train trip across the Polish Corridor, with its many changes, was fatiguing; but lapped in the solid comfort of the Hotel Bristol, Cristina recovered from it quickly. She did not wish to postpone her visit to a specialist; as soon as she could get an appointment, she wanted to take it. She went through the examination without a murmur, and emerged from the gynecologist's private office white lipped, but erect. He had found nothing wrong with her, she proudly told the Archduchess, who was waiting for her outside. There was no reason, that he could discover, why she should not have a dozen children, if that was what she wanted. He might like to see Hans Christian also, later on; but perhaps that would not be necessary. They might find, when they were reunited, that their separation had been of benefit. It was sometimes that way. He had congratulated her on her own courage and on her husband's exemplary patriotism. He believed both would be rewarded.

"We will hope he is right. If not, we will seek another opinion. You see, Cristina, that there is nothing unbearable about an experience of this kind."

"Oh, no. But shall we go back to the hotel now? That is, if there is nothing else you would like to do this afternoon?"

It had been almost unbearable for her, though she would not admit it. She had never before been unclothed and manhandled, and the indignity, as well as the pain of it, had appalled her. When she was back in her own bed, safe and secluded, she found she was shaking all over, as she had not trembled since her wedding night. And this time Hans Christian was not there to comfort her and uplift her. She had never so yearned for him, she had never felt the gulf of time that separated them to be so intolerable. She would gladly have given ten years of her life if she could have had him with her, even for ten minutes. She could not sleep, and finally, when she had controlled her quivering, she rose again from her bed and paced up and down her room until dawn. It was the first "white night" through which she had ever struggled. She was to struggle through a long succession of them before the next six months were over.

If the Archduchess suspected the inner conflict concealed by outward self-control, she gave no sign. She suggested the next morning that they might do a little shopping and sight-seeing, that they might communicate with a few relatives. Cristina acquiesced willingly. Madrid was the only large city where she had ever been before; she was impressed by the stateliness of Berlin, and eager to see more of it. She strolled with delight up and down Unter den Linden at Victoria Luise's side, and drove with her in a state of fascination through the Brandenburger Tor and the Sieges Allee and into the Tiergarten. Later in the day, after they had made a round of visits, all of them pleasant, she agreed that of course they should leave cards at the American Embassy.

Hans Christian had told her about the Rhodes and she was prepared to like them. But she had not foreseen that their proffers of hospitality would be so prodigal. The entire family immediately called in person, and it was actually with difficulty that she and the Archduchess resisted an effort to move them bodily from the Bristol to the Embassy. In the face of Victoria Luise's refusal to install herself there, Mr. Rhodes remained firm on other points.

"Remember what you told me about your traditions of hospitality when I came to Schönplatz, Highness! Why you wouldn't let me leave, not on a bet! Now you and this pretty young lady must let Mrs. Rhodes and Trixie and me take you out on the town!"

His idea of taking them out on the town was expansive. It included a lavish luncheon and a highly official dinner at the Embassy itself, repasts at all the most famous restaurants, and two evenings at the opera. Every time the Archduchess mentioned the advisability of returning to the country, he argued with her vehemently: When she had been so long coming to Berlin, she mustn't run away from it the minute she got there! It was an exciting time to be in the capital, just before an election. Had she ever been to a rally? Had she ever seen a torchlight parade? *What?* Well, didn't she want to?

"Mr. Rhodes, I have told you candidly that I'm not in sympathy with the present form of government in Germany. Like my son-in-law, Friedrich von Mitweld, I should like to see a return to the Empire. If that is impossible, then at least it should not be too much to hope that we might have some other kind of conservative and dignified government."

"I'm afraid it is, my dear lady, I'm afraid it is. The day of conservative, dignified government seems to be almost gone. I'm not in sympathy with what's going on here either—not that I can say so publicly, in my position, though I don't mind saying it to you. But that's all the more reason why I want to watch it. Don't you? Don't *you?*" he inquired, turning abruptly to Cristina and looking at her with appreciative appraisal.

"I should like very much to go to a rally. It would help me to understand better what my husband is doing."

She spoke as quietly as usual, but Mr. Rhodes did not fail to catch the longing in her voice.

"That's the idea— The *Sport Palast* it is then tonight, instead of the *Winter Garten.* It'll be a great sight and Goering's going to speak."

"He ought to diet, not talk," remarked Richard Eustis scornfully.

Cristina had not quite placed this personable young man. He appeared to be almost a perpetual guest at the Embassy. She supposed he must be a suitor for the hand of Beatrice. But then, it appeared to her, there was an endless number of such young men, with none of whom, as far as Cristina could discern, Beatrice was herself in love. Yet the Ambassador's daughter, whom Cristina secretly thought the loveliest-looking girl she had ever seen, was on terms of such easy friendliness with Richard Eustis that these seemed to bespeak a betrothal. Her curiosity, though not easily aroused, was piqued, and she was pleased when Beatrice at last spoke to her spontaneously on the subject.

"I suppose that someday I shall make up my mind to marry Card Eustis. He's been hanging around for more than nine years now. It will probably be the only way to get rid of him."

Cristina was increasingly puzzled. She had never heard the theory of marrying a man to get rid of him. And there was nothing in Beatrice's voice, any more than there had been in her manner, to indicate special affection. As if she divined Cristina's bewilderment, Beatrice linked her arm through her guest's and drew her towards the ping-pong table.

"We can't all draw prize packets, the way you did," she said gayly. "Some of the boxes at the church supper turn out to be duds. But we have to take a chance. Come on, let's have a game."

Her cordiality was clear, even though her speech was a mystery. Cristina, who was becoming more and more attached to her, decided to take her on trust.

The rally was certainly a great sight, as the Ambassador had predicted. His party reached the *Sport Palast* some moments before the program was scheduled to begin, but the area surrounding it was already thronged with people waiting to listen to loud-speakers. The Brown Shirts on guard saluted respectfully at the sight of Mr. Rhodes, and the gates were instantly thrown open to permit the passage of the official car, which was waved forward so fast that the close-pressing crowd had to choose quickly between being run over or being crushed against the wall. But swift as this progress was, the distinguished guests could see a tall young man charging through the multitude and plunging towards the gateway with every appearance of baffled rage. He began to argue with the guards, thrusting credentials in their faces. They answered with curt finality, which seemed to act as added fuel to his fury, and pushed him back. The next instant he was charging away again, and the Ambassador was following his flying figure anxiously.

"Too bad," he said, shaking his head. "That man's an American journalist, an able one. He's an angry one now too. I know what sort of story will be sizzling over the wires within the next fifteen minutes. Incidents of that sort do a good deal to upset the balance of friendly feeling, and it isn't too steady at best. Well I can't help just now, but I'll try to have a word with Hanfstaengl tomorrow— Come, we must get to our seats before this crowd gets any thicker. All right there, Highness? All right there, girls?"

It was the most remarkable spectacle Cristina had ever beheld. More than twenty thousand persons were packed into the vast arena, filling it to overflowing. Many of them, Mr. Rhodes told her, had been there since four in the afternoon, when the doors were opened. It was now after nine, and white-coated vendors of beer and sandwiches and chocolate moved slowly up and down the aisles. The audience patronized these vendors liberally, eating and drinking as they listened to the speeches, but this did not surprise Cristina, who had already noticed that German crowds seldom stopped eating and drinking, even in moments of tense excitement. That this was a moment of tense excitement she could not possibly doubt. Never had she heard such applause as that with which the Minister was constantly interrupted. Moreover, the twenty thousand kept rising as one man, with outflung arms and outstretched hands, which looked like endless flocks of birds suddenly summoned into flight. When at last Goering finished his speech, when the folded banners at the back of the stage were unfurled and swung out in the full force of their scarlet splendor, when the band began to play *Die Fahne Hoch* and every man and woman in the building began to sing, the sight, the sound, the surge of it all was almost overpowering. Even as an onlooker, even as an outsider, she was caught up in the vital current of force and feeling that flowed through the building.

What Goering actually said seemed comparatively unimportant, and Cristina could not understand why it roused such boundless enthusiasm. He attacked Communism, parliamentarianism, pacifism, the German Supreme Court, the Jews, and the Catholic clergy. She was puzzled and a little troubled by his remark about priests, but decided that perhaps her knowledge of German was not sufficiently thorough to enable her to understand him correctly. At all events, it was the unanimous force with which his remarks were greeted, rather than their own violence, which especially impressed her. That one man—even the Minister of a great country—should say what he did might have no portentous significance. That multitudes should applaud his words caused her to ponder deeply.

The following day she stumbled upon a gathering even more astounding. The Archduchess had insisted upon spending the election period secluded in her hotel suite. It was not until late in the afternoon that she consented to go out, accompanied by Cristina. Nowhere did the streets present the slightest sign of agitation. Indeed, except for a few casual Sunday strollers, these were entirely empty. At last, having traversed the entire length of Unter den Linden without any kind of provocative encounter, they turned towards the Lutheran Cathedral. Cristina might find a Protestant service interesting, the Archduchess said, if it was really true that she had never seen one. At any rate, they could sit at the Cathedral quietly for half an hour and rest before walking back to their hotel.

Instead, they were unexpectedly swept into the vortex of a throng of people who were streaming into the great building, and propelled into seats in a crowded gallery—the nave being already full to overflowing. A black-robed verger had thrust an Order of Exercises into Cristina's hand, and she studied it as she waited for those to begin. It bore the heading *Gottesdienst der Deutschen Sendung*—"A Service of the German Mission"—and this service began with a gospel reading taken from Mark 1:15: "The time is fulfilled, and the kingdom of God is at hand." She was slightly startled at the obvious implication which had been given to this famous quotation; but she became very much more startled as the exercises progressed. For this reading from the Scriptures was followed by two extraordinary songs. The first of these was sung with great feeling and fervor by the massed congregation accompanied by the splendid organ, and was entitled *The Time Has Come, The Time of Times.* Though it was not actually offensive, it was permeated with *double entendre.* The second was sung by a male choir, which, clad in flowing white garments confined by twisted and knotted girdles, advanced up the center aisle as it chanted slowly, without accompaniment and apparently with no sense of sacrilege:

Black is the cross that was borne by our Savior,
Black is the cross that God has laid on us.
Take it upon you, Germans, without complaint,
Carry it silently and strongly, as the Savior carried his.

After these two songs came numerous others, similar in type, as well as numerous other readings from the Scriptures. Cristina followed with amazement a passage from Matthew 24:29–31 for which were given correlative passages from Mark 13:24–27 and Luke 21:25–26:

Immediately after the tribulation of those days shall the sun be darkened, and the moon shall not give her light, and the stars shall fall from the heavens, and the powers of the heavens shall be shaken:

And then shall appear the sign of the Son of man in heaven: and then shall all the tribes of the earth mourn, and they shall see the Son of man coming in the clouds of heaven with power and great glory.

And he shall send his angels with a great sound of a trumpet, and they shall gather together his elect from the four winds, from one end of heaven to the other.

Even a person as inexperienced as Cristina, attending such a service on an election day, could not fail to be impressed by its extraordinary character. As they went down the steps of the Cathedral, the Archduchess remarked, somewhat satirically, that the peculiar partnership with God, which the ex-Kaiser so frequently voiced, still seemed to prevail, that the German people had apparently never been more firmly convinced that the Almighty was for them and that therefore they might safely assume that no one could be against them.

"I suppose it is this conviction which permits them to make comparisons and use similes which are very close to blasphemous," she continued. "But they do not appear any less shocking to me on that account. Indeed, they seem to lack sanity as much as they lack reverence. I am really very much upset. I feel that I shall have to return to my own room and lie down."

They had already agreed to go to the Embassy for that strange period called the "cocktail hour," and the Rhodes had sent the official car to the Bristol. In view of Victoria Luise's collapse, Cristina was obliged to take this alone; and after she had arrived at her destination, she found that there were apparently no other guests. Her light step made no sound on the carpeted stairway, so no one was instantly aware of her presence. But she could hear Beatrice and Richard Eustis carrying on an animated conversation in the drawing room beyond, and for a moment or two she was an involuntary eavesdropper.

"I always did think he had a screw loose, from the moment I heard about this crazy scheme of going away from Hamstead and making for Schönplatz. What man in his senses would leave a looker like Cristina to spend six months in a Labor Camp?"

"Lots of them. I don't mean that lots of them would leave lookers like Cristina, because there aren't so many in her class. But lots of them leave girls they're pretty fond of, just the same, when they think it's the square thing to do."

"Well, you must be taking leave of your own senses, Trixie. I never expected to see the day when you would stand up for a Nazi. And you know what those Labor Camps are like— It isn't as if you hadn't insisted on seeing one! Will you ever forget that hard-boiled sergeant that was detailed to take us out to the hideous 'hostel,' as they call it—the dreariest, drabbest building I ever saw in my life? Why, he looked like a vaudeville caricature of a German— I couldn't believe he was real! And don't you remember that dismal swamp and the fields of half-frozen ruts he ran us over, to show us the work of 'reclamation'? I was ready to drop in my tracks before I ever got to the hostel at all, and when I did get there, I wished I hadn't."

"I do think it was sort of bare and musty. Except for the Commons Room. You must admit the way the men had painted that was effective."

"Effective! I haven't forgotten the effectiveness of the plumbing—or rather the lack of it! No hot water and only one water closet. Latrines and showers in an outhouse and a limit put on the time you could use them!"

"Card, you're in a parlor, not a pullman smoker."

"All right then, I'll never forget the expression on the men's faces—all of them sober, some of them frightened and sick! Why, not one of them cracked a smile the whole time we were there. Of course I didn't see anything for them to smile about. But then I thought the alleged object of these hostels was to teach the nobility of labor and promote comradeship. Well, I guess the poor devils who go there learn something about labor all right, between five A.M. and ten P.M.—what with their ditch digging and ground clearing and tree chopping! The whole system looks to me like a convenient form of slavery! And if I'm not all wet they learn something about soldiering, too. The only books I saw lying around anywhere were biographies of military big shots and manuals of drill—besides that everlasting *Mein Kampf*, of course. But comradeship! Well all I can say is, it was the dreariest bunch of buddies I ever ran into."

"I hope that's all you will say, for the moment. You've monopolized conversation long enough. And as I have told you before, I wish you wouldn't shout so, when you're where the servants can hear you. We don't know how much of what they hear they repeat, or to whom. And whatever you do, don't do anything that could upset Cristina. She's tops. What's more, she's happy. She's got hold of the best man in the world, and she knows it. If you so much as look at her cross-eyed, I'll give you knockout drops."

Cristina purposely waited a minute before she went on into the drawing room. This was not only because she did not wish to distress Beatrice by betraying the fact that she had overheard Richard Eustis' remarks. It was also because she was thankful to catch at a chair, momentarily, for support. She was dreadfully dizzy. She had never fainted in her life, but she felt as if she were going to faint now. So this hostel which Richard Eustis had been describing was the sort of place where Hans Christian was voluntarily staying for six months! A dismal, dirty, evil-smelling spot where men slaved, but never smiled! Hans Christian, to whom gentleness was a point of honor, and cleanliness a cult, and beauty a creed! It made her sick to think of him there, it revolted her to realize that there he must remain for months and months, while she waited endlessly at home for him, wondering how much he would have changed when he was at last restored to her.

At first the change did not seem to be as great as she had feared, perhaps because she had schooled herself to meet it. She had gone back to Schönplatz the day after the disastrous episode of eavesdropping, and she had never left it again. She had resumed her studying and sewing, her letterwriting and flower fixing, and as the tranquil days flowed past, she recaptured her lost composure. The memories of what she had heard and seen in Berlin became mercifully blurred, and only the thought of Hans Christian remained clear. In her joy over their delayed reunion, she was blinded to any essential change in the image with which she had lived so long.

Little by little she saw him more accurately as he was, but always through eyes of infinite love. If he seemed somewhat sterner, somewhat graver, in his general bearing, what did that matter, so long as his attitude towards her was still one of ardent adoration? If his muscles and his mind had both hardened, were these not added indications of virility? She was still separated from him a great deal, for he was constantly called for conferences at Marienburg, at Königsberg and at Allenstein; and when he was at home, he spent endless hours over his correspondence, sitting at a huge flat-topped desk into which bookshelves were built along the sides. It was an inherited piece of great value and beauty; and when he found that he could trust Cristina never to talk to him at times when he was harassed, he caused another precious heirloom to be brought into his study and placed beside the desk: A high-backed sofa, upholstered in crimson velvet, with drawers built underneath the seat and at the two ends, leaving shelves on top where lights and ornaments could be placed. He told her that it had once belonged to a waiting lady of Queen Luise, who had doubtless slept on it in uncertain comfort at the foot of her royal mistress's bed, and kept her own belongings, as best she could, in the amount of drawer space it afforded. Probably she had felt cramped by it, and had longed for a *Himmelbett* and a Danzig chest of her own. Cristina loved it, however. She reclined contentedly on it for indefinite periods, busied with her needlework or looking out at the lake. But she never failed to be conscious of Hans Christian's eyes when he glanced up from his writing in her direction; and if he rose from his desk and came over to her, he always found her arms outstretched and her lips lifted, as she made room for him beside her.

The intervals in the study were subject to frequent interruptions. Hans Christian found his contacts greatly expanded, both because of his Party pursuits and because of his marriage. More and more people came to Schönplatz in these days, not only to meetings but to dinners and dances. In their turn, he and Cristina went to all the adjacent estates. The countryside had taken far more kindly to the bride on her arrival than it had to him when he came to East Prussia. Indeed, it was considerably impressed by her. She was gracious as well as beautiful, and her appearance caused something of a stir in a vicinity of dowdy women. She wore rare laces and rich brocades, high combs and ancient jewels, as no one in the neighborhood had ever worn them before. She carried a painted fan as naturally as she did a fine handkerchief. There was always a flower tucked in the V of her bodice and another in the waves of her hair. She was a great addition to any gathering. She danced divinely, and the light tinkle of her guitar, rising above the sonorous sound of a grand piano, enlivened the stodginess of many a musical evening and sent clear melody rippling through dark drawing rooms and along silent stairways. Though she was completely contented alone, she proved to have a faculty for friendship. Everyone warmed to her sweetness because it was sincere, and she in return found herself happily disposed towards all she met, from the most important *Junker* to the humblest peasant.

There was only one exception to this rule, and Cristina reproached herself because this was the case. There was a young woman named Trudchen in the village, whom she instinctively disliked, and of whose covert disrespect she became more and more conscious. At first she did not see much of the girl; but as the increase in Luischen's family gradually necessitated an increasing amount of extra service, Trudchen was summoned on occasions to the big house, where it appeared she had worked before her own marriage. She was a capable chambermaid, and she took excellent care of the rooms entrusted to her. Cristina's was not among these, but now and then Trudchen came in on some trifling errand, and eventually she brought a small basket of grapes, together with a little painted plate, and set them down on the bedside table.

"Why are you doing that, Trudchen?" Cristina inquired. "I did not ask you for any grapes."

"I know you did not, *Frau Baronin*. But the *Herr Baron* likes to eat them at night, before he goes to sleep."

"What makes you think so?"

"I do not think so, *Frau Baronin*. I know it for a fact. When he comes in, he will tell you so himself."

It was very late before Hans Christian came home from his meeting that night, and Cristina was already in bed when he reached their room. But as he moved about, preparing for bed himself, she was drowsily aware that he was standing beside the table helping himself to grapes. Their pungent smell was still on his lips when he kissed her. She asked him a sleepy question.

"Why did you never tell me that you liked grapes at night, *querido*? I would have seen to it that they were always in readiness for you."

"I haven't thought of eating grapes at night for years. I used to do it though. And when I saw them just now, they looked good to me. How did they happen to be here?"

"A new chambermaid, or rather a former chambermaid who has come back, brought them in. Her name is Trudchen. I suppose she used to take care of your room."

Hans Christian did not answer. Inexplicably, Cristina began to feel more wide awake.

"Did she?"

"Yes, I believe she did. A long time ago."

"Don't you remember her?"

"Yes, I remember her, now that you speak of her. I'd almost forgotten her until you did."

"She's rather a pretty little thing."

"Is she? It's so long since I've noticed anybody's looks except yours darling, and you're so beautiful——"

"But you must have noticed, when she was working here before, that she was pretty!"

"I suppose I must have. But I'd forgotten about that too— Cristina, you've hardly kissed me at all— Aren't you glad I'm back?"

She was very glad he was back, and she kissed him instantly; not long afterwards, she fell asleep. The next day, Trudchen brought grapes into the room again. Cristina said nothing and Hans Christian did not touch them. So the next morning she asked him whether he wanted them or not.

"I don't care," he said curtly.

He had never spoken to her in that tone of voice before. She was so puzzled that she did not know what she should do, and therefore she decided to do nothing. Trudchen continued to bring in the grapes regularly, and one evening, when she set them down on the bedside table, the painted plate hit the rosary that was lying there, and this slid to the floor. Trudchen picked it up and replaced it with abject apologies.

"I'm so sorry, *Frau Baronin.* It is such a pretty thing. I have never seen anything just like it."

"You've never seen a rosary, Trudchen?"

"No. Because I never had the honor of caring for Her Serene Highness's room. Of course I know she has one. I know that rosaries are used by Catholics. But she was the only Catholic here until you came. We are all Lutherans in the village, and the *Herr Baron* was a Lutheran also. There was never a rosary in his room when I formerly took care of him."

"The rosary is mine, Trudchen. I do not think the *Herr Baron* ever uses one."

"Ah— Then what they say in the village is not true. The *Herr Baron* did not become a Catholic when he married the *Frau Baronin.*"

"Yes, he became a Catholic when he married me. My uncle baptized him and he was received quickly into the Church because it was necessary that we should be married at once."

"But the *Frau Baronin* did not have a baby!"

"I'm afraid you did not understand me, Trudchen. It was necessary for us to be married very quickly because there was a revolution in my country, and the *Herr Baron* wanted to take me away from it to a place of safety. He became a Catholic because it simplified the arrangements for our marriage, and because it made me and all my family very happy to have him do so. But it did not mean much to him personally. I suppose that is why he never uses a rosary, as Her Serene Highness does, and as I do."

"I shall repeat what you have told me in the village, *Frau Baronin.* It will restore the *Herr Baron* to greater respect. I am sure that no one cares whether you and Her Serene Highness use rosaries. But for a leader in the New Party——"

Trudchen's face had resumed its usual blank expression, and Cristina wondered why she had troubled to enter into explanations with an empty-headed little chambermaid. But all her life she had been used to the friendly familiarity existing between Spanish servants and their superiors, and it had not been easy for her to break away from it and to assume the habits of Prussian discipline. Because she was slightly concerned at her own lapse from correctness, she mentioned the matter to Hans Christian later in the evening. He had not been obliged to go to a meeting that night, and they were walking quietly beside the lake when she told him. To her infinite surprise, he spoke to her even more curtly than he had when the subject of Trudchen came up before.

"I can't imagine what you were thinking of, Cristina! You shouldn't even speak to a little slut like that. You, of all persons!"

"What do you mean, *querido,* me of all persons?"

"You can't understand because you're so different. I worship you because you are. Please do as I say."

"So different from what, *querido?* And what makes you think Trudchen is not a girl of good character merely because she seems a little silly and forward? Why do you use such a dreadful word in speaking of her?"

"I could have used a much worse one. I shall if she ever comes into our room again. See that she is dismissed tomorrow."

"But, Hansel——"

"You heard what I said. I won't have her in the house."

Cristina had never dismissed a servant, she had no idea how it should be done. She tried to speak very kindly when she told Trudchen that they would not need her any more. But while she was worrying lest Trudchen's feelings should be hurt, she saw that a sly little smile was playing around the peasant's lips.

"I did not mean to displease the *Frau Baronin* by coming to her room. But it seemed natural for me to do so. I used to be there so much. And of course it makes no difference to me whether I work at the Great House or not. Because the *Herr Baron* has never ceased to send money to my family. He has kept his promise to me, he has done so for many years. He has always paid for his pleasure. I know that he always will."

Trudchen dropped a quick curtsey and was gone. Her sly smile was the last thing Cristina saw. Then she herself sat down unseeingly by the window and tried to be calm, tried to be composed, as usual. But she felt as if she had been cut to the heart, not by a clean swift dagger, but by a jagged knife which had stuck there, and which kept turning in the wound. All the flawless memories of her marriage to Hans Christian were suddenly smirched and stained. Now she understood why his first approach to her had been so skillful. He had not been guided by the instincts of love, as she had supposed; he had been schooled by sensual experience. And he had always paid for his pleasure. He had *paid*—for what she had gloried in giving him! How could she ever give him anything again? If only she could leave the Great House that very night and go to a convent—there must still be convents somewhere that were safe! If only she did not have to think of her mother's words, of which she had not thought since her wedding night, but which rose to haunt her now, that since she had spurned her vocation, she must accept her suffering! If only she already had conceived a child! Then perhaps she could reconcile her conscience to a withdrawal. But until she had given an heir to the Great House, she could not choose but stay there, she could not evade her duty. She understood that other saying now too, that a wife must submit to her husband, even under compulsion. Would Hans Christian use compulsion? Would he forget that he had said he did not want her to yield to his will, only to trust to his tenderness? She had trusted him unconditionally, and now her confidence had brought her to this pass——

She heard his step, the step for which she had always listened with such eagerness, and which now she dreaded to find approaching. She shrank back in her chair, wondering what she would do when he came up to her, how she would greet him, how she would tell him——

She did not need to try. He knew what had happened the instant he looked at her. He sank down on the floor at her feet, and took her hand and covered it with kisses.

"My darling—if I could only have spared you this——"

"But why couldn't you?"

She had thought she would not be able to speak to him. But now the cry came straight from her soul.

"It happened long before I ever knew you, before I dreamed that I ever would know you— Cristina, this is what almost every man has to confess, sooner or later, to the woman he loves."

"Almost every man? But I thought you were different from every other man!"

"I'm not. That's what I hoped you'd never have to learn."

"Have you— Was there ever anyone else beside Trudchen?"

"Darling, do you have to ask me? Do you have to keep on torturing us both? Can't you say to yourself, 'I'm the only woman Hans Christian has ever loved, the only woman he ever will love. He's mine now, body and soul. This is all that matters.'"

"Could you say that, if before I knew you, someone had——"

"No— No— No! But men are different, Cristina! It isn't the same thing, you must believe me when I tell you it isn't!"

Still clasping her hand he laid his head down on her lap. She could feel him clinging to her, she could hear his muffled pleading. Until then she had leaned on him, she had relied on him. Now he was leaning on her, he was relying on her. The jagged knife ceased to turn in her heart. She knew that she could not repulse him now, that he needed her as he never had before, that he was indeed all hers. Their interdependence was complete.

It was soon after this that Cristina began to believe she was going to have a child at last. But she did not want to tell Hans Christian until she was sure, to raise his hopes only to dash them again. She was eager to let him know that out of their mutual suffering had come the blessing which had been denied them as long as they had known only rapture; but she waited until she herself felt secure in her certainty. Then she decided to share her secret with him the first night that she felt his mood was propitious for such joyful tidings.

It was mid June when she concluded that she could not wait any longer, that her heart would burst with happiness if she did not unburden it. Hans Christian had been gone all day—a day of serene beauty, still and balmy. The roses were blooming in the garden, and the scent of them was lifted to her room. Early in the evening a young moon appeared in the sky, which was still blue as a sapphire; when the stars came out its color seemed only to deepen. Entranced by the beauty of it, arching in sparkling splendor over the trees and the lake, Cristina left her room in darkness to see it the more clearly, as she listened to Hans Christian's footsteps, her overburdened heart pulsing so hard that she seemed to hear its beating.

At last she heard him, too, coming up the stairs. In another instant he would have opened the door to their room, he would have caught her up and crushed her to him. She was sure of this, for he had never failed to do so as soon as he came home. But this time he crossed the echoing hallway in the opposite direction and rapped on Ernst's door instead. Ernst called out cordially from within, then came quickly to the threshold, flinging the door open.

"*Grüss Gott!* What can I do for you?"

"Ernst, wasn't your father in the War?"

"Of course, he was killed in the War. Near the very beginning, at Mülhausen."

"And your mother, what about her?"

"She died too. I thought you knew. Of heartbreak, I've always believed. She was an Alsatian, you know. Wars are always hard on these border people."

"What was her maiden name?"

"Weiller. Johanna Weiller. It's a common enough name. What makes you ask?"

"And what was *her* mother's maiden name?"

"Let me see– I've never known much about my forebears, never cared much. Poor people don't, Hansel, the way you *Junkers* do. But I think it was Bernstein– Yes, I'm almost sure it was Bernstein."

"Oh, my God!"

"Hansel, I don't know what you're driving at. Why on earth are you waking me up at midnight to ask me what my mother's maiden name was?"

"Because I've been asked myself what it was, by certain high officials. They think I should have asked you myself, when I suggested that you should come to Schönplatz to take charge– How many Aryans did you ever know whose name was Bernstein, Ernst?"

There was an interminable silence. Then Ernst began to speak again, very slowly and earnestly.

"Hansel, I don't know what to say. I swear to you that I never thought of this, that it never entered my head. I'd rather have cut off my right hand, I'd rather have died, than have made trouble for you. After all you've done for Luischen and me. After I've grown to care so for you."

"I know, Ernst, I know you're telling the truth, and I care for you, too. But——"

"Do you want us to go away? Do you want me to take Luischen and the children and go? If you do, we'll go at once."

"You'll go at once? You'll go where? Have you seen the signs posted in every village? If you were still living in Munich, if you'd never left there, you might be able to get away with staying. But to try to return——"

"We could go to Alsace. That's French now. We could take refuge among my mother's people."

"And what about Luischen? She isn't French, she isn't Jewish either. She's my own cousin. What about the children? You've got a son; he just escapes the three generation ban. He'll grow up a fine German boy, he's a fine German boy already. He'll be fitted, in a few years, to lead the Schönplatz *Jugend*. I've been counting on it, since I haven't a son of my own, or any hope of one! He's my next of kin in the family of the future— No, I won't have him go, I won't have any of you go. I'll keep you all here, no matter what's said to me— I've given in on enough other points, against my better judgment, against my conscience— Surely this time— Besides, how could I keep the place going, as far as that goes, if I didn't keep you? I can't be tearing from one end of Prussia to the other unless I've someone to leave here, someone that I can trust."

He stopped abruptly. His vehemence had spent itself. He spoke again shortly.

"I'm sorry I waked you up, Ernst, all for nothing. I was upset myself. It made me thoughtless. We'll find a way to fix things up. I'm very fond of you. Don't worry. Good night."

"Good night, Hansel. And thanks again for all you've done for me."

Hans Christian was crossing the hall, he was coming to his own room, which was still unlighted. But in the dimness he could see Cristina standing there, waiting for him, numb with horror. He switched on the electricity and looked at her searchingly.

"What are you doing? Eavesdropping?"

"I didn't mean to, Hansel. I couldn't help overhearing. This is the second time I've listened, when I couldn't help it, to something I'd have given my soul not to hear."

"And when was the other time? You better tell me!"

She told him, hesitantly, haltingly, struggling to keep back the tears as she did so. Dreadful as the details about the Labor Camp had once seemed to her, she could not even keep her mind on them as she talked about them now. She could think of nothing but Ernst, who was so tireless and faithful, of Luischen, who was so comely and cheerful, of the three children whom she so dearly loved. *The children!* How could she tell Hans Christian now that they were to have a child of their own? If she did, might it mean that after all he would send Ernst away? If she could only know that she would have a daughter, she might dare to tell him. She prayed that she would have a daughter. She who had prayed so long for a son. And distractedly, she went on talking about something else while she prayed, until Hans Christian cut her short.

"Richard Eustis was always a damned fool. I'm sorry you ever saw him. He's filled you full of lies. I'll tell you myself what a Labor Camp is really like, sometime, since you're so curious about it. But not to-night. I've got too much else on my mind. And I'm tired. God, but I'm tired! If I don't get some sleep, I'll go crazy myself, along with most of the rest of the world."

The next day he was called to Berlin. He did not tell Cristina why and she did not ask. After all, he had been called there often, now that so many dreadful things were happening in Germany. The Reichstag had been burned; all was not well with the Party; there had been suspicion of treason in high places. This much she did know and it was enough; she wanted him to be free to serve, and she had never lost her faculty for waiting. But the only hours that mattered to her were still the ones which she spent with him; and she had decided that this time, when he came home, she would tell him about the child. She had resolved to do that, no matter what happened.

His absence had not been protracted when he wired her that he would be home the next evening. All through the summer night she waited, thrilling to his approach. And still there was no sound of his car in the driveway or of his footfall on the stair.

When morning came, she went with a haggard face to Victoria Luise and together they tried to telephone. They could learn nothing. No one knew what had become of Hans Christian von Hohenlohe.

CHAPTER 27

THE AMERICAN AMBASSADOR sat in the palatial headquarters of the Gestapo on the Prinz Albrecht Strasse, facing a high official across a polished desk. His manner was completely controlled. But his voice, though that was controlled also, was edged with anger and anxiety.

"This is a very serious matter, *Herr Offizier*."

The *Herr Offizier* shrugged his shoulders, so slightly that the movement was hardly noticeable. He spoke civilly, with almost imperceptible contempt.

"It is regrettable, certainly. But as I have said already, there is nothing I can do about it."

"I believe it was Napoleon who said 'If a thing is possible, it can be done. If it is impossible, it must be done.' I am asking you to accomplish something that must be done."

"Many of Napoleon's maxims sound impressive. But he died in exile, on a lonely little island. It would seem, Your Excellency, as if escape from this would have been one of the impossibilities which he felt must be achieved."

The argument was unanswerable. Rufus Rhodes cursed himself inwardly for having laid himself open to it. He should have learned, long before, that he could not compete with men like this in adroitness. He had to try to cope with them otherwise.

"Hans von Hohenlohe is half American. His mother occupies a position of great power. She is very close to the White House, and the President has already protested, as you know. Now Senator Marlowe is on her way over here. I think it is highly advisable, from every point of view, that her son should be found before she arrives."

"Certainly it would be gratifying. Any mother is naturally anxious concerning the safety of her son; some mothers are overanxious. But that seems to me slightly beyond the present point, in common with most of your remarks, if you will permit the observation, Excellency. It would have been easy enough for Hans von Hohenlohe to become an American citizen. His own father paved the way for such an action. But he did not choose to do so. Instead he chose to come to Germany, to take over his ancestral estates, and eventually to affiliate himself with the National Socialist Party. I cannot conceive that if a man who was half German chose to go to the United States, establish himself on American soil, and become an active Democrat, that the President of your country would consider our Chancellor responsible provided this man was absent, without explanation, from his home. Neither can we accept responsibility for the case under discussion. As a matter of fact, our government has tactfully refrained from any official comment on many cases of kidnapping, lynching, and other American atrocities which seem to us uncivilized, to say the least. In return, we should be much obliged if your government would show similar restraint under much less provocation."

The high official picked up a folder which lay on the glass-topped desk and glanced at a neatly tabulated file which it contained. Then he spoke gravely.

"I am sorry to say that the record of the young man in whom you are good enough to show so much concern is not altogether commendable. His moral character, for instance, leaves much to be desired."

"His moral character!"

"Yes. He had hardly arrived in East Prussia when he seduced an innocent young peasant. Although she is now happily married to an honest villager, he still forces her to come to the *Herrenhaus,* ostensibly to work there. But the sums he continues to pay her are suspiciously large, and out of all proportion to his Party contributions."

"I know something about that case. I'd like to tell you the other side——"

"I should be interested in hearing it sometime. But for the moment, as our time is limited, suppose you permit me to go on. There is a young nurse in Nuremberg, whom Hans von Hohenlohe met when he first went there to a celebration of the Parteitag. Instead of attending its every function with fervor, he left his troop, whenever he could, to visit this girl. She is one of our most faithful followers. She noted down for us each of these lapses from grace."

"You mean she was deliberately set to spy on him?"

"I mean that we do not countenance laxity of any kind, Your Excellency, in our code of discipline and training. The new Reich must be cleansed of everything carnal and we are taking steps to see that it shall be. Hans von Hohenlohe has repeatedly disregarded our rules respecting this. His very marriage was an added affront to them. When he was given leave of absence to go to Spain, this was to recuperate from a severe wound; it was not to court the daughter of a decadent family. Yet he returned to it a second time, on the pretext of an emergency, and later it was revealed that this emergency was a hasty wedding. His attitude towards his wife is uxorious. He resents the slightest separation from her. And she is childless. By now she should have given three sturdy sons to the State."

"She's a beautiful, noble girl, who worships the ground he walks on!"

"I am not concerned with her beauty or her nobility or her senseless adoration. I am concerned only with her barrenness. And, I might add, with her religion. These Catholic women are usually a bad influence. Hans von Hohenlohe has been caught between two of them—one in her first and the other in her second childhood. The Austrian Archduchess is as bad as the Spanish princess. He also has an aunt who is a Carmelite nun in Cologne. And he has not had the sense to resist their wiles. He has become a Catholic himself! When, as he knew, we had millions of them to deal with already, to bring to heel, to exterminate!"

The official's expressionless face had suddenly become distorted. He brought his fist down on the desk with a bang. Then, controlling himself quickly, he picked up the file again and went on reading.

"The fact that Hans von Hohenlohe is a voluptuary and a Papist is lamentable enough in itself. But there are much more serious charges against him. He has repeatedly questioned Party principles. He had begun to do this even before Horst Wessel died. It required endless effort on the part of his comrades to keep him in line. He has, on occasion, failed to completely carry out orders, when these involved the forceful methods which our Leader knows to be necessary. Worst of all, he has harbored a Jew in his own house. This Jew's wife is the sister of Karl Welder, an avowed Communist and a ringleader at the Liebknecht Haus. He and Hans von Hohenlohe have been seen talking together in the street. Moreover, this woman's father is an unreclaimed monarchist, who spends half his time at Doorn hatching plots for the restoration of the monarchy. The whole setup could hardly be more damaging."

"*Herr* von Hohenlohe was completely unaware of Ernst Behrend's antecedents."

"He did plead ignorance on that score. But he was fully informed by the authorities, whom he next defied. They have been extremely patient with his shortcomings, because to offset these, he had a powerful position and certain commendable qualities. He inspired confidence in our cause, and he awakened the affection of his men, though he had never commanded the respect of his neighbors. But there is a limit to such patience. Possibly this has been reached. It would seem to be conceivable, under all the circumstances. But be that as it may, I cannot tell you what has become of Hans von Hohenlohe."

"You mean that you won't?"

"I mean what I said, Your Excellency, that I cannot. It is possible, of course, that he may have been taken into protective custody. It is also possible that he may have met with some unfortunate accident. In the latter case, his body will eventually be found and returned to his family by the authorities, with the usual recommendation that they should spare themselves needless suffering by refraining from opening the casket. In the former case, he will eventually communicate with his family himself, if he cares to do so. Correspondence is censored at concentration camps, but it is stopped only in very unusual cases."

"It never begins at all, does it, after certain 'examinations'?"

The high official rose, replacing the file he had been holding neatly in the folder. He bowed from the waist.

"I am afraid Your Excellency has been reading extracts from the American Jewish Press, which makes up in hysteria what it lacks in accuracy. I am sorry that I have not been able to be of more service. Some other morning perhaps— I know you will excuse me now. Unfortunately, I must leave you to keep a pressing appointment."

Rufus Rhodes had never seen Faith Marlowe, though he had read and listened to countless stories about her since she had become a legend on the American scene. He had heard that she was both lovely and beloved. But according to rumor, she had always been sought after vainly. Her marriage had been unhappy, her widowhood impregnable. In her youth she had been the inspiration of a great painter's genius and he had immortalized her beauty without benefiting by it. She owed her political progress to an obscure and grotesque local "boss," named Caleb Hawks. All this was more or less hearsay, like the tales of her estrangement from her son. All that Mr. Rhodes actually knew was that she had resumed her maiden name with her American citizenship; that she had shown herself an able member of the group self-styled as the "greatest legislative body in the world"; and that she "stood in well" with the White House.

He felt poorly prepared to meet her as he paced up and down at the airport, waiting for her plane to come in. She had made the quickest possible crossing, and had flown from London to Berlin. Trixie, who had gone out to the airport with him, did not seem to share his qualms. He often thought that if it had not been for her, he could not have stuck to his post, that he would have sent in his resignation long before. Only her cheerful and courageous acceptance of conditions as they were in Germany at present made them tolerable for him. And this last week he had been worried about her. She was very pale, she did not smile or say much; he missed her lovely color, her inconsequential chatter. But now, as she linked her arm through his, he felt vaguely comforted.

"I think we're going to like Senator Marlowe, Daddy. I believe she's going to be wonderful."

She was indeed wonderful. They saw that from the moment she stepped out of the plane. Inevitably, it was her beauty which struck them first, the beauty to which the thousands of pictures representing her had never done her full justice. Her face and figure were both flawless in their perfection, and no hat could hide the glory of her red-gold hair. She was a woman in her middle forties, but she could easily have passed for twenty years less, if her expression had not lacked the softness and her carriage the suppleness of youth. Her lovely lips closed in a line that was almost hard; there was a suggestion of sharpness in the contour of her cheeks, a look of lost gentleness in her eyes. She held herself erect and moved with dignity; she had great presence. Nevertheless, some quality essential to supreme charm was missing.

"She's putting up a brave front," Rufus Rhodes said to himself, "she's beside herself with fear and grief, and she's determined not to show it. That's what gives her such a look." But even before the thought was fully formulated, he knew it was not wholly correct. Faith Marlowe's air of defensiveness was nothing new; she must have had it a long time. Such lines did not come overnight into a woman's face, nor such rigidity into a fine figure. He must seek further back for their underlying reasons.

"Have you any news for me at all, Mr. Ambassador?"

"No, none. But don't be discouraged—that is, any more than you can help. I've got all sorts of lines out. And I've made appointments for you with several great personages, tomorrow. I'll tell you as we go along— Senator Marlowe, I nearly forgot. This is my daughter, Beatrice."

They shook hands, regarding each other with covert appraisal. It was approving on both sides. Trixie possessed herself of the Senator's dispatch case, speaking in a low voice as she leaned forward to take it.

"I'm driving the car myself, we'll have a chance to talk. A motor is about the only place where we can be sure we're not overheard."

Faith Marlowe nodded. She liked the way the girl faced facts, her brisk manner of walking, the effect of her clothes. Here, indubitably, would have been a desirable daughter-in-law, she reflected, as she got into the car and felt it start off, swiftly yet smoothly. Tense as the moment was, she could not help wondering why she had not achieved Trixie as such.

"Cristina is not in Berlin?" she inquired, indirectly following her own train of thought.

"No. She could not leave the Archduchess. The poor old lady's heart is in bad condition, and this shock has been too much for it. She is completely prostrated, and the end might come at any time. Besides, the entire management of the estate has fallen upon Cristina. Ernst Behrend felt, no doubt rightly, that if he were no longer in the picture, the situation might be eased, at least. He has taken his entire family and gone to Alsace. Of course he has not been able to carry any money out with him, and his French relatives were in straitened circumstances already. But possibly a way can be found to cope with that condition."

"Yes, of course," Senator Marlowe said quietly. "Everything possible should be done for Ernst Behrend and it will be— And possibly I may be able to help Cristina with the management of the estate and the care of *Tante* Luise. I have had a good deal of experience on my own farm, in Hamstead, and I have always been very fond of my mother-in-law— You think it would be well if I went on to East Prussia myself, do you not, as soon as I have kept the appointments you have made for me here?"

"Yes, that would be the best plan. Candidly, I am afraid the appointments may not amount to very much in the end. The Ministers you meet will be extremely civil and completely inactive. Presidential protests from America do not move them at all."

Mr. Rhodes spoke with angry contempt and deep concern. Faith Marlowe answered him with the same calmness she had shown before.

"I know. And of course President Conrad has always been bitterly opposed to the course Hansel took, and to my acceptance of it. He has been civil and correct in his behavior towards me during this crisis, as you say the Ministers will be. But I have known that he was saying 'I told you so!' to himself all the time."

There was not a break in her voice. But Mr. Rhodes found it hard to control his own as he took up the thread of conversation again.

"I'm sorry, but I'm afraid you're right. And I don't seem to get anywhere myself. Of course I've been to the *Polizeipräsidium*, to the Columbia Haus—in fact everywhere, for long conferences. I really don't believe that your son is in any of these places, or at Plötzensee or Oranienburg, or a concentration camp of any kind, for that matter. I think he really has disappeared. What happened prior to the disappearance, there is no way of telling. It is all the harder to trace the circumstances because he himself invariably said so little about his plans and orders. He never discussed them with his wife or his grandmother. He did not make mental companions of either one. He may have started for the prearranged meeting of the S. A. leaders at Wiesse, and never have reached there. Some men were arrested on the road in their cars, some at the railroad station as they got out of the train. Or he may have actually arrived, and come to grief afterwards. On the other hand, he may not have meant to go to Wiesse at all. Our lack of knowledge is very complicating. But at least we know what precipitated his disappearance—which is more than many people do under similar circumstances. Often a man's family and friends can't even find out of what he is accused."

"Would you mind telling me just what you mean by 'disappearance,' Mr. Rhodes? I promise you that I shall not have hysterics. Do you mean that you think that Hansel is dead already?"

He hesitated, but he believed her; she was the kind of woman who could take the truth. He decided to give it to her.

"I don't know, Senator Marlowe. There have been a good many cases where men under arrest were 'accidentally' killed. There have been some where there was no pretense that there had been an accident, when there was open admission that they had been 'punished' on purpose. You know that this latest episode is boldly called a 'blood purge.' If it would help to harrow you with tales of torture, I would tell them to you. But it would not. Just now there is a reign of terror in Germany. It is horrible for its victims, and it is even more horrible for the nation. The Third Reich can never retrieve what it has forfeited during this so-called 'Night of Long Knives.'"

"Then the accounts of this have not been exaggerated?"

"I do not see how they could be. There are about eighty acknowledged dead. I should not be surprised if the real number were ten times as large."

"But a few have escaped, Daddy. You know that two or three have managed to get away somehow. I am sure that Hans Christian has."

"What makes you think so, Beatrice?"

For the first time there was a trace of tenderness in Faith Marlowe's voice. The answer to her question came clearly and instantaneously.

"Because I know Chris. There's something about him that Hitler couldn't kill!"

Her conviction of this remained unshaken, at least outwardly. During the difficult days which followed, she went with Faith Marlowe to one Ministry after another, driving the car herself, and sitting patiently in antechambers, while the Senator was closeted with dignitaries. She insisted that she rather liked "waiting outside with the weapons," and she admitted that she sometimes struck up conversations with guards, partly to pass the time and partly on the off-chance of gleaning some valuable information. She also took Faith Marlowe to Friedrichshain, to the hospital which now bore Horst Wessel's name, to the Nicolai Friedhof, where "comrades" were constantly forgathering around his decorated grave, and to the Bomb Palast where the lost leader and Hans Christian had first met each other. One never knew, she kept saying insistently, when some helpful hint might stray in their direction. She declined to be discouraged, even when Oskar Kraus rebuffed them.

"He is really a very kind person," she said, as they drove unwelcomed away. "The first time I saw him was after I had been accidently hit in one of those wild street brawls they specialize in here. I was with Chris, and Oskar Kraus asked us both into his lodgings. He took care of me as kindly as if I had been a baby and he had been my nurse. And when Chris was in the hospital—why Oskar actually haunted it! Well, it does give you a queer feeling when someone who's shown qualities like that practically slams the door in your face. But there's something behind all this. We'll find out what it is yet."

Days passed, and still they did not. But she declined to admit either deception or defeat. She merely suggested that they might as well go on to Schönplatz.

"I'd love to drive you over there, I really would, Senator Marlowe. I've always wanted to go and Chris never invited me. Now this will give me a chance. And it will give us both something to do. There's nothing so bad as waiting around, is there, and feeling that nothing's worth while, as you go on pretending, buying new clothes, and making up your face and drinking cocktails before dinner? But Chris wouldn't want anyone to feel that way. He'd want us to make a stab at keeping up appearances. He wouldn't want these ruffians to have the satisfaction of knowing they'd got us down."

"I think you're probably right, Trixie."

"I know darned well I'm right. Besides, I know that the Archduchess and Cristina are simply counting the moments until you get to Schönplatz. In addition to worrying over Chris, they are grieving for Gabriel de Cerreno. His death wasn't unexpected, for he had been frail a long time and he'd been through a great deal in these last years. Still, it came as a shock, and they need comfort. Besides, I know they have a feeling that when you arrive and take charge everything will be better. Of course it will be, too— We could start tomorrow morning, if you like."

Faith Marlowe, secretly more sick at heart every day, agreed that it might be just as well, and neither Mr. nor Mrs. Rhodes put any impediment in their path. In fact, the Ambassador agreed with Trixie that Faith Marlowe was needed at Schönplatz and that there was nothing she could do, momentarily at least, in Berlin. So they started off without further delay. Trixie drove through to Danzig without difficulty in a day, and late as it was when they arrived there, insisted that they must go to Lauterbach's to dinner, that it was the best restaurant north of Paris, and that some *Danziger Goldwasser* would cheer them both up. The next morning she circled expertly around points of interest in the quaint old town before they took the road for Marienburg, deftly dodging various groups of *Hitler-Jugend* which were on the march.

"Talk about being more Catholic than the Pope!" she remarked. "This place is more Nazi than Berlin. The *Free* City of Danzig! It's about as free as a convict. And the Poles are about as popular as polecats would be. I was waked up at break of dawn by those Hitler kids singing under my window, weren't you? And I'd just drowsed off again when along came two brass bands. Do you know what I think, Senator Marlowe? I think if you can manage to thrust a German into some kind of uniform—it doesn't much matter what kind—and start him off behind a band, he'll go anywhere. Do you remember that story about the Pied Piper? Well, it looks to me as if the same sort of thing was happening now."

Faith Marlowe glanced at her attentively, struck by the shrewdness of the comment, and increasingly convinced that as Trixie herself might have expressed it, here was a "great girl."

"Perhaps I wasn't very tactful to talk that way about Germans," Trixie went on. "I keep forgetting you married one. Of course you know a lot more about them than I do."

"I didn't, when I got married." Faith Marlowe paused for a moment and then went on, with a candor curiously contradictory to her controlled voice, "If I had, I never should have married one, Beatrice. I like you so much that I can't help telling you I'm glad you haven't made the same kind of mistake."

"The only reason I haven't married a German is because the one I cared about didn't want me. If he had, nothing would have stopped me. I did everything I could think of— I don't mean vamping, I mean trying to improve. It wasn't any use. And then I made a terrible mistake. The first time he confided in me, when he was just on the point of proposing, I argued with him. I thought I knew more about what he was saying than he did. I still think so. But he couldn't take it. He was terribly hurt and terribly angry— After a long time, we made up, sort of. But only because he was sick, only because I was careful not to get controversial and he was too weak to try. And right after that, he fell for someone else. Hard, the way I had for him. Someone who'd never have a thought or a feeling that wasn't the same as his, someone who'd never try to find out what was on his mind unless he told her of his own accord, much less quarrel with him about it. Someone who'd just lie down and let him love her. I guess that's what Germans want out of girls, Senator Marlowe."

"I have often thought the same thing, my dear. And it is very fortunate you found this out before you married one, instead of afterwards. Though of course you will never believe this."

"Of course I shan't. If I'd only had him just for a little while— But never to have him at all—that's what hurts so, that's what I'll never get over. I can't seem to put him out of my mind. I'd like to get married, I never was cut out for an old maid. I'd like a lot of children too, and I bet I could take them right in my stride, without losing my health or my figure. But every time I almost make up my mind to go ahead, something stops me. I just can't do it. I've just written a man who's been proposing to me periodically for ten years that I never want to see him or hear from him again."

Faith Marlowe put out her gloved hand and lightly touched the bare brown one that held the wheel so firmly. There was affection as well as understanding in her voice when she answered.

"I know something about that too, Beatrice. Perhaps someday we'll talk it over—someday when we're surer we can keep calm than we are just now. We're both carrying a pretty heavy load. But I believe we're going to help each other carry it. I believe we're going to be great friends."

She turned away, pretending not to see the tears that had fallen from Trixie's eyes to her own gloved hand. But she did not overlook the generosity and justice in Trixie's next remarks.

"What I said a few minutes ago wasn't fair, Senator Marlowe. The German I care about didn't fall for this other girl because she was a door mat. She did think he was perfect— She still thinks so. But he thought she was perfect too, and she was— She is. She isn't beautiful but dumb. She's beautiful and everything else besides—gentle and gracious and good. I mean really good, not just namby-pamby. You'll see—of course you know whom I've been talking about. But I can't help it. I had to tell you."

"I'm so glad you did, Beatrice—so glad and grateful. And I am sure you are right, sure that this girl of whom you speak is—almost irresistible. You see, I knew her father."

It was a beautiful midsummer day. They lunched at Marienburg, and Trixie, completely calm again, suggested that they should stop to see the Stronghold of the Teutonic Knights before they went on. She felt sure that both the Archduchess and Cristina took siestas in the early afternoon; there was no point in pushing themselves; they might better plan to reach Schönplatz about teatime. Again Faith Marlowe agreed with her, and they made their way along at a rate surprisingly moderate for Trixie, talking to each other with increasing ease and intimacy as they went. It was nearly six o'clock when they skirted the vine-covered walls and turned in at the iron gateway leading to the *Herrenhaus.*

A young woman in peasant costume was standing at the door, evidently awaiting them. There was nothing strange about this, for Trixie had telephoned from Marienburg, announcing the approximate time of their arrival. But there was something surprising in the smugness of the servant's plump and pretty face. Both Faith and Trixie were conscious of it while she was still curtseying to them, before she had actually spoken.

"The *Frau Baronin* will be here as soon as possible to welcome Your Excellencies. But she may be delayed for a few moments. Something very sad has happened. Her Serene Highness has had another severe shock."

"What do you mean?" Faith Marlowe asked, almost sharply.

"Your pardon, Excellency. Will you not be pleased to enter the Great Hall? The *Frau Baronin* will be down at any instant and Fritz will come to occupy himself with the car and the baggage. It is this way: Her Serene Highness has seldom cared to read the papers in recent years. But this afternoon, for some reason, the radio was turned on, and she accidentally heard an announcement concerning the death of the Austrian Chancellor—Dolfuss, was that his name? Her Serene Highness became convinced that he had been murdered. Nothing could dissuade her. She cried out wildly that this was the beginning of the end in Austria. Then more news filtered through from the village. It seems that this Dolfuss was a Catholic, that he did not receive the last rites before he died. Her Serene Highness cried out still more wildly that his murderers must have prevented his absolution. She was quite unreasonable, quite beside herself. She began to talk about the *Herr Baron,* to say she was certain his fate had been similar, that such would be the fate of all those who opposed the Leader. The *Frau Baronin* did everything possible to quiet her, the doctor came as soon as he was summoned. But unfortunately——"

"Trudchen, what are you doing in this house?"

Faith Marlowe and Trixie both turned quickly, and through them both a simultaneous shudder ran. Cristina, dressed entirely in white, was standing on the dim stairway. There was something about her so closely akin to the supernal that neither of them could doubt for a moment that she had just emerged from a death chamber. But she did not seem to be bowed by grief. Celestial as she looked, she appeared more like an avenging than a sorrowing angel. She came slowly down the stairs without taking her eyes off the cringing servant. Then she took hold of her with slender hands that looked strangely strong.

"Have you forgotten that the *Herr Baron* gave orders that you were never to come here again?"

"No, *Frau Baronin.* But——"

"It appears that you did. It appears that you went into Her Serene Highness's room by stealth this afternoon when I myself had left her for a few moments. It appears you have done so before, since the *Herr Baron* went away. She told me so herself before she died. Now you have killed her by telling her truths from which I have shielded her. You talk too much, Trudchen. You talked about the *Herr Baron* in the village and he disappeared. You talked to the Archduchess in her bedchamber and she is dead. The doctor will come to your cottage in a few moments and talk to you. I do not know what he and other authorities will decide to do with you and I do not know yet what I shall decide to do myself. But I do know this. If you ever cross this threshold again, you will be pursued by a ghost. Perhaps by more ghosts than one. The Hapsburgs haunt their murderers, Trudchen. You had better remember that and you had better go before they rise up against you."

She relaxed her grasp, and with a little whimpering sound, Trudchen scuttled off into the darkness. Cristina put her arms around Trixie and clung to her for a moment. Faith Marlowe saw, and marveled in seeing, that there was no antagonism between the two, but deep affection. She saw too that this child of Sebastian de Cerreno had inherited his qualities of greatness no less than his qualities of grace. She put out her own arms as Cristina dropped quickly on one knee and kissed her mother-in-law's hand.

"I am grateful that you have come into this house of mourning, *madre mia,*" she murmured. "My father has always told me that you bring comfort and radiance wherever you go."

CHAPTER 28

Faith Marlowe did bring comfort and radiance to Schönplatz in the days that followed; but the unobtrusive foundation for these was the practicality of all her plans and the tactful efficiency with which she carried them out.

She did not commit the error, into which she might easily have fallen, of seeming to take over all the reins of government at the *Herrenhaus.* On the contrary, she deferred, and made it clear that everyone else must defer, to her son's wife. The Baroness von Hohenlohe was now the undisputed mistress of Schönplatz; her word and her wishes were law. But ready to reinforce and execute these, ready to shield her and smooth her path at every turn, stood Faith Marlowe. Cristina, so to speak, sat on the throne, and her mother-in-law stood behind it.

The result was order and harmony on every side. The respect which Faith Marlowe wrung from the neighborhood was unreluctant. There were even a few admiring individuals who spoke of her among themselves as *echt Deutsch,* a true German, sincerely believing that they were paying her the greatest possible compliment, and complacently unaware that she herself would have recoiled from the designation. They marveled at her perfect command of their language and her complete familiarity with their customs. Some of them recalled the time when she had first come to Schönplatz herself, as a girl of sixteen: How bewitching she had been then! She had not possessed the supreme repose and refinement which characterized Cristina; but she had been dazzling. And after she married Rudolf von Hohenlohe, her conduct, both as his wife and as his widow, had been irreproachable, as far as any of them had ever heard. It seemed strange, to be sure, that she should have resumed her maiden name, that she should long have affiliated herself so exclusively with American affairs, that she should have so completely alienated herself from her son. *Ach ja!* This was perhaps largely his fault. He had always had a queer streak, and finally he had succeeded in getting himself into deep difficulties. But if anyone could extricate him from these, it would doubtless be his mother. There was really something dazzling about her still; she had lost some of her former exuberance, but that was a change for the better; she had gained in dignity what she had lost in glamour. She was *prachtvoll.*

The ceremonies attending the funeral of the Archduchess were imperial, and her burial, between her three sons who had fallen in the World War, and her husband, who had been one of its greatest heroes, was impressive in the extreme. The monumental marble and the iron crosses in the woodland cemetery were wreathed in revived majesty as another mound rose beside them; the stillness of the forest became doubly profound as it engulfed another presence. Beatrice, wandering into Faith Marlowe's room, as she had been encouraged to do, late in the day after the services were over, made one of the seemingly random remarks that never failed to prove arresting to the older woman.

"Do you remember what Cristina said the afternoon we got here? To the blonde bitch who was lying in wait for us? That the Hapsburgs haunted their murderers?"

"Yes, Beatrice. Why?"

"Well, I believe it's true. And maybe not just the Hapsburgs, but the Hohenlohes too. Maybe not only when there's been murder, but in any case. Didn't you feel something strange out there in the forest? Don't you feel something strange here in the house?"

"Yes— I think there may be truth in what you say. I think the Hohenlohes as well as the Hapsburgs— But as for your feeling in the woods, that might all be due to murder after all. Everyone buried there is the victim, directly or indirectly, of the World War."

"And you believe war is just like any other murder, only on a larger scale?"

"How can I believe anything else now?— As for your feeling about Schönplatz itself— Well, you know:

> *'All houses wherein men have lived and died*
> *Are haunted houses.'* "

"Yes, I know Longfellow said so. But Schönplatz is different from any other house I've been in. Listen!"

Shivering slightly in spite of herself, Faith Marlowe listened. The silence was even more profound, even more engulfing, than that of the forest had been. She knew that if any sort of sound had suddenly penetrated it, she would have been obliged to stifle a scream.

"I know what haunts this house," Beatrice went on inexorably. "It isn't just dead people. It's a dead tradition, too. The tradition Chris thought was great. The one he was ready to give his life for. Maybe has."

Her lips were quivering, her eyes overflowing. Faith Marlowe put her arm around the girl.

"My dear, don't let it overwhelm you. Try to keep your heart and your manner both quiet. You may be right again. But don't forget this place has somehow survived for seven hundred years, through countless calamities. I hope it can survive still."

"I'd rather see a man survive than a house. I can't be quiet always when I think about Chris. Or Cristina either."

"Ah, yes, Cristina— I'm afraid we've been selfish enough to forget her temporarily. Do you know where she is, what she's doing?"

"I didn't forget her. I never forget her. She's in her room, lying down. She's terribly tired. She said she wanted to be alone."

"Very well, we will leave her alone for a time. But later, I think I had better look in on her. I'll be careful not to disturb her, in case she's asleep. But if she's awake, she might be glad to see me."

"No one could help being glad to see you, Senator Marlowe."

Faith's heart warmed to the girl's praise, as it had warmed from the beginning to her courage and sincerity. But, for the moment, her thoughts were preoccupied with Cristina. She was secretly worried about her daughter-in-law. It was natural enough for the girl to show signs of strain; but she had become abnormally pale, abnormally composed; there were deep circles around her eyes, and she seemed to hold herself erect with an effort. Faith wanted to see for herself whether Cristina was really resting. She continued to talk, in a friendly fashion, with Beatrice for another half an hour. Then she excused herself and went softly into her daughter-in-law's room.

She was relieved to find that Cristina was indeed asleep, on the ponderous bed which dominated its surroundings. Her parted hair fell in long braids over her breast, which was unconcealed by the fine laces that veiled it. Her hands were lightly clasped over the linen sheet with which she was partially covered. Her extreme pallor, enhanced by the whiteness of the linen against which she was lying, her complete stillness, and something about her posture, sent a fresh tremor through Faith; she steadied herself, almost angrily. This was not death, or any semblance of it, at which she was looking, she told herself resolutely; it was a revelation of life and love. Cristina was only sleeping as a consecrated bride might slumber at last, overcome by the manifestation of erstwhile mysteries; she was only sleeping as a potential mother might slumber, burdened already by the expanding blossom within her. All day long, even while the earth thudded down on Victoria Luise's coffin, Faith had been obsessed with the conviction that she was confronted not only with the end of an era, but with the beginning of one. Now, as she sat looking searchingly at Cristina through the twilight, she became increasingly sure of this.

The girl stirred slightly, as if conscious that she was no longer alone. With a fresh pang, Faith saw her turn on her side and stretch out her arms. As these reached only emptiness, she moaned a little under her breath, and half opened her eyes. Faith leaned over and spoke to her.

"It is I, *querida*," she said. "Hans Christian's mother. Have you had a good rest?"

Cristina sat up in bed, her eyes still heavy with sleep, her laces slipping still further from her shoulders. "I must have been dreaming," she murmured. "I thought——" Color came into her face and spread slowly over her snowy skin. Then, as she remembered realities, she emerged from confusion into composure. "Yes, I am rested now," she said gratefully. "Thank you for coming to see me. But this is not the way for me to receive you. Let me——"

"Please lie still, dear child. Let me go on looking at you just as you are. I have been happy, merely in doing so, as you slept. And happier still in thinking that my son's life has been beatified by yours. Wherever he is now, whatever he may be suffering, nothing can rob him of the memory of your bounty."

Cristina caught her breath, but she did not sob. And she lay still, as Faith had told her to do. Quiescence under control was still part of her creed, and she could hear her husband speaking to her through his mother.

"If you are really refreshed, I should like to talk to you for a little while. But let us speak very softly. However still a house may seem, its walls are sievelike— Have you thought at all what you want to do now, Cristina? You cannot stay alone at Schönplatz."

"I could, if it were necessary, *madre mia,* and I would. But I hoped it might not be. I hoped now that *Tante* Luise is dead, you would take me back to Spain."

"That I would take you? Back to Spain? Why, Cristina?"

"Because I am sure that when he is free, Hans Christian will seek for me in Spain. He will not try to come back here. That would be fatal."

"It might be dangerous. But are you sure that Spain is safe?"

"Can we be sure that any place is safe? At least it is quieter now than in a long time. My father writes me that with the change of government, from Left to center Right, there has been much improvement in his opinion. And though he has lost both Ventosilla and the Castello Viejo through the passage of the Agrarian Reform Laws, he still has the *caseria.* I do not think he will be molested there. It is such a small property, and so simple, compared to the others."

"Yes— It is small and simple, compared to the others. Somehow I cannot seem to see your father shorn of those. Is it partly because you are sorry for him that you want to go back to Spain, Cristina?"

"Yes, but only partly. I have not seen him, you know, since my marriage. And we were always very close to each other. Now that I have lost Hans Christian and he has lost *Tio* Gabriel, it seems natural to turn back to him. So I am thinking of myself, partly, too. But I am also thinking of someone else."

"Yes, Cristina?"

"I am going to have a child, *madre mia.* And after what has happened, I could not bear that it should be born a German!"

Her words came with a rush now. "Hans Christian does not know it. I did not know it myself until just before he disappeared. And the last night he was here, when I meant to tell him—that was the night he found out about Ernst, the night he could think of nothing else. He did not think of me at all, for the first time. He was frozen with horror, there was no love left in his heart. How could I tell him, on such a night, that at last—after we had hoped so long, and so vainly— No, no, I could not do it!"

"Of course you couldn't, Cristina. Of course you felt you must wait."

"Yes, and then I found I had waited too long. There was no other chance to tell him. And I did not know what to do. I was trapped. I could not leave *Tante* Luise all alone. I could not take her away with me, she was so old and ill. She failed very fast after *Tio* Gabriel died. And still I felt that if I did not go before others knew how it was with me, I might not be able to go at all, I mean, allowed to go. But now she has died, and you have come. I am not trapped any more. I am free. I can go quickly. No one has noticed, no one has guessed!"

"I had guessed, *querida*, I had noticed."

Faith leaned forward and gently traced the circles around Cristina's eyes; then she laid her hand lightly on the veiled breast, finding, as she expected, that it was full and firm under her touch. "Someone else would see what I have seen, very soon, if you stayed here. I was afraid today that you might faint at the funeral, and then— It is a mistake to suppose that only a changed figure can betray you. But do not be frightened, dear child. You are not trapped, as you put it, any longer. You shall leave at once, or at least within a few days, after all the funereal proprieties have been observed. There must be no look of flight about your departure. Now that the Archduchess does not need you any more, a visit to your father is quite in order. That is proper, that will arouse no suspicion. But as far as I am concerned——"

She stopped, and looked away for a moment. Then she went on, in a resolute voice, "I think I ought to stay here, Cristina. I think it is best that you should go, but I think it is best that I should stay. We must be practical. The dowry for which your father sacrificed is tied up here. It must be released. The sheep which have been the mainstay of the place for centuries—now that Ernst is no longer here, who would see they were shepherded, if I did not? And the horses—the beautiful white horses—what about them?"

"The beautiful white horses do not matter so much. But the dappled gray mare—the only one Hans Christian has bred—I thought, *madre mia*, that perhaps I could take her with me."

"Take her with you? How?"

"I could ride her, easily enough, from here to Danzig. I should not ride much now, I know. But that is not far enough to do me any harm.

And from Danzig I could go over the frontier into Poland. After that, anyone could take the mare safely into Spain. I thought, you see, that you and I could start together, as if we were out for the afternoon. The dappled gray mare means so much. She is a symbol."

"Yes, dear, I know. I understand how you feel. But so is Schönplatz. It is not just an estate, a valuable property. It is a legacy, a symbol, too. If Frau von Mitweld would have stayed here, perhaps I might have trusted it to her. But, as you know, it was hard to persuade her to come to her mother's funeral; it was impossible to persuade her to linger, after this was over. She feels too keenly about Karl and Luischen. And who can blame her?" Faith stopped again, remembering what Beatrice had said of Schönplatz earlier in the afternoon. This was no time for repeating that to Cristina; but with the thought of Beatrice, another idea entered Faith Marlowe's mind. "I do not think that I should leave here," she repeated. "Besides all the reasons I have mentioned, there is still the chance that Hans Christian might come here, instead of going to Spain, or at least that he might send a message. So one of us should be at Schönplatz on that account. Obviously you should not start out alone, however. Nor could you take the dapple gray with you, if you did that. But perhaps Beatrice would go with you. The American Ambassador's daughter, jaunting about the countryside, accompanied by a friend—what could be more in keeping with Trixie's character? I doubt if the frontier officials would even stop her, strict as they are."

Again it was a beautiful day when Beatrice Rhodes passed through Marienburg. This time Cristina was with her instead of Faith Marlowe, and she herself was not driving her sporty roadster; she was riding a snow-white horse, and wearing linen breeches and a soft shirt open at the throat, a sleeveless scarlet jacket, black boots. Her mop of brown hair was uncovered, her face and hands sun tanned, her teeth dazzling against the line of her lips as she laughingly greeted the *Kontroll Offizier* at the long bridge. He recognized her and gave her a gay salute.

"You are leaving us here in East Prussia, *gnädiges Fräulein? Schade!*"

"The *Frau Baronin* and I are dining with the High Commissioner of Danzig. We thought it would be amusing to go there on horseback. If we continue to have a good time, we may go farther. It is so pleasant to ride in the summer!"

He glanced from her to her companion. The *Frau Baronin—Ach ja!* That would be the wife—or the widow—of von Hohenlohe, who had disappeared, along with so many others, the night of the Thirtieth of June. Well— It was not for him to question the omnipotence of the Leader. On the other hand, he had received no instructions about the *Baronin,* and her papers, which he inspected, were entirely in order. Doubtless she was bent on seeing the High Commissioner to intercede for her husband, though what could the Commissioner of the "Free City" do? The *Kontroll Offizier* would have shrugged his shoulders if the *Baronin's* bearing had not somehow precluded him from such a gesture. Her type was not so much to his taste as the American girl's—there was a *Mädel* to warm any man's heart!—but it commanded respect, touched by reverence. She was mounted sidesaddle on a fine, dappled gray mare, and wearing a long gray habit, superbly cut. Her glossy hair was coiled in black braids under her gray beaver hat, her hands hidden in spotless gray gloves. And her eyes were gray too, clear and cool as crystal. She did not laugh, like the bare-headed, red-coated American; but she smiled and bent her graceful head as he handed her back her passport.

"*Glückliche Reise! Und auf Wiedersehen!*" said the *Kontroll Offizier,* saluting again.

Faith Marlowe sat alone among the stillnesses and the shadows of Schönplatz that evening. In a day or two, she knew, awkward questions concerning Cristina's absence might arise; she must be prepared to answer them convincingly and calmly. There were also endless problems to be settled concerning the estate. It was true enough that she had acquired experience on her own New England farm and in the management of her money; but was this wide enough to enable her to cope with endless acres, priceless stock, and tangled investments? She must not permit herself to doubt that it was. And when it came to the people who would surround her—"blonde bitches" like Trudchen, silly snobs like Frau von Edelblut—could she handle them with a touch seemingly light as foam but actually strong as steel? Well, she had never faltered yet in any human relation. Why should she now?

Briefly, and without concern, she considered her own career. At present, the Senate was not in session. When it reconvened, in December, the entire picture might have changed. If it had not, she could always resign. She was midway through her second term now, she had proved her mettle and redeemed her heritage, she had made the way easier for other women to follow, because of the trail she had blazed. It would not cost her anything to renounce an honor which had alienated her from her only child, and which had been empty from the beginning, as far as her personal happiness was concerned.

Her happiness! What happiness had life ever brought her? She could not answer that demand as easily as she had dismissed the question of a career. It became relentless, while the darkness deepened around the place where she was sitting. Her father's failure, her mother's disgrace, her shadowed childhood, the disillusionment of her marriage, the waste of her beauty, her renunciation of romance— She could not evade the mounting memories of these any longer. Was it enough for a woman, when she reached middle age, to know that her conscience was clear and her record remarkable? Bowing her head, since there was now no one left to see that it was bent, Faith Marlowe told herself bitterly that such knowledge was vain.

A board creaked queerly on the stairway, and through the open window, strange sounds seemed to mingle with the rustling of leaves. She heard them without heeding them. The White Lady of the Hapsburgs might have glided past her, so close that her ephemeral draperies fluttered in Faith's face, and Faith would not have noticed. The graves in the woodland cemetery might all have opened, disgorging the dead they entombed, and she would not have seen the ghostly file these formed: Hans von Hohenlohe, the younger, killed at the first battle of the Marne; Heinrich von Hohenlohe, dead in a Flemish hospital from wounds received at Ypres; Rudolf von Hohenlohe, fallen before Verdun; General Hans von Hohenlohe, father of these three, broken in body and mind by their loss, stricken here at Schönplatz; Victoria Luise, Archduchess of Austria, mother of these three, bearing herself like the daughter and consort of kings through a long life, but breaking at last with the betrayal of an empire. What a procession they might have made! If they marched before her that night, however, Faith was unmindful of them. Her vision was fixed, not on the ranks of the dead, but on the image of Sebastian de Cerreno as he had looked on the night when she first saw him, with a scarlet sash around his waist and the Order of the Golden Fleece encircling his neck.

It was nearly thirty years since that night, it was more than twenty since she had last seen him. But this was a memory that had never been stilled, and therefore it was not like those lesser ones, merely awakened. How had she ever withstood him, the greatest grandee of Spain, the greatest gallant in all Europe? He would have defied every law of Church and State to make her his, and still he had not prevailed against her will. To the very end, her chastity had been stronger than his charm. Yet now, sitting alone in the darkness, she asked herself one more question. It did not matter any more how she had withstood him. What mattered was, why she had withstood him, since in the end, she had come after all only to this extremity of frustration and isolation.

It was a long time before she even tried to control her weeping. But at last she rose and resolutely went from the dim drawing room up the obscure stairway and into her own chamber, determined that never again would she abandon herself to despair or say that all joy had passed her by. Not now, when she knew, beyond any possibility of doubt, that Cristina, riding the dappled gray mare, had gone safely past the Polish frontier, and that Hans Christian's child would not be born in Germany.

PART VIII

1936

The Strong Strain

CHAPTER 29

ANTONINA SAT in the kitchen of Bautista Ramirez' flat, with her apron flung over her face, rocking back and forth, and uttering low wailing sounds, like a wounded animal. Her own cries kept her from hearing the hum of the bombing planes circling over Madrid; they also made her oblivious for a long time to the noise of the bell buzzing above her own head. When she did hear it, she remotely remembered that the door of the house was unlocked in any case, since it no longer mattered whether this was fastened or not; if someone were seeking her, it would be easy enough to walk up the stairs and come down the corridor past the empty bedrooms and the *salita,* where the radio stood silent, into the kitchen where there were no more live coals burning in the apertures on top of the blackened stove.

After she remembered this, she bothered no more about it. What if someone were seeking her out—or if no one were? What did anything matter any more? She muffled her ears, already covered by her apron, more closely by placing her hands over them, and resumed her moaning. It was not until she felt a touch on her shoulder that she dully dropped her apron and looked up.

She did not recognize the man standing beside her. He was a cadaverous-looking creature, and a month earlier she would have screamed at such a sight. But she was used to horrible sights now. This man was only one of many she had seen. What he wanted with her, she did not know.

"You don't remember me, Antonina. But you were very kind to me once. I hoped you would be again. I thought perhaps you would make me some coffee, or a *refresco.* I'm terribly thirsty. I'm thirsty all the time."

As he spoke, the man tried to moisten his lips with his tongue, and seemed to fail. Antonina perceived now that he was not a Spaniard.

He did not talk like one, although his speech was quite intelligible, and he did not look like one. His eyes, staring out of the sockets in which they were sunk, were blue. Possibly they had been a bright blue once, though now this was glazed. His hair was a queer color, streaked and faded; but it had never been black. It might have been golden or even red before it became so drab. His skin, abnormally gray, was still untinged by brown; it must have had a clear red and white color, in happier times. In spite of her own grief, Antonina felt sorry for this stranger, who was suffering and thirsty, though still she did not recognize him.

"The fire is out. I have had no heart to light it. But if the *Señor* will wait, I will build it up, I will make him some coffee. And I think there are still two or three oranges in the larder. At least I can mix these with water at once, for a *refresco*."

She rose and set to work, forgetting to moan as she did this, so genuine was her solicitude. The stranger sank down on a chair and did not speak to her again until he had drained the last drop of the drink she had made him.

"Do you know when *Señor* Ramirez will be in?" he said at last. "I want very much to see him, the first moment I can."

Antonina shrieked, and began to cross herself, only to let her fingers fall quickly again to her side, as she tardily recalled that such signs, once instinctive to her, were now allied with evil in her mind. "Do I know when *Señor* Ramirez will be in?" she cried shrilly. "Where are you from that you have not heard? What did you want with him—not that it matters—now he is butchered! Who are you that you come here asking such questions, at such a time as this?"

The man sank down into his chair again and covered his face with his hands, moaning in his turn. It was the sound of the moan that made Antonina glance at him; but it was the sight of his hands that riveted her gaze. She had never seen such hands before, in the midst of all she had beheld in Madrid—so disfigured, so maimed, that she marveled he could still manage to use them. Pity welled up in her once more, drowning her own grief.

"It is a terrible story, *Señor*, but since I see that you yourself have suffered, I will tell it to you quickly—in order that you may be on your way to seek succor elsewhere. If my *patron* had only stayed in Madrid, all might still be well—who can say? The bombs fall down, hitting here and there as they come, but there are many they never touch. It may be they would never have touched him. However, he was fearful for the safety of his mother. The fate of women has been worse than the fate of men, *Señor*, whether they be old or young."

The stranger struggled to his feet, putting one of his maimed hands to his throat, as if he were choking. "Tell me your story faster," he muttered desperately. "If Bautista Ramirez can't help me, I must find someone else who can—some friend of his, someone who would be friendly to me."

"I am friendly to you, *Señor*, I will help you, if I can. I am all alone, I have no *patron* any more. I will put myself at your service. I am only an old woman, a servant, but I have a brother, and perhaps— It was this way, *Señor*, in the village where *Señora* Ramirez lived, as it has been in many others: Men and women were herded into the cemetery and shot down during the night, in groups. My *patron* and his mother fell side by side. There, I have told you, it is finished, my story. Will you tell me yours?"

"Antonina, don't you remember an unexpected guest to whom you were very good, you and your *patron* both, at the beginning of the revolution? A young man whom such a story would fill with sorrow? A traveling German who——"

At the word "German" the woman recoiled, as she might have shrunk from a snake. She shrieked again, and crossed herself, completely and unconsciously this time. "A German!" she screamed. "Do I remember? That smooth-faced boy who was set to spy on us? Who went back to his own country and spread lies about us? There are thousands of Germans in Spain now, fighting under Franco! I know, and my *patron* knew before he died, who sent them, who spread the poison, who the traitor had been——"

"Antonina, you're wrong, you're mistaken. Please listen to me! That boy wasn't a spy, he wasn't a traitor, he never said anything except that you'd been kind to him. He didn't even know there were any Germans in Spain now, fighting for Franco. He's—he's suffered himself, at the hands of the same men who sent them. He was taken out into the woods and told to run for his life. Then he was shot through and through, finally left for dead. When he came to himself, he managed to drag himself to a road. He was picked up by a passing car, borne away, nursed and hidden. Then he was found and clapped into a concentration camp and his rescuers with him. He escaped, but he was the only one that did."

"If he had died too, the serpent's nest would have been emptier! But we shall crush them yet, we shall kill them all, as they have crushed and killed us!"

"Antonina, you must listen to me, you must help me. I'm trying to get through to my wife, in Granada. I have a little son I've never seen. I was born in Spain myself, my baby was born in Spain. My wife's a Spaniard, all her people are Spaniards. The Cerrenos have lived in Spain for centuries."

"The *Cerrenos!* The intimates of Alfonso! The arch enemies of freedom! The people who are plotting, on the inside, to destroy the Republic and restore the Monarchy! The renegades who are shooting patriots in cemeteries and mowing them down with machine guns in bull rings!"

She was beside herself with fury. There was more than menace in her manner now, there was murder. A kitchen knife would have served her purpose as well as anything. She snatched at one, as Hans Christian eluded her. When the street outside swallowed him up, she was still pursuing him. Then another bomb burst, and her pursuit was over.

The American Embassy in Madrid was in an uproar. The distraught secretaries were striving to cope with a situation which was entirely out of hand in the midst of tumultuous conditions. The Chancery was filled with terrified tourists and enraged businessmen. One more man amid the scores storming the doors inevitably passed more or less unnoticed. Winthrop Ayer's nerves were already beyond the breaking point when one of these importunates actually took hold of him.

"What do you mean by doing that? What do you want?"

"I'm sorry, but I've been here two hours already, and I didn't have a minute to lose in the beginning. I've got to get through to the South, I've got to get to my wife."

"Are you an American citizen?"

"No, but——"

"Good God, what are you doing then? Get the hell out of here!"

"I'm Senator Marlowe's son. I have a right to ask for your help. I intend to have it."

"*Senator Marlowe's son!* The Nazi volunteer who was hoist with his own petard! So you escaped, did you, finally? And now you've come grovelling to get back what you gave up of your own accord! Well, let me tell you right here and now, there are plenty of men who've shown more sense and more sand than you did, who'll get help from this Embassy before you will."

"The American Embassy in Berlin didn't take that attitude. It was Rufus Rhodes who saw to it that I got this far. I believe he was your chief once. You must know something about his methods. He sent a wire to the Ambassador here."

"He sent a wire to the Ambassador here! Well, the Ambassador isn't here himself! He's in San Sebastian, or Biarritz, I'm not sure which. And what do you think wires amount to anyway, when civil war breaks out overnight?"

"We didn't any of us know civil war had broken out when I left Paris. We only knew that telephone service with Spain had been cut off, that radios weren't working. There were rumors that there'd been 'incidents' at Cuenca, a 'revolt' at Cartagena. But these were just reports. I didn't have any trouble about reservations. Then when I got to Hendaye, I couldn't get over the border. The trains weren't running and neither were the trolleys. Strikers were tearing up the rails. I lost a lot of time I couldn't afford to lose. But finally I heard that eight busses flying red flags as a badge of safe conduct were taking refugees from San Sebastian to Biarritz. They were supposed to go back empty, but I persuaded the driver of one to let me hide in it. The usual method of persuasion still works, though the rates are higher. I've used it all the way to Madrid. But apparently I got out of San Sebastian just in time. There are rumors that the Insurgents are upon it already."

Winthrop Ayer had begun to regard the interloper with reluctant admiration. Hans Christian, conscious that he had produced the effect necessary to galvanize the Secretary into action, went on more tersely.

"All this is beyond the point. The point is that I'm going to rejoin Mr. Rhodes in France as soon as I can get back there. I'm sailing for America on the same boat with him and his family. They're waiting for me at Versailles until I can get back. I'm taking my wife and child out of Spain with me. If there's any avoidable delay in carrying out this plan, you'll be responsible. You'll answer for it, eventually and officially, to the Secretary of State. And you'll answer for it to me personally right here and now and again after I become an American citizen. That won't be so long, either."

Hans Christian drew a deep breath. A different look came into his sunken eyes as he spoke. Winthrop Ayer, shrinking back from the sight of the hands laid upon his own, tried to shake himself free. But he knew he was caught and cornered. He knew that whoever else waited and for what, that this escaped exile who held him in his mutilated grasp must get through to Granada that night.

It was two hours later still before the *salvo conducto* from the War Office was actually in Hans Christian's possession. By that time the last scheduled train had left Madrid for the South, and in any case, no trains were running on schedule. Winthrop Ayer mentioned this, unresourcefully, as he and Hansel went down the steps of the Ministry together.

"Will you lend me your car? If I stop to buy one, that'll involve still more delay—even supposing I don't run into fresh complications in trying to make the purchase!"

"I'd be very glad to, of course, but you see——"

Hans Christian did not wait to see. He had always been a rapid runner, and weak as he was, he had no trouble in gaining the bottom of the steps before Winthrop Ayer grasped his purpose. The Secretary's car, bearing diplomatic license plates and flying the American flag, was parked at the curb. It was veering around the corner, with Hans Christian in it, by the time the outraged Bostonian had reached the sidewalk.

Hans Christian had been over the road from Madrid to Granada only once, when he had made the trip in Sebastian's "glorified gypsy wagon," lying down all the way and sleeping a large part of it. So he had nothing but instinct now to guide him in getting out of the city. But the sense of direction which comes with habitual driving stood him in good stead; he did not make a single false turn as he steered his way southward through the tortuous streets. He was determined not to stop, of his own accord, to ask the way, and thus lose still more time, if he could help it; and nobody attempted to stop him. There was no disorder in this quarter of the city. The populace was preoccupied, the police recognized the number plates, and a few Spanish soldiers actually saluted the flag. He gained the open highway without opposition or impediment.

As he sped over it, he drew deep breaths of relief and refreshment. A glance at the gage had shown him that the tank was full of gas; it would be hours before he would require more. He could afford to disregard the problem of refueling until it arose. It was hours since he had eaten, but he was not hungry, and he was conscious of no pain in his hands as these rested on the wheel. The summer night was bountiful in its beauty. The warm air stirred slightly; there was freshness in it, and fragrance. Stars shone overhead, and a full moon. The fields were filled with released radiance, the road was a silvery band between them, leading to Andalusia, "the land blessed by God"—"*tierra de Maria Santissima.*"

By this time Cristina would have had his messages—oh, long before this! He had sent her one the moment he had been over the Belgian border, another as soon as he had reached Paris, still another from Hendaye. She would be expecting him, waiting for him, watching for him. Probably he would see her as soon as he reached the outer courtyard, standing at the grilled gate leading to the patio, with a flower in her hair and the baby in her arms: His son, whom he had never seen, but whose birth had brought about his deliverance.

Pressing down harder and harder upon the accelerator, drinking in deeper and deeper drafts of the scented air, he put together the pieces which formed the pattern of this deliverance. He knew now that Cristina had kept in close touch with Trixie after she had gone back to Spain; and Trixie, in her turn, had kept going at regular intervals to the Bomb Palast. The first time, when Faith Marlowe had been there with her, Oskar Kraus had slammed the door in her face. But the second time, when she had gone alone, he had grudgingly consented to let her in. After that he had come to take her visits as a matter of course, eventually to look forward to them. Apparently she had been very tolerant and very tactful. She had managed to keep their conversations impersonal over a prolonged period. And when she had finally spoken of Hans Christian she had done so almost incidentally but very appealingly.

"I had a letter from Sebastian de Cerreno today—you remember, the Spaniard of whom I told you, who has suffered so much from the Communists. But this letter was almost happy. He has a little grandson—a real Christmas *Kindlein.* I do wish there were some way we could let Hansel know—if he is still alive. Don Sebastian says the baby looks exactly like him—golden hair, blue eyes, fair skin, all that. And at this season— If any of us only knew how to reach Hansel, or whether it was worth while to try again——"

After that she had spoken of other things. But when she had risen to leave, she had suggested that perhaps Oskar would come to the Embassy on Christmas Eve.

"Now that Hansel is not here to cook your dinner and trim your tree, I am afraid it is dismal for you at the Bomb Palast. I should like to try to give you a good time myself, since he can't. I have never forgotten how kind you were to me when I was hit on the head, the first time I met you. You have a very gentle touch, Oskar. You would be wonderful with children yourself. Well— My father and mother told me to say that they would also be very pleased to welcome you and Max on Christmas Eve. *Auf Wiedersehen.*"

"*Auf Wiedersehen, gnädiges Fräulein.*"

Oskar and Max had been genuinely touched by Trixie's invitation and they had accepted it. As the party was drawing to an end, Oskar whispered to Trixie in saying good night.

"Hansel is alive. He has been very ill but he is better. He was lost for a long time but I know where he is now, and I have found a way to send him a message about the *Kindlein.* Since it came at Christmastime, and since it is so like him, with golden hair and blue eyes, I felt——"

"I knew you would, Oskar. I can't tell you how grateful I am. You've made my Christmas a happy one too."

She had asked no questions, either then or later. When Oskar told her, eventually, that he thought he might get into closer touch with the prisoner, she had not pressed him for details. She had only nodded, and said she was very glad. More than a year had gone by, after that, before Oskar had asked her, without preamble, if she would be afraid to take a long ride with him at night, in her car, and whether she had large sums of money easily available. She had answered almost nonchalantly that she would be pleased to go out with him at any time, in her own car or any other, and that she always had large sums of money lying around and was always wondering what to do with them. As if to prove the point, the catch to her handbag had come unclasped, and a roll of bills had fallen to the floor. She had not picked them up.

All this Trixie had told Hans Christian herself, in her own words, on the night they met in the woods, and now he recalled every syllable she had spoken. It was not such a night as this, balmy and beautiful. A cold unseasonable rain had been pouring down, and the wind had lashed the trees about, and both wind and rain had stung them in the face. But Trixie had not seemed to mind. She was caped and hooded in scarlet cellophane, from which the water poured down, and she did not trouble to shake it from her face. She carried a big bag and a smaller one, both encased in waterproof covers, and she did not seem to mind the weight of these either. She talked quickly, but without any show of excitement.

"You must get into some of the clothes I have here. They're your own, they'll fit you all right. You'll get soaking wet, but that can't be helped. You can change into dry things on the train."

"What train?"

"The night express to Cologne. I have your tickets here and a compartment reserved for you. We've got plenty of time to catch it, if we don't dawdle. There's a passport in the envelope with the tickets—an American passport. We doctored up an old snapshot I took of you on the boat and had it rephotographed, and I copied your signature from one of the letters you wrote me when you first got to Schönplatz—just the Christian Marlowe part, of course. It's a pretty neat piece of forgery, if I do say so."

"Trixie—I—I——"

"Please don't try to talk, Chris. There really isn't time. Just one thing more. I won't say it before Oskar, then it will be true he never heard anything about your plans. I don't think you'll have a bit of trouble if you take a train at Cologne for Brussels. But if you'd feel any easier, go to the American Consul. He's a good scout, and I know he motors over into Belgium every day or so to buy vegetables. He'll take you with him. By the time you get to Paris, we'll be there too—mother and daddy and I. Meet us at the Meurice. We'll have a room engaged for you and your reservations all made to Madrid."

Again he tried to speak to her and again she interrupted him.

"I'm going back to the car now to wait for you. Here's a flashlight I brought for you in case you couldn't feel for your things. But don't use it any more than you have to."

Oskar was waiting in the car as well as Trixie when Hans Christian came up to it. They greeted each other briefly.

"Did you have any trouble getting out?"

"No. It was surprisingly simple—at the end. I won't go into all the rest. But finally it was merely a matter of *Trinkgeld* for a couple of troopers, and 'leave of absence' for an hour's rendezvous. They agreed, by the time they were half drunk, that even prisoners needed to have one occasionally." He could not have made such a statement before Cristina, but with Trixie it was easy and natural. "You're sure you're not going to get into trouble, Oskar, for your share in this?"

"I haven't had any share, beyond locating you in the first place and getting a few messages through to you. *Fräulein* Rhodes has done everything else."

It still proved futile to try talking to Trixie, so Hans Christian went on talking to Oskar instead, though nothing they said to each other was of much consequence. When they reached the station they said good-by in the car, so that they would not be seen together going through the waiting room or crossing the platform. But Trixie boarded the train with him and saw him safely into his compartment. He put his arms around her and clung to her, shaking all over, with tears of weakness and emotion streaming down his cheeks. For a few moments she steadied and supported him, until he had regained some measure of self-control. Then without apparent effort she disengaged herself.

"Good-by, Chris, I have to go. The train will start in a minute. But remember, I'll be in Paris when you get there. I'm going to take the morning plane. Don't worry, any more than you can help. And whether you worry or not, don't break down or back down."

He had done his best to meet her challenge, and on the whole, he had succeeded. He sped along now with no sense of shame and with one of increasing exaltation. At every village and crossroad he was stopped by guards, but the delay they caused him was brief. They raised their fists in the salute of the People's Front and said, "*Salud!*" They asked to see his credentials and gave these a cursory glance. Usually this was all, before they waved him on his way again. He made good time, for the road was almost empty. Then suddenly it was choked with soldiers. They were a sorry-looking lot, ill clad and ill armed. Most of them were clad in the dark cotton smock typical of the Spanish peasant. Some might have come straight from the fields, others direct from small shops. Several looked sick, a few really ruffianly. Scattered women, wearing rumpled blouses and dangling ornaments, marched beside them, and among these were girls, hardly more than children —younger than Cristina had been when Hans Christian first saw her, almost as young as Cecilia. Gay, impudent, rollicking Cecilia! How good it would seem to hear her laugh again!

The soldiers were going south, like himself. As long as he crawled along behind them, they paid almost no attention to him. But he could not afford to continue at this snail's pace. Neither could he take the risk of running one of them down, if he tried to cleave his way through their ranks without warning. He blew his horn, hoping against hope that they would part of their own accord and let him through. But he was instantly called upon to halt. The soldiers closed in around the car with a certain show of ferocity. Several shouted to him simultaneously to show his credentials and explain his errand. One of them raised a dilapidated musket in a threatening gesture. Hans Christian shut off his engine and spoke with the serious politeness to which he had never failed to find a ready response in Spain.

"*Buenas noches, amigos!* May I give three or four of you a lift? We seem to be all traveling in the same direction. You will see, *Señor Capitan,* by this car and these documents, that I am an American. And you will sympathize with my errand, I am sure of that. I have a Spanish sweetheart, whom I have not seen in some time. Since we parted, there has been a *niño*. I am hurrying to her, to assure her of my undying love, and of my eagerness to clasp our child in my arms."

The ferocious frowns changed to smiles; the man with the musket cheered. The ragged individual whom Hans Christian had addressed as *Señor Capitan* handed back the extended papers with a flourish. He had recognized both the seal of the War Office and the flag flying in front of the radiator. He did not even glance at the passport.

"*Por favor, camarad.* If you are in earnest, four of us will accept your offer and ride with you as far as Valdepenas. I will do so because it is imperative that I should reach there as soon as possible, and my friend Felipe, because he is lame and it pains him to march. While if two of these ladies who are with us and who are very tired—"

"It will be my pleasure, *Señor Capitan.* Let us be on our way. I too am in a hurry to reach Valdepenas. Can I buy petrol there, and a drink?"

"As to the drink, that is certain. But the petrol—I do not know. You will understand, *camarad,* that it is necessary to commandeer and conserve it. But I have a cousin who keeps a small garage there. He might be able to help you, in return for favors received."

They were off, shouting their farewells to the rank and file left behind. The Captain had seated himself in front, beside Hans Christian. Felipe, his lame leg extended, sat in the rear between the two "ladies," a steadying arm around each. One of them was a woman of thirty, with intense eyes and an aquiline profile. She spoke very little, and that through compressed lips; but the gaze she turned on Felipe was tender. The other was the very young girl who had made Hans Christian think of Cecilia. She had the same careless laughing manner, the same dark vivid beauty. There was nothing coarse or common about her looks. She had the basic refinement which Hans Christian had noticed in nearly all Spanish women. But she was plainly pregnant, and he marveled that she should have started out on such a march, when her hour must be so near. She must be passionately attached to her lover, indifferent to suffering, oblivious of danger. This also was the way of Spanish women, as Hans Christian knew.

He questioned them about the war. Did they know how far the Insurgents had penetrated already? The Captain became voluble. Cadiz had fallen first, that was where Franco, the Insurgent General, had landed with his foreign legions when he flew over from Morocco. Since then it had been bombed. General Queipo de Llano, commanding the garrison in Seville, had joined the Revolutionists. Indeed, he had sent an enthusiastic message to Franco saying that all the garrisons in Andalusia were going over to him, as well as the Navy. The message had ended with the words "No earthly power can check our triumphant movement."

"So he says," the Captain concluded almost gayly, "which shows how little he knows about the matter. For we shall check him—the men and women like those you have with you, *camarad*. What if Córdoba has been taken too? We shall recapture it. What if half Malaga is in flames? The other half still stands!"

"And Granada?"

"We are still holding Granada, though the Insurgents are very close. At any minute they may enter it. Was it to Granada that you were going, *camarad*?"

"Not into the city. To a *caseria* some kilometers this side of it."

"Ah, then all may be well. Let us trust that all may be well."

Hans Christian noticed that the Captain did not say "Let us pray that all may be well." But he himself prayed, silently mingling his petitions with assertions which he tried hard to believe. Oh, God, keep them safe! Don't let anything happen to them!— Of course they're all right. The Insurgent lines haven't spread to Granada. Even if they have the Cerrenos will be safeguarded. The only difficulty will be in getting through. The Safe Conduct will be of no value then. On the contrary, I shall have to hide it, it will be incriminating. But the American flag, the diplomatic license plates, the Special Passport—Christ, those are all any man would need! Christ, grant that they may be!

Felipe went to sleep with his head against the curving breast of the woman with the great intense eyes. She put her arm around him protectively, and gazed steadfastly ahead of her. Every now and then the young girl leaned forward to exchange a lingering embrace with the Captain. Their lips met hungrily and repeatedly, and finally he drew her forward and held her on his lap until they reached Valdepenas. Still holding her, he directed Hans Christian how to reach his cousin's shop, and when he descended from the car, he did not release her, but kept her close to him while he talked about the petrol. There was a difficulty, as he had anticipated; indeed, cars as well as gasoline were now subject to commandeering. But he told the story of the Americano's kindness, and of his purpose, graphically and sympathetically, and the cousin was much moved. It was forbidden, of course. But still— Enough petrol to get to Granada, was that the requirement? Well, probably it would never be missed. Motioning Hans Christian to drive inside the shed where their movements could not be seen by idle and curious passers-by, the man opened a large tin can and began to pour its contents into the tank. Meanwhile, the Captain and his sweetheart entered an adjacent house, and returning to the shed, brought with them beer and bread, cheese and olives.

Hans Christian had not known that he was hungry. Now he devoured the food ravenously and drank down the beer at one draft. It was necessary to wake and dislodge Felipe before he could proceed, but the cripple tumbled out philosophically. When Hans Christian climbed back into the car again, the older woman touched him gently on the arm.

"If I could be of service to you, *camarad*, I will go on with you. You have helped us so much— I know the road to Granada well, and the crossroads guards know me, and so do all our soldiers. You will not be stopped if you meet more troops, and you can go faster if you do not have to watch the way."

"But Felipe? Who will care for him while you are gone?"

"He will not lack for care, *camarad*, you may be sure of that."

The younger girl had spoken proudly. Hans Christian knew she was telling the truth. He tried, tactfully, to offer her a little present, "for the need she would soon have of it," and after she had looked at the Captain questioningly, she accepted it with a flash of white teeth and a volley of grateful words. When Hans Christian last saw her, she was standing with her arm linked through her lover's, shaking her curly hair back from her laughing face.

The moon had melted into the sunrise. The heat of the day had fallen early. It came and went in waves around the speeding car. The woman at Hans Christian's side was very quiet, completely controlled. Though there was no physical resemblance, something in her manner made him think of his mother, almost as poignantly as the young girl had made him think of Cecilia—his mother whom he had so tardily remembered. It had been only of Cristina whom he had thought, with any degree of concern, throughout the horrors of his imprisonment. Yet he had learned from Trixie, in Paris, that Faith Marlowe had come to Germany at once when she heard of his plight, that she had moved heaven and earth to secure his release, and that she had stayed steadfastly at Schönplatz until she had been literally dispossessed.

"As long as no one knew where you were she had the upper hand," Trixie explained. "The Gestapo chiefs were telling the truth when they said they couldn't give any information. Of course their original instructions had been 'Shoot to kill!' When the murderers returned to the scene of the crime and found the 'corpse' missing, they were pretty puzzled. It wasn't until they had tracked you down in your hiding place and dragged you off to prison that the *Regierungspräsident* of the Schönplatz area could write your mother to tell her that your property was *sichergestellt*. Did he send you a duplicate document? I believe that's supposed to be the correct thing, when the government becomes a 'benevolent custodian' prior to confiscation."

"Yes, I had the document, but I never heard from my mother, and I suppose none of my letters reached her. Is—is Schönplatz confiscated?"

"It must be, by this time. Confiscation seems to be automatic, if a prisoner flees the country. That and loss of citizenship. You're not a German any more, Chris."

"No, I'm not a German any more."

Trixie had said nothing further about that, knowing how it would hurt, and neither had he; but she had handed him the letters which Faith Marlowe had sent him in her care at the Meurice. It would be only a matter of days, perhaps of hours, his mother wrote, with characteristic brevity and reserve, before she would be called upon to surrender Schönplatz, now that his escape was known. The buildings and grounds were in good condition; she had kept them in the best possible repair. She supposed that the stud would be very valuable to the government; it might serve to supplement Trakehnen. And of course there were always the sheep. She hoped he would not reproach her for failing to save the property for him. She had staved off usurpation as long as possible. And she had become attached to the place herself, in the long quiet months she had spent there. She would regret to leave it. But she felt sure she could at least assure him that the woodland cemetery would always be respected.

Remembering the mocking laughter of Max, with whom he had once passed Stresemann's tomb in the St. Nicolai Cemetery, Hans Christian felt less certain of this, and his heart contracted. But this was not only because of the dead. It was also because of the living. He could see his mother, unshielded and unsupported, confronting the confiscators with the same courage which had enabled her to keep them so long at bay. He knew that she would have done it with firm lips and an unbent head, even at the very moment of turning over the keys. She must have gone through the paddocks and the pens, one last time alone, and through the fields and the forest, as well as from the top to the bottom of the house. But if her eyes had been blurred with tears as she walked, her step would still have been steady——

"She'll be at Hamstead waiting for you when you and Cristina and the baby get there," Trixie said, as if she had read his thoughts. "She'll feel better when she gets home. She sent me a letter too. About something I said to her once when she and I were talking about you. I told her I'd rather see a man survive than a house. She wrote to say I'd been right. I was, too, that time anyhow, Chris."

"There was another time when you were right, Trixie. The time when you talked to me in the Spreewald. I haven't forgotten."

She had not forgotten either, but she did not say so. She only urged him on, paving the way for his departure. Nothing that she could do had been left undone. But even Trixie had not been able to foresee the explosion in Spain.

As he thought of all this, Hans Christian turned to look at the woman beside him and was again struck by her spiritual resemblance to his mother. She had not spoken to him once, on her own initiative, since they left Valdepenas. But she had responded, sympathetically, every time he spoke to her. He felt increasingly drawn to her.

"Have you a son, *Señora?*" he asked impulsively.

She smiled, and as she did so, her face became beautiful. "*Si, camarad,*" she said in a glad voice. "He is a good son and a great toreador. I love him deeply and I am very proud of him besides, with reason. He has filled my home with joy and honor. A mother is blessed in such a boy."

"I shouldn't have thought that you were old enough to have a grown son, *Señora.* Is it your only one?"

"Yes, it is my only one. But you know what the lioness said to the jackal who taunted her: 'It is true that I have a cub instead of a litter. But that cub is a lion.'"

"I'm an only son too, *Señora.* I wish I thought my mother had reason to feel about me as you feel about your son."

"You may be sure she does, *camarad,* whether there is reason for it or not. That is the way with mothers."

She smiled again, and as if in afterthought, suggested that he should let her out at Jaen. She had relatives there, she could rest before she started back to Valdepenas. The rest of the way would be clear. There were no more troops on the march, and it was evident now that there would be no lines to pass through. She wished him well, and thanked him for his kindness. He thanked her a hundred times for hers. They kissed each other and parted as friends and allies, with the expressed hope of meeting each other again in happier times. He felt sure that from that time forward he would never instinctively regard a Communist as an enemy.

The perfumed patio had never looked more lovely than when Hans Christian entered it. Even the flow of the fountain seemed more musical than before, and on the bench beside it lay Cristina's guitar, carelessly laid down. But the patio was empty. Hans Christian called, and only the echo of his own voice answered him. He walked through the *galeria* and found it empty also. Then, frantically, he began to go through one room after another. Their vacancy mocked him as he passed along.

It was not until he reached the winding stair leading to the turret that he heard a small smothered cry. A great tapestry hung on the wall there, and underneath it was hidden a door leading to a small secret space. He wrenched down the drapery and flung the entrance open. Inside the hideaway Catalina was crouching, holding a child in her arms.

He needed no one to tell him that this was his son. Wide blue eyes looked up at him trustfully under a tangle of red-gold curls. He snatched the boy from the servant and hugged him hungrily to his heart. But at the same instant he asked a desperate question.

"What has happened? Where is everyone? What has become of your mistress?"

"*Disculpe, Señor* Baron. A detachment of the Red Forces has been this way. It was *Doña* Cristina herself who first saw them as they approached, who hid me and the *niño*. After that, I do not know. She made me swear by the memory of my mother that I would save him for you, whatever happened."

"And what has happened?"

"How can I tell, *Señor*? If the house is empty, everyone else is gone. But I have kept my promise. You see that the child is safe."

The old woman was crying bitterly. A puzzled expression came into the child's trustful eyes. Then he smiled, and crowing, leaned forward from his father's arms to pat her face. Her tears fell on his small rosy hand.

"You've done all you could, Catalina, I know that. But now you must help me search. We must find *Doña* Cristina, we must find them all."

"Have you been to the library yet, *Señor* Baron? You know that Don Sebastian is often in the library. We can look. He may have hid the others himself."

"No, I haven't been to the library yet. Yes, we can look."

He was already on his way up the stairs again, carrying his son. Something told him that he would find Sebastian there, and he was not mistaken. His father-in-law had not been mercifully killed. He had been bound hand and foot and left to starve. He was still conscious when Hansel reached him. But he was beyond speech.

"Where is Cristina? What has become of her?" Hans Christian was past coherent words himself. But Sebastian had collapsed utterly as he was released, and had fallen to the floor in a huddled heap. With mounting frenzy, Hansel stooped over him. "Sebastian, you must talk to me, you must tell me! Where shall I go? What shall I do?"

"It is too late. If you had only come yesterday! Cristina had your message, she watched for you all day. But now you can't go anywhere. You can't do anything. They have all been taken away."

"All? Not just Cristina? Cecilia and *Doña* Dolores too?"

"Yes. Cecilia and Dolores too. Cristina was playing her guitar, Cecilia was reading a funny story, Dolores was still at prayer when they took her from her *prie-dieu*. They were all brought in here after I was bound, stripped and raped before my eyes. Afterwards they were dragged away to the parish church. Don't go there, don't try to see the end. Take your child—the child Cristina saved for you—and flee before it's too late."

"Sebastian, you're beside yourself, you don't know what you're saying. Where is this parish church?" And as the only answer was a groan, he struggled to his feet again, and spoke sternly to the weeping woman beside him. "Catalina, you must tell me where this church is. Clearly, so I can find it without delay. And then you must stay with Don Sebastian and the *niño* until I can return. Do you hear? *Doña* Cristina trusted you and I do too."

"*Señor* Baron, do as Don Sebastian has said. Take the child and flee. I will stay here with Don Sebastian and care for him faithfully as long as we are both allowed to live. But do not go yourself to the parish church. It will be like the Church of Santa Maria at Baeza."

"And what happened at the Church of Santa Maria in Baeza?"

"It was there, *Señor*——"

"Yes, Catalina, tell me quickly!"

"We do not know for certain, but we have heard that it was there that all the women who resisted were butchered. May God have mercy on their souls and on us!"

He found the church fast enough. It was not far away. Its doors stood wide open. But they were blocked by corpses. Hans Christian stumbled over them and found the floor strewn with many, as he searched for one.

It was Cecilia he saw first. Then *Doña* Dolores. They were close together and though many were mutilated, they still retained in death a little of the look they had possessed in life. Horror had closed down so quickly upon them that Cecilia had not lost all her childish charm, or *Doña* Dolores all her pious precision. He could believe the one had been laughing, the other praying when she was overcome. There were some vestments lying near them, that had been torn asunder and trampled under foot. He picked them up, smoothed them out, and placed them reverently over the mother and daughter. Then he went on through the crowded nave.

It was not until he reached the altar that he found Cristina, lying on the steps. The crucifix and candlesticks had toppled over, but the altar cloth was still in place. He drew it off and laid it lightly over her. As he did so, he saw her eyelids flutter. Instantly he was on his knees beside her, calling to her.

"Cristina, I've come for you, I'm here. My darling, it isn't too late!"

Her eyelids fluttered again, her lips moved slightly, forming his name.

"I knew you would come, *querido*. It is never too late for your coming."

He put his arms around her, drawing her head against his breast, and as he did so, he saw a stain on the altar cloth grow brighter and deeper. But he saw too that she was still trying to speak, still trying to smile. He bent over more closely to catch the words.

"The child and the horse—they're both safe. I saved them for you—the strong strain."

"Yes, darling, I know. I know. I'll keep them both safe. I'll take them with me to America. But don't try to talk about them. Tell me that you love me. Let me hear you say that again."

"I'll say it over and over again, until the end comes. But there is something else besides——"

"Yes, Cristina?"

"There is my father. Promise me you'll make him go too."

"I promise. I'll make him go too."

"And ask Beatrice—if she would help you. She is so strong— I won't be afraid—for you—or the boy—if I am sure——"

"I promise you. I'll ask for her help. And take it. As much as she'll give me."

Cristina closed her eyes. The red stain was not spreading any more. She lay very still. But she spoke to Hans Christian once more, with her lips against his.

"It was like this—in your arms—that I found life—*alma de mi alma.* And now—in your arms—I meet death. What does it matter—that one follows the other? You have made them both—so sweet."

PART IX

1936

More Sacred Still

CHAPTER 30

"OF COURSE I never talk about it without being pressed, but I went over on purpose to be presented at Court. The Secretary of State suggested it to me himself, one evening when he took me in to dinner at the British Embassy. You know that's very exclusive in Washington nowadays, not at all like the French, where congressmen and writers and all sorts of queer people like that are invited. Well, as I was saying, Mr. Estabrook seemed to make such a point of it that I felt I couldn't refuse, though what I should really have enjoyed would have been a nice quiet summer in the country—one of those quaint villages in Vermont, for instance, where all the old houses have been reclaimed from the natives. Michael Trent, a great friend of the Secretary's, is our Ambassador to England now, and he and his wife, who is simply charming, did *everything* to make my stay in London pleasant. I went to the Royal Enclosure at Ascot, and to tea on the terrace of the Parliament Buildings, and—oh, everywhere! I didn't have a free moment, it was almost as hectic as Washington. I really think I'll have to go to a sanitarium for a few weeks before the season there begins, because I've been rushing all around the Continent too—Deauville and Carlsbad and places like that, so exhausting! And finally the usual siege with Paris dressmakers. They certainly are the most unmitigated thieves and liars in the world. I was disappointed in almost everything I bought, and still I don't know how I'm ever going to get through the customs. They're more arrogant and unreasonable every year, aren't they? Naturally, I wouldn't really smuggle, but——"

"I think I've kept pretty well within my hundred dollars. I don't expect to have much trouble. I don't go to the big houses—I've found the little ones so much more satisfactory. That's the way the French feel about it themselves, of course. And then I never waste much time on shopping. Our stores in Texas have all the latest styles, and besides, there are so many more important things to do in Europe than to spend days and days getting fitted. I came over as one of the delegates to the Biennial of the Women's International League for Peace and Prosperity. In fact, I don't like to brag, but I've just been elected one of its Vice Presidents by the largest vote any American's ever received for such an office. We had our meeting in Vienna this year, and I think it's simply ridiculous to talk as if any sort of trouble were brewing there. Why everything was just as pleasant as possible! The little sidewalk cafés all crowded, and orchestras playing, and nicely dressed people enjoying themselves. I've always heard it was one of the most delightful cities in Europe, and now I'm convinced of it. I took a wonderful side trip too, down the Danube to Budapest. There were special rates for the delegates to the Congress, and the Hungarian women gave us a marvelous welcome. I think it's very inspiring to realize how women from all parts of the world are coming closer together in these days, don't you? It makes one so hopeful for the future. Now there was an Esthonian lady I met—a most superior person—who explained to me all the reasons why the Baltic States would cling together and prevent aggression. Not that I believe there's going to be aggression. I think all those reports are greatly exaggerated. But I mean just in case——"

"Yes, I suppose so. I've never taken much interest in club work myself. You see, in Washington there's such a constant round—why last winter I didn't dine at home alone for six weeks running! And as I said, London's just as bad. Of course, I've always had a great many English friends, in fact one of my cousins married a member of the nobility. He's the most charming man you ever saw. His clothes have that *sculptured* look that make American men seem so unkempt. These cousins of mine have an enchanting place at Sussex, and I spent a week end there—Thursday to Tuesday, you know. The English certainly understand the arts of leisure better than we do. They make you feel it's vulgar to go tearing after money. Two English ladies—I mean real Ladies—who had been presented at the same time I was, were at this house party, and it was pleasant to talk over the Drawing Room with them. All the little details. For instance——"

"You don't suppose we're going to be alone at this table all the way over, do you? Of course I understand that the Captain never appears before the second or third day because of his duties, but certainly all the others he's asked to sit here can't be sick already. I wonder who they are, don't you? Frankly, as I looked around the deck this morning, I didn't see anyone whom I thought would be likely to receive such an invitation. I've crossed ten times now, in connection with my Peace and Prosperity Work, and I'm always struck with the ordinary appearance of most people on shipboard. I often wonder what becomes of all the distinguished persons who travel. But perhaps——"

"Good morning. I'm sorry to be a little late. My father and mother asked to be excused. They're rather tired so they're lunching on our veranda. But they'll be down to dinner."

The girl who had spoken so cordially slipped into one of the vacant seats at the Captain's table and began to study the menu, apparently oblivious of the fact that her two table companions were avidly studying her. It was painfully evident to them both that she had been having no trouble with dressmakers and that she had not been patronizing little houses either. Her powder-blue flannels were exquisite in both cut and color, and the molded felt hat, finished with a simple silk cord, which she wore with them, matched them perfectly as to shade and style. There were aquamarine clips at the neckline of her dress, and she had on a single ring which was also set with one large aquamarine. She looked up at the hovering steward with an agreeable smile.

"Can you recommend the caviar?" she inquired. "Yes, I'm sure it's delicious. I'll have that first, please. Then partridge, and lettuce with *pâté de fois gras*. A glass of sherry, very dry. Black coffee afterwards."

She laid down the card and turned again to the women beside her.

"This is Mrs. Delmaine of Washington, isn't it?" she inquired. "And Mrs. Brice of Fort Worth? The Captain told us we would have the pleasure of being with you—he's just dropped in to see us for a few minutes. He'll be here for dinner too. I'm sure you'll like him. We've crossed with him two or three times and we do, tremendously. Oh, I must introduce myself! My name is Beatrice Rhodes."

Mrs. Brice beamed. Mrs. Delmaine purred. Both spoke almost simultaneously.

"Miss Rhodes! Why I hadn't heard! I've wanted so much to meet your mother and somehow I've just missed her several times. Is the Ambassador going home on leave? I hadn't seen any announcement——"

"Yes, father's on leave rather indefinitely. We've been in Versailles more than a month, waiting for friends to join us. Their plans have been very uncertain, so ours have too. There hasn't been any announcement."

"But how wonderful that everything has turned out so pleasantly, and that you're on this boat! It's such a privilege——"

The caviar had come, beautifully imbedded in ice, surrounded by lemon delicately sliced. Beatrice soothed the solicitous steward, assuring him of its perfection in her eyes. But after she had tasted it appreciatively and broken into a piece of melba toast, she laid down her fork.

"Everything hasn't turned out as pleasantly as we'd hoped. Will you forgive me if I tell you a little about it? On such short acquaintance and all? Because I think perhaps it will be easier all around if I do. Especially as two of the persons whom the Captain invited to sit at his table may not feel that they can. I hope they will, but perhaps they won't. So I think you ought to know why—in a general way."

She picked up her toast again. She did not eat it, but neither did she crumble it. She held it firmly in her shapely tanned fingers.

"When father and mother and I left Germany," she said, "we joined a great friend of ours who had just gone over the frontier. You may have heard of him. He's quite well known. Some people call him Hans von Hohenlohe. Some people call him Christian Marlowe. It doesn't matter what you call him. He's one of the grandest persons in the whole world."

She was speaking quietly, attracting no attention at the surrounding tables. But there was a ring in her voice which had a strange effect upon her hearers. They both felt spellbound as they listened to her.

"We all came to Paris together and then Chris went on to Spain. His wife and his little boy were there, with his wife's family in Granada. He was very eager to get to them as soon as possible, and bring them back with him. The day after he left us, civil war broke out. He didn't even know it had started until he was almost to Madrid. By the time he could get to Granada, terrible things had happened. His wife's family had been practically wiped out—her uncle, her sister, her mother. She—died herself, just after he got there. But her father and her baby were still alive. Chris brought them back to us. They're on this boat with us now."

Beatrice Rhodes paused, and her listeners both managed, this time, to murmur something unintelligibly sympathetic as she did so. She went steadily on.

"The baby has an old Spanish nurse. He's well and happy. He's stopped crying for his mother already. But Chris—and Sebastian de Cerreno— I'm sure you'll understand why you may never see them, why it's better I should tell you the truth before all sorts of wild stories start circulating around the boat. You could both be a great help to me, if you felt like it. You could repeat what I've said to you, just as I've said it. Then other passengers would understand, they'd be kind and merciful. In what they said and what they did, too. It would be good for Chris and Don Sebastian if they could get out on deck, knowing they wouldn't be molested. It will be terrible for them if they have to stay in hiding all the way across the ocean. Not only because of what has just happened, because they've lost everyone that belongs to them except the baby. But because they've both been in hiding so long."

"Miss Rhodes, you know I'm very much honored——"

"My dear, if there is anything on earth I can do——"

"Thank you so much. I felt sure I could count on you. But I mustn't go on talking about this all through luncheon. I didn't want to depress you. Just to enlist you— Tell me about your presentation, Mrs. Delmaine— I understand London was unusually thrilling this year. And I want to congratulate you on your election, Mrs. Brice. Is it true that there are nearly a thousand new members in the International League of Peace and Prosperity?"

Beatrice Rhodes smiled and began to eat her toast again.

When luncheon was over, she sat on the veranda for an hour with her parents. Then she went across the corridor to the cabin which Christian Marlowe and Sebastian de Cerreno were sharing, and knocked on the door. It was Don Sebastian who opened it.

"I came to see if you two wouldn't come up on the boat deck with me for awhile. We could walk, or lie around in the sun, just as you like. And later on we could have a swim. The pool's very nice. I was in it this morning."

Hans Christian, who was standing by one of the portholes, neither turned nor answered. Don Sebastian, after glancing towards him, replied gravely.

"Thank you very much. It is thoughtful of you to suggest it. But not today, I think."

"Well, perhaps tomorrow."

"Yes, perhaps tomorrow."

When she returned the next day, however, the same episode was repeated. But the third time, after Don Sebastian had glanced towards Hans Christian's unresponsive figure, he made a different answer.

"It is very kind of you to think of us so constantly. I shall be glad to go up on deck with you, if you can find a secluded spot."

"I have one picked out already. I'm certain you'll like it."

When they reached it he assured her that he did, and he spoke sincerely. Two big lounging chairs had been drawn up high in the bow, and the place where they were had been roped off and marked "No Admittance." There was a small table between the chairs, on which a thermos jar stood, and a few books and magazines were scattered about. Beatrice poured out two glasses of orangeade, offered one to Don Sebastian, and sipped slowly from the other herself, making a casual comment from time to time. Then she picked up a book and began to leaf it through in the same desultory fashion. Eventually she read a few paragraphs aloud. When she stopped tentatively, Don Sebastian asked her if she would not go on.

It was nearly two hours later that she closed the book, glancing at her wrist watch.

"I have to go down. I can get into the stable about this time for a few minutes. And I always stay with the baby while Catalina has her supper. Don't you suppose you could persuade Chris to come up here when he finds there won't be anyone here but you?"

"I will try to persuade him, Be-atriz. So you stay with the baby every night while Catalina has her supper?"

"Oh, yes! We're great friends. He bounces around on my lap until he gets tired. Then he curls up and goes to sleep— Will you meet me up here tomorrow afternoon at three, Don Sebastian? I won't bother you by coming to your door and knocking first."

"I shall do so very gratefully and gladly, Be-atriz."

He was waiting for her when she reached there, and this time it was he who poured out the orangeade and made the initial remarks as they sat sipping it and smoking cigarettes. When Beatrice set down her empty glass, she asked if she should read to him again.

"The book is very interesting and you read well. Your voice is perfectly suited to reading aloud. But perhaps today we might go on talking for a time, Be-atriz."

"I should love to go on talking with you, Don Sebastian. And I love to hear you call me 'Be-atriz.'"

"Do you know the meaning of your name?"

"No— Names do have meanings, don't they? What does it mean?"

"It means 'making happy'— I believe you are well named. I believe you have acquired a gift for making people happy, Be-atriz."

"Oh, Don Sebastian, if I only thought so, I'd be the happiest person in the world myself! If I could only bring some happiness to Chris! But I can't reach him at all. He won't speak to me. He won't even look at me."

"Not yet. But someday he will. You must be very patient with Hans Christian, Be-atriz."

"Don Sebastian, I—I have been. I am. But——"

"When you remember what he has gone through——"

"But, Don Sebastian, haven't you gone through just as much? And you speak to me, you don't shrink away from me!"

"No, I do not shrink from you. I am thankful for your thoughtfulness, thankful to talk to you. But I have not been through as much, Be-atriz. Or rather, I have been through it in a different way. Though my grief is great, it is untinged by any sense of guilt. I have made many mistakes in my life, but none of them has destroyed my own standards or brought down destruction on those I loved. I am upheld, in a certain measure, by the knowledge of this, whereas Hansel has not even that cold comfort. Sincerely as he acted, he cannot escape from the consciousness that if he had been ruled by reason instead of swayed by impulse, he would never have become enmeshed in the Nazi web. He cannot forget that having made his initial mistake he might still have retrieved it. If he had returned to America, when I first urged it, he would have redeemed himself and saved Cristina. He cannot forgive himself because this is so."

"Don't you think he ever will?"

"No, never, any more than I shall ever recover from the desecration of my country and the slaughter of my family. I have terrible moments too. But I am not a young man any longer, I have learned more than Hans Christian. I know that I have not reached the end of endurance. Hans Christian believes that he has. That is the supreme tragedy for him just now."

"And you think it always will be?"

"No. I think that someday he will learn, as I have, that the only way to go through life is to keep beginning it over again. That is the one sure sign of vitality, the capacity that Americans, especially American women, have to such an ultimate degree. Even the revolutions in Europe are inspired by remembered wrongs. Americans may sometimes stumble in going ahead, but we Europeans stumble because we are always looking back. When Hans Christian forgets that he ever imagined himself a German and is conscious only of his Americanism, he will reach out again towards the realities of which you are a part."

"Don Sebastian, you said I had acquired a gift for making people happy. I believe you must have been born with one."

Sebastian de Cerreno shook his head. "No. On the contrary. I have failed in most of my efforts to create happiness. But for that very reason it will mean the more to me if I have given you a glimpse of it. All I have really done is to make you understand. When you do that, you do the rest yourself. The youth of Europe has been sacrificed, Be-atriz, to those remembered wrongs of which I just spoke. In Germany this sacrifice has taken one form, in Spain another. Both are horrible, and Hans Christian has been caught in the toils of both. He has a dual holocaust from which to rise. But he will—if you never fail him, if he comes to realize that you are standing by, whatever happens."

"I'll—I'll never fail him, Don Sebastian."

It was true that Beatrice and the baby were very great friends. Very often, after he had gone to sleep in her arms, she put him to bed herself without really rousing him from the comfortable torpor into which he sank after he had exhausted himself by bounding up and down on her lap. A crib had been set up for him beside Catalina's bed, in the small cabin that adjoined the one occupied by Hans Christian and Sebastian. Beatrice always stayed beside this crib until Catalina came from her supper, and sometimes she sang as she sat there, looking down on the sleeping child, and glancing across, every now and then, to the closed door leading into the next cabin.

It was not until they were almost across the ocean that the door finally opened, and Hans Christian came into his son's room while Beatrice was sitting there singing to the baby. He walked over to the crib without a word and stood looking down at it himself, still speechlessly. Beatrice rose and came to stand beside him.

"Don Sebastian wants us all to be very careful to talk Spanish to him, so he won't forget it, so it will always come naturally to him," she said without artificial preamble. "When I found this out, I asked Don Sebastian to recommend some books for me to read, some that would help me with idioms and conversation. I've studied Spanish before, but of course that wasn't the same. He told me about several. One of them is by Benavente—the man who won the Nobel Prize, you know, who wrote *The Kingdom of God.* There's a line in it that keeps running through my mind every time I sit here looking at the baby. May I tell you what it is? It may hurt you at first, but after you've thought it over, it will comfort you."

"Nothing will comfort me, but nothing will hurt me any more either. You may tell me if you like."

"'There is something more sacred than a grave: a cradle. There is something greater than the past: the future.'"

Hans Christian winced, but otherwise he gave no sign that he had heard her. She waited for a moment, and then she spoke to him again.

"Chris, won't you come up on the bridge with me for a little while? The Captain told me to go there whenever I liked. No one will speak to you, no one will disturb you. And it's so beautiful up there, between the sea and the sky."

"We can't leave the baby alone."

"I think Don Sebastian would stay with him, until Catalina comes back. I think he'd like to. I'm going to ask him, anyway. And I'm going to ask him if by and by he won't join us, when she's finished her supper. I think he'd like to watch the stars come out too, after the sun's gone down."

"Very well. Ask him."

Don Sebastian did not decline. Beatrice had felt very sure he would not. He answered her with characteristic courtesy when she inquired whether he would be willing to sit with the baby while she and Chris went up on the bridge.

"Certainly, if that will release you, Be-atriz. You have been faithfulness itself to our little boy."

"I think he's the most beautiful baby I've ever seen. It's all I can do to tear myself away from him. But I want Chris to come out in this glorious air with me. I want you to come too."

"Since I know you mean that, I will join you when Catalina has returned."

"I always mean what I say."

"That also I know, Be-atriz."

She opened the outer door of the cabin and held it ajar for Hans

Christian. Then she went swiftly down the long corridor and up a succession of gangways, at last leaping lightly over the barrier guarding the bridge. The officer on duty nodded, smiled and stood back. He did not speak to her and Hans Christian as they went by, and Hansel did not speak either, for a long time. When he did, it was to say something sad again.

"Do you remember the Captain on the other ship, Trixie? The one we came over on? He's lost it."

"Yes, I heard. But someday he'll get another."

"It won't be the same."

"It may be better. And the Captain of this boat won't lose his ship, Chris. He'll keep it, unless he does something disgraceful himself. He's an American. It's an American ship."

Again Hans Christian winced, and again Beatrice gave no sign that she had noticed this. She went on talking as if there were nothing unnatural about his silence, as if no strain existed between them.

"I think Don Sebastian is beginning to look better, Chris. I think he's beginning to realize what it will mean to find your mother waiting to welcome him, when the ship gets in."

"How can he think of such a thing? He wouldn't be coming, she wouldn't be waiting for him, if——"

"You told me yourself once, Chris, that a great scholar said there weren't any ifs in history. Perhaps there aren't any ifs in love. Anyway, I don't believe there ever have been for your mother. Even if Don Sebastian isn't glad he's going to see her, he must know how glad she'll be to see him. That must mean something to him."

"I don't believe it means much."

"Well, it will when he sees her, even if it doesn't now. And I don't agree with you. I believe it does already. We ought to hope it does, with all our hearts. Because, whatever else he's lost, he hasn't lost everything, as long as he's got her."

Hans Christian turned around at last and looked at Beatrice. There was no joy in his gaze, no radiance, no eagerness. But at least he did not flinch from her eyes, he faced her squarely and searchingly. He did not speak, and neither did she. But despite this, in one long triumphant moment, a question was asked and answered for all time. As they looked from each other out towards the sea again, their hands, clasping the railing, accidentally touched. Neither one drew away. They continued to stand, side by side, confronting the far horizon.